Praise for
SHERYL BROWNE

THE BABYSITTER

"Sheryl Browne seems to have a scary insight into the mind of a psychopath."　　　　—RachelsRandomReads.blogspot.com

"Sheryl Browne writes the most wonderful psychological thrillers. There aren't many thriller writers who can keep me reading, heart in mouth and pulse racing, into the early hours."
　　　　　　　　　　　　　　　　　—BeingAnne.com

"An author that does family tragedy, revenge and redemption as well as anyone."　　　　—CrimeThrillerHound.co.uk

"A highly addictive read."　　　　—TheBookReviewCafe.com

THE AFFAIR

"Simply superb!"　　　　—RachelsRandomReads.blogspot.com

"A twisty, dark, emotive, addictive, and utterly brilliant novel from Sheryl Browne."　　　　—TheWritingGarnet.wordpress.com

"It had both the mix of tension and emotion which had me hooked from the very first page."　　　　—JenMedsBookReviews.com

"*The Affair* is an addictive read that gives lies all their strength!"
　　　　　　　　　　　　　　　　　—ChocolatenWaffles.com

THE BABYSITTER

THE
BABYSITTER

SHERYL BROWNE

GRAND CENTRAL
PUBLISHING

NEW YORK   BOSTON

Grand Central Publishing
Hachette Book Group
1290 Avenue of the Americas, New York, NY 10104
grandcentralpublishing.com
twitter.com/grandcentralpub

Originally published in 2018 by Bookouture in the UK

First U.S. Trade Paperback Edition: July 2019

Grand Central Publishing is a division of Hachette Book Group, Inc. The Grand Central Publishing name and logo is a trademark of Hachette Book Group, Inc.

The publisher is not responsible for websites (or their content) that are not owned by the publisher.

The Hachette Speakers Bureau provides a wide range of authors for speaking events. To find out more, go to www.hachettespeakersbureau.com or call (866) 376-6591.

ISBNs: 978-1-5387-6428-2 (trade paperback)

Printed in the United States of America

LSC-C

10   9   8   7   6   5   4   3   2

To my family, who offered their love
and support unquestioningly when I needed it most.

To my little brother. I miss you.

To Drew. You are my inspiration. Without you, this book
might have had one or two plot holes.

I love you all.

PROLOGUE

EIGHT YEARS AGO

Oblivious to the slimy, wet mud oozing between her toes, Grace took a faltering step backwards, away from the house. Her huge cognac-coloured eyes illuminated by the light of the fire, she watched, mesmerised and helpless, as the flames licked hungrily at her parents' bedroom curtains. She'd tried to tell them what happened to Ellie wasn't her fault.

Constantly around her ankles, while their mum and husband number three had partied, her younger sister Ellie had been watching as she and her friends lit up their sparklers and drew their names against the dark blue ink of the sky. Ellie had wanted to do it, too. Later, Grace had promised her; anything to placate her and stop her "telling Mummy" she'd been smoking, which would only add to Grace's list of sins.

Ellie hadn't forgotten. Still awake when Grace had crept up to bed, her sister had whinged until, urging her to be quiet, Grace had given in and tiptoed back downstairs to fetch a packet of leftover sparklers from the box in the kitchen.

Her eyes like big brown orbs, Ellie had watched in awe as Grace struck the match and lit the sparkler, igniting a thousand crackling slivers of light in their bedroom. She'd squealed like the foxes that scream in the night when her flesh had singed, despite how hard Grace tried to shush her. Grace hadn't wanted to hurt her sister. But she knew nobody would believe her. They never did.

Grace took another step back, her heart skipping a beat as a figure appeared at the window, flames lashing at his flesh like hot vipers' tongues. It *wasn't* her fault. She'd *tried* to tell them. She'd *told* Ellie to hold the firework at arm's length. They hadn't been listening. Her mum's eyes had been as wild as the fire. She'd still been wearing her lipstick, blood red, like an angry red slash for a mouth, as she'd cursed and spat, "You stupid creature. Look what you've done. *Look* what *you've* done!"

She'd been holding Ellie in her arms, clutching her plump little hand in her own and pointing it out towards Grace like an accusation. Ellie's fingers had been blistered, her thigh, too, where the sparkler had landed.

Her stepdad had started after her as her mum swept past Grace to take Ellie to accident and emergency. "I'll drive you," he'd offered, but he hadn't wanted to. Grace could tell by the way his gaze drifted lewdly towards her that he hadn't wanted to.

"Don't be ridiculous!" her mum had snapped angrily. "You've drunk your own body weight in beer. Just… deal with her," she'd added, causing ice-cold dread to pool in the pit of Grace's stomach. She hadn't wanted to be alone with him, to watch him draw the blinds and turn from the window, that liquid, faraway look in his eyes as he unfastened his waistband.

Hearing the wail of the sirens growing closer, Grace tore her gaze from the window. Panic twisting her stomach and thick, choking smoke gripping her throat, she backed towards the denser foliage at the bottom of the garden.

☆

Pulling on the requisite hand and footwear protection, Mark sucked in a deep breath and braced himself to enter the premises. "DI Cain," he said, producing his ID and introducing himself to the uniformed officer in the hall, who was looking rather green around the gills. The guy was young—early twenties, Mark guessed, probably not long off probation. Mark had been about the same age, seven long years ago, when he'd encountered his first victim. He'd kept his breakfast down—just. This, though—a whole family incinerated, a young child included—was truly an initiation by fire. "DS Moyes?" he asked.

"Child's bedroom. First left at the top," the officer answered, and swallowed hard on his Adam's apple.

Mark nodded, glancing at him sympathetically. "Take a break," he suggested. "Grab some air." Not that the air out there was much less putrid than in here. As acrid as the smell of burned wood suffused with gunpowder was, it was doing little to hide the nauseatingly sweet stench of singed flesh. Like roast pork crackling on Sundays. Mark remembered well the times he'd looked forward to going to his gran's as a kid, escaping the end-less violent arguments at home. He hadn't been able to go near a roast joint since he'd attended a road traffic accident where the unfortunate driver, entombed in his car, had gone up in flames.

"I'm good, sir," the officer assured him stoically.

Mark was unconvinced. "Humour me," he said. "I've done my own fair share of contaminating evidence. Trust me, I know the signs."

"Sir," the officer said, his look now a mixture of embarrass-ment and relief as he turned for the front door.

Mark watched him go, and then, steeling himself, he climbed the stairs and headed directly for the child's room. Lisa Moyes, his detective sergeant, was there, looking down at the small form in the bed. Detective Sergeant Cummings was also there, though Mark was buggered if he knew why. First responder, he wondered? Unlikely. The man was a lazy sod. More likely he'd been on his way back from some seedy liaison in the city and had stopped by out of idle curiosity.

"Cummings." Mark nodded a curt greeting as he walked across to Lisa Moyes. He didn't like the man, a chauvinistic prick who obviously considered sexual harassment one of the perks of the job.

"What have we got?" he asked Lisa, who didn't meet his gaze. From the hand she ran under her nose, Mark guessed why. Petite in size, with blonde hair, which she purposely cropped short, and pretty, Lisa had had to work to prove herself in a largely male-dominated environment, determined to be as hard-nosed and detached as some of her male counterparts. As a mother herself, though, Mark suspected she didn't have a snowball's chance in hell of remaining detached now.

"A young girl," Lisa answered, eventually, "white Caucasian, aged approximately four. Cause of death—" Her voice catching, she stopped and fixed her gaze hard on the ceiling.

"Smoke inhalation," Cummings supplied. "The door was closed. She got lucky though, better than being burned alive. Can't imagine what must have been going through her mind hearing her mum and dad screaming. Poor cow must have been petrified."

At that, Lisa turned around. "You really are a prat, Cummings," she muttered, pushing furiously past him and heading for the door.

Cummings watched her go, confounded. "What was all that about?" he asked, looking clueless as he turned back to Mark.

Sighing, Mark shook his head. Married and divorced twice, Cummings had never had kids, but it didn't take a great leap of the imagination to guess what might have been going through that child's mind.

"Lisa has two children under five," he pointed out exasperatedly, and turned his attention to the little girl, his heart constricting inside him as he did. Curled into a foetal ball in her child-sized bed, she had her thumb plugged into her mouth and a one-eyed Pooh Bear clutched close to her chest.

Mark took a second to compose himself. He didn't have kids either. They had had a child, he and his wife, Melissa, and though his son's life might have been too short, Mark had grieved more than he would ever let on. Melissa had needed him to be strong, Mark had realised that as he'd watched her nursing their premature child in her arms. Her heart had been breaking as Jacob's weak lungs had stopped fighting. In those bleak weeks afterwards, Mel had fought to stave off a deep, dark depression born of carrying a child, giving birth to a child and then having that child cruelly stolen away. Mark had been dying inside. Probably the only person who'd guessed how much he was hurting, and how frustrated and angry he'd felt after two subsequent miscarriages, was Lisa.

No, it didn't need a great leap of the imagination to envisage how terrified in such circumstances a small child might be. Swallowing back a tight knot in his throat, Mark closed his eyes, offering up a silent prayer for the girl, before turning back to Cummings. "You might as well go home," he said tiredly.

"Oh? Why's that then?" Cummings asked, eyeing him warily as Mark headed for the door. Ever since Mark had caught him in the act of groping a female member of staff and attempted to wipe the floor with him, Cummings had been jumpy around him. More so once he'd realised Mark was on to his little transgressions with confiscated items. Drugs mostly, nothing major, but there was no way it could be overlooked. Cummings had also been quietly watching him, Mark was aware, as if waiting for him to slip up; probably looking for ammunition to use against him should Mark bring his suspicions to the attention of their superior officers.

"You're surplus to requirements," he clarified. "I'm thinking this isn't a crime scene."

Cummings looked doubtful. "But aren't there traces of accelerant?"

"It's bonfire night," Mark reminded him. "Judging by the embers outside and the obvious signs of alcohol consumption, the family were partying. Chances are the accelerant was to make sure the party didn't get rained off."

It had got the fire going all right, hadn't it, he thought jadedly. The idiots park the accelerant in the kitchen, a stray spark ignites the fumes, and bang, a fucking inferno. Mark quashed an overwhelming sense of anger. What were they thinking, taking that sort of risk with a four-year-old child in the house?

"I'll assess whether we need to drag the forensic specialists out of bed. DS Moyes and I can handle the rest. Once the coroner arrives, you might as well go and catch up on your beauty sleep. You look as if you could use it." The last was added acerbically, bearing in mind Cummings' penchant for touring red-light districts.

Mark turned away from Cummings and headed for the main bedroom. There, the smell was more cloying; the coppery odour of iron-rich burned blood suffused with barbecued meat turned his stomach over. Suppressing the urge to retch, Mark forced himself further into the room, almost stepping on what remained of one of the corpses as he did. The mother, he gathered. Burned where she lay, her body in much the same foetal position as the little girl, though through muscle flexion rather than fear, as she'd obviously been trying to get to the door.

Working to keep his nausea in check, he walked around the bed. The father had obviously headed for the window. Blackened and charred, clothes and curtain material melted into his flesh, his body was barely recognisable as human.

Mark couldn't begin to imagine the pain they must have gone through. Was smoke inhalation a less painful death, he wondered, his mind going back to the little girl. A forensic specialist had once assured him it was, marginally. Either way it was a fucking horrific way to go. *Dammit.* He needed to get out of here. He needed to breathe. Curtailing his anger, Mark headed back to the landing to concentrate on the practicalities of what needed to be done.

Gulping a lungful of slightly less stifling air as he exited the house, he glanced around, assessing the location. An isolated country property located on the Worcester and Herefordshire border. He'd already noted the absence of a fence or gate dividing the land from the road.

Pondering options for a perimeter, he was gazing into the woodland on the opposite side of the road when DS Moyes joined him. "How's it going?" he asked her.

"Slowly." Lisa sighed. "I sent one of the first attending officers to the local pub. The landlord was pissed off at being knocked up, but he confirmed he was here last night and that there hadn't been any arguments or suspect incidents. Guests were mostly local apparently. He's going to let us have some names."

"Right." Mark nodded. "I actually meant how's it going with you?"

"Good. I'm good," Moyes assured him, her gaze fixed to the front.

Mark noted the determined set of her jaw. "Bullshit."

Lisa's shoulders deflated. "Yeah," she said, running her hand through her short crop of hair. "Sorry about back there. It's just...Cummings can be a right tactless twat sometimes."

Mark sighed empathetically. "Tell me about it."

"I could imagine it"—Lisa tugged in a tight breath—"how terrified that little girl must have been. I don't know what I would do if I ever lost one of my children. I suppose the small plus is the parents won't have to go through the grieving—Oh God." She squeezed her eyes closed. "Sorry, Mark. I wasn't thinking. I—"

"It's fine," Mark said quickly.

Lisa obviously got the gist. "So, how's Mel?" she asked, her voice falsely bright.

"Good," Mark assured her, happy to talk about his wife. "Throwing herself into her work. She's managed to get a couple of commissions supplying local craft centres, so...Yup, she's doing okay."

Outwardly, Melissa and Lisa were as different as chalk and cheese. Taller than Lisa, with long, softly curled hair the colour of soft copper, Mel was meditative, rarely outspoken unless with good cause, caring. As was Lisa, but there the similarity ended. Lisa was definitely outspoken, and she could curse with the best of them. Inwardly, though, they were made of the same stuff, with a steely determination to keep going no matter what shit life dealt them. Having survived an abusive relationship, it was no wonder Lisa would have nil respect for a Neanderthal of Cummings' ilk. Mark wouldn't say it to her face, but having grown up in the midst of an abusive relationship himself, he had a profound respect for her. Lisa had been a friend to Mel when she'd needed one, and Mark had been grateful.

Mark smiled as his mind drifted to Mel, who of late could usually be found at her potter's wheel. Somehow, she'd pulled herself out of the pit of despair she'd fallen into and built up a business, albeit a fledgling one, from scratch. Mark was in awe of her.

"Excellent," Lisa said, looking pleased. "And are you two still…um…you know."

Noting the insinuating arch of her eyebrows, Mark got the drift. "Yes, we're still trying," he confided. And hoping, he added silently, that by some miracle one day they would be blessed with the child they both desperately wanted.

"You're a handsome bastard." Lisa smirked. "Who could resist?"

Mark shook his head. "I could think of a few."

"And modest with it. Be still my beating heart." Lisa fluttered her eyelashes theatrically. "Well, you know what they say, practice makes perfect and all that. It'll happen," she said, glancing over her shoulder as one of the first attending officers approached from the house. "Probably when you least expect it. Keep it up, Detective."

Mark's mouth twitched into a smile as she gave him a thumbs-up and turned to liaise with the uniform. Praying it would happen, for both of their sakes, Mark pulled in a sigh and turned his attention back to the task of setting up the perimeter.

"I'm heading back in," Lisa said. "They're removing the bodies."

Turning back, Mark arched an eyebrow, surprised she was so keen. He was all for facing fears head on—his biggest fear in his young life had been his own father, until he'd plucked up enough courage to confront him—but Lisa had been visibly upset in there. "You sure?" he asked her. "You can always take over out here while I go in."

Lisa nodded resolutely. "I'd like to be with her. Make sure she's all right, if that makes any sense."

"Perfect sense." Mark smiled, understanding. It was pointless, the little girl was dead, but making sure she was treated gently might possibly lay a ghost for Lisa.

Gesturing her on, Mark made his way around the side of the house to liaise with the officers out back, plucking his ringing mobile from his pocket as he went. It would be DCI Edwards calling, he assumed, wanting a progress report—i.e., checking up on him, after his psych report had labelled him borderline fit for work. Yes, he'd lost it with Cummings, and flooring a fellow officer hadn't been the proudest moment of his life, but the bastard had deserved it. And, yes, he might have been "borderline" at the time—his emotional state hadn't been great after the funeral—but he was fit for work now.

But when he looked at the screen, it wasn't Edwards. "Mel? What's wrong?" he asked, a knot of apprehension tightening inside him.

"Nothing's *wrong*," Mel assured him. "Does there have to be something wrong for a wife to call her husband?"

Mark glanced at his watch. "It's six in the morning."

"*Nooo*, really?" Mel said, in mock surprise. "Funnily enough, that's exactly what I thought when I groped for your body and came up empty-handed."

"Sorry," Mark apologised distractedly, his attention drawn by activity further down the garden. "I didn't want to wake you. I had a call-out. I left a note by the kettle."

"I haven't been down yet. I was too busy lying in bed contemplating the thin blue line."

"Sorry?" Mark said again, his attention now definitely elsewhere.

"Thin—blue—line," Mel repeated slowly. "Work it out, Detective."

"What?"

"Well, actually, I have blue lines and pink lines and . . . I'd say you've done a very thorough job, DI Cain."

Not sure he was hearing her right, Mark stopped walking. Was she saying . . . *Jesus.* Conflicting emotions assailed him, and he dragged a hand through his hair. He wanted to whoop and cry at the same time, to sound jubilant, for Mel's sake, but how could he? Here? Now? "Mel, I'm going to have to call you back," he said, his throat tight. "I—"

"Mark?" Mel cut incredulously across him. "Did you hear what I just said?"

"Yes. Yes, I did. It's . . . I can't talk now, Mel," he said, kneading his forehead in frustration as two officers walked someone towards him. "I . . ."

"Oh." Now she sounded deflated. Bitterly disappointed.

"It's a house fire," Mark explained quickly. "A family. There've been fatalities. I have to—"

"Oh no." Mel obviously realised his circumstances immediately. "Go," she urged him, as the officers, plus charge, stopped in front of him. "Call me back when you can."

"I will," Mark promised gruffly, realising the absolute impossibility of remaining detached as he looked into the tearful, terrified eyes of another child. A child they'd been unaware of and had obviously missed in the pandemonium. Still dressed in her unicorn-print pyjamas, she was shaking from head to foot. Her cheeks, smeared in crap from the fire, were tear-stained, her cognac-coloured eyes wide and utterly petrified.

"*Shit*," Mark uttered under his breath. "Where was she?" he addressed one of the officers.

"Hiding out in the bushes," he said, nodding at the trees behind him.

"Looks like she didn't want to be found," the second officer observed.

"I'm not surprised." His heart constricting for the girl, Mark looked back at her, unsure what to say, what to do that could possibly help. There was no way she would have even begun to process the enormity of what had happened. Nor would she for a long time to come—if ever.

"All right if we leave her with you, sir?" the first officer asked. "There's some debris needs shifting on the landing."

Mark nodded. "Go," he said. "Get another ambulance here pronto and alert DS Moyes on your way, will you?" he added, as the officers skirted around him. Apart from the fact that he hadn't got a clue how to handle this, protocol dictated he should have a female police officer present.

"Hi," he said, turning to the girl and trying to sound as reassuring as possible. "I'm Detective Inspector Cain." The girl peered at him through a straggle of mousey hair. "Mark for short," he added. "Do you have a name?"

"G...Grace."

"Grace. That's a nice name." Mark smiled again, wishing he could do more than just stand there. "Do you live here, Grace?" he enquired gently.

The girl glanced past him, nodded, and then hastily dropped her gaze.

Nice going. Despairing of his ineptitude in such a situation, Mark sighed inwardly, and then, removing his jacket, crouched down to her level.

She flinched as he moved towards her, her expression one of alarm, he noted.

"To keep you warm," he said. "You're shaking fit to break something loose." Again, he smiled and prayed he wasn't doing anything to add to her terror and confusion.

The palpable fear in her eyes diminished a little as he wrapped the jacket around her, making sure to hold her gaze as he did. "Can you tell me what happened, Grace?" he asked softly, pulling it close at the neck.

Warily, she searched his eyes. Her own were wide and dark, Mark noticed, as she glanced at the house and then back to him.

"I was asleep," she said, her gaze flicking guiltily away for a second. No surprise there. Skinny under her pyjamas, her demeanour that of a frightened five-year-old, she looked around twelve, thirteen maybe. Too young to have to deal with this, but old enough, he guessed, to have realised her family had possibly perished. "But something scared me," she said. "A crash."

"Like breaking glass?" Carefully, Mark probed a little further.

She nodded, then, gulping in a breath, dragged a sleeve under her nose.

A break-in, Mark wondered, or a window popping? The latter, he suspected.

"I smelled smoke," she said, swiping at her nose again. "I didn't know what to do. I shouted and screamed but no one came. I tried to get to out, but I *couldn't*, and I got scared and—"

"Hey, hey, slow down," Mark urged her, as the words tumbled from her mouth in a garbled, hiccupping rush.

"I didn't know what to do," she repeated, choking back a sob. "I was going to wake Mummy and Daddy, but…but…"

"Was there smoke on the landing, Grace?"

"Yes," she sobbed. "And fire. I couldn't get *past* it. I couldn't get through it. I didn't know what to do."

So she ran. *What else was there to do but fucking burn*, Mark thought furiously.

"I left them," she said, the sheer anguish in her voice cutting him to the core.

"You had no choice," he told her firmly.

"My sister. She was screaming. I couldn't save her." It came out little more than a whisper.

Useless. Feeling powerless as the girl's gaze hit the ground again, Mark ran a hand over his neck. *Stuff protocol*, he thought, getting to his feet, as she began to cry in earnest. It wasn't a criminal offence to hold a child while she broke her bloody heart, was it? Briefly, he hesitated, and then reached out to wrap an arm around her as another sob escaped her throat.

The girl, obviously in need of physical contact, moved towards him in an instant, her arms around him, her face pressed hard into his torso. Fresh, heart-wrenching sobs now wracking her frail shoulders, and Mark tried to soothe her, stroking her hair, offering her banal words of comfort.

"It wasn't your fault, Grace," he said throatily, but she only cried harder.

She was glued to him like a limpet when Lisa appeared, running towards them, to Mark's huge relief.

"The ambulance has arrived," she said, casting Mark a warning glance as she slowed her run to a walk.

Reading the look, Mark shrugged helplessly. Lisa was right, of course. This definitely wouldn't be listed as appropriate behaviour in the child protection and safeguard manual, but what else was he supposed to have done? "Grace," he said softly, "you need to go with Lisa now. Just to the hospital," he added quickly, as her startled gaze shot to his. "I'll be in trouble with my superior officers if I don't ensure you get adequate medical attention."

Again, the girl scanned his eyes, a new fear in her own.

"It will be all right, Grace." Mark tried to reassure her, his heart sinking as he realised it was utter bullshit. Things wouldn't be all right for this child ever again. How could they be? "I'll check up on you as soon as I can, okay?"

"Promise?" she asked uncertainly.

It meant he would get back home later than he wanted to, but…"Promise."

She seemed to accept that, giving him a small nod. "I'm frightened," she said tremulously, causing Mark's heart to constrict afresh.

"Don't be," he said, making sure to hold her gaze now. "You can always contact me if you need to, Grace. I'll always be there if you need someone to talk to or to protect you. That's an absolute promise."

CHAPTER ONE

MELISSA
PRESENT

"Mark!" Hoisting their six-week-old baby girl higher in the crook of her arm whilst simultaneously hanging onto their wriggling seven-year-old, Melissa called frantically after her husband, who'd set off at a run towards the burned-out cottage diagonally opposite their own. The fire was doused now, fire officers wearily reeling in hoses, but it couldn't be safe to go near the property yet.

"Mark, come back!" she shouted, and he hesitated for a split second, obviously debating his options before deciding on access to the back of the cottage via the garden gate. And then he was off, the distressed mewl of a cat driving him to instinctively react, as he tended to.

Oh God, what was he *doing*? Melissa held her breath as he scaled the back gate and disappeared over it, then her heart lurched violently in her chest as their daughter tore her hand from her own and made a determined dash to go after him. "Poppy!" she screamed.

"It's all right. I've got her." Moving faster than Melissa, their neighbour, the owner of the property that had caught fire in the night, went after her, sweeping Poppy up into her arms.

The fire officers had cordoned off the lane, and Melissa would have caught her before she'd gone far, but even so... Her world had gone off kilter for a nauseating few seconds. "Thank you."

Her heart rate returning to somewhere near normal, Melissa smiled gratefully at the woman as she walked back towards her. She'd moved in just before Evie had been born. Melissa had meant to pop over and see her, but then, with a new baby to care for and her business beginning to take off, providing she could fulfil her orders, she hadn't managed to make time. She should have. She was clearly the kind of person you would hope to have as a neighbour.

"I want to go with Daddy," Poppy whimpered, kneading her eyes tiredly with her knuckles. "I'm frightened."

"He'll be back in a minute, sweetheart," the woman assured her, gently coaxing her hand from her face. "I think he knows how terribly frightened my cat is, too, so he's gone to try and rescue her. He's a very brave man, isn't he?"

Poppy surveyed the woman uncertainly for a second, then she sniffled and nodded over the thumb she'd plugged into her mouth. "He's a policeman," she said shyly.

"Is he?" The woman widened her eyes, looking impressed for Poppy's sake. "Well, he's a very brave policeman indeed. I think he should have a medal, don't you?"

Poppy nodded happily at that. "Yes," she said, settling more easily into the woman's arms.

"I'll hold onto her, shall I?" The woman smiled and nodded towards Melissa's bundle. "You seem to have your hands full."

Melissa followed her gaze, down to the content little miracle in her arms, who, amazingly, had slept through the cacophony of noise around them. "Thank you," she said again, looking back to the woman, who was actually not much more than a girl in her early twenties at most. "Are you all right?" she asked her worriedly. Just a few short hours ago, Mark, having noticed the ominous orange glow through their bedroom window, had raced outside to find Monk's Cottage thoroughly on fire and her sobbing in the lane.

"Well, you know." Managing a tremulous smile, she shrugged. "I suppose there's always a bright side. At least I'm alive."

"Mummy, when's Daddy coming back?" Poppy asked, as Melissa pondered the stupidity of her question. Of course she wouldn't be all right, what with all her earthly possessions gone up in flames.

"Soon, sweetie," Melissa promised, glancing from her daughter's huge chocolate-brown eyes, which were so like her father's, every emotion dancing therein, and then back towards the smoke-blackened cottage, praying that Mark hadn't gone into the building. No, surely not. Distressed cat or not, he would be well aware of the dangers. Nevertheless, Melissa's apprehension grew as she watched one of the fire officers heading that way after him.

"I don't know your name," the woman said, chatting to Poppy, trying to distract her. Melissa was grateful.

"Poppy... What's your name?"

"I'm Jade. And I think your Daddy will be out very soon. Do you know how I know?"

Poppy furrowed her brow over the thumb she still had wedged in her mouth. "How?"

"Listen." Jade cocked an ear. "What do you hear?"

Poppy tilted her head to one side, the little furrow in her brow deepening as she concentrated. Then, "The cat's stopped meowing," she said delightedly.

"That's right. Which probably means your daddy's found her, which means your daddy's a hero."

"He is." Poppy nodded importantly. "He catches all the baddies and puts them in prison so we can all be safe."

"I bet he does." Jade exchanged a knowing glance with Melissa. "I bet he rescues all sorts of animals and people from all sorts of dangers, too."

"He does. *And* he shoos the scary bug monster from under

my bed," Poppy informed her, her little face earnest. "*I'm* going to be a policeman when I grow up, aren't I, Mummy?"

"That's right, sweetie." Melissa smiled distractedly, her gaze still fixed on the gate.

"Daddy's going to teach me, isn't—"

"Oh, thank God." Melissa blew out a sigh of relief as her husband finally reappeared, nursing the cat, which appeared to be subdued, miraculously. No doubt Mark had worked a little bit of his magic on it. The man was as soft as a brush when it came to animals and children. Melissa had no idea how he did the job he did, witnessing such despicable acts of cruelty sometimes, things that really could make a grown man cry. Mind you, she arranged her face into a suitably annoyed expression as he neared her.

Obviously sensing he might be in the doghouse, Mark did his usual trick, disarming her with that sheepish and far too winning smile of his, the look in his soulful brown eyes somewhere between contrite and teasing. DI Mark Cain obviously knew her too well, confident she would forgive him his sins—because she loved him, irrevocably. He was her rock, there for her when she'd been lost, gently helping her find the will to go on when depression had been a dark, cloying blanket threatening to suffocate her. She hadn't wanted to go on after losing Jacob. Wouldn't have, if not for Mark, whose heart had been quietly breaking too. Mark had loved their little baby boy, who'd been so outwardly perfect, but whose tiny lungs couldn't function independently. It had been there in his all-telling eyes. He'd so wanted the family she couldn't give him. The normal functional family that, with his awful, abusive childhood, he'd never had. He'd never made her feel inadequate, not with a look, not with a gesture, but she had felt inadequate. Especially after the miscarriages.

Mark had his flaws, a tendency to withdraw when he was immersed in some horrendous case, seemingly moody to those who didn't know the caring man underneath, but from the first time she'd met him, forcing herself to report her previous boyfriend, a manipulative excuse of a man who'd eventually shown his true colours and hit her, she'd known Mark was one of the good guys. He'd handled the case sensitively, checked up on her afterwards, become her white knight. He'd been a catch. This much Melissa knew, because, having told him that much once, Mark had never missed an opportunity to remind her he was. He didn't do a bad back massage either, she reminded herself, unable to stop her mouth curving into a reciprocal smile as he stopped in front of them.

"He's got her! He's got her!" Poppy exclaimed, bouncing excitedly in Jade's arms. "*Daddy!* You're a hero!" She extended her own small arms, obviously wanting to latch herself onto him, inconsiderate of the poor cat.

"Definitely a hero," Jade agreed emotionally, her eyes filling up as she stepped towards him. Blue eyes, Melissa noticed—striking ice-blue. The sort of eyes you couldn't fail to be mesmerised by.

"Er…" His arms full of her cat, Jade's full of his child, Mark looked nonplussed at how to make the swap. "Jump down a sec, Poppet," he asked Poppy, giving her a reassuring smile. "I'll pick you right back up as soon as Jade has her cat back."

"Is she your baby?" Poppy asked, dutifully allowing herself to be lowered to the ground while Mark passed Jade his furry charge.

"Yes." Jade nodded, reaching to take the cat gently from Mark's arms, and then leaning in to plant a soft kiss on his cheek. "She's my whole world. Thank you, Mark."

"My pleasure," Mark said, looking ever-so-slightly embarrassed as he bent to swoop Poppy up into his arms. And then he almost choked when Poppy locked her arms around his neck and announced, "Daddy's good at making babies, too. He made one with Mummy, didn't you, Daddy? He could make you a proper one if you asked him nicely, couldn't you, Daddy?"

"Um, I, er...*Ahem*." Mark clearly didn't know where to look as Melissa and Jade swapped amused glances.

"I think Daddy's a bit too busy, Poppy," said Melissa, deciding now might be a good time to rescue him.

"Busy causing chaos," the chief fire officer added, a despairing look on his face as he approached. "Don't do a solo again, hey, mate? You, above all people, should know it's not on. No one near the property until it's been cleared by the fire safety officer. I ought to report it. You'll land me in hot water up to my neck if you end up suffering from smoke inhalation."

"Yes, sorry." Mark looked contrite. "I didn't—"

"She wasn't inside. She was in the tree. She got scared and ran before I could catch hold of her," Jade interrupted, clearly seeing that Mark might need rescuing here too. "When will it be? The fire safety officer's visit, I mean," she added, neatly changing the subject.

The fire officer turned to her, and did a double take, literally. Melissa wasn't surprised. Wearing a nightie under the jacket one of the firemen had supplied her, albeit a modest winceyette affair, and with her long blonde hair tousled and just-got-out-of-bed gorgeous, Jade was undeniably attractive. "I'm not quite sure," he said, clearly taken with her. "Do you want to come over to the engine while I make a call?"

Melissa watched them go, Jade cuddling her cat, looking fragile and vulnerable, despite her well-developed curves, the fire officer unable to resist looking sideways at her. "Do you think he's trying to impress her?" she asked Mark.

"Undoubtedly," Mark concurred. "I doubt he'll get very far though."

"Oh? Because she's beautiful, you mean?" She idly wondered

if the girl had had Botox. Her lips and eyebrows were perfect. But then, she supposed, at her age they probably would be.

"Yes." Mark nodded, keeping his gaze fixed forwards. "And young," he added, his mouth curving into a mischievous smile as Melissa glared at him.

"Uh-oh," Mark said, winking at Poppy. "I think I might be in the doghouse, after all."

"Don't be silly." Poppy sighed expansively, giving him a despairing roll of her eyes. "Hercules doesn't have a house. He sleeps on my bed."

"I think he might need to move over to make room for me." Mark laughed, reading the now very peeved expression on Mel's face. "I meant that he's twice her age," he clarified, obviously realising he was on thin ice. "And, yes, Jade is pretty, as you've just pointed out, but not half as gorgeous as you, Mrs. Cain, is she, Poppet?"

"No's the right answer," he whispered, as Poppy looked doubtful, making Melissa laugh. She couldn't help it. The two of them together were mischief in the making. "Especially wearing my shirt," Mark added, rescuing himself this time. "Though I prefer it without the leggings under."

"Hmm?" Melissa wasn't ready to let him off the hook yet.

"You don't wear leggings," Poppy piped up, her huge eyes saucered in astonishment as she squirmed in Mark's arms to stare at him, which caused them both to burst out laughing.

"Only on Sundays," Mark assured her, hoisting Poppy onto one arm to reach in his pocket for his beeping mobile.

"You've met her then?" Melissa asked, easing the shawl to one side to check on Evie, who was still sleeping soundly.

"What?" Mark looked up distractedly from his phone.

Work texting him, Melissa guessed. "Jade." She nodded towards where Jade was gathering quite a uniformed fan club. "I noticed you knew her name, so I assumed you'd met."

"Out jogging. She runs around the same time I do," Mark confirmed, his mind clearly more on the text he'd received than their new neighbour.

"She is very young, isn't she? To own her own home, I mean?"

"That's what I thought," Mark said, his brow furrowed in concentration as he thumbed in a reply. "Her parents passed away recently, apparently. Left her a tidy sum."

"Oh no." Melissa immediately felt for her. Losing her own mum before she'd hit thirty was bad enough, but to lose both parents at Jade's young age would be terrible.

"You have to admire her pluckiness, buying a property, especially one in need of renovation." Mark glanced at Melissa and then back to Poppy, who'd clearly figured out that Daddy's mobile beeping early in the morning meant he would soon be leaving, and who was now fastening herself more firmly around his neck.

"Especially now," Melissa said, looking across to what had been reduced to an uninhabitable property and then towards Jade, who was walking back towards them, looking like a lost soul.

Noticing the fresh tears brimming in the girl's eyes as she reached them, Melissa's heart went out to her. "I take it it's going to take a while?" she said sympathetically.

Nodding, Jade dropped her gaze and nuzzled her cat. "It looks like it was probably an electrical fault, but they can't be sure until they've done all the checks."

"So, what will you do?" Mel asked, trying to make eye contact with Mark, whose phone was now ringing.

"Start the renovation over, I suppose." Jade sighed, and then clearly seeing that Mark needed to take his call and Melissa was struggling to manoeuvre Evie into the crook of her arm, moved to coax Poppy down with promises of chocolate.

Again, Melissa was grateful, if not overjoyed at the chocolate temptation. "She's allergic to dairy," she said, smiling neverthe-less. "But she can have a vegan chocolate bar, since she's being such a good girl, hey, Poppy?"

Amazingly, Poppy allowed Jade to unlatch her from her father, who was incapable of being strict with her.

"Allergic?" Jade looked utterly stricken as she lowered Poppy gently to the ground and took hold of her hand, as Mark stepped away to take his call. "God, how stupid of me," she said, closing her eyes.

"Don't look so mortified." Melissa laughed. "You weren't to know."

"No, but we covered food allergies on my course so it should have occurred to me to ask," Jade said dejectedly. "I did a childcare course in college," she supplied, as Melissa eyed her curiously.

"Well, it will next time." Melissa smiled encouragingly. "I actually meant where will you stay?" The girl was standing in the road with barely a stitch to her name.

Jade shrugged disconsolately. "I have a friend I could ring," she said, looking uncertain.

Again, Melissa felt her heart twist for her. "No family you can call?" she asked carefully.

At that, Jade quickly shook her head, and then looked down at Poppy with a reassuring smile. "I'll sort something out, don't worry," she said, giving her hand a squeeze.

Poppy, though, didn't look convinced. "You can't go out in your nightie," she said, her huge brown eyes aghast. "It's not allowed."

"Come home with us," Melissa offered. It was the least she could do.

"Yay!" Jumping on the spot, Poppy immediately gave that idea her seal of approval.

"I'm sure I can find you something to wear. We're about the

same size," Melissa went on, as Jade hesitated, "if you don't mind jeans or leggings, that is. I spend most of my life up to my eyes in clay when I'm not changing nappies or doing the school run, so it's jeans or evening wear, I'm afraid."

"She can't wear a sparkly dress in the day, Mummy," Poppy pointed out exasperatedly.

"Who can't?" Mark asked, a familiar faraway look in his eyes as he turned back from his call.

"Jade," Poppy informed him. "She's coming home with us. Mummy's going to share some of her clothes with her."

"Good idea." Mark smiled. "Sorry, got to go," he said, bending to plant a kiss on Poppy's nose and another gently to Evie's forehead.

"Um, haven't we forgotten something?" Melissa asked him, as he turned towards his car.

"Damn." Squeezing his eyes closed, Mark turned back to kiss Melissa, now looking definitely distracted, she noted. The call must have been important. She'd seen that look many times before.

"I actually meant your car keys," she said.

"Ah, right." Realising he was minus said car keys, and work jacket, and his ID, having dashed out when he'd spotted the fire, Mark headed swiftly past her back to their own cottage.

Rolling her eyes good-naturedly as he disappeared through the front door, Melissa beckoned Jade and—with Poppy skipping happily alongside her—they strolled more leisurely in the same direction.

Thirty seconds later Mark bowled past them again. "Bye," he said, spinning on his heel to smile apologetically. "Sorry, it's—"

"Urgent. I gathered. Go." Melissa waved him onwards.

"Bye, Daddy!" Poppy called after him. "Love you bigger than the sky."

"Bye, Poppet," Mark called. "Love you bigger than the sky

and all the stars." Blowing her a kiss, he shrugged embarrassedly at Jade and then climbed quickly in the driver's side.

"He's nice, your daddy, isn't he?" said Jade, as Mark started the engine and pulled away.

"Yes." Poppy nodded adamantly. "Mummy says he's too nice for his own good sometimes, but I don't really understand what she means."

"That people might easily take advantage of him," Jade explained, with a knowing smile.

CHAPTER TWO

MARK

Scratching his unshaven chin, Mark swung into the main office to find DCI Edwards pointedly checking his watch. "Problems on the home front, I take it?" he asked him acerbically, his expression one of despair as he looked him over.

Mark followed the man's gaze down to realise the front of his shirt hadn't fared too well after his encounter with the cat and his none-too-elegant scramble over the garden gate to rescue it. As if it mattered what he looked like, with a child on the missing list.

"House fire. Neighbour's," he explained, heading straight to his own office and his filing cabinet for the clean shirt he kept there in case of emergencies—of which there were many lately, with a new baby in the house.

DS Lisa Moyes was two steps behind him.

"Can you bring me up to speed, Lisa?" he asked her, tossing his jacket on his chair and reaching for his shirt buttons.

"It seems the girl was taken from home—assuming she was taken."

"Which is where?" Mark asked.

"Farley Village, close to the Herefordshire border."

Just twenty miles or so away from his own house, Mark realised. God, it could have been one of his kids.

"Parents were celebrating last night, apparently," Lisa went on. "Wife's birthday party. It all went a bit pear-shaped when hubby decided to give her a big surprise and shag one of the young female guests."

Mark arched an eyebrow. "Thoughtful bloke."

"Very. And doing it in their bed was a nice touch, I thought." Lisa smiled flatly.

Mark nodded, tugged off his shirt and reached for the clean one. "So, when did they notice she'd gone?"

"This morning." Lisa sighed. "Mum went up to check on her and found the bed empty. They checked the house and garden and then called us."

Which basically gave them a timeframe that was wide open. Mark tugged in a terse breath. "I take it they argued after the birthday surprise?"

"Volubly, according to the residents of the neighbouring property. At it half the night. Husband makes himself scarce at some point. Wife falls asleep on the sofa with a bottle for company. Fairly standard stuff."

In which case, it was possible the girl had slipped out, seeking to extract herself from what might have been one of many arguments, assuming the husband made a habit of screwing around. Mark's inclination as a kid had been to do the same. Knowing the shouting was a prequel to his father's violence, he'd been petrified. But wherever he went, whatever space he squeezed into, the bastard would always find him. He'd been terrified of the dark, imagining zombies or vampires lurking in shadows, but he'd felt a hell of a lot safer walking the streets at night than he had at home.

"We've searched all the likely places—house and garden again, gardens of properties within walking distance of the house, fields beyond it," Lisa continued. "And we've also managed to contact the wife's sister, who says that she poked her head around the child's door before she left. She confirms Daisy was still in bed."

Daisy. His thoughts immediately went to Poppy, imagining her missing and terrified in the company of some sick individual, and Mark felt something twist inside him.

"We've currently got uniforms going door to door throughout the village. And we're pulling up all local sex offenders," Lisa said, holding the door open for Mark as he hurried with the last of his shirt buttons. "There's something else," she added, as they walked towards the incident room. "Might be relevant, might not, but I'm thinking it makes the husband definitely worth checking out."

Mark read her expression and guessed he wasn't going to like it. "Shoot."

"The young female he was caught *in flagrante* with, she was very young. Just three days past underage, to be precise."

Mark felt his jaw clench. "Tosser. Find out whether he's on the sex offenders' register and make sure we have his PC and phone. If he refuses to hand them over, pull him in."

"On it," Lisa assured him. "Talking of tossers…"

Mark followed her unimpressed gaze to see DS Cummings strolling towards them, a sleazy smirk all over his face.

"Not interrupting anything, am I?" His gaze drifted from Lisa to Mark, who was hastily tucking in his shirt.

"Piss off, Cummings." Mark eyed the man disdainfully and moved past him, only to meet the now decidedly despairing glance of his DCI.

"Problem?" Edwards asked him.

Mark got the message. Even now, years after he'd communicated his feelings to Cummings regarding his sexual harassment of female colleagues, Edwards never missed an opportunity to remind Mark of his "tendency towards hot-headedness."

"Not with me," Mark assured him.

"Good," Edwards said. "DS Cummings will be working with you on this one. Given the gravity of the case, let's leave the personal feelings aside in favour of finding the girl, shall we?"

"Sir." Mark nodded, determined to do just that. Every second spent here was time wasted, as far as he was concerned. This would automatically be escalated as a high-risk case. The fact was, though, if the child had slipped out for whatever reason, with March temperatures averaging seven degrees, death from exposure was probable if she wasn't found soon. Time, therefore, wasn't a luxury they had.

CHAPTER THREE

JADE

Her day at school having been cut short when a water pipe burst, Poppy was chatting excitedly to Jade about her teacher, who'd apparently fainted in morning assembly, as Melissa led the way into the kitchen to dump the shopping bags on the island worktop.

"We heard the headmistress say it was because she was having a baby," Poppy said, attempting to scramble up onto a stool. "But we didn't see one."

Jade swapped amused glances with Melissa. "That's probably because baby wasn't quite ready to make an appearance yet, Poppy," she said, lifting her up.

Poppy nodded thoughtfully as Jade planted her safely on the stool. "Like Hercules' puppies, you mean?"

"Hercules had puppies?"

"Yes," Poppy informed her with a matter-of-fact shrug, as she peered into one of the carriers. "He's a girl dog, but Daddy got mixed up."

"Ah." Jade widened her eyes, which had Melissa laughing.

"He brought the wrong puppy home," she supplied, and then mouthed "rescue dog" in Jade's direction.

Jade nodded, getting the drift. Presumably, they'd decided to get a rescue, but Mark had had to change their choice at the last minute. Perhaps the dog they'd originally chosen had died, or shown unexpected aggression. He really was a lovely man. Poppy didn't know how lucky she was, growing up with a father who loved her like a father should.

"Poppy had already chosen the name, hadn't you, sweetie?" Melissa said, rescuing the eggs from Poppy before they ended up scrambled.

"Yes." Poppy extracted a pack of cookies from the bag—dairy free, as Melissa had pointed out in the supermarket. "I chose the name Hercules, because he had huge paws and Daddy said he was going to grow up to be big and strong," Poppy supplied. "Hercules' puppies weren't very strong though, were they, Mummy?"

"No, sweetie." Smiling sadly, Melissa reached to brush Poppy's too-long fringe from her face.

"They were teeny-weeny." Poppy demonstrated thus with her thumb and forefinger.

"Oh dear. Poor little things. I don't think they could have been ready to make an appearance either." Jade reached to give Poppy a cuddle, as Melissa pointed back to the front door, beyond which little Evie was still fast asleep in the car.

"They couldn't breathe properly," Poppy said, with a shuddery sigh, causing Melissa to hesitate at the kitchen door.

Jade smiled and nodded her on. "I bet that made you sad, Poppy," she said, as Melissa, duly reassured, went to retrieve the child she'd momentarily forgotten about.

"It did," Poppy said. "But I didn't cry too much, because I didn't want to make Hercules sad."

"Well, you're a very considerate, grown-up little girl. I'm impressed," Jade said. "Hercules is very lucky to have you as a friend. I wish I had a friend like you."

"But I *am* your friend," Poppy said, her face earnest as she turned towards her.

Looking into Poppy's huge brown eyes, framed by long, dark eyelashes—her daddy's eyelashes—Jade felt her heart constrict inside her.

She composed herself and arranged her face into a smile. "Well then, I'm very lucky too. And we'll stay friends, I promise. I'm not sure where I'll be living, but as soon as I find somewhere, I'll be in touch. Deal?"

Poppy knitted her forehead into a frown. "But why do you have to find somewhere? You can stay here," she said, splaying her hands to indicate the vast expanse of Melissa's kitchen, which, tastefully decorated, with children's paintings adorning the fridge and colourful height charts pinned to the walls, was comfortable and homey. Jade hated it.

"What, forever?" She chuckled indulgently. "I'm not sure your mummy would be very happy about that."

"Yes, she would," Poppy assured her, with an adamant nod. "Mummy says we should share with our friends and look after those less fortunut than ourselves."

"Fortunate," Jade corrected her. "I'd like to," she said, uncertainly. "We'll see how it pans out, shall we? If Mummy says she wants me to stay, then I'll think about it."

"She will," Poppy said confidently, stretching her arms out and leaning towards her to be helped down. "I'll tell her I want you to stay because you're my bestest friend ever."

"But only if Mummy suggests it first." Jade lifted Poppy off the stool, swung her round and planted her on her feet. "We don't want Mummy to think she's being ganged up on, do we?" she added, in answer to Poppy's obvious confusion.

Poppy shook her head sombrely. "No. Miss Winters says it's cruel to gang up on other people at school."

"Exactly." Jade smiled. "She's a wise woman, your teacher. And you're a sensible girl for listening to her. It's not nice being bullied, Poppy, trust me."

Poppy scanned her face. "Are you being bullied?" she asked her, her eyes clouding with concern.

"No," Jade assured her. "I was once, though, when I was little. It made me cry."

Poppy looked alarmed at that. "I won't let anyone bully you, Jade," she said, sticking her chin up determinedly.

"Nor I you." Jade reached out to brush her hair from her eyes. "We'll look out for each other. Okay?"

"Deal," Poppy said delightedly. "Would you like to see my room?"

Jade extended her hand. "I'd love to."

Poppy slid her own small hand trustingly into Jade's. "It's a bit messy. Nemo's water needs to be changed," she said, as they headed to the hall. "And Baby Annabell was supposed to tidy up her toys, but she forgot. You won't tell Mummy, will you?"

"My lips are sealed." Jade mimed zipping her lips.

"And mine are sealed about your secret chocolate supply." Poppy smiled up at her, doing likewise.

Jade smiled conspiratorially back. "I think we have an understanding." *Win the child over, win the parents over*, she thought, satisfied that she'd got the child on side. She'd felt a sliver of guilt for stuffing a whole chocolate bar down in front of Poppy while Melissa had been in the baby changing room.

CHAPTER FOUR

MELISSA

With Poppy and Evie fed and settled, Melissa gave Jade the guided tour of the house, before the poor woman was driven mad by Poppy's constant chatter and tea parties with an assortment of Peppa Pigs and scarily lifelike baby dolls. Poppy, it seemed, had taken to their guest, declaring Jade her "bestest friend ever." Jade had been wonderful with her, and Melissa could see why she'd chosen childcare as a vocation. She was obviously a natural.

"And this," she said, leading the way into the detached brick garage at the bottom of the back garden, "is what I grandly refer to as my studio. It still needs some work. The roof leaks when it rains and the window's rattling in the frame, but it's my sanctuary... when I can find time."

"Gosh, you have your own kiln?" Jade said, obviously feeling the blast of warm air as they went in.

"It is a bit stifling, isn't it?" Melissa said, as Jade fanned her face with her hand. "I normally have the air con on when I'm working." Reaching to flick the freestanding unit on, she bent to lift Poppy into her arms, lest she wander in the direction of the kiln. "I used to take my pieces to the art university to be fired, but they're extremely fragile once the clay's dried out. I did worry about the safety aspect of having my own kiln with little ones around, but at least it's away from the house. And, as Mark said, if I'm going to be a serious sculptor..."

"Impressive," Jade said, gazing around. "You even have a potter's wheel."

"And a husband who understands my artistic temperament." Melissa smiled, recalling how she'd caught Mark watching her from the doorway one night, before he'd wandered in and done a fair imitation of Patrick Swayze. It had been messy—gloriously messy—but hugely satisfying.

"Fortunately," Jade said, her gaze flitting over her, making Melissa immediately aware of the staple workwear she usually wore—leggings or jeans and tops that wouldn't be ruined by clay or baby sick spatter. Was Jade being the tiniest bit facetious?

But then, seeing Jade's warm smile, Melissa despaired of herself. It was *her*, feeding her own paranoia. She had wondered sometimes how Mark had stuck with her through the dark times. He'd never stopped reassuring her he loved her—down days, artistic temperament and all—but she couldn't help thinking he might wish he was with someone more glamorous, someone who preferred to wear something slightly more alluring to bed than one of her husband's old shirts. She was just someone who "scrubbed up well"—at least according to Detective Sergeant Cummings, who'd voiced such an observation at the last social function they'd been to together.

But then, Mark had been quite into her shirt last night. Melissa smiled quietly, recalling the wicked glint in his chocolate-brown eyes as he told her that imagining her naked beneath it was a serious turn-on, how he'd pinned her to the bed, with not much protestation from her, and worked excruciatingly slowly through each button, finally asking her to keep it on while he made deliciously slow love to her.

Phew. Stop. She'd be dragging him upstairs for a repeat performance as soon as he walked through the door at this rate. Dismissing her errant thoughts—which she absolutely shouldn't be having in company—she turned to her workbench to seat Poppy, who was growing heavy in her arms, at the end of it.

"And this is my latest masterpiece," she said, indicating the sculpture on the bench. It was ceramic dipped in bronze, a kneeling, naked couple embracing, and Melissa was particularly proud of it. Still, she felt a flutter of trepidation in her tummy at showing it to Jade, which was mad considering her work was already stocking the shelves of the local craft centres and Garden & Homes store. Hopefully, the latter would stock her nationwide at some point, depending on whether she could fill the orders.

"Wow!" Jade looked the sculpture over and then back to Melissa in awe. "That's really amazing, Melissa," she said, hesitantly reaching out a hand. "Can I touch it?"

"*Nooo*," Poppy whispered, turning aghast eyes in Jade's direction. "It's not allowed."

"Not allowed with sticky fingers," Melissa reminded her, reaching for the tissue she kept permanently up her sleeve, ready to mop the remnants of Poppy's coconut milk ice cream from her face, which would have the child wriggling like an eel in an instant.

"Go ahead," she said, nodding Jade on. "Sculpture is as much about tactile stimulation as visual, in my mind."

Tentatively, Jade traced the soft curves of the figures with her fingertips. "It's beautiful," she said, sounding genuinely impressed. "Nice pecs," she added, turning to give Melissa a mischievous smile.

"Yes," said Melissa, then, noting where her hand had come to rest, she laughed. "And I enjoyed sculpting that bit too."

"Mummy, what's pecs?" Poppy asked, temporarily distracted from Melissa's face-scrubbing endeavours.

"Muscles," Melissa supplied. "Large ones."

Poppy looked at Melissa, astonished. "But, *Mummeee*, that's a bottom," she pointed out, correctly.

Melissa and Jade exchanged glances and then both laughed out loud. "And a very tactile one, too," Jade assured her.

"What's tactile?" was Poppy's inevitable next question.

"Pleasing to the touch. Now, come on, young lady, scoot," Melissa said, lifting Poppy down from the workbench. "Go and choose a DVD. Daddy will be back soon to get you into your jim-jams. You can have one hour of TV before bed. And don't wake Evie. She's not due a feed yet."

"Yay! *Beauty and the Beast*." Poppy whooped excitedly, charging through the workshop door and up the garden path.

CHAPTER FIVE

JADE

"Do you work in the evenings then?" Jade asked interestedly, as Melissa checked her kiln. The temperature in the garage was now stifling. With that and all these toxic materials about, Melissa's "workshop" didn't appear to be a very child-friendly environment.

"To be honest, since having Evie, it's a case of grabbing time when I can. I have the baby monitor." Melissa nodded towards the monitor parked on another bench, the surface of which was littered with various modelling tools—some of them quite sharp, Jade noted. There was also a dustbin, full of slip-sodden clay. Extremely dangerous, with an inquisitive seven-year-old about. "I don't like to be too far away from her though," Melissa went on. "You never know, do you?"

"No, you certainly don't." Jade sighed, looking appropriately concerned. "You're not that far away here, though, are you? And little Evie's still at the sleep-and-eat stage. You might have to think about a babysitter later, of course."

Melissa looked thoughtfully at her. "Yes."

Bait taken, Jade thought, pleased. "So, you'll be working tonight then?" she asked, happy to leave the seed to germinate now it had been planted.

"I'm off to the university art class," Melissa said, surveying her "masterpiece" and then collecting up the workshop key from the bench. "They have a new life model so I thought I'd grab the opportunity to make a few more sketches."

Pausing before heading for the door, she looked around, as if checking all was in order, although there was precious little order in here. As far as Jade could see, the place was a mess. Not somewhere she'd want to spend time hiding away from her children. Jade would have cherished every second with her baby, if only...

Dismissing that thought, she smiled and widened her eyes in pretend surprise. "What, as in *naked* life model?"

"As the day he was born." Melissa smiled coyly. "Quite a tasty model too," she added, waggling her eyebrows suggestively, which was extremely irritating.

Jade smiled serenely. "The one you've modelled your sculpture on?" she asked, nodding back to the clay monstrosity adorning the workbench.

"The very same." Melissa looked pleased with herself.

"Hmm..." Jade cocked her head to one side, perusing the sculpture interestedly. "Well, I must say I wouldn't mind measuring him up with my pencil."

"You might need a big one," Melissa quipped, and blushed. "But whatever you do don't tell Mark I said that. I wouldn't want him measuring himself up and finding himself lacking."

"My lips are sealed," Jade laughed, zipping her lips. "It's nice of him to help out with the kids. I mean, I know he's their dad and everything, but..."

"Some men wouldn't," Melissa finished knowingly. "True, sadly. Mark can't always, of course, but he tries, depending on his workload."

Jade nodded. "Worth holding onto then?"

"Definitely. And I intend to," Melissa assured her, her expression smug. Like the cat that's got the cream—and knows it. Fittingly, she even had green eyes. They were quite nice, Jade supposed, in a beguiling, childlike way. It was no wonder Mark's natural instinct was to look after the woman. Jade had known him to be that kind of man the first time she met him. A good man. A caring man.

"Talk of the devil," Melissa said, worry creasing her brow as she checked the number on her ringing mobile.

Mark calling, Jade gathered. And what was Melissa's reaction? Delight that he was calling? Excitement? No. She was worried, plainly only for herself. Mark didn't need a vulnerable woman in his life. He needed someone who understood him. Someone to protect him from women like this one, who was clearly taking advantage of him.

"Oh, Mark..." Melissa sighed disappointedly into her phone. "I was just waiting for you to come..." Trailing off, she glanced at Jade, her expression changing to one of concern as she went on, "No, no, it's fine. Of course I understand."

Of course I understand, Jade mimicked silently. The woman wasn't capable of understanding anything but her own needs, as far as Jade could see. Presumably Mark's workload wasn't going to allow him to come home and babysit her children, after all. *Good*. That could work nicely to Jade's advantage.

"It's not the end of the world," Melissa assured him. "I can always reschedule. Just concentrate on what you have to do. Those poor parents. They must be going out of their minds..." Smiling in Jade's direction, she turned to walk down the path a little, in search of privacy.

As if Jade wanted to listen to her false sentiment anyway. Sighing contemptuously, she turned to close the workshop door. She was about to pull it to, when the cat that Mark had rescued slinked past her into the workshop. Jade glanced behind her to see Hercules, panting and prancing on the lawn. Obviously, the dumb animal had been chasing the cat, as if it could ever catch it.

"Scat," she hissed in the dog's direction, glancing quickly over her shoulder, lest Melissa hear her. Hercules might just ruin things for her, Jade had realised. Were it not for the fact that Mark clearly doted on the dog, even talking to the flea-ridden thing when he was out walking it, Jade would have rid herself of that particular problem. She was beginning to wish she had. Rat poison would soon put a stop to it growling at her.

Stepping back into the workshop after the cat, Jade was about to call it—though she wasn't sure by what name, as it was actually a stray—when, in one swift feral leap, it sprang from the floor up to the workbench. *Whoops.* Jade winced as the sculpture teetered. And then surveyed the cat thoughtfully as it padded to the end of the bench and back again to weave itself around the sculpture, which really was rather close to the edge.

Damn. Jade's plan to close the door and let the cat do its worst was foiled as she realised that Melissa had finished her call. She couldn't afford for her to peer back and see that she'd shut the bloody cat in with her precious works of art. However...

"*Shit!*" she said out loud, hearing Melissa coming towards her, and then moved—with the agility of the cat—across to the bench. "I've got it. Don't panic," Jade said, her best relieved expression in place as Melissa followed her in. "I saw it teetering." She nodded towards the sculpture, which was now on its side, resting on her hand. "Hercules chased Felix in." She hurriedly christened the cat. "I'm really sorry. I moved as quickly as I—"

"Oh God, don't be," Melissa cut in, her concern only for her sculpture as she stepped across to unburden Jade of it. "It was Hercules' fault. She's always up to mischief. It's like having another child sometimes, I swear."

Righting the sculpture on the bench, she turned to look at Jade. "Thank you," she said. "Thank God you were here."

Jade saw the woman close her eyes, clearly immensely relieved, and considered that she'd earned herself another brownie point. "But preferably catless?" she asked, turning to pluck the newly christened cat up.

"It wasn't Felix's fault, was it, Felix?" Melissa drew a hand down the cat's back as Jade cuddled it. "It was that naughty Hercules, wasn't it, sweetie?"

Oh no. Jade wasn't sure she could handle this woman baby-talking to animals, but she smiled brightly anyway.

"Bad Hercules," Melissa said, leading the way out again and making sure to lock the door once Jade had exited behind her. "Behave." She scowled in the dog's direction. "Or you'll be tied up."

Jade mentally shook her head. She would swear to God the woman was waiting for the dog to acknowledge her as she wagged a finger at it.

"Problem?" she asked, as they headed back towards the house. "Sorry, I didn't mean to eavesdrop, but I gathered it was Mark calling."

"He's been detained." Melissa sighed resignedly. "It can't be helped," she added quickly. "It looks as if it might be a child abduction case."

"Oh no. How heartbreaking." Jade's step slowed. She glanced at Melissa, suitably stricken, though she imagined the only people the abusive, alcoholic parents would be heartbroken for were themselves.

"Dreadful." Melissa shuddered. "Having little ones, Mark always takes these cases to heart."

"You're disappointed though, I bet," Jade ventured sympathetically. "I don't blame you. I would be. It can't be easy being cooped up with two little ones all day."

"I am a bit," Melissa admitted. "But then, I should really be counting my blessings. I can't begin to imagine what the parents of that little girl must be going through. What the poor child might be going through."

Stopping at the patio doors, Melissa wrapped her arms about herself, a troubled look clouding her eyes, as if she were imagining it. As if someone like her, living her perfect life, *could* ever imagine what it was like to be so traumatised as a small child that you prayed to God to make you dead and take you to heaven.

"Me neither." Smiling empathetically, though she was sure the little girl was better off where she was, Jade gently placed a hand on Melissa's forearm. "Poor Mark. I hope he finds her."

"Oh God, I hope so, too." Melissa pulled in a shuddery breath. "He'll be absolutely devastated. He can't bear even the thought of children being hurt in any way."

"I know." Jade sighed, recalling again the first time she'd met him, the genuine grief in his eyes. "You can see he's a caring man," she added quickly. "And he obviously adores his kids. I don't envy him. Look, it's only a suggestion, but why not let me babysit?"

Melissa looked uncertain.

"I have got my childcare qualifications, after all, so you might as well make use of me. And I can always call you if there's a problem."

"Of course you do," she said, still looking a little uncertain. "But...are you sure? It's a bit of a cheek."

"It's no problem at all," Jade assured her. "Like I said, I'm here anyway. It's the least I can do after all your kindness. And, to be honest, after this morning's events, chilling out with a DVD sounds like heaven."

Melissa glanced through the patio doors to check on Poppy, who was already sitting cross-legged in front of the TV in anticipation of *Beauty and the Beast*. "You've got the job," she said, smiling gratefully.

"I wish," Jade said, with a sigh. "I'm job hunting at the moment. But I've no idea how I'm actually going to apply for any jobs now I'm homeless."

CHAPTER SIX

MELISSA

"I usually let her catnap until eight, and then wake her for her feed," Melissa said, dashing into the lounge to grab her sketch pad and pencil case from the coffee table. She looked around for her shoulder bag and then remembered she'd hung it on the stairs. Honestly, she'd swear to God that giving birth had addled her brain.

"There's milk in the fridge. I generally warm it in a bowl." Realising she was running late, she checked her watch—and dropped her sketch pad. "You'll find one in—"

"Melissa, I can manage," Jade assured her, reaching to pick up the pencils that had spilled from the pencil case as Melissa bent to retrieve her pad. "And anything I can't find, Poppy can point me to. Right, Poppy?"

"Yeth," Poppy said, around the thumb plugged into her mouth. "You can go now, Mummy."

Dismissed, thought Melissa, eyeing the ceiling and then smiling gratefully at Jade as she handed her pencils back to her. "Don't miss me too much, will you?" she said, going over to plant a kiss on Poppy's cheek.

"I won't," Poppy said, attempting to peer around her at the TV.

"Well, that's reassuring." Melissa sighed, theatrically rolling her eyes at Jade.

But rather than feeling put out by Poppy's apparent indifference to her presence, Melissa was pleased. Jade, it seemed, had definitely won her over, which was a huge relief. Their last baby-sitter, the daughter of a friend, hadn't been a hit, and Melissa had been reluctant to bring in another, which wasn't conducive to she and Mark spending any quality time together. Jade had also been fabulous with Evie, feeding her earlier without a hiccup. She really was a natural with children.

"Bed by seven thirty at the latest, young lady," she said to Poppy. "And don't forget to brush your teeth."

"*Mummeee…*" Poppy sighed exasperatedly. "We're missing the film."

"Right, I can see where I'm not wanted." Shaking her head in amusement, Melissa headed for the door. "I'll be back in time for Evie's ten o'clock feed," she told Jade, and then stopped. "*Damn!* I forgot to get milk out the freezer for the morning."

"I'll do it." Jade spun Melissa back towards the front door as she turned in the direction of the kitchen. "Go. Not too much licking of pencils or drooling."

Melissa laughed. "I'll try not to," she assured her, and then hesitated again at the front door. "You know, you're quite wel-come to stay a while if you need to, Jade. I mean, I wouldn't want you to feel obliged to babysit just because you're here, but… Well, we have space if you need it while you sort yourself out."

Jade beamed. "I'd love to, as long as you're sure. It would be a huge weight off my mind."

"Positive." Melissa smiled warmly. "Just don't let madam here wrap you around her little finger." She nodded towards Poppy, who was listening eagerly from the lounge doorway.

"Does this mean you're staying forever and ever, Jade?" Poppy asked, her eyes wide with excitement.

Jade exchanged a knowing glance with Melissa. "Well, not forever and ever," she said, turning back to her charge. "But for the moment, yes."

"Yippee!" Poppy jumped with glee. "I told you. I told you."

"So you did," Jade said, steering her back into the lounge. She smiled at Melissa over her shoulder. "See you when you get back."

"Thanks, Jade. You're a godsend. I'm sure Mark will be pleased you're staying for a while," she called, dashing out.

"Oh, I'm sure Mark will too." Smiling, Jade settled down on the sofa, extending her arm for Poppy to snuggle comfortably under.

CHAPTER SEVEN

MARK

Driving home, Mark was thinking about Daisy Evans, the missing little girl. There had been no evidence of a forced entry, and he was considering the possible involvement of the parents in her disappearance, in particular the father's. Although Michael Evans had been caught having sex with a girl who was only just past the age of consent, Mark believed he hadn't known how old she was. The guy was an ex-footballer, and the girl was a member of his fan club. She was apparently besotted with him, and had told him she was eighteen. It didn't make what he'd done much more palatable, but her friends had corroborated his version of events. He'd had pornographic images on his PC, but nothing illegal. No suspect images or messages on his phone. He also had an alibi for the time in which his daughter disappeared. Mark wasn't enamoured of the man any more than he was of Cummings—who, laughably, had adopted a stance of moral outrage at Evans' "obvious sexual exploitation of a sixteen-year-old"—but the guy's anguish had been palpable.

The meeting with the mother had been harrowing. Mark's initial assumption on learning the parents had been arguing, so drunk they hadn't noticed their child was missing, had been a kneejerk reaction, one born of his own childhood memories of cowering in corners as arguments escalated. It had prejudiced his thinking. Daisy's mother had been beyond devastated, blaming herself. She'd broken down as they left. Pausing on the drive of the house, a detached country property worth a fair sum, Mark had heard her heaving sobs as the front door closed. Whatever the future of their relationship, if Daisy wasn't found, God help them, the parents would both blame themselves for the rest of their lives.

Dammit. Frustrated, Mark banged the heel of his hand against his steering wheel. They *had* to find her. But *where?* Sighing, he ran a hand wearily over his neck. He needed some downtime. He needed to check his girls were warm and safe in their beds, and touch base with Mel. He wished he could do more than touch base… her warm body up close was an appealing thought right now. Whatever shit he was dealing with, he always felt safe in her arms. She reckoned he'd been her white knight; that somehow he'd saved her, but Mark knew it was the other way around. He'd had relationships before her—too many, because with no role models in his life, he didn't know how to do relationships—but Mel had shown him how, made him believe that love was possible, that he was a fully functioning, normal person, despite his dysfunctional background and his conviction that bad blood would out and he would inherit the traits of his abusive father. She'd made him believe in himself, because she'd believed in him. She'd loved him. His love for her… it scared him sometimes. The all-consuming love he felt for his children terrified him. His family were his lifeblood. He simply wouldn't know how to be without them.

Noting Mel's car wasn't there as he pulled into the drive, it took a second before Mark remembered her art class. It looked like she'd gone after all. Who was watching the kids? Their last babysitter, though she'd come recommended, hadn't been up to much. Or rather, she had, if coming home early to find her in a steamy clinch on the sofa with her boyfriend had been any indication. Neither he nor Mel was prudish, but the cider the guy had brought with him was definitely not on. Emily, a mutual friend, helped out when she could, but weren't the Chandlers away on holiday?

Mark checked his mobile as he walked to the front door, only to find the battery had died, which might explain why he hadn't received a text from Mel. She would undoubtedly have sent him one. The lights were on, he noted. The T.V, too. Peering around the lounge door, he saw that it was empty, though the knot of worry in his stomach was quashed at the obvious signs of normalcy. He headed upstairs, figuring the kids would be in bed and the babysitter might be checking on them.

Poppy's door was ajar, and he could see her fast asleep in bed, Hercules curled up protectively at her feet. Mark breathed out a breath he hadn't realised he was holding in. Then, instructing Hercules to stay, he carried on towards the nursery, where he stopped and cocked his head to one side. Well that was a bloody relief. Tugging his collar loose, Mark listened for a second at the partially open door before going in. It seemed they did have a new babysitter, and she sang like an angel.

"*Hush, little baby, don't say a word,*" came a melodic voice from inside. "*Mama's going to buy you a mockingbird. If that mockingbird won't sing, Mama's going to buy you a diamond ring.*" Mark pushed the door open, and then, noting she had her back towards him, Evie nestled on her shoulder, he waited again rather than frighten her. He was mildly amused when she skipped straight to the last verse, obviously not knowing the words in between: "*Hush, little baby, don't you cry, Daddy loves you and so do I.*"

Smiling, Mark tapped on the door as she started the lullaby over. Jade spun around, the alarmed look on her face making it clear he had scared her, despite his efforts not to.

Shit. Mark stepped forward. "Sorry," he said. "I should have called up from the hall, but I thought the kids might be asleep. Are you okay?"

"Yes, sorry. My fault. I should have been paying attention."

"You were." Mark smiled. "To Evie." He nodded towards his baby girl, who was awake but sleepy, and perfectly content on Jade's shoulder. "I'll make sure to announce myself in future."

Jade smiled back, though she still looked rather flustered at him looming in the doorway. With good reason. Averting his gaze, Mark stopped short of moving further into the room to say hello to Evie. That possibly wouldn't be a prudent move, what with Jade wearing a strappy top and pyjama shorts under her dressing gown. Obviously she was staying with them, which given her circumstances was fine, but...Christ, this was awkward. Mark really wished he'd remembered to plug his phone in earlier.

"She's been as good as gold," Jade said, stepping towards him. "Haven't you, angel?"

Pressing a kiss to Evie's soft downy head, she looked back to Mark. "I was just about to pop her down for a nap before Melissa gets back, but I'm assuming you want to have a quick cuddle? Sorry about being in my PJs, by the way," she said, handing Evie gently to him. "I needed to wash the smoke out of my hair, so I grabbed a quick shower before I fed her."

And Mark felt like a bit of an idiot. Clearly, he was the only one feeling uncomfortable. And clearly it showed. "Thank you, I would very much like a quick cuddle," he said softly, marvelling afresh at the perfect wonder of his tiny child as he gathered her close.

CHAPTER EIGHT

JADE

Making sure Evie was safe in his arms, Jade nodded towards the door. "I'll just go and sort a few things out," she said to Mark, offering him another bright smile as she took her leave.

Once on the landing, she looked back, her heart flipping and her pelvis dipping as she watched this tall, dark, broad-shouldered man nestling his baby close.

He didn't yet know who she was, of course. Jade had made sure he wouldn't. She'd thought it better that way initially. He was fundamentally a good man, after all. She wouldn't want him to do anything that went against his nature. He would have to be persuaded gently that the life he was living was all a façade. That, as much as he loved his children, he could never be fulfilled living with a woman who'd used those children to trap him. He'd sensed her, though. It had been obvious from the appreciative look in his eye as he'd glanced at her figure—which Melissa's pyjama set enhanced quite nicely. He, too, felt the undeniable chemistry between them.

In time, he would know. Smiling fondly, she turned to the bedroom the bitch wife had said she could use. Soon, Mark would realise they were two souls connected, destined to be together forever.

CHAPTER NINE

MELISSA

Mark almost bowled into Melissa as he came out of the front door—on his way back to work, she assumed. "Hey." He smiled. "How's the new male exhibitionist?"

"Excellent," Melissa said, with a mischievous wink.

"That good, hey?" Despite his best efforts to look annoyed, Mark's mouth twitched up at the corners. "A lesser man might feel threatened, you know."

Melissa leaned in to press a kiss to his cheek, allowing her hand to stray around back to clutch a handful of his very pleasingly toned rear as she did. "Good job you're a bigger man then, isn't it, DI Cain?"

Mark furrowed his brow at that. "Er, thanks. I think."

"I take it this was a flying visit?" Melissa eased back to eye him seriously.

Mark nodded regretfully. "Afraid so. Sorry."

"No progress then?" Melissa asked, a shiver of apprehension running through her as she read Mark's gloomy expression.

"Not much, no," he said, sighing wearily. "I have to get back to the station. Organise available bodies for searches come first light."

He really did look tired. Melissa noted the shadows under his eyes as he leaned to brush her lips with a kiss and move around her. She wished he could stay.

She wondered if they would despatch police divers to the river. Organise fingertip searches in fields and woods? She knew from experience how these things progressed.

"I'll see you soon. Take care," she said, as he climbed into his car. It would be useless saying what she really meant: remember to eat, and try to get some sleep somewhere along the line. Learning the missing girl was around Poppy's age and knowing Mark as she did, she very much doubted he would be doing much of either.

"Oh, and Mark," she called, as he reached for his door. "I sent you a text earlier. Did you see it?"

"No, sorry. Mobile wasn't charged."

"Jade's staying for a while. I thought I'd better let you know in case you run into her wandering around upstairs when you get back."

"I've already had the pleasure." Mark smiled wryly. "She's qualified, presumably?"

"Abundantly," Melissa assured him. "She did a childcare course at college. I thought she might able to help out with the girls."

"Have you checked out her references?"

"Of course." Actually, she hadn't, but she could have hardly done that this evening. She'd do it first thing tomorrow. "Mark Cain, you're not questioning my judgement, are you?" Melissa cocked her head to one side, eyeing him pseudo-disparagingly.

"Never. Wouldn't dare."

Melissa laughed as Mark cringed in mock-terror and hurriedly closed his door. Watching him drive away, she turned to let herself in, trying not to mind that he was dashing off again. Policing was what he did, and she loved him for it, loved that he cared enough to want to try to make the world a safer place— but she missed him. And she worried incessantly for him, more so when he was dealing with cases involving children. With his own abysmal childhood, he seemed to feel their every hurt. But she wished he wouldn't blame himself when he couldn't fix that hurt. When he couldn't make their world a safer place.

He would slip out at night, sometimes, when sleep eluded him. Walking the streets, Melissa guessed, trying to get into the mind of a young child who might be a runaway, understanding why they might have run. He'd been reluctant to share his past secrets with her at first, imagining himself less of a man for admitting that his childhood ghosts haunted him still. He really was an enigma: strong and macho on the outside, yet deeply caring on the inside.

It had taken them a while to find each other again after Jacob. For her to come back to him. Mark had been patient—there to hold her when she'd needed holding, to catch her if she fell. And instinctively, no words necessary, he'd known when she'd needed him to move beyond holding. His lovemaking had been so gentle, so perceptive of her needs. And when she'd finally allowed herself to reach that sweet climax, he'd held her again while she sobbed in his arms. Held her like he might never let go.

She'd loved him more than she'd thought possible that night.

She hoped he was charging his phone. Dumping her sketch pad on the hall table and hanging her bag over the rail, she reached for her phone to text him again as she climbed the stairs to check on the children. She needed to remind him how much she still loved him.

Pausing at Poppy's door, she was about to go in when she noticed Jade emerging from the main bedroom. "Jade?" she said, surprised to see she was dressed in no more than a short towel.

"Ooh, hell." Jade whirled around. "Sorry. I didn't hear you come in. I was just about to take a shower but I couldn't find any shampoo in the main bathroom. I *really* need to wash the smell of smoke from my hair."

"Ah." Melissa nodded, relieved. For a second, she'd thought… She'd no idea what she'd thought, actually. "I'll fetch some from the en suite," she said, making a mental note to stock up on bathroom essentials other than baby products. And to leave more than a hand towel out.

CHAPTER TEN

MELISSA

"Morning," Jade said brightly, as Melissa came into the kitchen.

Melissa blinked, surprised to see everyone up and at it. "Good morning," she said, turning her gaze to Poppy, who, amazingly undistracted by early morning TV, was seated at the table, happily munching away on cereal—made with oat milk, of course.

"Morning, Mummy," Poppy said, equally brightly.

Bleary-eyed, Melissa wandered across to plant a kiss on the top of her head, peering into her bowl as she did. "I thought you didn't like cornflakes," she said, noting the distinct absence of morning must-have Coco Pops.

"I do now." Poppy shovelled in another spoonful. "Jade said it will make my hair grow like hers."

Melissa followed her daughter's wishful gaze to Jade's luxuriant blonde locks. It would certainly be some achievement, given that Poppy took after her father with her dark colouring and chocolate-brown eyes, but Melissa was happy to play along if it meant the battle of breakfast was no more.

Smiling, Melissa accepted the glass of fresh orange juice Jade handed to her, and headed towards the back door, where daughter number two also appeared to be content.

"She's had her early-morning feed," Jade said, as Melissa peered into the pushchair. "You were fast asleep, so I thought I'd bring her down. I wasn't sure whether you liked her to have a bit of fresh air, but it's such a beautiful day. I hope it's okay?"

"Perfect. Wonderful, in fact." Resisting the urge to plant a kiss on Evie's perfect cupid lips, Melissa tucked her shawl up and moved quietly away. She wasn't directly in the sun, but warm enough. Jade was right—it really was a gorgeous day.

Melissa looked her competent house guest over. Jade looked like a ray of sunshine, exuding vitality and health. She even made Melissa's clothes look good—a pre-baby striped yellow T-shirt, which Melissa didn't think suited her new, fuller breasted look, teamed with a pair of blue leggings.

"What do you fancy for breakfast?" Jade asked, heading to the toaster, where two hot slices popped on cue.

I'll have whatever you're having. Feeling the slightest bit wishwashy, and definitely mumsy, Melissa sighed inwardly. With her pale complexion and uninspiring ginger locks, which Mark kindly termed copper and which would be scarily frizzy at this time in the morning, she probably looked like one of the living dead by comparison. She couldn't believe she'd slept so long. The hot chocolate Jade had kindly made her last night appeared to have done its job. Obviously, she'd needed the sleep, but she didn't feel a lot better for it.

"I'll grab some cereal," she said, yawning widely—and receiving a reprimand from Poppy as she did for not placing her hand over her mouth.

"Sorry." Melissa stifled another yawn. "I'm obviously more tired than I thought I was."

"I'm not surprised, trying to run your own business with two little ones to look after—you must be absolutely frazzled," Jade said, glancing at her sympathetically as she sailed by with a tray, on which was the toast, Melissa noticed, along with a tumbler of orange and a black coffee. "Why don't you go and grab a shower? It might make you feel human."

Now Melissa definitely felt like one of the living dead.

"I'll just pop this in to Mark and then—"

"Mark?" Melissa gawked. "He's here?"

Jade stopped, looking puzzled. "In the lounge. He came home to get changed. He went to get a nightcap and the next thing I knew, he'd fallen fast asleep on the sofa."

Melissa glanced at her, confused. She felt as if she'd slept the clock around and woken up to find herself in another time zone. It was stupid—paranoid probably—but... Mark never went into the lounge for a nightcap in the middle of the night. He'd previously had a spell of drinking more than was good for him once. They both had, when life had been cruel. Since then, though, he'd have wine with his meal, but rarely a nightcap. If he was keeping the hours he was now, it meant he was working a case that needed him to be clearheaded. He would grab a cold drink from the kitchen and then come straight upstairs. If he couldn't sleep, then he would walk—with the dog, if he could coax her out without waking Poppy.

"He looked so exhausted I didn't like to disturb him," Jade went on. "I didn't like to think of him charging off again without eating anything either, so... Are you all right, Melissa? You look a bit pale."

Melissa was now feeling very baffled. She'd taken a paracetamol last night. At least she'd thought she had. She hoped to God she hadn't picked up the wrong packet. The sleeping tablets she'd been prescribed after losing Jacob were still in her bathroom cabinet. No, surely not. She'd checked the packet. Hadn't she? But still, she felt definitely woozy.

"What time did he come in?" she asked, aware it must have been after the last feed she'd given Evie. The baby had woken unusually early, at around two thirty rather than three thirty, which is when she'd taken the paracetamol.

"About five," Jade said, looking puzzled.

And she was up? Melissa was growing more confused by the second.

"I heard someone downstairs." Jade answered the question she hadn't asked. "I was worried about the children so I crept down."

"That was brave of you," Melissa said, in all sincerity. Jade wouldn't have known it was Mark.

"It could have been a bug monster!" Poppy said, aghast.

"In which case, I would have poked his beady bug eyes out," Jade assured her, looking fierce.

"With a big sharp knife," Poppy said, narrowing her eyes in an attempt to look fierce too.

"Probably not a good idea, Poppy," Melissa suggested, "unless you want to end up in prison. It's not allowed."

"But what about if it was a burglar?" Poppy asked, her eyes widened innocently.

"Still not allowed. In any case, it wouldn't be. Our house is very secure. Now, finish your breakfast, young lady. And then shoes on, please, or you'll be late for school."

"Sorry," Jade said, as Poppy huffed and went back to her cereal. "I *really* should have thought that one through."

Melissa looked up to the clock and wondered whether it would be acceptable to do the school run in her husband's crumpled shirt and leggings. Then she caught sight of Jade, still standing with the tray, looking uncertain and somewhat dejected.

And Melissa felt like a cow. The girl had let her lie in, obviously done her best to take over the helm while she'd been sleeping, and what had *she* done? Come over all proprietorial, as if her space were being threatened, and promptly burst her bubble. Her friend Emily had had a babysitter for a while, while she and Adam were busy setting up their holiday chalet business, and she'd once admitted she'd felt her nose had been put out of joint, even confiding she'd been the tiniest bit jealous at first, when the babysitter appeared to look after her child better than she did.

Chastising herself, Melissa smiled. "It's okay," she said, reaching to give Jade's shoulders a squeeze and then relieving her of the tray. It was nice of her to think of Mark, but if anyone was going to take him breakfast, it was Melissa. Not that he could expect such service on a regular basis. "Poppy has a vivid imagination," she said. "She's very good at storytelling. She must take after her mad, arty mother."

Jade looked relieved, though her smile was a little less zingy than it had been.

"I'll take this in and see if I can rouse my husband from his slumber," Melissa said, supposing she'd have to get used to setting boundaries, but perhaps more subtly in future. "You could do me a huge favour, though, if you wouldn't mind, and take Poppy to school. I'd hate to embarrass her in front of her friends."

Jade's smile widened at that. "You look fine," she said. "Great legs. But of course I wouldn't mind taking her. Come on, Poppy. Shoes on, sweetie. You can't possibly scrape that bowl any cleaner."

Extending her hand, Jade waited for Poppy to scramble down and latch onto it.

"Jade…" Melissa stopped her, as they headed for the hall. "Thank you. You've done an amazing job. I really would have been lost without you this morning."

"No problem," Jade assured her. "Poppy and Evie have been as good as gold."

Melissa hesitated. She hadn't been considering a babysitter just yet, though it was something she had on her future to-do list. She wasn't sure what kind of employment Jade might be looking for, but working here whilst overseeing the repairs to her own property might actually suit both of them, assuming she hadn't already scared her off. "Jade, it's just a thought, but if it's a babysitting job you're looking for, I could certainly use some help here."

"Really?" Jade looked hopeful.

"Really." Melissa looked around, indicating the general bedlam. "I was considering growing an extra pair of hands, but… I'd pay you the going rate, of course."

"That would be brilliant. Perfect, in fact. Yes, I'd love to." Jade beamed. And then she turned her smile on Mark, who had just appeared in the doorway, looking possibly more bleary-eyed than Melissa felt.

Smiling uncertainly back, Mark stepped aside to allow Jade to exit. "Ahem," he said, as Poppy skipped by without a word. "I thought you loved me bigger than the sky?"

Melissa heard Poppy's audible intake of breath as she realised she'd ignored him, and watched with amusement as she abandoned Jade's hand and charged towards her father. "I do!" she declared. "Bigger than the whole moon!"

"Glad to hear it." Only just managing to scoop her up as she threw herself at him, Mark laughed and smooched her neck, which had Poppy in wriggle mode in an instant.

"*Daddeee*," she said, rubbing her cheek as she pulled back to inspect his face, "you need to shave."

"Yes, *ma'am*. Immediately, ma'am." Lowering her to the floor, Mark planted her back on her feet, and then saluted. "Bye, Poppet," he said. "Have a good day, and remember the Cain motto."

"Be wise, stay vigilant." Serious-faced, Poppy repeated the motto Mark drummed into her every morning. Translated: *don't go near strangers*. "Wilco." She nodded, blew him a kiss, then turned to catch up with Jade as she opened the front door.

"Whoops. Hang on a sec." Mel put down the tray and turned to fetch a spare front-door key from the hooks on the utility door. "In case I'm in the shower or out in the garage when you get back," she said, handing the key to Jade.

"Brilliant." Jade smiled. "I might pop by the bank and order a new debit card, but I shouldn't be too long. Bye, Mark. You stay vigilant out there, too."

"I will," Mark assured her. Smiling as he watched them go, he turned to Melissa. "I think our temporary house guest's a hit."

"Um, actually, she might be more semi-permanent." Melissa quickly picked up the tray, hoping to distract him from the fact that she hadn't discussed hiring Jade with him first.

"Oh?" Mark arched an eyebrow curiously. "How so?"

"Well, I know we weren't thinking of taking anyone on just yet, but…" Melissa shrugged and smiled. "She's our new baby-sitter. I hope you approve."

Mark considered, and then nodded. "Absolutely," he said. "If it means I get served breakfast on a regular basis."

"Don't bank on it, Detective," said Melissa, pinching a slice of his toast.

With Evie settled back into her cot, Melissa finally stepped into the shower, allowing the hot water to cascade over her and wash her awake. She was soaping herself luxuriantly when Mark passed by the en suite door. And then stepped back for a better view.

"You do know that could be deemed provocation, Mrs. Cain?" he said, leaning against the doorframe, an arm across his chest, one hand grazing his unshaven chin as he watched her thoughtfully through the shower door.

Melissa smiled. God, he looked delicious, sexily dishevelled. "And that, DI Cain, could be deemed voyeurism."

"Guilty." Mark smiled, stepping into the bathroom. "I, er, don't suppose there's room for two in there, is there?"

"That depends on how good with the soap you are, DI Cain."

"Very," Mark assured her throatily, hastily stripping off his shirt and making short shrift of the rest of his clothes.

Melissa felt a thrill of anticipation as he stepped in behind her to demonstrate his skills. Burying his face in her neck, trailing his tongue over the already soapy wetness of her skin, Mark took his time, reaching around her to gently circle each sensitive nipple, touching her with slow, soft caresses and feather-light brushes with his thumbs, each touch so exquisitely pleasurable it was almost painful.

"Okay?" he checked with her, that alone almost bringing Melissa to sweet orgasm there and then, reminding her what a good lover he was, how caring of her needs. He hadn't been particularly sure of himself when she'd first met him—not surprising, given how his confidence had been knocked out of him. His uncertainty, though, had been nothing but endearing in a man so good-looking. And he'd learned fast. There was nothing they wouldn't do now, instinctively moving together as one. Nothing they hadn't done.

A low moan escaped her as he slid one hand over the soft round of her tummy.

"Have we got time for this?" she gasped, as he moved lower.

"Always," he said huskily, hitching her towards him. She ached for him; she needed him. She wanted to slide her hands over him, soap his broad shoulders, to trail them down over his chest, his taut stomach.

Feel his body up close to hers.

She caught her breath as he slid a finger carefully inside her, his thumb now expertly circling, building her to heights of ecstasy she wasn't sure she could bear.

"Beautiful," he breathed, with such intensity that, despite her baby blues self-doubt, she truly believed she was.

"Now?" he asked her.

Melissa could only moan her affirmation as he pulled her closer. With one hand propped against the wet tiles of the wall, his other supporting her, he eased himself inside her, pacing himself, checking with her, as if she were made of precious porcelain after all her body had been through. She loved him so much for that. And then he increased the rhythm, in tune with her, until he was plunging deep inside her.

CHAPTER ELEVEN

JADE

Bitch. Stunned, Jade backed silently out of their bedroom to press herself against the landing wall, her stomach clenching painfully inside her as she heard Mark's deep, throaty moan. Primal urges, that's all it was. He was a man. He had needs.

Jade tried to temper her fury, squeezing her eyes closed to block out the images of him making love to another woman. It was only because she was convenient. A convenient fuck! Why else would he?

Peeling herself from the wall, Jade tried to slow the rapid beat of her heart, and then, pausing at the nursery door, made her way quietly back to the stairs. She needed to be calm, she reminded herself. The epitome of niceness.

Notching up her chin, her back straight, Jade descended the stairs. Stopping in front of the hall mirror, she tried to compose herself, working to obliterate all emotion from her face.

Walking into the kitchen and calmly opening the dog food cupboard, she selected a chew from the plastic storage box therein and then headed for the back door, collecting the key for Melissa's workshop from the hook on the utility door as she went.

The cat was on the patio, basking in the sun. Whispering reassuringly to it, Jade picked it up. She actually couldn't wait to be rid of it. What was Melissa thinking, allowing a cat free run of the place? It could easily slink upstairs to lap at lips fresh with milk and end up suffocating her baby. Irresponsible cow.

The dog was on the lawn, its head plopped dejectedly between its paws. The stupid mutt had clearly realised the cat was too clever for it by far.

"Stay," she instructed it, and then headed to the workshop with the cat. Once inside, she placed the cat on the bench, using a sliver of the chew to entice it to stay there, and then went over to the window. Melissa was right, it was definitely in need of repair. Jade eased the latch and opened the window, and then, scanning the tools on the workbench underneath it, she selected a knife-like sculpting tool, which pushed easily between hinges and frame. It took a couple of heaves, but both hinges came away from the rotting wood fairly easily.

"Stay, Felix," she said sweetly, running a hand the length of the cat's back and up its tail as she passed it. Feeding it another nugget of chew, she moved to the sculpture, trailing a hand languidly over that, tilting it sideways, and then allowing it to fall and crash satisfyingly to the floor.

Alarmed, the cat jumped down, but Jade was already at the door, slipping sleekly out and closing it behind her. It didn't take much to push the window in. One hard shove was enough. Jade was impressed with the dog's agility skills, she had to admit, as she watched it sail through the windowless hole after the chew she threw into the workshop.

Jade furrowed her brow as she let herself out through the gate beyond the garage. Might it have cut its paws on the glass, she wondered. Briefly.

CHAPTER TWELVE

MARK

"I wasn't drinking on my own in the small hours," Mark assured Melissa, as he towelled his hair with one hand and checked a text from Lisa Moyes with his other. "We were out of coke in the fridge so I—"

Reading the text, Mark stopped: *Forensics back. Stain on stairs confirmed blood. DNA match to Daisy.*

Shit! Cursing silently, Mark tossed the towel aside. He was pulling on his clothes when he heard a distressed mewl and frenzied barking from the garden. Heading fast for the window, Mel close behind him, he looked out to see the cat scaling a tree as if its tail were on fire. Mark waited a second, expecting Hercules to come belting after it. More frantic barking but no sign of the dog. There followed a brief silence, followed by a sudden heart-flipping, high-pitched yelping that meant she was in trouble. Serious trouble, Mark realised, sensing the dog's escalating panic.

Turning, he raced to the landing, while Mel grabbed up her dressing gown, tugging it on and stuffing her feet into flip-flops to follow him.

"I'll go," Mark said, nodding towards the nursery. He was probably being neurotic, but his inclination right now wasn't to leave the children on their own, and out of hearing distance.

Once in the kitchen, Mark stopped to search for the workshop key, but it wasn't hanging from its usual hook.

Dammit! "Mel, the key!" he shouted, and headed out to the garden, where the dog's cries were growing more urgent by the second. What the hell had happened? All became clear as he neared the workshop and saw that the window—which he'd added to his mental to-do list but hadn't yet fixed—was missing. The cat must have gone in, chased by Hercules, who was now stuck inside the workshop.

"Stay, Hercules," he said, calmly but firmly, as he approached the empty frame. "It's okay, girl." Mark peered in, and swallowed, hard. "Okay, girl, stay. I'm coming."

"Mark?" Evie in her arms, Mel was behind him as he hitched himself up to climb through after the dog. "Where's the key?" she asked, as he was poised to drop the other side.

"Missing," Mark replied tersely, noting Hercules had sunk to her haunches and was emitting no noise now but a low, pathetic whine.

"What's happened? Is she all right?" Mel called urgently, as he dropped carefully down to crouch beside the dog, talking softly to her and trying to coax her to turn so he could reach to apply pressure to the wound.

No, Mark thought. *She's very much not all right.* How in God's name was he going to get her out without injuring her further? "She's bleeding," he said, as calmly as he could. He didn't want to panic the dog, or Mel. "Badly. Front leg. We need the key, Mel. Can you remember where you left it?"

"It's on the hook. I'm sure I hung it . . . Oh God." Evie clutched close to her, Mel peered into the garage after him, clearly shocked when she saw the fountain of rich red blood Mark was trying to stem with his fingers.

"Ring the vet," Mark instructed. "See if they can send someone urgently. I'll have to try and lift her back through—"

"Melissa!" It was Jade, shouting from the other end of the garden. "What is it? What's wrong?"

"Hercules!" Mel shouted. "She's injured. I've lost the key. We can't—"

"It's on the hall table," Jade cut in. "I'm sure that's where you put it. Hold on. I'll go and look."

Thank Christ for that. Mark thought, relief surging through him. The girl's timing was impeccable. From the amount of blood she'd lost, there was no doubt in Mark's mind the dog was going into shock. Lifting her back through the window would probably kill her. He should try to elevate the leg, he was aware, which would slow the bleeding. But how was he supposed to do that without an extra pair of hands?

Had Mel called the vet yet? Or the fire brigade, who could at least break the door down? A neighbour? Anybody would do. Where *was* the damn key? Frustrated, and trying hard to suppress his own panic, Mark leaned down to wipe the blood from his face against his shoulder. With combustible and toxic substances stored in here, the place was an accident zone. They'd discussed it. Agreed to keep the key on the hook, should it be required at short notice, and well out of Poppy's reach.

Yes, and he'd agreed to get the damn window fixed ASAP. If anyone was at fault here, he was. Mel had a million things on her mind with Poppy and Evie's needs to attend to alongside her work. Mark doubted he could perform the juggling act she did on a daily basis half as successfully.

"Hold on, girl," he said softly. "You're not called Hercules for nothing, you know." Praying silently, he glanced upwards, and then snapped his gaze to the door as it opened.

"Mel's rung the vet," Jade said, coming in and dropping down beside him. "He said to keep pressure on the wound and take her straight there. Mel's just popping Evie back in her cot. What can I do?"

Mark nodded. "I'll carry her. I'll need you to stay with me and take over the pressure bit. You'll need two hands, here and here." He indicated where his own hands were placed. "Are you okay with that?"

Jade immediately jumped to her feet. "I'm right by your side," she said determinedly.

Mark's mind was still on Hercules as he finally arrived at the station. And Mel, who was obviously blaming herself for what had happened. He shouldn't have been so short. He'd meant to apologise, but then he'd received another text from Lisa, informing him that DCI Edwards wasn't impressed by his absence, and Mel had slipped back to the workshop while he'd been replying.

At least it looked as if Hercules was going to be okay. Thank God for Jade, who'd certainly gone above and beyond her babysitting duties, even offering to pick the dog up from the vet's later while Mel tried to rescue what was left of her workshop and organise a glazier. Jade had only been with them ten minutes and already Mark was beginning to wonder how Mel had managed to keep all the balls in the air without her. She had though, allowing him to get on and do what he had to do. And by way of appreciation, he'd acted like a dickhead as soon as there was a blip on the domestic front, as if it was a major inconvenience to his work agenda. He'd left her in the workshop, plucking pieces of smashed sculpture from a pool of coagulating blood. She'd said it didn't matter when he'd asked her about it, but she hadn't looked him in the eye. She'd dragged her hair from her face, and kept her gaze fixed firmly on her task. Not sure what to do, what he could do, and running desperately late by then, he'd brushed her cheek perfunctorily with a kiss and said he had to go. No doubt Mel would quite like the freedom to sail out and leave someone else to pick up the pieces sometimes too. He really was going to have to apologise.

Pushing through the security door into the main office, Mark realised he needed to change the dressing on his hand. At first, he hadn't even realised he'd cut it while he'd been tending to the dog. But then, there'd been so much blood he'd have been hard pushed to identify any of it as his own.

"Crisis on the home front *again*?" DCI Edwards asked drolly as Mark headed past his open office door to the incident room.

That one was wearing a bit thin. Sighing inwardly, Mark offered an apology. He'd definitely been juggling crises on the home front at one point. With Mel ill, and everything falling apart around them, he'd taken to self-medicating, the odd nightcap growing into one too many. Mel had known it, which is why she was wary of him drinking late at night now. And Edwards had known it, reprimanding him on several occasions. He'd been right to—Mark's mind hadn't been on the job.

He'd lost sleep after messing up on a case, failing to notice one of his team hadn't followed the chain of custody, meaning evidence could have been contaminated. The vicious little shit who'd walked free had offended again, inevitably, kicking an old man almost to death because he'd refused to part with his phone. The old man had passed away a week later. Mark would never forgive himself for that. And Edwards, it seemed, would never let him forget it—which Mark couldn't blame him for, but he didn't need it, just as he didn't need Cummings constantly winding him up.

He hadn't lost too much sleep over his confrontation with Cummings. The man openly harassed women. He was a kerb-crawler. If anyone was a disgrace to the uniform, Cummings was. Mark couldn't prove it—yet—but he suspected Cummings had recently pocketed proceeds of a drugs bust he'd thought wouldn't be missed. The package he'd seen him passing to a sex worker had looked suspiciously like crack cocaine, which basically meant Cummings was fuelling the woman's addiction. Whether in exchange for sexual favours or information, Mark wasn't sure. Either way, the man was pond scum, end of.

Mark noted the cretin looking him interestedly over as he walked by his desk. He would swear the man was trying to goad him into losing it. Mark's guess was that Cummings knew he was on to him, and was trying to provoke Mark's "emotional volatility," thereby making any accusations he made against him questionable. Mark's only real hope of nailing Cummings was to get enough evidence to make sure he was at least suspended pending investigation.

"Blimey, hope it wasn't a domestic," Cummings commented behind him.

Shaking his head, Mark smiled sardonically. With supreme effort, he ignored Cummings and walked on. He had more important things to do right now than waste time on that prat.

"What have we got?" he asked, once in the incident room.

"The blood is definitely Daisy's," said one of the team, confirming what Lisa had already texted him. "She had an appendectomy about a year ago, so we were able to get a match from the hospital. I'm thinking we'll need to call the forensic experts back in."

That wasn't going to be news the parents would welcome. Mark sighed disconsolately. "Do the parents have an explanation for the stain?"

"She cut her foot in the kitchen a couple of weeks back, according to the mother," said Lisa. "The husband corroborates her story. We're still gathering information from possible witnesses, relatives and friends."

"Thanks, Lisa." Mark smiled wearily. "Anything on the garage CCTV footage?" he asked, ignoring Cummings, who'd wandered in with nil sense of urgency and was now slouching on the edge of a desk.

Cummings, though, wasn't going to be ignored. "Funny you should ask that," he cut in.

Kneading a temple, Mark glanced towards him. "Would you like to enlighten me?" he asked patiently.

"I've just been checking it," Cummings said. "I noted a car cruising past in the direction of the house."

Lisa was obviously as impressed as Mark at that really useful piece of information. "It's a road, Cummings," she retorted acerbically. "It's what cars travel on."

Cummings glanced at her indifferently and then looked back to Mark. "At four o'clock in the morning or thereabouts," he went on leisurely. "On three separate occasions over three consecutive weeks prior to the girl's disappearance."

"And?" Growing more irritated by the second, Mark urged him on.

"And it looked familiar," Cummings said, holding Mark's gaze.

"Oh, for fuck's sake, hurry it up, Cummings," Lisa snapped. "We haven't got all day."

Cummings' mouth curved into a slow smile. "It's a silver Audi Q5," he said, and let it hang. "Registered to one DI Mark Cain."

CHAPTER THIRTEEN

MELISSA

"She's fast asleep," Jade said, coming into the workshop. "Do you need a hand with anything here?"

Mel glanced up from where she was mopping the last of the blood from the floor. It seemed to have been smeared everywhere. Mark had been saturated in it. Some of it, Mel had realised when he got back from the vets, was his own. She'd fetched him a bandage and tried to help him wrap his hand, but he was rushing. Late. Keen to be gone. Mel couldn't blame him.

He hadn't said much about her sculpture, which had been smashed to smithereens. But then, that was understandable. He'd hardly have been taking stock of the damage while desperately trying to stem the flow of blood from the dog. The sculpture didn't matter. It *was* important, to her, and it being irretrievably broken before she'd had time to make a cast was obviously upsetting. It was the statue the Garden & Homes store was considering stocking nationwide. But it was insignificant in the great scheme of things. Poor Hercules.

More upsetting, though, was that Mark had been so obviously annoyed about her forgetting to put the key back. She'd felt like crying when he dashed off, giving her no more than a peck on the cheek after all that they'd done together the first time he'd showered.

It was the shock, she supposed, catching up with her. Plus,

she was still so damn tired. The fuzziness, like damp cotton wool in her head, just wouldn't clear. She needed to go for a brisk walk or something, get a grip. Mark was bound to have been frantic, and she was being oversensitive, her hormones playing havoc, more than likely. Thank God Jade had been there. Things could have been so much worse if not for her presence of mind.

"Mel," Jade prompted. "Do you need a hand?"

"No. Thanks, Jade." Mustering up a smile, Mel attempted to pull herself together. "You've been an absolute rock, I honestly don't know what I'd have done without you, but it's all pretty much cleaned up here now."

"I'm so sorry about your lovely sculpture." Sighing sadly, Jade walked across to where the remnants lay on the bench. "It's such a terrible shame."

Mel raked her hair from her face, which was a bedraggled mess. "It's not the end of the world." She shrugged. "But it could have been, if not for you. I'll just have to start over."

"Well, you just shout when you need some space to work," Jade suggested. "I feel so awful about it all. I'll obviously be more than happy to look after Poppy and Angel for as long as you need me to."

"Angel?" Mel looked at her curiously.

"Sorry—Evie." Jade shook her head apologetically. "I minded a baby about the same age until her parents moved away."

"Ah." Mel nodded. "Pretty name."

"Yes." Jade smiled. "She was a beautiful little girl. A lot like Evie."

Mel smiled at that. Evie was beautiful. The prettiest baby in the hospital ward, Mel had thought. But then, she had been the teeniest bit biased, she supposed. "Look, Jade, there's no need for you to feel bad about any of this," she assured her, leaning over to the bench and retrieving the key, which she would make sure to hang in its proper place. "It's hardly your fault."

"It is a bit. Felix was the cause of it," Jade reminded her, following Mel to help her out with the dustbin full of debris. "Hercules would hardly have hurled herself through the window if she hadn't been chasing the cat."

"True, I suppose." Mel took some small comfort from that. Glancing around, she satisfied herself that all that could be done was done for now, and pulled the door to.

"It's no wonder Mark was so snappy," Jade said, with another heartfelt sigh.

Mel glanced at her, as she helped carry the bin towards the designated rubbish and recycling area. "You noticed then?" she asked, her heart sinking.

"A bit," Jade admitted reluctantly. "But then, with everything that was going on and that woman constantly texting him..."

"Woman?" Mel arched an eyebrow as Jade trailed off.

"Lisa, I think I heard him call her from the bedroom when he went to get changed, before he left for work. I was passing, and I couldn't help overhearing," she clarified quickly, as Mel shot her a questioning glance.

Realising who she meant, Mel smiled amusedly. "She's a work colleague," she explained. God forbid Jade should think Mark was in the habit of ringing women from the bedroom. She'd be wondering what kind of household she'd agreed to work for at this rate.

"Ah, I gathered it must be something like that." Jade nodded. "She's a bit keen though, isn't she?"

Is she? Mel hadn't noticed. Then again, she didn't really give his many texts and calls much thought, other than that they were work-related and therefore necessary.

"I'd better get back to Evie," Jade said, stepping back to leave Mel to manoeuvre the bin into place. "Unless you'd rather...?" She nodded towards the house.

Mel followed her gaze. She'd like nothing more than to

retreat to the nursery, truth be told, to breathe in the reassuring smell of her little one and close her eyes for five minutes. Unfortunately, there was still the matter of the gaping hole where once was a rotting window.

"No." Smiling wearily, Mel ran a hand over her aching neck. "That would be great, Jade, if you wouldn't mind. I've still got to ring the glazier and I suppose I should tape something over the window until he can get here."

"No problem." Jade beamed her a smile back and turned to hurry back towards the house. "Oh, I wouldn't worry too much about covering the window," she called back. "I've got rid of the cat."

Got... What? Mel stared after her. "Got rid of it how?" she shouted, but Jade was already disappearing through the back door.

CHAPTER FOURTEEN

MARK

He wasn't serious? Was he? Looking from Cummings, who was slouching against the window ledge, to DCI Edwards, who sat stony-faced at his desk, Mark laughed incredulously. "You have to be joking," he said, bewildered that his DCI would imagine he'd be doing anything in the area but driving by.

"Doesn't look very amused, does he?" Cummings observed wittily.

"Sit down, please, DI Cain," Edwards instructed, casting a scathing glance in Cummings' direction, which was at least something.

Dragging a hand through his hair, Mark stayed where he was, his emotions swinging from disbelief to anger.

"We have to eliminate everyone from our enquiries, DI Cain. You above all should know that." Edwards' gaze flicked towards him and then to the chair. "Sit."

This was fucking *nuts*. Mark counted silently to five, lest he was tempted to give in to his urge to wipe the supercilious smirk off Cummings' face, and then did as bid, where he waited, infuriatingly, while Edwards finished writing up whatever was so uber-fucking-important he felt obliged to ignore him.

Finally, Edwards downed his pen, leaned back in his chair and laced his fingers over his chest. "Well?" he said, his expression impassive as he looked at Mark.

"Well, what?" Mark asked agitatedly. Did the man not realise what Cummings was up to? Looking for any and every opportunity to undermine him in front of Edwards. Obviously he didn't, because Mark hadn't yet filed his concerns about Cummings. Something he intended to rectify as soon as was humanly possible.

Edwards leaned forwards to eyeball Mark meaningfully. "Don't be insubordinate, Detective," he warned him quietly. "I'd like details, please, of what you were doing driving through Farley Village in the early hours of the morning on three separate occasions."

Tugging in a long breath, Mark curtailed his temper. "I was trying to get Evie to sleep," he said, locking eyes with Edwards and making damn sure to hold his gaze.

"Well, it's different," Cummings sneered, "I'll give you that. Definitely a new one on—" He stopped as Edwards glared in his direction.

"Would you like to elaborate?" Edwards asked, turning back to Mark.

Not really, no, Mark thought. But he had no choice, he supposed, galling though it was to talk about this in front of someone as contemptuous of marriage and children as Cummings was. "Evie went through a phase of not sleeping between her three thirty and six thirty feed," he explained, reluctantly. "Mel needed to sleep. She was exhausted. Evie tends to nod off in the car, so I drove around with her."

"Obviously going for father of the year award," Cummings drawled sarcastically. "In the habit of negotiating hairpin bends in the dark with your baby daughter in the car, are you?"

"I play music. Classical," Mark answered tightly. "It lulls her to sleep."

"Right. No doubt while being filmed. Pay you well, do they, Audi, for starring in their smoother ride advert?"

Mark clamped his jaw tight, and didn't retaliate. Cummings would just love that.

Edwards picked his pen up, his forehead creased thoughtfully as he tapped it on his desk. "And your wife will corroborate this, will she?"

"Bound to, isn't she?" Cummings muttered. "May I suggest we get the video enhanced, sir," he suggested, turning to Edwards. "Just to confirm that the child was actually in—"

"No, you may not," Edwards cut in bluntly.

Cummings stared at him, confounded. "But surely you're—"

"That will be all, DS Cummings. Thank you." Edwards turned back to Mark, something resembling a smile flitting across his face. "Mark, get Melissa to give me a call, will you?"

Mark was taken aback for a second. "Er, yes, no problem," he said, watching bemused as Edwards went back to his paperwork. "Is that it?"

"For now, yes," Edwards confirmed.

Cummings glanced between them, shaking his head scornfully. "I don't bloody believe this."

"Dismissed, DS Cummings," Edwards said, without looking up.

"What a fucking joke," Cummings griped behind him, as Mark headed for the door to get on with what he was supposed to be doing—finding a missing child.

"Oh, that you definitely are, Cummings," Mark grated, heading for his own office.

Lisa looked Cummings disparagingly over as she walked across to join Mark. "Someone piss on your firework, did they, Cummings?"

"Just doing my job," Cummings said, veering off towards his desk. "I doubt DI Cain would have hesitated if the shoe were on the other foot."

"Not for a second," Mark assured him, wondering whether it

might be worth an official warning in exchange for wiping the floor with the bastard.

Deciding positive action might be more productive than volatile reaction, Mark begged the use of a PC's personal vehicle that evening. He knew he should be using the time before the forensic specialist's report came back to be with his family, especially after the catastrophe that morning, but the cocky expression on Cummings' face as he'd sauntered out of the office had only made Mark more determined to catch the bastard in the act. Did the man really think that his car being picked up on CCTV amounted to anything? That he'd find *anything* in Mark's life or career—apart from the fact that Cummings' own repugnant activities had pushed him to the limit—that would make him a subject of investigation? Cummings had miscalculated, badly, if he'd imagined Mark would back off rather than risk being accused of pursuing a personal vendetta.

Following him at a discreet distance, Mark drove on by as Cummings parked up outside a 1960s high-rise, the seventh floor of which, Mark knew, was home to Tanya Stevens. Located just off the M5 into Birmingham on a notorious overspill estate, the decaying block of flats should have been demolished years ago, in Mark's opinion. Cummings wasn't paying Tanya a social visit, that was for sure. Normally to be found working the inner-city streets, Tanya only ever entertained her regular clients at home. Was Cummings one of them?

Driving around the block to allow Cummings time to go in, Mark planned to wait until someone turned up to allow him access into the foyer, but was surprised to find Cummings still parked up outside. So now what? Mark debated and then pulled into the car park of the adjoining block. There was a chance Cummings might have spotted him, but noting the open driver's side window and the billowing cloud of cigarette smoke, Mark thought not. The cocky bastard was clearly quite comfortable waiting there, for reasons which were pretty obvious in Mark's mind.

Sure enough, after a minute or so, Tanya appeared. She obviously didn't consider Cummings a regular, or else didn't trust him enough to allow him access to her flat. As a sex worker, Tanya was street savvy and choosy. Clearly, she had standards that excluded slimy, chauvinistic pricks like Cummings. Would she offer up any information about him, he wondered, given the right incentive? Mark doubted it. He'd first made her acquaintance after a girl who'd worked the patch next to her had gone missing, as, sadly, they sometimes did. Some of them had moved on, or more likely been moved on by their pimps. Some succumbed to drug abuse. Occasionally, missing girls would turn up having been hospitalised by their charming employers, or by the equally charming clients they hadn't been so streetwise about. Mark had a hard time convincing the girls he was more concerned for their welfare than how they earned a living. Realising he was on the level had earned him a grudging respect, and one or two informants. Not Tanya, unfortunately, who'd told him that, unless he could guarantee twenty-four-hour protection for her kid, she'd rather not piss off her pimp.

Watching as Tanya spoke briefly to Cummings through his window and then went around to the passenger side, Mark considered his next move. He had no wish to resort to taking snapshots of Cummings' nefarious sexual activities, but the fact was, if the man was passing drugs here, then he needed evidence of it.

Realising that Cummings had started his engine, probably to avoid whatever activities were about to go on in the vehicle being caught on CCTV, Mark did likewise. He doubted Cummings' "liaison" with Tanya would be a long one. She'd want to be in and out of that car ASAP. Then Mark would need to talk to her—buy some of her time, if necessary.

Surprised when Cummings' car slowed again as it hit the street, Mark idled behind him. Either that was the shortest hand job in history or there was some negotiation going on. Serious negotiation, from the look of it. Mark narrowed his eyes, reaching to unfasten his seatbelt as he noted the animated body language inside the vehicle.

What the—? He watched as Cummings turned to Tanya, his hand shooting out to clutch her by the throat and force her head back against the passenger-side window. Mark was out of his door in a second flat.

He was almost upon the car when the door flew open and Tanya spilled from it to hit the kerb hard. *Bastard.* Hearing the rev of the engine, and guessing Cummings was about to step on the accelerator, Mark deliberated, and then, noticing Tanya wasn't moving, he went instinctively to her.

She was out cold. "Tanya?" Seeing a trickle of blood on the road, Mark crouched down and quickly attempted to assess the damage before moving the girl. He blew out a sigh of relief as her eyelids flickered open.

"Hi. How're you doing?"

Tanya blinked, disorientated for a second, and then clearly registered who he was. "Fuckin' marvellous," she grumbled, her face creasing into a scowl. "How do you *think* I—*Ouch!*"

"Don't move," Mark said, as she tried to lift her head. "You might need an ambulance."

"Yeah, right. Blinding idea, Detective Cain. I'm lying in the gutter with me fanny on show and he says *don't move.*" Eyeing the sky, she heaved herself up regardless, amid much wincing and cursing.

Mark smiled, embarrassed, despite his years on the force. He debated whether to help her with the very short skirt she was tugging down, decided against, and offered her some assistance up instead. "You've had a nasty blow to the back of your head,

Tanya," he pointed out, as she hung onto his arm, attempting to right herself on the pavement. "You could be concussed."

"Well, I never. I wondered why I was bleeding. It's no wonder you're a detective." Sighing, Tanya rolled heavily made-up eyes, and then looked around for her missing stiletto, without which she was decidedly lopsided. "Do us a favour, will ya?" she said, nodding towards it.

Dutifully, Mark obliged, offering his arm again as she wobbled while stuffing her foot into the shoe. "I'll help you home," he said. He guessed he'd probably get a load of verbal for his efforts, but he wasn't about to let her make her own way like this.

"Thank God for the freakin' cavalry," Tanya muttered, as he steered her in the direction of his car. "Wanker..." she added disdainfully.

Mildly surprised—he wasn't sure what he'd done to earn that—Mark glanced at her, and then followed her gaze to where Cummings was cruising slowly by.

"*Fuck!*" Mark swore, noting the quick flash of a camera and the smile on Cummings' face as he drove away.

CHAPTER FIFTEEN

MARK

Pulling up on his drive, Mark sighed wearily. Tanya had wavered, just for a second, obviously tempted to shaft Cummings and give evidence about how he was passing drugs... "Yer living in la-la land," she'd told him outright. "What d'you think Eric'll have to say about me talking to the law, hey?"

Eric, the oily bastard that pimped her out, and had probably pumped her full of drugs in the first place, was highly unlikely to say anything, preferring to do his talking with his fists, or worse. It had been a non-starter. Cummings must have known he was behind him, and he'd played right into his hands. He'd obviously promised Tanya drugs as payment and then, knowing Mark wouldn't walk away, he'd decided to have fun of a different kind.

Idiot. Cursing his stupidity, Mark climbed out of the car and headed for his front door, trying to shake off the day as he did so. Mel really didn't need this—him miles away, contemplating where the missing girl might be, what Cummings might be up to. She needed him on board when he was home, focused on his family.

Wondering how the land lay, he let himself through his front door with a degree of trepidation. He'd checked in earlier, learning from Jade that Hercules was okay. He'd left a message for Mel, but she hadn't rung back, which was worrying.

"*Daddeee!*" Poppy, already in her pyjamas, immediately charged through to greet him from the lounge.

"Hi, Poppet," he said, sweeping her up into his arms. "How's my favourite seven-year old?"

"*Shhh.*" Poppy pressed a finger to her lips. "Hercules is sleeping."

"Is she?" Mark matched her serious look with one of his own. "In which case, I'll be as quiet as a mouse, I promise," he whispered, looking past her to Mel, who was smiling uncertainly in his direction.

Relieved, Mark walked towards her to offer a more affectionate kiss than he had this morning, although a rather awkward one, with Poppy sandwiched between them.

"How is she?" he asked softly, easing away.

"Good. She lost a lot a blood, but the vet thinks she'll be back to her old self in a day or two."

"She has to have lots of rest for the first twenty-five hours, though," Poppy informed him, with an important little nod.

"Twenty-five, hey?" Mark tried not to laugh, furrowing his brow thoughtfully instead. "In which case, we'd better tiptoe upstairs and read our story very quietly. I think it's past a certain young lady's bedtime, don't you?"

Poppy immediately scowled at that, and then brightened as Jade came down the stairs. "I'll take her," she said. Poppy whooped, then clamped a hand to her mouth, lest she wake the dog. "You look exhausted." Jade smiled sympathetically at Mark.

"Are you sure, Jade?" Mel asked. "You've already done more than your fair share today."

"Always happy to help out in a crisis," Jade assured her. "Plus, it will give you two time to catch up."

"Looks like we're outvoted," Mark said, as Poppy reached out, clearly quite happy to latch herself onto Jade in lieu of Daddy. "Night, Poppet," he said, pressing a kiss to her cheek as he passed her over. "Sleep tight."

"Night, Daddy." Poppy waved vaguely in his direction and then leaned back to study Jade's face as they mounted the stairs. "Will you tuck me in, Jade?" she asked her.

"But of course." Jade nodded reassuringly. "I'm an expert tucker-in."

"And Bedtime Peppa?"

"Well, Bedtime Peppa might cry if I didn't," Jade answered seriously.

"And will you check the bug monster's not there?"

"It wouldn't dare come near the place with me around. I've got my babysitter's bug-slayer badge. But, yes, I'll check anyway, just to make sure he hasn't snuck in."

"I love you, Jade." Poppy's voice drifted affectionately down from the landing.

Mark and Mel swapped amused glances. "Looks like I might be surplus to requirements," Mark said, loosening his collar as he headed for the lounge to check on Hercules, and actually feeling hugely grateful that Jade had volunteered after the day he'd had.

"Don't bank on it." Mel pinched his backside as he walked past her, and then yawned widely.

"I don't think you're up to the job, Mrs. Cain," Mark observed, smiling over his shoulder.

"I won't be after a glass of wine, which I think we've both earned," Mel assured him. "In which case, you'll have to do all the work. But you'll have to do it quietly." She lowered her voice as they walked into the lounge, where Hercules was snoring noisily on the sofa.

"Hmm?" Mark considered. "Could be an interesting challenge."

CHAPTER SIXTEEN

JADE

Poppy and Bedtime Peppa duly tucked in, Jade checked all was quiet in the nursery and then crept downstairs. She guessed they were in the kitchen, discussing their respective days over dinner together. How cosy.

Passing the lounge door, where the dog was still sleeping, which meant it at least wouldn't growl at her, Jade paused in the hall and listened.

"I really am sorry about losing the key," she heard Melissa say. God, why didn't the silly cow just grow a pair and stop apologising, especially for something she didn't do? It was no wonder Mark despaired of her. Well, the woman could forget offering him her body by way of recompense for her sins. She was going to be asleep before her head touched the pillow.

"It's me who should be apologising," Mark said, clearly about to take the blame. "I could have behaved a little less like an arsehole and slightly more sympathetically. I'm so sorry about the sculpture, Mel. I don't suppose it was salvageable, was it? As a cast, I mean?"

He was obviously interested enough in her arty-farty endeavours to know something about the process then. Jade scowled, not sure she was very pleased about that. But then, he would be, she supposed. He had such a caring personality. He couldn't change that about himself and nor would Jade want him to.

"No." Melissa sighed. "But I've started another. Jade was great, looking after Poppy and Evie while I was in the workshop."

Jade smiled to herself. She was all for Melissa singing her praises.

"I've been thinking though," Melissa went on, "maybe I should give up working. For a while, at least."

Oh please. Jade rolled her eyes sky-high at that blatant play of the sympathy card.

"What?" She heard Mark choke on his wine. And no wonder.

"I mean, it's not important, is it?" Melissa continued, nauseatingly selflessly. "Well, obviously it is to me, but it's not as if I couldn't put it on hold. Devote more time to the children."

There was a pause. Clearly Melissa was waiting for Mark to give the right response, which, Mark being Mark, of course he did.

"It's important to me, too, Mel," he said, with feeling. "Your art is who you are. You shouldn't give up a fundamental part of yourself out of guilt. You're a fantastic mother. Poppy's a shining example of that. And apart from the blip when Evie wouldn't settle into her routine, she's about as content as a baby can be. This morning was nobody's fault. Shit happens sometimes."

Melissa drew in a breath—and yawned. "I know," she said. "I'm just tired, I suppose."

"Looks like we've both had a shitty sort of day," Mark empathised.

"Oh God, I'm sorry, Mark," said Melissa—apologising, again. "I'm so busy thinking about me, I forgot to ask about how things went with you."

"Not great," Mark said.

Hearing him scrape his chair back, Jade was primed to bolt for the stairs, but relaxed when she heard him walk in the other direction. He must be fetching more wine from the fridge.

"What on earth was all that about with DCI Edwards?"

Melissa asked him, over the sound of wine being poured. If that was her glass, she would definitely be sleeping tonight. Like a dead thing. Jade only wished it were that easy. "I couldn't believe it when he asked me to confirm that you were driving Evie around rather than driving around on your own in the dead of night."

Mark paused, then said, "You did, though, right?"

"Of course," Melissa assured him. "I couldn't remember specific nights, obviously, but I told him you were driving her around to try and get her to go off to sleep."

"Might have looked odd if you could remember specific nights," Mark said, sounding distracted.

"So, why was he asking?" Melissa urged him.

Another pause, followed by a heavy sigh. "Cummings," Mark answered tightly.

"Your detective sergeant?"

"Unfortunately." Mark sounded tense now. "You remember we had an … er … altercation a while back?"

"Oh God, yes. The womaniser. I remember you told me. You hit him."

"Not hard enough," Mark replied angrily, and topped up the second glass. "He has a penchant for younger women, outside and inside of work. Harasses female members of staff. It's way beyond acceptable."

"But … has no one brought him to task? Reported him?" Melissa asked, disbelieving.

"Nope." Mark laughed sardonically. "Not even the girl who he was helping himself to a grope of when I clocked the bastard. Scared of losing her job. Long story short, I was reprimanded. Psychologically evaluated, not to put too fine a point on it."

And she didn't *know* all this? Jade gawped at the kitchen door. What an uncaring, self-centred bitch.

Melissa gasped. "What? Oh no …"

"It was just after Jacob. My emotions were all over the place." Mark sighed audibly.

"Precisely because you had just lost your son! They must have known that. They must have known that you wouldn't *attack* someone, however emotional you were, without provocation."

"He didn't exactly provoke me, Mel," Mark said, less passionately. "Pissed me off, severely, but in the eyes of my superiors, that wasn't provocation."

"Idiots," Melissa seethed. "DCI Edwards is well aware of how losing Jacob affected you. He knows that you would do anything for your children, including driving endlessly around at night to try to get your baby to sleep. I honestly can't believe someone could be so vindictive as to try to make that into anything but what it is."

"There's more to it than just the so-called attack," Mark said, and then paused. "This is just between you and me, though. I have no evidence."

"Of?" Melissa waited.

"I saw him kerb-crawling. I've been keeping tabs on him. I think, but I can't yet be certain, that he's helped himself to drugs, possibly from various crime scenes, the evidence room maybe..." Again, Mark paused, as if debating how much information to divulge. "It looks like he's supplying those drugs to sex workers, some of them clearly underage."

"You're joking," Melissa gasped, incredulous.

"I wish. Bottom line is, he knows I'm on to him. I suspect he's out to discredit me before I get enough to make sure he's kicked off the force and, hopefully, banged up."

"So, he's a sexual predator and a drug pusher," Melissa growled angrily. "What a disgusting individual. I can't understand how he's been allowed to get away with it."

Digesting this latest information, Jade gulped back a sudden overwhelming nausea. Hard though she tried not to, she felt it over again, the repulsion broiling in the pit of her stomach, the pain, the powerlessness of being at the mercy of such an individual, touching and pawing, salivating and thrusting and grunting. Closing her eyes, claustrophobic in the confines of the hall, she tried to block it out: the odious smell of him, body odour and beer; the look in his eyes as he studied her face, one of lust, his exhilaration fuelled by the fear of being found out, by her fear. The taste of him. She would never forget the sour, salty taste that would make her gag until she was sick.

Sweat prickling her forehead, her heart thrumming a drumbeat in her chest, she didn't hear the sound of Melissa's chair scraping back. She did register the sudden silence though. Sensing body contact in there, Jade snapped her eyes open. She couldn't allow that.

Time to announce her presence. Taking a few steps back up the hall, she started singing. It was the same song her mother had sung to her, a mother who actually couldn't have cared less if she'd cried. "*Hush, little baby, don't say a word, Mama's going to buy you a mockingbird. And if that*—Whoops! Sorry," she said, pretending embarrassment at finding Melissa on Mark's lap. She was kissing him! Stuffing her tongue down his throat probably, the slut.

Melissa shot to her feet when she saw Jade. And Mark—poor Mark—looked as if he wanted to drop through the floor. Gathering herself, Jade beamed in his direction. It wasn't his fault, she reminded herself. He was trying to be a good husband. He would continue to try until he saw Melissa in her true light. That was simply who he was: a good man right to the core. She hadn't needed to hear his revelations about his detective sergeant to realise that. Jade couldn't force it. She had to handle it carefully, peel the scales from his eyes slowly. He would realise eventually that to deny his heart's desire for a weak woman who was using him as a cash cow was a ridiculous waste of a life.

As for this DS Cummings, who was trying to ruin Mark,

Jade thought it was time the man got his comeuppance. She would make sure that Mark did get some evidence he could use against him. She couldn't entice the man to supply her drugs, as Mark would obviously become aware of her involvement, but Jade was quite sure she could entice him to other things. Yes, using his pathetic inclination to abuse women in order to ensure his downfall was entirely feasible. She needed to make the acquaintance of the delightful Cummings, Jade decided.

"No need to apologise, Jade," Melissa said, as Jade went to fill up the kettle. "We shouldn't have been canoodling in the kitchen."

Canoodling? How twee. Jade tried to hide her immense irritation behind a sweet smile.

"We got carried away, I'm afraid." Melissa smiled and yawned. And stretched, showing far too much boob over her low-cut top for Jade's liking. Mark could hardly avoid noticing them, could he?

"Why don't you go on up and run yourself a nice hot bath," he suggested, averting his gaze as he got to his feet. "I'll clear up down here."

"Good idea," Jade said, possibly a touch too enthusiastically. "You look absolutely exhausted," she added, fancying that, given the woman's age, saying she looked tired wouldn't go down very well. "I'll give Mark a hand and then bring you up a hot chocolate."

"Oh, don't bother, Jade," Melissa said. "It's really sweet of you, but you've done far too much for one day."

"It's no problem," Jade assured her, already on her way to the table to collect up the plates. "I'm making one for myself anyway. A good night's sleep is what you need, isn't it, Mark?"

"Looks like it." Mark smiled as Melissa tried and failed to suppress another yawn, and then, conceding defeat, headed sleepily for the door.

CHAPTER SEVENTEEN

MARK

She really was exhausted. Mark looked down at his wife, sleeping on her tummy as she usually did, her face turned towards him. *Ripe for kissing.* His eyes strayed to her lips, her glorious copper hair, which was splayed sexily around her. He would very much like to make slow, sensual love to her but, despite her suggestion that he do all the work, he guessed that waking her up might not be deemed pleasurable foreplay.

Undressing quietly, Mark thanked God again for Jade, who he'd left downstairs in the lounge, making sure Hercules was well tucked up. True to her word, she'd made hot chocolate for Melissa and brought it up to her, checking on Evie and Poppy as she did. She'd practically shooed him up to bed when she'd found him dozing in the lounge. She really was a godsend, arriving just when they'd needed her.

Safe in the knowledge that Jade would turn off the lights—he'd already made sure that everything was locked up, twice—Mark slipped carefully in beside Mel.

She didn't stir. Mark searched her face again, before turning off the bedside lamp. Not a flicker of the eyelashes. Slow, sensual lovemaking definitely wasn't on the agenda tonight. She was dead to the world. Ah well, there was always tomorrow. Mark pulled the duvet up over her shoulders and dropped a soft kiss on her cheek, at which Mel finally did stir, wriggling onto her side and into their usual sleeping position, her back facing him, her bottom tucked well into him. Smiling, Mark wrapped an arm around her and pulled her close.

He was drifting in and out of sleep himself—fitful sleep, broken by stark images of the missing little girl, curled into a ball in some cold dark place. And other images: another time, another place, another child, curled up, eyes milk-white and empty, screaming in terror from the depths of the smoke-blackened room he couldn't reach. He desperately tried to wrench himself from the dream. Her heartbreaking sobs were growing louder... too loud. Too much to bear.

Rolling over, Mark pulled himself upright. Blinking hard against the dark, sweat pooling at the base of his neck, he realised the cries were real. Here. Not inside his head.

Evie?

Scrambling out of bed, Mark checked the bedside clock and realised it was nowhere near feed time. Feeling panicked, and not sure why, he headed for the landing. He was outside the nursery door when he heard the soft lullaby: *"Hush, little baby..."*

Jade. Mark felt his heart rate return to somewhere near normal. She'd obviously beaten him to it. A godsend. Definitely. Mark sighed, relieved, and then, remembering he was stark naked, he about-faced and headed back to the bedroom, where he found Mel still sleeping, amazingly. Normally she would wake if Evie or Poppy so much as sneezed.

CHAPTER EIGHTEEN

MARK

Two weeks she'd been missing. Fourteen days and cold nights and they were still no nearer to finding her. Mark studied the latest photo of Daisy: a pretty, rosy-cheeked child, similar in colouring to Poppy, she didn't look unhappy, scared or lonely. There were no shadows haunting her smile. She was just a normal, trusting little girl. A little girl whose innocence had probably been irretrievably broken. Swallowing back the bile in his throat, trying to dismiss the images that thought evoked, Mark dragged his hands through his hair. He didn't know why, but he was sure she was alive. The pictures that flashed through his dreams every night, elusive and wispy at first, were now so clear he could almost reach out and touch her; her fear so tangible, he could feel it. He could even smell her surroundings: mildew, damp moss, leather. Definitely a property in the countryside somewhere, but it could be anywhere. Was he being fanciful? Some might call this a hunch. Mark worried it was just wishful thinking.

Feeling utterly jaded, he sat heavily back in his chair. So where did he go from here? Forensics had found other spatters of blood, but they were so small as to be insignificant, and possibly from the foot injury the parents had offered as explanation for the stain on the stairs. Whilst not ruling them out yet, the parents looked to have played no part in her disappearance.

Searches were continuing locally and nationally, but Mark was running out of ideas. Unable to ignore the nagging instinct that she was still alive, he'd taken it on himself to revisit some of the neighbouring properties. Hawthorn Farm, a mile or so from his own house, was on his agenda later. The owner, a recently bereaved widow, wouldn't welcome another intrusion into her life, but he had to do something. She had enough on her plate with the farm up for sale and a son who was amiable enough but not the brightest tool in the box. He'd once been arrested, nine years ago, according to the details on file. The charge, indecent exposure, had been dropped when a local guy had marched his fifteen-year old daughter into the station. Turned out she and her mate had decided it would be a "laugh" to remove "drippy Dylan's" clothes while he'd been skinny-dipping in the river. Dylan, sixteen years old at the time, had never lived it down. Kids could most definitely be cruel sometimes. Now living in one of the small cottages on the farm, he seemed harmless, with no other misdemeanours or mishaps on his record. Impressionable, gullible, but harmless. Still, though, Mark wanted to revisit the farm in the vain hope that something had been missed.

Sighing, he looked back to his computer. Rereading statements wasn't likely to produce anything new, but he had to do something. Pulling up another file, Mark scrolled through it, reaching distractedly for his ringing mobile as he did.

"Mark, hi, it's me," Mel said, over the noise of Evie crying, which immediately made Mark tense up. Evie was now waking several times most nights and Mel seemed permanently on edge. But then…Mark tried to suppress it, but the thought popped into his head anyway…Mel hadn't actually had to see to her at night over the two weeks since Jade had moved in. Jade's antennae always seemed to be on red alert. He'd met her on the landing a couple of times over the last week (he'd taken to wearing boxers at night now, just in case).

"Did you remember to book the table for tonight?" Mel asked him.

Crap. "No, sorry." Mark squeezed his eyes closed, realising he'd forgotten. They were supposed to be going out with the Chandlers to celebrate Emily's birthday, and it had completely slipped his mind. The broken nights, coupled with his increasing nightmares, were taking their toll on him too.

"Oh, Mark, honestly...I thought you'd done it days ago." Mel sounded utterly despairing.

"I'll do it now," Mark promised.

"Forget it. *I'll* do it," Mel said tetchily. "I doubt they'll have a table now anyway."

"Mel, I'll do it," Mark assured her, concerned by her obvious agitation. He'd been trying not to worry about it, putting Mel's irritability down to stress, but, frankly, he was alarmed. Whether or not she was getting up in the night to see to Evie, she was exhausted. She *looked* exhausted. And where previously Mel would have been unfazed by something like a dripping tap—grabbing the tool box, in fact, and changing the washer herself—the one that was constantly dripping in the utility was driving her mad. Mark had put it on his weekend to-do list. It was no big deal—but to Mel it obviously was. She'd looked... edgy. It was the only way to describe it. It just wasn't like her.

He was about to reassure her again that he would ring the restaurant and then call her straight back when Mel practically growled down the phone, "Oh for God's *sake*, now the bloody fuse box has blown. We really need to spend some serious money on this house, Mark, or move." And with that, she ended the call.

Staring askance at his mute phone for a second, Mark shook his head. Mel had chosen the house. A detached farmhouse in the peaceful countryside, but with neighbours close enough for it not to feel isolated, she'd loved it on sight, particularly the outbuilding, which was perfect for her workshop. A fantastic family home, she'd said, her glorious green eyes dancing with excitement as she'd viewed it. She'd been willing him to love it too. Mark had, but with reservations. Despite the obvious attractions—oak flooring, oak joinery, stone fireplaces and the airy feel to it, thanks to the many windows looking onto the spectacular Herefordshire countryside—it was going to need a hell of a lot of money spent on it. Even with the small trust fund Mel had been left by her mother, the renovation was going to have to be done as and when finances allowed, they'd both been aware of that. That hadn't been a problem either. Until now, apparently.

Mark swallowed back an uneasy feeling, wondering whether her recent behaviour might be symptomatic of something more, something he hadn't realised she might be struggling with. She hadn't suffered postnatal depression after having Poppy, but might she be suffering with it now? Mark had no idea. He was debating whether to suggest Mel make a doctor's appointment, which he was loath to do, recalling how hard she'd worked to be free of doctors and psychotic drugs after losing Jacob, but . . .

"Hello, earth to Mark," Lisa said, standing next to his desk.

"Sorry." Mark shook himself. "Miles away."

"I gathered. Coffee," she said, parking a mug next to his PC. "You look like shit," she added bluntly.

Running a hand over his unshaven cheek, Mark straightened himself up in his chair. He guessed he did, which wouldn't go down well with Edwards. "Cheers, Lisa," he said, then feeling in need of a caffeine kick, picked up his coffee. "You do my ego the world of good."

"I'm thinking a decent night's sleep might do you more good." Lisa cocked her head to one side, studying him thoughtfully. "I take it Evie's disturbing your beauty sleep? Not that you need much beauty sleep, obviously."

"Obviously," Mark concurred, his mouth twitching into a smile. "Her routine's gone to pot," he confided, glad, not for the first time, that he could talk to Lisa. It made life a whole lot easier at work, particularly now Cummings was back after his sudden mystery illness. It had been no surprise to Mark he'd gone off sick, probably hoping to avoid a confrontation with him. Mark's anger boiled afresh as he recalled his treatment of Tanya Stevens.

Rolling her eyes, Lisa empathised. "Babies." She sighed expansively. "If anyone had told me what I was in for, I'd never have had sex."

"Still, at least it was only the twice, hey, Moyes? Brave bloke," Cummings commented crassly, winking over his shoulder as he swung by towards the coffee machine.

Lisa settled for giving him a finger rather than verbalising her thoughts. "I take it you've tried all the usual tricks?" she asked Mark. "White noise, temperature, lighting, varying the rocking, breathing deeply if none of the above work?"

"Yup, pretty much everything. Or rather, Jade has."

"Jade?"

"The babysitter."

"Ah." Lisa nodded, but looked perplexed. "I didn't know you had one."

"We do now," Mark said. "Live in, thank God. She's amazing with the kids, but—"

"Night excursions in the car not working then, sir?" Cummings enquired sarcastically, as he sauntered back in the other direction.

"Fuck off, Cummings," said Lisa, obviously noticing Mark's agitation and answering for him.

Mark glanced disdainfully after Cummings. He really was a piece of work. "Do you mind if we, er…" Looking back to Lisa, he nodded towards the door, where he could hopefully grab some advice about Mel out of earshot of the creep. Lisa had been a friend to Mel when she'd needed one, and with two kids of her own, certainly had a good perspective on that side of things.

"With pleasure. There really is an obnoxious stench in here." Curling a lip in Cummings' direction, Lisa about-faced and headed for the door.

"So, what's up?" she asked Mark, once they were both in the corridor.

Mark started walking. The last thing he wanted was Cummings knowing any more of his business. "Not sure," he said, running a hand over his neck. "Maybe nothing."

"Which is why you're coming in late again, not shaving..."

"That obvious, is it?" Mark would have to do something about that. "It's Mel," he said. "I mean, it might be nothing to do with her and all to do with me, but she's...I don't know...tired all the time, edgy."

"Well, she's bound to be tired with Evie's feeding routine all over the place, Mark. It's bloody hard work getting up umpteen times a night."

"I know, I know." Mark sighed and massaged his temples. "It's just, she's not getting up at night. That's the point. She's dead to the world. Doesn't even hear Evie. Jade sees to her. She usually gets to her before I do. There's plenty of milk in the freezer, so it's not a problem, but..." Not quite sure how to communicate what the problem really was, wondering again whether there even was one, he trailed uselessly off.

Lisa scanned his face. "You're worried about her."

"A bit." Mark admitted, relieved. He felt like a traitor discussing Mel behind her back, but he really needed to know if he was being paranoid here—and Lisa would be the one to tell him if he was. "I might be blowing things out of proportion, but given what happened before, well, I wondered if you'd drop by on some pretext or other. Tell me what you think."

"Consider it done. I haven't seen her in ages. It'll be good to have a natter. I'm off early tonight—Anna's got a dance class. I'll pop by once I've dropped her off. And I'll check out that babysitter while I'm at it, see if she fancies a bit of moonlighting. She sounds too good to be true."

CHAPTER NINETEEN

LISA

Babysitter?! Lisa gawked as a girl who looked more like she was auditioning for *Baywatch* than babysitting answered Mel's door.

"Hi." Arranging her face into a smile, Lisa averted her gaze from the girl's breasts, not easily missed in the red tankini top she had on, which she'd paired with very short white shorts. Admittedly, there'd been a rare glimpse of early summer sun, but wasn't she a little underdressed for the job?

"Hi." The girl didn't smile back.

"Is Mel home?" Lisa asked, feeling a bit spare on the doorstep. As if she were a ten-year-old kid calling for her mate and definitely under scrutiny from her mother.

"She's having a lie-down." Waving vaguely behind her, the girl continued to look Lisa curiously over. "I'm not sure whether she's sleeping."

"Oh. Well, I'm sure she won't mind me going on up," Lisa said, nodding past her. "We're old friends. I'm Lisa, Mark's—"

"Work colleague," the girl finished, clearly not about to shift her pretty little arse and allow her access anytime soon.

Smiling patiently, Lisa waited a few moments before asking, "And you are...?"

"Oh God, sorry." The girl finally smiled back. "Jade. Mark's babysitter. And Mel's, of course. And I've obviously forgotten my manners." She moved aside at last, allowing Lisa access. "Come on in. I'll go and give Mel a shout."

"No worries, I'll just go on up," Lisa assured her, feeling uneasy as she stepped in, and not sure why—apart from the fact that Mel had obviously taken leave of her senses, dangling that sort of temptation under Mark's nose. But Mark wasn't like that. Lisa reminded herself of her tendency to label all men the same, having been married to the kind of abusive Neanderthal who made Cummings seem positively charming, and having more recently hooked up with a wanker who turned out to be shagging anything in a skirt, the younger the better. Mark was devoted to Mel. He'd never even looked in another woman's direction, as far as Lisa knew. It didn't make him a saint, but his dedication to his wife had been obvious when his life had been a complete shit fest.

"I've got to go and get a jacket for Evie anyway." She waved at Evie, who was in her stroller, all kitted up to go out. "We're off to the park while Poppy's at her friend's. Just wait there, won't be a tick."

Lisa watched her skip on up, trying hard not to judge her. She seemed friendly enough, after the initial hiccup on the doorstep. And she'd been right not to just allow anyone claiming to be a friend access to the house, Lisa supposed. She was obviously feeling the teeniest bit jealous.

Attempting to shrug off her concerns, Lisa crouched down to Evie's level. "We can't all be beautiful as well as brainy, can we, sweetheart?" She smiled, relieved to note that Evie looked healthy enough. The blip in the sleeping routine was clearly just that, a blip.

"So, what have we been up to then, Little Miss Mischief?" she asked her, crooking a finger to stroke her peachy cheek. "Are we keeping Mummy and Daddy awake, hmm? Would you like

Auntie Lisa to come and sing you a lullaby?" Evie's mouth widened into a delighted, gummy smile as Lisa jiggled her caterpillar stroller toy.

"You really are a gorgeous little girl, aren't you?" said Lisa, reassured by Evie's gurgles and chuckles and flailing little hands. There was nothing wrong in the baby department. And with Mel's sparkling green eyes and delicate features, she was going to be a knockout.

"Lisa?"

She turned at the sound of Mel's voice, but her smile slipped a bit when she saw her. Far from sparkling, Mel's eyes were heavy with exhaustion. She looked more knocked out than knockout. Whatever was going on, she needed to get to the doc's, and fast.

CHAPTER TWENTY

MELISSA

"I haven't seen you in ages," said Mel, smiling delightedly, despite that she felt a complete mess. She'd just climbed out of the shower when Jade came in to tell her Lisa was here, joking about her being Mark's frequent texter. Having been attempting to wash the cotton wool from her head, and failing, Mel had been ferreting through her wardrobe in hopes of finding something remotely sexy-looking to wear tonight. She'd given up when she'd seen Jade looking dazzling and thrown her leggings and old T-shirt back on. And now here was Lisa, looking trim and slim in her jeans, her short-cropped hair and huge blue eyes making her look like a little elf—a very attractive one.

Sighing inwardly, Mel brushed her damp hair from her face. She really was going to have to do something with herself. Take some vitamins, or energy pills or something. Go to the gym, or out jogging with Mark. Mel's heart dipped in her chest as she thought of him. She'd be surprised if he wanted to do anything with her. She'd been horrible to him on the phone. She really had no idea what was wrong with her. She felt like sleeping the clock around. They hadn't made love since the dreadful day of Hercules' accident, and Mark hadn't murmured a word. It was more than he dare do, she supposed, with her so snappy. When she wasn't sleeping or moaning or yawning, she was working. Or trying to. The blown fuse meant the kiln had stopped working, which had had her wanting to scream. She barely had time for the kids with her sculpture to remake, the casting of which still had to be done, and the orders to fill, which she hadn't even started on. It was a wonder any of her family wanted anything to do with her. Maybe she should go to the doctor's, Mel pondered. The thought didn't appeal. She'd steered clear of doctors and medication, even avoiding painkillers at the worst time of the month, since coming off her medication.

"My fault." Lisa moved to give her a hug as she reached the hall. "I've been so busy with work and the kids demanding my attention every two seconds. Anyway, I was passing after dropping Anna off at her dance class and I thought no time like the present. How are you?" Stepping back, Lisa looked her over, her brow furrowed. "You look a bit…"

"A mess, I know." Mel smiled and tried not to mind. Lisa tended to say it as it was.

"Frazzled," Lisa finished diplomatically, whilst looking her worriedly over again. "Are you okay, lovely?"

"Yes, fine," Mel lied, waving a hand dismissively. "It's a virus, I think. I can't seem to shake it off. I don't have an ounce of energy."

"Unlike some," Lisa observed, as Jade came bounding brightly back down the stairs.

"Got it." She dangled the jacket and headed for the stroller. "Come on, angel," she said, peering down at Evie and steering her towards the door. "Let's go and get some fresh air and leave Mel to catch up with her friend, shall we?"

"She's referring to you as Mel, not Mummy?" Lisa eyed Mel sideways as Jade tipped the stroller back and headed on out.

"Slip of the tongue probably." Mel smiled in Lisa's direction, and then scooted to catch up with Jade. "Hold on," she said, crouching to kiss Evie's perfect little cupid lips. The baby promptly wriggled and looked fretfully upwards in search of Jade. Trying not to mind that either—she was getting things so out of proportion lately, she'd drive herself as well as everyone else mad—Mel got to her feet, allowing Jade to go on her way.

"Have you got her water?" she called after her.

"Yes." Jade waved behind her. "And a spare nappy and the sunscreen. We'll be fine. You worry too much, Mel."

And lately she was worrying more than ever, when she wasn't too tired to think at all. Mel really did despair of herself. She had the perfect babysitter. A beautiful house, albeit in a constant state of repair. A good husband, whom she loved, very much. Two perfect kids. Everything in her garden should be rosy. So why did she feel so... down?

"Pretty, isn't she?" Lisa commented, as they watched Jade head jauntily off down the lane. "Slim, too. Makes me feel like a flipping heifer."

Mel laughed at that. "In which case I must look like the back end of a bus."

Lisa looked her over as they walked back in. "Hardly," she said. "You've lost weight."

"Have I?" Mel looked down at herself. That was a silver lining in the gloom, she thought, and then she felt her heart sink all over again. Why was she thinking this way? Feeling this way?

"I take it she's the new babysitter?" Lisa enquired, as they walked to the kitchen for coffee and a catch-up. "Live in, I gather?"

Information conveyed by Mark, Mel guessed. "That's right. She'd bought Monk's Cottage just up the lane—moved in with us after it caught fire. It was totally burned out. You must have noticed as you passed."

She checked the wall clock—aware it might take some time to make herself gorgeous—and then headed for the kettle, as Lisa parked herself on a stool at the kitchen island.

"I did," Lisa said. "She was literally on your doorstep then?"

"Yes." Mel spooned coffee into the mugs—or, rather, missed,

cursing silently. "We hadn't had much to do with each other really, but with her house going up in flames..."

"You got talking?"

"Obviously." Coffee successfully made, Mel picked up the mugs and carried them over, without spilling any, thankfully. "It was awful. All her worldly goods gone up in smoke. I offered her a roof for the night and, as we'd been considering a babysitter... Well, you could say she fell into our laps. I hate to say it, but the timing couldn't have been better, to be honest. She's an absolute godsend."

"So Mark says." Lisa sounded sceptical. "And she's qualified, presumably?"

"Of course. She has her childcare qualifications. I wouldn't have entertained the idea of employing her otherwise." Reminded that she hadn't got around to asking Jade about her references, she dismissed a flicker of guilt. The girl had more than proved herself in Mel's eyes.

"Right." Lisa nodded. "But don't you mind having another woman around?"

Mel eyed her with amusement. "You mean having a pretty young woman around?"

"Just saying." Lisa shrugged.

"Not all men do what Paul did, Lisa," Mel said, kindly, aware that Lisa's last boyfriend had dumped her for a younger model.

Lisa gave her a look as she dipped into the biscuit barrel. Her "Yes, and pigs fly" look.

Mel wasn't sure she liked the inference. Cautioning herself not to overreact, she pulled in a breath and reminded herself she'd been doing that a lot recently, reading things into things that weren't there. She'd even imagined that Jade had had the cat she'd supposedly loved put down. It had taken her ages to ask her. Jade had been horrified. She'd asked a friend to take it in, it turned out. Mel had felt awful.

"So," she said, mustering up a smile, "what else have you and Mark been discussing, apart from the attributes of the babysitter?"

Lisa's eyes flicked to hers. "Nothing much. This and that," she said vaguely.

"Such as?" Mel asked, watching her carefully over the rim of her mug.

Lisa put down her coffee and looked up to eye Mel levelly. "He's worried about you, Mel," she said, searching her eyes, a curious look in her own.

"Oh." Definite unease was now gnawing at Mel's stomach. "I see," she said, taking stock. "So, you've been discussing me then, clearly."

Lisa looked away awkwardly. "Well, yes, naturally you come up sometimes. But Mark was only confiding in me out of concern, Mel. He—"

"Our intimate relationship?" Mel felt her mouth go dry, her cheeks heat up. "Does that come under discussion during these cosy conversations you have?"

"No!" Lisa refuted. "Mark wouldn't do that. You know he wouldn't. He's just been concerned about you—"

"You text each other a lot, don't you?" Mel cut in angrily. It seemed to her that Lisa knew an awful lot about what Mark would or wouldn't do. And, clearly, *she* didn't. She'd never imagined her husband would discuss their personal details with all and sundry.

Lisa splayed her hands, looking incredulous. "Only on work matters. For God's sake, Mel, you don't honestly think that I—"

"Or, rather, *you* text him."

"Oh, come on, Mel." Lisa eyed the ceiling. "You know very well I only ever text him about work."

But she didn't know, did she? She trusted Mark, implicitly. Or she had. There had been something between Lisa and him once, at least Mel had suspected there had. He'd gone out with her, Mel had been sure of it. Her mind raced back to the first time she'd met Mark, when she'd been giving her statement about her ex. "Thanks for last night," Lisa had said. She'd threaded an arm around his waist as she passed him in the corridor and given him a squeeze. Thanks for last night! Mel had heard her, loud and clear. She'd assumed they'd had a thing. She'd been wrong, or so she'd been led to believe. She'd asked Mark about it, trying to sound casual. Lisa had needed a shoulder, he'd said. Still married to her abusive husband, she'd been having some problems. Yes, and what else had he offered her, Mel thought, fuming now at the obvious lie. Regular little white knight, wasn't he?

She narrowed her eyes. "Did he ask you to come here?"

Lisa didn't answer. Plainly not knowing how to. Plainly meaning he had.

"Well, did he?" Mel demanded, a distinct wobble to her voice.

"No." Lisa sighed, at length. "As I said, I was passing. I'm concerned about you, too, you know. I am your friend. I just wanted to check—" Lisa stopped as her phone beeped inconveniently in her pocket.

Or rather, bang on cue, Mel thought, humiliation bubbling furiously away inside her. That Mark had discussed the intimate details of their relationship at work, even with a supposed friend, was incomprehensible. Who else had he discussed it with? The entire police force? "Aren't you going to check it?" she asked Lisa, now studying her intently. "It might be one of the kids."

Knowing she had no choice, Lisa reluctantly retrieved her phone.

"Is it Mark?" Mel asked, cold certainty gripping her insides.

Lisa checked the text. Again, she didn't answer. Nor would she meet her gaze.

Mel tried very hard to hold onto her temper. "*Well?*"

Sighing heavily, Lisa closed her eyes and nodded.

Caught in the act. Seething inside, Mel didn't say anything, but coldly extended her hand.

Lisa waited a beat. "We haven't been discussing anything *intimately*, Mel," she said, reluctantly handing the phone over. "Mark was just worried, that was all."

Ignoring her, Mel took a breath and read the damn text that she didn't want to see, absolutely didn't want to read anything into. And her world shifted completely off kilter.

> *Off to Hawthorn Farm shortly. Hope all went well with Mel. Thanks for the ear. Talk to you tomorrow, preferably in private. Promise to be clean-shaven and looking my beautiful best.*

CHAPTER TWENTY-ONE

MARK

Leaning towards him, Mark planted his fists either side of Cummings' desk while he waited for whatever pathetic explanations the man thought reasonable for assaulting a woman.

"She's an informant." Cummings laughed incredulously, but Mark didn't miss the nervousness flitting across his eyes. They were alone, with no witnesses if he lost it big time this time and did what he really wanted to.

"And that justifies you forcibly ejecting her from your car how, exactly?" he said, through gritted teeth, making sure to hold eye contact with the detective sergeant.

"For *fuck's* sake, what is this? A bloody interrogation?" Cummings pushed his chair back and rolled his eyes at the ceiling. "She had a hold of my balls, all right!" He looked back to Mark, his expression one of humiliation. "What would you have done?"

If I were Tanya? You really don't want to know, Cummings. "Why?" he asked shortly. "Why did she have a hold of you?"

Cummings splayed his hands. "How the fuck do I know? Off her head on coke probably."

Yeah, right. Mark didn't believe a fucking word of it. Straightening up, he pushed his hands into his pockets. Still, he kept his gaze fixed hard on Cummings. "Supplied by you." It was a statement, not a question.

"Uh-uh. *No* way." Cummings got furiously to his feet. "I pay my girls cash."

Mark couldn't keep the contempt from his eyes. "Including the girls you have sex with?"

"Sometimes." He shrugged, looking back to Mark. "Some of us don't have the convenience of a wife to go home to, do we? *Sir.*"

Mark sucked in a breath. *Don't*, he cautioned himself, swallowing back the hard knot of anger climbing his chest.

"I'm presuming you have some evidence to back up your accusation?" Cummings asked, his eyes defiant, his tone holding a challenge.

Mark glanced away, disgust broiling inside him.

"Thought not," Cummings sneered, turning to reseat himself at his computer.

Mark counted, silently, steadily. He was an inch away from dragging the man back to his feet, stuff the consequences. "And the photos?" he asked, sorely tempted to forcibly retrieve the phone from the man's pocket.

Cummings looked disinterestedly up from his screen. "What photos?"

Mark clamped hard down on his jaw. "The photos I saw you taking, Cummings. You might do better to turn your flash off if you want to take covert photos in future."

Cummings knitted his brow, confused, supposedly, and then nodded as if realisation had just dawned. "It was my lighter. I was lighting a cigarette." He smiled flatly. "You could probably do me for that, since it was a pool car—depending how desperate you are."

Looking him scornfully over, Cummings dragged his gaze away, safe in the knowledge that Mark couldn't touch him.

Not yet. But soon, Cummings. Sometime very soon.

His gut twisting inside him, Mark turned to slam out of the office. His still had to check out Hawthorn Farm before hurrying home to shower before going out with Mel. Lisa was right, there really was an obnoxious odour around here.

CHAPTER TWENTY-TWO

JADE

"I still can't believe what he did," Dylan said, gazing down at Evie, who was contentedly sleeping after her feed. Jade sighed inside, wondering whether the idiot boy was worth the effort. He really was as thick as pig shit. He hadn't even recognised her from their school days. Mind you, with her changed facial appearance, blue contacts and once unremarkable mousey brown hair now a head-turning shade of blonde, he wasn't likely to. He even looked like a plank, with that perpetual gormless expression. But a pliable plank, she reminded herself, which was why she needed to stroke drippy Dylan's ego, along with certain other parts of his anatomy. When it was time to lose little Evie for a while—or, rather, for poor muddled Melissa to lose her for a while—Dylan could be trusted to keep his mouth shut. He'd already proved that much.

"I was young." Collecting up her baby bag, Jade walked across the barn, sighing wistfully as she joined him. "He was helping me out, really."

"What?" Dylan turned to her, his heavy forehead furrowed disapprovingly. "By making you have his babies?"

"Paying me, Dylan. I wouldn't have had a roof over my head otherwise," Jade reminded him. Dylan had offered her his roof, of course, when she'd tearfully confided in him. Thankfully, he'd realised it wouldn't be at all suitable for all of them, the cottage being so tiny and with basic amenities, and that, in any case, she couldn't possibly leave without her baby. More importantly, when she did leave, she had to be secure in the knowledge the child's father wouldn't try to grab her back.

"Yeah, well, it's still taking ad..." Dylan stopped, his frown deepening as he struggled for the word.

"Advantage," Jade kindly supplied.

"Yeah, that." Dylan nodded piously, puffing up his big barrel chest as he did. "It's just wrong, innit, him being a policeman and all. He should be setting an example. My mum always said that people in positions of authority should be beyond..."

Dylan trailed off, apparently at a loss for what policemen should be beyond.

"Reproach." Mentally rolling her eyes, Jade helped him along. "And your mum's right, Dylan. But I didn't have anyone else, did I. No mum. No dad. I only had him. You haven't said anything about the babies, have you?" she added quickly. "To your mum?"

Dylan shook his head adamantly. "No, Scout's honour."

Jade winced as he actually held up two fingers in a scout salute. "Or anyone else?" she asked, scrutinising him carefully. Dylan's cheeks flushed like a set of brake lights if he was ever embarrassed or uncomfortable. She'd soon know if he was lying.

"Haven't breathed a word," he assured her, with another exaggerated shake of his head.

"Good." Jade gave his cheek a pat, her other hand straying to his groin, causing Dylan to suck in a sharp breath. "We wouldn't want anyone to come between us, would we? And they would, you know, if they found out I'd had his babies before I was old enough."

"I didn't say anything, honest." Dylan's voice went up an octave as she gave his testicles a gentle squeeze, giving him an instant hard-on.

"You're a rock, Dylan." Jade leaned in, panting breathily in his ear, "I'm so lucky to have you as a boyfriend."

Dylan nodded. "I like being your boyfriend," he said, the flush to his cheeks indicating his awkwardness as his eyes flicked to hers and back. "You shouldn't be living with him, though, Jade. Not if you're my girlfriend."

Jade stopped her ministrations in favour of lifting his chin to gaze lovingly at him. Dylan might be pliable, but now he'd discovered what his penis was for apart from pissing, he was showing signs of becoming proprietorial. God forbid his male ego might drive him to do anything unpredictable. "It's only for a while," she assured him, blinking kindly. "Just until my house is rebuilt. And at least this way I get to see my children."

Dylan ran a hand under his nose. Still, he looked disgruntled. *Damn.* Jade hoped she wasn't going to have to go the whole hog and give him a blowjob by way of distracting him. It wouldn't take long but she really needed to be getting back. "And then you can move in with me, remember?" She dangled the prize carrot instead. The prospect of having her next to him in bed every night was enough to make sure he stayed on track.

"And the kids?" Dylan said, eyeing her uncertainly.

"And the kids," Jade assured him, smiling her sweetest smile. "And your mum can visit as often as she wants. She could even move in with us if she liked."

Dylan brightened at that. "She could cook our dinner."

"We'd be one big happy family," said Jade, though she was having to force the smile a bit now.

Dylan nodded happily, and then frowned, again. "But what about the other one?" he asked. "I'm not sure it's good for her, being away from you and all."

"Oh, she's fine." Jade waved a hand, irked now. Given how unemotional he was when it came to shooting vermin or snapping chickens' necks, she hadn't banked on him becoming attached to the girl. "She's much better off staying with you than with me."

Dylan didn't look convinced.

"You know *he* doesn't want her, Dylan." Jade blinked at him beseechingly. "It's best she stays where she is for a while. Just make sure your mother doesn't go poking her nose—*Shhhh*." Hearing a car drawing up in the farmyard, Jade cocked an ear.

Perplexed, since drippy Dylan and his depressing-looking mum hardly ever had visitors, she pressed a finger to her lips and tiptoed across the floor to peer through a popped knot in the barn door, and then...*Shit!*

CHAPTER TWENTY-THREE

MARK

Mark climbed out of his car, deciding to take a look around before knocking on the farmhouse door. If there was anything they'd missed, he was hardly going to fall over it, but he just couldn't shake the feeling that Daisy was still alive and being held close to home. She haunted his dreams. But then, the small girl who'd died in the cruellest way possible came to him at night too, her tiny form curled into a ball, clutching her one-eyed Pooh Bear close to her chest, calling out to him. And the smell, before the unbearable screams snatched him back to consciousness: thick, cloying smoke, scorching his lungs, suffocating him.

In dreams of Daisy, it was always the same rural smell. Mark had no idea why the nightmares kept coming, robbing him of what sleep he might get in between Evie waking. It was because he had children, he supposed. Because he lived in fear of something too unbearable to comprehend happening to his baby girls, and that, despite having police resources at his fingertips, he would be powerless to save them.

Shaking himself, Mark looked around. Once a well-kept, thriving dairy farm, the place was now abandoned, the cow house and stables sadly bereft of inhabitants. He decided to start with the smaller of the two barns, frightening scrawny chickens who'd obviously escaped the poultry yard into a flutter of wings and piercing skirls as he walked. Once inside, he wondered why he'd come. Like the rest of the farmyard, it was empty, dusty and derelict. Original beams supported the roof; ropes and chains hung from a crossbeam. Nothing much else inside; nowhere to hide.

The smell though—damp, earthy and pungent, of mildew and soft hay—was so familiar. Mark sighed, despairing of himself. He was supposed to be dealing in facts, not wild flights of the imagination. He was triggering childhood memories, that was all. One in particular, where he'd been selected as one of the school's deprived kids to go on some pony-trekking holiday. Turns out he hadn't been much safer away from home. He'd heard him before he saw him, his old man, pissed, ranting incoherently in the small office situated next to the stables—Christ only knew how he'd driven there. He'd come to fetch him back. Mark hadn't been about to go back though. Even as a kid, he'd known he wouldn't make it. Not that time. He'd hid instead— spent half his life hiding. Deciding the hayloft was too obvious a place, he'd bolted for the stable block, curling himself into the corner of one of the stalls. The stench of leather and hay and horse manure had been overpowering. He'd been more terrified of his father finding him than the horse's hooves, which had seemed pretty menacing to a ten-year-old-kid. He'd been lonely, too. The other kids' cruel taunts had intensified after that. *Forget it,* he told himself. It was the past, dead and buried.

Consigning it to history, telling himself he needed to stop chasing shadows, Mark turned to walk back across the yard, pained by the sense of isolation the disused property evoked.

CHAPTER TWENTY-FOUR

JADE

"Don't move," Jade whispered, her heart thrumming manically against her ribcage. Fear, and an undeniable frisson of sexual pleasure, surged through her as she watched Mark walk towards the barn. "He can't find me." Turning imploring eyes towards Dylan, whose face was now set in a hard scowl, she pressed a finger to her lips and stole a glance at Evie.

Hell! Why had she come looking for Dylan when she hadn't found him at the cottage? She'd already been pushed for time. She should have just left.

Please don't wake up, Angel. Seeing Evie twitch in her sleep, her eyelids fluttering, as if she might wake at any second, Jade prayed hard. He *couldn't* find her here. He absolutely couldn't. Panic mounted in her chest. She could lie through her teeth, but nothing would excuse exposing his baby to danger. He'd never forgive her. She couldn't risk that. There was also the risk that he wouldn't leave it there. That drippy Dylan might drop her in it, even though she'd coached him and coached him. And then what? Mark was a detective. He might take Dylan to the station, question him. How long would it be before Dylan spilled his guts and told him where the little girl—

Jade closed her eyes with relief, gulping hard, as she noticed the farmhouse door opening. Glancing over his shoulder, Mark turned towards it, and then stopped to fish his phone from his pocket.

Evie stirred as he spoke, as she naturally would on hearing the rich, deep timbre of her daddy's voice. Quickly, Jade turned to gather her from the stroller. "*Hush, little baby, don't say a word,*" she recited silently, rocking her gently. Then, grabbing her pacifier from the stroller tray and feeding it to her, she turned back to the barn door, hardly daring to breathe as she listened.

"Oh Christ... You're joking." She heard Mark's shocked tone. "But why the *hell* would she think that?"

Jade waited as Mark listened to whoever was on the other end of the line.

"But you told her the texts were only ever work-related?" Mark went on, running a hand agitatedly through his hair.

Jade felt a thrill of excitement spiking inside her. Melissa had obviously got the hints she'd been dropping about Lisa's persistent texting. And it was about time. Jade had been wondering whether she was going to have to paint the woman a bloody picture.

"Apart from the one I sent while you were there. Right." Mark sighed despondently and stared up into the sky. "Okay, thanks, Lisa. No, not your fault. I'd better get back."

Jade watched as Mark ended the call, studied the phone for a second, as if debating making another, and then walked towards Dylan's mother, standing in the farmhouse door. Poor Mark. She could almost feel his hurt. She so wished he didn't have to suffer all this. It was just so cruel. But then, she had to be cruel to be kind. There was no other way. They were two souls destined to be together. She would soothe away his troubles with sweet, tender kisses, take his seed inside her, gladly give birth to his babies. He would thank her, eventually, for opening his eyes.

CHAPTER TWENTY-FIVE

MELISSA

"So, what do you think?" Mel asked Poppy, turning from the front door after waving off Poppy's little friend and her dad, who'd kindly delivered Poppy safely home. He'd clearly appreciated her new look. Mel might have been out of circulation for a while, but she could still read the signs. Poppy, however...

Peering over Baby Annabell, clutched to her chest, she looked up at Mel uncertainly. "You look like Jade," she whispered, her huge chocolate-brown eyes filled with awe.

"Do I?" Mel fluffed up her new blonde locks, courtesy of a mad dash to the supermarket. "Well, there's a compliment."

Smiling, she held out her hand and waited for Poppy to take hold of it. Poppy hesitated for a second, which was only natural, Mel supposed, on finding a different-looking mummy greeting her at the front door. She actually wasn't trying to look like Jade. She'd been going more for the Lisa look, on the basis that Mark obviously preferred blondes. She'd stopped short of cropping her hair short, although she'd felt like it, closely followed by slicing into his shirts.

She toyed with the latter idea. But no. She was going to rise above it, she'd decided. She wasn't even going to question him about it. She was going to be the epitome of calm. Sitting in the corner sobbing like a baby wasn't an option. She had cried, bitter tears of hurt and soul-crushing humiliation. She felt too tired for this, too tired to fight it. And then she'd caught sight of herself in the mirror, looking pathetic, looking exhausted, and thought *fuck him*. And Lisa, her so-called friend. She wasn't going to scream and shout, she didn't want to hurl raging accusations in front of their children, she just wanted to get back to where she was a few short weeks ago. She wanted to feel well, to feel in control again. And to that end, she did need to fight. She'd stocked up on vitamins, throwing them in her shopping basket arbitrarily. Starting tomorrow, she would set her alarm and make sure to get up early. Eat sensibly, exercise, and then get back to work in earnest. She wasn't going to go down the medication route. There was absolutely no way was she going there again, so far down the bottomless pit she'd had to claw her way out of it by her fingernails. Wouldn't Mark love that, his wife comatose to the point of oblivion, enabling him to do what he liked, *who* he liked? But... She swallowed back a tight lump in her throat. He wouldn't. Not the Mark she knew. He'd always been dependable, there for her, the one solid thing in her life when everything else seemed to be sliding away from her. Her rock.

But he was human, wasn't he? Perhaps he was tired, too. Emotionally depleted. Perhaps he needed support, and she just hadn't seen it. She wouldn't fall apart, Mel promised herself. She wouldn't accuse him or attack him. She would wait. She would watch. And she would see. Because, if her worst fears were true, if he no longer loved her, which was possible—love wasn't forever, was it?—it would be there in his eyes.

Deep in her thoughts, Melissa hadn't realised Poppy was tugging on her hand. "*Mummeee*," she said, scowling up at her, "why are you standing in the middle of the hall crying?"

"I'm not," Mel said, blinking quickly.

"Yes, you are. You've got wet cheeks," Poppy pointed out, her innocent eyes wide and now dark with worry.

"I'm not crying, sweetheart," Mel assured her, quickly bending to pick her up. "I got shampoo in my eyes when I washed my hair, that's all."

Pressing her close, she gave her world-wise seven-year-old a firm hug, and tried to quiet her own rising panic. Poppy had looked at her as if she were mad. Was she? Or on her way to being? There had been a time when her grip on reality felt as elusive as sea slipping through sand. Simple, everyday tasks had been beyond her.

She couldn't allow that to happen again, to be so emotionally dysfunctional she couldn't care for herself, let alone her family. Her chest tight, she studied Poppy's confused little face and steeled her determination. She would not drift off to that faraway place and abandon her children.

Poppy leaned back, searching her face curiously in turn, as if she didn't quite know what to make of her. "Where's Jade?" she asked.

Mel mustered up a smile. She couldn't blame the child for that, she supposed, given her own odd behaviour lately. "On her way," she said. "She popped out to see a friend, but she'll be back before Daddy and I go out. Let's go and get your jim-jams on, shall we? And then you can help Mummy put some make-up on and make herself beautiful. What do you think?"

Poppy studied her for a second longer. "But you *are* beautiful, Mummy," she said, her expression concerned and earnest all at once.

Mel swallowed hard.

CHAPTER TWENTY-SIX

MARK

Mark drove home fast, cursing his thoughtlessness all the way there. He'd gone behind Mel's back. There was no point in denying it. The whys and wherefores wouldn't matter to Mel. He had. And he was sorry. But if Mel imagined, for one minute, that he would *ever* use anything that had happened between them as an excuse to...No way. Mel *must* know him well enough to know he would never risk losing his family, losing her.

Pulling haphazardly up on the drive, he took a breath and then pushed through the front door, cautioning himself to calm down. He was the one at fault here. He had no idea what was going on with Mel—he was worried about her, now more than ever—but, whatever his motives, he'd obviously made the situation a whole lot worse.

"Daddeee!" Poppy greeted him as usual, gleefully barrelling into him as he stepped into the hall, closely followed by Hercules, who seemed to be back on form.

Mark patted the dog and then scooped Poppy up into his arms. She was in her pyjamas, also as usual. The make-up though? Mark studied his daughter's glossy red lips and smoky grey eye shadow with bemusement.

"I'm beautiful!" Poppy announced, pressing her small hands to her blushed cheeks and beaming at him.

Mark widened his eyes. "Undoubtedly." He smiled, pressing

a kiss carefully to her nose so as not to smudge her. "Where's Mummy?"

"Trying her wardrobe on," Poppy supplied.

"Ah." Mark nodded. "Not sure it will suit her, but..."

"Not *really* the wardrobe, silly." Poppy rolled her eyes. "She's trying some *clothes* on so she can look gorgeous."

Mark quietly thanked God for the apparent normalcy—apart from Poppy's makeover—that seemed to prevail. "In which case, I'd better go up and make myself gorgeous in case I'm too scruffy to be seen out with her." He smiled, turning for the stairs.

"Wait." Poppy jiggled and pointed to the lounge, where *Scooby-Doo* was in full swing, judging by the sounds from the TV. "Mummy said I could watch the end of my programme."

"Bed as soon as it's finished," Mark said, lowering her to the floor. Straightening up, he watched her scoot back to the lounge, and then turned back to the stairs with a shake of his head—and stopped dead.

"Well?" Mel asked, searching his face as she paused partway down.

"Um..." Loosening his collar, Mark looked her slowly over, taking in the five-inch heels, the long shapely legs, the tight, short red dress that fitted her every curve, and which Mel had previously declared made her look tarty. Mark had disagreed, he recalled, assuring her it made her look red-hot. His gaze travelled higher, pausing at her breasts over the low-cut neckline, and then upwards to her face. She was wearing makeup—plenty of it, unusually. It was the hair that really grabbed his attention, though.

"Wow," he said.

"Wow in a good way, or a bad way?" Mel asked, studying him carefully. From her expression, however, Mark felt she wasn't seeking his approval.

"Good," he assured her. "You look...stunning." He didn't lie. She looked breathtaking. Slightly perturbing, though, was that she didn't look like Mel. Mark didn't dare say he'd loved her hair the way it was, a fiery hot copper.

"I thought I'd try a new look," Mel said. "Variety's the spice of life, after all," she added, holding his gaze as she joined him in the hall. "*Isn't it?*"

Noting the innuendo in her tone, Mark wasn't sure what to say. He'd hoped to apologise, but here in the hall, with Mel scrutinising him, a defiant expression on her face, and Jade looking on from the galleried landing, didn't seem quite the right time.

"I'd, er, better get changed," he said, nodding upwards. "I'll be two minutes." Smiling uncertainly, Mark headed on up, puzzling over this change in Mel. She'd smiled back, but…there had been something there, hiding beneath her cheerful expression. But she did look good, fantastic, and she seemed in control. Mark couldn't help thinking it was forced though, that she seemed to be working hard at it.

Meeting Jade at the top, on her way into the nursery, Mark followed her in to have a quick check on Evie. Finding her sleeping, he breathed a sigh of relief, and turned back to the door, almost falling into Jade in the process. He hadn't realised she was standing behind him.

"Sorry," he said, catching hold of her forearms as she stumbled backwards. "Did I hurt you?"

"No," she assured him. "*Shhhh.*" She smiled, pressing a finger to her lips and gesturing him out of the room.

"You'd better get a move on," she whispered, once they were on the landing, pointing down to where Mel was now heading for the lounge, calling Hercules to go out for a wee as she went, "or you'll be in even more trouble."

Clearly he was in trouble then. "Yeah, I think I might have some apologising to do." He smiled half-heartedly, guessing that Mel had "shared" with her what an idiot he'd been.

"Chocolates," Jade suggested. "They work for me."

Mark nodded and dipped his head in appreciation. Chocolates were a no. With Poppy's dairy allergy, they made it a rule not to have any in the house. Maybe flowers, he thought, and then wondered how they might be interpreted.

"If it's any consolation, I gathered you were just trying to get a female perspective," Jade offered astutely.

"I was. Backfired a bit, though, didn't it?" Mark rolled his eyes at his own ineptitude. "I'll try a grovelling apology, I think. And the most expensive thing on the menu. We shouldn't be too late back," he said, turning to the main bedroom. "You have all the numbers in case of emergencies, yes?"

"All to hand," Jade assured him. "I'll ring you if I need to, but don't worry. I'm sure there won't be any problems."

CHAPTER TWENTY-SEVEN

JADE

Well, there wouldn't be any problems here. As for what might happen in the restaurant...

Jade watched Mark walk towards his bedroom, looking troubled, as he would be by his wife's peculiar behaviour and trollopy appearance. Then, humming softly to herself, she headed along the landing to her own room, where she retrieved a shoebox from the top of her wardrobe. Pondering the side effects of the various drugs, she was replacing the packet of slow-release capsules under the few bits of memorabilia she kept there when someone tapped lightly on her door.

Quickly snapping the lid back on the shoebox, Jade stuffed it well back on the shelf. It was Mark at the door—Melissa always called out "just me" in an irritating singsong voice. Jade's mouth curved into a smile. Turning for the door, she hitched her T-shirt over her head, tugged it off and unsnapped her bra. Then, reaching for the dressing gown Melissa had so kindly provided her, she pushed her arms into it, holding it loosely enough at the front to expose a good expanse of milky white breast as she yanked the door open.

"Oh, my!" Jade blinked, suitably mortified, as Mark got the desired eyeful before turning away. "I'm really sorry," she mumbled, the door now partly closed as she peeped shyly around it. "I thought it was Melissa."

"My fault," Mark said, as a gentleman would. "Please accept my apologies. I'll announce myself next time." He was kneading his forehead in that way he did—flustered, obviously. Bound to be.

"Apology accepted," Jade assured him, tying her dressing gown tight to expose a lot less of herself. "I'm decent now. You can turn around."

Nodding, Mark turned back, looking decidedly uncomfortable. That was to be expected, she supposed. Jade continued smiling, her gaze grazing over him as he stood there, looking achingly sexy in a navy linen jacket with a light blue shirt underneath, dark jeans and leather belt. Her eyes rested briefly at belt level before travelling back to his face. Tall, dark and heart-stoppingly handsome; he was hers. Or he very soon would be.

"I just wanted to let you know we were leaving." He smiled nervously. "Poppy's still in the lounge. We'll be back around eleven."

"I'll come right down and fetch her. Enjoy," Jade said brightly, as he headed for the stairs. "Don't drink too much."

"I won't. I'm driving." Mark waved a hand as he went on down.

"All the more for Melissa then," Jade called after him. *The whole bottle would be good.*

Poppy fell asleep in record time, Bedtime Peppa tucked cosily up with her and Hercules lying protectively at her feet. Jade scowled at the dog and then tiptoed out. Then back in again to feed the goldfish. Sprinkling the requisite pinch of food into the bowl, she bent down to peer at the fish, eyes wide and making a guppy mouth as she did. The water was getting dirty again, she noticed. Sighing, she tipped another more generous dollop of food in. *Knock yourself out, Nemo.* What kind of a life was it, swimming around in circles in shitty water anyway? Cruel,

Jade thought. She gave him another sprinkle for good measure, and then, turning to poke out her tongue at Hercules, eased the door quietly shut behind her and crept out.

Peeping into the nursery, she noticed a little hand flailing in the cot and realised it was time for Evie's feed. "Coming, sweetheart," she assured her, and then, humming, she went back to her room to collect her Boots bag before carrying on down to the kitchen, where she picked up the sealed container of milk Melissa had left in the fridge and tipped it down the sink. It was a good job she'd started weaning Evie as soon as she'd moved in—she congratulated herself on her foresight as she prepared the formula. With her careless mother stuffed full of drugs, breast milk would obviously harm the poor little mite.

Milk in the microwave, she slipped back upstairs and lifted Evie out of her cot. She was now wide-eyed and alert, looking forward to her bath, followed by a warm, cosy feed and a soft lullaby.

"She'd probably let you slip through her hands and drown you in the bath, wouldn't she, Angel, hmm? Or stuff you in the kiln and fire you. Silly Melissa." In sweet singsong tones, she addressed Evie by her proper name, which suited her far better. She laid her carefully on the changing mat to undress her.

"You're a gorgeous little girl, aren't you?" Pulling her little sausage arms and legs gently from her pink stripy sleepsuit, she saucered her eyes and smiled down at her, laughing as Evie smiled back. Then she blew on her tummy, causing Evie to chuckle delightedly.

"Mummy's perfect little Angel, aren't you?" she said, standing up and hoisting the naked little baby high in the air. "Don't you worry, sweet girl, Mummy won't let naughty Melissa hurt you. Daddy would be heartbroken, wouldn't he, hmm?"

Holding her as high as she could, which Evie just loved, Jade twirled her around and around. "Piss off," she hissed over her shoulder, as Hercules growled at her from the landing.

CHAPTER TWENTY-EIGHT

MELISSA

"She's absolutely amazing. I have no idea how I managed without her," Melissa said, regaling Emily and Adam with tales of their perfect babysitter. "She's fantastic with the kids, isn't she, Mark?"

"Er, yes. You already said so, though, Mel." Mark looked worriedly from her to her wine glass.

Mel ignored him. She'd only had a couple of glasses. And someone had to fill the awkward gaps in the conversation, since Mark didn't seem to have much to say for himself, unsurprisingly. "She literally fell into our laps," she gushed on, talking to their friends, rather than to him. "I mean, it was just dreadful, her house catching fire like that, but the timing couldn't have been better from our point of view. Mark likes her too, don't you, Mark? Then again, he's quite partial to blondes. Thus…" Plucking up a strand of hair, Mel indicated her own transformed locks.

"It's different," Emily said, glancing between Mel and Mark. "I still think I prefer your own colour, though. In fact, I was saying to Adam I wished—"

"Can't afford to let things shlide, see, we women." Mel waggled her wine glass in Emily's direction. "I mean, having a baby's the most natural thing in the world, isn't it? We should just pop 'em out…" Poking a finger in her mouth, she attempted to pop her cheek. It didn't quite pop, but they'd get the drift. "And then bounce back to our beautiful, slim selves. Course, we'd have to be beautiful to start with. And slim." Mel furrowed her brow, pondering her pre-baby body forlornly.

"Good job you're both of the above then." Adam paid her a compliment, bless him, in the absence of one from her husband, whom she was obviously embarrassing, judging by the uncomfortable look on his face. Mel didn't much care. She was *so* bloody angry. How dare he sit there in judgement of *her*.

"But it has to be effortless," she went on determinedly, knocking back the contents of her glass and planting it on the table. "Lisa's effortless, isn't she, Mark? Like an adorable, natural little pixie."

Mark glanced down at that, drawing in a long breath—quite clearly embarrassed.

"I can't believe she can hold her own as a police officer. Ooh, pardon me, I mean a *detective sergeant*." Mel flapped her hand, pseudo-apologetically. "Probably holds everyone else's, as well," she added bitchily. Then, chuckling at her wit, whilst biting back a sudden urge to burst into tears, she reached for the wine bottle.

"It's all gone, Mel," Mark pointed out gently, glancing warily at Emily as he did so.

"Oh well, we'll just order another then." Mel waved the bottle by way of attracting the waiter's attention.

"The time's getting on, Mel," Mark started. "Maybe we should—"

"We'll have another Pinot Grigio, please," said Mel, smiling sweetly and fluttering her eyelashes at the waiter as he came across to their table.

The waiter nodded politely and, apparently oblivious to her subtle flirtations, reached to relieve her of the empty bottle. *Ah well, his loss.* He was probably gay. Far too good-looking not to be. Mel looked him over, giving Emily a conspiratorial wink. "Adam"—she turned to him—"another red?"

Adam glanced at Mark and then back to her. "No. Thanks, Mel, I've had more than enough," he said, with a gracious smile.

"But you're not driving," Mel reminded him. "You came in a taxi. What was the point of that, for goodness' sake, if you didn't intend to have a drink? Go on, go wild. You only live once."

Adam reached up a hand and scratched behind his ear. A habit he was prone to when he was agitated, Emily had once confided. He looked a bit agitated. Mel squinted at him. Probably because of Mark sitting there looking so bloody po-faced.

What had he got to be miserable about? It was *she* who was supposed to be miserable, wasn't it? Was *she* spoiling everyone's evening? No. Shooting Mark a scornful look, Mel reached to grab his still three-quarters-full glass. "Here then. You might as well finish Mark's," she said, pouring the remainder of the red wine into Adam's glass. "He's obviously not going to."

"Doesn't look like I am either," Adam pointed out, pulling back out of splashing distance as most of the contents of the glass spilled onto the pristine white tablecloth.

"Whoops, sorry!" Mel closed one eye and smiled wanly. "Never mind. I'll order you a single glass instead."

"Mel…" Mark caught hold of her arm as she waved the glass in the air. "He doesn't want one."

"Oh?" Mel turned to glare at him. "And *you've* decided that for him, have you? Clearly you're a mind reader now, as well as perfect in every other possible way and a genius when it comes to women's feelings. I mean you're just so flipping clever, I'm in awe. Particularly at how you *cleverly* managed to text Lisa about the little secret between you while she was sitting in *my* kitchen!"

The silence that followed was profound, made more obvious by all the diners in the restaurant seeming to stop clattering cutlery as one and turn heads in their direction. Mel didn't care about that either. Was *she* at fault here? For what, exactly? Making a monumental effort to have a good time when the man she'd thought she could trust implicitly had betrayed her? Did he really expect her to believe Lisa's feeble attempts to convince her they'd done no more than swap intimate texts? *Hah!*

Swiping a tear from her face, she snatched the new bottle of wine from the ice bucket as the waiter brought it across. "Come on—cheer up, everyone, for goodness' sake," she said, topping up her glass. "We're supposed be celebrating Emily's birthday."

Glancing at Mark, who wouldn't meet her gaze, and then at Adam, who averted his in favour of studying his phone, she leaned across to refill Emily's glass. "We should leave these killjoys here and go clubbing," she suggested, casting another meaningful look in Mark's direction. "Obviously, they've forgotten how to have a good time."

Emily, though, placed her hand over her glass. "Actually, I think we need to go, Mel." She smiled apologetically. "Kayla's not so happy with her babysitter. You know what eleven-year-olds can be like."

"Oh." Reminded of the fact that she had children of her own, Mel dropped her gaze. "Yes. Of course. Sorry, I...wasn't thinking."

"The taxi's outside." Emily reached to squeeze her arm. "I'll give you a ring tomorrow, Mel. Take care, hon."

Giving Mark a pointed look, Emily got to her feet and walked around to give Mel a firm hug. The two men stood simultaneously, leaving Mel feeling bewildered, still seated at the table. She had spoiled her friend's birthday. Spoiled everything. *No!* It was Mark's fault, not hers. She was only trying to be cheerful. What was the *matter* with everyone?

"I'll give you a ring. About that holiday chalet," Mark said, shaking Adam's hand.

"Do that." Adam smiled. "We have some new log cabins being built by the river. It would be great to have you and Mel over to dinner one evening. I'll give you the guided tour."

Emily went around to Mark then, giving him a hug. A very firm hug. Mel watched, jealousy and incomprehension warring inside her. Incomprehension at her own volatile emotions. Mark wouldn't. She *knew* in her heart that he wouldn't. His family were the world to him. So, why was she hurting so much? Why did she want to hurt him? Because it had been too good to be true? *He'd* been too good to be true? Her white knight had probably got tired of the battle. Tired of her. And who could blame him?

Adam and Emily left, and Mark rushed to settle the bill before she disgraced herself completely.

"Okay?" he asked her, slipping his wallet back into his pocket as he walked back to her, then leaning down to wrap an arm around her shoulders. He tried to make eye contact, but she looked away. She didn't want to see the pain in his eyes, the humiliation that would undoubtedly be there. She'd only been trying to have a bit of fun. It wasn't her fault. He'd caused all this, *not* her.

Her heart, which had been sinking steadily all evening, settled like a cold stone in her chest. She reached for the bottle of wine, drawing it proprietorially closer. People were looking. She could feel the prickle of their disapproving, hostile stares. But she didn't care.

"Go then. I'm staying," she announced, getting precariously to her feet as the too-handsome-not-to-be-gay waiter came over. "I'm going to dance on the tables with Miguel."

Stumbling forward, one leg decidedly shorter—it turned out she was missing a shoe—she snaked the hand still clutching the wine around the startled waiter's neck. "Dance with me, Miguel," she said breathily, attempting to lock come-hither eyes on his, but found she couldn't quite focus.

"Mel?" She felt a hand slide around her waist. Another trying to ease her arm from around the man's neck. "We need to go home, Mel," Mark said, close to her ear, as the room tilted and shifted. His voice wasn't angry. It was soft. Concerned. Frightened.

Oh, dear God. She was frightened.

Mel felt the floor shift violently beneath her, saw a thousand slivers of green glass shoot across the floor in slow motion as her legs melted, like soft butter, beneath her.

CHAPTER TWENTY-NINE

MARK

Mel didn't speak as Mark helped her into the car. She'd been subdued since the doctor at A&E had suggested that he might like to make sure his wife didn't drink so much in future. She'd looked out of it as they'd dressed the cut to her arm, which fortunately hadn't needed stitching. She still looked out of it, as if her mind was wandering to some dark, lonely place he couldn't follow. Mark had seen that look before. Guessing it would be fruitless to try to talk to her now, he made sure she was comfortable and went around to the driver's side. Climbing in, he reached gently around her to fasten her seatbelt, then took a breath, mentally steeling himself for what might be to come. "All right?" he asked her, not sure what else to say, what else he could trust himself to say.

Mel nodded, a small uncertain nod, but kept her gaze fixed on her hands, which were resting lightly in her lap. Sighing inwardly, Mark started the engine, wondering where the bloody hell they went from here.

As he flicked the wipers, which swiped hopelessly against the sudden deluge of late spring rain, Mel spoke. "Are the children all right?" she asked him, her voice barely a whisper.

You've finally remembered you have kids then? Mark thought, his emotions swinging from despair through anger to immense guilt. In truth, he felt like resting his head on the steering wheel and weeping. He had no idea what to do next. How to fix this. Bitter experience told him he couldn't, but he needed to. God help him, he couldn't let Mel sink so far down he was unable to reach her again. How had this happened? How hadn't he noticed the signs until now?

His jaw set tight, Mark gripped the steering wheel hard, reversed sharply and swung out of the car park. "They're fine," he said, after a pause, during which he'd had to work at composing himself. It would do no good to heap guilt on her shoulders, which would only add to the wretchedness she would undoubtedly be feeling. "Jade has everything under control. Don't worry."

She didn't look at him. Couldn't or wouldn't. Swallowing back a tight knot in his throat, Mark hesitated, and then tentatively reached across to squeeze her hand. "We'll talk tomorrow," he said gruffly. "Let's just get you home for now. You need to rest." He resisted saying that things would look better in the morning. He had a feeling that they wouldn't. That things wouldn't look better for a long time to come.

Mel didn't answer. Turning her gaze to the passenger window, she fell silent instead, watching the bleak night pass by as they drove.

Fat splodges of rain now plopping moodily against the windscreen, Mark concentrated on the road. Silently, he thanked God, yet again, that they did have Jade. As horrendous as the circumstances were that had forced her to move out of her house, Mark was bloody glad she'd arrived in their lives when she had. He'd managed last time Mel had been ill, but with two children to care for now, Mark doubted he'd cope without help. But wasn't he jumping the gun? Imagining the worst-case scenario? Her odd behaviour was reminiscent of her previous severe bout of depression, but his thoughtlessness at involving someone else in their problems had added to her upset tonight. She'd obviously convinced herself that he might actually be involved with Lisa.

He had to take things one step at a time. The first thing he needed to do was persuade Mel to get a diagnosis. Alongside that, he had to make sure she knew he was here for her. Shocked though he was by the sudden onset of symptoms, she had to know that she was much more to him than the mother of his children. She was the woman he loved. The woman who'd loved him back, despite his insecurities and flaws. If the sunny, independent person he knew her to be was momentarily eclipsed by the darkness, then so be it. He'd fight alongside her until the fucking sun came back out. He was here for the long haul. Somehow, he had to convince her of that.

Pulling up on the drive, Mark killed the engine and waited. Mel seemed reluctant to move. Guessing she would be struggling with her own conflicting emotions, Mark gave her a moment before softly prompting her. "Ready?"

Jade was waiting in the hall when they went in, her dressing gown belted tight, her expression apprehensive as she looked down at the shoes Mark was carrying. Mel had refused to put them back on, but even without them she was still unsteady on her feet.

Supporting Mel around the waist with his free arm, Mark shrugged, guessing he didn't need to communicate more than he had from the hospital.

Jade smiled sympathetically. "I'll make us some tea," she said, clearly attempting to give them some space.

"Thanks," Mark said, parking the shoes in the hall and steering Mel gently towards the stairs. He wasn't sure she would be able to drink any, but it might help. She'd vomited up what little food she'd eaten in the ambulance.

Mel stopped. "Are Poppy and Evie all right?" she asked, looking at Jade.

Jade stepped back, her concern obvious, as she looked Mel over. "Fine. Both fast asleep and dreaming happy dreams," she reassured her with a smile. Mark was grateful.

Mel nodded, smiling tremulously, and then wrapped her arms about herself and allowed Mark to guide her up the stairs.

She paused on the landing, looking first towards Poppy's door and then Evie's. Mark prayed she didn't insist on going in, and then breathed a considerable sigh of relief when she walked on. Aside from the fact that they would be bound to wake them, he doubted Mel would want Poppy to see her like this.

She still had her arms about herself as she walked into the bedroom.

"I'll get you something to sleep in," Mark offered, as she stopped in the middle of the room, seeming uncertain.

Walking to the en suite, he unhooked the shirt she wore from the door, considering whether to offer to help her to shower and quickly discarding the idea. His heart twisted afresh as he recalled the last time they'd been in there together, when everything had seemed so right between them. The morning Hercules had been injured, he reminded himself, realising now that things hadn't been as right as they'd seemed. He'd just been too damn wrapped up in his work to see it.

"I'll give you a hand," he said, walking back towards where Mel still stood, unmoving. "Fancy sitting on the bed?" he asked, standing behind her, ready to catch her if she stumbled. "It would make life a lot easier."

Still, Mel didn't move. "I'm sorry," she said instead, her voice so small and full of remorse, Mark felt like crying for her.

Briefly, he hesitated, and then wrapped his arms around her. "It's okay," he assured her, easing her towards him. "The world's still turning."

"So, *so* sorry," Mel said, her voice catching, causing Mark's chest to constrict.

"It's okay, Mel," he repeated throatily, turning her gently to face him as a sob shook through her. "We'll get through this, I promise."

Another sob escaping her, Mel leaned into him, dropping her forehead to his shoulder.

Mark pressed a hand to her hair—her gorgeous, copper hair, now blonde. Not Mel's. This illness was part of her, and Mark realised he'd have to accept it might always be. But it wasn't the biggest part of her, the person she was. Somehow, he'd deal with this. Help Mel deal with this.

"Can you promise me something, Mel?" he asked cautiously.

Mel nodded into him.

"Will you make a doctor's appointment?"

Mark prayed hard as he waited again. She hated the damn place. She would go for the kids, no qualms. But when it came to herself, she wouldn't go to the surgery unless she absolutely had to. He couldn't make her go, but hoped she would see that this was one of those times.

"Yes," Mel said at last, with some effort. "I will, I promise."

Breathing deeply, Mark pulled her closer. "Good," he said, overwhelming relief washing through him. "So, how about we get good and cosy together? I don't know about you, but I'm dead on my feet." Dropping a soft kiss to her head, Mark eased back, gently lifting her chin to look into her beautiful green eyes. The colour of ferns after the rain, they were peppered with such anxiety and uncertainty it tore him apart. "I do excellent cuddles." He mustered up a smile.

Mel laughed, a rather strangulated laugh. "My white knight," she said, her expression now one of immense sadness.

"At your service," Mark assured her, hoping he could be all she needed him to be. That he was strong enough. He would be. He needed to be. There was simply no other option.

Mark helped her wash her face, brush her teeth and get changed, the body-hugging dress being impossible to get off single-handedly even when stone-cold sober, he imagined.

Now, trying to find the balance somewhere between husband

and carer, he eased the duvet up over her. She was facing away from him, curled into a tight ball. Mark's heart wrenched inside him. Checking the baby monitor, which, mercifully, had remained quiet, he deliberated for a second and then switched it to mute, before quickly undressing and slipping in beside her. She might not need a lover right now, but she needed not to feel alone. He hoped she needed him.

Brushing her cheek with a soft kiss, he slid an arm around her. He closed his eyes as he felt the tension run through her body, heard her trying to stifle her tears. Mark wasn't sure what to do, what to say. He couldn't make it go away. "I love you, Mrs. Cain," he eventually murmured, close to her ear, wishing he could show her, but that would be insensitive beyond belief. He settled for holding her instead, waiting until her tears subsided and she relaxed into him. Waiting again, until he heard her breathing slow and felt the steady rise and fall of her chest, he eased quietly back out of bed.

He was desperately tired, but he needed to check on the kids. He also needed to let Jade know the monitor in here was switched off, at least for tonight. He'd heard her going back downstairs and guessed she'd been too disturbed by the evening's events to easily drift off. He just hoped she wasn't put off. He hadn't realised how much they would need her, but they did, now more than ever.

Mark found Jade in the kitchen, preparing a feed. And clearly, he'd caught her by surprise. She jumped as he came through the door, dropping the lid of the pedal bin faster than she'd intended and wincing as it clanged.

"Sorry," she said, blushing. "I didn't hear you."

"My fault. Sorry I startled you," Mark said, apologising for the second time in twenty-four hours.

Jade smiled brightly. "No problem. I was just making sure Evie's feed was ready. I didn't want her crying for too long and waking Melissa. How is she?"

"Okay...ish." Mark shrugged uncertainly. He wasn't sure how much he should divulge, given his mistake of confiding in Lisa, but, assuming Jade wasn't already thinking of moving out, she would have to be aware of at least some of what was going on.

"I made Mel some tea." Jade indicated the mug as he walked across to her. "It might need a quick blast in the microwave though."

"She's spark out," Mark said wearily. "I could use one though."

"Not this." Jade swept up the mug, tipping the contents down the sink before he had chance to reach for it. "Sorry. It's got loads of sugar in and I know you don't take it."

Mark furrowed his brow. Since when did Mel start taking sugar?

"She thought it might help with her energy levels," Jade said, though he hadn't asked. "I'll make you another."

Ah. Made sense, Mark supposed. As much as anything made sense tonight. "No need. Thanks, Jade, but I think I might have a nightcap instead." He shouldn't, but, frankly, he needed something stronger than tea. "Don't suppose you fancy joining me while you have your tea, do you?" he asked, noting her mug, which was still half full.

Jade hesitated for a second. "I'd love to," she said. "Evie's due to wake soon anyway. There's not much point going to bed."

"No." Mark guessed she wouldn't be getting a great deal of sleep tonight either. "Sorry about all of this, Jade. Mel doesn't make a habit of drinking. She has the odd glass of wine, but... Well, there's a bit more to it, to be honest."

Mark sighed despondently. He really didn't have a clue where to start.

Jade reached to squeeze his arm. "Come on," she said. "You can tell me all about it while you have your nightcap."

Picking up her mug, she headed for the lounge. Mark followed, grateful for her understanding, and for the fact that she didn't seem to be about to give her notice and bolt for the door.

Curled up on the sofa, Jade waited while Mark poured himself a large whisky. Taking a breath, he swilled the amber liquid contemplatively around the glass and then swigged back a large gulp.

"You looked as if you needed that," Jade commented, as Mark waited for the whisky to hit the spot.

"Yeah." Mark ran his hand through his hair and took a seat in the armchair. "Strange night."

"Do you want to talk about it? I mean, I know you probably feel like a bit of a traitor with Melissa lying asleep upstairs," she added intuitively, "but I'm a good listener, if you need one."

Mark nodded. Traitor pretty well summed it up, but what choice did he have? Jade clearly knew there was a problem anyway. He just hoped she wouldn't think it was too big a problem to deal with.

"I suspect Mel might be suffering symptoms of depression. I'm not sure yet, but the signs are there. She's suffered with it before. Severe depression."

He paused, looking at Jade for her reaction. The sad fact was, some people simply couldn't cope with mental illness, which was the basis of Mel's fury with him for discussing it behind her back. The rest, her imagining that he might be having an affair, was fuelled by the negative view of herself she would have right now. Mark was aware of it, but it didn't make it any easier to deal with.

Seeming to digest the information, Jade nodded.

Her expression was concerned, but not shocked, Mark noted. He took a breath and went on. "We lost a child. A while back. A son, six months old." Having studied the subject endlessly in his attempts to help Mel get through it, he was also aware that there might not be an apparent cause for the onset of symptoms, that the sufferer might not even be aware of it, but he felt Jade should know the circumstances around it, for Mel's sake.

Jade paled, now definitely looking shocked. "Oh God, Mark, that's awful. Poor Melissa."

"It was." Mark took a swig of his whisky. "Bloody awful, to be honest. There was a point where I thought I might lose Mel as well. I felt I'd already lost her emotionally. She came back to me, eventually, but…"

Mark trailed off. He hadn't realised he'd finished his drink until Jade walked across to relieve him of the glass. "Another?" she asked him kindly.

Mark glanced from her to the glass. Alcohol was small comfort, in reality. He'd depended on it too heavily in the past, but now he felt the need to anaesthetise himself, at least for tonight. "Better make it a small one." He smiled. "Thanks, Jade."

"You were saying?" Jade urged him on, as she poured a small measure.

"It's not something you just get over," Mark confided. "Mel really had to work hard at it. She took antidepressants, prescribed on a trial and error basis, had psychoanalysis. She hated it. Hated herself for it. She's lived in fear of slipping back there since. I suppose we both just hoped it had gone away." He'd certainly hoped, desperately. Obviously, he'd buried his head in the sand, rather than realise she might never be truly "cured."

Leaning forward, Mark dragged his hands exhaustedly over his face, and then looked up, surprised, as Jade placed a hand on his shoulder. "I'm sorry, Mark," she said sympathetically. "I know how difficult that must have been for you. It's hard on the sufferer, but it's hard on loved ones too."

Accepting the drink she offered him, Mark eyed her curiously.

"My mum," Jade elucidated, smiling sadly. "She struggled with depression for years. I do understand, honestly."

Mark felt a huge surge of relief, and then concern, as he recalled her personal circumstances. "That's not how she...?" He stopped, not sure how to ask whether she'd had to deal with the worst kind of loss possible.

Jade shook her head. "No, I lost my parents in a car accident," she said, heading back to the sofa. "The car caught fire, actually," she said, seating herself in the corner and drawing her legs up underneath her. "A gruesome coincidence."

Christ. A graphic flashback slamming violently into him: images of the dead child who haunted his dreams, calling ceaselessly out to him. Mark almost choked on his whisky.

"Are you all right, Mark?" Jade asked, unfurling herself and getting to her feet. "You look as if you've seen a ghost."

Mark drained his glass. "Yes," he managed, nodding. "Just exhausted." Definitely exhausted, he realised. He needed to sleep. And he really needed not to be drinking this stuff on top of endless nights broken with nightmares bordering on hallucination. "You must be, too."

"A bit," Jade admitted.

"I'm sorry, Jade. About your parents," Mark offered. "That must have been so hard to deal with."

"It was. But we cope when we have to, don't we?" Smiling stoically, she shrugged, and then turned quickly to the door as the unmistakable sounds of Evie waking reached their ears.

"I'll go," Mark said, dumping his glass on the coffee table. "You try and get some sleep."

Jade caught his arm as he joined her in the hall. "I have her feed ready," she reminded him. "Go to Melissa." She smiled reassuringly. "She might need you. And don't worry, Mark, I'm not going to run at the first family hiccup. The children will need support too."

Hearing her humming sweetly as he bypassed the nursery five minutes later, Mark couldn't help but be in awe of her. How she had coped, losing her parents like that and yet remaining positive and cheerful, he really didn't know.

He peered quickly into Poppy's room. Hercules was alert, looking up at him when he popped his head in, as usual. Everything seemingly normal. Yet normality was slipping away. Again.

Climbing in beside Mel for a second time, Mark reached gently for her. He needed to feel the wholeness of her, to reassure her he was here, though he doubted she would wake, given her sleep patterns over the last few weeks and the alcohol in her system. Mark was pretty sure she must have been hitting the booze earlier that day. The few wines she'd had while they were at the restaurant wouldn't have rendered her inebriated to the point of unconsciousness.

How long might she have been secretly drinking, he wondered. What might have precipitated it, caused her to reach for alcohol as a crutch, as she had done once before? He had no way of knowing. If only he'd been aware, been paying attention, then maybe, just maybe, he could have done something to help her.

Mel stirred a little in his arms. No more than that. Mark moved closer, pressing a soft kiss to her cheek, and then dragging a hand across his face to wipe a salty tear from his own.

CHAPTER THIRTY

JADE

For God's sake! What now? Jade was halfway through a phone conversation with drippy Dylan, who was fretting about the girl, who apparently looked "sickly," when she heard the commotion from the other end of the landing. Storming from her room, she only just managed to wipe the scowl from her face as Mark emerged from his bedroom. Looking worse for wear after his horrendous night out with his mental wife, followed by two sizeable whiskies, precious little sleep, and obviously panic-stricken, he hadn't bothered pulling on anything but his tracksuit bottoms.

Appreciating the view, Jade turned the flash off on her phone and took a photo to inspect more thoroughly at leisure, and then bolted after him as Mark headed for Poppy's room, where the child was howling like a banshee.

"Poppy? What on earth?" Mark faltered inside the bedroom door, clearly bewildered. Jade, one step behind—and contemplating poisoning the dog, who was emitting a low growl at the sight of her—could see why.

"What's happened, Poppy?" Concerned, as obviously he would be, Mark walked over to where Poppy was sitting cross-legged in the middle of the bed, cradling the goldfish bowl.

"Nemo's died," Poppy wailed, dragging an arm under her snotty nose as she looked up at him. "He's floating on the water. He's dead, Daddy. He's dead!"

Little brat. She'd make her eat the fucking fish for breakfast. Seething quietly in the doorway, Jade noted the foul-smelling water had soaked through Poppy's nightie and into the duvet beneath her, which would now have to be washed by yours truly, with Melissa about as much use as a fart in a spacesuit.

"Hey, hey. Come on, Poppet." Mark joined her on the bed, wrapping an arm around her and kissing the top of her head. It was such a tender gesture, Jade couldn't resist taking another photo. "Let me take a look," Mark gently cajoled her. "He might just be sleeping."

"He's not sleeping!" Fresh tears sprang from Poppy's eyes. "He's dead!"

Nodding understandingly, Mark squeezed her closer and then reached into the water.

Ugh. Jade recoiled as the slimy fish floated onto the palm of his hand. She watched in wonder as Mark blew softly on it. He really was the nicest, kindest person she'd ever known. He looked a bit crestfallen when it didn't twitch so much as a fin, despite several attempts at resuscitation.

"I think he might be, sweetheart," he eventually conceded, with a sympathetic sigh. "I'm guessing that means God must have wanted him for Baby Jesus' aquarium."

Mark looked down at Poppy, shrugging sadly.

Judging by the stubborn little crease in her forehead, though, Poppy wasn't buying it. "But why does God want him for baby Jesus' aquirum?" She looked querulously up at him.

To feed the five thousand, thought Jade, mentally rolling her eyes—though she had to admire Mark's ingenuity.

"Because…" Stopping, Mark furrowed his brow, clearly struggling for what to say next.

"Because Baby Jesus' aquarium is the ocean," Jade supplied, as he glanced helplessly in her direction.

Poppy looked towards her, blinking huge, hopeful eyes.

"One of the walls of his nursery is made of glass," Jade went on, walking across to kneel in front of her, rather than perch on the side of the wet bed. "He watches over the fish to make sure all the lost little ones find their mummies and daddies and swim in fish heaven together forever."

Poppy looked, awestruck, from Jade to Mark and back again. "Like Dory? She found her mummy and daddy," she whispered, and warming to the idea, judging by her expression.

"Just like Dory." Mark smiled at Jade, looking hugely relieved.

"They based the film on it, didn't they, Mark?" Her heart skipping a beat at the warmth in his decadent chocolate-brown eyes, Jade got to her feet before she melted in front of him.

"Yup." Mark played along perfectly. "It's a true story."

Poppy looked up at him and then to Jade—her wide eyes so trusting, it could almost be touching. "Will you help me bury him, Jade?"

"Of course I will," Jade promised with a reassuring smile. "I'll just go and see to Evie first." She indicated the nursery, beyond the door of which Evie was crying, having woken up far too early.

"And I'd better see to you, young lady." Mark placed the fish carefully back into the bowl and got to his feet. "We'll leave him there for now, where he's safe," he said, reaching to relieve Poppy of the bowl.

Parking it on the dressing table on the opposite wall, he gave Jade a conspiratorial wink as she headed for the door. Something deep within her swooped in response. Mark turned back to his daughter, who, in Jade's opinion, was demanding far more of his time than was healthy. "Come on, Poppet, up we come," he said, plucking her up from the bed. "We can't send Nemo to fish heaven wearing a wet nightie, can we? Arms up," he instructed, giving Jade another photo opportunity as he tugged the soggy nightie up over Poppy's head.

Jade didn't particularly want a wriggling, shivering, naked child in the photo, but with Mark's state of undress…How was a girl to resist? And Mark might like the photos, she supposed, later, should Poppy no longer be around.

Humming happily, she turned to the nursery, nipping deftly inside when she glimpsed Melissa stumbling from the main bedroom. Jade shuddered as she closed the door. Bleary-eyed and white-faced, and with her bleached blonde hair scarily all over the place, the woman looked like something the cat had dragged in. She thought fleetingly of the feline fleabag they'd assumed was hers. She really hoped Dylan didn't get it into his head to go poking around in the depths of his freezer. Preferring his mummy's home-cooking to his own culinary disasters, he wasn't likely to, and she had wrapped her parcel securely, first in polythene, then a carrier bag, before finally sealing it in a Perspex box and marking it Baby Milk. She'd told him it was imperative the box wasn't opened until the milk was ready to use, but still, she really ought to move it soon.

Jade hurried across to lift Evie from her cot. "Hello, my gorgeous baby girl." She flashed her a smile. "Let's get you changed and fed, shall we? We don't want silly Melissa interfering, do we, Angel? No, we do *not*." Jade's smile widened as, clearly delighted to see her, Evie chuckled gleefully and gave her a gummy grin.

Catching one excitedly flailing hand, Jade cradled her in the crook of her arm and pressed a kiss to her tiny fingers. "We want her gone, don't we, my precious?" she whispered. "Out of our lives forever and ever."

CHAPTER THIRTY-ONE

MARK

The local search for Daisy had now been widened, concentrating on woodland, orchards, beer factories and cider mills. Mark, meanwhile, was painstakingly going through historical maps and small-scale ordnance surveys, looking for abandoned buildings with basement access and properties that might no longer exist above ground level, in particular those with concealed septic tanks, or any conceivable place that might be used to secrete a small body.

"How's it going elsewhere?" Lisa asked him, coming back from a call-out to the town centre, where a group of local youths had decided to break the tedium of hanging around looking bored and had phoned in a sighting of the girl. Another false alarm.

Mark guessed she was asking after Melissa. Edwards had pulled him up twice this week for tardiness, now the norm for him with pandemonium on the home front. Mel had gone from sleeping heavily to waking several times in the night, thus insisting on taking over the night feeds. Mark would have been glad of it, grateful, were it not for the fact that he felt he had to watch her like a hawk, which really didn't make him feel great. Plus, it had thrown Evie's routine into chaos. Jade must have the patience of a saint, Mark had decided. She hadn't said so, but he'd guessed, from the look in her eyes, that she wasn't happy trusting Mel with the baby. Mel was also trying to catch up and fill the orders that had come in from Garden & Homes head office. Mark had been relieved, until he'd helped her load some ceramic stuff into her car, only to discover a carrier bag full of empty wine bottles.

"One day at a time." Mark smiled wearily in Lisa's direction, glad she was concerned enough to ask. He'd discovered from Lisa the full extent of Mel's reaction to his ill-timed text last week. Apparently, Mel had been reasonably calm, asking Lisa to leave and then telling her she didn't think for one minute he'd fucked her, because he preferred younger women with tits. Mark still winced when he thought about that scenario. Lisa obviously didn't text him early in the morning any more, which meant he was rarely up to speed when he did finally arrive at the station.

"He's still imagining the girl's alive," Cummings said as he walked past Mark's desk, heading for the door. Obviously, he had assumed they were discussing Daisy.

"There's always the possibility," Lisa pointed out.

"No chance," Cummings called back from the corridor. "She's pushing up daisies, mate."

"Crass bastard," Lisa tossed after him. "Can't we do something about him?" She turned back to Mark, visibly agitated. "I mean, do we have to share an office with the twat?"

"It's not easy when his old man's Edwards' golfing buddy, but, trust me, I'm trying," Mark assured her. Frankly, he'd rather work from the toilet than share an office with the man, but he was stuck with him, for now.

Sighing, he got to his feet. He'd pulled up a possible location—a pre-existing cottage on the perimeter of the Hawthorn Farm land. He needed to get uniforms together to check it out.

"Maybe I'll just hire a hitman," Lisa muttered moodily.

Mark's mouth twitched into a smile. "Nice idea. Not allowed, unfortunately."

"Plan B then," Lisa said.

Mark arched an eyebrow.

"Laxatives in his coffee, since he's so fond of spouting crap."

Mark shook his head as he collected up his jacket. "Messy," he said.

"Mark…if you need anything, an ear anytime, you know where I am. Right?"

"Cheers, Lisa." Mark nodded appreciatively. "I might take you up on that. But I think we have things pretty much under control for the moment."

Assuming Mel accepted help getting things under control that was, and kept her doctor's…*Shit!* Mark checked his watch and hurriedly pulled out his phone. He'd meant to call and remind her what time her appointment was.

CHAPTER THIRTY-TWO

MELISSA

After several unsuccessful attempts to feed Evie, to the exasperated stares of some of the patients in the waiting room, Mel gave up, close to tears. Hurriedly, she got to her feet, pressing Evie to her shoulder. She'd already tried rocking her, changing her, pushing her around in her stroller, waving the few toys they had in the surgery at her, walking around with her, but still Evie wailed as if she were being murdered.

Growing more and more fraught, Melissa almost had a heart attack when her phone rang, hurriedly grabbing it from her coat pocket. Seeing it was Mark, she hit answer and snapped into it, "*What?* I'm here!"

"I thought I'd just check," Mark said. "Make sure you made it okay."

"It's a trip to the doctor's, Mark, not an Antarctic expedition. I do *not* need checking up on."

"Right." Mark paused. "Is that Evie crying?"

Mel was tempted to end the call. Who the hell did he think it was? "Yes," she said shortly. "I'm trying to feed her."

Mark paused, infuriatingly. If he could hear Evie crying, why didn't he just go? "I take it Jade isn't with you then?" he asked cautiously.

"No. I don't need a babysitter either, Mark." Mel felt her hackles rising. "I'm an adult. I'm quite capable of driving myself to the doctors." She felt tears welling afresh, even as she said it. She *did* need a babysitter, for Evie. Clearly. But *she* was her mother. Why couldn't she seem to do anything right for her?

"You *drove* there?" Now Mark sounded disbelieving.

Pulling the phone away from her ear, Mel stared at it and then ended the call. Why didn't he trust her? Why did he keep watching her, as if waiting for her to fall? Was she falling? Had she only imagined she'd been happy and content such a short while ago? That Evie had? Her family?

Was it possible she was going mad? That she'd been the only one not to notice it, until now? Cold fear constricted her stomach, icy fingers tugging at her heart, at her mind. In this room full of people, she suddenly felt utterly alone.

"What is it, sweetheart?" she whispered, pressing her face to the top of Evie's soft, downy head, breathing in the smell that was supposed to bind mother and baby together forever. Yet Evie didn't want her. It was as if she could see, through her innocent child's eyes, that her mummy wasn't who she was supposed to be.

Mel wasn't aware of the fat tears sliding down her cheeks, the anguished sob escaping her throat. She didn't hear her name being called, until Dr. Meadows spoke right next to her, slid an arm around her shoulders and steered her gently towards one of the nurses' rooms.

Watching a nurse cooing to Evie, who was now gurgling happily, having drained a bottle of formula feed, Mel waited for Dr. Meadows to finish going through her notes. She almost hadn't come—but for Mark's insistence, she wouldn't have. She was glad she had now. Dr. Meadows had been kindness itself, somewhat restoring Mel's faith. Despite a growing queue of ever more disgruntled patients to see, he'd taken time out to make sure she was looked after, and, more importantly, that

Evie was. He'd waited until she was composed and then fetched her personally back to his office, thus allowing her to avoid the hushed whispers and sympathetic glances in the waiting room. Mel really didn't need those.

He'd listened while she'd garbled an apology, and waited while she explained that she had no idea why she was feeling this way, that things had been good in her life and that this feeling hadn't crept up on her so much as hit her like a bombshell.

He'd asked her to explain how she was feeling. After a brief hesitation, Mel had, summarising symptoms she knew only too well: lack of energy, exhaustion, sleeping too much, too little, loss of appetite. She was irritable, easily agitated, apathetic in turns. Each admission tightened the knot of fear inside her. She had problems concentrating and making decisions. Mel ticked all the boxes for the bleak depression she'd thought she'd escaped. The scariest box of all was the feeling that she was unable to look after her own baby. That she might even harm her own baby.

"And you're struggling with feelings of guilt?" Dr. Meadows asked astutely, turning towards her. His eyes were full of compassion, with no sign of the judgement Mel had been so worried about. She felt guilty all over again for not seeking help sooner.

Drawing in a long breath, she nodded.

"Feelings of hopelessness and self-blame? Thoughts of suicide or self-harm?" he probed gently. "It's nothing to be ashamed of, Mrs. Cain," he added quickly, when Mel dropped her gaze.

Again, Mel nodded. She'd tried not to allow her mind to drift down that path in the dark hours, tried so hard, but seeing the hurt in Mark's eyes, the confusion, yet perversely feeling compelled to hurt him more because of it, she had started to believe he would be better off without her. Knowing that he'd felt the need to talk to someone else, a female someone else, only compounded those feelings. Mel guessed Mark would never really understand how devastated she'd been, realising he hadn't been able to talk to her.

Dr. Meadows leaned back in his chair, his hands steepled thoughtfully under his chin. "I know you've struggled with these symptoms on a previous occasion, Melissa. The road to recovery isn't an easy one, is it?"

"No." Mel agreed wholeheartedly with that. The road she'd travelled had been a long and tortuous one, full of mountains to climb and potholes to trip her up.

"Half the battle is admitting it, of course," he went on. "People can be judgemental. It's human nature, I'm afraid." He paused and sighed. "Don't judge yourself through their eyes. That's the important thing to remember. Postnatal depression is common. If only mental health issues weren't still thought of as a stigma, I'm sure many women would admit to feeling like you do."

Would they, Mel wondered. Weren't new mothers their own harshest judges?

"We have the technology, we can fix it," he joked, winking.

Mel relaxed a little, which was obviously what he'd intended. If only it were that easy, though. "A brain transplant, you mean? Perfect." She smiled back. It felt good to do that. When did she lose her smile?

"A short course of antidepressants initially, I think," he said. "Counselling possibly, if you feel the need to talk. It might help. Is your husband supportive, Mrs. Cain?"

"Yes," Mel answered hesitantly. "But...he's been down this road before too." She let it hang.

He nodded. "If you don't mind my suggesting, I think you'll find he'd like to be. He arrived enquiring after you while you were with the nurse. He's waiting for you."

Watching Mark's expression change as he walked across to his child, Melissa felt joy tinged with unbearable, palpable pain. It felt as if her heart might tear apart inside her. This wasn't fair.

This wasn't Mark's fault. It was her. *Her* problem. *Her* stupid, dysfunctional brain.

And now, where once he had been free to walk away, he would feel obliged to stay, because his love for Evie and Poppy was unequivocal. But could he really cope with this? Again?

"Hey, little miracle," he said, taking Evie carefully into his arms and gazing wondrously down at her, as if he couldn't quite believe her. Mel swallowed a tight lump in her throat.

"She's beautiful," the nurse said, sighing audibly as Mark bent to place a soft kiss on Evie's forehead.

Mark smiled, the kind of warm, adoring smile fathers reserve for their children. "Like her mother," he said throatily, turning to face Mel.

Seeing the love in his eyes, peppered with crushing anxiety, Mel caught a sob in her throat. She *had* to get better. For Mark's sake, for her children's sake, she had to get well.

CHAPTER THIRTY-THREE

MARK

Unfastening Evie's car seat, Mark lifted her out, and then breathed a sigh of relief as Mel's car turned into the drive.

"Here she is, baby," he said softly, waiting for Mel to pull up before he went inside. He couldn't stay. Lisa had covered for him, but he needed to get back soon. He wished Jade was home. He wished to God Mel wouldn't insist on driving. The last thing Mark wanted was for Mel to think he was trying to take away her independence, but, in his estimation, she shouldn't be, particularly with a child in the car. She was exhausted and distracted, and he also feared that she'd started drinking during the day.

As if to demonstrate his point, Mel climbed out of her car, walked past him to the front door, and then went back for her keys. And then back for a second time for Evie's baby bag.

"Thanks for coming, Mark. We'll be fine now," she said, walking past him again to unlock the front door. She reached for Evie's carrier, as if expecting him to hand it over and go back to work.

"I'll bring her in." Mark smiled and stepped towards the house.

Mel nodded tightly, but moved aside, allowing him to carry Evie through. "Shall I take her up?" he asked, as Mel followed him into the hall.

"No." Mel returned his smile, but still she seemed miles away. "I thought I'd have her with me in the kitchen for a while. I've missed her company."

Mark hesitated, thinking that Evie might be tired after all the excitement, which would probably make her fractious later.

"I'll take her up in a little bit," Mel said, pulling off her coat.

Mark nodded and carried Evie through to the kitchen, heading for the island in the middle of the room, where he hesitated again. Would she be all right parked up there? Of course she would, he chastised himself. Mel wasn't likely to accidentally knock baby plus sizeable car carrier onto the floor. Still, though, he pushed the seat well into the centre of the work surface.

"Have the assessors been yet?" Mel asked, coming in after him as Mark eased Evie out of her coat.

"Sorry?"

"The fire assessors. I wondered if Jade had managed to get the go-ahead on the work to her house?"

Mark tried to think. He'd noticed that Jade didn't seem to show much interest in the house. She'd barely been near the place. But then, it couldn't be easy sifting through the burned-out remnants of your life, future plans turned to ashes. "A couple of weeks ago, I think. She said she was getting some estimates together. Why?"

"No reason. I just wondered." Mel shrugged, looking preoccupied as she walked across to the kettle. "Do you like it?" she asked out of the blue, leaving Mark struggling to keep up.

"Like what?" Checking Evie didn't need changing, he headed for the fridge for her water.

"My hair." Mel turned to him, her pretty green eyes awash with worries Mark had no clue about and felt powerless to help her with.

He looked her over, noting her pale complexion, which the hair colour did nothing to improve. "Truthfully," he said, hoping he wasn't about to put his foot in it, "I prefer your natural colour."

Seeming unperturbed, Mel nodded. "Coffee?" she asked, turning away.

"No. Thanks." Concerned at the seemingly random conversational leaps, Mark watched her carefully. "I have to get to work."

"Sorry. Yes, of course you do." Mel paused. "I'm thinking of changing it back."

The hair, Mark assumed. "Good idea," he said, going back to Evie, who Mel hadn't so much as glanced at since she'd come in.

"Would you lie to me, Mark?" Mel asked, completely out of left field.

"Never," Mark answered straight off. In actual fact, he felt he was lying, right there, going along with her insistence in ignoring the elephant in the room. He wanted to talk to her about what was happening, not skirt around the issue, having this stilted, staccato conversation. How could he hope to help her if she wouldn't confide in him? "Where did that come from?"

Mel ignored that, too. Or maybe she hadn't heard him. From the impassive expression on her face, Mark wasn't sure. Making her coffee in silence, she wandered to the back door, opened it and went out to sit at the patio table.

Minus coffee. Mark noticed it still sitting on the work surface. "Back in a minute, sweetpops." Evie seeming to have satisfied her thirst, he grabbed a paper towel to mop up the drips, and then followed Mel out with her drink.

"I have to go soon, Mel," he reminded her, placing the coffee on the table and checking his watch, debating whether he should ring in and claim some emergency. But how many times could he do that? Perhaps he should keep it up his sleeve, in case there was another day when Mel needed him more. He shook off the thought. "Will you be all right?"

She didn't respond.

"Mel?"

"Yes, fine," Mel said, looking up at him but not seeming to see him.

"Evie's had some water," he tried, wishing she would talk to him; wishing that by some miracle this would all go away.

Mel smiled. "Good," she said.

Exasperated, Mark glanced back to the kitchen, where Evie was on her own, content for the moment, though he doubted she would be for long. He wasn't happy about leaving her there and Mel out here. "Will Jade be back soon?"

"Should be," Mel said. "She went to the dentist with a tooth. She's picking Poppy up on the way."

A toothache, Mark presumed. And she must be picking Poppy up from school on the way home, not the way there. Growing more concerned at Mel's emotionless responses, Mark pulled out a chair to sit opposite her. "Are you okay with the medication, Mel? The antidepressants?"

Mel answered with an indifferent shrug.

"Have you taken any? Your first dose, I mean."

Mel's answer this time was a shake of her head.

And yet, she seemed more out of it than ever. Frustrated, Mark pressed on. "Do you think it's a good idea to drive on them, Mel?" He had to broach the subject of her driving, whether she might think he was being controlling or not. His only other option was to take the car keys, and he really did *not* want to do that.

Mel looked at him at last, guardedly. "If I felt I couldn't drive, I wouldn't."

Mark nodded. "You'll have to report it to the DVLA if it does affect your driving."

Mel frowned, and then shrugged again, as if only half-interested, which increased Mark's apprehension. So, what now? This was getting him nowhere.

Deciding he had no other option, Mark breathed in deeply and took the bull by the horns. "And you'll avoid alcohol, yes?"

"Avoid…?" Snapping her gaze to his, Mel searched his face. "Are you serious?" She laughed incredulously.

Mark held her gaze. "Deadly," he assured her. He would do anything and everything for her. He believed, hoped, that she knew that to be true. Risking his children, though, was something he couldn't do.

"Since when did getting drunk, *once*, for the first time in I don't know how long, become a criminal offence?" She stared at him, her expression somewhere between bemused and angry.

"Spectacularly drunk," Mark reminded her, for want of a better word.

"Yes, spectacularly!" Mel's voice rose. "And I'm sorry I embarrassed you. Sorry that, for whatever reason, I couldn't handle it, but…Oh, for God's sake, Mark. How many times am I supposed to apologise? I haven't had so much as a sip of wine since."

"Right." Mark sighed, heavily. He hadn't expected her to admit it, but he'd hoped she wouldn't deny it outright.

"What does *that* mean?" Mel asked, her anger obviously escalating.

Mark ran a hand over his neck. "Nothing. I'm just concerned, Mel, that's all."

"About me driving while taking medication?"

"Obviously." Mark locked eyes with her. Mel's gaze was fiery, her eyes slightly bloodshot. He studied her, noting her pupil reaction time seemed to be slowed, and steeled his resolve. "I don't want you taking risks while—"

"Driving under the influence of alcohol?" Mel finished furiously.

"Both of the above," Mark supplied disconsolately.

"I *don't* drink and drive!" Mel snapped, her tone now aggressive. "I never have!"

Tugging in a terse breath, Mark squeezed the bridge of his nose hard with his thumb and forefinger.

"*Mark?*" Mel waited for him to answer, but he couldn't say what he truly felt: that he couldn't trust her, and it was killing him.

"I don't bloody believe this!" Mel shoved her chair back and stormed into the kitchen. "Why don't you bloody well breathalyse me and be done with?"

Berating himself on his abysmal handling of the situation, Mark hurried after her.

His heart dropped as he watched her banging around, opening cupboards. All of the fucking cupboards.

"Take a look," she said. "Go on!"

"Mel, don't." He glanced towards Evie, who had been startled by the loud crashing of doors opening and shutting.

"Don't forget the fridge." Mel marched over to it, yanking that open too. "I mean, I'm bound to have a bottle chilling in there for..." She stopped, staring hard at the contents, and then slammed the door shut. "*Fuck!*"

Mark bit back his own anger. He wasn't sure where this was going, but wherever it was, it wasn't happening in front of Evie.

"Who turned the fridge off?" Mel yelled, as he walked across to her.

Mark stopped, confused. "What?"

"The fridge. It's off at the wall!" Mel waved a hand in the direction of the socket and then reached for the freezer door. "*Shit,*" she muttered. "Shit, shit...*shit!*"

Oh Christ. "Mel..." Hearing the sob in her throat, and realising immediately what was wrong, Mark started towards her. But he stopped as Jade came in, with Poppy, wide-eyed and wary, holding tight to her hand. She was holding a goldfish in her other hand, Mark noticed, his heart sinking further as he realised his little girl's bubble was about to be rudely burst.

"What's happened? Mark? Mel?" Obviously puzzled, Jade trailed off.

Mark held up a quieting hand. Then, seeing Jade had understood, he nodded towards Evie and then went over to Mel.

"It's ruined," she said, crying now in earnest. "All of it."

Mark reached out, gently stroking her back, attempting to ease her towards him. He had no idea what else to do. He couldn't fix this.

"Why is Mummy crying?" Poppy asked Jade in a worried whisper.

"I think she has a headache," Jade answered quietly, moving towards Evie, who was now demonstrating her distress vocally.

Mark nodded his appreciation and tried to comfort Mel, but she was fighting him, pulling away from him. "Did you do it?" she asked, swinging around to level an accusing gaze at Jade.

"Do what?" Jade looked confusedly from Mel to Mark. "I'm not sure, I..."

"The freezer," Mark explained, feeling worn out already, to his very bones. "Someone's switched it off."

"Not me." Jade looked alarmed. "At least I don't think I—"

"Well, someone did!" Mel snapped, causing both Jade and Poppy to step back.

Glancing at Jade apologetically, Mark wrapped an arm around Mel's shoulders. "It was an accident, Mel," he said softly, aware of how distraught she would be. Determined to breastfeed Evie, she'd expressed milk religiously every day, making sure the freezer was always stocked up.

"It's all ruined," Mel said again, her sobs stilling to a shudder as she heaved air into her lungs.

"I'm so sorry, Mel." Mark tried to pull her closer, but Mel didn't want to be held. Didn't appear to want him near her. Her body language was stiff, her emotions all stuffed precariously inside. Like a watch spring, Mark felt, wound way too tight and ready to uncoil in an instant.

"It's okay." She drew in a shaky breath. "I was going to wean her anyway. I can't feed her myself now, can I? That would really be putting my child at risk, wouldn't it? You'll be pleased to know I'm in possession of enough of my faculties to have thought that one through, Mark."

The medication. Mark squeezed his eyes closed. *Dammit.* It hadn't even occurred to him, but it had to Mel. And she was devastated. She shrugged him off and walked away.

Mark hesitated for a second and then, hearing her climbing the stairs, he moved to go after her. He couldn't leave her, not like this.

"I'm sorry," Jade said tearfully, as he walked past. "I honestly don't think I did switch it off, but if I did..."

Noting how crestfallen she looked, as if holding herself responsible, Mark stopped and placed a hand on her shoulder. "It was an accident," he repeated firmly. "Anyone could have inadvertently knocked the switch." Even Mel. In her present state, Mark had to concede that she might have done it herself.

Jade nodded, still looking unhappy. Very. Mark hoped this didn't cause her to leave.

"I'll go to the chemist," Jade offered, dredging up a smile from somewhere. "Get some formula. I'm sure Evie will be fine, Mark. Don't worry."

Mark closed his eyes, relief surging through him. If anyone knew what to do here, it was Jade. "That would be great. Thanks."

"No problem," she assured him. "Do you want to come with me, Poppy?"

"Uh-huh." Poppy nodded quickly, looking as if she'd rather be anywhere than home right now.

"I could take Evie, too," Jade suggested. "We shouldn't be too long. It might give you a chance to..." She nodded diplomatically towards the stairs. "If Mel wouldn't mind me taking her car, that is?"

"I'm sure she won't." Mark nodded to the keys on the work surface, and then crouched to give Poppy a firm hug. "Be good, Poppet," he said, his heart twisting as he noted the bewilderment in her eyes. "And remember, Jade's in charge while Mummy's not feeling well. Make sure to do everything she tells you to. Okay?"

"I will," Poppy promised, with a brave little nod.

"Good girl." Mark kissed her forehead and straightened up.

Hearing Jade shushing Evie and chatting to Poppy as he went up the stairs, assuring her that Dory would be fine, left in her special fish water in the sink, Mark counted his blessings. He'd worried about her qualifications when Mel had employed her so quickly. That had been one long month ago, and clearly his worries had been unfounded. Not only was she competent enough to care for the children in a crisis, she was caring enough to want to. She was indispensable. Mark knew that now with certainty. He'd need to do all he could to make sure she had access to everything she needed, including Mel's car. If Jade stayed—and he prayed that she did—she would need to drive it on a regular basis.

Mark's first reaction when he woke in the small hours was surprise at the complete silence. His second was panic as he reached for Mel to find her side of the bed empty.

He threw back the duvet, almost falling over it in his scramble to pull on his tracksuit bottoms before heading for the landing. Seeing no glimmer of light from downstairs, he went straight to the nursery, glancing into Poppy's room as he did. She was fast asleep, Hercules lying loyally at the foot of her bed. She'd obviously been fighting with the duvet too. Bidding Hercules to stay, Mark crept quietly in to ease the covers back over his daughter's small form.

The nursery door was closed, unusually. Both he and Mel preferred it left open a fraction. Warily, Mark listened outside and then, hearing no sound, he pressed down the handle and went inside, looking apprehensively over to the cot as he did.

Evie, lying on her tummy, one tiny hand to the side of her face, appeared to be sleeping. Needing to reassure himself, Mark took a breath and stepped further in. Seeing his baby girl's eyelids flutter as her mind chased her dreams, he closed his own eyes and allowed himself to breathe out.

Mel was standing in the middle of the room, though she gave no indication she knew he was there. She was quite still, her arms wrapped tightly about herself. Not sure what to do next, wondering whether she might even be sleepwalking, Mark hesitated for a second, watching her watching Evie, and then, noticing her shoulders tense as she breathed deeply in, he walked quietly across to her.

"I wouldn't hurt her," Mel murmured, as he stopped behind her.

"I know." Hearing the wretchedness in her voice and wondering how long she'd been standing here, quietly crying, Mark felt his heart hitch. "I know you wouldn't, Mel," he said, placing his arms around her and desperately trying to quash the feeling that, if he let go, he might lose her.

CHAPTER THIRTY-FOUR

MELISSA

Melissa willed her body to respond, her mind screaming. Her heart constricted inside her; she tried to run, to breathe, but her feet were weighed down by the swirling nothing beneath her. The air was too thick, too putrid; choking smoke seared her lungs. Petrified, she tried to reach Evie. Tried to push and prise them away, the hands that clutched and clawed at her legs, disembodied arms rising and writhing like pale grey vines from the mire. She was crying. Pitiful whimpers turned to terrified tears—her baby was crying. Someone was shaking her, hurting her, and she…couldn't…

Hush, little baby, don't say a word…

Jade?

"Morning," Jade greeted her cheerily.

Prising heavy-lidded eyes open, Mel blinked hard against the bright light the girl seemed to be bathed in.

"Morning," Jade said again, standing over her. "I brought you some tea."

Attempting to focus, Mel gulped hard against the parched dryness of her throat, and struggled to lever herself up.

"Hold on," Jade said, taking a step to the side.

Squinting, Mel registered the sunlight filtering through the slatted blinds. Her blinds at her bedroom window, she realised, immense relief washing through her.

"You were sleeping like a baby." Jade bobbed back into view. "We didn't like to wake you, so—"

"We?"

"Mark," Jade clarified, leaning down to help her with her pillows. "He said you hadn't fallen asleep until after three, so we thought it was best not to disturb you."

There was that "we" again. Mel wasn't sure she liked it. Or being left to sleep until some ridiculous time. Her sleep patterns had been erratic, to say the least, when she'd been unwell before. She'd had no reason, not even the will, to get out of bed then. But things were different now. She had a family, and suddenly, paranoid though it might be, she felt excluded from it. Routine was what she needed, to get up and get on with it. She didn't want to give in, to lie in bed, battling nightmares that seemed too real to be dreams and slipping further into her black hole. "Where is he?" she asked, pushing the duvet back and attempting to pull herself into a sitting position, no easy task with her brain and body seemingly immersed in soft treacle.

Jade reached a hand out to steady her. "He's taken Poppy to school. And Evie's due her check-up, so he—"

"Mark's taken her?" Mel asked, surprised. "But doesn't he need to be at work?"

"He said he wanted to spend some time with her. I was ready to take her, but—"

"Wanted to keep her out of harm's way, more likely," Mel growled. Seeing the alarmed expression on Jade's face, she felt immediately guilty. Again.

"He means well, Melissa," Jade said, tentatively, obviously wary of being interrupted or snapped at. "I know how you feel, honestly I do. Sometimes you just want people to go away and not treat you as if you're incapable, but he is trying to be helpful."

He was. She knew he was. Mel sighed inwardly, and then

looked at Jade curiously as her thoughts caught up with her. "Do you? Know how I feel?"

Jade hesitated, and then reluctantly nodded. "I was on medication, too," she admitted, now looking awkward. "Only for a short while, after my parents…" Mel searched her face, attempting to digest this new information about her babysitter. "I'm fine now. I probably should have mentioned it before, but…" Dropping her gaze, Jade trailed embarrassedly off.

"You thought I wouldn't employ you?" Mel finished, empathising completely. There was more understanding of mental illness nowadays but still there was prejudice and fear of the unknown. Mel had experienced it herself. She'd never imagined Mark might think her incapable of looking after her own children though.

Jade nodded slowly. "Sorry," she said, in a small voice.

And Mel despaired utterly of herself. The girl had been efficient, genuinely caring towards Poppy and Evie, falling over herself to help out. More than that, she was prepared to stick around when many people wouldn't. Most people, in fact. And how had she shown her appreciation? By accusing her of sabotaging her milk supply, when it had obviously been just an unfortunate accident. Jade must feel awful.

"Don't be sorry." Mel reached out to take her hand, and the poor girl looked as if she might burst into tears. "For the record, I would have employed you, and, also for the record, you're doing a fantastic job, Jade. I'm immensely grateful."

"Really?" Jade beamed at that. She had a gorgeous smile.

"Really." Mel gave her hand a squeeze. "It's me who owes you an apology. I shouldn't have jumped to conclusions about the freezer. The switch is in the perfect place for getting accidentally knocked. I've done it myself with the kettle. Anyway, I'm sorry."

"Apology not necessary," Jade said, reaching for the tea and passing it to her. And then the tablets. Mark must have given them to her. Plainly, he was worried she'd forget to take them, or leave them lying around. Mel dearly wished she could forget to take the bloody things. She already felt woozy to the point of drunkenness. It was no wonder he'd thought she was secretly partaking of the odd tipple. She wished he hadn't accused her of that though. It felt as though he didn't trust her.

Mel stared at the tiny, innocuous-looking tablets Jade offered her.

"They'll help," she urged, as Mel hesitated.

"Not for the next few weeks." Aware of what the side effects were, which would only get worse before she got better, Mel sighed, but took them anyway and washed them down with the tea. "As long as you don't mind coping with the mood swings," she said, feeling a little easier confiding in Jade now that Jade had confided in her.

"I'll look the other way if you throw a wobbly," Jade promised.

Mel smiled. "I'd walk the other way, if I were you. I might be about to throw one."

Jade widened her eyes worriedly. She had nice eyes, Mel thought. True baby blue, and as innocent as a baby's too.

"The hair." She rolled her eyes upwards. "What on earth am I going to do with it?"

Jade cocked her head to one side. "Dye it back," she said. "In fact, I might join you. I quite fancy going copper. Meanwhile, wear it up. Come on, I'll show you."

Taking hold of Mel's hands, she pulled her to her feet and steered her towards the wardrobe mirror, where she proceeded to gather her hair and pull it into a topknot.

Ouch! Rather too roughly, Mel thought, but felt it impolite to point out.

"Like this, see?" Jade smiled, and waited for her reaction.

Mel studied her reflection. It was an improvement, she supposed, but she doubted she'd look as bright and bouncy as Jade any time soon. *Jaded* is how she looked—pale and drawn. How had this happened, she wondered again, her resolve waning a little, which wasn't helped by the room spinning in slow revolutions around her. Mel wondered about that, too. How it was she'd felt so spaced out before she'd even started the medication.

"You should wear some blusher," Jade said, surveying her thoughtfully. "Until you get the colour back in your cheeks."

So she'd noticed her sallow complexion too. "I can imagine what Mark will think about that," Mel said, with another roll of her eyes. Other than a little concealer beneath her eyes, she hardly ever wore make up around the house, clay spatters on top of blusher not being a good look. He'd probably think she was off to proposition another waiter. Recalling her drunken endeavours at seduction, the waiter's horrified expression and Mark's clear mortification, Mel winced inwardly.

"Think about what?" Mark asked, eyeing her curiously as he came through the open bedroom door.

"Mel wearing her hair up," Jade supplied, diplomatically leaving out the pale and uninteresting bit. "What do you think?"

Mark looked at Mel through the mirror as Jade demonstrated her proposed up-do. "Sexy," he said, smiling.

It didn't reach his eyes, though, Mel noticed. There was no mischievous glint there, no subtle innuendo. He looked wretched, as pale as she was, and utterly exhausted.

"I, er, should go. Running late," he said, reaching for his mobile. Out of habit, Mel wondered, as he pocketed it again without checking it, or did he not want to check his messages in front of her? "Will you be okay, Mel?"

"Yes. Why wouldn't I be?" Irked by what felt like his patronising concern, Mel replied sharply—and then immediately regretted it.

"I'll go and see to Evie," Jade said, tactfully excusing herself from the situation. "Is she still in her carrier, Mark?"

"In the lounge, fast asleep," Mark confirmed, turning his

confused gaze away from Mel towards Jade. "She's due a feed soon, so I thought I'd leave her for the moment."

"Brilliant." Jade headed towards the door. "That'll give me a chance to get it ready."

"Thanks, Jade." And this time his smile was one of relief, tinged with palpable sadness.

Mel felt her heart sink. He didn't want to be here. How could he? And then her stomach lurched as she noticed Jade reach out to brush his arm with her hand. Bewildered, Mel turned away from the mirror. Why would she do that? Commiseration? Reassurance? It was too intimate a gesture. She must know that. *He* must. Right here in front of her. In her *bedroom*.

"Mel? Are you all right?" Mark asked, as she turned swiftly to the en suite.

"I'm fine! For God's sake…" *Please, just stop asking.* Mel closed the door and turned to lean against it, desperately trying to hold back the useless, *pathetic* tears. To convince herself it was just her paranoia at play, misinterpreting things, yet again.

CHAPTER THIRTY-FIVE

JADE

Jade had no idea why she hadn't got rid of the girl sooner. She'd felt sorry for her, initially. How could she not, with her mother seething and raging, embarrassing her in the middle of the supermarket? The woman had been a complete witch, dressed like a trollop: short skirt, tits on show, blood-red lipstick, like an angry red slash for a mouth. Watching from across the aisle, seeing the woman's rubbery lips exaggeratedly moving as she'd cursed and berated the child for accidentally knocking over a display stand—"You stupid girl! Look what you've done!"—Jade had felt goosebumps prickle her skin. She recognised the child's fear. The same fear she'd felt when her own bitch mother had snarled and scorned and walked away, leaving her with *him*. She felt again the ice-cold dread pooling in the pit of her stomach, the repulsion, the pain; the powerlessness as he'd pushed into her, groaning and thrusting and grunting. The hopelessness, trying to make her mother understand. *It wasn't her fault!*

Daisy had said the same thing. "It wasn't my fault, Mummy," she'd cried, huge, salty tears sliding down her cheeks as she'd looked beseechingly up at the spiteful, self-centred cow. Looking for comfort, where there was none.

It could have been her.

Irresistibly drawn, Jade had followed them, cruising past the house in the car she'd since disposed of—a car of her own being superfluous to requirements once she'd secured employment with the Cain family. Approaching on foot on her subsequent vigils, she'd watched and she'd waited. She'd seen the hysterical mother hurling accusations at the father, so drunk after a boozy party she couldn't stand up straight. "You're disgusting," she'd screamed, lashing out at him, her face twisted, her eyes full of hatred. "A fucking disgusting paedophile!"

Jade had made her decision then. They didn't deserve to be parents. They didn't deserve Daisy. They deserved to burn in hell. First, though, they needed to learn, to realise what they'd done. They needed to lose the child, whose innocence they were stealing, whose childhood they were breaking, whose love and trust they were abusing.

Obviously frightened of them, Daisy had come willingly when Jade had told her she was going to keep her safe—which she'd every intention of doing then. The girl had reminded her of her little sister. Annoyingly, just like her little sister, she was becoming a nuisance. Poppy had, too. But Poppy, of course, had also turned out to be spoiled beyond belief and far too demanding of Mark. Jade still hadn't come to a decision about her. She'd so hoped Poppy would have some redeeming features. She didn't want Mark to go through the unbearable grieving process of losing another child unless he absolutely had to.

This one, though...It was hard work, keeping the girl occupied and fed with Dylan constantly fretting and ringing her. And now things were moving on with Mark, she'd become a liability Jade didn't need.

Jade sighed as Dylan fussed and twitched behind her, scared to death his mummy would discover his secret and realise what kind of a pathetic idiot he really was. She peered down at the girl, who was sleeping contentedly enough, thanks to a large dose of Tylenol. "She's fine," she told him, turning from the bed. "It's just a cold. She'll feel better after a nap."

Dylan stared at her stupidly for a second and then, wiping his shirtsleeve under his nose, he followed her to the bedroom door. "You sure?" he asked, once on the landing. "It's just, she didn't seem to be breathing right when I looked in on her last night. Chesty-like, you know?"

Jade looked him over, taking in the worry lines furrowing his brow like a five-bar gate, his jeans which were an inch too short—obviously turned up by his mother—and the wet patches under his armpits, and suppressed her immense agitation. "I'm her mum, Dylan. I'm also a qualified nursery nurse. I think I should know, don't you?"

Smiling sweetly, she stroked his cheek—God forbid she should have to stroke any other part of him today—and then, feeling nauseated at the stench of body odour mingled with pig shit that seemed to permanently emanate from him, she turned quickly for the stairs.

Grabbing up her bag, she headed across the tiny living room and straight for the front door.

"You going already?" Dylan asked, following her like an annoying little lapdog as she stepped out and breathed in some blessed fresh air.

"I have to pick Poppy up from school."

Jade sighed as she watched him lumbering after her, wondering again how a man who was built like a brick shithouse came to be scared of his own shadow. It was useful, of course, along with the fact that he'd obviously been born stupid, but she did worry it might be her downfall. Dylan would undoubtedly spill the beans if he were cornered—he couldn't lie convincingly to save his life. Jade would probably have to do something about him too, which was a shame, but needs must.

"So, will you be taking her soon?" Dylan asked, shrugging his huge round shoulders awkwardly. "It's just that me mum comes out to talk to the pigs sometimes." He nodded to where the disgusting creatures were snuffling and grunting in the field adjoining the cottage,

Jade had to stifle a laugh at that, the image of his sour-faced, frumpy mother talking to the pigs. Mind you, she wasn't surprised, with only Dylan for company.

"I will, I promise. It's just…" Jade faltered. "You know he doesn't want her," she went on, looking tearfully back at him. "He's bound to do something awful to her. She really is much better off here for now."

"He" being Mark, who Dylan believed to be the father of the girl, and who was as capable of doing something awful to a child as he was his needy wife. His inexhaustible patience was becoming a bit of a concern. Jade needed Mark to realise that Melissa was nothing but a ball and chain around his ankles, pulling him down. He needed to leave her. Jade had no intention of sharing him for much longer.

Puffing up his chest manfully, Dylan looked her over and nodded. "I know," he said sympathetically, placing a huge paw around her shoulders. Jade's skin crawled. "It's okay," he said gruffly. "She can stay a bit longer. I'll try and keep me mum away."

"Thanks, Dylan." Jade smiled at him, and silently thanked God she'd convinced him to change the locks. With his miserable mother wandering around, she was going to have to do something about the girl sooner rather than later, she realised. "I knew I could depend on you. I'll see to her soon." Checking her watch, she sighed regretfully. "I'd better go."

Giving him a peck on the cheek, Jade turned, resisting the urge to wipe her mouth. She wasn't sure how, exactly, she would see to her. Feed her to the pigs? Pondering her options, Jade hummed softly to herself as she went. *Hush, little baby…*

CHAPTER THIRTY-SIX

MARK

"Hey, Poppet." Mark swept Poppy up as he came through the front door. He was late. Way later than he'd expected to be, having been on site at a demolished property within the search radius for Daisy Evans. Discovering the building had a basement, it had been worth checking out, but to no avail. Now, Mark felt exhausted and frustrated. "Shouldn't we be in bed?" He nodded to the hall clock, where Poppy could see that the big hand was way past the half past seven mark.

"I *was* going." Poppy made huge eyes at him as he put her down. "But Mummy said she would come up and tuck Dory in."

"Ah, I see." Mark nodded, then furrowed his brow, pondering how, exactly, one tucked a goldfish into bed. "So where is Mummy?"

"Working," Poppy said, following him towards the kitchen. "She'll be utterly sausted," she added, with an elongated sigh.

"Exhausted," Mark corrected her, looking curiously towards Jade, who was busy loading bottles into the steriliser.

"She's been in the workshop since this morning," Jade explained, turning to flick on the kettle, which was now plugged into a socket well away from the freezer, he noted.

"She's been working all day?" Mark was surprised. He'd worried the side effects of the drugs, which he knew to be difficult to handle for the first few weeks, might make it impossible for her to work. But then, Mel was a fighter, he reminded himself. He'd never known her to give up on anything easily, an attitude of which their two beautiful kids were evidence. Plus, she found her work therapeutic, which might actually help. Staying out there the whole day and half the evening, though? He hoped she wasn't overdoing it.

"She's been in to check on Evie once or twice but that's about it," Jade said. "Do you want me to take Poppy up and read her a bedtime story while you go out and have a chat with her?"

"That'd be great. Thanks, Jade." Mark guessed Poppy wouldn't be too devastated at having Jade read her a story in lieu of him. Mark was grateful for Jade's help, and amazed at how adaptable she was prepared to be. Grateful also for the effort she made to be a friend to Mel. She would certainly need one, particularly now her friendship with Lisa had cooled. Mark still couldn't get his head around what the hell had been going through Mel's mind. But that, he suspected, was probably a subject best left alone for now.

"Yay! *Lily the Little Mermaid*!" Poppy clapped her hands gleefully.

Definitely not devastated. "I take it she does Lily better than me?" Mark asked.

"She's a *girl*, silly. Lily's a girl mermaid," Poppy informed him.

Mark sighed theatrically. "A lesser man would be crushed, you know."

Poppy pressed her hand to his cheek as he leaned down to kiss her goodnight, searching his eyes worriedly, and then giggling when Mark went cross-eyed. "You're teasing," she said, trying very hard to do likewise and make her pupils meet in the middle.

"A bit," Mark said, planting a kiss on her cute button nose. "Good job I know you love me bigger than the sky, isn't it?"

"And the moon."

"And all the stars. Night, Poppet. I'm assuming you've had no further trouble from the bug monster?"

"No. Jade slayed him," Poppy said airily, as Jade led her to the door.

"With a single blow of my bug-slayer sword," said Jade, rolling her eyes good-naturedly over her shoulder.

"A single blow? Wow. You're a braver man than I am," Mark said, looking suitably impressed as he headed for the back door.

"*Daddeee*, she's a *girl*!" Poppy called from the hall.

"I know, I noticed," Mark called back.

Rather than barge in and possibly frighten her, Mark tapped on the workshop door and waited.

"It's open," Mel shouted, after a moment.

"How's it going?" Mark asked, going in.

Mel stepped away from the sculpture she was working on. "Truthfully," she said, brushing her fringe from her face with the back of her hand, "crappily."

Mark looked her over, hopefully not too obviously. She had clay on her face. He might have wiped that off with his thumb, a few weeks back, brushed her soft lips with his own. Now? He felt he was walking on eggshells, never quite sure how she'd react. He might do better to check how the land lay first.

"You're probably pushing yourself too hard," he ventured. "You should take a break."

Mel glanced at him despairingly. "Thanks for the advice, Detective," she said, with a definite hint of sarcasm. "In case you hadn't noticed, I'm miles behind with my orders. But then, you've obviously been too busy elsewhere to notice."

It looked like the ground underfoot was going to be tough going. Mark sighed. "Which means?"

"Nothing." Mel shrugged, picked up a modelling tool and went back to her work. "It's just you've been a bit distracted lately."

Mark looked at her askance. "That's hardly fair, Mel," he said, wondering how to point out that the only thing he'd been distracted from was his job.

"No, nor is being treated like an invalid." Mel shot him a look, a flash of fury in her eyes. "*Or* an idiot."

Mark staggered inwardly at that. He hadn't been. Had he? He sifted through his memory—though he was so bloody tired, he could hardly think—and realised he probably had. Her *I don't need a babysitter* comment came to mind, her obvious annoyance at him asking her if she was all right every two seconds. He needed to pull back. Give her some space. Stop acting as if *he* was her babysitter.

"Right." He nodded, running a hand through his hair. "Well, if I have, I'm sorry. I'm concerned, that's all. You can't blame me for that, Mel."

Mel looked him over—guardedly, Mark noticed. "So why so late?" she asked him. "If you're so concerned, I mean, why work so late?"

Because I have to catch up, too. I'm not exactly having a picnic here myself, Mark thought. "Work," he said. "The missing girl. We located a property that might have been a possible location. I needed to check it out."

Mel looked momentarily saddened by that. Then she frowned. "With Lisa?"

And there it was, whatever was eating away at her. "Yes, with Lisa," he said exasperatedly. "I work with her, Mel. What do you want me to do?"

"Tell the truth," Mel suggested, with another casual shrug.

"The truth?" Mark stared at her, completely confounded. She really did think he been screwing around, didn't she? "*Jesus Christ*, Mel! I have no idea what's going on in your head, but—" He stopped, realising that what he was about to say would seem way below the belt.

Mel didn't speak. Just carried on sculpting.

This was useless. "I should go and check on the kids." Kneading his temples, Mark sighed heavily and turned away before he said something he would certainly regret.

He got as far as the door before Mel stopped him. "I'm sorry!"

Mark took a slow breath and turned back. He needed to stay calm, he reminded himself, however bloody angry he felt. The fact was, Mel wasn't likely to be rational right now. He knew that. It didn't make it any easier though.

"The kiln's still not working properly, and everything seems to be going wrong—even the sink's blocked up." Mel waved a hand in that direction. "And... *me*! Me, Mark! I'm going wrong," she shouted, clamping a clay-caked hand to her breast. "I can't do a thing right for Evie. She seems to think Jade's her mummy, and Poppy seems to prefer Jade's company too. I... I can't *think* straight any more!"

Mel looked at him, her eyes beseeching, her chest heaving, clearly desperate for understanding.

Mark wished he did understand. That he could. Right now, he felt confounded, shut out, utterly impotent. "I love *you*, Mel. You! I don't *look* at anyone else, I don't *want* anyone else. Can you *please* try and hold on to that?"

Mel pressed the heel of her hand to her forehead. "I know," she said eventually. "I know you do. It's just..."

She looked back at him, scanning his face hard.

Just what? Apprehension twisted inside him. She hadn't said she loved him. Did she? Love didn't come with a lifelong guarantee, did it? Might she want out? Could that be part of what was going on here? Mark took a step towards her—and there was a loud thump on the door behind him.

Fuck! He cursed silently, glanced back to Mel and then, arranging his face into something less than a scowl, turned to open it.

"Sorry. I had to kick the door, rather than knock it," Jade said, holding a tray aloft. "Hope I'm not interrupting, but I brought Mel some tea out. She said her kettle wasn't working earlier." She smiled past Mark to Mel. "I brought your tablets out, too, Mel. Just in case you forget to take them."

CHAPTER THIRTY-SEVEN

JADE

Jade wasn't surprised to find Mark still in the lounge, drinking what appeared to be his second glass of whisky. He'd drained his first when he'd come downstairs, looking dishevelled yet sexy in his tracksuit bottoms and a T-shirt. Mel had drifted off to sleep before he'd come out of the bathroom and he hadn't wanted to disturb her, he'd said. He really was a kind, caring man. Selfless. His own nights had been disturbed constantly, first by Evie waking, then by needy Melissa insisting on seeing to her and only succeeding in making her more fractious, and now by the silly bitch's screaming nightmares. Still, though—Jade tried to be charitable—she couldn't help those. Considering the amount of medication she was on, she'd been surprised Melissa had stayed the pace today, working on her stupid pottery in the garden. Jade did hope she was swallowing all the tablets. She'd have to keep her eye on that.

"Do you mind if I join you?" she asked, going on in. She couldn't leave the poor man sitting there on his own, looking so utterly dejected, so desperately lonely. He was studying the bottom of his glass as if looking for answers. He needed company, the comfort of a good woman's arms around him. *Soon, my love. Soon.*

Mark looked up at her, smiling wearily. What Jade would give to press her lips softly against his and soothe his worries away. "That bad, hey?" he asked her.

"No." Jade smiled reassuringly back. "I thought one red wine wouldn't hurt, though, if that's okay? It might help me to relax. Busy day." She yawned and stretched, making sure to expand her chest, showing off her breasts, covered only by a flimsy strappy top, to maximum advantage.

Mark looked at her, his eyes travelling fleetingly lower before moving back to her face. He smiled again, obviously having appreciated the view. "Help yourself," he said.

Jade was *so* tempted to invite him to do the same, but…it was too soon. He was clearly worrying himself silly about Melissa, imagining himself responsible for her, indebted to her in some way for giving birth to his children, as if she'd done something miraculous. Well, Jade supposed it was a bit of a miracle that she'd managed to produce two, given that the woman was useless at the fundamentals. He must have been so relieved when she did finally manage to get pregnant and hang on to it—he wouldn't have to keep going through the mechanics of having sex with her. Jade doubted he would have got much satisfaction there. And he certainly wasn't getting any now.

Jade might have to do something about that, she decided. Fuck him long and slow. Jade's insides clenched at the thought of him coming hard inside her. She could almost feel it.

"Another?" She turned, waving the whisky bottle, sure he would see the burning desire pooling in her eyes, possibly throw his principles to the wind and stride across to take her there and then. Mark's gaze, though, was unfortunately elsewhere, studying the happy-fucking-family snaps lined up on the mantelpiece. Bloody Melissa. Jade reined in her irritation. It wasn't his fault. It was *hers*, digging her claws in and holding on to him, manipulating him. The sooner the man stopped torturing himself and made up his mind to leave her, the better.

"Mark?"

"What?" Mark snapped his gaze back to her. "Oh. Sorry. I, er…" He looked from her face to the bottle, taking in her breasts, which she was holding the bottle strategically in front of, and then back to her face. "Why not?" he finally said, handing the glass to her.

The poor man was beyond exhausted. He needed a massage, firm hands to ease away the knots in his muscles. Pouring his usual small measure, then adding another good splash, Jade carried the drink over. His fingers brushed hers as she handed it to him, sending an electrifying jolt of sexual tension right through her.

"Thanks," he said, such longing in his eyes as he smiled up at her that Jade was tempted to throw her own carefully laid plans to the wind and peel off her top there and then. But no. The decision had to be his. She couldn't rush it. She couldn't give him cause to lay the blame at her feet should he lose his children. Though that was highly unlikely—there was no way Melissa would be deemed capable of looking after them, assuming she didn't do them all a favour and end her sad little life before custody was an issue—but it was still better to err on the side of caution.

Offering him an encouraging smile, Jade walked across to the seat opposite him, making sure to swing her hips seductively, but not too overtly, as she did. Curling herself up on the chair, she watched him pondering for a while—probably questioning how he'd come to be trapped in such a destructive relationship. "I'm a good listener," she said.

Mark turned his attention back to her, his expression pensive. "I hadn't realised how bad things were," he said quietly.

Jade waited, hoping he'd say more, but Mark fell silent, kneading his temple instead.

"I'm glad I can be here," she said. "To help."

Mark nodded, once.

"And how's the investigation going?" she asked, keen to show some support with the obvious lack of any from his wife.

"Not great." He sighed and took a large gulp of his drink. "I thought I was on to something, a possible location on Hawthorn Farm, but..."

Oh shit! Alarm bells rang loud in Jade's head. "No luck, I take it?" she asked, trying not to sound too interested, as her brain scrambled for a plan. She'd have to speak to Dylan, enlist his help, bribe him or goad him. It wouldn't be a problem, she assured herself. The man was as malleable as Melissa's clay, but she'd have to do it soon.

"No." Mark shook his head disconsolately. "Turned out to be a wild goose chase. I was so bloody sure."

Sighing again, he got to his feet and walked to the cupboard to top up his glass.

"Is that why you were late?" Jade asked.

"Yeah, sorry about that. I was later than I thought I'd be. If I'd known Mel was working I would have tried to get back sooner."

"It's not a problem," Jade assured him. "I get that you'll be detained sometimes. I mean, with a missing child investigation underway it's bound to happen." She hesitated, then decided to go for it. "I'm sorry Mel didn't seem to understand."

Mark looked at her quizzically as he sat back down.

"I overheard, when I brought the tea out."

Mark nodded, his jaw set tight. "She used to," he said, taking a small sip of his whisky. "For some reason, she doesn't seem to trust me right now. I'm still not sure I understand why."

"Does that worry you?" Jade probed carefully.

Mark hesitated, as if not sure how much to confide. "Frankly," he said, after a second, "it bloody terrifies me."

"Why?" Jade asked, gently urging him on.

Mark ran his hands up over his face. "I don't...I know she's ill, but I'm beginning to wonder whether she still..." He paused, picked up his whisky, put it back down, then got to his feet.

"She seems to be pulling away from me," he said eventually. "I'm not sure how I'd handle it if we split."

What? Her heart flipping violently inside her, Jade stared hard at him.

"I've seen the damage a broken home can wreak," he went on, plunging his hands in his pockets and walking to the window, staring out at nothing. "I don't want that for my kids," he admitted, his voice tight.

And Jade's heart settled clunkily back into its moorings.

And he wouldn't have to, she decided, steeling her resolve. There would be no broken-home scenario. Angel was hers. She loved her. She was *her* child. She would *never* see her without her father. He must know that. Poppy, who was now grating seriously on her nerves, she hadn't made up her mind about yet, but she could tolerate her, at least for a short while, if Mark was really going to be so heartbroken without her.

"Crap!" Mark said suddenly, moving away from the window and heading for the door.

Jade started after him, and then, realising Evie was crying, rushed into the hall. "I'll go," she said, catching his arm as he mounted the stairs. "You've had one or two whiskies," she pointed out kindly, searching his eyes. Such troubled eyes, it tore at her heart.

Mark nodded and stepped back down, a little unsteadily on his feet, Jade noted. "One or two too many," he admitted, looking ashamed.

"I think you probably needed them," Jade sympathised. "I'll look in on Melissa as soon as I've settled Evie. Why don't you have a lie down on the sofa? You're obviously a bit tiddly. It might be an idea not to disturb her tonight."

Knowing Melissa would be cooped up in the workshop for some time, Jade finished her tasks in the kitchen the next morning. She'd struggled a bit with the U-bend under the sink, but the lump of clay was now successfully wedged in place.

Having realised she needed to bring things to a head, Jade had lain awake in the night pondering how, and finally come to a conclusion. She had to shatter Mark's white knight image once and for all, make Melissa believe that he wasn't the perfect husband she had always thought. But the woman wouldn't go of her own volition, not without the children, and Jade would never allow her to take Angel. Nor would Mark. He was obviously scared for his fragile demented wife, but his children came first. If Melissa wasn't going to leave willingly without them, then Jade had to make sure she left unwillingly.

To which end, she had to make sure that Mark started being less concerned for his wife and more concerned for himself. He had to get good and angry, and Melissa needed to see it, to realise how utterly disillusioned with her he was. She had to learn that he was concerned for his children, as any caring father would be, and that having her sectioned might be his only option. Melissa would react, of course—irrationally and violently, hopefully. Yes, the more she pondered, the more she liked the idea. Melissa would go, and soon, one way or another.

And Jade would step seamlessly into her shoes.

We'll all be together soon, sweetheart. She mentally addressed her precious Angel. *Just you, me and Daddy. Won't that be lovely?*

But what about Poppy? She was already a needy child, and she would only get worse with her mother gone. Jade knitted her brow. She hadn't considered that until now. She would have to get rid of her. There was no other option. But... Mark doted on her. He would be inconsolable.

Yes, but then he would need an awful lot of comforting, wouldn't he? Jade's mouth curved into a smile at the prospect of that. And if she got pregnant soon, which she would, after sex, sex and more sex, Mark would soon have something else to occupy his mind.

Checking the wall clock—she needed to be off soon if she

was going to enlist Dylan's help in getting rid of Daisy—Jade made the tea, and then reached up to the cupboard to extract Melissa's tablets, popping one in the cup and one on the tray, which Melissa would dutifully swallow.

She'd take her a biscuit, too. There wasn't a lot of point in the woman watching her figure, after all, when Mark was clearly appreciating the view elsewhere.

Now, what had she forgotten? Ah, yes. The vodka, Melissa's tipple of choice—the perfect drink for an alcoholic trying to hide the smell of booze on their breath. Humming happily, Jade went to the hall to extract the half-litre bottle from her handbag, one of several she'd purchased, and then, removing the top, she headed to the downstairs toilet to tip a good measure down the sink. Going back to the kitchen, she placed what now appeared a half-drunk bottle in the under-sink cupboard, far enough back to be hidden. Until one emptied the cupboard, that was, which Mark would have to do in order to unblock the pipe and avert a disaster.

CHAPTER THIRTY-EIGHT

MELISSA

"It's open," Mel called, hearing a tap on the workshop door, and then, realising it could only be Jade, who'd no doubt come bearing tea and biscuits, she wiped the clay from her hands and walked over to open it.

"How's it going?" Jade asked, with her usual radiant smile.

Mel smiled back, rather less joyously. "Painfully."

Holding the door for Jade to come in, she beckoned to Hercules, who'd decided she preferred curling up in the workshop during the day, rather than in the kitchen with Jade. Mel couldn't fathom why the dog had taken a dislike to the poor girl, growling if ever she was around her. As Jade had said, it was probably because she was nervous around dogs, having been bitten by one as a child. The dog obviously sensed it, she'd suggested. Still though, it was a bit of a mystery, Hercules being such a placid animal.

"Come on, girl, outside." She beckoned again to the dog, who was watching Jade warily as she deposited the tray. "Hercules, come *on*," Mel tried, patting her thigh when the dog didn't budge. She was growing irritated, she realised. She was doing that a lot lately—not surprising, when she was so perpetually exhausted. She felt like a zombie. Maybe she should ask Dr. Meadows about changing her medication, or reducing the dose? Her nightmares were terrifying, and so real, as if she were living the dreams and the daytime was an illusion. Mel knew she'd terrified Mark, too, on several occasions, screaming out in her sleep. The last thing she wanted, though, was to resort to taking sleeping tablets on top of antidepressants, which was her only option if either of them were going to get a decent night's sleep.

"All right. You can go out later. But don't blame me if you end up crossing your paws." Mel sighed, closing the door, and walked across to where Jade was looking her sculpture over, probably coming to the same conclusion Mel had.

She was sculpting like a zombie too.

"You've finished it," Jade said with enthusiasm. "Well done, Mel."

"Finished, yes, but unfortunately not so well done." Emitting another sigh, Mel surveyed her endeavours with a critical eye. Her couple seemed to be holding on to each other in petrified desperation, rather than loving embrace. Where was the passion? The sensuality? The desire?

"But it's beautiful." Jade sounded surprised. "Really evocative."

"Evocative of what though?" Mel said glumly. "They're supposed to be in post-coital ecstasy, limbs, hearts and bodies entwined, two lovers as one, not two people grieving."

Jade considered her passionless lovers quietly for a moment. "Maybe he wasn't up to the job."

It took Mel a second to catch up. "Oh God." She laughed. "More work needed then?"

Jade shrugged noncommittally. "Well, I think it's fab, but I know it won't be right until you're happy with it. I'll leave you to massage his ego," she said, turning for the door. "I thought I'd go out for a while before collecting Poppy."

"Oh?" Mel tried to quell an immediate sense of panic. Panic that she'd be left alone to care for her baby, she realised, with an overwhelming sense of dismay.

"I'm off to the DIY store," Jade went on, oblivious. "I thought

I'd try and get a few ideas for the cottage, if ever the work gets underway. Don't worry, I'll take Evie with me so you can get on."

Mel's panic gave way to relief, followed swiftly by trepidation. What would she do when Jade wasn't here on a permanent basis? How on earth would she cope?

Jade paused at the door. "What do you fancy for dinner? I could pop by the supermarket and get something nice, if you—"

"No!" Mel said quickly. And then she stopped herself, taking a deep breath. What the bloody hell was wrong with her? She had to get a grip! Of course she'd *cope*. Evie was *her* child. She loved her with her very bones. She'd lost her way, that was all. Postnatal depression wasn't something she should feel ashamed of, or guilty about. She simply needed to find her way back, to regain control of her emotions, her life, her child. One step at a time.

Calming herself, she glanced towards Jade, who was blinking bemusedly in her direction. "I thought I'd cook tonight," Mel explained. "I'm really grateful for all your help, Jade. I'm sure we'd have starved without you, but it's not fair to expect you to do it every night. You're already doing far too much."

"I don't mind."

"I insist," Mel said, with a decisive nod. "It will give you a break, and, to be honest, I could do with a break from my moody lovers."

"No problem," Jade said, smiling understandingly. "So, what will you cook?"

Mel thought about it. "Spaghetti bolognese," she decided. She could defrost the mince in the microwave and she probably had the other ingredients in. Enough to make a reasonably tasty dish anyway, served up with garlic bread, which Poppy and Mark both adored.

"Perfect," Jade said, looking impressed. "And I'll be around, so you can give me a shout if you need a hand."

Mel steeled her determination to do nothing of the sort as Jade bounced brightly out of the door. She could manage to produce a meal in her own kitchen, for God's sake.

Meanwhile... Her clay man needed more than his ego massaging, she fancied. He needed major surgery.

With the kiln still not working properly—meaning she'd have to transport everything to the university and beg the use of their kiln—she'd be more behind than ever if she started over, but... It was no good. The piece was substandard. Sliding her sad lovers reluctantly into the bin, she went to fetch a fresh lump of clay, which she could at least knead in readiness to start afresh tomorrow. Leaving the biscuit unguarded, however, with a Labrador in sniffing distance, turned out to be a fatal mistake.

"Hercules! Bad girl!" Mel scolded the dog, dumping her clay and tugging at her collar. But the dog resisted her attempts to heave her away, knocking the cup over and lapping greedily at the dregs. "Out. Go on, out!" She marched the dog to the door, ready to throw her out. She was furious, and no one could accuse her of getting this out of proportion. What if Hercules jumped up to snatch at Poppy's food? Or, God forbid, she tried to take food from Evie?

That dog really was getting away with too much. Sleeping on Poppy's bed with Evie only yards away across the landing might even be too risky. But Mark seemed to have this hare-brained idea that Hercules would protect her if they were broken into. The only chance of that would be if the dog licked a burglar to death.

Honestly, if Mark was going to allow her the run of the house the least he could do was train her. If he couldn't do that, then he should think about rehoming her. Jade had rehomed her cat quickly enough, after all, she thought crossly, retrieving the cup from the floor and finding it was cracked. Muttering, Mel crashed the cup back onto the tray—and then stopped, and breathed, realising her anger was escalating. It was a cup. Not even an expensive cup. God, was she really getting things so out of proportion, again, that she was contemplating letting Hercules go to complete strangers?

She thought of the ease with which Jade had got rid of her cat. Mel still couldn't help wondering how the animal had disappeared so quickly. Surely she wouldn't have had the poor thing put down? No, she said friends had taken it.

Feeling more guilty than ever that she'd considered Jade capable of having the cat disposed of in such a way despite her determination to give that particular emotion short shrift, Mel turned to mop up the tray, only to realise the capsule she should have taken was soggy with tea, its powdered contents spewing out.

On the bright side, at least Hercules hadn't swallowed it. Despairing of herself, Mel shifted the tray out of the way and set about taking her frustration out on her lump of clay. She'd take another tablet when she went in to make dinner, which hopefully wouldn't turn out to be as disastrous as everything else she attempted to do.

CHAPTER THIRTY-NINE

JADE

Oh, you have to be joking! Jade stopped short of the cottage, realising that Dylan's mother really *was* talking to the pigs. And not just in a "Who's a pretty porkie?" sort of way either. She was having a whole fucking conversation with them. Obviously, she was as soft in the head as her drippy son was.

"Careless farming they said it was, Inky," the woman was saying mournfully. "Said we'd managed our farm in a way that encouraged floods. I've never heard the likes. Killed my Charlie, they did, worked him to death, with their rules and regulations. Left me with nothing. Except our Dylan, of course."

Sighing forlornly, the woman stopped and gazed off over the fields. Probably contemplating suicide, Jade thought despairingly, if Dylan was all she'd got.

"I'll be glad to see the back of the place," the woman went on, bending to pick up a metal bucket full of foul-smelling swill to chuck to the beasts.

Ugh, disgusting. Jade screwed up her nose. It was probably the leftovers of the piglets they'd given birth to. Where the hell was Dylan? Realising there was no sign of the man—who was obviously more moronic than she'd suspected, allowing his mother to wander around with the girl not thirty feet away—she stepped quickly forwards. The woman hadn't got a key, but God forbid she got it into her head to go peering through the windows.

"Morning, Mrs. Jackson," Jade said brightly, at which the woman jumped, literally, and whirled around, dropping her bucket in the process.

"Is Dylan here?" Jade asked, wearing her sweetest smile.

A hand clutched to her ample chest, Mrs. Jackson took several slow breaths and then narrowed her eyes. "Why?" she asked suspiciously.

"I thought I'd ask him if he fancied going into the village," Jade improvised. She wouldn't be seen dead with him in the village, or anywhere else for that matter.

"Why?" the woman repeated.

"Because we're friends, Mrs. Jackson," Jade said patiently.

Mrs. Jackson folded her arms and cocked her head to one side. "Right. And my Inky's priming his wings as we speak," she said, attempting to be clever, which really didn't suit someone dressed in crap-covered dungarees and whose personal hygiene was obviously on a par with her son's. Mind you, Jade could understand her cynicism. Dylan, who only ever attracted the wrong sort of attention, had about as many friends as he had brain cells.

"He looks out for me, Mrs. Jackson," Jade explained, less patiently. Evie was asleep in the car. The window was open, so she'd hear her if she cried, but even so, she hadn't got all bloody day. "I feel safe with him when other idiots come sniffing around."

Mrs. Jackson arched an eyebrow at that, obviously trying to work out whether Jade was being sincere.

"Is he home?" Jade asked again, growing perturbed now. Surely Dylan hadn't actually gone off the premises and left the girl on her own?

"He's fixing the barn roof," the woman said, turning disinterestedly away.

Jade stared at the rude bitch's back. And then—*oh fuck*—past her to a movement at the cottage's upstairs window. The girl was walking around. If she looked out of the window, the woman was bound to spot her.

Irritated, having been delayed while she took necessary action to ensure Mrs. Jackson didn't discover the girl, Jade parked outside the pub and texted Dylan back. He was worried, because his mother had apparently gone out without telling him. Definitely tied to her apron strings. Jade shook her head despairingly.

She obviously couldn't find you. She's probably visiting friends, or gone shopping or something. Bit tied up with children today. See you tomorrow first thing.

She would have to be there early, she decided. She couldn't have him throwing a wobbly now. She needed him. As well as helping her move the girl, she had other plans that required Dylan's participation. He was tall and dark, and therefore easily mistaken for Mark at the wheel of Mel's car. He was going to need careful handling, though, with lots of physical and emotional reassurance.

One eye on the entrance to the pub, she waited patiently for her phone to ping back a reply and then breathed out a sigh of relief when it did.

Okay. C U then. Xxx

Rolling her eyes at his use of abbreviated text words, and fully expecting him to text again before the day was out, Jade sent him a smiley face back, with three reciprocal kisses, and then emitted a sigh of relief as DS Cummings exited the pub, bang on cue. Having googled his details and then followed him, she'd learned he liked a pint with his lunch, and one or two once he was off duty. He was also obviously everything she'd overheard Mark confiding to Melissa he was—a womanising, sexist wanker, led by his penis, which, Jade suspected, would make him just as malleable as Dylan.

Waiting for the right moment, Jade watched him pause in the car park, picking his teeth and leering after two scantily clad girls half his age as they teetered on vertiginous shoes towards their car. "Hope you've been watching your alcohol intake, Taylor," he called after them. "Wouldn't want me having to arrest you now, would you?"

"Depends..." said one of the girls, smiling coquettishly back over her shoulder.

Yeah, depends on how much he's paying. Jade curled a lip and sighed inwardly, supposing it was time to flash her own assets in his direction. Clearly the man couldn't resist a pair of tits. Glancing over her shoulder to check on Evie, who was soundly sleeping, bless her, Jade adjusted her plunge bra and tugged down her strappy top to show off maximum cleavage, and then climbed out of her car. Her phone clutched to her ear, she swept her hair from her face and stared down at her flat tyre, looking suitably flustered. And then, bending from the waist, she leaned to examine it. As she was wearing her tightest skinny jeans, she guessed he'd be enjoying the view.

"An hour?" she said despairingly, talking to no one into her mobile. "No, it's just that I have a baby in the car and I have to get her back to her parents. Yes. Okay, I'll wait. No choice really, have I?"

Sensing a certain someone approaching, Jade sighed and ended her "call."

"Problem?" Detective Sergeant Cummings said behind her, not that Jade had imagined he would be the slightest bit concerned unless he fancied getting into her knickers.

Jade turned, making sure to look girly and wary for a second, and then hugely relieved when he flashed his ID. Plainly, he was thinking she'd be impressed, the full-of-himself prat. "Slow puncture," she said, with a helpless shrug. "I don't have a car pump with me, unfortunately, and I have to get my charge back to her parents."

DS Cummings followed her gaze to Evie in her baby carrier. "Can't you ring them?" he asked.

Clearly *not* Sir Galahad then. "Well, I will, obviously, but her mum's due to go out soon." Jade checked her watch. "*Hell!* I'll probably get the sack."

His gaze roving over her, Cummings ran a hand contemplatively over his chin. "I don't have a pump in the car, but…" He glanced at her tits, then down to her tyre, and then nodded behind him. "Tell you what, I'll go and ask in the pub. The owner's bound to have one."

"Would you?" Jade all but wilted with relief. "That would be so kind. I'd be really grateful."

"No problem," Cummings assured her, glancing down to the hand she'd placed on his arm and then back to her face, lingering appreciatively at her breasts again on the way up. "Why don't you wait in your car? You never know what sort of cretins might be hanging around a dive like this."

Oh, I have a pretty good idea. "Thank you, I will." Jade fluttered her eyelashes and turned back to the car.

Cummings held the door open, all the better to ogle her as she climbed demurely inside, bum first, threading her legs slowly in and smiling suggestively up at him.

"Don't go anywhere." He winked, looking pleased with himself, as he turned to jog keenly back to the pub.

Five minutes later, Jade looked on in suitable awe as DS Cummings inflated her tyre. "So strong," she said, smiling coquettishly, God help her. "You have a wonderful pumping action," she breathed, her voice loaded with sexual innuendo.

He paused in his wonderful pumping action to scan her eyes questioningly. "So I'm told," he said hopefully, and most definitely weighing his chances.

Jade lowered her eyes, perusing the length and breadth of him slowly before coming back to his face. "I can see why," she said, running the tip of her tongue provocatively over her lips.

At which the guy looked positively orgasmic and pumped harder.

"You're an absolute hero," Jade said, once she was good to go, her eyelashes now unashamedly in overdrive. "I honestly don't know how I can thank you."

At that, his mouth curved into a lurid smirk. "Oh, I can think of a way," he said, taking the bait. "How about you let me buy you a drink?"

"It should be me buying you one," Jade pointed out.

"Tomorrow night?" he said, pushing it. "I could pick you up, if you'd like?"

"Better not. I'm a babysitter—live in. Might not go down well with my employers. I'll meet you here. Seven thirty."

"Excellent," he said, having a last inspection of the goods he no doubt fancied sampling. "I'll look forward to seeing you then."

Job done. Jade was going to enjoy seeing this disgusting, drug-pushing creep get his just deserts. "See you tomorrow," she said, planting a soft kiss on his cheek and noting his sharp intake of breath with satisfaction.

CHAPTER FORTY

LISA

"In your own time, Cain," DCI Edwards said, drumming his fingers impatiently on Mark's desk and looking hugely unimpressed.

"Yes, sir. It's here somewhere." Mark scrolled through his inbox again, obviously not finding what he wanted, and looking like shit. Dark circles under his eyes, four o'clock shadow, he looked as if he hadn't slept for a month. The distinct whiff of whisky Lisa had already caught wasn't going to go down well either. Edwards, who had a nose like a sniffer dog, was bound to notice that.

Lisa glanced across to Mark, rolling her eyes as Edwards exaggeratedly checked his watch, as if he'd been waiting half an hour rather than a couple of minutes. "Got it," she called across. "Sending it over now, sir," she said, emailing the forensics report Edwards had asked for across to him.

"Thank you," Edwards said curtly. "My office, DI Cain. Now, please," he added, twirling around to march in that direction.

Leaning back in his chair, Mark thumped the heel of his hand against his forehead, and then looked royally pissed as Cummings, who'd just strolled in late from lunch—a liquid lunch, by the looks of him—walked past with a smug smirk on his face.

"Sleeping on the job, sir, *tsk, tsk*. More water with it, mate," he suggested. "And maybe a few less night-time excursions?"

"You should do stand-up, Cummings, you really should.

Preferably in the middle of the motorway," Lisa snapped, reaching into her desk drawer for her emergency supply of extra-strong mints. She'd had occasion to sit up pondering her problems through the bottom of a glass herself. Mark, however, looked as if he'd been brooding over his at the bottom of the bottle.

"Make sure you swallow it before you go in," she advised, tossing the mints across to him.

"Cheers, Lisa," said Mark, getting wearily to his feet.

"Fancy a drink after?" Lisa asked as he bypassed her desk, thinking he might need to offload a few things.

Marks smiled wryly. "Probably not a good idea, but thanks. And Mel's cooking anyway."

"Ah." Lisa nodded. "Another time then. Good luck," she added, as, running a hand through his hair in a vain attempt to smarten himself up, Mark headed for the high jump.

Cooking? Lisa knitted her brow. Well, that was progress, she supposed. From what she'd gathered from Mark, life on the home front had lurched from bad to worse, though she only had to look at his dishevelled appearance to realise that. His decision-making was a bit awry, as well. Yesterday he'd deployed uniforms to premises that had already been thoroughly checked. Walking away from his computer and leaving confidential information on the screen, Lisa had noticed that too. All of which had given her cause to worry, particularly about Miss Baywatch Babe, who'd appeared on the scene around the same time things started going pear-shaped. It had been convenient for Mel and Mark that she'd just happened to be there—a homeless, fully qualified babysitter, looking for a job—but Lisa couldn't help thinking that the situation had been extremely convenient for Jade as well.

Could the au pair, whose house renovations seemed not to be imminent anytime soon, be causing problems between them? Mark loved his wife and kids more than life itself, Lisa had no doubt about that, but it was a bit of a coincidence that Mel was suddenly imagining that Mark was having an affair—albeit with *her*. Mark Cain was a good-looking bloke, and under other circumstances, Lisa might have been tempted, but they were nothing more than good friends. She wondered at Mel's madness, allowing a pretty young woman to live with them. And, although she really shouldn't be judging her, from what she'd seen when she'd met her, the babysitter had been a little underdressed for the job.

She glanced towards Edwards' office, where Mark was shuffling awkwardly on the spot as Edwards bollocked him, loudly, to Cummings' amusement. She might be barking up the wrong tree, probably fuelled by the fact that she was upset about her own cooled relationship with Mel, but…

Lisa was only marginally surprised when Google coughed up sweet FA about Jade Hart. Had Mel done all the checks? Had Mark? Had they actually seen the woman's paperwork? Though, she wouldn't have any paperwork, would she? Not hard copies anyway. All burned to a cinder, presumably—and also too conveniently for Lisa's liking. Mel might not have pursued it once they'd decided Jade was an angel sent directly from heaven.

Guessing at Jade's age, Lisa was checking yearly college student intakes when she heard Edwards raise his voice. He wasn't happy. By the sound of it, neither was Mark. "I was out last night," he yelled heatedly back. "Yes, I had a few drinks. Since when did that become a criminal offence?"

"Since you're obviously so hungover you can't see straight! You're exhausted. Go home!"

Wincing, Lisa glanced in Cummings' direction. He was just loving this, the smug bastard.

"Immediately, DI Cain," Edwards called after him, as Mark emerged furiously from his office.

Lisa closed down her search window and hurried over as

Mark yanked his jacket from the back of his chair. "That went well then?"

"It just gets better. I'll text you...ring you tomorrow." He stormed to the door, and Lisa saw his jaw clench as Cummings stood to open it for him.

CHAPTER FORTY-ONE

MARK

Attempting to calm down, Mark selected some soothing music as he drove around for a little while before going home. Chopin's "Piano Sonata No. 2," though, served only to heighten his anger and frustration. Was he being monitored on overhead cams by Cummings, he wondered, for whatever perverse reason that would no doubt become clear? Probably. Bastard. Blowing out a frustrated sigh, Mark selected Vaughan Williams' "The Lark Ascending" instead—one of Evie's favourites—and tried to get some perspective on his life. Edwards was right, of course. He wasn't capable of doing his job. Mark dearly wished he hadn't dragged him over the coals in earshot of that wanker Cummings though, who would probably get off on it.

He *was* exhausted, weary to his bones. He needed to do as Edwards had advised and take some time. He was no use to anyone like this. At least he wasn't being put on "voluntary" gardening leave for the foreseeable future, as he'd half expected to be. That was something.

Feeling more in control, Mark turned for home. He couldn't help wishing it felt more like a home, that he could turn the clock back, or forward. That he could make this whole mess go away. He couldn't. No one could. All he could do was be there. And he would be. If Mel was fighting, he'd fight alongside her.

Mel's car wasn't there, he noticed as he pulled up, which meant that Jade and the kids weren't back yet. That was good. As much as he loved his children, it would be nice for Mel and him to have some space.

Mark parked up and let himself in, and his heart nose-dived. Cosy conversation wasn't going to happen, he realised, any more than dinner was. Clangs and curses were coming from the kitchen, followed by "For God's sake, Hercules, get out of the way!" Mark headed in that direction, stopping confounded in the doorway as a scene of utter chaos greeted him.

"Mel?" he said. The first thing he noticed was the open red wine bottle on the island, half empty, he noted, his heart plummeting further. Warily, he turned his gaze towards Mel, who appeared to be fishing wormlike spaghetti from the overflowing sink. "What's happened?" he asked, trying hard to reserve judgement.

"This bloody house happened!" Mel swiped her hair from her face, clanged the colander on the drainer, and turned to glare at him. "The bloody sink's blocked up. I *told* you the plumbing was packing up. Everything's packing up. Hercules! Get out!" She scowled down at the dog, who was helping herself to the spaghetti on the floor.

Mark's heart skipped a beat as Mel grabbed her roughly by the collar and attempted to drag her out.

"*Jesus*, Mel, don't." Mark stepped in, herding Hercules towards the back door. "She's just doing what dogs do."

"Yes, scavenging!" Mel snapped, dropping down to scrape up the spilled spaghetti. "Because *you* didn't take her to training lessons, because you were too busy working! As usual. She's been asleep in the middle of the kitchen floor for the last hour. I've had to keep walking around her while I'm trying to cook. She's completely out of control."

What? Mark definitely couldn't get his head around that one. The demands of work meant he'd missed one or two sessions, but the dog had been to training lessons. Not eating spaghetti off the floor hadn't been covered, but he decided for the sake of argument not to point that out. *Christ!* About to help her clean up, he headed fast for the gas hob instead, where he realised there was a pan close to catching fire.

"Shit!" he cursed, grabbing the handle without thinking and then dropping it as fast as he'd picked it up. It landed with a crash, spewing the contents across the ceramic tiles to add to the mess already there.

Mel looked up sharply. "Why in *God*'s name did you do that?"

"It was hot!" *Dammit.* Shaking his scalded hand, Mark headed for the sink to run it under the cold tap. He cursed silently when he realised he couldn't.

"Are you hurt?" Mel asked, concerned now she'd realised he'd hurt himself.

Mark reached for the tea towel, wetting it and wrapping it around his hand. "No," he said tightly, turning to face her. "Have you been drinking?"

Mel shook her head, confounded. "What?"

Mark looked at the ceiling, willing himself not to lose it. "The wine?" He nodded towards the bottle.

Cocking her head to one side, Mel studied him curiously. "It's one you opened. I put a spoonful in the bolognese sauce. Would you like to breathalyse me? Scrape some up from the floor and get your forensics team to test it?"

Great. Mark blew out a long breath. "Mel…" He stepped towards her. "I'm sorry. I just…"

"Assumed?" Mel finished.

Sighing, Mark nodded wearily. "Wrongly," he admitted. "I'm sorry. I…" He trailed off, not sure what else to say.

Mel studied him a second longer. "So am I," she said disappointedly, pulling her unimpressed gaze away from his and walking into the hall.

Mark had cleaned up, fetched his toolbox, and was about to investigate the situation under the sink when Jade and the kids arrived, Poppy chattering excitedly as they bustled through the front door. About her teacher's big belly, Mark gathered, as they came towards the kitchen.

"But how did the baby get *in* there?"

Mark winced as he heard her ask.

"Little baby Jesus put it there to keep safe and cosy until it's fully grown," Jade answered smartly.

"Like we put Dory in the fish bowl to keep safe and cosy till she's grown?" Poppy asked.

"Just like that."

Well done, Jade, Mark thought, smiling as the babysitter and her charges arrived in the kitchen. He wasn't sure how he would have fielded that one.

"Daddeee!" Poppy did her usual and flew over to him, regardless of the under-sink paraphernalia Mark had in each hand.

"Hi, gorgeous girl. How was your day at school?"

"Good." Poppy nodded, unhooking herself from his neck and allowing him to straighten up. "We felt Miss Winters' tummy. It's huge!"

So were Poppy's eyes. Mark couldn't help but laugh.

"They're learning about the birds and bees early," Jade said, as she lowered Evie carefully down in her carrier.

"God, I hope not."

"The child-friendly version, I think." Jade smiled as she walked over to him, and then frowned as she peered in the sink. "Oh." She eyed him sympathetically.

Mark shrugged, feeling for Mel. He owed her one hell of an apology. He just hoped she'd accept it, once he'd unblocked the sink and sorted out an alternative to spaghetti bolognese.

"What's for dinner?" Poppy stood on tiptoe and peered into the sink.

"Takeaway McDonald's," Jade said, steering her away. "You can come with me to fetch it."

"Yay!" Poppy whooped, obviously all in favour of that.

Mark breathed a sigh of relief. "Thanks, Jade," he said, feeling indebted, yet again.

"No problem," Jade assured him. "I'll take Evie too. She's not due a feed for another hour or so. We should be back by then."

Grateful, Mark went back to the under-sink cupboard. "Fuck," he uttered, extracting something that didn't belong there.

"Daddy!" Poppy whirled around. "That's a really naughty word."

"I, er... It is. An extremely bad word. Sorry, Poppet. I banged my head." He smiled tightly, his eyes travelling to Jade, who'd clearly gathered the reason for him cursing out loud.

"Oh no!" Looking alarmed, Poppy hurried across to him. "Does it hurt?" she asked, her little brow now creased with sympathy.

"Yes. It does. It hurts quite a lot," Mark said throatily, turning to park the bottle of vodka he'd fished from the cupboard on the work surface.

CHAPTER FORTY-TWO

JADE

Noting the number of the incoming call, Jade left Poppy to her cereal and dashed out the back door to answer it.

"It's my fault!" Dylan blurted in her ear, before she had a chance to speak. "It's my fault. She's just lying there, and I—"

"*Whoa*, Dylan, slow down. What's happened? What's your fault?"

"Me mum! She's ... *not moving*! She's ..." Emitting a guttural sob, Dylan broke off.

"Stay where you are," Jade said firmly. "Don't touch anything or say anything. Not to anyone, Dylan."

Dylan choked back another distraught sob. And another.

Hell, he was losing it. "Dylan!" Jade felt panic twisting inside her. "Do you hear me?"

"It's my fault!" Dylan repeated, sounding like a distraught parrot.

"Dylan, it is *not* your fault! You weren't even *there*," Jade barked. "Were you?" she tacked on quickly.

Dylan sniffled snottily. "No," he said timidly, after a second. "I was fixing the barn roof, and when I finished I couldn't find her. I thought she'd gone out, like you said, but ..." He broke off with another sob.

"No one will blame you, Dylan, I promise." Jade softened her tone. She needed him to get a grip. God forbid he should get it into his thick head to dial 999. "But you have to listen to me. You need to stay calm, stay there and not talk to anyone—don't even use the phone. Can you do that for me?"

There was a hiccuppy pause. "Uh-huh," Dylan replied uncertainly. "Will you come?"

"Of course I will. I'll be there as soon as I've dropped Poppy off at school," Jade assured him. "It will be fine, my love. I'll help you sort it all out. Just make yourself a cup of sweet tea and sit tight. Okay?"

"Okay," Dylan said, sounding somewhat relieved.

Thank God for that. Dylan subdued, for the moment, Jade hurried back inside to finish making Mark's coffee. She needed to be gone, but first she needed to check how the land lay here. They hadn't kissed and made up, she was aware of that. Other than to say goodnight to Poppy and Evie, Melissa had stayed in her bedroom. And no wonder. Clearly, she'd decided to keep a low profile. Mark had been white with anger when Jade had left to fetch the McDonald's, and then subdued when she had arrived back. She'd learned from Melissa when she'd taken her some warm soup, with the necessary extra ingredient, that they'd argued about the catastrophe that was dinner. He'd been avoiding her since, Melissa had said shakily, meaning Mark had valiantly restrained himself rather than tackle the ridiculous woman about her drinking habit. Probably because it would lead to the inevitable argument, which Jade knew Mark desperately didn't want his children to witness. He really was a lovely man. After helping Poppy with her Peppa Pig construction kit before her bedtime, he'd spent the rest of the evening listening to his music—trying to distract himself, Jade guessed. Then he'd spent the night on the sofa, fetching a pillow and sheets from the airing cupboard this time, which meant it might be becoming a more permanent arrangement.

Perfect. Jade hummed happily to herself. Who would have thought a little lump of clay could wreak such havoc?

"All finished?" She smiled brightly at Poppy as she passed by with the coffee.

"Yup," Poppy said, picking her bowl up and tipping the last dregs of milk towards her mouth.

"Good girl," Jade said, though she felt sorely tempted to slap her. Ill-mannered glutton. She really did have to go. "Go and get your shoes on then, sweetheart," she urged her. "I have an appointment this morning. If you're really quick getting ready, I'll bring you some sweets later. How does that sound?"

"Yay!" Poppy clapped delightedly, slid off her chair and skipped happily to the stairs.

Spoiled little brat. Quashing her irritation, Jade went quietly into the lounge. There was a chance Mark might still be sleeping. After all that had gone on, Jade doubted he'd had a very restful night.

But she found him sitting on the sofa, contemplating the bottle of vodka on the coffee table, obviously debating how to tackle his self-centred, needy wife about it. *Poor Mark.* Jade's heart went out to him. "Morning," she said, toning down the cheeriness. She didn't want to appear insensitive.

Mark dragged his hands tiredly over his face and got to his feet. "Morning." He forced a smile, for her sake, bless him.

"I made you a coffee," Jade said, walking across to put the mug on the table. "With extra caffeine. I thought you could use it." Glancing at the vodka, she smiled sympathetically.

"I could." Mark sighed, a world-weary sigh. "Cheers, Jade," he said, moving to bundle up his sheets, which were in a bit of a tangle. Definitely not a restful night then, Jade deduced.

"How are you feeling?" she asked, reaching to help him.

"Okay," Mark lied. "A bit tired." He paused, a wretched look in his eyes. "I'm sorry about all this, Jade," he said, glancing embarrassedly away and back again. "If you wanted to hand in your notice, I'd quite understand."

"And leave you in the lurch? I wouldn't dream of it. The children need stability above all else right now. I don't want to add to their troubles." She flapped a sheet and folded it briskly. "I could cancel my arrangements, though, if it would help. Under the circumstances, I mean."

"Arrangements?" Mark's expression was one of confusion. And mild panic, Jade noticed, gratified. He was going to miss her. But not half as much as she would miss him.

"I mentioned it to Mel. My friend, Samantha…she gets the result of her biopsy today. I said I'd go with her."

"God, no, don't cancel," Mark said emphatically. "Go. I'm sure we can manage for…?" he trailed off on a question, his look now hopeful.

God love him. He really was in an intolerable situation. The sooner Jade could get him out of it, the better. "Just the one day," she assured him. "She lives in London though, so I wouldn't be back until quite late."

"No problem." Mark smiled, relieved. "I'm off for a couple of days, so I can look after Evie and collect Poppy. I'm guessing you could use a break anyway, although that's probably not much of a break. Give your friend my best. I hope it all turns out okay for her."

Even now, he was thinking of others. Jade's heart fluttered inside her. A gem, he really was. "I'll take Poppy to school on my way," she said. "Evie's fast asleep. She's due a feed at nine. You have my mobile if you need it. Good luck with…" Pausing, Jade glanced again at the vodka. "Everything."

"Yeah, thanks. I might need it." His look now, Jade noticed with quiet satisfaction, was one of utter despair.

*

Seeing Dylan standing at the far side of the pig field, Jade called to him as she climbed out of the car. When he didn't respond, she called out again, and then cursed and heaved the gate open to head towards him.

"Dylan!" Jade was seriously irritated now. Squelching through mud and pig shit in her trainers was most definitely *not* on her list of favourite things to do.

Finally, he turned towards her as she skirted around the pig house, careful to give Inky and bloody Oinky a wide berth. "It's my fault," he said pitifully, his face the colour of damp putty and slick with sweat.

"Dylan…" Jade tempered her tone and tried to hide her annoyance. Could he not hear himself? He sounded like a two-year-old, for God's sake. "Whatever's happened, it is *not*—"

Jade stopped, gulping back a violent bout of nausea as she followed his gaze down to the ground. *Bloody hell.* They'd eaten half her face.

"Oh my God! Dylan!" Jade looked away from the woman, genuinely horrified. She was going to step carefully amongst those carnivorous little fuckers in future. "What the hell have you done?"

"Nothing!" Dylan widened his eyes in obvious terror. "She was upset," he blurted defensively. "We had a row, yesterday morning. She wanted me to phone Uncle Bob and ask him for a job, but I didn't want to work on a building site. I told her I wanted to stay here, on the farm. Uncle Bob doesn't like me and Eric is always taking the mickey. I don't *want* to work in Birmingham. I told her and she got all upset. She wasn't talking to me and I—"

"Dylan, stop." Jade moved closer, clutching his shoulders with both hands. He was blinking rapidly, close to hyperventilating or wetting himself. "Slow down. Who's Eric?"

"Me cousin. He's always winding me up." Dylan dragged an arm under his nose and glanced embarrassedly down.

Gosh, I wonder why. Suppressing a sigh, Jade arranged her face into suitably annoyed. "He's obviously an idiot," she supplied what he needed to hear, whilst bracing herself to bend down and examine the woman at closer quarters.

"She's gone, Dylan." Hoisting herself quickly to her feet, she looked at him, oozing sympathy.

"Dead?" Dylan squeaked.

Yes, idiot, dead. Jade nodded solemnly. She looked dead enough, but, having found the faintest of pulses at the base of her neck, Jade suspected she wasn't yet, quite. So, what did she do with her now? Finishing the job would be the kind thing to do, but she could hardly do that with Dylan looking on. The pigs would probably chomp their way through the rest of her eventually. But that would take time and they could hardly leave her here meanwhile.

"It's my fault." Dylan gulped hard.

Jade gritted her teeth. If he said that one more time, in that wimpish tone, he'd be joining his mum as the bloody pigs' lunch. "Dylan, it's not," she stated firmly. "But…it is possible they might blame you."

Holding his gaze, Jade tried not to notice his Adam's apple bobbing grotesquely in his throat. "She probably passed out or had a heart attack or something. Did she mention she'd been having pains in her chest?"

Dylan's face drained of what little colour he had. "After Dad died," he said, his voice now a croaked whisper. "She said her heart was hurting."

"Well, there you go then. It wasn't your fault. It might even have been brought on by Mark Cain sniffing around again."

"Cain?" asked Dylan, his thickset brow furrowing. And then a spark of fury glinted in his eyes. *Good*, Jade thought. That's what she needed—Dylan angry, not cowering and bawling like a baby. Ready to do whatever it took. She had a plan, and it involved Mark being "seen" to be driving around certain areas. If Dylan pulled it off, she'd succeed in tarnishing Mark's "white knight" image in Melissa's eyes. She had to get that bloody woman off the scene before it was poor Mark who ended up on medication.

"With all the stress she's been through, worrying about why he's snooping around could easily have caused her to have a heart attack. Bastard. He might even come back," she said, forcing the point home.

"Oh shit." Dylan looked fearfully past her, as if expecting Mark to arrive any moment, blue lights flashing.

"We have to move her." Jade nodded determinedly.

"But..." Dylan looked uncertain. "Shouldn't we call an ambulance or something?"

"She's dead, Dylan," Jade reiterated. Or she soon would be, judging by how much blood she'd lost. "And we don't have much time. He might come back," she reminded him. "We can't just leave her here for him to find, can we? Even if he doesn't blame you, he's bound to set you up, especially if he has an inkling about us, and he must have. Why else does he keep coming here?"

Glancing back at his mum, Dylan thought about it. He was going to go for it. Jade could almost hear the cogs creaking. "And we have to move Daisy, too. Today. We'll take her in the car and put your poor mum in the barn where she'll be nice and safe until we can bury her properly. How does that sound?"

Dylan still didn't look a hundred per cent certain, but he seemed placated by the "bury her properly" bit.

"Don't worry." Jade pressed a kiss to his cheek, though with Dylan's sweat glands in overdrive and that faceless old hag staring up at her, she actually felt like vomiting. "I'll help you, I promise."

By which she meant she would offer moral support. Jade had no intention of getting her hands dirty. She was meeting the delightful DS Cummings tonight. And, as much as the thought of being anywhere near him made her skin crawl, she intended to look her provocatively enticing best.

"We have to go, Dylan," Jade said gently an hour or so later, watching him sobbing in earnest, chest heaving and huge round shoulders shaking as he looked down at his poor soon-to-be-deceased mother.

Realising he'd be there for the foreseeable future if she didn't hurry him up, Jade stifled a despairing sigh and attempted to comfort him. Placing a hand on his arm, she rubbed it gently, sending goose pimples up her own—and not in a good way. "Come on, my love," she coaxed, encouraging him away. "We need to move Daisy. Your mum's at rest now."

"Do you think she's happy?" Dylan looked at her beseechingly.

Delirious, I should think. Jade really had to work at keeping her face straight. "Of course she is. She's with your dad now, isn't she? Her heart won't be hurting any more, Dylan. She won't be in pain."

Appeased, Dylan nodded slowly. "Bye, Mum," he said gruffly, running a hand under his nose and finally turning away. *Thank God*, Jade thought, taking his hand as they walked back towards the cottage. They needed to get a move on if they were going to get this done while Mark was collecting Poppy from school. Melissa shouldn't be a problem. She'd dosed her up with enough drugs to knock out a horse.

CHAPTER FORTY-THREE

MELISSA

Mel was lying down when Mark finally came into the bedroom. She didn't want to be. She'd tried so hard to get up, to get dressed. But with the room spinning around her, she'd made it halfway to the bathroom before giving up and crawling back to bed.

"Mark?" Mel struggled to sit up. She was desperately trying to piece the events of the last few weeks together, trying to work out how in God's name she ended up here, but everything was fragmented, disjointed. She couldn't seem to separate dream from reality any more, memories slipping away from her like wisps of smoke on the air.

Easing her legs over the edge of the bed, Mel summoned up what little energy she had and heaved herself to her feet. Taking a step, she stumbled, and her heart, already heavy with guilt and confusion, plummeted like a lead weight in her chest. Mark didn't move to help her, as he would have done a short time ago. His face white, his expression inscrutable, he stayed where he was by the door, watching. Waiting? For her to fall? Mel swallowed hard.

"Here," he said, walking across the room after a second, during which time Mel had sunk heavily back down on the bed. "If you need it so badly, take it."

Stopping in front of her, he lifted his hand and tossed a bottle onto the duvet.

Vodka? Mel glanced at it, bewildered. "I don't…" She drew her gaze back to his. "We don't drink vodka."

"Apparently one of us does," Mark said, scanning her eyes, his own dark, thunderously dark, and… *accusing?*

She blinked at him, stupefied for a second, before the disturbing realisation dawned. "You think it's mine?" she asked, incredulous.

"It was in the cupboard under the sink. I sure as hell didn't put it there," Mark said coolly. "So, tell me, Mel, who else might have?"

Mel stared at him, stunned. He didn't really think…? No, surely not. She never drank vodka. She didn't even like the stuff. "It's not mine. Whoever put it there, it wasn't me."

Mark held her gaze. Apart from a telltale tic in his cheek, his expression didn't flinch. "Right," he said, shortly, and turned away.

"Mark! I didn't. It's not mine!" Mel sounded desperate, even to herself.

Mark stopped.

"It's not, Mark. I swear it's not."

Mark pushed his hands into his pockets, his shoulders tensing.

"Why would I put it there?" Mel implored him. "Why would I do that, and then tell you the sink's blocked? Why would I *do* that, Mark?"

Mark shrugged. "Because you forgot you'd put it there?"

"It's not mine!" Mel screamed it.

Mark whirled around. "So, who *did* put it there then, Mel?" he demanded angrily. "Hey? Jade? Poppy? Evie?"

Mel shook her head, confused and scared—by the tone of his voice as much as the nightmare her life had become. She was losing him. He was pulling away from her. Second by second, right there in front of her, he was pulling away. And there was nothing she could do about it.

"*Hercules?*" Mark shouted when she didn't answer, causing her to jump. "The *fucking* fairies?"

Mel bit back her tears. She wouldn't. She wouldn't cry in front of him. Her heart twisted painfully, because, truthfully, she knew he wouldn't come to her now if she did. "I...I don't know," she stuttered, desperately scrambling through her dysfunctional brain, acknowledging, not wanting to acknowledge, that there was only one person it could be. "Jade," she whispered finally. "It must have been Jade."

"Right." Mark laughed bitterly. "Without Jade," he said, his eyes now burning with fury, "this house would be falling apart."

The comment hit her like a low blow to the stomach. Mel didn't speak. She couldn't.

Mark sucked in a breath and looked away, absolutely disgusted. "I'm going," he said hoarsely. "I can't do this."

"Who *else?*" Mel shouted, behind him. "Who else could it have...Oh God." She stopped, cold foreboding sweeping through her. "It was you."

Mark didn't answer. His step faltered, but he didn't turn around.

"You want me gone, don't you?" Mel swallowed back a sick taste in her throat. "Is that it, Mark?" she asked him, her emotions swinging violently. "Is that why you're trying to convince me I'm going out of my mind? Why you're driving me away? So you can be with Lisa? Someone else, if not her? Who, Mark? How many other women do you have *intimate* conversations with?"

Still Mark didn't say anything. Her heart now beating a rapid drumbeat in her chest, Mel watched as he walked calmly out of the room without uttering even a word.

CHAPTER FORTY-FOUR

MARK

Mark sat at the kitchen island, his head in his hands, wondering whether it was him who was going out of his mind. She believed it. She really did believe he was having affairs. Worse, she believed him capable of such horrendous manipulation. And to what end? To move someone else in in her place? *Jesus*.

Swallowing hard, he pulled himself to his feet. Going to the kitchen cupboard, he extracted the prescription drugs, pulled out the leaflet and studied it, yet again, desperately trying to find some explanation as to what was happening.

His wife was delusional, paranoid to the point of insanity. Hallucinating. Having screaming nightmares most nights, for most of the night, and then suffering insomnia when she wasn't. The drowsiness, dizziness, obvious depression and irritability, those symptoms could be put down to the medication, but not this. This was extreme. He needed to speak to her GP; he hoped data protection wouldn't prevent Meadows from speaking to him. Somehow, though, Mark doubted changing the medication would make any difference. She needed help, more help than he or her GP could offer. She needed professional help. God help him, she might even need sectioning. Mark could hardly stand the thought, but if he had to, for the sake of their children... How much was this damaging them?

Thanks to Jade, Poppy seemed almost oblivious, although she

had asked him why Mummy was strange when he'd read her a bedtime story the other night. Last night, she'd prayed to God to "make Mummy smile again." Mark swiped angrily at an errant tear on his cheek. Evie was fine, sleeping better than she had been. She'd sat in her bouncer for a good hour after her eleven o'clock feed, smiling and gurgling and reaching a hand towards her mobiles. Her hand–eye coordination was good. She was content. She was unaffected. For now.

Deliberating whether to take Mel a drink up, he decided against it. She'd been out of it, dead to the world, when he'd retrieved the lunch she hadn't eaten. He'd taken the opportunity to check the bathroom cabinets. He'd never imagined, even when she'd been at her lowest ebb, after Jacob, that she would ever contemplate taking an overdose, but he was imagining it now.

Time to bite the bullet, he supposed. Searching the house for hidden bottles—Mark had never imagined himself doing that either. He didn't want to prove anything, confront her again—he just needed to know.

Three bottles, all partially drunk. Feeling sick to his soul, Mark lined them up in the kitchen. One stuffed down an armchair—Mel's chair. One in the airing cupboard, nestled between the sheets. Another secreted in a Perspex storage box in a rarely used cupboard. Mark might have missed it, if he hadn't been looking. How many more were there? One under the mattress maybe? A couple in the workshop? No doubt she would have booze hidden away there. *Fuck!*

Grabbing the first bottle, Mark squeezed his hand hard around it, sorely tempted to smash it against the nearest wall. Only Evie's presence in the house stopped him. Breathing hard, he unscrewed the top. Mel wouldn't hurt her. He recalled her saying it. But *why* had she said it? Because the thought had occurred to her? Because the urge had possessed her? Not bloody surprising, putting this lot away on top of the pills. Mark furiously ditched the second bottle, and then the third, down the sink that had been blocked.

Blocked with clay. Mark stopped, the final bottle still poised. How had it been blocked with clay? From Mel washing her hands there, he'd thought. Hadn't she said the sink in the workshop had been blocked too? From washing her tools there, he'd thought. He'd assumed the clay had accumulated in the U-bend. Except it hadn't been particles of clay, collecting at the bottom of the bend like sand. It had been a solid lump.

Mark thought about it as he headed for the back door to dump the bottles and search the workshop. He was halfway out when he paused, thinking of Evie. She *wouldn't* hurt her, he assured himself, carrying on out.

Still, though, Mark searched with haste. He checked the kiln, the shelves and cupboards, workbenches and the spaces beneath them. He was heading back to the door when he remembered the clay bin. She wouldn't, would she? But then, it was precisely what addicts did. Mark had been a copper long enough to know that. Crouching, he made sure his sleeve was out of the way and delved down into the slip-sodden clay. *Bingo*, he thought bitterly, as his hand made contact with what felt like a polythene-wrapped package.

Tightening his grip, Mark attempted to pull it out, but the clay seemed reluctant to part with it. Bloody hell, what was it? A two-litre bottle? He pulled harder. The package finally unsuckered itself with a squelch, causing Mark to fall back on his haunches. Retrieving the parcel from where it had landed on the floor, he eyed it curiously, wiped some of the muck from it, and then dropped it, scrambling backwards.

Jesus Christ. Mark's heart slammed into his ribcage, his stomach turning over as his mind registered what his eyes refused to believe. The cat's eyes were wild, wide and terrified, its fanged mouth wide open, the polythene clinging to its face.

Mark's hand shook as he poured a whisky. Knocking it straight back, he poured another and was about to swallow that when he remembered what time it was. *Shit! Poppy.* Mark pressed the heel of his hand against his forehead, breathing in hard and trying for some kind of composure, some equilibrium in a life that was fast careering out of control.

Attempting to pull himself together, he dumped the glass back on the table and headed for the kitchen, where he heaped coffee granules into a mug. He made it strong and black, topping it up with cold water so he could swill it down as fast as he had the whisky. How much had he had? Two fingers? Three? Mark couldn't recall. His hands were still shaking. Badly.

He raced for the stairs, cursing the creaking floorboards on the landing as he approached the main bedroom door. He wanted to check Mel was all right, but he desperately didn't want to wake her. He couldn't have a conversation of any kind with her until he'd got his head around what was going on. As if he could. As if anyone other than a trained psychiatrist could make sense of any of this.

His breath hitched in his chest as he went quietly into the bedroom. Mel was on her stomach, her normal sleeping position, and not one that would normally worry him, except he couldn't tell whether she was breathing. Going closer, Mark hesitated, and then crouched down and studied her face. Seeing the rapid eye movement behind her eyelids, he dropped his head to his hands, relief sweeping through him. He wanted to cry. He wanted to scream. To berate the god he wasn't sure he believed in. A god who could do *this*! *Why?*

He needed to be at the school. He needed to take Evie with

him. There was no way he could leave her here, not now. Quickly rechecking the bathroom, praying he hadn't missed anything, Mark went into the baby's room, talking softly to her as he gathered her warm, fragile body from the cot. Evie whimpered sleepily, but she didn't cry. Mark was grateful for this smallest of mercies.

The tablets. He couldn't risk leaving them. But he couldn't empty the whole house of possible suicide tools either. What the hell was he going to do? Thinking of the long row of carving knives in the kitchen, Mark knew he couldn't do it. Not on his own. Glancing down at Hercules, who was nervously wagging her tail, Mark closed his eyes against the stark image of the startled, petrified cat. Was it even safe to leave the dog?

CHAPTER FORTY-FIVE

JADE

Jade very nearly had a heart attack as she saw Mark pulling out of his drive. Parked in the lane, her skin prickling with apprehension, she held her breath and waited. Then she closed her eyes with relief as Mark turned in the other direction. He must be running late to pick Poppy up from school, Melissa no doubt demanding his attention. As if the poor man hadn't got enough on his plate without having to deal with his drug-addled wife's drink problem. Jade understood why he felt he should stay—of course she did, she knew him—but surely he must realise by now that exposing his children to that kind of environment might be worse than the damage a broken home could wreak? But Mark would carry some guilt if he simply walked away from the needy cow. He couldn't help his caring nature, which was obviously why he hadn't sought further professional help yet. She would talk to him about it, subtly, when the time was right. Meanwhile, she had to up her game. If Mark was reluctant to do what it was blatantly obvious he should do and get her sectioned, then Jade had to make damn sure Melissa had every reason to leave him.

"Are you sure it wouldn't have been better to just take her in? You know, just tell him," Dylan asked, irritating Jade immensely. Hadn't she already explained in great detail that Mark didn't want the child?

Curtailing her impatience, Jade turned to him. "It would be

too risky, Dylan," she said, arranging her face into a suitably sad smile. "He's...unpredictable. And don't forget, he'll have his colleagues behind him whatever I say. Trust me, it's better this way. She'll be safer at my house, for now."

"But...Isn't your house burned out?" He was looking in the direction of her cottage, which was little more than a blackened shell. God, he really had been the last in the queue when they handed out brains.

"I've made a nice space in the basement," Jade assured him. "I've got her favourite duvet and all her favourite toys. She'll be fine."

"She looks a bit pale," Dylan said, glancing worriedly back to the girl.

Jade had to concede she definitely looked peaky, her complexion the shade of a delicate white lily. But the Tylenol would help. And she'd probably feel better after a nice sleep. At least she wasn't suffering at the hands of the bitch mother and paedophile father who'd made her short life such a misery. With any luck, she might slip off quietly, which had to be better than being stuffed in a kiln while still alive.

"She needs some sun on her face, that's all. And she'll soon have it. As long as you do your bit tonight. I can count on you, can't I, Dylan?" Sighing soulfully, Jade made sure to look uncertain and vulnerable.

Dylan melted. "You can rely on me, Jade," he said manfully, reaching out a big paw for her hand. "I won't let you down, I promise."

"Nor I you." Jade smiled tremulously. "I just can't wait for all this to be over. For us to be together, as we should be." Aware he might need a little reminder of what their being together meant, she moved closer, one hand pressed to his cheek, her other seeking his groin, which had Dylan squeezing his eyes closed and emitting a low throaty groan in an instant.

Shit! Jade's eyes sprang open as Dylan pressed his lips hard against hers and, clearly excited, proceeded to stuff his tongue deep into her mouth. Shuddering inwardly as he probed deeper, his tongue sliding around like a repellent slug, Jade moved her hand lower, applying just enough pressure to his balls to leave him wanting more, rather than with irreparable damage. "Tomorrow," she said breathily, easing away before he got it into his head that she was going to go the whole hog and give him a blow job.

Dylan emitted something between a wince and a moan. "Promise?" he asked hoarsely.

"Most definitely," Jade said, lowering her eyelashes and leaning in to press a placatory kiss to his overripe cheek. "Now, you know where you're going, yes?" she asked him, unclipping her seatbelt and climbing out.

"Uh-huh." Dylan nodded, climbing across to the driver's side of Melissa's car, grimacing a bit as he went. "I'm following the satnav, and then when I reach my destination, I'm going to drive around a bit."

"And?" Jade prompted him.

Dylan knitted his brow. "I'm going to drive slowly," he managed, with a decisive nod.

"That's right. And what else?" Smiling, Jade encouraged him on.

"I'm going to stay close to the kerb," Dylan said, looking pleased with himself.

"Perfect." Jade beamed him another smile. "And remember, you're doing this for your poor mother too, Dylan. We owe it to her to make sure that DI Cain gets hurt where it hurts most. We need to make sure his reputation is under suspicion. That he's labelled unfit to be a policeman and a father. They'll take him in for questioning. And as soon as they do that, I'll be free. I can take my children and leave. No one will believe his word against mine once they realise what kind of person he is. Especially when I have a stable home with you if social services come snooping, which they're bound to."

She hoped the halfwit didn't mess this up. Evidence Mark had been touring red-light districts was all Jade needed. She knew Melissa couldn't possibly tolerate it.

"Don't forget to drive past the speed cameras fast," she reminded Dylan. "But not too fast." She wanted him to clock up a speeding ticket or two in the suspect part of the city, not get stopped. If that happened, Jade would have to claim he stole the vehicle, or kill him.

"I won't." Dylan fastened his seatbelt and clutched the steering wheel, his expression now one of steely determination.

Man on a mission, Jade thought wearily, rolling her eyes as she walked around to the tailgate to collect the bag Mark would have assumed was for her London trip, but which, in fact, had contained her necessary change of clothes for her meeting tonight. The question was, what to do with him when he'd accomplished his mission and she had no further need of him? A fall from the barn roof, possibly? No. She'd have to climb up there with him, or drug him and haul him up, which would be nigh on impossible without winching equipment. Hauling him over a beam in the barn, however? Yes, that might be an option. He'd murdered his mother, after all. That he'd chosen to hang himself rather than live with his conscience would be the natural tragic conclusion.

CHAPTER FORTY-SIX

MARK

Dr. Meadows wasn't being majorly helpful. And with Evie in his arms, Mark was attracting attention he could do without. He moved away from a group of mothers, all of whom were smiling indulgently in his direction, no doubt thinking he looked lost, like a fish out of water. If only they knew how lost he was.

"I'm not asking you to break patient confidentiality, Dr. Meadows," he said into his hands-free as he walked. "I'm asking you to listen. She needs psychiatric evaluation. She needs it now. I'm concerned. Very."

"Is she a danger to herself, Mr. Cain?"

"Yes. No." Mark sighed heavily. "I…don't know."

"Has she tried anything?"

"No, but I think she might," Mark answered honestly.

"Has she had any psychotic episodes?"

What the fuck defined psychotic episodes? With one eye on the school gates whilst trying to placate Evie, who was growing fractious, Mark tried to think. How to explain. Where to start. How the hell to get some urgency injected into this.

"Hallucinations?" Dr. Meadows went on. "Delusions?"

"Both of the above," Mark confirmed.

"Do you think she might be a danger to her children, Mr. Cain?" Meadows asked pertinently, causing Mark to draw in a sharp breath. "I'm sorry to ask these questions," he went on when Mark hesitated, "it's just that in order to make a proper evaluation..."

Mark glanced down at Evie, catching hold of one of her tiny hands as she flailed it, pressing a soft kiss to her hair. Mel's hair. She was going to be just like Mel. Beautiful.

"There was a cat," he said throatily, after a second. The words, the thought of what he was doing, almost choked him, but Mark knew he had to. He might be wrong, hoped to God he was, but the risk was one he just couldn't afford to take. "In her workshop. Wrapped in polythene. Suffocated, I think." Mark didn't dare imagine when she'd done it, or where she'd stored it, the episode with the freezer still stark in his mind. "I was searching for hidden bottles. She's...drinking—a lot—and I..."

Mark stopped. This sounded insane. It was insane.

Dammit. Seeing kids spilling out into the playground, Mark headed quickly back the way he'd come. "I have to go. I'm picking my daughter up from school," he said, determined not to leave Poppy waiting, or for her to overhear. She didn't need to know any more than she already did, not yet.

"Get your wife to make an urgent appointment, Mark," Dr. Meadows said, sounding more understanding. "Or better still, make one for her and try to make sure she keeps it. I'll text you some numbers. Psychiatric crisis intervention team, helplines, et cetera."

Mark's heart plummeted to the pit of his stomach. What choices did he have, though? None, it seemed. If only Mel would talk to him. Let him in. If only she would be honest with him.

CHAPTER FORTY-SEVEN

MELISSA

Realising the shrill cry piercing the silence wasn't part of her nightmare, Mel snapped her eyes open. Her phone was on the bedside table, its persistent ring dragging her from sleep, sleep that was no escape from the insanity her life was becoming.

It stopped as she reached for it. Lethargic, her limbs too heavy, she couldn't even manage to take a phone call. Close to tears, Mel summoned up what little energy she could and disentangled herself from the duvet, woozily sitting up and reaching for the phone as it started ringing again. She'd almost hit answer when she realised who was calling. *Lisa.*

Anger and humiliation welling up inside her, Mel let it ring. Staring at the phone as it went again to voicemail, she wiped a salty tear from the screen, swiped another determinedly from her face, and then steeled herself to listen. Both voicemails were from Lisa, along with several texts. The gist of it all was that whatever Mel was thinking, she was wrong. Mel swallowed back her heart, which seemed to be wedged painfully in her windpipe, seeing again the fury in Mark's eyes, the coldness, the accusation. She hadn't got that *wrong.* She hadn't imagined the vodka bottle he'd tossed at her, the disgust on his face. She hadn't imagined that, any more than she'd imagined she *wasn't* drinking.

Sinks blocking up, kilns breaking down, the freezer...A hand going involuntarily to her breast, Mel drew in a long breath. The key. Poor Hercules.

She breathed out. Mark confiding in another woman, the excessive texting between them, the lies. She had not *imagined* any of it.

The only thing that was *wrong* was this house, which she'd once loved the very bricks and mortar of, and everything in it. Mark was wrong. What he was doing was *wrong*. He had two children, for God's sake. Evie was so tiny, so vulnerable. Poppy worshipped the ground he walked on. Why would he do it? Why would he send the woman she'd once considered a friend to check up on her, and then blatantly text her while she was in the house? Why would Lisa go along with it? Were they colluding to drive her out of her mind, or to leave? *Why?* She had no money. Her inheritance was tied up in the house. Unless it was the house he wanted? She had nothing else, nothing worth...

The children?

Was that it? He knew she would never part with them. *Ever.* And he wanted—needed—to be part of a family. But if he didn't want her, as a wife, as a mother to his children, what better way to eliminate her from that role than to label her an unfit mother? To label her insane? Have her sectioned? Take power of attorney over her affairs. Take everything. Mel's stomach tightened, certainty running coldly through her like ice in her veins.

She had to get out.

Mel pulled herself to her feet, nausea immediately washing over her. She had to go. Reeling, she forced herself unsteadily on, another bout of dizziness assaulting her as she made it to the bathroom. She needed to shower, but there was no time. Jade would be back soon with Poppy. She needed to be ready.

She needed not to take the *fucking* tablets.

Leaning over the toilet, Mel tried to make herself regurgitate those she had taken, but only managed to retch painfully. Her stomach was empty and raw. As raw as her heart.

Evie. Turning to the sink, Mel ran the taps full force and splashed cold water over her face. Stumbling back to the bedroom, she tore off her shirt, Mark's shirt, feeling as though her chest might tear in two as she did. She pulled on jeans and a clean T-shirt, and stuffed her feet into her flip-flops. She would come back for the rest. All that mattered now, though, all she wanted now, was her children.

Going to the nursery, mentally listing the few essential baby items she would need to take, she went straight to the cot—and stopped dead. *Empty.* The cot was empty. But where...? Jade hadn't taken her. She'd heard her crying earlier, and *not* in her dreams. She'd heard her.

Mark. He'd been here when he should have been at work. She'd lost track of time, but she was sure of that. He'd taken her. But where? Would he come back? Again, she saw the impenetrable coldness in his eyes, dark and unforgiving. He would keep Evie close, hold on to her. She couldn't fight him physically. She couldn't call the police. Couldn't call anyone. Couldn't...

She couldn't fight him.

Oh God... A sob escaping her, Mel clamped her hand to her mouth and stepped away from the cot. *Please don't let him do this.* Sick, giddy with nausea, she staggered back another step, felt for the wall behind her and sank to her haunches. *Make it stop. Please, make it stop.*

CHAPTER FORTY-EIGHT

MARK

Hearing Hercules whining sorrowfully upstairs, Mark parked Evie in the hall. "Go and get yourself some ice cream, Poppet," he said, nodding Poppy towards the kitchen.

"Yes! Vlanilla and Gorilla." Poppy dumped her bag and shot off.

"Yup, that'll do," Mark called after her, knowing that was a safe food option for her. "Just the one though."

Going on up, he paused apprehensively on the landing. Realising where the sound was coming from, he closed his eyes and offered up a silent prayer. But when he stopped at the nursery door, a mixture of disbelief and relief washed through him.

She was crying. The dog's head resting gently in her lap, she was sitting on the nursery room floor, quietly sobbing.

"Mel?" His heart breaking for her, Mark crouched down in front of her, as Hercules looked dolefully up at him.

Mel met his gaze. Her eyes, frantically searching his, were swollen and red, awash with hurt and confusion. "Where is she?" she asked him, running a hand shakily under her nose.

"Who?" Mark asked gently. Noting the way she was looking at him, guardedly, mistrustfully, he felt the foundations beneath him shift another inch. "Where's who? Mel, what's—"

"Where's my *baby*?" Mel shouted desperately over him. "Where *is* she?"

"Downstairs!" Panic gripping him, Mark answered quickly. "She's downstairs," he repeated, as Hercules sat up and barked, clearly as concerned as he was. "I'll fetch—"

"Mummy," Poppy interrupted worriedly from the doorway, "what's wrong?"

Mark snapped his gaze to her. Her ice cream was dripping, little white rivulets running down her chin, down her hand. She was close to tears. "Nothing's wrong, Poppet." Mark got to his feet and went to her. "Mummy's..." *What?* What could he say to explain this away?

"I'm fine, sweetheart." Wiping a hand over her eyes, Mel smiled shakily towards her daughter. "I tripped over one of my flip-flops, that's all. I landed on my bottom. *Ouch!*"

Frowning, Poppy surveyed her uncertainly for a second. "Are you hurt?"

"A little bit." Mel's voice caught in her throat.

"Don't cry, Mummy." Propelled by her obvious anguish, Poppy flew towards her, throwing her arms, plus dripping ice cream, around Mel's neck. "Daddy will rub it better. He has magic hands. He can make the hurt go away."

They would have laughed at that once, until they'd both cried. Together. But now, Mel didn't even glance at him.

"I think I prefer cuddles from you," she said instead, burying her face in Poppy's hair and hugging her tight.

He'd lost her. Mark's heart cracked in his chest. There was no way to reach her. "I'll fetch Evie," he said, turning for the stairs. He didn't feel comfortable leaving Poppy alone with her, but she was safe, he felt, for now. Still, he unbuckled Evie quickly.

CHAPTER FORTY-NINE

JADE

"So, you're thinking of running your own nursery then?" the delightful DS Cummings asked. Taking a huge gulp of his pint, he wiped his hand across his mouth and addressed Jade's breasts, prominently displayed in her minuscule top.

"Eventually," Jade said, leaning forward to offer him plenty of cleavage as she picked up her wine, which she'd made sure he paid for. She'd already had to fork out for a taxi to get to here. Still, it would be worth it. She was sure their meeting would be productive. "It really depends on whether I can get the planning requirements through."

"Ah, well"—Cummings finally focused on her face—"that's where you'll find me a handy copper to have around. Friends in the right places," he said, tapping the side of his nose and then giving her a slow wink.

"Really?" Jade said, looking hugely impressed.

"I know a few people. Reckon I could pull a few strings." Cummings picked up his glass, swishing the contents around and holding her gaze meaningfully.

His meaning was clear: he would coerce a few people and expect to be amply rewarded for his efforts. Jade got the not-so-subliminal message. "That would be amazing," she gushed. "I'd be *so* grateful for any help you could offer."

Lowering her eyelashes coyly, Jade looked up at him with eyes full of innuendo.

Cummings' mouth curved into a slow smirk. Clearly, he'd got the message: you scratch my back, and you get certain parts of your anatomy serviced in return. "Let me have the details. I'll make sure any requirements go through," he said, his gaze drifting lustfully down again, before coming back to her face, or rather her lips.

"You're an absolute hero," said Jade, and then, smiling appreciatively, she flicked her hair back and adjusted her top, thrusting her breasts forward and further whetting his disgusting appetite. God, the man was transparent, and utterly loathsome. The thought of him slobbering and sucking away at her caused her stomach to recoil, but needs must.

"At your service." Cummings winked again and picked up his glass. "So, where are you working now?" he asked, tipping his beer to his mouth.

Jade hesitated for a second, and then decided that, contrary to being put off by her disclosing who she worked for, the cocksure bastard would probably be turned on.

"For a colleague of yours, I think," she said, taking a casual sip of her wine. "Detective Inspector Mark Cain and his wife. Do you know them?"

At that, Cummings promptly choked on his beer. "*Shit!*" he spluttered, lowering his glass and wiping a dribble from his chin. "Sorry," he mumbled. "Er, yes, I do. He's my boss."

Jade noted the look: irritation bordering on contempt, though he tried to hide it. "Your boss?" She widened her eyes, feigning surprise. "Oh." She paused, chewing worriedly on her bottom lip. "I hope that's not going to be a problem. It's just, well, I like you, and..."

"No, no problem. My personal life is my own," he assured

her, folding his arms as he leaned back in his chair to appraise her once more; the look in his eyes, Jade detected, now one of quiet triumph. He was definitely getting off on the thought of fucking his detective inspector's babysitter.

And fuck him she would. Entice him to games that even in his most perverted fantasies he wouldn't have dreamed of. And then she would gain her own satisfaction from presenting herself at the station with substantial bruising as evidence of his sadistic attack. Given his reputation, Jade suspected his colleagues, particularly his female colleagues, would believe him capable of anything. *No one messes with my man and gets away with it, soon-to-be-ex detective.*

"Good." Holding his gaze, Jade ran a finger around the rim of her glass, dipped it into her wine and then pushed it slowly into her mouth.

No one.

CHAPTER FIFTY

MARK

Mark had worried about leaving Poppy and Evie with Mel, even for the time it took to fetch Mel's tablets. Now he was regretting it bitterly.

"Mel, for Christ's sake, open up!" He banged on the bedroom door again, aware he'd be frightening Poppy, but not sure what else to do. *He* was frightened. He thought about ringing one of the numbers Dr. Meadows had texted him, and felt himself free-falling into a dark place from which there would be no return.

"Mel, please," he begged. "Just for one second. I need to talk to you. I don't want to shout it through the door. The kids..."

No answer.

He could hear Poppy whispering inside. Mel was telling her it was a game. *A game!* Trying to stay rational, Mark pressed his hands either side of the door and leaned his head tiredly against it. What could he do? Force it? He felt like dropping to his knees and weeping. Who else could he call? Talk to? He'd lied to Edwards—said he was fine, just overwrought, would be back at work within the week. He'd avoided telling Lisa too much in case she tried to talk to Mel, which would only make matters worse.

For the sake of Poppy and Evie, he couldn't let this go on.

Resigned to make the only call he could, Mark tugged in a deep breath and took a step away. Then the door squeaked open.

"I want the children with me. They're staying with me tonight," Mel said coolly.

Seeing the gritty determination in her eyes, knowing there was no way to get the kids out of there without arguing in front of them, Mark nodded slowly and looked away.

"Okay," he said, his throat tight. "Okay. Just…" He looked back at her, imploring her, through whatever madness was in her mind, to understand. "Please don't lock the door, Mel."

Mel didn't say anything, just looked him over as she might a stranger.

"I'm terrified there'll be a fire, Mel," he admitted hoarsely. "Please, don't lock the door."

CHAPTER FIFTY-ONE

JADE

Finding the house in semi-darkness, Jade was intrigued. But finding Evie and Poppy's rooms empty and Mark sitting on the landing floor, his head resting on his arms and apparently fast asleep, she was furious. What had that pathetic excuse for a wife been up to now?

Jade crouched to gently shake his shoulder, and Mark almost shot out of his skin.

"*Christ.*" He ran his hands over his face and glanced towards the bedroom door beside him.

"Mark?" Jade looked him over, concerned. "What's—?"

Mark pressed a finger to his mouth, and quietly eased himself to his feet, gesturing her to follow him to the stairs.

She'd follow him anywhere. To the ends of the earth. The poor man looked like death, he really did. That *bloody* woman. Jade might bring all this to an abrupt halt and strangle her and be done with it.

His gaze constantly flicking towards the bedroom, Mark outlined what needy Melissa had been up to, telling her about the extra bottles he'd found. It confirmed Jade's suspicions, she admitted reluctantly, that she had been a bit tipsy on occasion.

"There's more," Mark said, looking suddenly nervous, as if scared what her reaction might be. "The cat..."

"Felix?" Jade prompted him, a surge of excitement running through her as she guessed what he might be about to confide.

"Mel said you, er...She said you got rid of him?" Mark looked at her questioningly.

Jade furrowed her brow. "I said he'd run away," she said, pondering appropriately. "It was a bit strange, because he was a homey sort of cat. I wondered if he'd been run...Oh no." She clamped a hand to her mouth. "Has something happened to him?"

Nodding sadly, Mark closed his eyes. "He...It looks like he was suffocated. I'm sorry, Jade."

"Suffocated?" Jade repeated, aghast. "But...how? Where?"

"Polythene," Mark said, his voice almost failing him. "I found him in the workshop. In the clay bin. Jade, I am so, so sorry. I couldn't not tell you. I..." Blowing out a breath, Mark trailed wretchedly off.

"Oh God." Looking horrified, Jade searched his face and then allowed her grief-stricken gaze to fall slowly to the floor. "Poor Felix," she said tearfully. "Poor *Mel*." She glanced back at him, and then came over quite faint.

Mark reached for her immediately, helping her as she lowered herself shakily to sit on the stairs. "I'll fetch you some water," he said, as she clamped her hands to her tummy and dropped her head to her knees.

Smiling gratefully, Jade took the glass when he returned, sipping the water and taking several slow breaths.

"Okay?" Mark asked, his expression so anxious, it was all Jade could do to stop herself reaching for his hand.

She nodded sadly, as if accepting the tragic news about her beloved cat bravely. "I'm all right, Mark. Honestly, I'm fine. It's Mel we need to worry about. Has she had her medication?"

Mark trailed a hand through his hair and shook his head. "She's refused it," he said, looking sick to his soul. "She's refusing to eat. I think she thinks I'm trying to poison her. She won't let me near the kids."

He stopped, squeezing the bridge of his nose hard between his thumb and forefinger. "I have no idea what I'm going to do, Jade," he admitted, his tone wretched. "None."

Jade got to her feet and stepped towards him, her heart aching. She couldn't keep his children from him! That was just too cruel, the callous bitch. "Let me try," she said, keen to ease his obvious anguish. She was also keen to find out just how far needy Melissa was from the edge. A few more little pushes in the right direction and she would do something drastic—jump or leave him. It was a matter of days. Jade felt a bubble of sweet anticipation growing inside her.

"I'll make her some soup. She might take it from me, and she'll at least keep that down," she said, taking the opportunity to press a reassuring hand to his worried face. She looked into his eyes, the pain she saw there cutting her to the core. He didn't look convinced, but he nodded wearily.

Yearning to wrap her arms around his broad shoulders, which were far too burdened with the weight of all this, Jade restrained herself. "I was thinking…" she said, her brow knitted thoughtfully. "You might not agree, but… You don't have any sleeping tablets, do you?"

Mark looked curiously at her. "They're in the top kitchen cupboard. Why?"

From his wary expression, though, Jade guessed he was one step ahead of her. "I think it might be an idea to crush one up and pop it in her soup," she suggested, making sure to look reluctant. "I know that looks like you're doing exactly what she thinks you are, but… At least she'll sleep, until morning hopefully." Or longer. Jade had no intention of putting just one tablet in there. "Which means Poppy and Evie will get a decent night's sleep, too. God knows they must need it."

Mark drew in a tight breath and eyed the ceiling. Obviously, he would be unwilling, being such a naturally kind man, but eventually he acquiesced with a tired nod.

Jade tapped lightly on the bedroom door. "Mel," she called, "it's me. Can I come in?"

There was a brief silence before Melissa padded to the door to pull it open an inch, peering warily past her as if expecting to see Mark about to charge in. This was good. The woman was definitely close to cracking or leaving. But she couldn't take Evie with her. Jade couldn't allow that.

"I brought you some soup," she said, going in as Melissa eased the door further open.

Melissa wrapped her arms about herself, eyeing the mug suspiciously as Jade turned to face her.

"I know a bit of what's happened." Jade smiled at her understandingly. "Mark's version, at least," she said, hinting that she didn't necessarily believe him, which would hopefully encourage Melissa to open up and spill her guts.

"It's kind of you, Jade, but…" Still eyeing the mug, Mel hesitated, and then shook her head. "I don't think I should."

"You can't stay up here without any sustenance, Mel," Jade pointed out, oozing compassion. "You need to stay strong, for the children."

She nodded over her shoulder to where Poppy and Evie were tucked up on the bed, fast asleep. It really was a heart-warming scene, Poppy with her thumb plugged in her mouth, one little arm protectively around her tiny sister. Such a pity they'd have to be separated.

Melissa turned to the bed, and stopped. "He's trying to drive me away," she blurted out tearfully. "Or drive me insane. I'm not sure which. Both probably."

Well, she was well on the way to the latter, Jade thought, following her to put the soup down on the bedside table—and make damn sure she drank it. She looked demented. A bedraggled mess. Not quite the bright-eyed, bushy-tailed, smug cow Jade had first met.

"*Mark?*" Jade feigned disbelief. "But…he seems so nice. So normal." She blinked confusedly. "I can't believe he's—"

"Been overmedicating me?" Mel turned to her, her eyes full of hurt.

Jade looked at her boggle-eyed. "Really?"

"You don't believe me." Melissa searched her face, her hope fading.

Jade stepped towards her. "I didn't say that," she said, placing a hand on her arm. "I've been in an abusive relationship myself, Melissa. The man was a complete control freak, a sociopath. Presented a perfectly respectable front to the outside world, but behind closed doors…Believe me, I know how deceitful and hurtful men can be."

Melissa studied her, her pale face flooding with obvious relief. Then, nodding, she closed her eyes and sat shakily down on the bed. "He's accused me of drinking," she confided. "Excessively. But I haven't been. He's even planted bottles."

"Bloody hell." Jade widened her eyes in mock horror.

"He was vile—so angry, so cold." Melissa tightened her hold around herself. "I think…he's trying to get me certified. Trying to take the children away from me." Her expression was now one of fear. A bit like the fleabag cat, Jade recollected, as she'd pressed the polythene bag over its pretty, green-eyed little face.

Melissa notched up her chin. "I won't let him."

You won't have much choice. Jade sat down as a cold shiver ran through Melissa's body, which was looking a bit scrawny, Jade noticed. She really ought to drink the soup.

"Thank God you alerted me to his affair with Lisa." Melissa

looked miserable. "He might have got away with it if you hadn't. Oh, God"—she gulped back a sob—"what am I going to do, Jade?"

Jade squeezed her shoulders and held her tight for a second, which was frankly a second too long for her own liking. "Drink your soup," she said. "Get a good night's sleep, and then make a doctor's appointment."

Melissa turned tear-filled eyes towards her.

"You need to change your medication," Jade went on firmly. "Whether or not Mark is feeding you drugs, God forbid, the medication you're on obviously isn't helping your symptoms. You need to change it, and stay on top of it yourself. You also need to let your doctor know what's happening, for your own sake, so he'll have it all on record."

Jade prayed it sounded plausible. The ridiculous woman couldn't just stop taking her medication. That would be a complete disaster.

"You have to get yourself right, Mel. For the children." Jade passed her the mug, and then gave her shoulders another squeeze. "If you need some support, I could always come with you."

"Would you?" Melissa's hopeful look was back.

"If you want me to, yes. Don't worry, I'm on your side, Mel."

"Thank you." Melissa breathed out a heavy sigh—and took a sip of the soup. "I was going to go. Take the children and leave," she said, glancing uncertainly towards Jade. "But you had my car."

"Oh, Mel, I'm so sorry," Jade said, looking suitably distraught. "If I'd known about any of this, obviously I wouldn't have taken it. I wouldn't have gone."

"It's all right. I shouldn't be driving anyway, not like this, not with the children. In any case, I don't think I should."

"Oh?" Jade felt suddenly apprehensive as Melissa took another sip from the mug.

"I've been googling it, on my phone."

Googling what, for fuck's sake? Jade was growing agitated. Immensely.

"I shouldn't leave the marital home. I would if I thought the children were in danger, but I honestly don't think Mark would hurt them. So"—she took a heartier drink of her soup—"I've decided. I'm going to fight back. I'm staying."

Shit.

CHAPTER FIFTY-TWO

JADE

Thank God for that. Jade offered Melissa her new tablets with a smile. She'd eased off the drugs she was feeding her, but she couldn't hope to up them again without drawing suspicion if Melissa wasn't taking any medication at all. She'd been able to continue with the sleeping tablets, however. She couldn't watch her 24/7, and Mark desperately needed some sleep. He could do with a good meal inside him, too. He'd said he would get himself something for dinner, but Jade doubted he had actually eaten anything over the last two days while she'd been babysitting his needy wife. He looked dreadful. He would make himself ill at this rate.

"Why don't you have a nice bath," she suggested, "light some candles and put loads of bubbles in. You could dye your hair back, too." She nodded towards the copper dye Melissa had purchased from the chemist, determined as she was to try and "get back to normal," as if she ever had been normal. Listening to the nonsense the woman had spouted in the surgery this evening had been painful. The doctor had nodded in sympathy, given her various abuse helpline numbers, but he'd clearly thought she was off her trolley. Jade had made sure to back up his inclinations, looking appropriately concerned and doubtful in turns.

Melissa, who was now sitting on the bed, feeding Evie, to Jade's annoyance, looked up at her, smiling wanly. "Nice idea," she said, "but Poppy needs bathing. Then there's her bedtime story."

"I'll see to Poppy." Jade smiled warmly, though she could cheerfully strangle the woman for alienating Mark from his children in his own home. He'd have to learn to live without Poppy eventually, but she didn't want him further upset now, on top of all of this. Jade had tried to convince her that Mark wouldn't just snatch them, that he'd know how upsetting that would be for Poppy, but still Melissa was wary, insisting on moving the cot into the main bedroom and telling Poppy she could sleep with her because she was feeling lonely with Daddy sleeping downstairs because he wasn't feeling well.

"Or...you could let Mark help out," she suggested, deciding to try again. If Melissa had decided to "fight," then Jade had to up her game. She had to ensure there was no doubt in Mark's mind that this woman was a danger to Poppy and Evie. To which end, Jade needed him to be hands-on with the children.

"No." Mel shook her head adamantly as she lifted Evie to her shoulder. "If he insists on staying here, he stays on my terms. He's given up any rights to his happy family life. I still can't believe he's done the things he's done. He ought to be locked up. If only I could prove it." Stroking Evie's back, she pulled her possessively closer, and Jade's heart constricted inside her.

"I know," Jade said, turning to get her little angel's cot ready, her face flushing with jealousy and anger as she did. "The thing is, though, Mel, it's Poppy who's suffering. She doesn't understand. She misses him."

Melissa stood, turning to lower Evie into the cot. Jade couldn't quite read her expression, but suspected she was wavering. "Where is he?" she asked.

"Out running." Trying to run his frustrations off, she knew. He couldn't hope to, though, when the source of it was under his roof. "You're not on your own with this, Mel," she reminded her. "You can rely on me to keep an eye on things."

"I know." Melissa smiled sadly. "Okay. I'll have a bath," she relented.

Good, Jade thought. Pity she hadn't taken her sleeping tablet. With a bit of luck, she might have drowned in it.

"And make myself beautiful while I'm in there." Mel rolled her eyes. "Well, presentable, anyway," she said self-effacingly, causing Jade to wince. "Even though there doesn't seem to be much point any more."

Jade moved to give her a hug as the inevitable tears welled up. God, she really was a weak specimen. "You're doing it for *you*, Mel," she said forcefully. "For the children."

Mel nodded. "Thanks, Jade," she said, smiling gratefully this time. "I don't know what I'd do without you."

"No problem. That's what friends are for," Jade assured her, squeezing her hand and turning for the door. "Indulge and enjoy. I'll go and extract Poppy from in front of the TV before she gets square eyes."

CHAPTER FIFTY-THREE

MARK

"How are things?" Lisa asked, when Mark picked up her call.

"On a scale of one to ten, eleven." Coming through the front door, Mark sighed and wiped an arm across his forehead. He'd run until he thought his lungs would give out. He'd thought it would help channel some of his anger and sheer bloody frustration. It hadn't.

"That bad, hey?"

"And some," Mark answered honestly. "How're things with you?"

"Wonderful. I love being in an office with Cummings strutting about like a dog with two dicks. Seems there's a new lust in his life, poor cow. She's obviously short-sighted or in serious need of counselling."

Mark laughed, and then wondered when he'd last done that. "Any developments on the Daisy case?" he asked her seriously. Even with the madness his life had become, he hadn't been able to stop thinking about the little girl, to shake the nagging feeling that somehow, somewhere, she was alive.

"Nothing. It's gone cold. Looks like the powers that be will be scaling the investigation down. Sorry, Mark," Lisa said, dashing his hopes that someone might come forward with fresh information, that one of the team might come up with something in his absence.

Mark's stomach knotted inside him. He'd let the girl down. He should have been on top of it, he thought, his frustration growing. He should have been on top of what was happening here, too, right under his nose, before it spiralled out of control. Before he lost the woman he'd loved with all of himself. Still loved.

"Look, Mark, I've been meaning to ring you about something else. It might be nothing, but…"

"Clearly you think it's something," Mark prompted her, tugging his damp T-shirt over his head as he headed for the kitchen for a cold drink.

"I've been doing some digging and—"

But Mark cut her off mid-sentence. "I have to go. I'll call you back," he said quickly, abruptly ending the call.

"Lisa?" Mel asked him, from where she was standing by the fridge.

Mark cursed inwardly. "A work call," he said, feeling guilty, with no clue why.

"Of course it was." Mel's tone was flat. She didn't look at him so much as through him. "Just orange," she said, indicating her glass pointedly, and then walked past him to the hall.

"Shit…" Mark muttered, fetching himself a coke from the fridge, and finding himself wishing he could have a whisky—or several. Consume so much alcohol he'd be comatose and oblivious to any of this. "Sod it," he said, parking himself heavily at the kitchen island. What happened? What in God's name went so wrong? *How?* He stared upwards, as if there were a God up there who might answer him.

He wasn't aware of Jade coming into the kitchen behind him.

"Oh dear, I take it things are getting to you?" she asked him sympathetically.

"Just a bit." Mark smiled disconsolately.

Jade pressed an arm around his shoulders. Being half-naked,

Mark felt somewhat awkward, but wasn't sure how to extricate himself without offending her.

Jade saved him from any potential awkwardness. "Poppy's ready for her bath," she said, giving his shoulders a reassuring squeeze and then moving towards the cooker. "She wants *The Wheels on the Bus* for her bedtime story."

Mark looked at her with surprise.

"She said to tell you to hurry up." Jade smiled and nodded him towards the stairs.

He was being allowed contact with his own kids? That was something, Mark supposed.

CHAPTER FIFTY-FOUR

JADE

"And then we had gymnastics..." Jade could hear Poppy chatting to Mark about her school day as she crept along the landing. "But I don't like it." Jade peeked around the bathroom door to see Poppy wearing her petulant, annoying little frown.

"Oh, why's that then?" Mark asked.

"Because I like swimming better," Poppy said, her little face pointing upwards as Mark carefully rinsed the soap from her hair. "Miss Winters calls me her little mermaid," she informed him importantly. "Cos I can hold my breath for seven whole... *Ouch! Daddeee*..."

"Oops, sorry, Poppet. Hold on a sec." Mark got hastily to his feet as Poppy clamped her hands to her soap-stung eyes. "Damn," he muttered, turning for the towel to find it wasn't there.

The missing towel in hand, Jade took a step back down the stairs as he emerged from the bathroom to head for the airing cupboard, Poppy whingeing behind him. "Daddy, it's *stinging*."

Jade sighed and, covered by the outwardly opening airing cupboard door, stepped quickly back up towards the bathroom. She didn't have to dunk her, thankfully. Poppy had already taken it upon herself to look like a drowning mermaid.

Disappearing in the nick of time, as Mark reappeared, Jade waited at the top of the stairs. And sure enough... "Poppy!" Mark shouted urgently. *"Poppy!"*

"What the *hell* were you *doing*?" he snapped angrily, plucking her from the water and swinging Poppy towards him, who clearly *wasn't* drowned. More was the pity. Peering back around the door, Jade watched jealously on.

Startled by his tone, and the shocked look on his face, Poppy squirmed in his arms, attempting to wriggle away from him.

"Poppy, stop." In danger of dropping her, Mark tried to hang onto her. "Poppy!"

"I was holding my breath!" Poppy cried, and promptly burst into tears.

"Christ…" Mark hugged her close. "I'm sorry, Poppy," he murmured throatily into her wet hair. "I thought…"

She was rewarded, of course. Melissa fussed and fawned all over the little brat, while Mark, who'd almost suffered a heart attack, lingered awkwardly in the background, looking shocked—and guilty. As if it was his fault. Honestly, did the woman who'd promised to love and cherish him really have to work so hard at compounding his guilt? Obviously, if the child had drowned, it would have been an accident. Yet, Melissa, who'd previously thought Mark was her knight in shining armour, was looking at him as if he were a complete monster, nothing but contempt in her eyes, which was all to the good, Jade supposed.

Poppy, oblivious to the trouble she'd caused, was now busy licking her bowl free of vanilla ice cream. Little pig. They ought to have christened her Pinky.

"Come on, sweetie, let's get you tucked up in bed." Melissa, who still had a towel wrapped around her hair, shot Mark another venomous look as she plucked Poppy from the stool at the island, as if the child had lost the use of her legs.

Mark said nothing, just kneaded his forehead in that frustrated way he did. Jade knew why. He was trying to avoid arguing in front of his children. Did the woman not have eyes? A brain in her rusty-haired head? Could she not see how much he cared for his children?

Jade pulled in a breath, blowing it angrily out through her nostrils, as she headed for the kettle. "I'll make some hot chocolate," she said, working to keep her tone in check. "Would you like one, Mark?"

But he just stood there, looking for all the world like a lost soul. A lost, lonely soul.

"It wasn't your fault," Jade said, walking across to him and pressing a hand softly to his chest. "She didn't come to any harm."

Mark glanced down. He didn't seem to mind her hand there. "She could have done," he said, his tone hoarse, as if he were holding back tears. "I shouldn't have left her."

The kettle boiled behind them. Jade smiled again affectionately and turned to it. She had no idea what to say to him. Words couldn't make his pain go away. He needed comfort, holding. He needed to be loved. To be needed. She was treacherously close to telling him the truth; that bitch had never wanted him for more than his seed, his money, his status. That she'd used him, mercilessly. Never loved him. Not like Jade loved him.

"Chocolate?" she said instead, the kettle poised over a mug.

"What?" Mark looked up distractedly. "Oh. No, thanks." Smiling sadly, he turned to the lounge.

For something stronger, Jade suspected, and she didn't blame him. How she wished she could sit next to him, lie next to him, press her ear to his chest and listen to his poor heart beating. Sighing, she popped two pills into Melissa's hot chocolate, stirred longingly, and then froze. *The hot chocolate wasn't dairy-free, was it?*

CHAPTER FIFTY-FIVE

MELISSA

"Poppy, shuffle over, sweetie." Mel came out of the bathroom, where she'd finally managed to rinse the colour from her hair, to find Poppy lying sideways across the bed.

"Poppy?" Glancing at her through the mirror as she gave her new copper locks a last rub with the towel, Mel guessed she must have fallen asleep—not surprisingly, after the evening's events. She knew, in her heart, that Mark would never hurt their daughter. And she'd done it herself, dashed out of the bathroom for a towel or a toy, she thought guiltily. She hadn't admitted that to Mark, of course. She didn't want to give him any more ammunition to use against her.

Why was he doing this? Mel paused, gulping back the heart-ache, the horror and disbelief that she could have been so terrifyingly wrong about him. Why didn't he just *go*? Be with Lisa, if that's what he wanted? Accept that, in destroying his marriage, he'd be giving up his children? He was crushing her, little by little. Killing her. She hated him for it. Hated herself for allowing him to.

"Poppy, come on, my lovely," she whispered to her daughter, who was well and truly asleep. Mel walked across to her, bending to ease her around. And she stopped dead, her heart lurching violently in her chest.

"Poppy!"

Her lips were swollen. She wasn't breathing properly.

"*Poppy!*" Mel screamed, hoisting her into her arms. "*Mark!*"

Hearing a distinct wheeze in her chest—*Please, God, no, not my baby!*—Mel turned, nausea sweeping through her, her heart beating as though trying to burst from her body.

Mark banged through the door before she'd reached it.

"*Jesus Christ!* What's happened?" He reached immediately for Poppy.

Mel didn't protest, but fed her into his arms. "I don't know. I thought she was asleep. I...She..." She gulped back a sob. "She must have eaten something. I don't *know*."

"She has a rash." Mark's eyes flicked quickly over Poppy. "Fetch her auto-injector."

Shocked, Mel was frozen to the spot.

"Mel. Go!" Mark shouted urgently, bending to lower Poppy quickly to the floor.

Mel turned, and flew. They had several. Emergency supplies. *Where?* She tried to fit her disjointed thoughts together in her head. Bathroom. Poppy's schoolbag. *Handbag!* Her gaze falling on her bag hanging from the en suite door, she seized on it, fumbling with it until finally turning it over and spewing the contents on to the floor.

Clutching two EpiPens, she raced back to where Mark was putting Poppy in the recovery position. Her throat hard and tight, Mel watched him. His face was pale, but his movements were precise and calm. Her own hands shaking, her legs feeling as if they might fail to support her, Mel passed him the pen. Mark injected it, straight through Poppy's pyjamas and into her thigh.

"Mark?" Jade appeared, hovering uncertainly behind him on the landing. "Oh my *God*, what's happened?"

"Dial 999," Mark instructed, his gaze still on Poppy as he held the EpiPen in place for the required ten seconds. Would Mel have remembered to do that?

"Just say anaphylaxis. A child," Mark added, as Jade punched the number into her mobile. His tone was quiet but authoritative, his expression taut with worry as he pulled the injector pen out, concentrating his efforts now on massaging Poppy's small thigh.

"Baby?" Mel dropped to her knees, stroking Poppy's sweat-dampened hair back from her face.

"Come on, baby. You can do this," Mark said, his voice cracking as he gently took their daughter's tiny hand in his own.

He closed his eyes briefly, massaged her back, checked his watch, trying to stay composed, Mel knew. "We need to know what's caused it," he said, checking his watch again. "The ice cream?"

Mel shook her head. "No. It's safe." She could barely get the words out. But what? Searching frantically through her sluggish mind, Mel tried to think. She hadn't had anything that might cause... "Oh no." Poppy had chocolate stains around her mouth.

Mel scrambled to her feet and stumbled to the bedside table, and her insides turned over. But... Poppy wouldn't. "The drinking chocolate," she said shakily, cold fear running the length of her spine as she turned back to her unconscious child. "She's—"

"Oh, sweet fucking Jesus." Mark heaved in a breath and snapped his gaze to Jade, who'd come quietly in to take Melissa's place, softly caressing Poppy's cheek with the back of her hand. "Did you...?"

"No." Jade shook her head adamantly.

"Mark?" Melissa moved falteringly towards them. This was her fault. *Hers.* She needed to know what to do. She needed to do *something.*

"We need to get her to the hospital. Now!" Mark said tersely, gathering Poppy into his arms. "Jade, go and start my car. Mel, make sure you have another EpiPen. You might need to use it on the way."

Mel focused through her guilt and confusion. The paramedics would have oxygen, but Mark, who'd grown a shade paler, must be thinking they might be too late.

CHAPTER FIFTY-SIX

JADE

"*Hush, little baby, don't say a word…*" Pressing a kiss to Evie's forehead, Jade lowered her gently into her cot. "Mummy will be back soon, my sweet Angel," she said, caressing her peachy cheek as she smiled down at her.

She really was a content little baby, Jade thought, which was thanks to *her* calming influence in a sea of madness, obviously. She really did despair. If she phoned social services herself, she'd bet they'd whisk the children away from their demented mother in a flash. But she couldn't do that, of course. The vicious cow would no doubt hurl accusations at Mark, making him out to be anything but the good, loving, patient father that he was, and he would be denied access to them too. But not to worry: Melissa was almost at breaking point. Jade almost felt sorry for her.

Humming, she made her way downstairs, reaching into her pocket for the credit card she'd slipped from Mark's jacket during the pandemonium. Now then…which sites to browse, she wondered. Nothing extreme, she'd decided. She didn't want Mark to get into serious trouble. They would have to be sites with sexually graphic images though, where she would purchase certain goods used in the pursuit of certain pleasures—or rather Mark would, before saving the sites to his bookmarks. Melissa would be bound to go apoplectic, undoubtedly leave or demand that Mark did. Undoubtedly also, Mark would refuse to leave without his children. At which point, Jade would step valiantly but reluctantly in to help him remove them to a safe place. Or one of them, at least, depending on the evening's outcome.

Mark could save himself all the hassle if only he'd intervene and have his mental wife sectioned. In time he would see it was the only kind thing to do, for her own and everyone else's safety. Meanwhile, though, Jade had no choice but to ramp up her efforts, even if she did have to manufacture the proof that Mark found his needy wife about as exciting as cold tapioca.

Collecting Mark's laptop from the hall, Jade extracted the luxury bar of chocolate from her handbag, peeling back the enticingly shiny wrapper and settling down at the kitchen island to browse at leisure. Mark and Melissa would be ages at the hospital, which gave her plenty of time.

Popping a chunk of chocolate in her mouth, Jade sucked slowly. *Mmm.* It really was as delicious as she'd mentioned to Poppy. Hopefully, after the trauma of her collapse and hospitalisation, the brat wouldn't remember eating it, but if it came out, then Jade would just play her part—innocent and apologetic. And of course, it had never occurred to her to imagine the thieving little brat would sneak into her bag and help herself to it.

Up bright and early the next morning, Jade hovered at the kitchen window, intending to catch the postman before Mark or Melissa came down. They weren't likely to surface early after the dreadful night they'd had at the hospital, opting to stay by Poppy's side.

She'd survived, probably due to Mark's quick thinking in getting her there. Mark had rung her, as he would, to let her know they were keeping her in for observation for at least eight hours. He really was so thoughtful, assuming she'd be worried. Her blood tests had been clear, he'd also told her, which had perturbed Jade a bit. Having given his consent to Jade spiking needy Melissa's bedtime drink once, he'd perhaps suspected Jade might have thought he was condoning it on an ongoing basis, therefore inadvertently feeding Poppy a sleeping tablet. As if she would. It was tempting. Very. But it would have been monumentally stupid, when he plainly loved Poppy, as a father should love a daughter.

Quashing a pang of jealousy twisting inside her, Jade spooned coffee into the mugs and popped a pill into Melissa's.

She'd been hoping the chocolate might do the job. But… *c'est la vie*. Jade had been disappointed, naturally, but pleased for Mark, who, despite being exhausted to the point of dropping when they'd arrived home, had look so heartbreakingly relieved, Jade could have cried.

Aha, at last. Noting the postman heading for the front door, Jade took the eggs she was scrambling off the heat. She was going to feed them a hearty breakfast—and Melissa another pill—after their traumatic experience.

"Good morning," she said brightly, beaming the postman a smile. He smiled delightedly back, his eyes trailing lustfully over her—as men's eyes did—and handed her the post.

Moron, Jade thought, her smile widening nevertheless as she closed the door and looked at the envelopes, one of which contained a green document, which, if she wasn't mistaken, was a certain speeding ticket.

Glancing quickly up the stairs, as she heard someone rising, Jade tore the envelope open, quickly scanning the contents. *Oh, well done, Dylan.* The man had excelled himself. Clearly, he did have a brain cell rattling around inside that dense skull of his. Jade noted the perfect location and timing of the speeding offence, which was well after she'd arrived home—courtesy of a lift to the end of the lane from "Call-me-Pete" Cummings—and everyone had been tucked up in bed, apart from Mark.

CHAPTER FIFTY-SEVEN

MARK

"Morning," Mark said, tugging his shirt on as he came into the kitchen.

Jade, fixing them up a late breakfast, turned to smile tremulously at him. "Morning," she said quietly, and then turned sadly back to her task.

Narrowing his eyes, Mark looked her over as he walked across to the fridge for orange. "Something smells good." He nodded towards the bacon cooking under the grill.

Jade didn't look back at him. "I thought something a bit more substantial might help, after spending the night at..." She broke off, looking close to tears. "I'm so sorry, Mark. I had no idea there was dairy in the hot chocolate powder. I—"

"No...It wasn't your fault."

Mark ran a hand wearily through his hair as he noted a tear slide down her cheek. He'd thought...As he'd watched Mel with Poppy, not letting go of her tiny hand, not moving from her side for a second, he'd wondered just how accidental the shit that kept piling on top of them really was. His imagination had run riot. He'd got it wrong, looking for someone to blame, he guessed. There wasn't anyone. Not even God.

Sighing, he pulled his beeping phone from his pocket to mute it, wondering only briefly why Lisa would be texting him to "chat" when they'd agreed to send no texts unless it was urgent.

Jade was chopping at the mushrooms. Chopping blindly, if the now steady flow of tears was anything to judge by. "I prefer less salt with mine," he joked, attempting to lighten things.

Clearly not appreciating his efforts, Jade just cried harder, dabbing at her cheeks, before going back to the mushrooms with a vengeance.

"I'm not into fried fingers much either," Mark tried.

Jade stopped chopping. "I'm so sorry, Mark," she said again, looking utterly miserable. "I'll go if you want me to. I'd understand. I . . ."

Mark hesitated as she heaved in a breath and pressed the back of her hand to her nose, and then he reached out to tentatively wrap an arm around her shoulders. "I'd be in one hell of a mess if you did," he said truthfully.

Jade turned and buried her face in his shoulder. "I'm sorry," she repeated, with heart-wrenching anguish.

"I think I got that." Awkward though he felt, Mark gave her a squeeze, and then carefully moved to put a little distance between them. "Poppy's home safe now. Let's just put it behind us, shall we?"

Jade nodded and smiled up at him. It wasn't her usual radiant smile, but at least she didn't look consumed with guilt any more. "How's Mel?" she asked.

"I think she's feeling as guilty as you seem to be, to be honest."

Mel hadn't actually said much while they'd waited at the hospital, but Mark had read the body language, the arms wrapped tightly around herself, seen the torment in her eyes. She didn't need him to drive it home. "Stuff happens." He shrugged. "At least she's relented a bit on the accident in the bath. I think we've both realised we could lose her."

Jade looked up at him. "You're a nice person, Mark Cain. Do you know that?"

"Yeah." Mark smiled ruefully. "I only wish my wife thought

I was." Mel hadn't looked at him much either, apart from with sheer relief when they'd realised Poppy was going to pull through. She hadn't come to him, ruling out any body contact between them, if only to offer each other comfort. But at least she had finally looked at him. Maybe there was hope, he thought wearily.

Reminded of his close proximity to Jade, which might be misconstrued, given Mel's current suspicions, he moved quickly away from her.

Jade looked at him confusedly.

"It's probably not a great idea for Mel to see us... Well, you know," Mark explained, finishing clumsily. Offering Jade a reassuring smile, he prayed that they could all put this behind them, that the small improvement he'd noticed in Mel's physical symptoms might mean they could move forwards and somehow find their way out of this nightmare.

"I'll take Mel's breakfast up," Jade said, her smile definitely brighter as she turned back to the chopping board.

CHAPTER FIFTY-EIGHT

JADE

So, they'd had a little bonding session at the hospital, had they? Well, she'd soon nip *that* in the bud. Jade restrained herself from banging things into the dishwasher, placing them just so, lingering over the extremely sharp knife she felt like chopping certain little fingers off with.

Spoiled, that's what she was. *A wilful, overindulged little...*

"Do we need anything?" Mark said behind her, pulling his jacket on as he came back into the kitchen.

"Meds," Jade said, quickly stuffing the knife in the cutlery basket and turning to retrieve Mel's prescription from the notice board. "I thought as you were going to the chemist..."

"Cheers," Mark said, smiling a little more easily than he had earlier that morning. Jade doubted he'd be doing that for long. "I'll only be half an hour or so. The kids are in with Mel."

Where else, thought Jade, suppressing her growing urge to tiptoe in and suffocate that woman with the pillow, take her baby and be done with. But that wasn't a good idea. Being a detective, Mark was bound to cotton on to something.

"See you soon," he said, heading towards the front door, obviously feeling safe to go out for five minutes now he didn't think he was in danger of being thrown out.

Closing the dishwasher with a bang, Jade went to the window, making sure Mark had pulled out of the drive before retrieving the speeding ticket from behind the toaster.

Now to do the deed, while Melissa was disorientated, which she would be by now, and still shell-shocked after almost losing her precious Poppy.

Collecting up the rest of the post—plenty for Melissa about her arty-farty crap—Jade went upstairs, tapped on the bedroom door and went on in to find Melissa sitting on the edge of the bed, her hands pressed to her forehead and plainly feeling woozy. Evie was fretting, Jade noticed despairingly. The woman really was a useless cow.

"Hi, Mel," she said, making sure not to sound too cheerful in light of last night's events. Placing the post on the bed, she went across to lift Evie from her cot. "How are you feeling?"

"A bit queasy, to be honest." Mel smiled feebly in her direction. So she wasn't about to start pointing fingers for a tragedy which was clearly her own fault, which was a relief. Jade needed Melissa on side if she was going to pull this off.

"Would you like some tea?" she asked her. "You haven't eaten much." She'd picked at her toast earlier, but had eaten a good portion of the egg, thank goodness.

"I'm not very hungry, Jade." Mel offered her another weak smile.

"I'm not surprised after last night." Jade pressed Evie close to her shoulder; she'd stopped fretting the second she had picked her up. Clearly, she knew whose shoulder she preferred. "I'm really sorry about what happened, Mel."

"Not your fault. Poppy's curiosity obviously got the better of her. I still can't believe it..." She brushed Poppy's hair lovingly back from her face, causing the little brat to stir in her sleep. "She's all right, that's the main thing."

"I'll go and change Evie," Jade offered, heading towards the door. "Give you time to get yourself together." She'd only had half the day already. God help the woman's family if they had to rely on her for sustenance. "Oh . . . I brought your post up."

Melissa glanced at the envelopes on the bed half-interestedly, noting the one on top was from her Garden & Homes store and emitting a soulful sigh, which possibly had something to do with the orders she hadn't managed to fill. Aspirations beyond her dubious talents, that was Melissa's trouble, Jade thought with a satisfied smirk. Perhaps she should have channelled more of her energies into looking after her husband, rather than ensuring he looked elsewhere.

"I, um, opened one of the envelopes in error," she said, looking apologetic as she nodded towards them. "I thought I'd better let you know in case you wondered."

"Oh?" Melissa leafed through the envelopes.

Jade stepped back towards her. "It's just . . . Well, it's a speeding fine, and I was worried you might think it was me. It was your car, you see."

Melissa looked at her in surprise. "*My* car?"

"It's dated two o'clock in the morning," Jade went on, as Mel found it and read it. "And as I was back here by ten thirty, obviously I was concerned."

Melissa scanned it, her expression growing more puzzled by the second.

"Particularly when I noted the location."

Melissa still looked puzzled. Gormless cow, she probably wasn't familiar with the area, even though she was a policeman's wife. Honestly. "It's in the red-light district." Mentally rolling her eyes, Jade waited for the significance to sink in.

"I thought maybe someone had stolen the car. You know, for joyriding or something."

Got her, Jade thought, supremely pleased as Melissa's expression turned to disbelief, swiftly followed by palpable fury.

"What, and then returned it?" she seethed. "No doubt they washed and valeted it too! That absolute bastard!"

Poppy, who'd been blissfully sleeping, oblivious to the trouble she'd caused, shot up. "Mummy, what's wrong?" she asked, kneading her eyes worriedly.

"Nothing," Melissa said shortly, finally managing to stand upright. Pretty quickly, all credit to her. Jade watched interestedly.

"But *Mummeee*, why are you angry?" Poppy whined, shuffling towards the edge of the bed to go after her.

"I'm not!" Melissa snapped. Then she closed her eyes and drew in a tight breath. "I'm not, sweetheart," she said, attempting a smile. "Mummy has a headache, that's all. Go with Jade, darling. I have some things I need to do."

"Come on, Poppet." Jade extended her hand. "You can help me feed Evie."

Poppy's gaze flicked worriedly to Jade. "But I don't want to," she whimpered, bringing her knees up and shuffling towards the headboard, as though trying to make herself smaller. Yes, and Jade knew why.

"Go!" Melissa barked. "Now, Poppy, before I lose my temper."

"Come on, Poppet, come with me." Smiling reassuringly as Melissa turned back to whatever mad mission she was on, Jade walked towards the bed. She plucked up the speeding ticket, stuffing it in her pocket, before grabbing hold of the disobedient little brat's arm. Poppy was shuffling further away, her face set in that infuriating petulant scowl she had.

"We'll watch a nice DVD later. How does that sound?" Jade asked her sweetly, all but dragging a tearful Poppy to the door. Melissa, fortunately, was too busy pulling Mark's clothes out of the wardrobe and going through pockets to notice.

Once on the landing, Jade whirled Poppy around to face her and leaned in to eyeball her meaningfully. "Who did your father say was in charge?" she hissed, squeezing the child's arm hard.

Poppy gulped back a sob. "You," she answered tremulously.

"That's right," Jade growled. "Now, do *not* cause me any trouble, *sweetheart*. Not unless you want me to tell your daddy you've been stealing. And, trust me, you don't want me to do that. He's already *very* annoyed with you."

CHAPTER FIFTY-NINE

MARK

As he came through the front door, Mark knew there was something wrong. Poppy didn't come bounding excitedly to him. Instead, thumb in mouth, she sloped dejectedly towards him, glancing warily over her shoulder as she did.

"What's up, Poppet?" Dumping his carrier bag, Mark crouched down to her level.

Poppy scanned his eyes, her own uncertain and...*guarded*?

"Poppy?" Mark eyed her questioningly.

"Mummy's angry," Poppy whispered, her wide eyes now brimming with tears.

Mark looked to Jade, who had appeared in the kitchen doorway. Evie in her arms, she shrugged helplessly and then looked nervously upwards as something crashed onto the floorboards above them.

"Stay here, sweetheart," Mark said, giving Poppy a reassuring smile. "Do as Jade says. I'll be back in a minute."

Heading swiftly up, Mark went straight to the main bedroom, not bothering to knock.

"Mel? What in God's name are you doing?" he asked, bewildered, as he saw Mel picking up clothes from the pile strewn on the bed. *His* clothes. "Melissa..." Anger unfurled inside him as he watched her go through his pockets, tossing aside a pair of trousers and picking up another pair. "Would you like to tell me what's going on here?" he asked, now trying very hard not to lose it.

Mel didn't answer him, just kept right on searching. But for what?

"Melissa! What the hell are you looking for?"

"I don't know!" Mel's expression as she glared at him was one of sheer contempt. "Why don't *you* tell *me*?" She threw one of his jackets down and picked up another item. Realising it was a shirt and would yield nothing, she dropped that to the growing pile on the floor

Mark felt his jaw tense, felt his life slipping away from him, like sand through a timer. "You need to stop this, Mel—*now*," he said, making no attempt to hide his growing fury.

Mel ignored him. "What will I find, Mark, hey?" She walked stiffly over to his dressing table drawers, dragging them out to spew the contents onto the shirts. "Condoms?" she spat. "Lube? Tell me"—she whirled around—"what other dirty little secrets am I likely to find?"

What the...? Mark was stunned, in utter disbelief at this new twist in the madness. "Mel, stop," he said shakily. "You need to talk to me."

"You do *use* condoms, I take it?" Mel spat venomously. She was killing him. She was fucking well crucifying him.

"Mel! Stop!" Mark caught hold of her arm, but Mel yanked it away.

"Or is it more of a turn-on fucking prostitutes naked?"

"For God's sake! Where the *hell* is this coming from? You're completely insane."

"Ha! Oh, yes, of *course* I am," Mel yelled, gesticulating wildly. "It's all in my mind, isn't it? I'm imagining it all, aren't I?"

Mark didn't speak. He couldn't. His temper was way too close to spilling over.

"Just like I imagined your sordid little affair with *Lisa*!"

Mark ran his hand hopelessly through his hair. He had no idea what to do. None.

"Did I imagine you've been overmedicating me? Putting extra drugs in my drinks? Did I imagine *that*?"

"*What?*" Mark looked sharply back at her. "Look, Mel," he moved towards her, felt the foundations rock this time, crumbling beneath him. "I don't know what you think I've done, but can we please—"

"Do *not* try to deny it!" Mel stepped back. "I have evidence!"

"Evidence of *what*?" Mark yelled, torn between guilt and gut-wrenching despair as he watched his wife dementedly dragging clothes from the bed, fumbling around, picking up envelopes, tearing them up.

"*God!*" She stopped, clutching handfuls of her hair. "Evidence of your nocturnal activities," she seethed, turning towards him. "Your therapeutic trips out at night, kerb-crawling."

Kerb-crawling? Mark felt his stomach turn over. "Fuck," he uttered, his anger shifting as he realised there was only one place any sort of so-called evidence could have come from. Cummings, the bastard. The photos he'd taken. It had to be. "It's bullshit, Mel," he said. "Whatever you've seen or heard, it's—"

"You make me sick." Mel looked him over, disgusted. "Get out."

"Mel, you need to listen," Mark tried, taking another step towards her. "There is *no* way—"

"Get out!" Mel screamed, reaching for whatever came to hand from the bedside table. The alarm clock. Her aim was good. Mark winced, his hand going to his face as she hit her target. "Just take your bloody things and go! Or I swear to God I'll call the police."

"And tell them what, Mel?" Mark asked calmly. "That I assaulted you?"

Mel held his gaze. "Yes," she said, her expression resolute, her eyes burning with hatred.

"Right." Mark pulled his bloodied fingers away from his cheek. "It wouldn't be true though, Mel, would it?"

His heart free-falling into the vast space between them, Mark shook his head and turned away.

"I want you out, Mark," Mel said coldly behind him.

Clearly, she was prepared to believe a slimy piece of shit like Cummings over him. Had her illness caused *this*? Caused her to be so suspicious of him, so paranoid, she'd believe such complete crap, even *knowing* him? Or were they headed this way anyway? Mark had no clue. Maybe he didn't know her. Maybe he never really had. Either way, he was going nowhere. She really must be insane if she thought he'd leave his kids to this.

"No way, Mel," he said, squaring his shoulders as he walked away. "Call who you like. I'm staying."

CHAPTER SIXTY

JADE

What did she have to do to get him to leave? Get her to plunge a knife through his heart? And did Melissa have a victim mentality or what? Jade was feeling a need to lie down, she really was. Skidding away from the door as it opened instead, she made as if she'd just been settling Evie as Mark emerged from the room, the look in his eyes one of pure murder.

Oh no! He had blood on his cheek. Jade noted the sharp cut on his cheekbone and her anger boiled inside her. What had the bitch done to him now?

"Did she receive any calls?" Mark demanded. "Did Melissa receive any telephone calls or texts?"

Jade, uncertain where this was going, didn't immediately answer. "I . . . I'm not sure," she stammered. "Possibly. I don't pay much attention to Mel's calls."

"Right. Of course, you wouldn't. Sorry, I er . . . Sorry."

"It's fine," Jade assured him. "I realise you're a bit fraught. You're, um, bleeding." She indicated his cheek, which really did look sore. Jade could see it swelling already.

"Yeah." Mark pressed his fingers to his wound. "Steadily." He eyed her thoughtfully for a second, before hurrying down the stairs.

His heart. Jade placed a hand over her own. He meant his poor broken heart. She really didn't think she could bear it.

CHAPTER SIXTY-ONE

MARK

Poppy had been missing when he'd come down after the fiasco upstairs. His mind conjuring up all sorts of worst-case scenarios, Mark had felt sick to his gut when he'd finally found her, curled as tight as she possibly could be, hiding behind the armchair. Hiding from him.

Gulping back a large swig of whisky, Mark looked across to the chair now, his breath hitching in his chest as he saw again his baby's face. Obviously, having heard the argument and sensed the unbearable tension between him and Mel, she'd been petrified. So she'd tried to find a safe place to hide in, just as he'd once done. She wouldn't budge when he'd asked her to come out. "No. I want to stay with Mummy," she'd insisted, her child's eyes so vulnerable, her voice so small, Mark had felt another piece of himself die. It was Jade who'd persuaded her out in the end. Mark wasn't sure how. He'd gone into the kitchen, not wanting his baby girl to see his heart break. And Jade had taken her up to Mel.

He glanced to his phone on the coffee table, which beeped with another incoming text. It was probably Lisa again. She'd texted him several times, wanting to talk to him about something important, but "not work-related." Whatever it was, it could wait. Mark simply hadn't got the heart. Doubted very much he could talk coherently now anyhow. He lifted his glass to take another swig of whisky, realised he was empty and walked across to the cupboard for a refill, grabbing the bottle and placing it on the table in much the same place as the vodka had been.

Sinking heavily back down on the sofa, the irony that he was doing exactly what he'd condemned Mel for—getting so drunk he couldn't function—wasn't lost on him. The fact was, though, he wanted not to function. He wanted oblivion, escape from the nightmares, both sleeping and waking.

He wanted to confront Cummings in some secluded place, knock his teeth so far down his throat he'd be shitting them for a week. But he couldn't, of course. If he left the house, he'd come back to find the locks changed. The claims Mel was making might have been based on something concocted in her feverish imagination, but it was all way too coincidental. Mark had no doubt that Cummings had taken photos, and that he'd always intended to use them in some way. But he'd been braced for something work-related. He hadn't realised how clever the twisted scumbag was, how low he would sink to destroy him.

What hurt most was that Mel was all too willing to believe it. Kerb-crawling? She clearly thought he was on a par with the sick fucker.

Reaching for another top up of the poison, and knowing it would only make everything look worse in the cold light of day, Mark paused, his hand seeking Hercules, lying faithfully at his feet. "At least you don't think I'm a complete bastard, hey, girl?"

Mark stroked her velvety ears as she looked dolefully up at him. It could be worse, he supposed. His shirts hadn't parted company with their sleeves. Yet. Picking up the bottle, Mark laughed cynically, and then he began to weep.

CHAPTER SIXTY-TWO

JADE

He didn't hear her come in, unaware of her presence until she sat quietly down beside him. Mark immediately tried to compose himself, pulling himself upright and taking his hands away from his face. He didn't want her to see his weakness, as he thought of it; for her to realise he'd been quietly crying when he'd thought there was no one to hear him,

"It's all right," said Jade, squeezing his hand gently. "It's all right, Mark," she repeated, her heart thrumming excitedly as she realised it was time to show him, to reassure him that it would be. "We can get through this."

Closing his eyes, his dark luxuriant eyelashes wet with tears, Mark nodded tightly. "Can we?" he asked, his throat hoarse, his demeanour so very tired as he squeezed her hand back. But then eased himself away and got unsteadily to his feet.

"Of course," Jade said, watching him walk across to the window. "We have to think about the children and do what's best for Mel, but—"

"Which is?" Mark asked, drawing a hand tensely across the back of his neck.

Jade hesitated. *Put the needy bitch in the mental ward* wouldn't be quite the considered, sensitive response he was looking for. "That has to be your decision, Mark," she said instead, her tone hopefully indicating that she would understand, whatever decision he came to.

"I know," he said, staring out of the window as she stood up and walked towards him. "I'm not sure I can make it, though. The right one, I mean."

Shrugging disconsolately, he heaved out a heavy sigh and dropped his gaze to the floor.

She wanted to tell him that there was only one decision he could make if he wanted to end the sheer purgatory his life had obviously been for far too long, but... it wouldn't be a decision a man with a conscience could make easily. Reaching a hand out instead, she trailed it lightly over his shoulders as she moved around in front of him.

"You have to think of the children," she said carefully. "I just want you to know, I'm here for you. Whatever you need."

She smiled encouragingly as Mark looked at her. His eyes were slightly unfocused and full of such obvious torment that Jade felt her heart break for him. It was clear what he needed: someone to hold him, to take him to a place where he could abandon his inhibitions and forget all his anguish. He needed to lose himself, with her, inside her.

"Thanks, Jade." Mark managed a smile back, albeit a smile tinged with sadness—not surprising, given the agony his wife was putting him through. "I have no idea what I would do without you." He reached out then, placing a hand softly on her forearm and causing every inch of Jade's skin to prickle with sweet anticipation.

Jade's hands trembled as she made him coffee—strong and black he'd said, when she'd insisted on making it for him. He could barely stand up straight, and his eyes were heavy with exhaustion.

She was killing him. That bitch upstairs, she was slowly killing him. He wouldn't leave her, nor would he have her sectioned. He might realise there was no other choice eventually, but Jade was growing tired too. She'd waited too long for him to come back to her. For her sweet little angel to come back to her.

Waiting for the kettle to boil, Jade walked across to the island, where Mark's jogging top was still draped on one of the stools. Picking it up, she pressed it to her face, breathing in the smell of him, the masculine essence of him, suffused with the woody aftershave he wore. She wanted him. She would have him. She would have her baby.

He was fast asleep when she crept back downstairs to check on him, his coffee cold and untouched on the table. Standing over him, Jade's eyes travelled the length of his broad-shouldered physique, semi-naked and bathed in soft moonlight from the window. He cried out as she watched him, struggling with the dark demons that were haunting his dreams.

She would help him chase them away. It was safe to, now that he'd acknowledged his need for her. Jade could still feel the tingle of his fingers brushing her skin, sending shock waves the entire length of her body. It was time. She had to show him. His pain was her pain. She would soothe him with soft kisses, not empty promises. She would stand by him, be there for him, right by his side. A shoulder to cry on. A warm body to comfort him, to make love to. And yes, to take out his frustrations on, vent his emotions, if that was what he needed. She would love him as he needed to be loved.

Freshly showered, her body oiled and perfumed, Jade reached for the shirt she slept in, one of Mark's, and slid it over her shoulders, allowing it to fall softly to the floor.

Gently, she straddled him, careful not to wake him. Her heart ached for him, her pelvis yearned to feel him inside her. *Slowly*, she cautioned herself, through the warm mist in her head, the aura that was Mark in her soul. He would need encouragement initially, gentle persuasion to push aside any guilt he might feel. But it was time.

His eyelids fluttered as her hair brushed his cheek. His poor, bruised cheek. Jade's fingers strayed to his face, her lips following in their wake. A hair's breadth from his, she could almost taste his tongue searching for hers, probing deep into her mouth.

Slowly.

She registered a shift in his position, a stirring in his groin as she allowed herself the sweet taste of him, tracing the thin film of sweat at the base of his neck. Moving downwards, she paused to gently caress a nipple with her lips, the taut muscles of his stomach, his hips; finally reaching her prize. She felt him move as she took him into her mouth, heard him utter a throaty expletive as she worked on him expertly with her tongue.

"*Shit.*" She heard him groan again.

Jade increased her efforts, ignoring the question on his lips— "Mel?"—and the sound of feet stumbling towards the bathroom overhead. Why was he whispering *her* name? Why wouldn't he let her go?

She couldn't ignore the hand he wove through her hair, the violent expletive that exploded from him as he yanked her sharply up.

"What the *fucking* hell are you *doing*?" Seizing her shoulders, his fingers digging hard into her flesh, Mark shoved her away and scrambled to his feet.

Shaken, Jade crossed her hands over her breasts, watching, stunned, as he hastily rearranged his tracksuit bottoms and reached for his top. "I...I was lying with you. I—"

"*Why?*" Mark stared incredulously at her.

Seeing an unmistakeable flash of fury spark in his eyes,

Jade shook her head, bewildered. "Because...we're meant to be together. We... You *said*. You said you needed me. That you wouldn't know what to do without me. You promised. The first time you held me, you said you would always—"

"You need to go," Mark interrupted, pulling his furious gaze away.

But he looked towards the stairs, Jade noticed, relief washing through her. He was worried about being caught. "It's all right," she whispered reassuringly, getting to her feet and moving towards him. "I understand. It doesn't matter. We have the rest of our lives to—"

"*What?*" Mark turned back to her, his expression now one of astonishment.

"To be together," Jade finished, her mouth going dry. "To—"

"I don't want to be with you." Mark was looking at her now as if she were something abhorrent. "I want to be with my wife!"

No, he didn't. Jade stared at him, confounded. She'd felt his body stirring, his heart beating. He was confused, tired. The alcohol—

"I love my *wife*, Jade. I don't want anyone else. I never will."

Liar! Anger rose like liquid bile in Jade's chest. "You wanted *me!*" She pointed out this all-too-obvious fact. "You wanted to make love to *me*. You can't deny *that*."

"*Jesus.*" Mark shook his head, pressed his fingers hard against his temples. "I was practically fucking unconscious!"

"But not too out of it to lie back and enjoy a free blow job!" Jade retorted, fury now burning like acid inside her.

Mark's studied her, his eyes darkening dangerously, and then he moved suddenly past her. Jade flinched. "I thought you were Mel. It was Mel I wanted."

Retrieving her shirt from the floor, he shoved it at her, barely looking at her as he did.

He's lying. Jade's heart stopped beating. *He's lying.*

Desperate to rescue the situation, she stepped closer. She'd got her timing wrong. Moved too fast. He was scared. "It's all right, Mark. I understand, really I do." Arranging her face into a seductive smile, she reached to graze a hand across his cheek, and then leaned closer, attempting to press her lips against his.

Mark stopped her, roughly grabbing hold of her wrist. "You're fucking *insane*. I want you out. Get your things and go."

He *meant* it. Shocked, Jade searched his eyes. Eyes that were no longer kind and caring, but cruel, contemptuous and cold. Humiliation and hurt churned inside her. It wasn't her timing she'd got wrong, it was her estimation of *him*, a man she'd imagined to be strong, to be her saviour. But he wasn't strong. He was weak, weaker than his pathetic wife. A user, an abuser, just like all the others. The absolute *bastard*.

Swallowing back her rage, pushing it down to that deep, dark place where so much hurt already festered, she told herself to bide her time until she had more suitable opportunity to vent. "It's the middle of the night," she said, composing her features and looking tearfully back at him. Her nakedness, she was aware, would add to her obvious vulnerability. He wouldn't send her out now, a woman on her own in the dark.

Breathing hard, Mark appeared to debate with himself, and then picked up his mobile from the coffee table and selected a number.

Jade watched in disbelief as he spoke to the taxi firm.

"You have ten minutes," he said, his gaze flicking back to hers as he ended the call. "Get dressed."

Jade felt her heart settle like a stone in her chest. "What about my things?" she asked, notching her chin high.

"I'll send them on," Mark said impassively.

Noting the unflinching look in his eyes, his utter indifference to her feelings, Jade nodded slowly. He'd shown himself in his true colours. They all did, eventually. So be it. He would live to regret this. She would make damn sure of it. Peeling her eyes away from him, she wrapped the shirt tightly about herself and turned to walk to the door.

She stopped as she realised he was actually *following* her. Clearly, he was going to make sure she left with nothing other than the clothes on her back. Without her baby. *Her baby*, who she'd loved and nurtured far more than his useless bitch of a wife ever had. She wouldn't abandon her, and DI Mark-bastard-Cain had badly underestimated her if he imagined she would. If he imagined for one second he wouldn't suffer for feeding her empty promises, keeping his options open and then callously abandoning her.

Hush, little baby, don't say a word. Jade hummed silently as she walked past the nursery ahead of him. *Daddy loves you, and so do I . . . Mummy will be back, my sweet Angel.*

CHAPTER SIXTY-THREE

MELISSA

Mel had debated whether to take her medication. She was feeling woozy, again, as she had every morning in what seemed like forever, but she'd set the alarm and dragged herself out of bed, determined to get some control back over her life, her emotions, for the sake of the children. She would take the tablets, she'd decided, but later, once Poppy was at school. She would speak to the doctor again too. If she hadn't needed counselling before, she thought she might need it now, to help her through the break-up of her marriage.

Willing herself not to go there, not to think about any of it, for fear she might never stop falling, she was stepping into the shower when Mark came into the room. She reached hurriedly to close the door, wishing she could close the door so easily on her emotions, the memory that immediately sprang to her mind causing her stomach to clench painfully: the last time they'd made love. Right here, in the shower. Such meaningful love, she'd thought then. Mark being so gentle, so caring of her needs. She'd thought she'd known him, all of him, every inch, inside and out. But she hadn't. She hadn't known him at all. Mel lifted her face, allowing the cool water to wash the tears from her cheeks.

He was sitting on the bed when she came out, his hands hanging loosely between his knees, looking utterly dejected, so exhausted, Mel's heart would have bled for him, once.

"Where's Poppy?" she asked, noticing the empty space in the bed as she looked past him.

Mark looked at her, his expression one of tired despair. "Playing in her room," he said quietly.

Mel nodded, relieved, her gaze flicking to the cot, where Evie was still sleeping.

"I'm not going to take them, Mel." Following her gaze, Mark sighed hopelessly. "I just don't want to leave them."

"With a madwoman?" Mel added facetiously.

"You're not mad, Mel." Mark rubbed a hand tiredly over his eyes. "You're depressed."

"So I'm told. Don't worry, I'm taking the tablets," Mel retorted, walking across to the dressing table to brush her hair and at least put some foundation on. She had no intention of walking around looking how she felt. Not any more.

"Did you want something?" she asked him. "It's just that I need to get dressed."

Mark obviously got the message that she'd no intention of getting dressed in front of him. But he didn't move. "It's Jade," he said after a second. "She's gone."

"Gone?" Confused, Mel turned to face him. "Gone where?"

"To her friend's in London." Mark looked up at her, his expression now uncomfortable. "She, er, won't be coming back."

Won't be... Mel stared at him, stunned for a second, and then her anger, her sheer bloody fury with this man she'd thought was her rock, unleashed. "You know, I'm really not surprised," she said, her voice loaded with contempt. "Learning that the man she's working for, the respectable Detective Inspector Cain, is a serial-shagging bastard is enough to drive any vulnerable young woman away!"

"Oh, for *fu*..." Mark heaved himself to his feet. "Can we not do this now, Mel?" he said, his voice tight with anger. "The kids," he added, glancing towards Evie.

Using the fact that she was prepared to argue in front of them against her? Mel looked him over, scarcely able to believe that this was the man she'd once trusted implicitly.

"I came to see if there was anything I could do to help." Mark shrugged, pushing his hands in his pockets and dropping his gaze, clearly unable to meet hers.

Mel was about to tell him there was; he could collect his things and leave, when Poppy spoke timidly from the door. "Daddy, are you still annoyed with me?"

CHAPTER SIXTY-FOUR

MARK

Mark snapped his gaze towards where Poppy stood on the land-ing, looking warily at him over her Bedtime Peppa clutched to her chin, and his heart sank to a whole new level. He looked questioningly at Mel, who looked as confused as he felt.

"Poppet," he said, walking across to her and crouching down to her level, "I'm not angry with you. Why do you think I would be?"

Poppy didn't answer, merely pushed her chin further into her soft toy, her huge uncertain eyes searching his—right down to his soul, it seemed to Mark.

"Poppy?"

"Are you going to send me to prison?" she asked, her brow knitted worriedly.

"To prison?" Mark laughed incredulously. "Why on earth would I do that?"

"Because of the chocolate," Poppy said, her voice barely a whisper, her eyes now welling with tears.

Was that all? Mark's laugh this time was one of sheer bloody relief.

"I don't want to go to prison, Daddy. It's dark and cold. And they don't let you take any toys, or play, or *anything.*" Poppy's voice quavered and her face crumpled, and Mark reached out for her.

"You don't go to prison for something like that, sweetheart." He squeezed her tight; felt like crying with her. "You shouldn't have done it, but I'm guessing you've already figured that out. I'm not angry with you."

A sob shaking her small shoulders, Poppy didn't answer.

Mark reached to wipe the tears from her cheek with his thumb. "I love you, Poppy," he said firmly. "More than all the stars and all the fish in the sea. Got that? I will never stop loving you, no matter what."

Poppy flung herself at him, almost knocking Mark backwards. "I love you bigger than a whole whale," she snuffled into his neck, locking her arms firmly around him.

"That's a lot." Mark hugged her hard. "Come on, sweetpops. Let's go and get you ready for school."

Taking her small hand in his as he got to his feet, he turned to Mel. "Shall I drive her there?" he asked hopefully.

CHAPTER SIXTY-FIVE

JADE

It was enough to melt hearts, it really was. Under cover of the trees on the opposite side of the lane, Jade watched Poppy skipping happily to the car alongside her precious daddy, her Bedtime Peppa clutched to her chest. Obviously he'd won her over with his false kindness and oh-so-caring persona. *Lies.* Little did his precious little Poppet know it, but he would hurt her too, abuse her, *lie* to her, just as he had Jade.

Naively, her body not yet grown, her emotions so vulnerable, Jade had forgiven him for abandoning her that first time, despite the initial doubt that had niggled inside her. She'd dismissed it. Made excuses for him, as women did for the despicable, abusive men in their lives. And she'd waited for him. Remade herself for him. Offered herself to him on a plate, and he'd rejected her. The bastard, as if he hadn't enjoyed her going down on him. As if he wouldn't have taken full advantage of what was on offer and fucked her senseless if needy Melissa hadn't stumbled to the bathroom overhead. He was a user. An abuser of the worst kind. Jade's humiliation simmered furiously inside her. It was time Mark Cain realised the grave consequences of using his position to exploit vulnerable young women.

He thought he could just walk away from it. Get away with leading her on and then crushing her under his feet, all the while hiding his deviant nature behind his family, his career, his respectability. He had no idea what the word *respect* meant. Now it was time to strip away his veneer and show the world what a deceitful, manipulative excuse for a man he was. The public weren't safe with him. His children weren't safe with him. *Her* baby wasn't safe—vulnerable to his twisted whimsies, his wife's mental instability. It was time to redress the balance, turn the tables. To have Mark Cain disgraced and removed to a place where he'd have a lifetime to ponder all that *he'd* lost. It was time to take back what he'd stolen, to ruin him as surely as he'd ruined her.

She sneered as she watched Poppy the spoiled brat chatting to her podgy-faced little pig, her fingers intertwined with her father's.

Time to put away childish things, my lovely.

Mark would never hold his daughter's hand again.

CHAPTER SIXTY-SIX

MARK

Coming back from a jog, which he'd hoped would clear his mind, Mark was turning into his lane when his heart slammed into his ribcage. *What the . . . ?* His gut twisting violently inside him, he didn't hesitate, sprinting towards the house.

"Sorry, sir, I can't allow you through access." A uniform barred his way as he approached the sea of blue lights. "There's been an incident. We need to cordon off—"

"Fuck off, this is my house," Mark shouted, attempting to push his way past the man.

The guy pushed back hard, sending Mark staggering.

"Let him through! It's DI Cain!" Lisa shouted, emerging from his front door. Mark righted himself, his head reeling, blind panic almost choking him.

"Who?" The uniform glanced confusedly back at her.

"Mark Cain!" Lisa bellowed. "The baby's father! Let him through."

Evie? No! Feeling something break inside him, Mark scrambled past the officer. His baby. *Christ, please not his baby.*

"Sorry, Mark, he's the new probationer," Lisa said, looking him over apprehensively as she ran to meet him on the drive.

Mark nodded tightly. "What's happening?" he asked, his tone short as he desperately tried to keep a rein on his spiralling emotions.

"I'm sorry, Mark…It's Evie. She's been taken."

Lisa moved quickly forwards as his legs almost failed him. "Take your time," she said sympathetically, moving to wrap an arm firmly around him as Mark bent, clutching his thighs and attempting to draw air into his lungs.

Nodding again, Mark straightened up. "When?" he asked, barely able to get the word past the hard knot in his throat.

"Ten fifteen, give or take a minute," Lisa said, her tone quiet and measured—a hopeless attempt to reassure him.

Mark reeled inwardly. He'd forgotten to take his mobile with him. He'd been five minutes into his run when he realised, and had debated going back for it, but had decided against it. He'd been out, running, without his mobile while his child was being abducted.

"Melissa fastened Evie into her seat and then went back inside to pick up a box," Lisa explained.

"A box?"

"A sculpture. She was taking it to the university to be fired," Lisa clarified, as Mark frantically tried to make sense where there was none. "She'd left the boot open, so the car was unlocked. When she came back…" Lisa stopped, her voice catching.

Their child had gone. Nausea churning his stomach, Mark closed his eyes, feeling every one of Mel's emotions, every second of the agony she would have gone through. "Witnesses?" he asked gutturally.

Lisa shook her head. Mark guessed there wouldn't be. The lane wasn't a useful through road to anywhere, providing access only to the local farm and a few houses.

Mark half-turned away, no clue what to do at a crime scene that involved his own family.

"We've been trying to locate Jade." Lisa cut through his deliberations. "I asked Mel, but she's not making much sense. Any ideas?"

"Jade," Mark repeated, cold foreboding washing through him. Could she…? *Would she?* "She's gone."

"Gone?"

"Fired," Mark said tersely. "Find her."

"I'm on it," Lisa assured him. "Do you have any details? Previous employers, addresses? Relatives we can start with?"

Mark's heart nosedived into the pit of his stomach.

"You did run a background check, right?"

Hopelessly, Mark shook his head. "Mel said she would. I… didn't push it."

Lisa drew in a sharp breath, but didn't comment. "I'll get everyone I can on it," she said. "Don't worry, Mark. We'll find Evie."

Cursing his idiocy, his sheer bloody incompetence at not running the check himself, Mark nodded. "Where's Mel?" he asked, attempting some sort of focus as he glanced towards the house, their dream home, which had become a house of horrors. Mel would be broken, utterly destroyed.

"Lounge. Distraught, obviously," Lisa said, and then hesitated. "She thought you'd taken her, Mark. I thought you should know."

The news didn't surprise him. It hurt, but it didn't surprise him.

"I've telephoned the health centre and asked her GP to come out." Aware of Mel's resistance to visit the surgery, Lisa's tone was guarded. "I thought, under the circumstances…"

Mark nodded. He didn't like the idea, but sedation was probably the only way Mel would get through the first few hours. After that… nothing would help her, nothing but her child safe in her arms would pull her back from the abyss. Mark knew that with certainty.

"We've called in forensics," Lisa called, behind him. "And obviously Edwards has all available bodies on it."

Mark nodded again, grateful for that much. He needed to be at the station, on top of this, but not before he'd seen Mel, tried to reassure her, though he doubted he could.

"Poppy?" He turned back to Lisa, a new fear twisting his stomach.

"We've despatched a squad car to the school. I'll let you know as soon as—Hold on." Stopping, Lisa checked her radio. "She's safe."

And Mark allowed himself to breathe.

CHAPTER SIXTY-SEVEN

LISA

Her heart breaking for them, Lisa paused between calls, watching as Mark walked across to where Melissa stood by the window, her arms wrapped tightly about herself, as if trying to keep the emotion inside. She didn't seem to be aware of Mark's presence, jumping as he reached out to touch her.

"I'll find her, Mel," he said quietly. Cautiously, he moved closer, gently coaxing her around to face him. "I will find her, I promise," he repeated, his voice thick with emotion.

Poor bastard, he looked worse than Lisa had ever seen him. Even after losing little Jacob, when he'd been struggling on all fronts, drinking too much, sleeping little, he hadn't looked so utterly drained.

Clearly as exhausted as he was, Melissa allowed him to pull her closer. Lisa hoped to God they could find some comfort in each other. They didn't deserve this on top of everything else. Relieved as she saw Mel drop her head to Mark's shoulder, Lisa was about to discreetly leave when Melissa spoke.

"Why?" she asked sharply, pulling away from him. "*Why*, Mark?"

Lisa's heart sank as Melissa glared up at Mark, her expression a toxic mix of raw pain and pure anger.

"*Why* did you trash everything?" Melissa demanded. "Throw

your family away? Try to drive me half out of my mind? You *bastard*!"

Shaken, Mark struggled to answer. "Mel, don't," he tried, attempting to close the space between them.

"I can't do this. I *can't*. I want her back! I want my *baby*!" Backing away from him, Melissa screamed it.

"Mel, please…" Desperation in his voice, Mark stepped back towards her. "Please, don't—"

"No!" Melissa lashed out, landing a blow to Mark's arm. "I want her back! Do you *hear* me?" She hit him again, the flat of her hand curling into a fist, thumping into his chest. "Where *is* she?"

Mark didn't defend himself or attempt to stop her; he just waited until her blows became useless, ineffectual flails, and then, gently, he caught hold of her wrists. Still, he didn't speak. Silently, he pulled her close and lowered his forehead to hers. "I'll find her," he said hoarsely.

Guessing now was a good time to leave them alone, Lisa turned for the hall, pondering the whereabouts of Jade as she went. She couldn't believe Mark hadn't pushed Mel regarding the background check. If only he'd answered her texts. But then, he had been preoccupied, she supposed. And the "perfect" babysitter had soon installed herself in their lives and made herself indispensable. It might be nothing to do with her, of course. She might be the angel sent from heaven that Mel had seemed to think she was. In which case, Lisa would be extremely interested to find out why she'd been fired. She'd ask Mark as soon as she could. At the station would probably be best. He would undoubtedly want to be hands-on with this, the alternative being to go slowly insane.

CHAPTER SIXTY-EIGHT

JADE

"Jade?" Cummings sounded surprised when he answered the phone. "What's happening, babe? Where are you?" He sounded caring—as if he gave a damn in reality. The man was a chauvinistic Neanderthal of the worst kind, to whom women existed only to satiate his perverted appetites. He hadn't needed much persuading to play games in the bedroom, throwing himself into his role with gusto. Oh, how Jade would have enjoyed bringing this sadistic little prick down. Her plans regarding the delightful Cummings, however, had changed.

"Babe? Talk to me," he urged her, an impatient edge to his voice now. "You need to let me know where you are. You know we have people out looking for you?"

"Looking for me ... Why?" Jade made sure to sound puzzled.

"Cain's kid." Cummings hesitated, as if he might be having an actual thought about anyone but himself. "She's gone missing. You need to come in and—"

"*Poppy?*" Jade cut over him, alarmed. "Missing?"

"Not Poppy. The baby," Cummings went on. "We need to know what time you last saw her. Whether you saw anyone prowling—"

"*Evie?* Oh God, no." Jade squeezed her eyes closed, getting into the role as she emitted a heartfelt sob. "When? *How?*"

"This morning," Cummings supplied. "We need to know what time you last saw her. Whether she was—"

"I haven't. I didn't," Jade cut in quickly. "Not this morning. I...left. Suddenly," she said cautiously, as if not quite sure how much to disclose. "Last night. I had to get out. I didn't want to leave the children, but I was scared and I didn't know what else to do, and—"

"Whoa—scared? Why?"

Jade gulped back a huge breath and sniffled for effect. "They had a row," she continued, after a second. "A dreadful argument."

"About?"

"I'm not sure. What started it, I mean, but I think..." Again, Jade paused, not wanting to appear keen to divulge.

"It's okay, Jade. Take your time," Cummings said, attempting to be sympathetic. "You know you can confide in me."

Jade rolled her eyes at that. Yes, right. *Hurry up and dish the dirt, you silly bitch,* was more likely what he was thinking, desperate as he was to get something on Mark.

"Melissa," Jade went on falteringly, "I think she had an affair. Mark...He'd been drinking, heavily. He was shouting. Really angry. I was upstairs, with the children. I couldn't help but overhear."

"Overhear what, sweetheart?"

"He was calling her names, awful names. He..." Jade paused for another timely sniffle. "He thinks the children might not even be his."

"*Bloody hell!*" Cummings gasped, astonished. "Well, well, that explains a lot. Poor bastard," he commiserated—and then chuckled. Clearly, he was highly amused.

Excuse me, distraught victim of crime on the line here, Jade thought, disgusted.

"He turned on me," said Jade, cutting his merriment short. "When I came downstairs. Melissa had gone out. I'm not sure where, and he...He turned into an absolute *monster*. I tried to run, to fight him off but he's so much heavier than me. I...I didn't have any choice, Pete. Honestly, I didn't. He..."

Jade trailed off, waited, and sure enough...

"Are you telling me he *raped* you?" Cummings asked, his tone a mixture of utter disbelief, outrage...and excitement. Definitely excitement. He would be orgasmic, Jade had no doubt, revelling at the prospect of using the information to destroy Mark Cain.

Result, she thought. Then, "*Yes*," she cried, emitting a wretched sob.

"You need to come in," Cummings said brusquely. "I'll come and fetch you."

"No, I'm...with a girlfriend. I'll come to the station."

"As soon as possible," Cummings instructed. "We can't let the bastard get away with this. Don't wash away any evidence, babe," he said, tempering his tone to something near concern. "And keep this between you and me for now, will you? I don't want him getting wind we're onto him before we can bring him in. Okay?"

"Uh-huh," Jade said timidly.

Perfect, she thought, ending the call and turning her attention to the police exiting Mark's property.

The timing would be crucial. She had to get Melissa alone. Which she soon would, it seemed. Jade smiled as one of the officers turned at the squad car to ask Melissa whether she was sure she would be all right on her own, informing her that the family liaison officer would be with her soon.

Jade waited as the squad car drove off and then, checking the road was clear, took a step towards the house, cursing as her phone vibrated. It was Dylan calling, again.

"*What?*" Jade hissed, moving back under cover of the trees.

"What do I do if she wakes up?" Dylan asked. "Her little cheeks are still all flushed. I'm worried she might start crying again and I—"

"For God's sake, Dylan, she won't wake up. I've given her some Tylenol," Jade snapped. She was anxious to get back into the house while there was a lull in police activity. With Dylan fussing and clucking about like a mother hen, thinking Angel looked a bit peaky, she'd miss her opportunity. He'd even suggested he take her out in her stroller for some fresh air. *Moron.* Jade had paid cash for the room, but the last thing she wanted drippy Dylan doing was perambulating about the Travelodge car park, which would be bound to draw attention. "I'll be back soon, my love," she assured him, softening her tone.

Once she'd filled Melissa in about her deceitful bastard of a husband, that was. Which she would need to do soon, before Mark gave anyone his version of events. Clearly, knowing he'd be dropping himself in it if he confessed why he'd thrown her out like so much rubbish, he'd decided to keep that information to himself.

She had to get to Melissa now. There was no other time. Having carelessly endangered her child while she pissed about with her stupid clay statues, Melissa would be teetering dangerously near to the edge. Her grip on reality would be fragile, and she would be susceptible, ready to believe her husband capable of anything. And once she'd seen the indisputable evidence of his perverted sexual preferences, then the weak, self-obsessed woman would fall, and so would Mark Cain.

Letting herself quietly in through the back door, Jade found the kitchen was empty. Poor Melissa must be having a little lie down, she deduced. And no wonder, if she'd popped a few of these little beauties. Seeing the sedatives, Zopiclone, at the back of one of the work surfaces, Jade hummed contentedly and turned for the hall.

Mark's laptop was there. *Oh, deary me.* He really was careless. Though it was only his personal PC, one really would think that, as a policeman, he might have it better protected. Quickly plugging in her phone, she uploaded the desired photo to his desktop. Most of the pictures she'd taken were innocent enough, but the one of him in Poppy's bedroom, the dreadful day her poor little goldfish had died, that could easily be wildly misinterpreted. Mark half naked, removing Poppy's nightie? That would certainly look suspect, particularly in combination with a few of the more risqué sites she quickly saved to his bookmarks— definitely extreme, most definitely illegal, and enough to have Melissa and his colleagues reeling with shock.

Job done, Jade replaced the laptop in its usual position and turned for the stairs, humming silently as she went. *Hush, little baby…*

Hearing a sound from the nursery, she guessed that's where she'd find Melissa, no doubt regretting having neglected her baby. Jade was heading that way when Poppy's door squeaked open and the girl peered out to stare at her like a startled sparrow.

Smiling languidly, Jade pressed her finger to her lips, which was enough to have the brat backing back in and closing the door in a flash. Presumably the dog was in there with her. And it had better stay in there too, or the next noise it emitted in Jade's presence would be a gurgle.

In the nursery, Melissa was standing with her arms wrapped about her in the protective stance she'd adopted since her perfect little world had started falling apart. Rolling her eyes at the woman's complete inability to do anything other than feel sorry for herself, Jade tapped lightly on the door. "Mel?" she said, her voice loaded with fake concern.

CHAPTER SIXTY-NINE

MELISSA

It took a second for Melissa to register the voice behind her. When it did permeate the thick fog in her head, she wondered whether she was imagining it. She'd imagined she could hear Evie crying in here every time she lay back on her bed.

"Mel? Are you okay?"

Jade? But hadn't Mark said she'd left? Mel could only assume because her situation here had become intolerable.

"I'm so sorry, Mel," Jade said, tears streaming down her face. "If I'd been here... If I hadn't run off like that... Oh God, I'm so sorry. I didn't know what else to do. I should have stayed. I—"

Jade gulped back a wretched sob, and despite her own pain, which if God was merciful would surely kill her, Mel felt for her. Jade wasn't to blame. If anyone was, she was—though, in truth, she blamed Mark.

"It's not your fault, Jade. They'll find her." Even as she said it, the hopelessness, the tidal wave of grief she'd felt since Evie had gone, washed through her afresh, leaving her weak and empty in its wake.

Her sobs stilling to a shudder, Jade nodded. "I had to come back. I have to tell you something, Mel," she said, her innocent blue eyes—child's eyes, almost—clouded with confusion and worry. "I wasn't sure whether to say, but I think you need to know."

"Know what?" Noting the nervousness now in Jade's eyes, Mel felt an immediate sense of uneasiness.

"I ... need to show you," Jade said hesitantly.

"Show me?"

"Mark's laptop," Jade said uncomfortably. "I needed to do some online banking so I borrowed it and ... I should have asked him, but ..."

His laptop? Icy trepidation running the length of her spine, Mel was already halfway out of the door, heading for the hall, where she knew Mark always left it.

Staring in disbelief at the screen, Melissa felt repulsion flood every pore in her body. It couldn't be true. *It couldn't!* Yet it was there, right in front of her eyes: every sordid detail, every vile pornographic image.

Dear God, not children.

Nausea gripping her stomach, Melissa dragged her horrified gaze away from the graphic images, which would be forever imprinted on her mind, and ran to the downstairs toilet, where she retched the dry contents of her stomach until her insides were raw.

Poppy? Why was that photo on his desktop? *Only* that photo? He wouldn't. *He wouldn't!* Melissa snatched at the toilet roll, pressed a wad to her mouth, trying to stop the violent trembling that shook her entire body.

"Melissa?" Standing behind her, Jade barely whispered it. "Here," she said, two small pills in her outstretched hand. "Take these. Dr. Meadows left them, remember? They'll help with the anxiety."

"*Anxiety?*" Melissa laughed—a laugh bordering on hysteria. It was going to take more than two pills, she thought, desperately trying to quell the nausea as she reached for them, swallowed them quickly down and headed back to the kitchen.

"I've warmed you some milk," Jade said. "It'll help line your stomach," she added, offering her the mug cautiously, as if Melissa might throw it at the nearest wall. She wanted to. She wanted to tear the whole house apart, brick by brick, and everything in it. Erase the nightmare. Dear God, she wished she could erase it.

Melissa took the mug, swilling the contents back for Jade's sake as she sat down and braced herself to browse the rest of Mark's internet history.

Flicking through his bookmarks, her stomach clenched as she realised there were many such sites. Then she turned her attention to his emails. It didn't take long to find a folder marked "x-receipts," making it the last folder listed in his favourites. Mel's insides turned over afresh as she realised what kind of online purchases he'd made. He couldn't have. Surely to God... She *knew* him. Or she thought she had.

"There's something else, Melissa," Jade said tentatively as, trying to still the palpitations in her chest, the dizziness in her head, Mel closed the laptop.

What? What else *could* there be? Melissa looked questioningly up to where Jade was standing opposite her, fiddling nervously with her hair.

"The reason I left." Looking tearful again, Jade went reluctantly on.

She looked more than upset, Mel thought, studying her face. She looked fearful. *Ashamed?* "Jade?" Her heart thudding painfully now, Melissa urged her on. "Tell me."

"He'd been drinking a lot," Jade said quickly. "Because of the problems between you, I think."

Was she defending him? Against what? What had he done?

"I didn't know what to do." Jade looked beseechingly at her. "He came to my room. I wasn't sure why. I thought it was to do with the children. I tried to get him to leave. I begged him to, but…" Jade stopped, her face flushing as she glanced quickly down. "He's much stronger than I am."

"No." Melissa reeled. She felt the room shift around her.

"I tried to fight him off, I swear. I should have said something, I know I should, but you were going through so much. I thought it would be better if I just left. I wish I hadn't. I wish…" Swallowing, Jade dropped her gaze back to the floor. "Evie might still be here, if only I'd said something."

Melissa stared at her, shocked to the core. She'd loved him. With her whole heart, she'd loved a man who was a complete monster.

"You think he's taken her, don't you?"

"I honestly don't know," said Jade. "If he has, I'm sure he won't hurt her, but…"

Pausing pointedly, she glanced at the laptop and then back to Mel. "Knowing what you know now about his… activities, I really think you should tell the police. For Evie's sake."

CHAPTER SEVENTY

MARK

Mark had been going door to door with officers, targeting sex offenders and investigating any known links to child trafficking for sexual exploitation or the babies-for-sale trade. They were also visiting parents who'd recently lost babies, in particular bereaved mothers without a support network who might be prone to depression.

As if any parent wouldn't be. Mark had empathised completely as some of them had relived their experiences, his mind playing over memories of his own son, outwardly perfect while his small lungs had struggled to draw their last breath. His tiny white coffin. He'd had to excuse himself as one mother had recounted how she'd nursed her seven-month-old baby in her arms until God had taken her for an angel. Leaving the woman in the care of a female police officer, Mark had sought the sanctuary of his car, where he'd sat with his head on the steering wheel, his heart bleeding steadily inside him.

Glancing around the woodland adjoining the local beauty spot, every square foot of which could conceal a small body, Mark felt a sinking sense of hopelessness. He'd trodden this route looking for Daisy. He'd never imagined he'd be walking it again in search of his own missing child.

Clamping down on his thoughts before his mind wandered too far, Mark reached into his pocket for his ringing mobile.

"Mark, I managed to get hold of Jade on her mobile, finally,"

Lisa said, when he picked up the call. "She's going to come in and give a statement, but I thought you should know her alibi checks out. We have her on the bank's security cameras at the time she says she was there."

"Ten fifteen." Mark sighed. Given her unceremonious departure from the house, he'd thought... But he'd been wrong. He wasn't relieved at the news, however. Jade had definitely formed an attachment to Evie, but if she had taken her for whatever reason, Mark had doubted she would hurt her in any way. "Okay, Lisa, thanks. I'm on my way to see Mel. I'll be back at the station as soon as I can."

"See you later," Lisa said. "Oh, and Mark, about Jade... I couldn't get much sense out of Mel, for obvious reasons, but why did you say she'd left exactly? It's just, it was a bit sudden, wasn't it?"

"Very," Mark said, and sucked in a breath. He had to give some kind of explanation, but what? *She took advantage of me while I was drunk* would sound pretty lame. And unbelievable. Mark was well aware of that. "I haven't said anything to Mel yet, but..." He faltered, feeling acutely embarrassed. "She, er, came on to me. Heavily."

Lisa was quiet for a moment. "And you're surprised?"

Not surprised; shocked. And angry, bewildered and humiliated. Ashamed. He wondered whether he'd been responsible, whether he'd led her on in some way. All of the things he'd told victims of sexual crime they shouldn't be feeling, and none of which he wanted to become general knowledge. Cummings would have a field day.

"A bit," he said instead, glancing up curiously as two officers approached him. "Looks like I'm needed. I'll catch you at the station, Lisa."

"DI Cain." One of the officers looked at him apologetically as Mark ended his call. "We have instructions to accompany you to the station."

Accompany him? "Why?" Mark asked, his stomach tightening as he braced himself for news of Evie.

"DCI wants to have a little chat," the other guy said, his tone arrogant.

So it wasn't about Evie. Mark felt himself go weak with relief. He looked the guy over, deciding to seek him out later regarding his attitude. Right now, he hadn't got the time or the inclination. "What about then?" he asked.

Shooting his colleague a disparaging look, the first officer spoke. "I'm afraid I can't say, sir. We've just been asked to make sure you get there."

"Sorry, it will have to wait," Mark said, reaching for his car door. "I'm going home to see my wife."

"It's not a request, sir," the officer responded, his expression hardening as he moved to prevent him opening the door.

Mark looked at him, thunderstruck, and then turned to the second officer, who'd walked around to position himself on his other side. "We've been told to escort you," the man said dispassionately. "We also need to take possession of your phone."

"*What?*" Mark laughed incredulously. "You have to be kidding?"

"Never been more serious in my life. *Sir,*" the second officer assured him, his tone now definitely disrespectful.

The officers disclosing nothing on the drive in, other than to tell him there were no developments regarding Evie, Mark still had no idea what was happening. He had a distinct feeling, however, that his colleagues did, as the two men insisted on escorting him right to the DCI's office door. The silence as he was walked through the main office was so profound you could have heard a paperclip drop. The scornful glances didn't do much to alleviate Mark's uneasiness, and the contemptuous sneer he registered on Cummings' face caused his step to falter. It was Lisa's expression, though, one of palpable shock, that stopped him in his tracks.

"Lisa?" he said, his apprehension growing tenfold.

Cummings got to his feet. He didn't speak, didn't utter a word, simply moved to stand by Lisa's side.

Lisa glanced at Cummings, back to Mark, and then looked embarrassedly away.

"Sir." One of the officers urged him on, taking hold of his arm.

"I know what I'd do with paedo pervs in our own ranks," someone muttered, as Mark walked on. "Castrate the bastards and make an example."

"What the *fuck* is going on?" Mark demanded, as Edwards swung his door open.

"Sit down," Edwards said shortly, banging the door shut and marching past him to his desk.

Mark stayed put. "Look, I have no idea what the hell this is all about, but—"

"That's an order, DI Cain. Sit!" Edwards eyed him furiously. "Now!"

Mark tried to temper his own fury. "My daughter's missing," he said, walking reluctantly across to the chair. "Whatever this is, can't it wait?"

"No, Cain, it can't *wait*," Edwards assured him, glaring at him until he sat.

Edwards stayed standing, still staring unnervingly at him. "Now then," he said, finally, "would you like to tell me what the hell this shit is all about?"

Mark's first reaction was revulsion as Edwards twirled the laptop on his desk to face him.

His second, overwhelming panic as he realised the laptop was his.

CHAPTER SEVENTY-ONE

JADE

Melissa was taking longer to succumb than Jade had anticipated. She eyed her suspiciously as she blundered up the stairs ahead of her, having dutifully taken her regular meds washed down with a cup of strong, extremely sweet tea. Had she thrown up again when she'd gone to the loo? She really was an irritating cow. Mark was welcome to her. Except, he wouldn't have her ever again, apart from in his pathetic little fantasies.

"I need to go to Poppy," Melissa said, making her way clumsily along the landing. "I need to talk to her."

Talk to her? Jade rolled her eyes sky high. The woman was barely coherent.

"Whoops." Her mouth curving into a smile, Jade caught Melissa as she appeared to lose the use of her legs and reeled sideways into the wall. "I've got you," she said, easing her up and steering her in the direction of her bedroom.

"Poppy," the woman mumbled, dragging her feet, to Jade's immense annoyance.

"You've had a terrible shock, Mel," she said caringly. "You really should lie down. Come on. Let's get you on the bed and I'll fetch Poppy. She can snuggle up with you while I make you both something to eat. How does that sound?"

Mel nodded, pressing her hand to her forehead as she stumbled onwards, her brow furrowed and her expression pained, as if her perfect little world had disintegrated. She was probably contemplating how to end it all. As if she need worry her pretty little rusty-haired head about that with her babysitter here, ready to take care of everything.

Jade was debating whether to bring Poppy in or lock her away when Melissa babbled something about tiny toes and plaster casts, and weaved towards her bed.

Jade watched her go, perplexed. *Bonkers*, she thought, shaking her head. Complete basket case. She really had no idea what Mark had ever seen in her.

The hair was quite pretty, she supposed, looking closely at it as she helped needy Melissa lie back on the pillow. Wavy and lustrous, the copper suited her better. Why she'd ever sought to emulate her by dyeing it blonde, Jade couldn't fathom.

Still, she couldn't blame her for trying.

Turning to the door, having decided to fetch the brat, Jade fluffed up her own hair in the mirror, pouted her full lips and admired her breasts. Mark Cain had missed out big time. She'd have taken him to heights of ecstasy he couldn't imagine in his wildest fantasies.

His loss.

His very great loss indeed.

She was halfway along the landing to Poppy's room when her phone rang. Dylan, again. Jade tutted tetchily, accepted the call, and answered in her sweetest tones.

"It's on the news," Dylan squeaked in her ear.

Jade stifled her agitation. "It doesn't matter, Dylan," she said patiently. "He'll be in custody by now." Reviled by his colleagues. Spat on, probably. Jade got immense satisfaction from that. "They won't believe another word he says."

"But they're looking for her." Dylan sounded panicked.

"Not for long," Jade said, less patiently.

"But what if they believe him? He's a policeman, ain't he?

One of their own." Dylan was talking fast, thinking in clichés. "And he is their father. What if they come—"

"They won't!" Jade snapped, gritting her teeth hard. God, she was so sick of mollycoddling him. She should have fed him to Inky and bloody Oinky. Though it would probably take them a month to chomp through the useless great wimp.

"They won't, Dylan," she said, more kindly, when she realised he'd gone quiet. "The CCTV footage and speeding fine *you* clocked up will see to that." Emphasising the "you," Jade thought it better to leave out the one or two other sordid activities the disgraced detective inspector would be charged with.

"CCTV?" Dylan whispered, aghast.

"They do have cameras in red-light districts, Dylan," Jade pointed out. "But don't worry, you're the same colouring and height as him. And if anyone should ask, not that they will, I'll vouch for you, obviously."

"Will you?" Dylan asked, sounding like an uncertain child.

"Of course, my love. I couldn't have done any of this without you. We'll be free soon. Together forever. But you have to keep your head and do everything I tell you."

"I will. I am," Dylan replied defensively. "It's just..."

"Just what?" Jade felt a prickle of apprehension.

Dylan went quiet again. Jade contemplated garrotting him. "Daisy," he blurted out. "I'm worried about her. She—"

"Oh, she's fine," Jade assured him airily. "We'll all be together soon." She glossed over that inconsequential problem in favour of changing the subject. "How's Angel?"

"Still sleeping," Dylan said. Jade could hear the bed squeaking under his huge bulk, which meant he was checking on her. "She looks pale though," he added worriedly. "I think she needs a bit of fresh air. Me mum always said a bit of fresh air would put the colour back in my cheeks."

"Dylan..." Jade tried very hard not to scream.

"I could take her to my house as well, if you like. It wouldn't matter if she cried there, and—"

"Dylan! No!" Jade stopped him in his excited flow, and then sighed inwardly as Poppy's bedroom door squeaked open. She scowled at the child, who was peering at her through the crack in the door with one eye. It was like something from a horror movie, it really was. "I have to go. If she wakes up, just give her more Tylenol," she said to Dylan, and rang off.

Poppy backed away as Jade advanced towards the door, as if she were some kind of evil witch.

Irked, Jade thrust the door open and marched in. The room was an absolute pigsty, as usual, spoiled little brat. "Your mother wants you in the bedroom." She gestured her that way. "And behave." She glowered at the girl as she skirted around her, her silly Peppa Pig clutched babyishly to her chest. "Or I'll eat your fucking goldfish."

CHAPTER SEVENTY-TWO

MARK

"For Christ's sake, they're websites!" Sweat prickling his forehead and saturating his shirt, Mark dragged his hands exasperatedly over his face and got to his feet. "Anyone could have accessed them!" He looked desperately from Edwards, seated at his desk, his expression impassive, to Cummings, who'd laughably been drafted in to question him.

"Right." Folding his arms, Cummings exchanged meaningful glances with Edwards. "And the image of your daughter? Someone *accessed* your computer to post that too, I suppose."

Attempting to control his temper, Mark clamped his jaw tight. He could already hear the cell door clanging shut behind him. "That was *not* taken by me!" he said, his patience fast evaporating. Could they not see the fucking obvious here? That, if he hadn't taken it, then someone else had. Someone who had access to his family and his home computer. Someone who undoubtedly now *had* his daughter. What the *hell* was the matter with them?

"Yeah, you said." Shaking his head, Cummings looked him over scathingly. "So, leaving the Category A pornographic images of kids aside for the moment, since we're clearly not getting the right answers, perhaps you could explain this?" He picked up a piece of paper and dangled it in Mark's direction. "And, just so you know, 'it wasn't me' won't cut it."

Mark noted the colour of the form, green. "A speeding fine?"

"Correct." Cummings smiled superciliously. "Clocked up at two in the morning"—he paused, smirking as he held Mark's gaze—"in the heart of the red-light district. So much for the father of the year award, hey, Cain. Play classical music while you're doing the business, do you?"

Mark stared incredulously at him. "No way," he said vehemently, his heart rate spiking as he realised he was being set up from all angles. "I haven't been anywhere near there—on or off duty."

"We have photographic evidence, DI Cain," said Edwards, still watching him in that supposedly non-judgemental way he had. But the pen he was tapping rapidly on his desk and the fact that he was addressing him formally told Mark he was being judged—and found guilty. Of *this*. "CCTV images," Edwards went on, now eyeing him steadily, as he leaned back in his chair.

He waited.

Mark kneaded his forehead. He didn't answer. How could he, other than to say *It wasn't me*?

"We also have a photograph which shows you apparently assaulting a sex worker," Edwards added, laying the pen down on his desk, as if demonstrating that he'd considered the facts and found him guilty. "Do you have an explanation for that?"

Tanya Stevens. Mark fixed his gaze hard on Cummings. "Provided by?" he asked, bile rising in his throat.

"A fellow officer who felt obliged to draw my attention to it."

"I bet he did." Laughing disdainfully, Mark dragged his gaze away. "It was a different time, a different place."

"To the one you weren't in," Cummings added drolly.

Mark looked contemptuously back at him. "You bastard," he seethed, fury burning impotently inside him.

Cummings nodded, almost imperceptibly, a smirk playing at the corner of his mouth as he turned to perch himself on the edge of Edwards' desk. "Bit of a shitty thing to do, wasn't it,

DI Cain, using your wife's car to fuck prostitutes? Get off on it, do you?"

His wife's? Mark was confused, for a split second. She'd had access to that too. Access to their lives and everything in it. Free access to Mel and Poppy, while he was being detained for Christ knew how long. "I have to get out of here," he said, his stomach knotting painfully. "I need to leave."

"You should know we've called in a forensic specialist to examine the car, DI Cain," Edwards said dispassionately.

"A *forensic?*" Mark was astounded. "Looking for what?" he asked, his panic escalating.

Edwards didn't answer.

"You've been on top of the Daisy Evans case from the outset, haven't you, Cain?" said Cummings. "Obsessed, almost." He paused, as Mark's shocked gaze shot back to his. "One can't help but wonder, given your... shall we say, sexual preferences... were you obsessed with finding her, or making sure no one else did?"

Mark felt the blood drain from his face. "Are you serious?" He looked in utter disbelief between the two men.

"We've been doing some digging," said Cummings. "Had a difficult childhood, didn't you, DI Cain? Abused at the hands of your father. That must have been hard to deal with."

Now he *had* to be joking. Mark shook his head, repulsed by the man and the implication. "Not in the way you're implying," he said, his throat tight, his voice calm.

"Really?" Cummings' accusing gaze strayed to his. "Still fucked you up, though, didn't it, DI Cain?"

"This is *crazy!*" Mark clenched his fists. "You're way out of order, Cummings, and you know it!" He was now dangerously close to exploding.

"Getting a bit irate, DI Cain? Not thinking of getting physical again, are we?" The perverse pleasure Cummings was taking in this was written all over his face.

Mark was close, too close, to taking a swing at him, and the bastard knew it.

"Back off, DS Cummings," Edwards ordered, his expression now one of complete disillusionment as he stared at Mark. "We found something in the car, DI Cain," he informed him solemnly.

"Such as?" Mark asked, his throat dry, his mind racing as he ran through the possibilities, blood being the most likely.

"One of Daisy's shoes," Cummings provided. "How did that get there, Cain? I mean, one would assume you'd never met the girl before she went missing."

Oh, sweet fucking Jesus, no. The news hit Mark like a thunderclap. This wasn't happening. It couldn't be. *Please, God, don't let this be happening.*

"No doubt the forensics examination will yield more," Cummings added.

"Do you have *anything* to offer in your defence, DI Cain?" Edwards asked him, agitatedly. "Anything at all that might give me pause for thought before cautioning you?"

Reeling, Mark swiped at the perspiration tickling his forehead. Mel had obviously handed over his computer. Gulping back his nausea, Mark recalled the hatred in her eyes, the way she'd looked at him when she'd believed him capable of manipulating her, drugging her, kerb-crawling, for fuck's sake. And now this. She wouldn't alibi him. She couldn't. He'd been sleeping on the sofa. Panic now tightening his gut like a vice, Mark closed his eyes.

"You've been having a few problems at home, haven't you, DI Cain?" Cummings went on matter-of-factly. "Arguments, concerning the children? Are they yours, DI Cain? Or was your wife claiming they weren't so you didn't try for custody?"

Mark eyed him, completely bewildered.

"Just wondering," he said, shrugging, "whether it might explain why your daughter's gone missing."

"Where is she, DI Cain?" Edwards asked quietly. "Where's Evie?"

"Jade," Mark squeezed the word past the parched lump in his throat, his emotions going into free-fall as he realised where this was leading, "I have to find her," he said throatily, turning for the door.

"Jade. This would be the girl who says you raped her?" said Cummings.

Feeling as if an express train had just slammed into him, Mark stopped dead in his tracks. She was framing him, knocking nails into his coffin, one by one, and he could do *nothing*? He hadn't got a snowball in hell's chance of convincing anyone that he'd had no part in any of this. *Christ.* His baby? His family?

He needed to get out of here. A sluggish pulse beating prophetically at the base of his neck, he continued towards the door.

"You really are a lowlife piece of scum, aren't you, Cain?" Cummings said disgustedly. "Spouting your holier-than-thou crap. Lording it over everyone, hiding your sick perversions—"

"Enough!" Edwards cut him short. "DI Cain, you might like to take this opportunity to call a solicitor."

Mark sucked in a breath, knowing what was coming next.

"Mark Cain, we are legally obliged to inform you that we are arresting you on suspicion of child abduction and offences contrary to the Sexual Offences Act 2003." Mark could feel Cummings' satisfaction as he cautioned him.

"You do not have to say anything, but it may harm your defence if you fail to mention when questioned something which you later rely on in court. Anything you do say may be given in evidence. Do you understand, DI Cain?"

Mark nodded slowly, his jaw clamped tight. "I need to go,"

he rasped, reaching for the door despite knowing he stood no chance of getting through it and out of the station.

Cummings was on him in a second, locking an arm tight around his neck. "You're going *nowhere*, mate," he snarled in his ear.

Two officers bursting through the door to flank him either side, Mark tried to stay upright as Cummings landed a vicious blow to his side.

Mark stopped struggling as he was manhandled through the main office, the hostile glances of his supposed colleagues telling him all he needed to know. In their eyes, he really was the lowest of the low. His only hope was Lisa, who knew him almost as well as his wife did—or had. Mark prayed harder than he'd ever prayed as he was escorted past where she stood amidst the audience who'd gathered for the show, wilting with relief as he noted her expression. Not open disdain. Confusion, but not repugnance.

Mark didn't speak. He doubted he could get the words past the fractured pieces of his heart, which were now wedged like shards of glass in his windpipe. He prayed again instead, that Lisa would read the desperation in his eyes.

Lisa nodded. "I'm on it, sir," she said simply.

CHAPTER SEVENTY-THREE

JADE

Jade had to work at maintaining her façade as she assured the family liaison officer at the door that Melissa was fine, that she was sleeping and that she would be here for her when she woke. A thought had occurred to her: Mark might well have been charged by now, in which case it was possible police would soon be crawling all over the house like flies over dog shit, searching for evidence. Something else was worrying her, too: her conversation with drippy Dylan. She hadn't been able to properly concentrate, what with the brat peering at her through the crack in the door. He'd said something about taking Angel to his house. He'd also said "as well." What had he meant? God, the man was a liability. If he'd got it into his thick skull to do anything off his own bat, she'd boil his balls and make him eat them.

The officer finally handed her a card and told her she'd call back. Jade smiled sweetly, closed the door calmly and then turned to the stairs spitting with rage.

Everything had been going nicely to plan, albeit an alternative plan, and now she was under pressure. She needed to get this done. She needed to get out of here and get to Dylan, who infuriatingly wasn't answering his phone, before the moron messed everything up.

Mounting the stairs, her eyes fixed upwards, her mind on the woman who'd stolen her life, Jade didn't notice the dog until it emitted a low growl behind her. Would the stupid beast not just lie down and die? Seething, Jade carefully back-stepped. And then laughed. The pathetic animal's attempt at a snarl was more a drool, disgusting creature. She noted the whites of its eyes as the dog's eyes rolled, the distinctly wobbly legs. "*Awww*, what's the matter, Hercules? Did the drugs make you feel poorly, hmm? Can't you make it upstairs? Tough *shit*!"

Lunging forward, Jade caught hold of the dog by the collar and heaved it through the kitchen to the back door. She might have been impressed by its loyalty, its heroic attempts to dig its claws in, if it hadn't snapped its head around and bitten her.

Now she was annoyed. *Very*. Assisting the animal out with a vicious kick, Jade slammed the back door and returned to the stairs, blood popping through the teeth marks on her wrist.

Flinging the bedroom door open, Jade locked eyes with the brat, who immediately scurried closer to her mother, as if the woman was capable of doing anything other than lie slumped on the bed. She was still attempting to keep her eyes open, Jade noted, her fuse fizzling steadily. She was obviously fighting the drugs. *Silly bitch*. Could she not just get it into her head that it was time to give up? This was *her* bed. It was *her* man the slut had been sleeping next to. It was time Melissa learned a few home truths, since she was insisting on being so bloody obstinate.

"Out!" Jade glared at Poppy, enough fire in her eyes to let the brat know she meant business. "Now, or there'll be trouble." Eyeballing the girl meaningfully, she waited while, sniffling irritatingly, Poppy shuffled off the bed to sidle to the door, where she paused to look pleadingly back at her.

Heartbreaking, it really was. Jade smiled nastily, and then tipped her head back, raised her hand and made swallowing goldfish gestures that had the brat scuttling out in a flash.

Turning back, Jade walked across to the bed, her brow furrowed in concern. "Oh dear, you haven't drunk your medicine," she said, looking down at the cold tea on the bedside table.

Melissa tried to raise herself.

She was a fighter, Jade conceded wearily, pushing her back down. "Not to worry," she said, leaning down to peer into Melissa's pretty green eyes, noting the hugely dilated pupils with satisfaction, "you've had enough to ensure you sleep soundly. I'd give in to it, if I were you. The alternative might not be very pleasant. Still, on the bright side, at least you won't have any more nightmares."

Clearly as stubborn as her brat child, the woman stirred again, attempting to lift her rusty-haired head from the pillow. "Mark. Where's Mark?" she mumbled, wiping the smile from Jade's face in an instant.

"Bitch!" Jade spat, bringing her hand back to slap the slut's face hard. "He doesn't want you! Haven't you seen what's been going on right under your nose? *Stupid* cow! It's *me* he wants." Placing a hand the other side of Melissa, she glared down at her, almost eyeball to eyeball with her. "*Me* he's been fucking, for months. Right here, in *this* bed."

Her chest heaving with anger, Jade jabbed a finger into the pillow right next to the woman's face. "Anywhere and every-where, and every which way. In the nursery, Poppy's room, the kitchen, the lounge, even your precious fucking workshop," she snarled, making sure to paint a graphic picture for the useless cow to contemplate as she drifted off.

Melissa attempted to focus on her, but couldn't, finally clos-ing her eyes as the truth sank in.

Satisfied, but not finished, Jade straightened up. "He needs a real woman, a proper mother for his kids," she went on, driving Melissa's failures home, "not some whingeing, weak, pot-making freak."

Jade curled her lip in contempt as Melissa made a last valiant attempt to sit up, groping sideways as she did, presumably in search of her phone. Sadly, it was just out of reach. Calmly, Jade nudged it away.

"Useless." She sighed, and then turned away, humming. *Hush, little baby, don't you cry...* She headed to the dressing table, extracting a piece of paper from her pocket as she went. It was a nice touch, Jade thought. A goodbye note addressed to Poppy, showing the poor little mite her mother's last thoughts were with her.

Jade smoothed it out carefully, and then, smiling at her own thoughtfulness, she turned back to help Melissa finish her tea.

CHAPTER SEVENTY-FOUR

LISA

Instinct telling her to proceed with caution, Lisa peered through the lounge window. Poppy was standing in the middle of the room, one hand twisting her hair into tight ringlets, her thumb plugged in her mouth. Lisa tapped lightly on the glass. Finally managing to attract the little girl's attention, she smiled encouragingly and gestured towards the front door.

Peering through the letter flap, Lisa mentally crossed her fingers as Poppy cautiously approached. The girl looked traumatised. She desperately didn't want to scare her. "Hello, Poppet," she whispered, hoping to put her at her ease. "Where's Mummy, sweetheart?"

"Sleeping," Poppy said, around the thumb she was still sucking nervously on.

Leaving her daughter wandering around on her own? Whatever shit Mel had been through, however depressed she was supposed to be, the Mel Lisa knew would never do that.

"I need to see her, Poppy, urgently. Do you understand?"

Poppy nodded. Her eyes were full of trepidation. Picturing her own daughter at that age, feeling how she was feeling, Lisa prayed inwardly. "Do you think you could be a big girl, Poppy, and help me?"

Again, Poppy nodded.

"Good girl," Lisa said. "I need you to open the door, Poppy. Can you reach it?"

Poppy gave another short nod, before she promptly turned around and scooted towards the kitchen.

Not sure where she'd gone, or whose unwanted attention she might attract, Lisa prayed harder, and then blew out a sigh of relief as Poppy reappeared, dragging a chair slowly but determinedly behind her. "I have to do the bolt," she said.

Minutes later, Lisa was in, immediately crouching to pull Poppy into a hug. "Well done. Daddy will be so proud of you," she said, close to her ear. "Now, I need you to do something else for me, Poppy."

Taking her personal mobile from her pocket, Lisa eased back, holding the little girl's gaze with a reassuring one of her own. "I want you to go to the lounge and stay there. If you hear or see anything that worries you, I want you to press nine three times on my phone, and then the green call button. Can you do that?"

"Uh-huh." Poppy's nod was resolute.

"Show me where the nine is, honey." Lisa held the phone up and Poppy duly pointed.

"Good girl," Lisa said, a wave of relief washing through her. "Tell them who you are and don't end the call until Daddy's friends get here. Promise?"

"Promise." Poppy crossed her heart.

Hoping to God she would be safer there than wandering about outside on her own, Lisa steered her gently in the direction of the lounge, quickly checked the other downstairs rooms— the kitchen, downstairs cloakroom and study—and then made her way quietly upwards. Poppy's bedroom door was open; the nursery door too. That room was empty, obviously. Lisa's heart constricted.

The main bedroom door was closed. Beyond that was Jade's room, she assumed. The door was ajar, too tempting an invitation for a detective. Praying a floorboard wouldn't squeak at the crucial moment, Lisa headed that way, aiming to have covered all bases before going into Mel's bedroom.

Jade's things were still there, everything neat and tidy. Way too tidy. Lisa noted the lipsticks on the dresser, lined up like soldiers on parade, the bed made up to hospital standards. Bypassing the dresser in favour of the wardrobe, Lisa flicked through the few clothes hanging there; Mel's mostly, apart from the skimpy babysitting gear the girl was fond of wearing.

Lisa glanced upwards. Seeing a shoebox on the top shelf, she checked over her shoulder and then lifted it quietly out. It was stuffed full of memorabilia—pieces of jewellery, odd bits of make-up, a few old photographs. Lisa wasn't surprised, until she came across one photograph in particular: a little girl, aged around four. A little girl Lisa wasn't likely to forget. But she was very much alive in this picture, giggling as she posed with her older sister, a one-eyed Pooh Bear clutched close to her chest.

Lisa dug deeper, finding a stash of what she recognised as antipsychotic drugs. Her blood ran cold.

A sick feeling in her gut, in her soul, Lisa turned, charging towards the main bedroom. Pausing only long enough to register Melissa lying unmoving on the bed, she sprinted across the room, fumbling to call it in as she went. Shaking Melissa with one hand, she'd got as far as telling the police operator they needed to check out the babysitter when an almighty crack to the back of the skull cut her call short.

CHAPTER SEVENTY-FIVE

JADE

Maybe those crappy sculptures weren't so useless, after all. Jade watched fascinatedly as the blood oozed from the copper's wound, staining the cream carpet a deep crimson. Served her right, interfering cow. Jade had no doubt DI Moyes, with her suspicious eyes, had fancied shagging Mark. She wouldn't be shagging him now, would she?

Jade gave the hopeless policewoman a prod with her foot and then, satisfied she wouldn't be causing any more trouble, she turned towards the door. Some women really were complete bitches, happy to hop into bed with a man knowing full well he was already taken.

Time to clean up, she supposed. Get rid of the whole sorry mess.

CHAPTER SEVENTY-SIX

MARK

Mark had had enough of being questioned, cross-questioned and clearly disbelieved. "Charge me or let me go," he demanded, challenging Edwards as he came back into the interview room.

"Sit down, DI Cain," Edwards said, glancing down at the table, ostensibly to pick up his papers. "Your claims will be investigated, along with everything else. Meanwhile, try to stay calm."

Mark stared incredulously at him. "My daughter's missing!" he shouted, his anger way off the scale. "I'm stuck here, about to be remanded into custody for serious offences I didn't commit, while I believe my family to be in danger, and you want me to sit down and stay *calm*?"

Edwards turned to walk back out without uttering another word. Had he despatched anyone to his house yet? Even forensics pulling the place apart would be better than Mel and Poppy there on their own. Was he doing *anything*? Mark dragged a hand furiously over his neck. *Fuck it*, he thought, heading towards the door after Edwards, only to find Cummings blocking his way.

"Move." Mark eyed him levelly.

Cummings smiled flatly. "You're under arrest, Cain. You know how this works. You're going nowhere." He grabbed hold of Mark's arm and attempted to shove him towards the seat. That did it. Blind fury driving him, Mark shoved him, hard.

Caught off guard, Cummings stumbled, crashing heavily to the floor. "You *prat*," he growled, heaving himself upright.

Mark clenched his fist at his side, itching to punch the bastard's lights out as Cummings advanced on him. "Don't," he warned him.

"And who's going to stop me? You?" Cummings taunted. "Finally lost it, haven't we, Cain? Knew you would, eventually. Didn't have to do much other than wait around, did I?"

Mark looked him over, making no attempt to hide the contempt in his eyes. "Like falsify evidence, you mean? You're a fucking disgrace, Cummings."

"That's rich," Cummings sneered, "coming from someone who gets his kicks fiddling with kids. I would say your own kids, but you don't know they *are* yours, do you?"

Mark narrowed his eyes. Where was this shit coming from?

"So why rape the babysitter?" Cummings asked, goading him on. Just couldn't resist, could he, the arrogant prick. "I'd have thought she wouldn't do it for you, given she's over the age of consent?"

"Does it for you though, doesn't she, Cummings? Did she make this allegation before or after you two had had sex, I wonder?" Mark put two and two together and presumably got a correct four, judging by the now smug look on the other man's face. "You really are a gullible git, Cummings. She's been using you, feeding you information. Wrong information. Do you honestly think she wanted you for your sexual prowess?"

Cummings smiled languidly, still every inch the cocky bastard he was. "At least I don't have to resort to raping women and kids."

Mark clenched his jaw. "You'll get yours, Cummings. It's only a matter of time before someone realises you're lifting drugs from the evidence room."

Cummings shrugged indifferently. "Nothing major. No one's

likely to miss it. I must admit you did put the wind up me a couple of times. You got way too close to catching me in the act when I picked up Tanya Stevens."

"Which is why *you* assaulted her presumably?" Mark asked casually. "Distraction technique?"

Cummings smirked. "Worked, didn't it?"

"It might have done, Cummings," DCI Edwards said calmly behind him. "If you hadn't got quite so cocky with it."

Paling, Cummings shot around to face him. "It was self-defence, sir," he said quickly. "I had to use force to restrain her. She—"

"Out!" Edwards ordered him.

Cummings hesitated for a second, then, noting the livid look in Edwards' eye, stepped past him and walked apprehensively towards the door.

"Mark." Edwards looked at him, his expression not quite so openly scathing as it had been. "The doctor's arrived." He glanced awkwardly away again. "If you're ready?"

"Would it make any difference if I wasn't?" Mark asked him disappointedly.

There was definitely sympathy in the man's eyes now, probably because he was about to undergo the humiliation of being swabbed, prodded and poked. But when Edwards turned to the door, it was to find a uniform barrelling into him from the other side.

"Sorry, sir," the man said quickly. "Moyes called in. DS Moyes. The call was cut short, but she said something about a babysitter? There's also been an emergency call. A little girl. We managed to keep her on the line for a while. Looks like she was calling from the same location."

His house. Mark's blood froze in his veins.

CHAPTER SEVENTY-SEVEN

JADE

"There you are." Jade smiled down at Poppy, crouched behind the chair, her knees tucked up to her chin. "My, you were hard to find," Jade said kindly, moving to heave the armchair away from the corner and flush the little brat out.

Extending her hand, her smile frozen on her face, Jade waited.

Obviously realising there was no way to hide, Poppy reluctantly emerged, plugging her thumb into her mouth and nervously taking Jade's hand. Was the poor little mite worried about her mum, Jade wondered, or her soon-to-be-boiled goldfish? Her goldfish, more than likely. The child was just like Melissa, self-centred, no thought for anyone but herself.

"Good girl." Squeezing her hand, Jade led her across to the sofa, where she could keep an eye on her while she attended to the business of cleaning up. "Now, you stay there while I get a nice warm fire going, and then we can go for a little walk in the fresh air. How does that sound?"

Poppy didn't answer. Jade let it pass. She was obviously tired. It was way past her bedtime.

"She really is a careless cow, your mum, leaving all these hazardous materials lying around in her workshop." Jade chatted companionably to the girl, sprinkling liberally as she did. "Lord knows what she was thinking. I mean, white spirits, on a low shelf? Honestly, it's a wonder social services didn't cart you off years ago. Being a drink-addled druggy's no excuse for child abuse, is it?"

The first armchair thoroughly doused, Jade walked across to the other, smiling reassuringly at Poppy as she went. "You're better off without her, my love, and that deceitful father of yours. Trust me, having no parents is better than having abusive parents. They scar you for life."

The second armchair wet enough for her purpose, Jade ditched the bottle, picked up another containing heating oil, and headed for the sofa. "Almost done," she said cheerily, unscrewing the top, and then pausing. Cocking her head to one side, she looked the quaking girl over. No, she decided. It was tempting, but she needed the brat for insurance purposes, at least for now.

"Come on, sweetheart," she said, offering Poppy her hand. "Let's get you out in the fresh air. These fumes really aren't any good for you." Tsk-ing at the irresponsibility of a mother who would expose a child to this, let alone the clay and glaze dusts, which must surely be highly toxic, Jade poured out the last of the oil and led the little girl to the safety of the hall.

"Stay," she ordered. "If you move, I'll saw your feet off."

The girl let out a ragged sob. Jade sighed, pulled her matches from her jeans pocket, and held onto her patience. It wasn't her fault she was the product of her dysfunctional parents, she supposed.

"Here we go," she said, bending as she struck the match, watching the flame dancing in the little girl's watery eyes.

Mesmerised for a second, Jade jumped to her feet before the match burned down, and then, tingling with anticipation, she tossed it into the lounge. "*Whoosh,*" she whispered, closing her eyes, a thrill rushing through her as it caught.

Jade hesitated, making sure the flames leapt and furled before pulling the door to. "It's going to be the most beautiful bonfire ever. Much bigger than the others I made. There's lots of wood in your house, you see," she confided conspiratorially to Poppy, taking her hand firmly in her own. "I'll let you get closer to the next one," she promised.

The girl was crying in earnest now, gulping back huge snotty sobs as Jade led her to the front door.

She'd feel better after a good cry. Not that Jade ever had. She'd stopped crying once she'd realised tears were pointless when there was no one who cared enough to hear them.

"You really need to feel the heat of the fire on your face to realise the true cleansing beauty of it," she said, attempting to mollify the child as she pulled the front door open—and then stopped, fury uncoiling inside her as she saw several blue lights rotating outside. The interfering bitch upstairs had got her call through.

Jade's faced darkened as she watched another squad car screeching towards the house, her supposed hero spilling from the passenger door as it careered to a halt halfway across the lawn.

"Too late, copper," Jade spat, clutching Poppy's hand tighter and stepping back.

CHAPTER SEVENTY-EIGHT

MARK

Undiluted terror gripped Mark's stomach as he took in the scene before him in surreal slow motion. Splintering wood. He could hear beams falling. Hear his house burning.

Windows shattering. Flames crackling. People shouting. Sirens screaming. His daughter's cries—he sucked in a breath, couldn't breathe out—they reached inside him and ripped his heart right out of his chest.

He tumbled forwards, his emotions colliding, his world exploding.

And then he ran.

Wrestling free of the arms that tried to hold him back, ignoring his DCI yelling behind him, he ran.

He kicked at the door, ramming his shoulder, his whole body weight against it—"Give, you fucking thing!"—and then he was in. Falling into the hall, choking back the fumes that seared the back of his throat, he righted himself, pressing his arm to his mouth as he made his way through the smoke to the stairs.

Noting the open doors on the landing, he didn't pause, but he prayed, a prayer that came from his soul, as he crashed into the main bedroom, his lungs raw from the effort of trying to breathe. Needing to assess the situation, to think strategically through the debilitating panic, Mark closed the door to buy some time, and registered the horror in front of him.

Lisa, facedown on the floor, bleeding from a head wound, unconscious at best.

Poppy...alive. Mark silently thanked God. She was sobbing, tugging hard on Mel's arm. "Mummy, please, you *have* to get out of bed."

Mel was barely responsive.

A potent mixture of fear and fury raging inside him, Mark snapped his gaze to the tall casement window where, standing precariously on the ledge, her back to the concrete drive twenty long feet below, was Jade. The smile on her face was triumphant, her movements controlled. She knew that Mark knew he had a decision to make: her or his wife? If she fell, if she died, his baby's whereabouts would die with her.

Mark took a faltering step forwards. She edged dangerously back.

"Don't do this, Jade," Mark begged her, his voice hoarse. "Please, don't do this."

"*Why?*" she snarled. Her face, illuminated by the sweeping blue lights outside, was twisted with rage. "Because you *care*?"

"I care." Marked took another cautious step. "I care very much. You need help, Jade. Please, let me—"

"Liar! You pretended you did, but you didn't! You promised me you'd always be there. Made me an *absolute* promise. And you weren't!"

"When? Talk to me, Jade." Mark moved closer. "Tell me. I don't understand."

"Oh, here we go." Jade laughed. "The 'I'm sorry, I never meant to hurt you' crap."

"I am sorry!" Mark said, fear slicing through him afresh as she teetered. "If I did something—"

"I'd lost everything! My whole life burned to ashes! You told me it was going to be all right. You held me and you *told* me, and it wasn't! You lied to me! You left me. You left me to be with that slut of a wife because *she* was pregnant!"

Mark stopped, bewildered. There was no reasoning with her, no talking to her. She was utterly insane.

"*I* was pregnant! Made pregnant by him!"

"*Who?*" Mark shouted, groping desperately for some comprehension, some inkling of what she was talking about.

"It was *her* fault! That spoiled brat of a sister, always whining and seeking attention."

Mark ran a hand over his face. No idea what to say. What to do.

"It was only a blister from a sparkler, and she screamed like she was being murdered!" she ranted on, sounding more insane by the second. "She asked for one, over and over, she kept whining: *I want to play sparklers. I want to play sparklers.* I only gave it to her to shut her up, stop her moaning and tittle-tattling, telling tales. She *told* them I'd given it to her. She knew I'd get in trouble. She was always getting me into trouble. She told them I burned her, so I fucking well did!"

"Your sister?" *She...?* Mark reeled incredulously, as the horrific implication of her disjointed ramblings became clearer to him.

"Yes, my *sister,*" she spat. "Their perfect little princess, who could do no wrong. All of them! Tucked up in their beds, snoring away like they hadn't got a care in the world: her, Miss Goody-two-shoes, lying there with her pathetic thumb stuck in her mouth, looking like butter wouldn't melt. And *her,* that bitch-mother. She knew! She *knew* what he was doing. Every time she left me he did it, touching me, hurting me, grunting and thrusting and apologising—and that whore of a mother just let him! She took that snivelling little brat to the hospital with a tiny little blister, and she *let* him."

Oh, Jesus. Mark was beginning to see... the images from his dreams, recollections from a call-out he could never quite forget. A little girl curled into a foetal ball in her child-sized bed, her one-eyed Pooh Bear clutched close to her chest. Her older sister, still dressed in her unicorn-print pyjamas when they'd found her, had been shaking from head to foot. Her cheeks, smeared in soot from the fire, had been tear-stained, her cognac-coloured eyes wide and utterly petrified.

Mark swallowed hard. *Grace.*

"You burned them alive?" Astounded, he searched her face, looking for some shred of conscience, some indication she understood the horrendous thing she'd done, was doing.

"I hurt them like they hurt me! I went to the kitchen, and I struck the match and I killed them. And you said it would be all right. You pretended you cared. But you didn't! You're all the same, liars! Users and abusers," she screamed, over a deafening crash from the landing.

The stairs going? Mark kept his gaze on hers, prayed it wasn't. Sweat wetting his eyelashes, pooling at the base of his neck, he tried to focus as the lightbulbs popped. His heart was thundering so loudly he could almost hear it above the cacophony of sirens outside. He risked another step towards her.

Jade twisted around, ready to jump.

"Jade, wait! What happened to her?" Mark shouted urgently. "Your baby. What happened to her? *Tell* me. Make me understand."

"*Hah!*" Jade laughed cynically. "As if you could."

"Try me," Mark begged.

Jade didn't speak for a second. "I thought she was an alien growing inside me," she said quietly. "But she wasn't. She was beautiful. So tiny. Blue. Her skin was tinged blue."

Premature? Oxygen starvation? Mark felt another violent twist in his chest.

"I knew God would take her for an angel when she died. I sang to her when her eyes closed...*Hush, little baby, don't you cry*...She smiled at me. I'm sure she did. My perfect little Angel. I knew she'd come back to me."

"Evie." Full realisation finally dawning, Mark almost choked the word out.

"Angel!" Jade glared back at him, her eyes smouldering with hatred. "*You* abandoned me. Tried to take her away from me. I have nothing to live for without her. Now she'll die too. And when she does, remember it was *you* who killed her, Mark Cain."

Mark didn't dare move, other than to brace himself and pray harder as she moved closer to the edge.

"I'll see you in hell," she snarled.

Intent on her aim, she didn't notice the hand snaking around her ankle, her calf.

The woman whose child she'd stolen wasn't about to let her go.

"Hell can wait for you, Jade."

CHAPTER SEVENTY-NINE

JADE

He'd grabbed her. Wrapped his hand around the waist and yanked her away from the window. He'd hurt her. Curled into a ball in the corner where he'd flung her, Jade watched as he handed the brat down through the window. He didn't even glance in her direction as he helped needy Melissa out. She was protesting, of course, whingeing, always whingeing, wanting her precious little baby.

Jade couldn't believe it when he walked past her to gather the policewoman from the floor, the scheming cow who wouldn't have hesitated to steal him from her. Carefully, he carried her to the window, searching her face, as if he was already in love with her, the bastard. It was *she* who needed him. She was choking to death. Couldn't he hear her?

Finally, he turned his attention to her, and Jade shrank back. His breathing laboured, his expression pure thunder, he simply stared at her. There was no compassion in his eyes, nothing. He didn't move to help her when she coughed again—so hard, she was sure her lungs would turn inside out. He barely flinched when the door cracked, and thick grey smoke furled further into the room.

Jade looked frantically towards it. She was going to burn. He was going to let her. Her skin would be blackened and blistered, her eyes would pop. *Oh God…* "Mark?" she croaked, her throat parched and sore from the fumes.

"Where is she?" Mark spoke quietly, his eyes never leaving hers. "Evie, where is she?"

Jade looked at him, pleadingly, beseechingly. She couldn't tell. He must know that. If she did, he would have no reason to save her.

Jade's thoughts were cut short as the door blew. "Mark!" she screamed, as hungry flames rushed petrifyingly towards her.

CHAPTER EIGHTY

MARK

She was barely recognisable as the young girl he'd met eight long years before. An innocent young girl, Mark had thought, and one he'd inadvertently sent out the wrong signals to. She'd obviously had cosmetic surgery as she grew older. Disguised her striking cognac-coloured eyes with blue lenses. She'd been beautiful—on the outside. Broken on the inside. Whether from birth? No one would ever know the workings of a mind that had compelled a young girl to burn her family alive.

There was nothing for him here. The doctors had confirmed cerebral hypoxia from the fire, meaning that, if she survived, lack of oxygen to the brain would result in severe and permanent damage. Despite the full-scale investigation now underway, with absolutely nothing to go on, they weren't likely to find Evie. Mark knew it, but he hadn't said so to Mel. He'd hardly spoken to her, desperate though he was to hear her voice, which had always seemed to anchor him in his darkest moments. He'd been too scared to, knowing it would be a conversation he couldn't bear. She was never likely to forgive him for doubting her, judging her, readily accepting a diagnosis that was wrong. Being involved, albeit unknowingly, in a plan to drive her steadily out of her mind. Accusing her, and then getting so paralytic himself he'd allowed a woman to take advantage of him, manipulating him to the point where he was the accused, locked up like the worst kind of criminal while…He didn't dare imagine what might be happening to Evie. Melissa could never forgive him that. He would never forgive himself.

Swallowing back the grief and guilt weighing too heavily in his chest, Mark turned away from Grace's hospital bed. He didn't really know why he'd come. To see with his own eyes, he supposed. He'd tried to save her, blistering his hands and his arms dragging her out, but it had been too late. He'd gone over that until he'd driven himself almost out of his mind. Lisa had tried to reassure him, telling him she could never have been truly saved. It didn't help. The fact was, crucial seconds had sealed her fate. Sealed his baby's fate.

He couldn't undo it. Couldn't make any of it right. Jade, Grace, whoever she was, had achieved her aim. She'd set out to have him or destroy him, and he'd assisted her every step of the way. *He'd* killed Evie. He was the one who'd destroyed his family.

Kneading the back of his neck, exhausted—sleep only came now to torment him, Mark was deep in thought as he walked the length of the hospital corridor, thinking now about Poppy. He'd let her down too, failed in his most fundamental obligation as a father to protect her. The child psychiatrist had been hopeful, but Mark wondered whether she would ever recover completely from her nightmare. She'd need lots of support and reassurance, and to know without doubt that she was loved. Mark had plenty of that to offer her, so much it hurt. But how was he going to love her from a distance? He'd have to, but how would Poppy cope? She'd locked her arms around his neck and sobbed when he'd told her he had to leave, after visiting her at the Chandlers' house, which was where Mel was staying. How would his little girl know he wasn't deserting her again?

Heading into the reception area, Mark didn't hear Lisa at first, calling him across the foyer. He barely acknowledged her when she yelled, "Oi, superhero, look up." In other circumstances, Mark might have smiled. His new label down at the station was better than "paedo scum," he supposed, but Mark really didn't feel like a hero. He'd saved Mel and Poppy, but part of his family was missing. Part of himself was missing.

"Mark!" Lisa yelled, clearly determined to get his attention. "I know you have a lot on your mind, but will you please stop feeling so sorry for yourself."

Not sure he was hearing her right, Mark snapped his gaze up.

"There's someone here to see you," Lisa said, a teasing smile on her face as she approached him. "I've got a feeling you might want to see her too."

Following her gaze, Mark's dormant heart kicked to life in his chest. The woman he loved, had always loved, would always love, was walking towards him. And in her arms, nestled close to her breast, was his baby daughter.

Mel stopped and offered Evie to him. She opened her mouth to speak, but faltered as Mark gathered Evie into his arms, neither much caring that they were crying openly in front of an audience.

"They were left in the foyer at Herefordshire Hospital Reception," Lisa explained. "Evie's been checked over. She's fine, but—"

"Wait..." Mark tried to process. "They?"

"Daisy. She's alive." Lisa squeezed his arm. "Barely, but there's a chance. Her parents are with her now. Obviously, they'll need some support. Social services will make an assessment of her home situation, but... She's found, Mark."

Mark tugged in a tight breath, blinked hard and looked heavenwards.

"There's more," said Lisa. "We found Jade's baby. Buried in a shallow grave in her grandmother's garden. It looks as if she was born prematurely. Her grandmother died suddenly, apparently, from a fall. As Grace stood to gain from an inheritance, we're looking further into that."

Mark nodded. Despite all that had happened, he still felt sick to his soul that Grace had been abused so consistently as a child. That her circumstances had gone unnoticed, meaning she'd never received the help she obviously desperately needed.

Lisa paused, waiting while Mark caught up. "Whether she played a part in that, or not, she was sick, Mark. Or else pure evil. None of what happened was your fault."

"I know," Mark said throatily. Truthfully, though, he would always wonder whether he could have helped her more, followed up on her progress after visiting her at the hospital, been there should she need someone to talk to, as he'd promised he would.

"Go home, Mark," Lisa urged him. "Your family's waiting."

Mark looked down at his daughter, and then turned to his wife. And he knew. Seeing the look in her beautiful green eyes, the colour of ferns after the rain...there was hope.

"I'll leave you three to it," Lisa said, turning to give Mel a hug and then sauntering off looking quite pleased with herself. "Oh." She turned back. "Take your time, but when you've kissed and made up, do you think you could collect your dog? She's adorable, but she's giving my kids ideas."

Lisa rolled her eyes and carried on, as Mark and Mel ignored her in favour of beginning the healing process.

CHAPTER EIGHTY-ONE

DYLAN

Dylan watched from his truck as Mark Cain and his wife left by the front entrance of the hospital. "I think Jade might have lied to me," he said, seeing how the man gazed lovingly down at little Angel as he carried her. How his wife kissed his cheek and then threaded an arm around his waist and leaned her head against his shoulder. "Do you think she lied to me?" he almost shouted, glancing upwards.

She didn't answer him. He didn't expect her to. That was okay. He knew his mum was watching over him. She always had.

Watching them walk to their car, Dylan ran a hand hard under his nose. "It doesn't matter. I still love her," he said, with a determined nod. "And I know she loves me. She showed me how much she loves me."

Dylan thought about it and made a decision: "We need to bring Angel home. Be a proper family, just like Jade wanted."

LETTER FROM SHERYL

Dear Reader,

Thank you so much for choosing to read *The Babysitter*. I really hope you enjoyed it.

If you would like to keep up to date with my latest book news, please do sign up at the website link below. Your email address will never be shared and you can unsubscribe at any time.

www.bookouture.com/sheryl-browne

This wasn't the easiest story to write, as it does touch on subjects that some might find difficult to deal with—loss and mental issues around bereavement in particular. I tend to gravitate towards family, family dynamics and just how strong a family unit can be when faced with adversity. Yes, I do sometimes write from personal experience. Even then, though, careful research is called for in order write about such issues sensitively and honestly. I would like to thank those people who have shared their stories with me and also those people who have been there for me: my family, my friends, not least my wider circle of friends that now includes wonderful bloggers, reviewers and readers who encourage me every step of the way.

Thank you. I really could not do this without you. If you have enjoyed the book, I would love it if you could share your thoughts and write a brief review. Reviews mean the world to an author and will help a book find its wings. I would also love to hear from you via Facebook or Twitter or my website.

Keep safe everyone and happy reading.
Sheryl x

 sherylbrowne.com

SherylBrowne

 SherylBrowne.Author

ACKNOWLEDGEMENTS

I would like to offer a massive thank-you to the team at Bookouture, without whom *The Babysitter* would never have been born. Special thanks to Helen Jenner, whose patience, enthusiasm and editing skills have made the story the best it can be, and to Peta Nightingale for loving the initial idea enough to give the book its wings.

Special thanks also to Kim Nash for her quiet determination, absolute professionalism, unstinting support and belief in me, and to all the other lovely, friendly and super-supportive authors at blogger and author events organised by Kim. We share the highs and the lows and realise we have one thing in common that drives us on—our love of writing.

I owe a huge debt of gratitude to those bloggers and reviewers who have taken time to read my books, review those books and shout out endlessly for me. I so often say I couldn't do this without you. I simply couldn't. Your passion leaves me in absolute awe. Thank you! Huge thanks, too, to Shell Baker, who led me by the hand around the maze that is often Facebook groups—gave me a push in the right direction when I needed it and who works her socks off for authors.

Final thanks to every single reader out there for your tremendous support—every book sold, every positive comment and every review spurs a writer to keep on writing when the going might get tough—and to Drew, who was there, quietly encouraging his mad mother on, when it did.

One thing that I have learned from these special people around me is to never be afraid to reach out. So often when you do, you find someone has been there, and that that someone cares.

THE
AFFAIR

SHERYL BROWNE

PROLOGUE

I had never imagined what it would be like to hold a life in my hands. Once, I would have been shocked by the realisation that I was an inch away from killing someone. No more. Strangely, I feel nothing, as if I, too, am in a state of limbo, suspended in this moment, somewhere between life and inevitable death.

We're fifteen long floors up, the muted throb of the city, lit up at night, reaching me as if from another dimension. The ground below, hard and unforgiving, looms closer for an instant, as if silently urging me to let go.

Can I? I waver. Am I capable? I'd imagined, in my darkest hours, when dreams only ever came to haunt me, how lost love could drive a person to acts of despair or even madness. How cold-blooded murder might have its basis in love, or unrequited love. In being unloved, spurned or wronged. There is no other way.

I feel it, the undiluted fear emanating from the individual over whose future I have control. This person is petrified, literally: dissociated, yet aware, unable to speak, move or control their own body. Incapable. *Powerless*. Mine to do with what I will. We think that we're immortal, that nothing can touch us, but in reality, we're fragile creatures. Flesh and blood. On impact, the skull will smash like an eggshell.

Obliquely, I wonder what thoughts will occur as the body plunges, its downward trajectory stopped suddenly, violently. It's said a person's life flashes before their eyes when close to death, because the parts of the brain that store memories are among the last to shut down. Some who've had near-death experiences describe a loss of all sense of time—life events that last for a second or a century. They relive moments of sublime happiness and extreme pain, feeling also the pain they've caused others around them. I've heard it described as close to purgatory. Will this person live a century in purgatory? I hope so.

CHAPTER ONE

JUSTIN

Pulling wearily into the drive after a double shift on call at the hospital, Justin was relieved to see Alicia hadn't yet left for work. They rarely argued, preferring to talk things through. They'd come close to arguing last weekend, though, and hadn't yet resolved the issue. His issue, he'd realised. Justin hadn't much liked himself for acting like a suspicious prat and obviously upsetting her. He'd been sure he'd heard her crying in the bathroom, and that had gutted him. At the time, given he'd been inwardly fuming, he'd thought he'd been quite restrained. But thinking about it since, no matter how restrained he'd imagined himself to be, the unspoken accusation had been there, and that was bloody unfair. The last time she'd cried heartbroken tears, it had been for him, when his family had been so senselessly murdered. She'd been there unstintingly for him ever since.

She was there whenever he relived that awful night in his dreams, sweat pooling at the base of his neck and saturating the sheets beneath him. Unable to contact his parents or his sister, he'd gone to their house and let himself in with the key he still had. The first thing he'd noticed was the smashed mirror on the hall wall. Justin closed his eyes, feeling afresh the cold fear that had settled in the pit of his stomach when he'd realised the blood at the epicentre of the fractured glass belonged to his sister. She'd tried to run. Her assailant, not fit to be labelled an animal, had left her bleeding out from her knife wounds on the hall floor.

He hadn't been able to cry. He'd been numb, incapable of processing his emotions, unable to reach out to Alicia, until she'd forced him to, holding him like she would never let him go and crying with him. He had no idea what he would have done if she hadn't been there for him then. They'd not long been married. He'd been so wrapped up in his grief, he'd shut her out. She'd had every reason to walk away, yet she hadn't. He needed to apologise, end this awkwardness he'd caused between them. Grovel, if necessary. Luke was only six months old, for Christ's sake. Her sister's birthday party, which she'd needed some persuading to get dressed up to go to, had been Alicia's first night out after a complicated caesarean section that had nearly cost her and Luke their lives. What in God's name had possessed him to end up spoiling it for her?

"Whoops, sorry." He found himself apologising prematurely as he opened the front door and narrowly missed hitting her with it.

"My fault." Alicia shuffled around from where she was strapping Luke into his carrier. "I'm a bit disorganised, as you might have gathered. We're running late, as per usual." Pressing a kiss to Luke's soft, downy head, she smiled up at him, somewhat guardedly, Justin noted, which made him like himself even less, and then got to her feet.

"There are croissants in the oven. Still warm, just about. Don't forget to eat," she said, heading for the kitchen, and then back-stepping to call up the stairs, "Sophie! Clock's ticking."

"I'm coming!" Sophie yelled from her bedroom. "Do you want me to go to school naked or what?"

That would be minus her make-up, Justin gathered. Shaking his head amusedly, he crouched down to say hello to Luke, who jiggled happily and offered him a delighted, gummy smile.

"Pandemonium reigns." Justin gave him a conspiratorial smile back. "So, how're you doing, little man, hey? Keeping a low profile, I hope." Catching hold of one excitedly flailing hand, he marvelled again at the miracle of their surprise arrival. He was doing well—healthy and strong after a worrying premature birth. His mind drifted to the baby who'd undergone a complicated procedure in the early hours of the morning. Would she be strong enough to survive, he wondered? Admitted with an extradural haemorrhage caused by a head injury, and with no paediatric surgeon available, Justin had had no choice but to drain the blood off, thus reducing cranial pressure, himself. The next twenty-four hours would tell. She was a fighter though. All Justin could do now was pray she didn't succumb to any infection.

Reminding himself of all he had to be grateful for, Justin stroked Luke's peachy cheek in lieu of giving him a cuddle and got to his feet.

Massaging his aching neck, he turned tiredly to the stairs. His fifteen-year-old daughter was descending, clearly disgruntled about school days that started at such an ungodly hour they didn't allow time for her morning beauty regime.

"Good morning," said Justin, as she stomped past to pick up her schoolbag.

"It's not. It's raining," Sophie huffed moodily.

Justin smiled and waited, and sure enough, Sophie back-stepped to plant a kiss on his cheek. "Morning, Dad," she said, with a sheepish smile. "Oh." Looking him over, her forehead creased into a concerned frown. "Fun night, I take it?" she enquired, obviously noticing his weariness.

"I've had better," Justin admitted, and reached to give her shoulders a squeeze. "You'd better get a move on or you'll be getting a black mark."

"Again." Sophie mumbled, hitched her bag over her shoulder and turned to the front door.

"Do you think you could help carry something, Sophie?"

Alicia called after her, emerging from the kitchen, Luke's juice in one hand, handbag and baby bag in the other. "I'm running out of hands."

Sighing, Sophie turned back to relieve Alicia of the juice, rolling her eyes as she did.

Justin gave her a "don't push it" look, and Sophie looked suitably apologetic. "Bye. See you later," he said to Alicia, hoping she'd make proper eye contact with him.

Alicia nodded. Her smile was tremulous, her eye contact brief. Justin inwardly cursed himself again. He really had acted like an idiot, cross-questioning her because some ex–work colleague had made it obvious he was interested in her. He wished they'd had time to talk properly since, but their conflicting schedules hadn't allowed it. His, mostly. As clinical lead in accident and emergency, his job was demanding—soul-destroying, sometimes—with insane targets to meet. The rewards of helping outweighed the endless bureaucracy and the heartbreak of losing patients, but it took its toll. Double shifts were a killer, meaning their time together suffered.

He should have made time. He'd been jealous, there were no two ways about it. He'd been furious when this guy, Paul Radley, had tried to get her to dance with him, grabbing her hand and dragging her away from her sister, sliding his arm around her waist—crossing the lines, in Justin's book. Alicia had pulled away, left him standing on the dance floor, and Radley had looked nonplussed, agitated. Justin had watched him watching Alicia walk away. He'd met him at the bar afterwards and there was something…the way the guy had looked at him—a challenge in his eyes, almost. It had caused Justin to wonder, just for a second, if something had gone on between Alicia and him, possibly because he'd been preoccupied with his own problems around the same time she'd worked with Radley in financial services.

He'd ring her at work, he decided. Order some flowers to

be delivered beforehand. Hope she was available and ask if she fancied having lunch with a sad, jealous bastard. Meanwhile, if he had any hopes of being at his scintillating best, he needed to catch up on some sleep. After a demanding night, he was utterly exhausted. All he wanted to do was crawl into bed. Yawning, he climbed the stairs, tugging off his jacket as he went, and then stopped, as Sophie trudged back through the door.

Puzzled, Justin turned back. "I thought you were late?"

"I am now." Sophie sighed, with an obligatory roll of the eyes. "Mum's outside calling the breakdown service. The car won't start."

CHAPTER TWO

ALICIA

"Nope, it's not going anywhere," Justin confirmed. "You're out of petrol." He nodded towards the dash and then glanced sympathetically up at Alicia.

"Oh no." Alicia sighed inwardly. She'd been so het up when the engine had spluttered and died, she hadn't even noticed the petrol gauge. Her first job this morning was to arrange urgent accommodation for a young mother whose toddler had been assaulted by the child's father. She couldn't let that child down, or let her mother down, who wasn't much more than a child herself. With more families on their caseloads than they could cope with, there were no other social workers to cover for her. Alicia felt suddenly too close to crying the tears she'd been desperately trying to hold back since she'd realised the grave danger her own family was in, and how much Justin would hurt, her children would hurt, because of her.

Swallowing hard, she turned to the rear passenger door to start unbuckling Lucas, her precious baby boy. Justin would die to protect him, to protect Sophie. *She* would. Whatever hold Paul Radley imagined he had over her, she would kill to protect them. All of them, including her husband, who'd done nothing to deserve having the foundations of his life ripped from beneath him. Closing her eyes, she tried to still the image that Justin would see: another man's breath hot on her neck, his mouth close to her ear, whispering his love for her as he pressed himself into her, assuring her that her husband need never find out. It would destroy him. She *wouldn't* allow it. *Couldn't.*

"How long before the breakdown service gets here?" Justin asked, climbing out.

"An hour," Alicia said quietly, lifting Lucas out, easing him close to her shoulder and breathing in that special smell that binds baby and mother together forever. "Sorry, sweetheart. Mummy's been a very silly mummy, hasn't she?"

Silly and weak, and unforgivably deceitful. Her heart squeezing inside her, Alicia eased back to drink her little miracle man in, marvelling at the perfectness of him, his softly curled eyelashes, his perfect cupid lips.

"I'll drive you," Justin offered. "The only alternative is to fetch petrol from the garage and that will probably take just as long."

"It's okay, Justin," Alicia assured him, noting the dark circles under his eyes. He looked utterly exhausted. His job was demanding enough without her troubles to contend with. Her heart twisted as she thought about what he'd already had to deal with, the awful loss in his life. What he might still have to face, unless she could stop whatever was lurking, ready to twist and weave its insidious way through the fabric of their marriage.

"You've been working all night," she reminded him, as if he would need reminding. "You're possibly not even safe to drive. I could take your car." She glanced towards it. "As long as you don't need it before I get home?"

"I don't, but…" Justin looked uncertain. "You haven't driven anything but an automatic for years, Ali. I'm not sure I'd get much sleep, worrying about you having an accident."

"I'll be fine. I'll get the hang of it once I get going." Alicia waved away his concerns.

"It's a forty-minute round trip. I won't die of sleep deprivation, I promise," Justin assured her. "I'll take you. I'm only going to be texting you otherwise."

Guilt immediately lodged itself like a hard stone in Alicia's chest. He would text her. He always did, checking she'd arrived safely. *Just wanted to remind you I love you*—that was his latest subtle way of enquiring.

"Thanks." Alicia glanced away. She couldn't meet his eyes, just then. How would he cope, if he knew? Losing his family all over again—how would he ever be able to deal with it? He couldn't find out. Whatever she had to do, she had to make sure he never found out.

"Are you getting in?" Justin asked her, his head cocked bemusedly to one side as he looked her over, clearly noting her mind was elsewhere.

"Yes, sorry, miles away." Alicia turned to the door he'd opened in his own car, quickly strapped Lucas into the carrier that was already there and then hurried around to the front passenger side. "Where's Sophie?" she asked, climbing in.

"Waiting in the hall rather than get rained on," Justin supplied, smiling wryly as he climbed into the driver's side.

"Sorry about forgetting to fill it up," Alicia said, for want of something to say, as she fumbled for her seatbelt. "I meant to do it yesterday, but I completely forgot."

"I'm not surprised." Justin started the engine. "You obviously have a lot on your mind."

Alicia felt her heart thud. What did he mean?

"I did the same thing myself last week," Justin went on, clearly attempting to make her feel less incompetent, rather than make any insinuation. "It's not a problem. I can catch up on my sleep later."

"I'll have to pin a note on the fridge or put an alert on my phone or something. My head's like a sieve these days. I swear pregnancy addled my brain." Plugging in her seatbelt, Alicia babbled inconsequently, desperate to stay on safe ground.

"All done?" Justin asked her, checking she had belted up. He was always attentive in that way, making sure she was safe. That Sophie and Lucas were. Alicia had hoped to do the same for him, keep him safe, when he'd been floundering after losing his family in the cruellest possible way. A hope doomed to failure. Part of her had known that the truth would come out, causing her world to unravel. She'd ignored it. Hoped it would go away. And now Paul Radley had come back. The lie she'd told was in danger of being exposed. She couldn't ignore it. Not any longer.

"Good." Justin went quiet, and then turned to glance towards the house, presumably checking for signs of Sophie.

For a long second, silence hung heavy between them, like a yawning chasm, and then he turned back to her. The icy chill running the length of her spine told Alicia he was about to broach the subject she'd prayed he wouldn't. She wasn't ready. He wasn't. He would never be. Her heart sank hopelessly. "Alicia," he started hesitantly, "about the other night, I was—"

The passenger door being yanked open cut him short, allowing Alicia to breathe out the breath she hadn't realised she was holding in.

"God, what is it with this rain?" Sophie moaned, throwing herself into the back seat. "It's totally ruining my hair."

"Don't worry, Sophie, you're still irresistibly gorgeous, even with totally ruined hair." Justin eyed her amusedly through the rear-view mirror as he pulled out of the drive. "But not as irresistible as your mother, obviously."

Alicia felt her heart drop as if down a lift shaft. "I assume there was some kind of innuendo in there?" she asked him quietly.

"What?" Justin looked across to her, surprised. "No," he said quickly. "There wasn't meant to be. Look, Alicia"—he glanced again in his mirror, careful of Sophie in the back—"about the other night: I was out of order. Overreacting. A touch of the green-eyed monster, obviously. Can you blame me? You're a beautiful woman."

Astonished by that, Alicia simply stared at him.

"So, have you two kissed and made up then?" Sophie asked, clearly aware of the awkwardness there'd been between them. "Only Luke reckons all this not talking to each other crap is really juvenile, don't you, Luke?"

"I don't know." Justin turned questioningly to Alicia as he slowed at the traffic lights. "Have we?"

Alicia studied him, bewildered. How could he imagine she was beautiful? How could he ever have? Her heart felt too big in her chest, stuffed full of regret, of overwhelming love for this man, who actually had made her feel beautiful—even immediately post pregnancy, he'd told her she was gorgeous. Small lies, little white lies to make her feel better, whereas hers...Feeling as if it might be for the last time, she leaned towards him and pressed a soft kiss to his cheek. She wished there was a way to tell him, before his love turned to hatred, how deeply she loved him.

Justin reached to squeeze her hand, and then, a warm glint in his eyes, leaned towards her to steal a kiss of his own.

"*Urgh*, cover your eyes, Luke," Sophie advised her baby brother. "The parents are doing lovey-dovey stuff in public. *So* embarrassing."

Alicia felt a laugh bubble up inside her. It felt good. For the briefest moment, everything felt normal. If only she could hold on to it. Never let it go.

"Sorry," Justin mouthed, giving her an apologetic smile.

Gulping back her heartache, Alicia smiled back and cupped her hand to his face, needing to feel the solidity of him. Soon it would be gone. Soon her man—her strong, dependable man—would recoil at her touch.

"Er, excuse us, children present." Sophie sighed disapprovingly, and then said, "Dad, lights. You're stopping traffic."

"Hell," Justin mumbled, checking the lights and then pulling hurriedly out.

Alicia was still looking at him when her blood froze in her veins. "Justin!" she screamed, clutching his arm hard.

Instinctively slamming his foot on the brake, Justin swung his gaze to the side window. "Dear God..." The words died on his lips as the full impact of the collision hit the family.

CHAPTER THREE

JUSTIN

Justin saw nothing but deep, dark red. Heard nothing. Felt nothing but numbness throughout his entire body.

Then all his senses assailed him at once: searing pain in his ribcage, a cacophony of noise, too loud in his head. Horns blaring. People shouting. Petrol spilling. Sirens plaintively wailing.

Alicia. Screaming.

Sophie, her voice high-pitched, hysterical. "Dad! Oh God. Oh God. *Dad!*"

Luke . . . No sound at all.

Justin's heart kicked hard. White-hot pain shooting through his shoulder, down his spine to his pelvis, he turned towards Alicia, registered the palpable shock on her face, the blood on her forehead, matted in her hair, tracing the contours of her face.

"Justin! The *children!*" she yelled. "Please, God, don't do this. Not my children. *Please!* Not my *children!*"

Justin was already fumbling with his seatbelt, grappling with it, tearing at it. *Come on!* "Fucking . . . *fucking* thing!"

"Dad!" Sophie's voice was the terrified sob of a child as he twisted to face her. "Luke!"

Jesus Christ, no. Please, no . . . Twisting back to his door, Justin reached for the handle, cursing again loudly as he realised the locking mechanism was engaged. Reaching to release it, he tried again, only to find the door was stuck. Justin shoved his shoulder against it, his whole body against it, pushed with all his might, finally spilling from his car to land heavily on the pavement.

Blinking bloody sweat from his eyelashes, his breaths coming in short, sharp rasps, he planted his hands on the concrete, heaved himself up to all fours, reached for the buckled metal of the door to pull himself to his feet.

His legs almost failing him, aware of the bedlam of traffic around him, the shocked faces of onlookers frozen in time, Justin groped for the rear passenger door.

He was vaguely aware of other hands helping him to wrench it open. Justin couldn't see whose. His focus was on Sophie. She was choking back sobs now, close to hyperventilating. *Luke.* He couldn't get past her. Couldn't make her hear him.

"Sophie!" He seized her shoulders as she attempted to climb out, locked his eyes hard on hers as she screamed over and over, petrified, soul-crushing screams of pure fear. "Keep still! You're okay! *Please...*" He moderated his tone "Don't move, Sophie. You might have a neck injury."

Luke. Someone was reaching into the other side. "Don't!" Justin screamed it. He needed to get to him before they moved him.

Swiping at the droplets of crimson clouding his vision, Justin galvanised himself into action and made his way around the back of the car. It took a second, a slow thud like a death knell, before he registered the impossible angle of the carrier.

CHAPTER FOUR

ALICIA

Petrified, Alicia watched as a flurry of medical staff attended him, her tiny baby, lost on a hospital trolley made for an adult, monitors beeping and pinging around him. He looked so small, so fragile against the vast expanse of white sheet. His little face wasn't damaged. He still looked perfect. Her perfect little boy, his softly curled eyelashes brushing his cheeks as he slept. His perfect cupid lips. His little hands curled into fists. His tiny chest rising and falling. Breathing. *He's breathing.* Squeezing her eyes closed, Alicia felt the room shift, breathed in and out with him. *Please keep breathing, baby. Please keep breathing.*

She could hear someone talking about the positioning of his carrier in the car. *Back passenger seat, forward-facing.* The words reached her as if muffled by endless fathoms of swirling, icy water. *Responsive to pain.*

Oh please, God, no.

Folding her arms tightly across her midriff, Alicia felt the tear rip steadily through her heart, felt the tug in her womb where she'd carried him, kept him safe and warm until he was grown enough to come into the world. He was hurting! Her baby boy was hurting, and he *wasn't* grown. He was *tiny.* He was hurting, and she couldn't make it go away, couldn't keep him safe. She needed to. She was his *mother*!

"Please help him," she begged, her voice catching on the sob in her throat. She didn't want Lucas to hear her crying. It would scare him.

Swiping a hand across her face, she gulped back another wretched sob. "Please do something," she pleaded. "Don't let him be in pain. *Please...*"

A nurse came to her side, speaking gently, as if cajoling a child. "We're doing everything we can, Mrs. Cole. Why don't you come and wait in the visitor's room?"

Alicia felt the woman's arms close around her shoulders, trying to coax her away.

No! Did they think she would *leave* him? Did they think she would leave her baby? She needed to stay. She needed to talk to him. He would respond to her voice. He *would* respond. Oh God, she needed to hold him, feel his warm body next to hers, his tiny heart beating. "Please help him. Somebody, please help—"

Justin. Her gaze shot to the resuscitation room doors as they crashed open.

"You need to step away, Dr. Cole," someone ordered, as he moved towards Lucas. "It's too personal. You have a possible pneumothorax. You're in no fit state to—"

"He's my fucking *son!*" Justin shouted, struggling to get past two colleagues who were attempting to hold him back.

"Pulmonary contusions evident," another doctor said, as he pressed a stethoscope to their baby's small chest. "Get hold of paediatrics. Tell them—"

"He won't make it!" Justin screamed. "He's about to go into respiratory arrest. You need to intubate. Now!"

The doctor looked towards Justin and then, his expression foreboding, back to the other medical staff gathered around him. "Tell paeds to stand by," he instructed a nurse, as Alicia's heart slowed to a dull thud inside her. And then to another, "Get me an EZ-IO drill. And get the fast scanner here now."

Alicia knew what he was about to do. She couldn't bear it.

Didn't think she could stand to hear the sound of the drill whirring and cutting.

She felt Justin's arm around her. Instinctively, she turned to him, felt his other arm enclose her, pulling her towards him. Guilt rose inside her, her mind screaming what she already knew. It was her fault. All of it, *her* fault! This was her punishment for the wicked thing she'd done, the dreadful mistake she'd made. But it was *her* mistake. The punishment should be hers, not her baby's. Not Justin's. Not Sophie's. Hers alone.

"You shouldn't touch me!" She pulled away from him, feeling she might taint him. Everything she'd ever done had shaped his life, had brought him to this terrible place. He shouldn't be with her. She should never have made him be. "You shouldn't be anywhere near me!"

Justin stepped towards her, tried to ease her back. "Alicia, don't..." He stopped, drawing in a harsh breath. Hearing the wheeze rattle his chest, Alicia looked sharply up, saw the agony in his eyes, the perspiration mingling with the salty tears on his cheeks as he looked towards his broken baby. He was hurting. Hurting so badly. How could he ever forgive her? How would she ever forgive herself?

He would never come back from this. He would blame himself. He would never stop blaming himself if...

"Blood pressure's dropping."

CHAPTER FIVE

ALICIA

Feeling closer to him there, Alicia had stayed in the same place for two solid days since coming home from the hospital: sitting in the chair in the nursery. It was an antique rocking chair. Justin had bought it—to make feeding times easier, he'd said. Lucas had been easy to feed, a contented baby. It was a perfect chair for cuddling and snuggling him, though.

Her heart squeezing painfully, Alicia caught a breath in her throat as she recalled how she'd woken from an exhausted sleep shortly after bringing Lucas home, panic immediately engulfing her when she realised it was past his feed time and he wasn't crying. Her heart rate had slowed to somewhere near normal when she'd found Justin's side of the bed empty; she'd crept tentatively along the landing to find her husband nestling his son in the crook of his arm, humming softly as he rocked him gently back to sleep.

He'd done it many times since, when he hadn't been working. Alicia accused him of quietly hoping she would sleep through, so he could spend precious alone time with his son, and Sophie made merciless fun of her dad getting in touch with his feminine side. Alicia had pointed out he'd taken his fair share of night-time feeds with her too, the only difference being they hadn't had a rocking chair. At this, Sophie had bemoaned her deprived childhood.

Alicia smiled at the memory, and then swallowed hard against the cold stone wedged like ice in her chest. Shivering involuntarily as Lucas's wind-chime mobile tinkled the softest of sounds, she eased his patchwork quilt higher towards her face, breathing in the smell of him. His smell was everywhere: on her clothes, in her hair. She couldn't bear to wash him away. He permeated every surface, every wall, every pore of the house.

Looking towards the mobile, sure she could hear his delighted chuckles and gurgles as it jangled, she realised Justin was standing on the landing, watching her, not moving. He didn't come in. He hadn't come into the room once since he'd been discharged. Because he couldn't cope with it. Because his pain was too raw. Alicia could see it. It was etched deep into his eyes.

He needed her. He needed his family, his baby. She couldn't bear it. Alicia looked away.

"Can I get you anything?" he asked hesitantly.

Alicia shook her head. She couldn't eat. Couldn't swallow. Couldn't breathe.

"Some tea or hot chocolate?" he tried.

"We'd only just started weaning him," she said, for no reason other than she could see the confusion in Lucas's beautiful summer-blue eyes when she'd first fed a spoon into his mouth. "He opened his mouth for the spoon on Sunday. Soft fruits. He liked soft fruits mixed with his milk."

Justin breathed in. "I know," he said throatily.

Another minute stuffed full of silence passed by, then, "You should try and eat something, Alicia. At least let me get you some tea?"

Alicia smiled sadly. Her mother had always gone for the kettle in a crisis. A tradition passed on from her gran. A "cure-all cuppa," her gran had called it. It couldn't cure this, couldn't take away the ache in her chest where her heart should be. Her hand strayed to the soft round of her tummy. The emptiness where her baby had grown.

She wished her mother was here. That God, in whatever infinite wisdom it was, hadn't seen fit to take her away from her too. She would have judged her, no doubt she would have done that, but she would have kept loving her. It was selfish, but she needed that love. She desperately needed the love of someone who could know all there was to know and still keep loving her. To be held until her heart had stopped breaking and the unbearable pain went away.

But it wouldn't go away. Couldn't. Ever.

Justin, would he hold her? Could he bear to, now that he suspected? And he did. She could feel it. How could she let him? Only to tell him she'd betrayed him in the worst possible way a woman could betray a man? He was bleeding too, just as steadily as her, and she had no idea what to do.

She needed to try. Needed to help him get through this. Could she at least do that, before she broke him completely? Glancing away, she wiped a tear from her face. "I'll come down soon," she said, though she had no idea how she would. She couldn't bear to see Lucas's things in the kitchen—his little bowl and his feeding cup. Couldn't conceive the idea of throwing them out. Here she was, surrounded by his things, his tiny baby clothes, his toys, by him. There were no surprises, nothing that would leap out at her and force the air from her lungs.

Alicia listened to the landing clock ticking, loud against the silence, as Justin nodded defeatedly and walked away. How she wished she could wrench the hands of the clock back, eradicate time, her mistakes—and the cruellest second of all, in which God had taken their baby away.

Not God.

Her. Getting unsteadily to her feet, she walked towards the

window. She'd been responsible for Lucas's death. If not for her lies, her weakness, none of this would have happened. She might have remembered to fill up her own car had she not been so distracted by Paul Radley. Justin wouldn't have been driving her. If only she'd been honest, neither of them would have been distracted that day from what mattered most in the world: their family. Justin wouldn't be facing pain after insurmountable pain. She should have told him the truth. It was too late now.

"Where are you, baby?" she whispered glancing up at the stars, twinkling brightly against a vast canvas of black. "Where are you, my beautiful baby boy?" Closing her eyes, she pressed his little quilt close to her face and allowed her tears to finally spill over.

She wasn't aware Justin had come back until he reached for her. Alicia leaned into him as he eased her to face him. She couldn't help herself. She didn't deserve him, but she so needed him, wanted to morph into him, never let go of him. Knew, as the hand of the clock ticked past this moment, that he didn't want to let go of her either.

But he would. He was blaming himself. It wasn't his fault. None of it.

She'd wanted to save him and now she would destroy him.

Pressing her face hard into his shoulder, Alicia tried and failed to still the sobs that shook through her body. "I'm sorry," she choked wretchedly, blinded by snot and tears. "So, so sorry."

"Shhh," he murmured, softly stroking her hair, as if she were a child in need of comfort. And she was. Oh God, how she was. "You have nothing to be sorry for."

Alicia heard a sob catch in his throat.

And her heart cracked wide open.

CHAPTER SIX

JUSTIN

She'd decorated the nursery herself, as she had most of the house—an old Victorian property, which had been badly in need of renovation when they'd moved in. Steeling himself to venture into the room on his own, once Alicia had finally gone downstairs, Justin recalled how he'd almost had a heart attack when he'd found her halfway up a stepladder in her fifth month of pregnancy. She'd laughed away his concerns when he tried to dissuade her.

"I know this is your protective gene kicking in, but I'm only two rungs up," she'd pointed out. "Being pregnant doesn't mean I'm suddenly made of porcelain, you know? I'm fine, Justin, I promise. Go on, shoo. Go to work."

Still, though, with Sophie staying over at a friend's to work on the lyrics of their latest "going to be phenomenal" pop song together, Justin had been reluctant to leave her.

"Justin, go. You're making me feel self-conscious," she'd urged him, blushing as he'd continued to watch her. With artistic flair, she'd been using a template to paint the pale blue wall with white seagulls, her tongue protruding in that cute way it did when she was concentrating.

Justin had smiled, and then stepped instinctively forwards, as she'd stepped down to deposit her paint tray. With her wild, caramel-coloured hair piled on top of her head and wearing one of his shirts as an overall, she'd looked possibly more beautiful in his eyes then than she ever had. "You look utterly gorgeous, Mrs. Cole," he'd assured her, leaning in to brush her lips with a soft kiss.

"And so do you, Dr. Cole," she'd said, sweeping her eyes over his business suit—compulsory attire when meeting with the hospital trust, and which Alicia apparently considered a "bit of a turn-on." There'd been a far too enticing look in her eyes as they'd come to meet his.

Unable to resist, Justin had eased her towards him, kissing her this time most enjoyably thoroughly. "I may have to take this further later," he'd said hoarsely, when they'd finally come up for air.

"I'll consider that a promise," Alicia had replied, delicious innuendo dancing in her eyes as they'd lingered on his. "Now, be gone, Dr. Cole. You're late."

Checking his watch, Justin had winced. "Damn. I was obviously having too much of a good time. I'm gone. Be careful not to overdo it," he'd said, helping himself to another quick kiss. "Be good, baby Cole," he'd added, bending to kiss her tummy, should baby Cole feel neglected, and then heading fast for the landing. "And make sure not to overstretch," he'd called back.

Now, gulping back the emotion climbing inside him, Justin's gaze strayed towards the cot. He'd found the baby butterfly wind chime hanging over it when he'd come home.

She'd painted the ottoman that day too. It had been her mother's, and Alicia hadn't wanted to part with it when she'd lost her, but they'd never quite found the right place for it. She'd rubbed it down and painted it white, topped it off with two cushions and a traditional teddy bear dressed in a blue striped nightshirt and nightcap. That had been the night Justin had learned their baby's name. Lucas Cole. She'd stencilled it on the front of the ottoman, leaving space for his date of birth underneath.

She'd added that the week after they brought him home—six months, almost to the day, before his short life was stolen away. Justin swallowed as he looked towards it. He wasn't sure whether it was his heart, or the wound from the tube they'd inserted to drain the fluid from his lung, that ached so incessantly. Whatever it was, he felt he deserved it. He'd been behind the wheel, exhausted, distracted. He'd been responsible for what had happened to their son.

Dragging an arm across his eyes, Justin walked out of the room, easing the door closed behind him, and then stopped and pushed it ajar again. Alicia preferred it open. She didn't want to shut him away. She didn't have to say it.

Stopping on the landing, Justin glanced at the ceiling, blinking hard, wishing he could do something to ease Alicia's pain. *Can I get you anything?* He laughed scornfully at the thought of the banal question he kept asking her. *Yes*, she should tell him. *You can get me my baby back.*

God. Heaving in a breath which stopped somewhere short of his chest, Justin dropped his gaze, squeezing the bridge of his nose hard in a vain attempt to suppress the rage burning inside him. He couldn't bring Luke back. Couldn't undo the godforsaken day on which he'd been responsible for the death of her child. He would die himself, right here, right now, in exchange for his little boy's life back, if only God were merciful and would let him.

CHAPTER SEVEN

SOPHIE

Seeing her dad on the landing, obviously upset, Sophie had stepped back into her bedroom. He hadn't cried though. It was like he wouldn't allow himself to. Her mum, too. She'd been sitting in Luke's room mostly. Whenever she did come out, she moved around the house like a ghost, her arms wrapped around herself, as if keeping everything in. Keeping everyone out. She'd been shutting out her dad. Blaming him, obviously, because he'd been driving, which was just so fucking unfair.

Since he'd broken the news to Sophie at the hospital, his voice cracking and his face deathly white, her dad hadn't spoken to her much either, other than to ask if she was all right.

Her mum kept asking her the same question, as if she could ever be. As if any of them could. Or else she snapped at her if she moved anything of Luke's. And then she would apologise. Why didn't they just let it out? Stop tiptoeing around each other and scream at each other, if that's what it took?

She kept assuring them she was okay. How could she not, when they were hurting so much? But she wasn't okay—stuck here in her room, because wherever else she went, she felt in the way, as if she were somehow intruding. They'd be devastated if she said it out loud, but that truly was how she felt, like she daren't say or do anything that might touch a raw nerve.

Her teacher, who had rung her to see how she was, had suggested she write down her feelings. She needn't show it to anyone, she'd said. Some things, on reflection, are better left unsaid, but it might be therapeutic, she'd told her. It did help. Sophie glanced down at the notebook she'd been scrawling in, the contents of which would definitely devastate her parents, and then plucked it up and stuffed it well under her clothes in her chest of drawers.

She debated whether to ring her mate Chloe, but then decided against. Chloe had been texting her constantly. She made the right noises, but she didn't understand, not really, that she felt as cold and empty as the house did without Luke in it. That with his funeral somehow to get through, she didn't want to go out, to the cinema, clubbing to "lose herself on the dance floor," or anywhere else. She didn't want to sing either. She listened to her music—Adele, mostly, whose soulful emotion fitted her mood. Sophie wished she might be as good as her one day. She didn't sing along though. She didn't have the heart. All she wanted to do was stay cocooned under her quilt, left alone, preferably. But she couldn't even do that for her mum or her dad coming up every two minutes, like they were on a rota or something, to ask the perpetual question.

Sighing heavily, Sophie wandered back to her bed, picked up her phone and plugged her earphones in. She was selecting her playlist when there was an inevitable tap on the door. Her dad, she guessed. He usually waited before entering—"at his own peril," he once would have said. Would he ever joke again, Sophie wondered, or smile or laugh?

"Yup, I'm here," she called. She wasn't sure why she'd said that. Because part of her suspected they were frightened she wouldn't be. That something terrible might have happened to her too.

Her dad did smile when he came in. A forced smile. He looked at her, worriedly, as Sophie had expected he would, as if she might fall apart or self-combust on the bed or something. "I thought I'd get some food," he said, trying to sound normal.

Sophie shrugged. She wasn't hungry. None of them were.

"I thought pizza, maybe?" Scratching his forehead with his thumb, her dad shrugged in turn, as if he knew that it would stick in her throat, whatever it was.

"If you like." Sophie offered him a small smile back, when what she really wanted to do was go to him and hug him. She couldn't though. She'd tried that when he'd arrived home. She'd gone to him, wrapped her arms around him. She'd hurt his chest. She could tell when he'd winced. He'd said he was fine, just a bit sore from where they'd inserted the tube; that was all. *Bullshit.* He wasn't fine. It was utter bollocks, pretending he was coping, when he quite clearly wasn't.

"Veggie with extra peppers?" he suggested, his voice tight, trying so hard not to crack it was heartbreaking.

"Sounds good." Knowing he needed her to, Sophie played along.

Her dad ran a hand over his neck, nodded and turned to the door. And then turned back. "Sophie," he said, walking across to her, "if you want to talk about anything…" He faltered. "About Luke… I'm here. You know that, right? I'm listening."

Glancing down at her phone, Sophie swiped a hand under her nose. She didn't say anything. She wanted to. Wanted desperately to talk about Luke, about what had happened, but with her mum and dad clearly unable to, how could she?

"Sophie?" Her dad hesitated, and then sat down on her bed. "It's okay to cry, you know," he said softly, taking hold of her hand.

He had nice hands. Sophie swallowed. Clean fingernails. A surgeon's hands, those of a man who saved lives. But he hadn't been able to save his own son. Sophie had heard him at the hospital, cursing himself, cursing the "fucking bastard" who'd hit them and run. Blaming himself.

Sophie looked up then, searching his eyes. Steel-blue eyes,

Sophie would term them. She'd always been able to read them: a soft twinkle therein when he'd tease her, usually about her "tarantula" eyelashes or her eyebrow stud—her face jewellery, as he called it; when he hugged her, which he'd always done often. Now they were stormy, almost gunmetal grey. Uncertain, tortured eyes. "Is it?" she asked him.

Her dad looked away, which pretty much communicated that he didn't think it was okay, not for him anyway.

"Have they found him yet?" Sophie asked. "The man who cut the lights?"

Her dad took a breath and shook his head. "Not yet, no." Sophie could feel his frustration.

"Will they?" She kept looking at him, willing him to look at her. To let down his guard and look at her properly.

"I'm not sure. I hope so," he said, pressing a thumb hard to his forehead.

"Will they prosecute him? If they do find him, will they charge him?"

"I don't know, Sophie." Again, he faltered, looking awkward, as if he wanted to protect her. But he couldn't. This was happening to her too. She wasn't a child. She read the newspapers, watched the news. Knew that, if they did find him and they did prosecute him, he might get no more than a slap on the wrist. "It depends on whether they have enough—"

He was cut off as the telephone rang, yet again. Saved by the bell, Sophie thought wearily.

Her heart sank as her dad got to his feet, going to answer the bloody thing, talk to people who didn't have a clue what to say. *Talk to me!* She wanted to scream after him. *I'm listening!*

Her mum knocked and came straight in, catching Sophie unawares. She'd been going to watch Netflix stuff on her iPad, but nothing seemed appealing. She'd given up eventually and curled up under the duvet.

"I brought you some pizza," her mum said, as Sophie poked her head out.

"Thanks." Sophie nodded, squinting against the sudden light from the lamp.

"You will eat it, won't you?" her mum asked, worry flitting across her eyes as she placed the pizza on the bedside table.

Realising she looked worse than she had when she'd last seen her—drained and definitely in need of some sustenance herself—Sophie straightened herself up. "I'm not really very hungry, but I'll try," she promised.

Her mum didn't look convinced. "You have to eat something, Sophie. You need to keep your strength—"

"And so do *you!*" Sophie snapped, and then felt immediately guilty. "Look, I'll eat it, Mum. Okay? I don't need to be mollycoddled or treated like I'm incapable."

Her mum looked bewildered at that. "I wasn't aware I was treating you like anything."

"Seriously?" Sophie widened her eyes. "You're bringing me dinner in bed? I'd have to have been dying for you to do that normally."

Shit! Shit, shit, shit! She hadn't meant to say that.

Seeing the stunned look on her mum's face, Sophie felt tears stinging the back of her eyes. "Sorry," she mumbled, dropping her gaze. "I didn't mean…"

"I know." Perching herself on the edge of the bed, Alicia reached out to place a hand on her arm. "It's okay to grieve, Sophie," she said softly. "It's natural to be—"

"So *grieve* then!" Sophie yelled over her. She couldn't stand this any more. "Talk to *each other*, why don't you—not me. Stop trying to act like you're not crucified inside!"

Alicia snatched her hand away, as if she'd been burned.

"You're angry," she said, understandingly, deflecting the conversation away from herself. "It's natural. You're bound to—"

"Yes, I'm angry!" Sophie shouted louder. "Bloody angry!" Dragging her hair from her face, she glared at Alicia, whose face had now drained of the little colour she'd had. Sophie knew she was hurting her, but she couldn't stop. They needed to be told. They needed shaking out of this...stupor. To be there for each other. "I'm angry at the injustice of it," she went on furiously. "The cruelty! Angry with *you!*"

"Me?" Alicia asked shakily.

"Both of you." Sophie looked past her mum to her dad, who, clearly having overheard, had appeared on the landing. "You're treating me like a *child*. Sparing me the details. I don't want to be spared! I want to *know* what's going on. I don't want you wrapping me up in cotton wool! Don't you understand?"

"Sophie..." Justin stepped in, his face taut, definitely angry. Good! She wanted him to be angry. She wanted him to do *something*. Shout, swear, throw things. Anything but walk around here like a dead-inside zombie.

"*What?*" Sophie turned on him. "Luke was my *baby brother*. I might have said he did nothing but eat, puke and poo, but I loved him, Dad. I *loved* him. I miss him, and my heart is hurting so badly, and I can't talk to you, because we're all walking around on *goddamned* eggshells."

Sophie glared at him, her expression defiant, her shoulders heaving.

Nodding slowly, Justin walked across to sit on the edge of the bed next to Alicia. He hesitated for a second and then reached out to take Alicia's hand.

Her mum curled her fingers around his, Sophie noticed, relief washing through her.

Pressing his thumb against his forehead, in that way he did, her dad took a breath and then reached for her hand too. "There are several stages of grief, Sophie," he said, glancing at Alicia. "I think we've both been in the denial stage. We're getting there." He tried to sound reassuring.

Sophie wasn't sure she was reassured entirely, but at least they were acknowledging it.

"I think you might be in the anger stage—with good reason," her dad went on. "I'm sorry if I ... *we* appear to have been distant. Sometimes, I ..." He hesitated. "I find I struggle to say how I feel, because I think it might trigger emotions I'm not sure other people can handle. I suspect that might be true for your mum too, just now."

Smiling sadly, he squeezed her hand. "You're right, though: we do need to talk. We're not other people, are we? We're a family. We need each other."

Sounding choked, he looked again at Alicia.

Sophie followed his gaze, to where her mum was sitting with her head bowed. Crying. She was crying. *Shit!* Sophie saw one tear plop from her chin, and then another.

"Oh God, Mum, I'm sorry." She shuffled across to her. "It's okay," she said, sliding her arms around her. "You can cry on my shoulder. I don't mind a bit of snot on my T-shirt, honest I don't."

Sophie swallowed hard as her mum emitted a strangled laugh.

CHAPTER EIGHT

JUSTIN

Justin hadn't been sure why he'd decided to come to the hospital the day before his son's funeral, but once he'd arrived, he'd realised he needed space, to try and get his emotions under control. He'd worked hard at that over the years, since he'd discovered his murdered family and almost lost his sanity. Whenever his thoughts went there, images like sick movie stills playing through his mind, his moods swinging violently from the same paralysing panic he'd felt then, through despair, to angry disbelief that the bastard responsible—an opportunist thief needing to feed his drugs habit—had never been caught, he employed the coping mechanisms he'd learned: calming deep breaths; counting when he felt himself too close to the edge. Tiles on floors, fluorescent lights on ceilings, he counted until he was able to reach some kind of detachment. But the tidal wave of grief, shot through with sheer fury, that crashed over him every time he thought about Luke, about what kind of person could hit a car, clearly causing serious injury to a family, and then run—Justin stood no chance of detaching from that. From the fact that he was also culpable; driving whilst tired and distracted.

As hard as he tried not to dwell on why he'd been distracted, he couldn't help himself. Perhaps because of the irony of Radley resurfacing days before the incomprehensible cruelty that had taken Luke from them. Justin knew he needed to let it go. Alicia and he had taken a step forward since the accident, with Alicia, at least, no longer keeping all her grief inside—Justin knew how destructive that could be. She still seemed unable to talk properly to him though, hold eye contact with him, and he badly needed her to. He was assuming it was because he'd been driving, that there was part of her that couldn't help blaming him. Still, though, his mind would wonder about Radley. He simply wouldn't go away.

Taking a breath, Justin realised the parents of the six-month-old baby girl brought in with brain trauma would probably wonder what he was doing, staring down at her, and snapped his attention back to her.

He'd performed emergency surgery on this child the day before his own little boy had died. She was alive. A small miracle in the bleak madness his life had become. *Untouched, untroubled, untarnished.* He couldn't help recalling what he'd thought when he'd first gazed down in wonder at Sophie. At Lucas. He'd sworn to keep their world safe. To keep them safe. He'd failed. Failed in his most fundamental obligation as a father.

Swallowing hard as a new wave of grief sucked the air from his lungs, Justin tried to breathe through it, focussing on checking the little girl's vital statistics. And then, satisfied she was doing as well as she could be, he stroked her cheek softly with his finger and was rewarded with a delighted gurgle, which almost broke his heart all over again. "She's going to be a knockout," he said, composing himself and turning to offer the parents a reassuring smile.

"Thanks, Dr. Cole." The young father smiled awkwardly and then glanced away.

Justin guessed they'd heard the news about his son, which had travelled like wildfire around the hospital. He should go. He hadn't meant to make them feel uncomfortable, which inevitably they would be, but he'd needed to see for himself that she was thriving. "I'll leave you in the capable hands of the nursing staff," he said, smiling again as he turned for the door.

"Dr. Cole," the mother said, behind him.

Justin had only half turned back when she launched herself at him, throwing her arms around him, dropping her head to his shoulder and squeezing him hard. "Thank you," she said emotionally. "For everything. For coming to check on her. You're a very special man."

Justin didn't feel very special. No matter how hard he tried, no matter how much he counted, anger was all he felt. So much anger and guilt stuffed inside him it was fucking choking him. He managed to make it to one of the patients' toilets along the corridor before he gave vent to his tears.

CHAPTER NINE

ALICIA

Breathing out a sigh of relief, Alicia came from the kitchen to meet Justin as soon as she heard his key in the front door. "Are you all right?" she asked him, almost before he'd stepped through it.

Justin glanced at her confusedly.

"I was worried," Alicia said, trying not to sound accusatory. God knew, that was the last thing she should be. "You've been gone a while. I rang the hospital. They said you'd left. And when you didn't come home, I wondered...I thought..." She trailed hopelessly off, the words she wanted to say to him dying in her throat.

He could talk to her—that was what she wanted to tell him. *Should* tell him. She was here for him. Every thought she had now was muddled. Everything she said to him would add an insult to the injury that would inevitably be caused when the truth came out. She could feel it, like a guillotine casting a long shadow over them, ready to drop, when Paul Radley chose to let it.

"Sorry," Justin said, with an attempt at a smile. "I should have thought. I was out walking, lost track of time. I meant to call."

"But you're all right?" she asked again, knowing he couldn't possibly be.

Justin took a second, a long second, to hang his coat up, and then finally turned to look at her. "Under the circumstances"—he paused, holding her gaze—"yes, as well as I can be, I suppose."

Alicia scanned his eyes. Usually so bright and intelligent, twinkling amusedly whenever he smiled and always full of compassion, there was nothing there now other than deep-rooted pain.

"Dad?" Sophie called apprehensively to him from the landing, breaking the silence now hanging between them. "Are you okay? You've been gone ages."

Justin snapped his gaze away from Alicia to look up at her. "Yes," he said, quickly. "Sorry, Pumpkin. There was a patient I needed to check on. I should have rung. I'm okay, honestly."

Wiping a hand quickly across her cheek, looking small and vulnerable, and about as convinced as Alicia felt, Sophie looked him anxiously over, and then padded quickly down the stairs to throw herself into his arms.

Justin held her, hugging her back hard. "We'll get through this, baby, I promise," he said hoarsely, dropping a soft kiss to her hair and then looking back to Alicia.

Alicia saw a question in his eyes. Fear, too. The same fear that was eating away at her. *Will we get through this?* Alicia had no way to answer.

Justin turned his attention back to Sophie. "Have you eaten?" he asked her, easing back to scan her face.

Looking pale and drawn, Sophie hesitated. She hadn't, but clearly she didn't want to tell Justin that. She wouldn't lie to him either, so she simply shrugged instead.

"How about some soup?" Justin suggested, talking to her encouragingly, as he might have done when she was a small girl tucked up in bed with some childhood illness.

Sophie nodded then. "I'll have some if you will," she said, turning to the kitchen.

"Deal," Justin said. "Alicia?"

Alicia felt all her emotions bubbling to the surface as he looked at her, with such uncertainty in his eyes, it tore another piece from her heart. She should eat. She should at least try—for his sake, for Sophie's—but what she really wanted to do was curl up under her duvet until the unbearable tightness in her chest went away. The duvet on the bed where she slept with the man she'd loved with her very soul since she'd first met him. The bed in which they'd talked, about important and inconsequential things, laughed and made sweet love, he sensitive to her every need, touching her to her very core, creating the child God had called back to heaven too soon. Alicia held on to that thought: that that's where Lucas was, safe with her mum and his great-nanna, who would be making endless cure-all cups of tea. It was what sustained her when she woke in the darkest hours, feeling so lonely and empty, desperate to turn to the man she knew would offer the comfort she so badly needed. Yet, how could she? She *had* to tell him. Everything. What alternative was there?

"Soup?" he asked her.

Alicia swallowed. "I'll join you in a minute." She smiled, though her voice caught painfully in her throat. "I'm just going to grab the blouse Sophie needs ironed for tomorrow."

Halfway up the stairs, Alicia saw him glance down, massaging his temples hard. Staying where she was, she watched as he turned his gaze upwards, as if contemplating... How would he ever survive the day he buried his six-month-old son?

CHAPTER TEN

ALICIA

Alicia didn't have to shout upstairs to hurry Sophie on the next morning. Joining Justin in the hall, she looked towards her daughter as she descended the stairs. Her face was pale, her eyes awash with unshed tears. She looked frightened, lost and so very lonely.

Wanting to cry for her, wishing she could take her pain away, Alicia moved towards her as she reached the hall. Offering her a small smile, she held her gaze for a moment, trying to reassure her. She shouldn't have to go through this. No one should. It was too cruel. Crueller still for a fifteen-year-old girl who was struggling to be an adult because she felt her parents needed her to be.

Sophie was going to do the eulogy. It would be one of the most heartbreaking things she would ever do in her life, but Alicia hadn't tried to dissuade her. Justin had agreed it was something she needed to do, for her baby brother. He'd said he would step in if she couldn't get through it. Alicia wondered, though, how *he* would get through it.

He looked dreadful, more exhausted than she'd ever seen him. Even at his lowest ebb, she'd never seen him look so utterly bereft. Dark shadows under his eyes—in his eyes—he looked like a man who might never sleep again.

She didn't ask him if he was all right, reaching for his hand to squeeze it reassuringly instead. Justin squeezed hers back, briefly, and then pulled in a long breath and went to the front door to check whether the cars had arrived. Alicia didn't want them to arrive. Didn't want the moment to come when she would have to say a final goodbye to her child.

Gulping hard, she glanced down and then looked back to Sophie, whose eyes were now full of trepidation. Alicia reached for her hand. "Okay?" she asked her, brushing a stray curl from her face. Cascading over her shoulders, Sophie's long, sable hair was darker than Justin's. Her eyes were a deep, rich chestnut brown, where Justin's were blue. Yet, in so many other ways, she was so like him. Her mannerisms, her deeply caring nature— these were the things they shared. Justin adored his feisty, funny daughter. He would kill to protect her, Alicia knew that to be true. She hoped Sophie knew that she would, too. That she knew in her heart that her mother loved her with all of herself, no matter what else happened.

Sophie nodded, and gave her a small, tremulous smile.

"You're a beautiful, special person and I love you very much. Never forget that, Sophie," Alicia whispered, squeezing her into a firm hug.

Sophie hugged her hard back, and Alicia felt her heart hitch in her chest. It was enough, that hug, to sustain her. She would get through this. Somehow, her legs would carry her. She would keep standing. Sophie would need her to. And Justin, her husband, a good, honest man, who would never knowingly hurt anyone...Whatever the future held, he needed her now, and she would be there.

"Ready?" he said softly, behind her.

Bracing herself to face the worst day of her life, alongside the two people who mattered most in the world, Alicia nodded and turned to him, her gaze dropping from the immeasurable heartbreak in his eyes down to his tie. It was slightly askew, she noticed. She imagined his hands shaking as he'd tied it.

Instinctively, Alicia reached to straighten it, another intimate gesture between them that sent an unbearable wave of sadness right through her. He used to smile when she fixed his tie—that languid, slow smile that would make her fingers all thumbs—and then invariably steal a kiss. He'd tugged it loose once, a glint in his eyes that told Alicia they were both going to be late for work.

Alicia dropped her gaze. She couldn't bear it, the hurt she could now see there.

Justin surprised her, reaching to gently lift her chin, so that she had no option but to look directly at him. "We'll find a way through this, Ali," he said, his voice hoarse. "We have to."

Pressing his forehead to hers, he tugged in a ragged breath.

Feeling his hand softly tracing the length of her back, Alicia moved towards him, threaded her arms around him and held him tight. He needed her to. And she needed it too.

They stayed like that for one long, precious moment, before someone tapped on the front door. She felt Justin stiffen, pulling himself upright as he eased away from her, turning to face the insufferable heartache to come.

CHAPTER ELEVEN

ALICIA

Alicia watched Justin carry Lucas in his arms, his gaze focussed on the catafalque. She wanted to scream at the injustice of it—right here, right now, in front of all the people gathered to mark the passage of their son's short life in respectful silence. She wanted to drop to her knees and sob. Or run as far away as she could from the nightmare that was never going to end.

But she couldn't.

She had to be there.

Her family needed her.

Her throat closing, her heart beyond breaking, she watched as Justin lowered the casket. "Bye, little man." She read the words on his lips as he placed a hand briefly upon it, wiped his eyes with his other hand and turned away. He didn't look at anyone as he took his seat. Alicia guessed why: he couldn't bear to see the sympathy in their eyes. He simply wouldn't be able to cope with it.

She reached for his hand, gripping it hard. She heard nothing of what the minister was saying beyond "God has walked with Luke since before he was born." Sophie took hold of her other hand and Alicia held on tight to her daughter.

It took a second to realise Sophie was easing away. Alicia couldn't breathe past the pain in her chest, couldn't focus through her tears, as her beautiful, brave daughter took her place at the pulpit.

She felt Justin's hand on her back, his arm sliding around her as she bowed her head, gulping hard against the sobs she couldn't seem to stop.

Haltingly, Sophie began. "'Do not stand at my grave and weep; I am not there, I do not sleep. I am a thousand winds that blow, I am the diamond glints on snow...'"

Alicia looked up, her heart breaking for her, as her baby paused, trying to compose herself.

"Luke did sleep." Sophie glanced upwards, wiped a tear from her cheek and went on, as Justin got half to his feet. "He slept a lot." She laughed tremulously. "I wondered what the point of him was at first. And then I realised. Seeing the pure innocence in his eyes, the little hand he trustingly offered me, his smile"—again, she stopped, her voice quavering—"simply because he was delighted to see me. Luke taught me how to love, unconditionally and with all of me. He's nestled safe in an angel's wings now, but he will never leave me. He's here." She pressed a hand to her heart. "He will always be."

Easing her daughter to her when she made her way back, Alicia kissed her temple, and then turned to Justin. His gaze was fixed downwards. She saw the tears spill onto the order of service resting on his knees, his other hand going to his forehead as he drew in a deep breath, trying to contain his emotion.

Outside, she would tell him how much she loved him. Would always love him. She had no idea what tomorrow would bring, but today, she was Justin's wife. He was her husband. His heart was tearing inside him, and he needed her to be there for him.

CHAPTER TWELVE

JUSTIN

Once outside the church, Justin's strength almost failed him. People were spilling out, glancing over to him, talking in hushed whispers about the beautiful service, the flowers, debating whose cars to follow to the reception. Alicia's sister had stopped her on the way out. Watching her sobbing now in Jessica's arms, Justin thought his presence might be an intrusion. Deciding to give them a minute, he waited, shaking hands and thanking people for coming.

Seeing someone approach her, seemingly without hesitation, Justin felt his already fractured heart splinter. It wasn't jealousy that consumed him as he watched Paul Radley, the man from Alicia's past, place a hand on her arm and lean intimately towards her. It was desolation. Standing there, amongst people he knew, people who cared deeply, Justin suddenly felt more alone than he ever had in his life. He had no idea what to do. How to be. He wasn't sure he even knew who he was any more, what his role was. He felt utterly and hopelessly lost.

Kneading his temples, desperately trying to hold back his tears, he turned away. He couldn't do this, stand here, feeling as if he was on the outside. The man had worked with Alicia aeons ago, for what, six months? A year? It had been a small financial services company. She hadn't really liked her job, she'd said, and had eventually left to retrain as a social worker. As far as he knew, she hadn't seen this man since. So what the hell was he doing *here*?

Realising his anger was way too close to the surface, Justin started walking. Whether he was getting things out of proportion or not, he couldn't handle this. Not now.

"Dad?" Sophie said behind him, as he reached the path heading towards the exit.

Justin turned back. The guy was still there, his hand still on Alicia's arm, his face close to hers. Too close. Justin looked away. He couldn't breathe.

"Justin?" He heard Jessica hurrying towards him. "Justin, are you all right?"

Ineffectually attempting to compose himself, Justin nodded shortly.

Jessica stopped in front of him, placing a hand on his arm, as he glanced again towards Alicia. "He's just an old acquaintance," she said, looking kindly into his eyes.

Was he? Justin's gaze flicked again to Alicia and back. He was beginning to very much doubt that that's all he was, not least because her sister had just felt the need to convince him of it.

"I need to go," he said, restraining himself from going over there and establishing the facts for himself. "I have to...walk. Clear my head."

Jessica looked surprised, and then nodded sympathetically. "You need some alone time. I can't say I blame you. Go on, take all the time you need. I'll let Alicia know. I'm not sure she'll understand entirely"—she glanced anxiously back over her shoulder—"but I'll make sure she knows you're okay."

Justin laughed drily at that. Deep in conversation with her "old acquaintance," he wasn't sure Alicia would even notice he'd gone. "Will you take care of Sophie for me?" he asked Jessica.

"Of course I will," Jessica assured him. "Do you want me to tell Alicia you'll see her at the reception?"

Justin hesitated. He would be there: Radley, being way too intimate with *his* wife. And he was supposed to do what? Stand by and watch? "Just tell her I'll see her later."

"At home?" Jessica asked worriedly.

Justin nodded, and turned to Sophie, who was looking at him in bewilderment. "Stay with your mum, Sophie, will you?" he asked her throatily. "Please. Can you do that for me?"

Her expression now a kaleidoscope of confused emotions, Sophie nodded uncertainly, as Justin turned around again and walked away.

CHAPTER THIRTEEN

JESSICA

Jessica glanced after Justin and then back to Alicia, who was still talking to Paul Radley. Seeing him there was clearly more than a little disconcerting for Justin, given the attention Paul had paid Alicia at her party. She really couldn't blame Justin for leaving, after seeing the man attempt to monopolise her again, here of all places.

She should intervene, she supposed. Clearly, Alicia needed rescuing. Her daughter needed her right now. Jessica doubted she would do in lieu of her mother.

Seeing Sophie was extremely upset, Jessica placed an arm around her niece's shoulders and eased her towards her.

"Why is he going? Without Mum?" Sophie asked, tears cascading down her face. "I don't get it?"

Jessica hugged her closer. "I think he just needs some space, sweetheart," she said. "Don't worry, he'll probably be at home when you get there."

"They're not coping." Sophie cried harder. "They're avoiding talking about him, about anything meaningful. I don't know what to do."

"They're hurting, lovely," Jessica said soothingly. "Probably both feeling guilty and not sure how to reach out to each other. I know you want to help, but there's nothing you can do in reality. Just give them some time, and remember they love you however preoccupied they might seem."

Sophie nodded. "I don't want to go to the reception either," she sniffled. "Not without Dad. People I've never even met will be trying to talk to me about Luke, and I know they'll mean well, but they didn't know him, did they? It's just…"

"Too much?" Jessica suggested.

Sophie's nod this time was one of relief.

"I tell you what, why don't you come and stay with me for a few days? We could have a good natter, try to put the world to rights, watch romantic films when that fails, and then have a good cry together."

Sophie didn't look sure.

"It would be good therapy," Jessica said. "We could even go out for the odd pizza, or whatever you fancy. What do you say? I could use the company. I'm a bit fed up of knocking around my empty house on my own, to be honest, and it might give your mum and dad a bit of space."

"I don't know," Sophie said hesitantly. "Do you think Mum would mind?"

Jessica glanced towards where Alicia was still talking to Paul Radley. "I shouldn't think so. She'll understand you need some space, too. She's going to be tied up at the reception anyway from the looks."

Sophie followed her gaze. "Who's he?" she asked, perturbed.

"Just a friend," Jessica supplied. "An old work colleague. He's been working in Dubai for a few years. They've obviously got things to catch up on. Look, if you really can't face the reception, we'll have a word with your mum and slip off now. We could go and grab your stuff on the way. Your dad's probably headed off home, so you might be able to have a word with him before you leave. Sound like a plan?"

"But how will mum get to the reception?" Sophie asked, clearly concerned about her mum, which was commendable. Sophie was turning out to be a very caring young woman. Jessica would be proud to have a daughter like her. She couldn't help but feel a pang of jealousy as she recalled her own lost babies. The man who'd been in her life back then had seemed to think she shouldn't even grieve over them, since she'd never managed to get past the crucial three-month stage of her pregnancies.

She had grieved for them, silently. She'd even grieved for their indifferent father, pathetically, since a man who'd walked out on her while she'd been losing their child hadn't been worth wasting a single tear on.

Shaking off her sadness, because here wasn't the place if she wasn't to end up sobbing like a child herself, Jessica turned her attention back to Sophie. Alicia really should be paying her a bit more attention. She was bound to be emotional after standing up there and giving the eulogy so beautifully. But then, Alicia wouldn't know whether she was on her head or her heels right now. And Paul Radley reappearing certainly wouldn't be helping her emotional state.

"She'll travel in the funeral car," she said, smiling reassuringly. "And if she doesn't want to do that, I'm sure one of the guests won't mind taking her."

Paul Radley, for one. Jessica debated the wisdom of allowing Alicia to be alone in his company for too long. But she clearly did need to talk to him. As Alicia had said, when he'd turned up at her party uninvited, she needed to establish why he'd reappeared after so long. She could hardly bury her head in the sand and ignore the fact that he was here.

She actually might be doing Alicia a favour, taking Sophie off her hands for a while. And with a bit of luck, they would catch Justin at home. Plainly, he'd been upset and angry, seeing Paul Radley here. Jessica really couldn't blame him. The least she could do was offer him a shoulder and try to reassure him.

CHAPTER FOURTEEN

ALICIA

"I really am so sorry, Alicia," Paul said, his face earnest.

Alicia didn't answer. She was too stunned.

"I'm taking up far too much of your time. I know you don't want to hear about my reasons for not being able to get back to the UK until now, but if there's anything I can do." He smiled kindly. "Anything at all..."

Yes, there is, Alicia thought. *Please, please leave me alone.* "No, there isn't," she said quickly, her stomach tight with nerves as she looked past him again in search of Justin, who would be as confounded as she as to why Paul was here.

"I couldn't believe it when David told me your news." Paul shook his head in commiseration.

David? Alicia tried to think past the chaos of jumbled thoughts in her head. One of Jessica's old flames. She recalled what Jessica had told her at the party, insisting that, though she'd been quite close to Paul Radley when they'd all worked together, socialising with him along with this David, she hadn't invited him to the party. He'd apparently arrived with David, who also worked in financial services. Presumably, they were friends. It made sense. But it didn't make her feel any better about him turning up out of the blue—again.

"I wanted to call by and pay my respects," Paul went on,

apparently oblivious to her growing desperation to end the conversation and get back to her family.

His respects? Alicia was doubly stunned at that. He didn't know the meaning of the word. If he had any respect at all, for anyone, he would *not*...Her thoughts ground to a halt as her gaze fell on Sophie, who was walking away from the church with Jessica. She couldn't see Justin. Panic clutched at her stomach. Where on earth was he?

"Paul, I have to go. My family needs me," she repeated firmly, moving past him, now frantically scanning the immediate vicinity of the churchyard, the groups of people heading towards parked cars, preparing to go on to the reception. Where *was* he? She'd lost sight of him when Jessica had stopped her as they'd filed out of the church.

Hurrying towards Sophie and Jessica, she caught up with them. "Sophie, sweetheart..." Her heart plummeted as Sophie turned towards her, tears now flowing unchecked down her face. "It's all right, baby," she said, her voice catching as she pulled her towards her. "It's all right."

"It's not though, Mum, is it? How *can* it be?" Sophie mumbled into her shoulder.

"She doesn't want to go to the reception." Stroking Sophie's hair, Jessica filled Alicia in. "I said she didn't have to, I hope that's okay? Justin's already left, by the way."

Left? Oh God, no. Because of Paul Radley? "When?" Alicia asked, panic tightening her chest.

"A few minutes ago. I think he needed to be on his own." Jessica met her eyes, an attempt at reassurance in her own, and then glanced past her to Paul Radley, who was walking towards them. "I've told Sophie she can come and stay with me for a few days, if that's okay with you. I said I'd take her back to fetch her things."

Alicia shook her head, bewildered. "I should take her," she

said. "I should be with her. With Justin. Is he all right? I mean, did he seem..." She trailed hopelessly off. Of course he wasn't all right. How could he be? She looked at her sister in desperation.

Jessica wrapped an arm around her. "He's fine. Well, as fine as he can be. He just needed some time alone," she assured her. "He'll probably go on to the reception."

Alicia searched her face, unconvinced.

"Why don't you go straight there," Jessica suggested. "People will expect to see you. It was Justin's colleagues who paid for the buffet, after all. At least you can be there in lieu of him until he turns up. I'm sure he will, Ali."

Alicia hesitated. She should, if only for a short while. Searching Sophie's face worriedly, she debated her options.

"I'll be fine, Mum," Sophie said, wiping a black track of mascara sideways across her face. "I'd like to go to Jess's for a few days, to be honest. You know, away from...things at the house."

Alicia felt her heart wrench inside her. Away from reminders of Luke, she meant, which were far, far too painful for her. "As long as you're sure," she said slowly. She couldn't bear the thought of Sophie being on her own and hurting. How could she let her daughter out of sight of her right now?

Nodding, Sophie smiled weakly.

My beautiful daughter. She had to keep her safe. Had to.

Squeezing her hard, Alicia reluctantly let her go. Reaching to brush her hair from her face, she cupped her cheek with her hand and gently kissed her forehead. *It will be all right, baby. It will be.* Even as she thought it, Alicia felt the thread snagging, as if her life was already unravelling. "I'll ring you," she promised.

"I've called a taxi. Why don't you get off before everyone starts leaving," Jessica suggested.

"I can give you a lift, if you like?" Paul offered, standing suddenly by Alicia's side.

Taken by surprise, Alicia jumped, and then glanced warily at him.

"No," she said quickly, preferring him to have as little contact with her family as possible. "Take the funeral car, Jess. I'll take the taxi."

"Are you sure?" Jessica eyes flicked between her and Paul.

Alicia nodded. "I'd be happier knowing Sophie's left safely with you," she assured her, hoping her sister would get the message.

"Okay," Jess said, looking a little reluctant. "Watch what you're doing, Ali." Giving her a firm hug, she slid an arm around Sophie's waist and led her on towards the car.

Her heart going into freefall, Alicia blinked her own tears back, determined to hold herself together, to harness the strength to try to hold her family together. She *had* to.

"The offer still stands," Paul said, as Jessica and Sophie headed off. "My car's just over there." He nodded towards it. "It will save you waiting around for a taxi."

Hesitant to go anywhere with him, Alicia tried to read his expression. His dark eyes were intent, determined. His smile, though, was sympathetic—no innuendo, she noted, somewhat calmed.

Guardedly, she nodded. It would be a chance to talk to him alone, perhaps her only chance, and she needed to. She had no choice but to. She had to find out what he wanted and then get him out of her life, out of Justin's and Sophie's lives, whatever it took.

"Good," he said, leading the way. "It's the least I can do, after all."

Alicia followed him, bemused by the fact that he didn't seem to realise the least he could do was to stay away from her, from her family.

"Do you want to give me the address?" he said, once they'd climbed into his car.

Alicia gave him the details, and then waited while he fiddled with the satnav.

"Bear with me." He smiled in frustration. "It's a rental car. I'm not quite sure where everything is yet."

The address finally entered, Alicia looked out of the window as they drove slowly out of the cemetery. She wouldn't talk to him here, where she'd just laid her beautiful, innocent baby to rest. It would be a desecration of his memory to even begin to discuss something that would hurt his father so badly.

Bye, little Lucas. Mummy will be back soon, sweetheart. Alicia closed her eyes as they passed through the gates, feeling afresh the wound in her chest where a piece of her heart had gone with him.

Ten minutes. She swallowed, calculating the time she must spend with Paul Radley until they reached the hotel, then steeled herself and turned towards him. "Why are you here, Paul?" she asked him. Though calm on the outside, her emotions were in turmoil.

Paul glanced at her and then back to the road. "On holiday," he said, repeating what he'd told her at the party. "Looks like it's going to be a bit of an extended stay now though."

Alicia's heart sank. "Oh, how so?" she asked, bracing herself for what he might say.

"I've been offered a contract to stay and head up some investment seminars by Graham & Young Investments." Paul turned again to look at her, his gaze lingering this time. "Obviously, they value my expertise. Just a short-term contract," he went on, smiling inscrutably and looking back to the road. "I should be on my way back to Dubai fairly shortly.

"Okay?" he asked her kindly, a second later, as Alicia wiped away another tear, this time one of relief.

CHAPTER FIFTEEN

JUSTIN

Counting steadily, his gaze fixed downwards, Justin kept walking. He didn't much care where. He just needed space to think. He *had* to be getting this out of proportion. There was no way Alicia could have had an affair! He would have known. He *would* have known!

Had he read all the signs but refused to acknowledge it? He'd certainly wondered about her staying over at a girlfriend's more than once. The evasive eye contact when he'd asked her which friend. He'd dismissed it. Told himself he was being paranoid. His biggest fear, when he'd woken up to the fact that he'd been so wrapped up in his grief over his family that he'd barely paid her any attention, had been that he would lose her. So, what if she had? Justin felt his heart drift free from its moorings. What then? He had absolutely no idea what he would do. None.

Reaching his road, he was surprised to see Jessica's car parked outside the house. They must have left the funeral soon after he had. Probably *because* he had. He shouldn't have, but how could he have stayed? How could he have made polite conversation when he felt as if he were dying inside?

Groping for some sort of composure, Justin let himself through the front door, where he found Jessica and Sophie in the hall.

"Dad!" Relief flooding her face, Sophie flung herself towards him. "Are you all right?"

Wrapping an arm around her, Justin squeezed her shoulders. "I'm okay, Pumpkin," he assured her, his throat tight. Glancing past her, he looked along the hall, and then, seeing no evidence of Alicia, looked questioningly back to Jessica.

"I think Alicia's gone to the reception to thank people," Jessica supplied. "Sophie was upset, so I offered to drive back with her."

He shouldn't have left his daughter. Justin glanced down at her, his gut wrenching as he noted her swollen eyes and smudged make-up. He hadn't been thinking straight. Then again, maybe he had. Maybe he was now acknowledging something he'd refused to see before.

"Why don't you go and grab your stuff, Sophie?" Jessica smiled encouragingly in Sophie's direction. "I'll have a quick word with your dad."

Sophie looked uncertainly between them, and then nodded. She was halfway up the stairs when there was a knock at the front door.

Justin opened it to find Sophie's friend Chloe standing there. "I just wondered if Sophie was okay," she said, glancing towards the stairs. "I can come back if you're busy."

"It's okay, Chloe," Sophie called, coming back down. "Ten minutes," she said to Jessica.

Justin smiled, feeling relieved, as she headed past him to go outside, probably wanting to talk in private. He was glad she had a friend who obviously cared. She would need one—perhaps more than she knew.

Jessica waited until the front door had closed. "She's coming to stay with me for a while, if that's okay?" she said, smiling sympathetically at Justin. "She was actually very upset after you'd gone. And Alicia was... Well, you know, busy talking to people. I thought it might be a good idea to get Sophie away from the house for a few days."

"Right." Justin nodded tightly, guessing Jessica had diplomatically stopped short of stating the obvious: that Alicia had been too busy talking to her "old acquaintance" to notice how upset her daughter was. "And is Sophie okay with that?" he asked, concerned that she might feel pushed out in some way.

"I think she could use some breathing space, to be honest," Jess said, obviously well aware of the emotional toll all of this would have had on her. "I thought we'd watch some girly films together, go out for a meal maybe. You know, do normal stuff. It might do her good."

Justin guessed it probably would. Things had been far from normal here. Judging by their conversation the other night, pushed out was exactly how Sophie did feel.

"She needs you, Justin," Jess reminded him—as if she needed to. "Alicia's bound to be a bit preoccupied now, but Sophie's going to need someone to talk to."

Preoccupied with what, exactly? "So it would seem," Justin said, heading past her to the lounge. He didn't want to have this conversation in the hall.

"I can't even begin to imagine what you must be going through," Jess said, following him. "I mean, I know Luke's death has devastated you both, but it must be so much harder on a man, when you're supposed to be the strong one, holding everybody else up. I could see how upset you were today. I just wanted you to know you have a shoulder, if you need one."

"Thanks, Jess," Justin said distractedly, and then, running a hand wearily over his neck, he headed for the drinks table.

Pouring a large whisky, which he felt badly in need of after the day's events, his gaze fell on one of their old Adele CDs that Sophie had left on the table. Would she get through this? Would he ever hear her sing again? They'd never derided her ambition to be a pop artist. She emulated Adele so beautifully; if Justin closed his eyes, he really believed it was her. She was good, though she probably needed to hone her individuality. He'd been partway through converting the basement into a studio—that was going to be his present to her for her sixteenth birthday. Now, he had no idea what the future would hold.

Taking a long drink of the whisky, which burned the back of his throat but did nothing to warm him, he placed the glass back on the table, stared at it for a second and then braced himself. "Can I ask you something, Jess?" he said, looking cautiously towards her.

"Anything," Jess assured him.

Justin doubted she'd be so ready to answer when she heard the question. "Sophie..." He paused, not sure he actually wanted to hear the answer. "Is she mine?"

"What?" Jessica paled.

"You're closest to Alicia, Jess," Justin went on quietly. "I have to know. Am I Sophie's father?"

Hearing himself speak the words, Justin felt like a complete bastard. How was he supposed *not* to ask though? He'd gone over and over it. Radley had worked with Alicia sixteen years ago, when she'd been with the financial services company. Justin remembered it well, the details brought sharply back into focus by the man's reappearance. It had been then that he'd lost his family. Then that, spiralling into a depression he couldn't seem to climb out of, he'd pushed Alicia away, rather than reach out to her. He'd finally woken up to the fact that he'd been so immersed in his grief he was paying no attention to her needs when she'd started staying out: spending nights with a girlfriend, she'd said. He'd hated himself for it, but he had wondered whether that was the truth. She'd had every reason to give up on him. With his emotions all over the place, he'd been impossible to live with. He'd tried to convince himself he was being paranoid, his suspicions based on nothing but the fear of losing her, too. They'd got through that rocky period. They'd been a strong family unit ever since. He'd thought they had. It had taken him a while, though, to stop looking for the signs.

Something else had also occurred to him as he'd walked, something which had turned his gut inside out. Justin had noticed it when Radley had been watching him, a challenge in his eyes, at that fateful party: the man's eyes were brown. Striking brown. Sophie's eyes were a rich chestnut brown, where his and Alicia's were blue. Genetically speaking, it was rare, though it was possible. He'd tried to rationalise it, but now... Was he being paranoid all over again? The fact that Radley seemed to pop up wherever Alicia was, was he imagining that? Imagining the fact that the man was all over her? Justin thought not. He hoped to God he was wrong.

His heart constricting painfully, he waited for Jessica to answer.

Jessica, though, didn't seem to want to answer, looking away instead, looking anywhere but at him. Looking guilty. "You need to talk to Alicia," she said, eventually.

And Justin knew. Without a doubt, he now knew what he so desperately *didn't* want to. Already bursting with grief and guilt, his heart damn near exploded.

CHAPTER SIXTEEN

SOPHIE

Sophie stopped in the hall, hardly able to breathe as she tried to digest what she'd just heard. Shaking her head in bewilderment, she swallowed hard and stepped closer to the partially open lounge door.

"Why the *hell* didn't she tell me?" she heard Justin say angrily from inside.

"I don't know," Jess answered, sounding frantic. "I don't know if there's anything *to* tell. I know she was unhappy at one point, but she never talked to—"

"Bullshit!" Justin cut furiously across her. "What am I supposed to do with this, Jess, hey? I mean, *what*? Carry on as if it's an inconsequential little detail she forgot to mention? Be there for her and pretend it's not killing me that I've lost my son *and* my daughter? Jesus Christ. *How?* Does she even want to be with me?"

"Justin, *please* . . . You need to ask Alicia. Now's not the time to go into any of this."

Justin laughed cynically at that. "No, you're right," he said bitterly. "There never was a right time, I suppose. Not when she was carrying the child she forgot to mention wasn't mine. Not when she gave birth to her. Not when I held her for the first time, swore to devote my life to protecting her. How about before I walk her down the aisle? How about then, Jess? Will she tell me, do you think, as the bastard who had his eyes and hands all over her steps in to take my place?"

"Justin, what am I supposed to say?" Jessica beseeched him. "She's my sister. I can't betray her trust."

"How long did it go on?" Justin demanded, and then laughed again bitterly. "Christ, I must be fucking blind. It's still going on, isn't it?"

Sophie stopped listening. Clamping her hands hard to her ears, tears streaming unchecked down her face, she whirled around to fly upstairs to her bedroom.

He wasn't her father. She felt as if her world had just been ripped from underneath her. Gulping back a sob, she clutched her tummy tight. She felt so nauseous she was sure she was going to throw up. How long had he suspected? How long had he been reluctant to talk to her, to look at her properly? And he had. She'd sensed it. When she'd needed him most, when she'd had nothing but ghosts for company, Luke haunting her dreams, he'd been distant. Not just distracted, but different.

And *she*... her so-called *mother*... Sophie had been so worried for her, hurt so much for her, but *she* obviously didn't care about anyone! *Liar!* Lies. All of it.

Who, then, was her father? Who had her mother had some furtive, dirty affair with, while married to the man she'd passed off as her dad? Was it someone Sophie knew? The milkman? The postman? The fucking odd-job man?

It was sick! Sick and disgusting and sad. Why would he put up with that? *Why?* Stuffing things randomly in her overnight bag, Sophie snatched it up, swiped a hand across her cheeks and headed for the door. She couldn't talk to him. She just couldn't. She couldn't bloody well breathe. Stopping halfway across the room, she paused and scrutinised herself in the mirror. She didn't even look like him.

She had no idea who she was.

Choking back another sob, she wondered at the cruelty of this happening on the same day they'd buried her baby brother. Half-brother. That realisation hitting her like a blow to the chest, Sophie determined she would never trust either of them again. *Ever.*

She had to get out. Going with Jessica was her best hope of avoiding him, her father who wasn't her father and was clearly furious at being deceived into thinking he was. He was probably planning how fast *he* could get away.

Away from her.

She needed to speak to her mother. She wanted explanations, as if there could possibly be any. But not here. Not now. They'd probably be so busy arguing, or more likely not talking to each other, they wouldn't even notice her.

CHAPTER SEVENTEEN

JUSTIN

Justin wasn't happy Sophie had left before he'd had a chance to ask her how she was feeling now that the funeral was over. As if he needed to ask. Devastated—that was how she would be feeling.

Choking back an angry knot in his chest, he considered this new twist in their lives, and how it was going to affect Sophie. Because if not now, at some time it would have to. Had Alicia not considered how many times she might be asked for her parents' medical history throughout her life when she'd decided to keep this huge secret to herself? *Jesus Christ*. It had been so many years. Everything—their whole relationship, as well as his relationship with Sophie—was based on a lie. To her, plainly, this had been too trivial to mention. How many other things might she have lied about? How many other details might she have neglected to tell him? Like the fact that the long-lost lover hadn't just *happened* to turn up after the funeral, for instance? Or that *fucking* party? Wasn't it more likely that she'd had contact with him over the years?

Following Jess and Sophie to the front door, Justin dragged a hand furiously over his neck, attempting to curtail his building anger. They would have exchanged emails, no doubt. Text messages, phone calls—the added thrill obviously being that it was all going on behind his back. Had they met up when Radley had visited the UK, which surely he would have done? She'd been away a couple of times over the years. On residential training courses pertaining to her ongoing social work training, she'd said. More probably she'd been in that bastard's bed, the topic of post-coital conversation being their future plans.

Christ, he felt sick.

Breathing in hard, he forced a smile for Sophie's sake. "Bye, Pumpkin," he said, wishing she'd unplug her earphones so he could say goodbye properly before she left. Seeing that she was distracted, obviously into her music, which she probably found therapeutic, he settled for giving her shoulders a squeeze and kissing her cheek instead.

Sophie offered him the briefest of smiles and followed Jess out.

Justin watched as, head bowed, she walked to Jess's car and climbed inside the passenger side. He'd thought she might wave as they drove off, but...

Oh God, no. Justin's heart flipped over. He'd thought she'd been outside. He'd seen her and Chloe through the window, walking away from the house. Might she have come back earlier than he'd realised, heard him and Jess talking? *Dammit!* He'd needed to speak to Jess, desperately needed to speak to her, but why hadn't he thought before broaching the subject with Sophie around?

Cursing himself, Justin pulled out his mobile and selected her number, hoping she would pick up, relief surging through him when she did. "Sophie, I just wanted to apologise," he said quickly.

"For?" Sophie asked guardedly.

"Leaving you earlier. I'm sorry, Sophie. It was a selfish thing to do. I just—"

"It's fine," Sophie said over him. "You're dealing with shit. I get it."

"We all are," Justin reminded her gently.

"And some," Sophie replied quietly, after a pause.

"Are you sure you're okay?" Justin asked, trying to read the inflection in her voice. He could feel her slipping away from him already. "Staying with Jess for a while, I mean?"

"Yeah, it's fine. Me not being in the way will give you two some space, won't it?" She sounded so indifferent. "Crap, battery's dying. I'd better go."

"Okay, but ring me when you get there, will you?" Justin asked, feeling extremely concerned by her reluctance to be drawn into conversation. Was he reading too much into it? She'd seemed all right when he'd come home, or as right as she could be under the circumstances. When she'd left, though…

"Sophie?" Realising she'd gone, Justin tossed his mobile onto the hall table and stared at it, uncertain what to do next.

He couldn't lose her. Above and beyond Alicia's deceit, which was crucifying him, his gut-wrenching fear was that he would lose Sophie. She would have to learn the truth eventually. Parental medical history was so important, for pregnancy as well as future health issues. He couldn't keep this information from her—as a doctor as much as anything else. Once she found out, he might become peripheral to her life. Imagining that *bastard* taking over his role, being there for her when she needed a father, was destroying him. He loved her, irrevocably. He'd loved her since he'd gone with Alicia to her first scan and glimpsed her tiny form on the monitor. She'd been his reason for focussing on the future, not dwelling on a past that was too painful to contemplate. Losing his family had almost destroyed him. He *couldn't* lose Sophie. Whatever her biology, she was *his* daughter.

He'd need to take a test. His heart wrenched again as that sickening thought occurred. Should he do that before confronting Alicia? He didn't understand. Why had she stayed with him if she was still involved with this…whoever the fuck he was? Why the *hell* hadn't she told him?

Kneading a temple, he reached for his phone, selected Alicia's number and then hesitated. She'd just buried her son. *He'd* just buried his son, he reminded himself, his grief almost choking him as he realised the death of the child he'd loved with every fibre of his being was in danger of becoming secondary to all of this. *Was* Lucas his child?

He stopped, feeling the foundations of his life crumbling beneath him as that thought occurred. He couldn't do this. He couldn't talk to her. Hear her voice. Feel another part of him die inside when she lied.

CHAPTER EIGHTEEN

JESSICA

"All right, lovely?" Warily, Jessica glanced sideways at Sophie. Jessica had heard her outside in the hall, and knew she'd overheard. She'd expected her to say something at the house. Or at least mention it when Justin had rung just now. Instead, she'd got off the phone fast and immediately texted someone. So much for her battery being dead.

God, she hoped Sophie would be all right. She'd have to try and talk to her. Jessica didn't agree with what Alicia had done, deceiving Justin all these years, to say little of putting her in an impossible situation. Obviously not as adept as her sister at subterfuge, she'd found herself completely unable to lie to Justin's face when he'd had asked her outright. She hadn't actually confirmed his suspicions—it wasn't quite as clear-cut as he'd imagined it was—but she was glad he knew now. Alicia loved him, Jessica was sure of that, but it wasn't fair to keep a man under false pretences. Frankly, she didn't think Alicia deserved him. It wasn't a little lie she'd told, after all. It was humungous. She should have told Justin the truth straight away, as Jessica had urged her to. Back then, after Paul Radley had disappeared off the scene, there had been no reason not to. Honesty was surely the best policy, given the risk that Justin would find out one day. If Alicia had just been honest, they might have been able to get past it. She would never, ever have wished Sophie to find out third-hand though.

"Sophie?" Jessica reached out, giving Sophie's arm a squeeze when she didn't answer.

Sophie tugged an earphone loose and looked at her questioningly.

"All right, sweetie?" Jessica asked.

Sophie shrugged. "You know," she said, and fixed her gaze on the side window. "Can you do me a favour, Aunt Jess?" she said, after a second. "If Mum rings, can you tell her I'm asleep or something?"

"Of course," Jessica assured her, her heart skipping a beat. "Are you okay?"

Another shrug from Sophie. "I just don't want to talk to anyone. Not yet."

Jessica felt a prickle of apprehension run through her. Sophie would definitely need some space now, and Justin would most definitely need a shoulder.

CHAPTER NINETEEN

JUSTIN

You need to come home. It's urgent.

Justin placed his phone precisely down, lining it up perfectly with the edge of the table, as if that could somehow put his world back in order. Then he paused. He was less puzzled by the tiny screw on top of the hall table than the fine dusting of plaster around it.

Instinctively, Justin glanced towards the alarm box to the side of him, and then reached to open it. It took a second to register what he was looking at; to realise, cold foreboding sweeping the length of his spine, that the two crucial wires were disconnected, meaning there'd been someone in the house. *Jesus.* Justin's mouth ran dry. When?

While they were at the funeral?

While they'd been here?

While Sophie had been upstairs...

"*Fuck!*" His gut clenching, his gaze automatically shooting to the far corners of the hall, Justin froze. Images of his sister, her blood bleeding into the hall carpet, his parents, walls and white sheets stained impossibly crimson, emblazoned themselves on his mind. He took a faltering step forwards.

And then, snatching his phone back up, he ran.

Propelling himself into action, he slammed into the front room. Scanning it as he jabbed 999 into his phone, he registered that nothing seemed to be missing, checked the other downstairs rooms and then raced to the back door.

Locked. He noted the key, hanging well out of sight on the hook in the utility.

No broken panes.

They'd come through the front door. Through the fucking *front door*!

His heart rate escalating, a pulse thrumming rapidly at the base of his neck, Justin grabbed hold of the banister and swung himself upstairs to push the nursery door open. Undisturbed. Everything as still as the grave.

Sophie's room? It was a mess: dresser drawers open, T-shirts spewing out like hungry tongues. More mess than usual? Taking in the clothes-strewn bed, Justin had no way of knowing.

Backing out, he headed for their own room. His pulse rate slowing, his adrenaline still pumping, he banged the door wide, stepped inside—and stopped dead.

His blood freezing in his veins, he stepped towards the dressing table and closed his eyes. When he opened them, it was still there, scrawled in red lipstick on the mirror, scorched indelibly on his brain.

SORRY FOR YOUR LOSS

Justin tried to breathe, but he couldn't pull air past the fury lodged like acid in his chest. "Bastard," he seethed, trying and failing to obliterate the image of the smashed mirror in the house of his parents from his mind. "*Bastard!*" Slamming his fist into the glass, ignoring the cut from the sharp shard that sliced through his flesh, he turned away, heading for the landing. His anger simmering steadily inside him, he went up to check the third floor.

Having scoured the whole house, including the bathrooms,

and checked every window on the basis that the scum who'd broken in might just get it into their fetid minds to come back, he went back into Sophie's room and sank heavily onto the bed.

They'd refurbished this room together, he recalled obliquely, he and Alicia. Sophie hadn't wanted prissy pink walls and florals, she'd said. She'd wanted grungy, whatever that meant. Street art style, an industrial theme, Alicia had knowledgeably informed him. He'd come into his own on the DIY front, putting the metal bedframe and wire storage lockers together. And then he'd put his foot in the paint tray, which had had Alicia in hysterics, coaxing the scowl from his face and making him laugh at his own ineptitude. She had a knack for doing that. They'd fallen into bed exhausted that night, taken time to make unhurried love together, despite their exhaustion, falling asleep with bodies and limbs entwined. Had it been less satisfying for her than for him? Had he been inadequate in some way? Had he always been?

His mind went back sixteen years, to the day he'd asked her about the girlfriend she'd supposedly been staying with. She'd stayed three, maybe four times. She hadn't been well after the first time she'd stayed over. A hangover, she'd said, and maybe a bug of some sort. She'd also been subdued. He remembered that well. That was when the doubts had first surfaced. She'd originally said they were going out. Then she'd said they'd stayed home, preferring girl-talk and a film. He'd asked her what on earth they found to talk about. "This and that," she'd said vaguely. He'd asked her what film they'd watched. She'd looked panicked for a second, before she'd come up with a title. It was a film he and she had already seen together. It was nothing, he'd told himself. She'd clearly drunk enough to make her recollection hazy. Yet, there was something: her body language had been tense. He'd noticed the slight flush to her cheeks, as she'd turned away from him. He'd found himself watching her and, far from the evasive behaviour he'd expected, he'd found her looking back at him, her eyes wide and uncertain, locked right on his. He'd wondered whether it was because she was uncertain about him, his commitment to a marriage he'd been emotionally absent from.

He should have paid closer attention to his instincts. Maybe then, he wouldn't be sitting here now, watching his life fall apart. Everything, piece by piece, was disintegrating around him and he had no way to stop it. No one to turn to.

Staying where he was, trying to get a grip, he counted the words repeated on the graffiti-print wallpaper, starting with one strip, reading to the top, and then travelling down the next. His gaze snagged on a notebook lying on the floor, and Justin stopped counting and reached for it.

Idly, he flicked it open, his eyes immediately falling on a poem written in Sophie's neat handwriting, and his breath hitched painfully in his chest.

I say I'm fine, but I'm crying inside.
I daren't let you see, the tears that I hide.
I'm hurting.
It's like he didn't exist.
Why can't you talk about him?
Tell him how much he is missed.
They say time will heal pain.
But time can't bring you back again.
I'm hurting.
Truly, how I feel is heartbroken,
For your short life stolen.
The words left unspoken.
I miss you, Luke.
We all do.
Stay safe with the angels, sweetheart.
Until I find you.

Pressing a thumb and forefinger to his eyes, Justin gulped hard. She would be devastated by this. Already broken-hearted at the loss of her brother, Sophie would feel that everything that defined who she was, everything dear to her, had been stolen away from her. She might never recover emotionally. If she couldn't trust her own mother, her own father—if he wasn't honest with her, she might never trust anyone again. How would he tell her? How the *hell* was he going to talk to Alicia? What would he do if she said she was leaving? Would he beg her to stay?

No. Justin dragged an arm across his eyes and got to his feet. He wasn't going to do that. An affair he might have forgiven, given his own erratic behaviour. But the deceit, the lies she must have told since—he could never forgive that. How could he live with someone who couldn't possibly have loved him? Alongside the knowledge that Sophie might not be his daughter, that's what hurt most of all: realising that she probably never had.

Ignoring the rich droplets of blood on the carpet, which were his own, Justin made his way back to the hall. He was halfway down the stairs when he stopped, noting a darkly dressed figure approaching, visible through the opaque glass in the front door.

CHAPTER TWENTY

ALICIA

All sorts of scenarios having raced through Alicia's mind when she'd received Justin's text, her first terrifying thought that something might have happened to Sophie, she'd accepted Paul Radley's offer of a lift home. Once on the way, she'd debated the wisdom of arriving with him, but her first instinct had been to get here as soon as she could.

Arriving at the house, she fumbled her key into the lock and almost fell through the front door. Relief sweeping through her when she saw Justin standing on the stairs, she took a step towards him. "Justin? What's—" *Oh God!* He'd been injured. Her heart lurching against her ribcage, Alicia flew towards him. And then she stopped uncertainly.

His face white, his expression inscrutable, Justin didn't move. He simply looked at her as if she were a stranger, and Alicia's heart, already heavy with guilt and unbearable sorrow, plummeted like a lead weight in her chest.

"Justin, you're hurt." Her gaze dropped to the spatters of blood on his shirt, then back to his face.

"I'm fine." Justin scanned her eyes, his own thunderously dark, and then looked past her, his expression hardening.

"Sorry," Paul Radley said from behind Alicia. "I wouldn't have come in, but I saw the door was open. You dropped your phone in the car, Alicia."

Oh no. Alicia felt her stomach turn over. She'd asked him to let her out of the car away from the house. He must have known why she had. And now he was walking into the hall as bold as brass. Why would he *do* that?

"Paul gave me a lift to the reception." She fumbled hopelessly for an explanation. "He came to the funeral and when I got your—"

"Right. Well, now he's played the hero, *Paul* can just fuck off again, can't he?" Justin cut in angrily, his gaze fixed stonily on Paul's.

Cold fear pierced through Alicia like a knife. "He offered me a lift, Justin," she said, falteringly, willing God to strike her down dead if it saved her husband any more hurt. "Jess brought Sophie back and I didn't have any transport, so—"

"Drives a taxi then, does he?" Justin interrupted bitterly.

"No, I..." Alicia shook her head, confused and, above all, frightened. He was *bleeding.* She needed to know why. She needed to know what had happened. "Justin, *please,* the text. "You said it was urgent. Please tell me what's happened. Where's Sophie?"

Justin's eyes flicked to hers. "She's fine, I *think,*" he said, emphasis on the "think." "She's with Jessica."

Thank God. Alicia closed her eyes.

Looking between her and Paul, Justin finally came down the stairs. "We've been broken into," he said bluntly, causing Alicia's world to shift further off-kilter.

"Broken into?" She stared at him, shocked. "But...how? *When?*" Not last night. They would have noticed. As devastated as they had all been this morning, they would have noticed a break-in.

"Today," Justin supplied, glancing away. "The police are on their way." He looked back to her. "I suspect *Paul,* who has an uncanny knack for turning up uninvited, might be better off out of the way, if you don't mind my suggesting."

His gaze travelled pointedly back to him.

Paul nodded understandingly. "Of course. My timing couldn't have been worse, could it? This is unbelievable, when you already have so much to contend with. Please accept my sincere condolences. This must be a very difficult time for you both."

"It is," Justin assured him.

Someone had broken in while they were at the funeral? While they were burying their child! Alicia felt anger unfurl inside her. *The absolute bastards!* "Have they touched anything?" she asked, her blood running cold as she imagined the things they might have touched, desecrated, stolen. Memories broken. Her children's things. Her baby's. Please ... not her baby's. She swallowed back a jagged knot in her throat. "Have they taken anything?"

His hostility seeming to wane, Justin turned his attention to her, focussing on her at last. "I'm not sure. I've looked, but—"

"Have they been in the nursery?" Feeling sick now to her very soul, Alicia stepped shakily towards the stairs.

"Alicia, wait." Catching her shoulders, Justin stopped her. "You need to wait, Alicia. The police said not to go into any of the upstairs rooms. They said not to touch anything."

Alicia wavered, every one of her emotions colliding. This was her punishment. She'd lost her dear precious child, but she would not let the lowlife who'd done this sully her baby's memories. She prayed his tiny space hadn't been invaded. It still smelled of him. Her baby!

Clamping a hand to her mouth, she pushed past him. She had to see. She had to know.

"Alicia!" Justin was right behind her as she stumbled up the stairs.

Finding the nursery untouched, Alicia gave way to the sobs climbing her throat, and thanked God for this one small mercy. Her next thought of her daughter, she squeezed past Justin to Sophie's room.

Seeing nothing obviously missing or touched, she allowed herself to breathe out, and turned to go to the main bedroom.

Close behind her, Justin caught her arm as she neared the door. "You shouldn't go in there, Alicia," he said quietly, his eyes now holding a warning.

There was something he didn't want her to see. Something he knew would upset her. She searched his face. There was no anger there now, just heartbreaking bewilderment and so much pain. Concern also, for her. Guilt consuming her, Alicia dropped her gaze. "I need to, Justin," she said. "I have to know."

Once inside the door, she stopped dead. Studying the mirror in disbelief, reading the cruel message left there, realising it was Justin's blood at the smashed centre of it, that her husband would be suffering because of it, because of her, Alicia felt her heart falter.

It wasn't whoever had broken into their house who'd sullied their memories.

It was her.

CHAPTER TWENTY-ONE

JUSTIN

It had taken every ounce of Justin's willpower to control himself when Alicia had come home with the man who might well be Sophie's father. Now he was restraining himself from asking her to stay, instead of going to her sister's and leaving things hanging between them. But then, knowing what he now did, Justin guessed it was him, rather than a houseful of tainted memories, she might prefer to be away from.

He supposed he should be grateful, given the lack of police resources, that the detective in charge of the hit-and-run case had turned up personally. They were giving the break-in some priority, but the scene of crime officers seemed to be taking their sweet time trying to establish whether they might have any forensic evidence to go on, meaning Alicia would most likely take up Radley's offer of a lift to her sister's. How ironic that when Justin had asked him to leave, wanting the bastard out of his house and away from his wife, the police had requested he wait around—to eliminate any fingerprints he might have left, they'd said.

He'd gleaned from Radley's expression that he'd been more than happy to oblige, eager to hang around Alicia. Was he getting some perverse kick out of it, humiliating the man whose wife he was having a seedy affair with? Justin glanced contemptuously to where he stood in the middle of *his* lounge, looking at him as if he were weighing him up. *Prat.* Justin sucked in a terse breath and turned his attention to Detective Inspector Taylor, willing him to hurry it up.

"What about the writing?" Alicia asked him, as DI Taylor scribbled in his notebook.

"We might have been able to get a handwriting analyst on it. Unfortunately, now the mirror's smashed and spattered with blood..." Shrugging hopelessly, Taylor looked regretfully towards Justin.

Justin glanced down. It had been a kneejerk reaction. Probably the only one who would understand why he'd reacted that way was Alicia, because she knew the circumstances under which he'd found his family.

"So, it's just the items you mentioned that you think are missing?" Taylor double-checked, referring to his notes. "One half-carat diamond ring; one ladies' Radley watch; one ladies' nine-carat gold bar-and-chain bracelet; and one yellow gold locket, enhanced with a white gold floral motif?"

Alicia nodded. "I'm not sure about Sophie's things. I'll have to speak to her," she said, sounding and looking more exhausted than Justin had ever seen her. "The locket," she added, as Taylor closed his notebook, "it has photographs of my children in it. The one of Lucas was the last one we'd taken of him."

Hearing the heartbreak in her voice, watching the tears slide slowly down her cheeks, Justin choked back his own emotion. He had the photo of Luke on his phone, but it was the significance of it being stolen on the day of his funeral that was breaking her heart. He was halfway towards her when Mr. Magnanimous himself beat him to it. "I'll take you to Jessica's, when you're ready," Radley said, smiling sympathetically.

Alicia looked up at him, and then got to her feet.

And Justin felt her slip away from him another inch.

"No," she said, taking him by surprise. "It's kind of you to offer, but I think I'd rather take a taxi."

Radley also looked surprised, Justin noted, or possibly slightly irritated. "Oh," he said, his smile now on the tight side. "Are you sure? It's no trouble."

"Positive," Alicia said, nodding adamantly. "I have some things I need to do. You might as well get off."

She wasn't looking at him, Justin noticed, but Radley was looking at her, definitely perturbed. The man was obviously a cocksure son of a bitch who wasn't used to being turned down.

"I'll show you out," Justin said, pushing his hands in his pockets and nodding towards the front door. He would quite like to physically escort him out, but he guessed that wouldn't be a smart move with police in the house.

Closing the front door behind him, having declined to shake the hand the bastard had the gall to offer him, Justin took a second and then went back to the lounge.

Finishing her call, to a taxi company, it sounded like, Alicia wrapped her arms about herself in that way she'd adopted. She looked cold, haunted, alone with her grief.

She shouldn't be on her own, not now. He had to stay here until the forensics officers had finished their business, but... "Why don't you call Jessica?" he suggested. "She won't mind coming to fetch you."

Alicia shook her head. "I'd rather she didn't leave Sophie. And I don't want Sophie coming with her and seeing police here."

Justin understood. Sophie would have to know, but they could break this news to her gently, he supposed. There would be no way to soften the blow regarding her parentage.

Swallowing back his anger, which would serve no purpose right now, he walked across to Alicia. Whatever was happening between them, she needed not to feel the kind of emptiness he knew she would be feeling. The kind of desolate loneliness that would drive her further into herself. He'd been there. He might not have surfaced, if not for her. If he wasn't misreading things here, which clearly spelled out that three was a crowd—and he didn't think he was—then maybe he should be the one to bow out.

Not gracefully though. He would fight for Sophie. Though he felt jaded to his very bones, he would never give up on his daughter. *Never.* As long as she needed him, he would be there. And if one day she didn't... Justin quashed a stab of anguish in his chest. He would cross that bridge when he got there.

Alicia didn't relax into him as he eased her into his arms. She didn't tense, though. Justin didn't read too much into that, but he was taken aback when she rested her head lightly on his shoulder, staying like that for a second, before looking up at him, her eyes awash with such raw emotion that it tore him apart. "Will you ring me?" she asked him, her voice small and defeated. "If you hear anything?"

Feeling a sharp lump slide down his throat, Justin nodded. "I will, I promise," he said hoarsely, and pressed his forehead lightly to hers.

CHAPTER TWENTY-TWO

SOPHIE

Sophie hesitated, her thumb hovering over her phone when she saw it was her dad calling. But she couldn't call him Dad any more, could she?

Was he ringing to break the news, say, *Hey, how're you doing? Oh, by the way, I'm not your father?* He could hardly just leave it, could he, now he'd finally found out something that was basically a life changer?

Her heart missed a beat at the thought that he would want to change his life—but he'd have to, wouldn't he? It's not like he'd want to stay with a woman who'd turned out to be a cheating, lying bitch.

She placed the phone on the bed and let it go to voicemail. Jessica's spare bed in her spare room, pretty and prissy and nothing like her own. Sophie missed it already. She missed him. Missed Luke so much it hurt. It felt like her intestines were all twisted up inside her. Turning away from the phone, she curled herself into a ball, clamping her hands to her tummy and wishing the cramps would go away, that everything would go away. Especially her mother. All of this was her fault. *All* of it.

Plucking at a loose edge of wallpaper, she ignored the phone when it rang again. He was a bit keen, wasn't he, to drop another bombshell in her life? She didn't have a life any more, though, did she? Not one worth living. Sophie's anger intensified, twisting itself into a tight knot, like a snake squirming around in her belly. She'd never hated her dad. She'd been pissed off with him sometimes, yes, but he'd never been a rubbish dad, distant like some of her friends' dads were, or overbearing: laying down the rules, expecting her to jump to his command. He'd always tried to talk to her, even when he completely didn't get it. He'd smiled when she'd needed him to, making her think that whatever trauma she was going through maybe wasn't such a big deal after all. She didn't hate him now, though she wanted to. She just wanted him to do what he'd always done—make things all right. He'd always looked out for her, taking the little dickhead who was bullying her at junior school aside and making him stop with no more than a succinct word. Wiping away her tears and bathing her knees when she grazed them, which she always seemed to be doing when she was small.

He'd taught her to ride her bike on her own in the hall, she recalled, rather than risk her skinning her knees again on the icy pavement outside. Sophie's mouth curved into a small smile as she remembered how he'd whooped like a big kid when she'd finally got the hang of it. His eyes had been so full of pride, she felt like she'd climbed a mountain. And then he'd gone slightly cross-eyed when one of the rugs that covered the flagstones had slipped from underneath him and he'd landed flat on his back.

She pictured herself dropping down to clamp her hand to his cheek. "Are you hurt?" she'd whispered fearfully.

He'd lifted his head and given her a wink. "Nothing damaged but my pride, Pumpkin," he'd assured her. He had been hurt though. He'd dislocated his shoulder, they learned later, but hadn't said anything, in order to protect her impressionable five-year-old's feelings.

She wished she could be small again, his little girl, safe in the unshakeable belief that her dad would be there for her forever.

He'd never lied to her either. Was he going to now? Would

he try to soften the blow with more lies, she wondered? Would he quietly distance himself from her, or just wash his hands of everything and walk away?

Unfurling herself as her phone rang for a third time, Sophie leaned her back against the wall, brought her knees up to her chest and reluctantly picked it up.

"Hi, Sophie, it's Dad," Justin said when she answered, causing the icy dagger to inch further into her heart. "Are you busy?"

"No. Just sleeping." Sophie plucked nervously on her eyebrow stud. "Sorry, I muted my phone."

"Are you okay?" Justin asked, immediate concern in his voice.

"Yeah, just stomach cramps." Sophie shrugged. "You know."

"Ask Jess for a hot water bottle," Justin advised, sounding like he always did, as near normal as it was possible to be in the abnormal shit-fest their lives had become. "Take a couple of paracetamol and curl up under the duvet for a while."

"I will," Sophie said, thinking that a truckload of paracetamol might be the only thing that would make this pain go away. "So, why the call?" she asked him, bracing herself for bad news—which it would be, whatever he said. If he didn't tell her, he'd be lying, leaving her with the uncertainty of when the bomb would drop. And if he told her... Sophie tucked her knees closer to her chest. She didn't think she could bear it.

"I just wanted to let you know your mum's on her way over," Justin said, causing her to immediately uncoil.

"Why?" she asked apprehensively. "I mean, why's she coming here now? I've only just got here."

Justin hesitated. "There's been a problem...at home," he said carefully.

Sophie almost laughed. That was one way of describing a total fucking catastrophe, she supposed. "What kind of problem?" she asked warily, praying that if he couldn't tell her the whole truth, he wouldn't give her a load of bullshit. He'd be struggling with it as much as she was, after all. His pride would be badly bruised this time. His heart pulverised, all thanks the woman who had vowed to stay faithful to him. *Cow.*

"A break-in," Justin supplied, after a pause. "Nothing major taken," he added quickly, obviously trying to reassure her. "Some jewellery: your mum's gold locket, a few other things. No items of yours, as far as we can see. I think your mum will feel safer there with you and Jess though."

"A break-in?" Sophie felt goosebumps prickle her skin. "But... *when?*" she asked, disbelieving. How? How did this shit just keep happening?

"While we were out. At the funeral."

It took a second for Sophie to digest. *While we were saying goodbye to Luke, someone had...* Tears springing to eyes, she glanced upwards.

"Okay, Pumpkin?" Justin asked softly, which only made it worse.

"Yes," Sophie blurted quickly. She couldn't cry. All the hurt stuffed inside her would come tumbling out if she did. She couldn't talk to him either. How could she? From him, at least, she wanted honesty. She didn't want to be pacified. She wanted the *truth*. The unedited, ugly truth.

"You didn't notice anything missing or moved in your room, did you, Sophie?" Justin asked her.

Shaking her head, Sophie tried to focus. She hadn't. But then, she'd been in such a state of shock that she probably wouldn't have noticed if Santa Claus plus his reindeer had dropped down the chimney. "No," she said. "What about you? Are you coming here too?" She hoped her broaching of the subject sounded innocuous.

"I, er..."

Sophie tried to suppress her growing sense of dread as Justin searched for an answer.

"No," he said, eventually, over a long intake of breath. "I'll, er, be staying in a hotel, just for a while. I . . . have a work trip, a conference," he went on falteringly. Lying badly.

And Sophie's heart splintered. "Right," she choked, feeling the knot in her stomach tighten into a fist. "I have to go. Dinner's ready. I'll see you . . . whenever."

CHAPTER TWENTY-THREE

ALICIA

Alicia gazed out of the taxi window, seeing nothing of the normality going on around her, her mind instead full of disjointed snapshots of her life: Justin in the delivery room, nestling Sophie gently in his arms, swearing to his new baby girl that he would die to protect her.

His awe when he'd watched Sophie take her first steps. His fierce sense of pride as she'd accomplished each achievement in her life, big or small. The adoration that shone from his eyes whenever he quietly listened to her singing. The same adoration she'd seen in his eyes for Lucas, as he'd watched his baby boy grow.

The tortured, terrifying heartbreak when he'd realised he couldn't save him. Alicia would never forget that look in his eyes.

The thunderous look, bordering on hatred, she'd seen when Paul had followed her into the house. She would take that memory to her grave.

He knew—at least part of it. He would be beyond devastated, and she didn't dare hope he could ever forgive her, but if he ever found out about Sophie, the possibility she might not be his, it would kill him. At least Paul couldn't disclose that to him, though. He couldn't reveal what he didn't know. She'd never told him about her pregnancy. For Justin's sake, she'd sworn she never would.

Realising they'd arrived at Jessica's, Alicia paid the taxi off and climbed tiredly out. She needed to be with Sophie. To hold her close and never let her go. To try somehow to stop the hurt, the immeasurable pain her daughter would be going through. She had no idea how she could, apart from simply being there for her. She knew she hadn't been, through all of this. And now some heartless animal had invaded their home. Sophie would be terrified by that knowledge.

She'd barely taken a step when a car drew up as the taxi pulled off. *Paul Radley.* Alicia's blood turned to ice as she recognised his car. How in God's name did he know Jessica's address? Jessica had gone out with his friend for a while, not him.

"Alicia," Paul called, winding his window down.

Alicia glanced towards the house, and then took a breath and walked towards him.

"I just wanted to check you were okay," he said, smiling as she approached.

"So you followed me?" Alicia looked at him, astonished.

Paul furrowed his brow. "Why would I do that? I know where your sister lives. I dropped David off here from the tennis club several times. I was just concerned, that's—"

"What do you want, Paul?" Alicia asked him tersely. Maybe he was genuinely worried—she'd always been rubbish at reading the signs where Paul Radley was concerned—but whatever his reasons were for hounding her, he must know that he was putting her marriage in jeopardy.

"Look, Alicia." He sighed. "I know I took off suddenly, and that you probably don't want to see me..."

Probably? Alicia laughed incredulously.

"Can we talk? Please?" he asked her. "Five minutes. No more, I promise."

Alicia glanced nervously back to the house. She didn't want him anywhere near her daughter.

"We can drive around, if you like? Or we can just sit in the car."

Alicia hesitated, and then braced herself. "Just five minutes. And we'll stay here," she said, walking around to his passenger side. "So?" she asked, climbing in.

Paul looked her thoughtfully over. "I'm concerned, Ali, that's all," he said kindly. "I know asking you if you're all right is ludicrous. Clearly, you're not going to be, after all that's happened. I'd just like to help, if I can."

Alicia glanced warily at him. Surely he must know that the only thing he could possibly do to help would be to leave her alone? "There's nothing you can do, Paul, really," she assured him. "Thank you for the lift to the reception, and for bringing my phone back—it was kind of you—but I really think it's best if we don't have any further contact. I have my family to think of."

Letting out another heavy sigh, Paul nodded. "Your daughter," he said.

"And Justin," Alicia reminded him. "Look, Paul, I really should go inside. I need to talk to Sophie."

"Right," Paul said, as she reached for her door. "Give her my love."

Her heart immediately skipping a beat, Alicia froze.

"Sophie," Paul clarified, as she looked cautiously back at him. "Give her my love, will you?"

"*What?*" Alicia stared hard at him.

Paul looked away, placing his hands on the steering wheel and fixing his gaze straight ahead. "I've been wondering... about the timing of your pregnancy." He paused pointedly. "I talked to Jessica at her party. She mentioned she'd been thinking of having a joint party with Sophie for her upcoming sixteenth. Naturally, that gave me pause for thought."

Alicia's heart stopped dead. *Jessica?* But, surely she would have realised she wouldn't want him to have her date of birth?

"Is she mine, Alicia?"

Alicia didn't answer. She wasn't capable of formulating an answer.

"I have a right to know, Alicia. If she is my daughter—"

He stopped, his grip on the steering wheel tightening. His eyes were dangerous, when they came back to hers. "Well?" he demanded.

"I...I don't know," Alicia stammered, completely destabilised. "I..."

Paul sneered. "I see. But you didn't think to mention the fact that you were pregnant?"

"No, I...You went away. I—"

"I rang you! I emailed you! You didn't return one of my calls. Not one! Why? I *loved* you. I couldn't stop thinking about you. *Why* didn't you—"

"*Loved?*" Alicia stared at him, stunned.

Paul tugged in a terse breath. "I've missed her childhood, Alicia," he growled, his jaw tightening. "Those years of watching her grow up, they were mine."

"That's rubbish!" Alicia countered, her anger unleashing. "What happened between us was a mistake. It was wrong—you know it was. And what if I had told you? You left! Went off to your bright new career in Dubai. Why would I have imagined you would have been remotely interested in a child you might have fathered?"

"I didn't leave voluntarily," Paul said, after a second. "I had a spot of bother. With the Financial Conduct Authority." He paused, embarrassed. "An investment complaint. It was all cleared up eventually, but...The point is, I *was* interested. I asked you to join me. You didn't even bother to reply."

"Join you?" Alicia studied him, now utterly bewildered. "I was *married*. I loved my *husband*."

"But you still came back. Made love with *me*," Paul retorted. "What we had was good, Alicia. Special. You can't deny that."

Alicia laughed incredulously. To him, it had been. He'd kissed her tenderly before she'd left the hotel room that first time. He'd sent her flowers, she remembered, to the office. He really had thought it was special. A relationship. "You're mad," she said, and turned to shove her door open.

Paul idled for a second, after she climbed out. Alicia felt the hairs rise on her skin as she wondered whether he might try to follow her in. Then, at last, he eased away from the kerb.

"I'll be in touch," he shouted through his window as he drove off, causing cold terror to rip through her.

Justin was going to find out, from *him*, and there was nothing she could do to stop it. She'd never said the actual words—told Justin that Sophie was his. Why would she? He'd trusted her, God help him. He'd never questioned her. He'd been the best father to Sophie that a man could be. She had to pre-empt Paul, talk to Justin before he did.

It would kill him. His heart would be utterly broken.

Swallowing back her deep sense of shame, the shame she'd carried, and which had intensified every time she'd lied, whether with words or by omission, she swiped a tear from her cheek and turned to the house, ringing the bell urgently, only to find Jess already swinging the door open.

"Ali..." Jess's face was white, her eyes filled with apprehension as they searched hers. "Justin... He knows."

Alicia felt her legs go weak beneath her. *Oh God, no.* "How much?" she asked, her voice hoarse. "How much does he know?"

Stepping back to let her in, Jessica glanced guiltily down. "Sophie. He knows about Sophie," she said, looking wretchedly back at her.

Alicia stared at her, uncomprehending. Surely Jess hadn't...?

She'd *sworn* she wouldn't. She'd urged Alicia to tell Justin the truth years ago, but she'd promised she would never take it upon herself to do so.

"I didn't tell him," Jess said quickly. "I would never have done that, I swear to God I wouldn't. But when he asked me outright... I was vague, but couldn't lie to him, Ali. I'm just no good at it. He guessed. I think he'd half guessed already. I'm so sorry." She looked at her beseechingly. "So, so sorry."

Alicia nodded, the floor seeming to shift underneath her as she tried to digest, tried to imagine what unbearable heartbreak Justin would be going through right now. "It's all right," she said, closing her eyes. It was her fault. Not Jess's. Hers. She should never have expected her to lie for her. "I need to ring him. Talk to him."

"There's something else." Jess caught her arm as she fumbled shakily into her bag for her phone.

Alicia looked sharply up. *What?* What else could there be?

"Sophie." Jess's eyes were wide with fear. "I think she might have overheard."

Alicia felt the breath being sucked from her body, her world unravelling, her marriage crumbling. Her husband's life ruined. Her daughter's.

CHAPTER TWENTY-FOUR

SOPHIE

She was here. Having watched her mum climb out of the car and come through the front door, Sophie stepped back from the window. A car driven by another man, she'd noted. She obviously had him at her beck and call, just like she'd had Justin.

Sophie was disinclined to talk to her—what could she have to say, after all, that was worth listening to? On the other hand, what she did have to say would be important. For one, Sophie would quite like to know who her father was. She would also like to know why she'd decided it was okay to lie to her, as if she had some God-given right to fuck up her life because she'd given birth to her.

She intended to have an exit strategy in place, however. If her mum fed her more bullshit, as Justin just had, she wanted to be well away from them both. Justin could bugger off on fictitious business conferences as much as he liked, and her lovely mother could stew in her own mess.

Checking she had all she needed in her overnight bag, she glanced at her phone as it signalled an incoming call. Justin again. She'd guessed it would be. Obviously he'd heard the disillusionment in her voice when she'd ended their last call and was concerned. Or maybe he now realised that she knew what a complete screw-up her life was. Well, that was tough. If he were genuinely concerned, he wouldn't have lied—end of. Rejecting the call, she selected Chloe's number, and then waited worriedly as she took ages to answer. *Please pick up, Chloe,* she prayed silently, as she heard Jessica and her mum talking in the hall. She would be up in a minute, Sophie guessed.

Was she contemplating dropping the news casually into the conversation, Sophie wondered, saying, *Hey, what do you fancy for dinner? Takeaway?* And then, *Oh, and you're the product of a seedy affair I had, by the way, but I decided to pass you off as Justin's. Fancy some onion rings?*

Finally, Chloe picked up. "Hey, what's happening?" she said warily, aware from Sophie's texts earlier about her mum's dirty little secret that the shit was about to hit the fan.

"Everything," Sophie said shakily. "It's a complete nightmare. Mum's just arrived. I swear, if she tells me one more lie…" Sophie stopped and squeezed her eyes closed. "I need to talk to you, Chloe," she went on tearfully, despite her best efforts not to waste tears on people who obviously didn't give a damn about her. "Can I come over?"

"Crap, I'm not in tonight, Sophe," Chloe said worriedly. "I'm babysitting."

Shit! Panic twisted inside her as Sophie heard someone coming up the stairs. "I have to go. Can you meet me somewhere?" she asked her. "Please, Chloe. I really need to talk to you."

Chloe hesitated. "I'll get something sorted," she said, after a second. "Where and when?"

Sophie blew out a sigh of relief. "Brum town centre. An hour? I'm taking the bus. I'll meet you in the Bull Ring, outside H&M, second floor."

"Okay," Chloe said uncertainly, as Sophie rang off.

Pushing her phone into her bag, she braced herself, turning to face the door as there was a light tap on it. If a single untruth came out of her mouth, if she tried to justify what she'd done in any way, Sophie would be out of the door, and *she* could rot in hell.

"Hi." Coming cautiously in, her mum looked at her uncertainly. "How are you?"

Sophie almost laughed at that. "Ecstatic," she said shortly. "How would you be?"

Her mum's face paled.

"So, who is he?" Sophie asked bluntly, careless of the fact that her mum actually looked like shit. As far as she was concerned, she deserved to. "The man you cheated on Justin with," she clarified, as her mum grew an impossible shade whiter. "You know, my father—as opposed to the man you passed off as my dad for the whole of my life!"

Her mum flinched, as if she'd just slapped her. Through narrowed eyes, Sophie watched the swallow slide down her throat, her arms going protectively around herself. It wasn't going to work. The fragile, defensive body language wasn't going to cut it. Not this time. "*Well?*" she demanded.

Alicia's eyes scuttled for the safety of the floor. "I don't know," she said weakly. "Not for sure. I—"

"You don't *know?*" Sophie stared at her, incredulous. "You mean it was a one-night stand?" Lie number fucking one. She'd heard Justin asking Jess how long it had gone on. Whether it was still going on. So, obviously he thought it was. How could she do that to him? *How?*

"No! I didn't mean…" Stumbling over her words, Alicia shook her head. "I meant I wasn't sure whether—"

"*Who*, Mum?" Sophie kept eyeballing her.

"A colleague," Alicia finally said.

"Ah, an office romance," Sophie said facetiously. "How boringly predictable."

"No. It wasn't like that," Alicia said, looking more flustered by the second. Trying to remember her lies, Sophie thought angrily. "There was an after-work thing. A birthday party. I—"

"An office jolly." Sophie widened her eyes girlishly. "So, obviously it was perfectly reasonable to end it with a fun shag with the nearest bloke. *What*, was it *his* fucking birthday?"

"No! I didn't intend for it to happen, Sophie. I'd been drinking. I lost track of how much. Your dad...Justin wasn't well, and I—"

"Oh, nice one," Sophie sneered. "He's not well, so you feel sorry for yourself and decide to get a little attention elsewhere?"

"No. I didn't decide anything. I...He..." Alicia trailed off, tears spilling down her cheeks. "Sophie, please...You've every right to be angry, but please sit down and let me try to explain properly. I know how it looks, and I did lie to Justin, but—"

"Who is he, Mum?" Swiping tears from under her own eyes, Sophie stayed standing. "The man at the funeral, the man Justin was staring at, was that him? Is that why he left so suddenly?"

Alicia didn't answer. She didn't need to. The guilt in her eyes said it all.

"You're a real bitch, do you know that, Mum?" Sophie said quietly. "He's just buried his baby! And now he has to deal with this shit! Of course, that's assuming Lucas *was* his baby."

Alicia looked up sharply. "Sophie, stop it," she begged. "Please stop."

"I wish I could," Sophie said, her heart pounding so hard she was sure it would burst right out of her chest. "I wish I could stop my fucking life and get off!"

"It was never meant to happen!" Alicia sobbed. "I didn't mean to hurt Justin. I didn't want *any* of this."

Sophie studied her mum hard. "So you regret it then?"

Alicia looked at her bewilderedly. "Of course I do. I wish to God I could turn back the clock, but I can't!"

"Cheers, Mum," Sophie said, her heart sinking without trace.

"You know what, you don't regret it half as much as I do. Have a nice life." Swallowing hard, she turned away.

"Sophie, wait!" Alicia tried to stop her as she grabbed up her bag and turned to push past her. "I didn't mean I regret having you. I've never for one second regretted—"

"I wish I was fucking dead!" Sophie spat.

Did her mum honestly think she wanted to listen to this crap? That she would want to hang around while they split up, tearing her apart in the process? Well, stuff that. She wasn't about to stay here *or* with her bitch mother—no way. And Justin was hardly going to want her living with him. He'd want out of the whole crappy situation. At least they had that much in common, she thought cynically, as she thundered down the stairs.

CHAPTER TWENTY-FIVE

JUSTIN

"Chloe, slow down." Holding the telephone close to his ear, Justin tried to make sense of what Sophie's friend was saying. "Where and when were you supposed to be meeting her?"

"In town, but I'm babysitting." Chloe still wasn't making much sense, frustratingly. "She rang me earlier, and then she rang me again, and she sounded so upset. I'm worried about her, Mr. Cole. I can't take the baby with me and I—"

"*Whoa.* Chloe, please, slow down." Justin felt a knot of panic climb his throat. "Take the baby where? Why was she upset?"

Chloe didn't answer.

Justin pressed his fingers to his temple. "Chloe, this is really important," he said, working to keep the immense agitation he was feeling from his voice. "I wouldn't ask you to share anything you thought was confidential otherwise."

"Birmingham. The Bull Ring shopping centre. Outside H&M, on the second floor. Sophie said she was catching the bus in. She's probably already halfway there by now."

"Okay." Justin nodded. He needed to go. But first, he needed to know why she'd taken off. "Can you tell me why she was upset, Chloe?" he urged her gently. "Is it to do with Luke and the funeral?"

Again, Chloe was reluctant. "She heard you, Mr. Cole," she confided, eventually. "She heard what you were saying...about her not being yours. She was really upset. I should have told her to come here, but I didn't think, and now—"

"*Jesus Christ.*" Why hadn't he done something? He'd *known* she had. Cold dread pooled in the pit of Justin's stomach.

"I thought you should know. I wasn't sure what else to do." Chloe was talking fast now, sounding scared. "I'm sorry, Mr. Cole. I—"

"It's okay, Chloe. It's fine. I'll find her," Justin reassured her. "Let me have your number and I'll text you." He snatched up the newly delivered loan car keys and his mobile, noting several messages from Alicia as he did so. "Meanwhile, will you let me know if she gets back to you?"

"Uh-huh, yes, I will, I promise." Sounding relieved, Chloe reeled off her number. "Do you want me to text her?" she asked tentatively. "I thought maybe if I told her I was coming, but I was running late, that, you know, it might buy you a bit of time."

"Good idea. You did the right thing, Chloe." Justin quickly keyed in her number and sent her his. "I'll be in touch."

He was halfway out of the front door when Alicia rang. "Justin, it's Sophie—she's gone!" she said frantically when he picked up. "She heard...what you and Jessica were discussing. She... She's taken her overnight bag. She's not answering her phone. I've tried her a hundred times. I don't know what to do. I—"

"*Fuck!*" Justin's chest constricted. If she'd taken her overnight bag, she clearly intended to stay away from Jessica's. Would she come back here? Justin very much doubted it, now that he knew what she'd overheard. She had her key, but... *Dammit*! He needed to find her.

"I know. Chloe rang me." Drawing in a tight breath, he braced himself. "Is it true?" *Do not lie to me, Alicia.*

An agonising second ticked by, before she delivered the blow that would surely kill him. "I...I don't know."

"I see," Justin said quietly. He felt close to exploding. "So, what did you expect her to do, Alicia? Sit down and have a nice, calm conversation over a fucking cup of tea?"

"Oh God. Justin, I…" Alicia broke off with a sob. "I'm sorry. I am so, *so* sorry. I never intended to hurt you or Sophie, I swear I didn't."

"Right." Yanking his car door open, Justin threw himself behind the wheel. "That's not how it looks from here, Alicia."

"I know. I'm sorry." Alicia sobbed harder. "I know you can't forgive me. I know you won't ever, but please, please help Sophie."

"*Jesus!*" Justin slammed the car door. "Did you honestly think I *wouldn't*?"

"No. I…" Alicia's voice caught wretchedly in her throat. "I'm so sorry."

"So you said." Justin breathed in hard. "Just tell me one thing, Alicia. Was he worth it? Was he worth *this*?"

Alicia didn't answer. Justin guessed from her choking sobs that she couldn't. "I have to go. I have to find my daughter," he spat. He simply didn't have it in him to be anything but angry. It was too late for apologies—way too late. The cold, hard fact was that her deceit had led to this. If he didn't find her tonight… anything could happen by morning. He might never find her. That thought slicing through him like a knife, Justin cut the call, started the engine and screeched the car out of the drive.

CHAPTER TWENTY-SIX

JESSICA

"Ali?" Jessica said tentatively, walking to where Alicia stood motionless in the hall.

"He hung up." Alicia looked tearfully down at her phone. "I've destroyed him. Destroyed my whole family."

"Come on, Ali. Tears won't help anything. Let's go and sit down and think about what to do—calmly." Sliding an arm around her sister, Jessica attempted to lead her towards the kitchen. She decided not to point out that Alicia wasn't the only one feeling terrible right now. Alicia might have brought this on herself, but Sophie had done nothing to deserve this. Justin definitely hadn't, and he'd no doubt be feeling awful. She would ring him, Jessica decided, as soon as she could. The poor man would be gutted, thinking he hadn't got a soul in the world to talk to.

"He'll call back," she tried to reassure Alicia. And he probably would, because that's the kind of man he was: caring. "He's bound to be shocked and upset. You need to give him some time, Ali. It's an awful lot to take in."

"He hates me! He has every reason to. I *lied* to him, Jess, about the most important thing in his life! Even knowing he might find out, I kept on lying to him."

"I know." Jessica nodded sympathetically. "I did warn you what might happen, but you were so adamant. You know, sometimes the biggest lie of all is the lie we tell to ourselves, sweetheart." She sighed sadly, aware of her own propensity to do just that.

She'd lied to herself for years, telling herself Michael, the would-have-been father of her children, had they survived, wasn't a complete misogynist. He was—a controlling, self-centred woman-hater. He hadn't liked her friends, hadn't wanted her to meet his friends, the way she'd dressed, the things she'd said whenever they were in company. He clearly hadn't liked her very much in the end, as proven by the fact that he'd walked out on her when she'd realised she was miscarrying—again. She must have been mad, and obviously attracted to bastards. She hadn't known any man that wasn't a bastard in some form, apart from Justin.

She wished she'd spotted him before Alicia had called first dibs on him. She and Alicia had been working for the same company then, alongside Paul Radley. In fact, it was Jessica putting in a word for her that had got Alicia the job. In gratitude for which, Alicia had nabbed the only decent man for miles from right under her nose. Justin had been coming out of a seminar at the same venue in which they were holding their sales conference, and had walked right into her. They'd practically fallen into each other's arms, and that had been that. Jessica wouldn't have ended up with the misogynist if he'd walked into *her* first, and Justin wouldn't have ended up with his heart broken. But, of course, in falling into Alicia, Justin had fallen for her. It had been obvious that he was immediately smitten by her rosy blushes and self-effacing apologies. Alicia, with her complete inability to see her own attractions—to see that her shyness obviously *was* an attraction—had wondered what the handsome young doctor saw in her. Jessica couldn't help thinking that Justin might be asking himself the same question right now.

Alicia wiped a hand across her eyes. She really did look wretched. Jessica doubted she'd had a wink of sleep since Paul

Radley had turned up, and this was without losing dear little Lucas. She couldn't help but feel for her.

"Convincing myself I was doing it for Justin, you mean." Alicia clearly got the gist, another crop of tears spilling from her eyes. "He'd been wounded and broken and lost, and I made it my excuse to tear his heart out. He will never, ever forgive me. How can he? And Sophie...Dear God, Sophie."

"You did it for the right reasons, sweetie," Jessica assured her, stepping in front of her and taking hold of her hands. "He'll call back." She locked her eyes on hers. "Whatever he feels about *you*, he loves Sophie, Alicia. He'll be there for her. You know he will."

Alicia nodded, squeezing her eyes closed. "I know. But that's what makes it so cruel, don't you see? He would have loved her anyway, if only I'd found the courage to tell him, been honest from the outset and given him a chance."

"Possibly," Jessica conceded, though he would have to be a saint to have stayed with her, in reality. It wouldn't be easy for any man to accept his wife might be carrying another man's baby, even someone as family-orientated as Justin, and that was obviously Alicia's real reason for not telling him. She should have been honest with herself and with him, given him a chance at another relationship, if that's what he'd wanted. "We can't undo history, though, can we, sadly?"

Alicia glanced upwards. "I wish to God I'd listened to you." A shudder ran through her. "I might as well have taken a knife to his heart."

"You're being too hard on yourself. He will be hurting. Of course he will. But you know him well enough to know his thoughts will be on Sophie," Jessica repeated firmly. "Let him concentrate his efforts on finding her. It's better he's focussed on that."

Shakily, Alicia nodded. "You're right," she said, making a visible effort to stem her tears. "There's no point trying to offer him explanations—not now. He won't want to hear them."

"Just give him some time," Jessica said, giving her a hug and finally managing to lead her to the kitchen. "Do you have any idea where she might be?"

"Thankfully." Alicia nodded, running a hand under her nose. "Chloe rang him at home. Sophie spoke to her, apparently. She probably felt she had no one else to turn to."

Including her. Jessica felt sad and angry about that. She would never wish any harm on her niece. She'd been put in an impossible situation. Sworn to keep Alicia's secret for her, she'd lost the trust of people that mattered to her, too. One day, when she was less fragile, Jessica really needed to point that out to her sister.

"That's probably where she is then," she said reassuringly, pointing Alicia towards the kitchen table and making sure she sat down. She looked very wobbly on her feet—unsurprising, given the shock she'd had. "Don't worry too much, Ali. She might not want to come home right away, but Justin will make sure she's okay."

"But what if she's not at Chloe's?" Alicia looked fearfully up at her. "What then?"

"Then we start ringing around anyone else she might know. We'll find her, Alicia," Jessica said adamantly.

"But what if we don't?"

Noting the look in Alicia's eyes now was one of palpable terror, Jessica felt icy trepidation sweep the length of her spine. She wouldn't wish that on her. On poor Justin. She needed to ring him, as soon as possible. Make sure he knew that she'd been absolutely sworn to secrecy. She couldn't bear the thought of him being angry with her, thinking she'd condoned Alicia's behaviour.

CHAPTER TWENTY-SEVEN

JUSTIN

A mixture of guilt and anger gnawing away at him, Justin keyed in a text to Alicia as he headed towards the shop Chloe had mentioned. As furious as he was, he couldn't leave her worrying herself sick. She would be beside herself with grief, feeling bereft twofold, as he was. Sorrow weighed like a cold stone inside him as he thought of his innocent baby boy, whose soul they'd laid to rest just a few hours ago. It seemed like a lifetime had passed since then. *I'll call you as soon as I know anything*, he typed, and then hesitated, not sure how to sign off, dearly wishing it was possible to turn back the clock to a time where their lives weren't irretrievably fractured and he would have ended his text with a single X, as always. Not any more. It was all gone, everything they'd ever had together, slipping through his hands as surely as water through his fingers.

Not Sophie.

He couldn't lose her. *Wouldn't.*

Leaving the message as it was, he hit send and quickly selected Sophie's mobile for the umpteenth time since he'd left home. His heart hitching, he slowed as the call began to ring, his gaze shooting towards a coffee shop ahead of him. Her ringtone: Adele. The tune that rang constantly around the house. It *had* to be hers. She was there, somewhere.

Shit! He ground to a halt as the phone stopped ringing. She was here. He could sense her. But where? Dragging a hand through his hair, his desperation mounting, he scoured the seated crowd—and his heart almost stopped pumping.

Looking every bit as vulnerable and lonely as he knew she must be feeling, Sophie was sitting on the far side of the coffee shop.

Dammit. He cursed silently as a group of kids scraped their chairs back, simultaneously rising from a table directly in front of him.

His gaze fixed on Sophie, Justin mumbled an apology and squeezed past them, and then faltered as she turned to him with a look of alarm. A feeling of sick trepidation clenched his stomach.

"Sophie," he said, making sure to keep his tone calm.

Time seemed to freeze for one agonising second as she locked eyes with him, and then, as Justin took another tentative step towards her, Sophie shot to her feet, grappling her overnight bag from the back of her chair and almost stumbling over a table as she backed away. Backed away from *him*.

"Sophie, *wait*! Please," he called desperately, as she turned away. "Sophie!"

"No!" Sophie whirled back around, her expression now one of near hatred, which shook Justin to the core. "Go away! Leave me alone!"

"Sophie…" Bewildered, Justin took another hesitant step. "Please. Don't do this," he begged. "Come back. We'll talk, just you and me. We'll sit down and—"

"No!" Sophie dragged her hair from her face and glared furiously at him. "I'm not going *anywhere* with you. Why the hell should I?"

"Because I'm telling you to!" Justin snapped, his frustration, coupled with gut-wrenching fear, spilling over. If she took off now, he'd have absolutely no idea where she was. And the way she was feeling... He couldn't allow that. "Come back here now!"

"Fuck off! You've no right! I don't *want* to!" Sophie shouted tearfully. "I don't want to be anywhere near you. Don't you get it? I just want you to go away and leave me *alone!*"

Justin felt the ground shift beneath him. He wanted to go to her, hold her, let her scream, kick him, punch him, if that would help. Anything. "I'm your father, Sophie," he tried, his voice catching. "I'll always—"

"You're not!" Rage now emanated palpably from her. Justin could feel it, like an icicle through his heart. Rage, hate, hurt—all directed right at him. "You're a liar! Both of you! *Liars!*"

Uncertain what to do—go forward or back off—Justin watched helplessly as two concerned women stepped towards her, one placing an arm around Sophie's shoulders, drawing her further back, further away from him.

"He's not my father. He's *not*." Gulping back a sob, Sophie addressed the women, and then, seeing Justin step towards her, wrenched herself away from them.

His blood turning to ice in his veins as she turned to flee, Justin moved fast, almost colliding with the women as he raced after her, only to find two security guards blocking his path.

"I wouldn't if I were you, mate," one of them said, the menacing look in his eyes telling Justin he wasn't about to let him get past.

"She's my daughter," he said, holding the man's gaze, praying he would see the desperation in his eyes.

"Yeah, and he's mine," the man quipped drolly, nodding towards his sidekick. "Back off, mate," he warned him. "The police are on their way."

The police? Given how efficient he'd found them so far in finding any link that might lead to who killed his son, Justin might have laughed, had he not felt like crying. "She's upset," he attempted to explain, tried hard to hold on to his temper. "I need to go to her."

Fuck this, he thought, as the two men stood their ground, like immovable mountains. Arms folded, feet splayed in a Neanderthal display of aggression, it was clear they weren't going to let him go anywhere. Determined to get past them any way he had to, Justin's attempt to push through was cut short by someone grabbing him from behind, seizing his arm and twisting it high up his back.

Christ. "Sophie!" Ignoring the pain ripping through his bicep as his arm was pushed impossibly higher, Justin struggled to stay upright.

"Sophie!" He screamed it, his heart splintering as, brought heavily to his knees, he watched his daughter disappear into the crowd.

CHAPTER TWENTY-EIGHT

SOPHIE

Choking back her tears, Sophie kept going. What had she done? She'd wanted to hurt him. She'd wanted to hurt them both as much as she could, but not like this. She should have stopped those security guards. Instead, she'd made them think he was a bloody paedophile.

Oh God, she hadn't meant to do that. Pausing to catch her breath outside the shopping centre, Sophie squeezed her eyes closed, seeing again the hurt and confusion on Justin's face. They'd forced him to the floor. Held him down like the worst kind of criminal. And he'd done *nothing*. He might be ready to walk away from the nightmare his life had become, from the deceit and the lies her mother had fed him—she could hardly blame him for that—but he'd always loved her as a dad should love a daughter. He couldn't feel that way any more, that was clear to Sophie, but she couldn't stop loving him as a father so easily. Part of her, the biggest part of her, would always love him, yet there was another part of her that hated him for being naive enough to allow himself to be deceived. It didn't matter much now though, did it? She would never see him again. She didn't want to. Hearing him say out loud that he'd lost his daughter, listening to his lies, his invented reasons—work conferences, whatever—to extract himself from her life now Luke was no longer part of his, that would have been too much to bear.

Suppressing a sob, she wiped the back of her hand shakily under her nose and tried to think about what her next move should be. Where she could go. Chloe had obviously told Justin where she was. Realistically, she couldn't have gone there in any case. Chloe's mum would have been on the phone in a flash.

Holly! She'd moved away when her parents had decided to run a caravan park in Herefordshire somewhere. Sophie wasn't sure where, exactly. Holly had been a good mate, though. She might be able to crash there for a few nights, until she got her head around what to do. Holly might even be able to sneak her into one of the caravans, which would buy her some time. She'd be sixteen soon. She could get a job then. An office temp job or something in a shop, maybe. Anything. Stacking shelves in the supermarket would do until she'd secured some accommodation—a single room somewhere or even a bedsit. Then she might be able to apply for a student loan to cover her fees and living costs while she went to veterinary school, which is what she wanted to do.

It was a plan, at least. She didn't need them—treating her like a child one minute and then like she wasn't even a person the next, like she didn't have feelings. Knowing her mum, she'd probably flipped a coin: heads, an abortion; tails, she passes her off as Justin's and crosses her fingers. Pity she hadn't kept her bloody legs crossed, Sophie thought furiously. *What am I supposed to do with this*, Justin had said. What had he thought *she* was going to do?

Scrolling through her contacts, she found Holly's number and rang her. She couldn't go over there tonight, as Holly was out with her family celebrating her brother's birthday, but, after a quick catch-up, she arranged to meet up with her in the morning, which left her with nothing to do but wait around. She could kill a few hours at the train station, she supposed, where she wouldn't look too conspicuous; check out the train times and then download something to read on her phone.

She was sitting in Starbucks at the station, wondering whether she could get away with hiding in the loos for the night, when her phone beeped an incoming text alert. From her bitch mum or her dad, she presumed, wavering for a second when she thought it might be him, and then steeling herself to ignore him if it was. She felt bad about what had happened at the shopping centre—none of this was his fault, after all—but he'd been pretty quick to announce he didn't have a daughter when he'd learned Alicia's secret, hadn't he? Warily, Sophie checked the number—one she didn't recognise.

> *Hi, Sophie, hope you don't mind me contacting you. I would like to have got in touch sooner, but Alicia begged me not to. I realise this all might be a bit overwhelming for you, but could we talk, possibly? I'd love to hear from you, if you'd like to. All best, Paul Radley, your father.*

Stunned, Sophie stared at it, and then knitted her brow. How the bloody hell had he got her number? And why the contact now?

Thinking it might be some kind of scam, Sophie hesitated for a second, and then dismissed the idea. Given the content, it couldn't be anything other than genuine. Fiddling worriedly with her eyebrow stud, she debated and then texted back.

> *Were you the guy at the funeral?*

> *Yes. I wanted to speak to you then, but it didn't seem appropriate. I'm so sorry for your loss. Px*

Sophie chewed on her bottom lip, hesitated briefly again, and then—"Sod it"—she phoned him. It couldn't do any harm, could it? Thanks to her bitch mum, the harm had already been done. And at least he'd acknowledged she'd had a loss.

"Sophie?" he asked, when he picked up.

"Uh-huh," Sophie answered guardedly. He'd said Alicia had begged him not to contact her, which smacked of the truth, knowing now what a deceitful cow she was, but... "How did you get my number?" she asked him.

"I've been talking to Alicia, hoping I could come to some arrangement about having some contact with you. Fifteen years is a long time to be denied access to your own child. I've missed you growing up." He drew in a breath. "She's okay with me having your number, apparently, so I guess she's relented for some reason."

Yeah, and Sophie knew why. Because she wanted to pass the shit she'd caused on to someone else to clear up.

"It's great to hear from you, Sophie," he said, sounding as if he might even mean it.

"Why?" Sophie asked cynically.

Paul laughed. It wasn't a derogatory laugh though, more an amused chuckle. "I get why you'd be cautious," he said. "I've missed you," he added simply. "There's never been a day when I haven't thought about you."

Sophie wasn't wholly convinced by that, but he sounded sincere.

"So why didn't you get in touch before then? I mean, you didn't have to just... *not*, did you?"

"No," Paul conceded. "Truthfully, I didn't want to mess up your mother's marriage. I cared too much about her to do that. I'd hoped we'd be together. Things weren't going too well between her and Justin... But that's history—probably stuff I shouldn't be repeating. I knew Justin was a decent guy, which actually didn't make me feel great about falling in love with his wife, and...well, I thought I was doing the right thing, for everyone. I didn't think it was the right thing by you, to be honest, and I didn't bargain on missing you so much it hurt, but it did—a lot. And then I lost my wife and kids in a boating accident—I think that was a wake-up call."

"Oh, shit," Sophie murmured, shocked. "That's rough."

"It was," Paul said quietly. "It took me a while to get over it—not that you ever do. I realised then that I needed to see you, make sure you were okay. Do you think we could be friends, maybe? Meet occasionally? It would be great to catch up. Not that fifteen years is going to be easy to catch up on." He stopped, sighing heavily.

"Sixteen," Sophie pointed out.

"Right. Ninth of October. Happy upcoming sixteenth, Sophie."

Sophie raised her eyebrows at that. "You've been marking days off on the calendar then?" she asked drolly.

"I think that might be deemed a touch obsessive." Paul laughed. "No, I just remember that date, that's all." He paused. "So, how are you, generally?"

Sophie went quiet. "Generally," she said, after a second, "crap."

"Oh, how so?" Paul asked, sounding concerned.

"Stuff." Sophie shrugged vaguely. She wasn't actually sure she wanted to share her sad life story with him. "Mum and me had a fight."

"Oh," he said, sounding as if he got it. "A bad one?"

"Very."

Paul paused, then said, "You're not within earshot of her then, I take it?"

"Nope. I'm at New Street Station. Wanted to give her some space, you know, so I'm going to stay with a friend—just for a few days," she lied. She wasn't sure she would ever want to see her again. "Trouble is, my train's not until morning, so I'm killing some time."

"You're there on your own?" Now Paul sounded surprised.

"Yeah. I'm a big girl now," Sophie reminded him.

"Have you eaten?"

"No, not yet. I might grab some chips or something."

"Look, it's only a suggestion," Paul said, "and you can say no—I'm not likely to be offended, since you don't even know me—but do you fancy meeting up? I could come and get you. We could grab a pizza or something. You could even crash here, if you like. Once you've established I'm not too weird, that is."

Sophie wasn't sure about that.

"Or just share that bag of chips, if you don't fancy doing anything else. On me, obviously."

"Last of the big spenders." Sophie smiled. "Okay," she said. He sounded all right. Normal. And she couldn't sit around here all night. She'd already seen a few homeless people being moved on.

"Great," Paul said. "I'll be with you in half an hour. Maybe forty minutes. I just have to have a quick shower. I've been in the gym. Don't want to make a bad first impression, do I? Oh, where are you?"

"Starbucks, or else just outside. I'll keep an eye out for you."

"I'm the tall, dark and handsome one," Paul joked.

"And modest." Sophie laughed. "See you soon."

She liked him, she thought, ending the call. He definitely didn't seem weird.

CHAPTER TWENTY-NINE

ALICIA

Hearing Justin come through the front door, Alicia stopped breathing.

He'd already told her what had happened over the phone. "She ran from me," he'd said hoarsely, and then stopped. "I tried to…" He'd stopped again. Alicia had heard his voice crack, felt his unbearable, palpable pain, and her heart had torn apart inside her.

Sophie had worshipped him. She'd had the best relationship it was possible for a daughter to have with a father.

Alicia clenched her fists. Why had she *done* it? *Why* had she waited, knowing this would eventually come out? That when it did, it would tear her beautiful family apart. Jessica had been right. She'd lied to herself and everyone else. She was everything Sophie thought she was—a selfish, unfeeling bitch.

"So, she already had her overnight bag packed?" DI Taylor asked her.

Alicia hardly heard him, her gaze going past him as the lounge door opened—hoping to see what, she didn't know. If he met her gaze, which Alicia was petrified he wouldn't, there would be nothing but hurt and disappointment in his eyes. Open contempt, too—that would be there. How could it not?

Seeing the gash on Justin's cheek, his dishevelled appearance, Alicia felt another part of her curl up and die. "Justin…?" She moved instinctively towards him, and then stopped as he fixed her with a stare that could freeze an ocean.

He didn't speak as she faltered, turning his gaze quizzically towards DI Taylor instead, obviously wondering why he would come again personally.

"What happened to you?" DI Taylor asked, turning to look at him.

Justin smiled ironically. "Security guards weren't too keen to let me go," he said, his expression wary as he glanced between Taylor and the woman police officer with him.

He looked utterly exhausted, jaded to his very bones. Alicia wished there was some way to take his pain away, but there was none. She couldn't go to him, hold him. Dear God, how much she wanted to do that. There was nothing she could do but take herself, the cause of his pain, away. Her guilt threatening to choke her, she glanced down as Justin's gaze came back to her. She could feel his eyes on her, studying her, obviously looking for some clue as to who this stranger he'd lived with, loved with all of himself, was. In the edge of her vision, she saw him walk across to her, stand a foot away. The space felt like an iceberg between them.

Tentatively, Alicia reached out to him, placing a hand on his arm, and Justin flinched, physically flinched at her touch, and Alicia knew. She'd lost him. There would be no going back. Even if their beautiful, precious daughter walked through the door right now, there would be no going back for any of them. She'd done that.

"So, what do you propose to do?" he asked DI Taylor. His tone was tight with pent-up emotion. Emotion that surely had to be vented, if he wasn't to go the same route he had once before, driven slowly and steadily out of his mind by grief.

"I'm afraid there's nothing much we can do at this juncture," DI Taylor said, with an apologetic sigh.

"*What?*" Justin reeled where he stood. Alicia knew this was too much to take on top of his frustration with the police's lack of progress in regard to Lucas and the crash. "My daughter is *missing* and you're telling me you're going to do *nothing*?" Raking a hand furiously through his hair, he stared at Taylor, stunned.

DI Taylor's expression was sympathetic. "It's too soon to register her officially missing," he explained. "And then, the first thing we have to establish is the level of risk to the person who is missing. If she—"

"My daughter!" Justin's voice rose. "The person missing is my daughter! Jesus!" He banged the heel of his hand against his forehead. "She's fifteen! Doesn't that make her at risk? What the hell is *wrong* with you people? Why aren't you out looking for her?"

Taylor looked regretfully to Alicia, before turning uncomfortably back to Justin. "We have your statement, Dr. Cole," he said quietly. "We're doing all we can for now."

"Which, as you've just pointed out, amounts to nothing," Justin said furiously.

Again, Taylor glanced away, plainly unable to meet his gaze. "She went of her own volition, according to Mrs. Cole."

Alicia nodded. There was no escaping the fact that Sophie had been driven out, her life shattered and her heart broken, by her own mother.

"Which means what, exactly?" Justin asked, his jaw tightening.

"If a person goes missing voluntarily, then it's generally an indicator of a problem in that person's life," Taylor explained patiently. "And you've obviously been having a few problems..."

"Obviously," Justin said, his tone now bitter with contempt. "Meaning, in your expert opinion, she's classed as a low-risk case?"

"For now, yes." Taylor nodded ruefully. "We have a list of her friends and acquaintances. I gather Mrs. Cole has already contacted most of them, but we will contact them again and keep you posted if anything new comes up."

"Right. Such as my daughter being found raped or murdered?" said Justin. Alicia's stomach tightened like a slipknot.

Taylor glanced quickly in her direction. "We could use a recent photograph," he said, offering her a commiserating smile.

Nodding, Alicia swallowed back the jagged glass in her chest.

"I have one in my bag," she said, fighting tears as she turned to the sofa to retrieve the photo she carried in her purse. She couldn't cry. Though she wanted to curl up and weep like a child—for her children, for Justin, who once would have comforted her—now was not the time. Now, Justin would hate her as much as she'd known he'd once loved her—and it hurt. It hurt so very much.

Shoving his hands in his pockets, Justin watched as Taylor looked at the photo and then passed it to his colleague. "So, have you made any progress in regard to whoever murdered my son? Just wondering whether you're even trying. You know, out of idle curiosity," he said, his tone scathing.

"We don't take the death of a child anything other than seriously, Dr. Cole," Taylor assured him. "We're following every lead, I can assure you. I'm afraid we don't have much to go on, other than the colour and type of the car."

"A black Land Rover," Alicia said.

DI Taylor nodded, and then sighed. "Unfortunately, black Land Rover doesn't really give us much to go on without at least part of the registration. And, as we have no witnesses to the road traffic accident, we're—"

"No witnesses?" Justin almost choked.

"No independent eye witnesses who can provide a description of the driver of the car," Taylor clarified. "We've appealed for people to come forward with any information, but without a clear identification or fingerprints, we can't check the national database, which means we're at a bit of a loss, I'm afraid."

"A loss?" Justin stared at him, incredulous. "I don't believe this! You mean the bastard is going to get away with it?"

"What about CCTV footage?" Alicia asked, feeling as desperate as Justin looked.

"Not much use, I'm afraid." Glancing apologetically at her, Taylor shook his head. "We don't have a clear image of the driver's face and, unfortunately, the angle of the camera doesn't show us the number plate. I'm sorry, Mrs. Cole. I can't give you any further information, as yet."

He *was* going to get away with it. Nausea rose rancidly in Alicia's chest. She looked at DI Taylor in disbelief, while Justin simply laughed, a short, derisive laugh, and then walked away. He stopped at the door. His frustration was tangible, his anger emanating from him. Breathing out, eventually, he reached to knead his forehead, and then, "Stuff it!" he growled, slamming the heel of his hand hard into the lounge door.

"Dr. Cole." DI Taylor took a step towards him, a warning edge to his voice. "I realise how frustrated you must feel, but I'm not sure getting aggressive is going to help, is it?"

"He's upset." Alicia went to Justin, placing a hand on his arm.

"Upset? *Jesus!*" Justin pulled his arm away, looking at Taylor in bemusement. "You know what," he said, after a second, his expression somewhere between cynical and bitterly disappointed, "I think getting 'aggressive' might just help, actually. Then again, maybe you're right. I mean, my son being murdered and my daughter going missing is hardly worth getting upset about, is it? I tell you what, why don't we go shopping instead, hey, Alicia?" he suggested flatly. "Or maybe we could catch up with a few old 'work colleagues' for a drink. What do you think?"

"Justin!" His words cutting her to the bone, Alicia called after him as he strode out, shaking his head at Jessica who was standing in the hall, looking alarmed.

I'm sorry! she wanted to scream, to break down right there, right then. But she didn't deserve his forgiveness. She'd ripped his life apart, thrown everything he'd ever given her—his love, his commitment—right back in his face.

Desperate, feeling utterly anchorless without him, powerless to help him, she stayed where she was as Justin slammed through the front door.

CHAPTER THIRTY

SOPHIE

"Nice pad," Sophie said, glancing around the open-plan living area. It was a brand-new Central Plaza apartment, decorated in white and greys, with a hardwood floor, great globular chrome lights and a huge L-shaped leather sofa. It must have cost a bomb.

"It is pretty cool, isn't it?" Paul said, closing the front door and nodding her on in. "It has a residents' gymnasium, twenty-four-hour concierge service and a fantastic view over the city centre. Not mine, unfortunately. I'm flat-sitting for a friend."

"Ah. Nice friend," Sophie commented, her eyes boggling at the size of the flat-screen TV, which had to be seventy-five inches at least.

"There are plenty of flats available though. Out of most people's price range, I guess. The building's still practically empty. I might buy one when I move back from Dubai." Paul followed her awestruck gaze thoughtfully. "With a bedroom decorated to your specifications, of course—assuming you'd like to stay over occasionally?"

"Yeah, maybe," Sophie said, smiling in his direction.

Looking pleased, Paul smiled back. He really did seem all right. She'd been a bit worried when he'd suggested she crash at his—she'd never met him before, after all, and weird stuff happened—but she'd figured she was safe when he'd turned up with a bag of chips, looking like a nervous schoolkid. Handsome, but definitely nervous.

"What do you fancy?" he said, walking over to a table lined with so many bottles of booze that Sophie's eyes boggled all over again.

"Something seriously strong," she said, "but I'd better not. Mum and Dad would go ballistic." Realising what she'd said, Sophie dropped her gaze. She was missing home already. Missing Luke so much, she didn't think her heart would ever stop hurting.

"How about a small wine?" Paul suggested. "I promise I won't tell if you don't."

Sophie nodded, but kept her gaze fixed down.

"Hey." Paul walked across to her, placing a hand on her shoulder as her eyes filled up. "It can't be that bad, can it?"

Sophie sniffed hard and dragged a hand under her nose. "It's my fault," she blurted. "What happened with Justin. It's my fault." She hadn't told Paul that Justin had found out he wasn't her dad—somehow she'd felt she would be betraying him—but she'd told him some of what had happened in the Bull Ring. "I shouldn't have run. I should have at least gone back and told them it wasn't what they were thinking. Do you think they might have called the police?"

"I very much doubt it." Paul smiled reassuringly. "And, in any case, Justin's an articulate man. He would have soon put them right."

Sophie shrugged. "I suppose."

Paul reached to ease her chin up. "I have no idea why you would think any of this is your fault, you know," he said gently, his smile now bemused. "The problem is your mother, not you."

Gulping hard, Sophie nodded. He didn't have the whole picture, but he was right. She'd done nothing wrong except be born. Lately, she'd been wishing that she hadn't been.

"Do you want me to drive you back home?" Paul asked her, his brow furrowed with concern. "I don't like the idea of you going off to your friend's upset."

Sophie scanned his eyes. Like hers, they were dark espresso-brown, sympathetic and kind. Justin's eyes had always been kind. She couldn't remember him once ever losing his rag. Why had her mum done it, strung him along for so many years? Sophie got that people had affairs, but she didn't get why her mum would have built such an elaborate web of lies. She must have known it was bound to come tumbling down like a house of cards.

And why had she done it in the first place—not just lie, but have an affair at all? It wasn't like they'd didn't get on or had monumental rows or anything. They'd had their mental moments, but mostly they'd been solid, or so Sophie had thought. Justin definitely loved her mum. Sophie only had to think of the way he'd looked at her, that quiet smile in his eyes, to know that. Whenever her mum had been upset about a child at work who'd been abused in some way, he would go to her and massage her shoulders, kiss the side of her neck and hold her. Her mum always turned to him, buried her head on his shoulder and told him how much she loved him.

She was a kind person. That's why she kept on doing the shit job she did, even though she said the traumatised kids, who had to live their reality while she was tucked safely up in her bed, haunted her dreams. What she'd done to Justin was plain cruel. It just wasn't her. It was no wonder he'd been so shocked. Sophie's mind went to him, and she tried not to hear the words he'd said about how he'd lost his son *and* his daughter. Whatever he was feeling, she knew he'd loved her too. She'd felt it. He could hardly love her now though, could he, the spawn of her mum's affair with another man?

Sighing, Sophie shook her head. "No," she said, though she wished more than anything that she could go back, to a home that felt like a home, like it used to. But that place didn't exist any more. Her baby brother was dead, her mother was a lying bitch, and Justin…After what she'd done to him at the shopping centre, Sophie doubted he'd ever want to set eyes on her again. "They're going through shit," she said, still not wanting to divulge too much. "The house got broken into while we were at my little brother's funeral." Trailing off, she shrugged and forced back her tears. There was no way to go home, as far as she could see. No home to go back to.

"I'll be okay." She smiled tremulously up at him.

Paul didn't look convinced. "You really are going through it, aren't you?" He shook his head in commiseration. "Tell you what, how does a holiday sound? It might do you good to get away from everything for a while."

Sophie gawked. "A holiday? Where?"

"Wherever you'd like," Paul said, going back to pour the drinks. "Florida, maybe?"

"*Florida?*" Sophie's eyes grew wide. Accepting the glass of white wine, she drank thirstily. "But…what about my passport?" She knitted her brow. This was happening way too fast. "And clothes and stuff."

"Well, now Alicia knows we're in touch…" Paul took her glass and walked back to the table to top it up. "I'll ask her about it. I'm thinking, under the circumstances, she might think it's a good idea, a way of allowing you all some space."

Sophie was happy to give them as much space as they needed—and then some. Still, she wasn't sure. A holiday to Florida? Was he made of money? Yeah, she was his daughter, but he hardly even knew her. It sounded a bit too good to be true. As far as he knew, she could be a total brat.

"And I'll buy you some new clothes," Paul offered, causing Sophie to do a double take. "You won't need much anyway, in that climate."

Sophie searched his face, puzzled.

"I can see you're a bit cautious," Paul said, handing her back her glass. "I don't blame you. You're right to be. But I'd like to make up for some of the things I haven't been able to do for you. Why don't you ring her yourself, if you're worried? Put your mind at rest."

Sophie took another drink. "I suppose I could text her. I don't really want to talk to her."

Placing her glass on the coffee table, she dropped her bag on the floor and delved into it for her phone. And then, her heart skipping a beat, she delved deeper. "Shit," she muttered, dragging the contents out of it.

"What's wrong?" Paul asked, watching as she searched.

"It's not here. My phone." Sophie swept her hair from her face. "Crap. I must have left it in the station."

Paul sighed sympathetically. "Looks like there's a new phone to add to that shopping list then."

He obviously was made of money. Sophie didn't turn down the offer. She already felt lost without her phone.

"Do you want me to ring her?" Paul asked, just as Sophie was debating whether to ask to use his phone. "It might save you some hassle if I speak to her."

"Would you mind?" Sophie was actually grateful for the offer. Her mum would only text back, and then she'd be obliged to answer. She didn't really want to get into dialogue of any sort right now. Wasn't sure she would ever want to.

"No problem. It's probably a good idea to clear things with her before getting anything booked anyway. I have to go into town first thing tomorrow to see my bank manager. I was thinking of doing it then." He smiled and crouched to help her collect up her stuff. "Then, after everything's booked and I'm out of my meeting, how about we head off somewhere for the day? The weather's going to be mild, apparently. We might as well make the most of it."

"Like where?" Sophie eyed him curiously.

"Your choice. Somewhere fun," Paul suggested. "It might help take your mind off your problems."

Sophie thought about it. "Blackpool," she said. "Maybe the theme park?"

"Okay. Sounds good." Paul nodded, getting to his feet. "But you might have to hold my hand."

Sophie frowned at him.

"Scared of heights," Paul explained, shrugging embarrassedly.

Sophie smiled, feeling more at ease with a man who would admit to his vulnerabilities. "Don't worry, I'll look after you," she said, checking her jeans and jacket pockets for her phone, just in case, though she knew it wasn't there. "But don't you have work?"

"I'm on leave," Paul said, offering her another reassuring smile. "And I'm more than happy to devote my time to getting to know you. Shall we check out where you'll be sleeping?" he asked, reaching to pick up her bag.

CHAPTER THIRTY-ONE

ALICIA

Trembling from head to toe, Alicia stood under the freezing-cold shower until her skin started to turn blue. It did nothing to numb the raw pain in her chest, the emptiness inside her where her babies had grown. A whole night she'd been gone. A whole *night*! Where was she?

Wiping away the tears, mingled with water, that were cascading down her face, she turned off the shower and climbed out, her body moving on autopilot; her mind on Sophie, imagining where she might be. In some dark, desolate place, as cold as she was? Her skin tinged blue? Wet and hungry, crying tears of anger and hurt, rather than fear and shame?

Please let her be safe. Clamping down hard on an image of her lying somewhere too lonely to contemplate, her body bruised and broken, Alicia clutched up a towel, pressed it hard to her face and suppressed a sob. She'd just heard someone pass on the landing. She hadn't been sure whether it was Jess or Justin, but she didn't want him to hear her. No doubt he'd think she deserved to cry on her own, but it would be another tug on his emotions, which were already in turmoil.

Staying where she was, she tried to think what to do, where to look. Sophie hadn't been in contact with any of her friends, other than Chloe. After that—nothing. It was as if she'd disappeared off the face of the earth.

Please don't let anything have happened to her.

Gulping hard, Alicia glanced upwards, praying that God might take pity on her for the sake of her daughter. Might Sophie call Justin, she wondered. If she couldn't—wouldn't—ring her, then surely, once she'd stopped to think, she would realise that Justin cared deeply. That whatever *she'd* done, he would never stop caring for her.

Contemplating sending her another text, her heart leapt into her mouth when her phone pinged on the shelf, echoing around the tiled walls of the bathroom. Not daring to hope, Alicia snatched it up and hastily read the message. And then reread it, her heart somersaulting in her chest.

I need to speak to you. I was going to call round, but I realise that might not be a good idea. I don't want to cause any upset, Alicia, I promise you. I just want to do what's best. Could we come to some arrangement perhaps?

Feeling her whole world shift, Alicia placed the phone back, staring at it as if it might bite her, and then scrambled, still damp, into her clothes. How had he got her number, she thought, as she pushed her feet into her flip-flops and squeaked open the bathroom door. She hadn't...he must have taken it from her phone, she realised, anger tightening inside her, which he'd so magnanimously returned to her, completely careless of the fact that he was walking into Justin's house uninvited. Squeezing her eyes closed, Alicia took a breath and hurried downstairs, moving silently so that Justin and Jessica, who were talking in the kitchen, didn't hear her.

She had to speak to Paul Radley. Whether or not she wanted to, she had no choice now. She couldn't have him coming anywhere near her. She had no idea how Justin might react if he did. Cold foreboding snaking the length of her spine, she eased the front door open, slipped out, walked away from the house, and then steeled herself and called him.

"Hi, Ali," he answered on the fourth ring. "I take it you got my text? I would have rung, but I guessed that might be a bit awkward."

"Why are you doing this, Paul? What do you want?" Alicia snapped.

Paul avoided the question. "Alicia, don't you think it might be an idea to discuss this face-to-face, rather than over the phone?" he said instead. "Why don't we meet up and have a nice relaxed lunch, and then—"

"*Why*, Paul?" Alicia demanded.

Paul didn't answer immediately, then he said, "Hold on a sec, I need to go somewhere more private."

Alicia waited for what seemed like an eternity.

"Sorry," he said, finally coming back on. "I was in the foyer. There's still work going on in the building, workmen all over the place. I didn't want everyone overhearing our personal conversation."

Alicia continued to wait silently. If he thought she was going to be drawn into actual conversation, he was wrong.

"I think we need to come to some arrangement, Alicia," he said, obviously getting the message and getting to the point.

Her heart thudding, Alicia closed her eyes. "What arrangement?" she asked him, attempting some level of calmness until she'd heard him out.

"A mutually agreeable one. I'm assuming you don't want Justin to know?"

Nausea churning her stomach, Alicia didn't answer.

"Look, Ali, I really don't want to cause any upset, especially to Sophie," he went on—sounding concerned, Alicia noted with disbelief. "I'm sure there's a satisfactory way forward that will suit us both."

"Which would be?" Alicia asked, drawing in a tight breath and holding it.

"Like I say, I think it would be better if we discussed it face-to-face. How about I book a table at our favourite hotel? I could be there in, say, an hour? We could have something to eat and—"

"It won't work, Paul," Alicia cut in evenly, determined not to give him the satisfaction of knowing how upset she was. "He knows about what happened between us."

Ending the call, she tried to still the palpitations in her chest. Unable to believe that he would do this, on top of all that they'd suffered, that Justin and Sophie had suffered, she stayed where she was for several minutes. The past had come back to haunt her. Almost in the blink of an eye, her life, and Justin's along with it, had unravelled. As if she'd made an arrangement with the Devil himself, she'd known deep down that one day it would. And it wouldn't stop here—Alicia could sense it. Paul Radley presumably didn't know that Justin was aware that Sophie might not be his. As far as he was concerned, he had one more ace up his sleeve. Would he try to use it? Would he cold-heartedly try to destroy her husband completely? She wouldn't let him. The twist in all of this was that Paul Radley knew she wouldn't.

CHAPTER THIRTY-TWO

ALICIA

Alicia watched Justin checking his texts, trying Sophie's mobile for the thousandth time that morning, pressing his fingers hard to his temples when he got no reply. Dragging in a long breath, he went back to staring out of the lounge window, undoubtedly seeing nothing but the same petrifying images she was.

Where was she? Why weren't the police doing anything? Why had they classed her as a low-risk case when, if she was out there on the streets, she was clearly at risk. It was *her* fault. All of it. She was the reason Sophie had left, the reason her husband couldn't look at her. Could hardly bring himself to speak to her. How could she ever have risked her child's future, her life, been naive enough to imagine that if she closed her eyes to it, it would all go away? She'd made bad decision after decision. She'd been so stupid and weak.

Justin would have no life without his children.

She glanced towards him from where she sat uselessly on the edge of the sofa. He hadn't slept, not a wink. Neither of them had even considered going to bed, watching the clock instead, endlessly pacing and hoping and praying. Jumping, physically, whenever a phone rang. When a floorboard had creaked overhead in the night, it was as a ghost had trodden lightly over their graves.

"Justin…" Tentatively, Alicia got to her feet and walked

towards him. "I'm sorry," she murmured—a short, useless word that couldn't possibly convey the deep remorse that she felt.

Justin tensed, his broad shoulders stiffening. "Don't, Alicia," he said, after a second, his voice hoarse. "Please don't. I can't deal with this right now. I just can't."

"Please, talk to me," she begged him. *Tell me to go if you want me to.* She couldn't bear the thought that she might be torturing him even further by being anywhere near him.

"About what?" Justin shrugged, his back still to her. "What is there to say, Alicia? Luke's gone. Sophie's missing. Out there somewhere because of some *fucking*…" He stopped, breathing hard.

"Because of me. I *know*." Alicia sobbed. "I'd undo it if I could. I didn't mean for—"

"But you *can't*!" Justin turned towards her, his eyes smouldering with raw anger. "You can't undo any of it! There's nothing to talk about, don't you *get* it? We have no past that I can contemplate even thinking about, let alone talking about. No future. There is *nothing* you can say that will make any of this—"

The ringing of his mobile cutting him short, Justin immediately answered it.

Alicia felt as if her heart might turn inside out as she watched him, praying it was news of Sophie.

Justin glanced at her. His disappointed expression told her it wasn't. "Yes, thanks for calling back," he said into his phone. "I need to take some extended leave for personal reasons. Do you think you could organise someone to cover as clinical lead?… I'm not sure. Dr. Paton, possibly?"

He waited, squeezing the bridge of his nose hard between his thumb and forefinger. "Okay, thanks. Tell her to call me if she gets stuck on anything." His frustration tangible as he ended the call, he glanced up at the ceiling.

"Justin, please believe that I never meant to hurt you," Alicia tried cautiously, knowing how ludicrous it sounded even as she said it. Still, she had to try.

"Right." Emitting a guttural laugh, Justin dropped his gaze. "I need to go," he said gruffly, turning suddenly to the hall.

"But where?" Panic gripping her afresh, Alicia followed him.

"To look for her," Justin said, grabbing his jacket from the banister and heading for the front door. "I can't just stand around here doing *nothing*, for Christ's sake."

"Wait," Alicia said, as he yanked open the front door. "I'll come with you. Let me get my mobile and—"

"No," Justin said adamantly. "Not because..." He stopped, sighing heavily as he turned to her. "It would probably be better if we split up," he suggested, his eyes flicking briefly to hers. "I'm going to be walking the streets, in the town centre, anywhere I can think of. You might do better to concentrate on local areas, places she might be known—cafés, clubs she might have been to. And you could speak to her schoolfriends."

Alicia glanced uncertainly away.

"It would look less suspect than a man hanging around the school. The police may have covered it, but..." Again, he stopped, making proper eye contact with her at last, albeit guardedly.

But they might not have. Alicia understood. And Sophie's schoolfriends might be more likely to talk to her mother than the police, particularly if they frequented the same clubs she and Justin both guessed Sophie snuck into. It made sense. She was sure he wouldn't want to be in her company, but he wasn't making a point. His thoughts were on Sophie's welfare. As she had known they would be.

Swallowing hard, Alicia nodded. "Be careful," she said, holding his gaze, wishing he could see inside her heart to understand how truly sorry she was.

CHAPTER THIRTY-THREE

SOPHIE

"It's Britain's highest rollercoaster," Sophie said excitedly, her nerves tingling with anticipation as the car trundled to the top of the ride. "Wow! Look at that!" Breathing in the crisp, salty air, she glanced out over the bird's-eye view of the seafront they had from almost sixty-five metres up. It had been raining when she and Chloe had come before, grey and gloomy, but today, with the sun bouncing like jewels off the water, the sight was spectacular. She was really glad she'd come now. She'd felt like crap when she'd finally woken up, woozy and headachy, having slept really heavily. She'd been sure she was coming down with the flu. Paul had said she'd feel better for a day out. He'd been right.

"You'll have to hold on tight." Her adrenaline pumping, her chest now about to burst with anticipation, she turned to Paul as they reached the dizzying summit of the climb, from where they would hurtle back to earth, leaving their stomachs behind them. "We're going to drop at, like, eighty miles an—Oh."

Paul was holding on for grim death. She noted his white-knuckled grip, his eyes squeezed tight, his complexion, which was a sickly shade of green. *Shoot.* He really was scared of heights.

Sophie was about to try to reassure him when her breath was snatched from her mouth, her insides turning inside out as they plunged, rolled, twisted and spun.

"*Shit.*" She regurgitated her tonsils as they swooped to a stop, her heart thumping so manically she was sure it would leap right out of her chest. "Are you all right?" She turned quickly to Paul, who was grappling to get out of his seat.

Scrambling out when the safety bars were released, Paul didn't answer, heading fast away from what had obviously been pure torture for him.

"Paul?" Sophie caught up with him where he'd stopped, clutching his thighs and taking deep breaths. "Are you okay?"

"Yes," Paul managed, and nodded.

"Are you sure? You look terrible. I didn't realise you were that scared. Do you want to go and find somewhere to sit—"

"I'm fine!" Paul snapped, causing Sophie to take a step back. He'd been really cool up until then, laughing and joking. He hadn't minded at all about getting soaked on the spooky water ride and he'd been fine on the Grand National. To Sophie, the ancient wooden rollercoaster, clunking and grinding, was way scarier than the ride on the Big One.

"Sorry," he said quickly, straightening up and arranging his face into a smile. "I felt a bit nauseous for a minute. I'm fine now," he reassured her, placing an arm around her shoulders. "Come on, let's go and do something tamer, where we can keep our feet on the ground."

Sophie had quite fancied seeing the Tower, but maybe that wasn't such a great idea, given his phobia. "Go-karting?" she suggested.

"And that's supposed to be tamer?" He arched an eyebrow.

"Oh, right." Sophie guessed he probably wouldn't want to be whizzing around bends and stuff. "The casino?" she ventured.

Paul didn't look impressed. "I don't really approve of gambling, Sophie, sorry. How about the *Star Trek* exhibition?"

"Sounds good." Sophie nodded. It wasn't exactly her first choice, but she supposed he was paying.

"Excellent." Wrapping an arm around her shoulders, he gave her a smile and led her on. "And then food," he suggested. "Hopefully, I'll have got my appetite back by then."

Paul wasn't enthralled with the exhibition, Sophie gathered. It wasn't as exciting as she'd expected, but it was okay. She'd thought sitting in the captain's chair of the original Starship *Enterprise* was cool. Paul, though, didn't seem to rate it much.

"So what did you think?" Noting his pensive expression as they walked out, she tested the waters.

"Not worth the entrance fee, in my opinion," Paul said. "Considering how vast the *Star Trek* universe is supposed to be, the exhibition was extremely small, wasn't it? And I didn't see any evidence of the *Star Trek: Discovery* props as promised by the signage outside."

He was obviously a Trekkie. Shrugging, she quickened her pace to keep up with him as he strode off.

"What do you fancy to eat?" he asked her, his smile back in place a second later.

Sophie plumped for chips. "You have to have chips at the seaside."

"Really?" Paul's smile dwindled. "Well, it is your day out. Okay, chips it is."

Five minutes later, his smile dwindled further as Sophie pointed out the pier-front burger and chips kiosk. "I think I prefer to eat mine with a knife and fork," he suggested, obviously not keen to eat his chips walking along the seafront, which Sophie had quite fancied. There was nothing quite like eating chips drenched in salt and vinegar straight from the paper, as far as she was concerned.

Noting his unenthusiastic expression, she shrugged easily.

"Okay," she said. They'd probably come in a cone anyway, and that wasn't quite the same.

"How about here then?" she asked, pointing out a Burger King a few minutes later.

Again, Paul didn't look that taken with the idea. Sophie was beginning to wonder whether he even wanted chips.

"Kentucky?" she tried, another few shops on.

Paul looked no better impressed. "What about over there?" He nodded across the road. "It looks a bit more salubrious, don't you think?"

Sophie didn't quite get why eating chips had to be done salubriously, but the curiosity coffee shop he was indicating looked kind of cute, and now at the point where her belly was thinking her throat had been cut, she'd go for anywhere that served food.

Grabbing a window seat, Sophie perused the menu hungrily, though she'd already chosen her order from the board behind the counter. Veggie burger and chips—had to be. She was practically fantasising chips now. "Done," she said, handing the menu to Paul with a smile. "What do you fancy?"

Paul frowned. "A clean table," he said, wiping two fingers along the surface of it, examining them and then sighing audibly. Taking the menu with a shake of his head, he scanned it leisurely, finally deciding on beef stroganoff.

Sophie wrinkled her nose. "I don't know how people eat meat," she said. "I mean, I wouldn't judge anybody, but personally, I couldn't eat another living creature if my life depended on it."

"It's dead, Sophie," Paul pointed out, his smile a bit short this time. "And I doubt many carnivorous animals would give you the same consideration if the situation were reversed."

Oops. Sophie reprimanded herself. He probably thought she was criticising him. "I know. It's just a personal choice and, like I say, live and let live. Or rather, eat and let eat." She shrugged and gave him a bright smile.

Paul's smile was more relaxed then. "I'll order," he said. "Why don't you go and wash your hands."

Sophie followed his gaze as he nodded towards the loos, and then looked back at him, perplexed. She didn't need to go to the…Ah. She got the gist as he turned to summon one of the waiting staff. He meant *actually* wash her hands. A bit fastidious, wasn't he? She knitted her brow. But then, she supposed she had been hanging on to rides where a million other sweaty hands had been clinging on for dear life.

Fair enough. Hoping the food wouldn't be long, she humoured him.

Her hope faded when she came back to see a coachload of old-age pensioners coming in. Looked like the service was going to be slow. Sighing inwardly, Sophie took her seat and tried to ignore her rumbling tummy. "So, what do you do in Dubai?" she asked him, distracting Paul from checking his watch.

"Investment advice," he said. "All a bit dull really, unless you're into financial planning."

Sophie tried not to look too bored. "Do you mind if I ask you when you lost your family?" she ventured.

Paul looked down at that. "It's a bit painful, to be honest," he said. "Maybe another time. We don't want to spoil the day, do we? Tell me about yourself. What do you want to do when you leave school?"

"Veterinary surgeon," Sophie answered straight off. "I was hoping to do my undergraduate course at the Royal Veterinary College, but I'm thinking that might depend on whether I can get a student loan now."

Paul eyed her interestedly. "Oh, how so?"

"Stuff," Sophie sighed. "You know, at home."

"Ah, I see. I wouldn't worry too much about that, Sophie. I can cover your study costs," Paul said, smiling benevolently.

Sophie's eyes grew wide. "Really?"

"I'd have to run it by your mother first, but yes, I don't see why not. I'm supposed to be looking out for you, aren't I?"

"Well, yes, but…" Her uni fees? *Wow.* How cool would it be to have those covered?

"Unless you want to have a word with your mother, that is?" Paul asked.

"No." Uh-uh. She absolutely did not want to have a word with her mother. Not any words, any time soon. But what about Justin? How would he feel?

She was debating whether to broach the subject with Paul when she noticed he was checking his watch again and looking agitatedly around for signs of their food.

Justin would feel relieved, Sophie guessed, turning to gaze out of the window. He wouldn't want the responsibility now, would he? He'd hardly want to pay out thousands of pounds for someone who wasn't his daughter. It might have been different if he'd known she wasn't his from the outset. He would have had a choice then. Who knows, he might have decided he wanted to be her father. Her mum had taken that away from him, though, hadn't she? She should seriously consider Paul's offer, she decided. Show them that the choices about her life weren't theirs to make.

Paul was growing more agitated, she realised. He was rearranging the cutlery on the table, lining up knives and forks and condiments and then checking his watch again. Finally, breathing in a tight breath, he gestured a beleaguered-looking waitress over. "Is there any chance of actually getting served today?" he asked her irritably. "We have a long journey home."

The girl, not much older than Sophie, a student probably, looked flustered, and offered to go and hurry it up.

Five minutes later, smiling apologetically, she placed their meals in front of them.

Sophie had started ravenously on her chips when Paul plonked his knife and fork down, clinking his plate as he did. "Waitress," he called—loudly. "This is lukewarm, undercooked and, frankly, inedible."

Sophie shifted uncomfortably as the now embarrassed girl retrieved his plate and scuttled back towards the kitchen.

"Sorry about that," Paul said, his smile back again as he wiped his mouth on his napkin, folded it up and looked in Sophie's direction. "I hope it didn't spoil your meal."

"No," Sophie assured him. Hers had been fine. She was about to suggest he maybe should have had chips after all, but then thought better of it.

"Good," he said, reaching for the hand in which she was still holding her fork and giving it a squeeze. "I'd hate my daughter to be disappointed on her special day out."

CHAPTER THIRTY-FOUR

JESSICA

Having had no news of Sophie all day, Jessica considered it the least she could do to help Alicia hand out leaflets that evening. It was freezing cold though. She wished she'd put her thicker coat on.

Shivering in a sudden deluge of rain, she glanced towards Alicia, and then, sensing trouble, sprang after her. Obviously despairing of people either declining to take the leaflet or else accepting it with barely a glance, Alicia had got it into her head to chase after a commuter from the rush hour train, which was possibly a bad idea.

"You could at least have looked at it!" Alicia yelled at the man, as Jess reached her, catching her by the arm. "It's my daughter! She's *missing*!"

"Come on, sweetheart." Jessica urged her away. People were beginning to stare. There was no point in shouting at random strangers. That wouldn't bring her daughter back. Jessica swallowed back a knot of guilt in her chest. It wasn't her fault she'd gone, of course—this was Alicia's own doing—but Jessica wished she'd warned Justin that Sophie had heard them talking. Sophie might not have wanted to discuss it, but it might have given him a chance to try and initiate a conversation with her. Justin would never get over the heartbreak if anything happened to her. Never.

Walking shakily back with her, Alicia stopped, crouching to

fish the leaflet from the puddle it had landed in when the man had tossed it aside. Then she dropped her head to her knees and let out a wretched sob.

Jessica joined her, as people rushing homewards skirted around them. Taking the leaflet from her, her heart wrenched for her sister as she noticed the print had smudged, causing a black track to wend its way down Sophie's cheek. No wonder she was upset. Whatever she'd done, Jessica wouldn't wish this on her. "We'll get some laminated posters made up," she suggested, slipping an arm around her and helping her to her feet. "I can get them done at work."

"Thanks, Jess." Alicia nodded tearfully. "I have no idea what I would have done without you. Gone mad, probably."

"Madder, you mean?" Jessica smiled, hoping to coax Alicia into doing the same. "You're soaked." Jessica squeezed her sister close and attempted to rub some warmth into her as they walked. "Let's go and have a hot drink," she suggested, nodding towards a McDonald's. "And then, when we've warmed up a bit, we'll come back and hit the pub crowds. How does that sound?"

Tugging in a shuddery breath, Alicia nodded more determinedly.

"That's better," Jessica said, squeezing her tighter. "You have to hold it together, Ali, for Sophie's sake."

"I know. I'm trying, but…" Another fat tear spilling down her cheek, Alicia brushed it away. "I'm sorry, Jess. I just feel so bloody *raw* inside. So empty."

"You're bound to." Jess sighed understandingly, leading the way into McDonald's and steering her disorientated sister towards a seat.

"Not here." Alicia stopped short. "Do you mind if we grab a seat at the window?" She nodded towards the high stools and headed towards them. "I can watch people passing by then."

In hopes that Sophie walked past, Jessica realised, glad that Alicia did still seem to be functioning and thinking, albeit sluggishly. She didn't want her having a breakdown. Justin would be bound to be sympathetic—it was in his nature—but it wouldn't do him any good.

"I'll go and grab us a drink. Won't be a second," she said, leaving her leaflets and coat with Alicia, but taking her phone with her. Having Alicia privy to all her calls out of work hours, she'd found, was a touch awkward.

Coming back with toasted bagels and two hot chocolates, she noticed Alicia was staring vacantly into the distance. Not much people-watching going on here then.

"I'm so relieved Justin's keeping me updated on where he is," Alicia said, as Jessica deposited the tray and hitched herself up next to her.

"He said he would, didn't he? He's always been dependable, Ali."

Alicia looked immediately guilty. "He must absolutely hate me."

"He doesn't hate you." Jessica reached to squeeze her hand. "He's not going to recover from this easily, but I don't think he hates you."

Alicia didn't look very reassured by that, but she could hardly tell her he'd forgive her and that they'd walk off into the sunset together. That was highly unlikely. The man's whole world had collapsed around him.

"Eat something," she said, pushing the bagel towards her. "It'll make you feel better."

Alicia shook her head. "Sorry, Jess, I really don't have any appetite."

"You have to eat, Ali." Jess looked her over worriedly. "You'll be no use to anyone if you make yourself ill."

Alicia gave her a small smile. "I will. Later."

Jessica wasn't convinced. "Have you tried to talk to him?" she asked, wondering what explanations Alicia might have offered

Justin—not that she imagined Justin would be receptive to anything she had to say, if his reaction to her attempts to apologise to him yesterday was anything to judge by.

Alicia placed the hot chocolate back down. She'd barely taken a sip. "There's nothing I can say that will detract from the fact that I deceived him, Jess—horribly. I lied to him. He's not likely to want to listen, is he?"

"No," Jessica started, with a sigh, "but—" She stopped as Alicia's phone rang, causing Alicia to jump.

Scrambling to retrieve it from her bag, her face hopeful, she checked the number. "It's Paul," she said, debating for a second and then answering it.

Jessica had guessed as much from her expression. She was only surprised Alicia was taking the call. She picked at her bagel and tried to listen without making it too obvious.

"What do you want, Paul?" Alicia asked him. "Why do you keep ringing me?"

She listened for a second. "But I don't want to see you," she said adamantly. "Or talk to you. If you have anything to say, then I suggest you say it through a solicitor." And with that, she ended the call.

A solicitor? Oh dear, it looked as if Paul was intent on laying some claim to Sophie then. God, how dreadful. Jessica certainly hoped she was going to tell Justin about that.

CHAPTER THIRTY-FIVE

SOPHIE

"Sorry about that," Paul said, coming back into the lounge area, having gone to his study to make an urgent phone call. "Business, I'm afraid. An irate client. Clearly, he thinks I'm available even when I'm on leave. Some people never cease to amaze me."

Shaking his head, he walked across to the drinks table, dropping his phone on the coffee table as he went, Sophie noted.

"Wine?" he asked her, waving a glass in her direction.

"No, thanks." Sophie smiled. "I think I've still got a hangover from last night."

"I doubt that. You only had two small glasses. It's probably motion sickness from the rollercoasters. Maybe later, yes?"

"Yeah, maybe." Sophie thought not. She'd thought she must have been coming down with something last night, but the wine, which she hardly ever drank, had made her feel so woozy, it had been all she could do to undress and crawl into bed. And then she'd had some really weird dreams. "Do you mind if I watch some TV?" She nodded towards the telly.

"Help yourself," Paul said, glugging back a red wine and topping up his glass. "There's Netflix on there, if you fancy selecting us a film for later. I'm just going to take a quick shower and then how about I cook us a proper meal? You haven't tasted anything until you've tasted my creamy mushroom linguini."

"I'm impressed," Sophie said, flashing him another smile as

she located the remote and seated herself on the sofa. "I don't know my cannelloni from my spaghetti."

Paul looked pleased at that. "It's perfect with parmesan," he said, pulling off his trainers, and placing them by the front door. "And garlic bread, of course."

"Can't have pasta without garlic bread," Sophie concurred, watching him over her shoulder.

"A girl after my own heart," Paul said, stepping away from the trainers then cocking his head to one side and surveying them. He stepped back again to arrange them just so.

"Won't be long," he said, walking between her and the TV.

He straightened the magazines on the table and the cushions as he went, Sophie noticed, knitting her brow; one cushion, in particular, required much realigning, and he then stood back and studied it as if it were a piece of art or something. He was obviously a perfectionist. She'd have to remind herself not to leave her crap all over the place, but that was no big price to pay for crashing here for a while. It was a hell of a better option than a caravan in Herefordshire, assuming Holly had been able to swing it. She doubted she would have been able to stay there for long, in any case, and her job options would have been far fewer than in Brum. Here would do nicely, until she could find a place of her own, and if her mum didn't like it, that was tough after treating her with nil respect. It would certainly show her that she was perfectly capable of managing without her *or* Justin, and the shit they'd dumped on her because they thought they had a right to.

"Help yourself to anything you need," Paul said. "There's Coke in the fridge if you don't fancy anything stronger yet."

"Will do. Thanks," Sophie called, noting him refilling up his glass as he headed for the bedroom area. He drank a lot. Again, not a big deal. It's not like it was whisky he was knocking back, and he was okay—good fun, bar the perfectionist thing. Sophie could live with that. She'd survived a lot worse lately.

She hadn't asked him about the new phone. She'd thought that might be pushing her luck after all the money he'd spent on her and his offering to pay her uni fees. She was still slightly gobsmacked about that. But then, he was her father and he wouldn't have offered unless he'd wanted to.

She eyed his phone on the coffee table, wondering whether she should maybe send her mum a text, just to let her know she was okay. On the other hand, she'd never given a stuff about her feelings, had she? Her deliberations were cut short as Paul reappeared, heading swiftly across to the table to sweep the phone up.

"Forgot to mention something to the client who thinks I've got nothing better to do," he said, glancing despairingly up at the ceiling. "Work—I swear I'm thinking about it 24/7. Selected that film yet?"

"Not yet, no," Sophie said, flicking through the list. "How about *10 Cloverfield Lane* or *American Psycho*?"

Paul looked doubtful. "Aren't they 18s?"

Sophie swung her gaze towards him. Was he serious?

"Don't look so alarmed, Sophie." He laughed, obviously noting the look. "I'd hardly allow you wine and then censor your TV viewing. In any case, *Cloverfield Lane*'s a twelve, I think."

Sophie blew out a sigh of relief. "You're bit of a Netflix geek then?"

"I watch a lot of TV, yes," he said, smiling sadly. "I tend to have a lot of time on my hands, without the woman I love."

Oh, shit. Raw nerve. "Sorry," she said. "I imagine that's really hard."

"It is." Drawing in a long breath, he glanced down.

"So, which one?" Sophie asked, guessing he didn't want to go there.

Paul thought about it, a not very enthusiastic look on his face. "I don't really like psycho stuff, to be honest," he said, reaching to relieve her of the control and flicking through the genres. "How about we compromise and watch *Once Upon a Time in Venice*? John Goodman stars in that, too, and Bruce Willis. It's supposed to be pretty good."

Sophie had quite fancied *10 Cloverfield Lane*, but she could compromise. That's what being an adult was supposed to be all about, after all. "Sounds good." She nodded, feeling pleased when his smile brightened.

"Five minutes," he said, heading jauntily off to the bathroom. "And then I'll get that pasta on."

"Food is served, Madame," Paul called from the dining area an hour later.

"Cool," Sophie said, flicking off the TV and going to where Paul was placing the plates down. Blimey, he really did things in style, she thought, noting the fancily folded napkins and what she supposed were crystal glasses on the long chrome and glass table.

"I feel like the queen," she said, as he took the tea towel from his arm, dusted her seat with it, and then pulled the chair out for her.

"Nothing but the best for my daughter," he said, tucking her in and going around to pluck up her napkin, flick it with a flourish and place it on her lap.

"I thought an unoaked Chardonnay to complement the meal," he said, topping up her already half-filled glass. "I find the earthy flavours from mushrooms can leave mild wines tasting like water," he added knowledgeably, placing the bottle down and taking his seat at the other end of the table.

Sophie looked warily from her glass to him. "I'm not sure I should," she said uncertainly.

"You can't have creamy mushroom linguini without a good

white wine," Paul said, nodding at her glass as he took a mouthful of his food. "Sip it. I promise you'll appreciate it. Don't worry, I'll keep an eye on your intake."

Just the one wouldn't hurt, Sophie supposed. And now he'd poured it... Picking up the glass, she took a sip and squeezed her eyes closed as the fruity, acidy flavour hit the back of her throat. *Wow*, that was seriously strong.

"Well?" he asked, clearly interested in her view.

"Excellent," Sophie said, not entirely sure whether it was. "It's kind of..." She had a think, not wishing to sound like an ignoramus. "Sharp and crisp, and fruity."

"You obviously have a nose," Paul said, leaving Sophie perplexed. "You'll probably notice there's no buttery vanilla taste. Some people call it the naked wine."

Now Sophie was definitely perplexed, but he clearly knew his stuff. Obviously, he had lived the high life, which was fair enough, since he'd earned it. Plus, he'd had a shitload of tragedy on the personal front, problems even worse than hers, and he was getting on with his life. And *that*, Sophie decided, picking up her glass and taking a larger swig, was exactly what she intended to do. "Cheers," she said, nodding him a toast.

Paul did likewise. "Eat up," he said, indicating her meal with his fork. "Don't want all the chef's hard work going to waste, do we?"

Grabbing her fork, Sophie dug in, swirling the linguini around and taking a huge mouthful. "Do you think I should ring Mum?" she asked conversationally between chews. "Just to let her know I'm all right?"

"Probably a good idea," Paul said, taking another sip of his wine. "Maybe not tonight though. Don't want to ruin our film night, do we?"

"No." Sophie slowed her chewing, knitting her brow as a realisation began to dawn.

"I've spoken to her anyway. She's fine with you being here, as long as you want to be."

Sophie stopped chewing, grabbed up her wine, took a huge gulp and swallowed hard. It had meat in it. She'd just swallowed part of a pig. *Shit.* What did she do? She felt sweat prickle her forehead. She couldn't not eat it, not after all his careful preparation.

Reaching for her glass, she took another drink, feeling definitely nauseous as she did.

"All right, Sophie?" Paul eyed her curiously over his glass.

"Yes," Sophie said quickly, looking down at her plate, and then, seeing the small chunks of ham there, feeling dangerously close to actually being sick. "I, um…'Scuse me," she said, scraping her chair back. "I feel a bit…"

Getting to her feet, Sophie turned for the bathroom, and found herself groping for the walls as the room shifted worryingly off-kilter.

"Sophie?" Paul was behind her, sounding alarmed.

"Sorry," she mumbled, her head reeling, her stomach churning. "I'm not feeling very well. I…" Trailing off, she stumbled forwards, and the walls tilted. Attempting to stay upright, the room now revolving steadily, like a merry-go-round on slow spin, Sophie tried another step, but her limbs felt heavy, sluggish.

"Sophie!" Paul caught her as her legs gave way like butter beneath her.

"I thought you were coming down with something." Her eyes shut tight, Sophie heard him as he swept her up into his arms and carried her towards the bedroom. "You probably have a vitamin deficiency. You really should be eating meat, you know."

CHAPTER THIRTY-SIX

JUSTIN

A whole week he'd been searching. Seven dark, grey days and cold nights. Tonight, it was raining. Icy, slashing rain, which seemed to be seeping into his bones.

Debating whether to ring Alicia again, Justin decided against. He had no news, and with each passing day, that was definitely bad news. Alicia had promised to ring him the minute she heard anything from Taylor, which might be never. The police had had no sightings of Sophie, though that didn't surprise Justin. She was obviously going to stay a low-priority case. Bitterness, like corrosive acid, rose painfully in his chest.

Alicia was out there too, handing out leaflets, visiting the various places they'd discussed, talking to kids at the school. Endlessly searching faces in the street. Justin had no doubt she would be doing that. He wished he could talk to her properly, communicate on anything but the most basic level. The fact was, though, he simply couldn't talk about anything that touched on who they were before. Who he'd thought they were. Couldn't bear to allow his mind to think about the future they didn't have. He needed to stay focussed on finding Sophie. It was the only way he knew how to get through each day.

Concentrating his efforts, Justin walked on through the city streets, counting paving stones as he went, which at least occupied his mind if it did nothing to help calm him. Sleep might help, but that only ever came now to haunt him. Reaching the area he'd been heading for, where young and old slept rough in the city centre, Justin pulled out his photo of Sophie, showing it to a few people, getting no information. Then stopped, his chest constricting as he noticed a young girl around Sophie's age.

She was a drug user. Justin noted the paraphernalia around her but didn't judge her. One week observing the people here had altered his thinking. These kids were hooked. And once they were, it seemed there was rarely any going back. No going forward either, becoming the people they could be. They were stuck—slaves to their addiction. It was a lesson well learned in regard to the drug users who came into accident and emergency.

Seemingly oblivious to him as he walked towards her, the girl concentrated on her endeavours. Her head shot up as he stopped directly in front of her, her expression one of alarm.

"Sorry," Justin said quickly. "I didn't mean to scare you."

"Are you after my stuff?" she asked, a panicky look in her eyes.

"No," he assured her. "I'm looking for my daughter. I wondered whether—"

"Haven't seen her," she said immediately.

Justin sighed and massaged his forehead. "I haven't shown you her photo yet."

She shrugged and continued with her task, drawing her brew up into a syringe and flicking the needle. A long-term user then, Justin surmised, a knot of anger tightening his stomach. No matter how much he counted, he couldn't seem to reach a point where his emotions weren't pivoting between fury, fatigue, fear and despair.

"Do you mind if I sit?" he asked her.

She looked up again, seeming to measure him. "Not if you don't," she said chirpily.

She was pretty. Unusual coloured eyes, somewhere between hazel and green—pupils constricted, meaning she was possibly a heroin user. Lowering himself down beside her, Justin felt his heart constrict. Seeing the eyebrow stud, in the same place as Sophie's, he looked away, trying hard not to see his daughter sitting in the same place as this young girl. If she was still alive. He clamped down hard on that thought.

"Is she missing?" she asked him. "Your daughter?"

Justin nodded wearily and dragged a hand over his neck.

"So why did she split?"

"We had some problems. Her mother and me. We argued. Things were said. Things that Sophie overheard. Things she shouldn't have." Justin paused, his gut aching, tears too damn close, he realised, gulping back a lump in his throat. "Do you ever wish you could turn the clock back?" he asked her.

"Every day," she assured him, with a wry smile.

"I should go," Justin said, attempting to compose himself.

"Do you have that photo?" she asked, as he got to his feet.

Relieved she was prepared to at least look at it, Justin pulled it from his inside pocket and handed it to her.

She scanned it, then looked back at him. "I think I might have seen her," she said, her brow furrowed thoughtfully. "About a week ago, hanging around New Street Station. I remember thinking she shouldn't be. She didn't get on a train though."

"Oh?" Justin said, his heart rate spiking.

"She left with some bloke, eventually."

Fuck. Justin swallowed hard. "Can you remember what he looked like?" he asked, hoping against hope that she might.

"Not really. An older bloke, quite tall, dark. They left eating chips together, so I figured she must know him."

"Do you remember what clothes he was wearing?" Justin tried to keep the desperation from his voice.

She shook her head. "Jeans and trainers. I can't remember what jacket. They were clean though. He'd didn't look like a deadbeat."

Tall, dark; wearing jeans and trainers. Justin sighed inwardly. She could be describing half the male population.

CHAPTER THIRTY-SEVEN

SOPHIE

Sophie awoke with absolutely no recollection of where she was. Panic slicing through her, she pulled herself to a sitting position, squinted hard against the thin, wintry sunlight filtering through the blinds and then glanced hurriedly around. *Paul's.* Closing her eyes, she breathed a sigh of relief. She was at Paul's apartment, in his guest room, though how she'd got here from the lounge, she hadn't the slightest clue. No, not the lounge, the dining table. Sifting through her dysfunctional memory, she eased her legs over the edge of the bed and felt immediately woozy. A dull throb, like a band slowly tightening, pounded at the base of her skull. She massaged her neck, trying to recall anything beyond taking her seat at the table, but the images were grey and wispy.

Shit! He must have put her to bed. She certainly didn't remember getting into it herself. Glancing quickly down at her attire, she emitted a huge sigh of relief, and then jumped to her feet as there was a tap on the door, only to end up plopping heavily back down again. "Yes," she called croakily. God, her throat felt like sandpaper. What the hell was the matter with her?

"Are you decent?" Paul called, pushing the door open a fraction.

"Uh-huh," Sophie said, guessing she was decent enough for his eyes, being dressed, though had no clue what she must look like. Had she been sick? She'd definitely caught a whiff.

"Morning—or rather, afternoon." Paul smiled as he came in, bearing a tray. "Are we feeling a bit better?"

"Ugh, no, I feel awful," Sophie said miserably, blinking against the light that flooded in from the lounge. "What happened?"

"At a guess, the flu bug going around happened. It's a nasty one, apparently."

He could say that again. "Did I pass out?" she asked, guessing she must have.

"You don't remember the doctor coming?" Paul placed the tray on the dressing table and turned to her, surprised.

"Doctor?" Sophie's eyes boggled. "No." She shook her head, bewildered. She was obviously sicker than she thought she was.

"You were running a fever," Paul said. "She gave you a shot."

A shot?

"Just something to bring your temperature down," Paul said, as her eyes drifted to the small pinprick on her arm. "She said to call her again, if you got worse, but I'm guessing you must be slightly improved, since you're back with us. You had me really worried there, I can tell you. I must have checked on you at least ten times in the night."

Oh. "Thanks," Sophie said weakly, feeling grateful and guilty. "Sorry for all the trouble I seem to be causing."

"It's no trouble," Paul assured her. "I think you might need to take her advice though."

"Which is?" Sophie asked, wondering whether she could make it to the bathroom. She seriously needed to shower.

"She's in agreement with me about you possibly being lacking in essential vitamins and minerals. If you really can't face eating meat, and I'm guessing you can't, you need to supplement your diet. I've bought you some vitamin pills. I've left a couple on the tray." He nodded towards it. "There's scrambled eggs there, if you're up to it. And then I'm thinking you might want to get changed."

"Thanks," Sophie said again, feeling still puzzled. He must have remembered she didn't eat meat if he'd discussed it with the doctor, so why had he put meat in the meal? She shrugged it off. He must have forgotten, and then been reminded when she'd thrown up.

"Like I say, no trouble. You can't help being ill, can you? I've rung your mum, by the way. She sends her best."

Her best? She passes out and her mother sends her best? *Cheers, Mum.* At least she was finding out how wanted she really was now. The cow was probably out there having a ball. Shagging the latest boyfriend and test-riding a few more from Tinder.

Sophie shrugged. As far as she was concerned, she and Justin were well shot of Alicia. Her eyes suddenly filling up, Sophie hurriedly wiped her nose.

"I'll come in and strip the bed while you're in the bathroom," Paul said, heading for the door.

"Strip it?" That was a bit unnecessary, wasn't it? She didn't stink that much.

"Mascara." Paul turned, nodding past her to the pillow, upon which, Sophie realised, were several tell-tale black patches. "You might want to not bother with it while you're ill."

"Oops. Sorry," she said, wiping a hand under her nose again.

"Oh, and Sophie?"

She looked sheepishly back at him.

"Use a tissue to blow your nose, yes? There's a box on the bedside table."

"Oh, right." Sophie plucked one and fiddled with it. She didn't actually want to blow her nose.

"Your bag's over by the window," he reminded her. "I'll leave you to it. Shout when you're ready and I'll give you a hand to the bathroom."

"Okay, thanks," Sophie said, as he went out. "Oh, where are my boots?" she called, assuming he'd taken them off last night.

"You were sick on them." Paul poked his head back around the door and gave her a sympathetic smile. "Looks like we'll have to get you a new pair, when you're up to it."

Crap. Sophie's heart sank. She found a use for the tissue after all, dabbing at the tears that sprang from her eyes, despite herself. She shouldn't feel bereaved over a bloody pair of boots, but those were her new Red or Dead boots. More importantly, Justin had gone with her to buy them the week before their world had been blown apart. It shouldn't matter. But it did.

Testing the floor with her feet, Sophie heaved herself up, feeling in need of Luke's little pink elephant toy, the only link to her past and something she had made sure to bring with her.

Wobbling as she went, she dropped to her knees and delved into her bag, and then delved deeper. It wasn't there! She did the whole pulling-stuff-out thing all over again. She'd had it here. She was sure she had. Hadn't she? And now it wasn't here.

She'd lost it. The one thing she'd wanted to keep above everything else.

"I'm so sorry, Luke," she whispered, tears spilling down her cheeks. "So sorry." She was sure she could hear his happy little gurgles above the distant rumble of traffic, that she would see her beautiful baby brother again soon. She missed him so much. Sometimes, she would close her eyes, sure that when she opened them, he would be here. Sophie's heart twisted inside her as she remembered Luke's flailing little arms, his squeals of delight as she laughed and cooed at him and pressed his pink elephant to his cute button nose, the way his true baby-blue eyes would grow wide with excitement when they alighted on her coming into his nursery.

She'd been sure she could do this, survive on her own. She had no choice but to.

But now, her chest felt so tight she could hardly breathe.

CHAPTER THIRTY-EIGHT

ALICIA

"Paul again?" Jessica asked, obviously noting Alicia's wary expression as she checked her incoming call.

Alicia nodded, her heart, already heavy with guilt and confusion, plummeting like a lead weight in her chest.

"Persistent, isn't he?" Jessica gave her an unimpressed look. "Are you going to answer it?" she asked, turning to fill up the kettle.

She had no choice but to, Alicia realised. However much she told him she didn't want to speak to him, have anything to do with him unless through legal channels, he just wouldn't stop. *Why?* What could he possibly hope to gain? He didn't want to suddenly take an interest in Sophie. He hadn't even enquired after her, for God's sake. And if, by the remotest, most unbelievable chance, he did want to figure things out with Sophie, then surely he must realise that this way wasn't going to achieve anything.

Hesitating for a second, Alicia steeled herself and took the call.

"Why are you doing this, Paul? Why are you harassing me?" she said, before he could speak.

"Harassing?" Paul laughed, incredulous. "I'm not harassing you, Alicia. I'm simply trying to have a civil conversation with you about my daughter. Surely you have to concede you owe me that much?"

His daughter? Hearing him speak the words, laying claim to her as if she *was* his, not even caring enough to ask how Sophie might feel, how she might be, *where* she might be, Alicia swallowed back her contempt. *She's not here!* She wanted to scream at it him. *She's not here—because of you!* She would never let him near her. Never.

"Look, Alicia, I just want to see you." He sighed heavily. "I don't want to cause you more heartache. That's the last thing I would ever want to do. I just want to talk, that's all, one-to-one, not over the phone. We can sort this out, surely? I'm not an unreasonable man."

Didn't want to cause her more heartache? Alicia could hardly breathe.

"You said your husband knows about us," Paul went on.

Alicia didn't answer. How could she, without playing into his hands?

"Does he know there's a possibility Sophie might not be his?"

Alicia gripped her phone hard, praying this conversation wasn't heading where she thought it might be.

"Look, all I want to do is to see you and to talk, Alicia. That's not too much to ask, is it? We had something good once. We shouldn't be pulling each other apart. We can work together on this, can't we?"

"I don't want to see you, Paul," Alicia repeated forcefully. "There are no circumstances under which I want to meet you, don't you see? I love my husband."

Paul went quiet.

Alicia waited. He was still there. She could hear him breathing.

"I think you might want to see me, Alicia," he said, eventually, "given the results of the paternity test."

Oh God, no. Alicia closed her eyes, feeling sick and claustrophobic, the noise of the kettle boiling and the clink of the cups behind her grating on her nerves, as the room closed in on her.

"I don't want to cause any upset, Alicia, I promise you. I just want to do what's best," Paul continued, sounding quite calm. Kind, almost. Reasonable.

Feeling as if she might be going slowly insane, Alicia scrambled feverishly through her muddled recollections. He couldn't have. How could he have, unless... Had he been in touch with Sophie?

"How?" she asked him, her mouth dry, her throat parched. "How did you get a test done? You'd need to have something of hers." *A toothbrush? A strand of her hair?* She tried to think, hoping that he was lying. Yet, there was a part of her that was desperately hopeful that he might have seen her in the past week.

"Her hairbrush," Paul supplied, killing all hope Alicia might have had dead. "When I was at the house."

After they'd been burgled? When they'd just laid Lucas to rest?

"You left me no choice, Alicia. I have a right to know. I think your husband has a right to know, too, don't you?" Paul said, as if anything could excuse the vileness of his actions. "I'll leave it with you. I really do think we need to meet though, don't you? For Sophie's sake."

Realising he'd ended the call, Alicia felt her blood run cold. What did he mean? A hard kernel of apprehension knotted inside her.

"Not a good outcome then?" Jessica enquired, glancing at her worriedly as she carried the tea to the table.

"No." Struggling to draw air past the lump in her throat, Alicia shook her head wretchedly. "He claims to have had a paternity test," she murmured, her mind still reeling, her heart plummeting to the depths of her soul. "He's calling her his daughter,"

"Oh my God!" Jessica stared at her, aghast. "You have to tell Justin, Alicia. He needs to know."

CHAPTER THIRTY-NINE

ALICIA

Coming into work had been a bad idea. If not for the little girl on her caseload who'd rung in claiming her father had deliberately burned her, she wouldn't have. How could the mother have blamed the child, she wondered, bewilderedly. How could she have demanded that the child be removed from the family home, rather than the father, even after the hospital had concluded the injuries were non-accidental? Looking away from the manager who was heading the team meeting, Alicia swiped away a tear.

She couldn't do this any more, she realised. How could she hope to remain detached, to try to hold families together—which had been her naive reason for wanting to do this in the first place—when she'd been responsible for tearing her own family apart? When her own daughter was missing? She'd often felt upset after the type of visit she'd had today, but this time she'd been devastated. She'd rushed straight from her car to the toilets, where she'd locked herself in a cubicle and sobbed her heart out.

She wasn't any help to anyone like this, least of all the children. They needed someone who was level-headed, and strong enough to fight back for them.

Lost in her thoughts, her heart leapt in her chest when her phone buzzed. Justin, she realised, her pulse racing—though in a very different way to how it always had whenever he'd texted her before. Grabbing up her bag, she mouthed an apology to the manager and hurried towards the office exit, collecting her coat as she went.

Clutching her coat around her against the cutting wind, her thoughts immediately going to Sophie and how cold she might be, Alicia made her way to where Justin had said he'd parked and scoured the road, left and right. It was only when he flashed his lights that she remembered he wasn't driving his own car any more, which had been written off the day their baby boy had died.

A crushing wave of grief washing over her, Alicia closed her eyes, working hard to compose herself before heading towards him. She felt as if she were hanging on by her fingernails, but she couldn't let go in front of him. She knew that would only compromise him into offering her comfort he couldn't possibly want to.

Sliding into the passenger seat, her heart missed a beat as she looked Justin over. He looked dreadful: unshaven, exhausted, his eyes those of a haunted man.

"How are you?" he asked her awkwardly.

She had no way to answer. "Getting through the days," she said, turning forwards as Justin fixed his gaze on the windscreen. He still couldn't look her in the eye. Alicia didn't blame him. She couldn't look herself in the eye.

"Have you spoken to him?" he asked after a second, resting his hands on the steering wheel.

Alicia swallowed. "Yes," she said, and took a deep breath, bracing herself to tell him what she desperately didn't want to. Lies hadn't kept him safe. She had no idea how she'd ever hoped they would.

Justin simply nodded. "Do you think he might have been touch with her?"

"I don't know," Alicia answered honestly. "I think not, from the things he said. He hadn't spoken to Sophie before she left. I'm not even sure he knows she's missing."

Justin ran his thumbs pensively along the steering wheel. "You're not having in-depth conversations then?" There was a sarcastic edge to his voice.

Alicia's heart dipped an inch lower, if that were possible. "No," she said simply. To try to explain would mean to explain everything, and Justin had given her no indication he wanted to hear it. "I texted him this morning." On the back of what he'd said, she had no choice but to contact him. *For Sophie's sake*, he'd said. She'd gone over it and over it. She thought he'd been talking about Sophie's future, but there'd been something in his tone that she couldn't quite figure out… "To ask him whether he'd been in contact with her," she went on. "He didn't answer."

Justin glanced at her, his expression a mixture of wariness and surprise.

"His voicemail said he was at a one-day conference. I confirmed it with his office. He seems to be behaving perfectly normally."

Again, Justin nodded. "You know where he works then?" There was that sarcastic edge again to his tone, though now clouded with weary resignation.

"Jessica knew, through her friend, David," she supplied, wanting to soften the blow she was about to deliver; knowing she couldn't possibly. She'd never before reached a place where she'd thought life wasn't worth living. Now, whenever she dozed, in the hours between the thin light of dawn and daylight—the only hours that sleep allowed her some escape—she would open her eyes to the harsh truth of an existence without the people she loved, and she simply didn't want to be in this reality any more. If not for Sophie, for the further pain she would cause Justin, she doubted she would be.

"There's something I have to tell you," she said, feeling

physically sick at the thought of delivering another knife wound to his chest. "Something he told me."

Justin didn't respond, stilling his hands on the wheel and seeming to brace himself instead.

"He said he'd had a paternity test." There was no way to soften the news that would surely crush him. She waited, praying, futilely. How would he not be destroyed?

Justin didn't react immediately. And then, shaking his head, he emitted a short, scornful laugh. "And he's had the results?" he asked, his tone flat.

"I believe so, yes." Her throat tight, Alicia looked away. If he looked at her now, if she saw what was in his eyes, she would crumble. "He threatened to tell you," she whispered, using her sleeve to wipe her eyes, rather than delve into her bag for a tissue. "Or at least he hinted he would, so yes, I suppose he must."

"Threatened?" She felt Justin turn to her. "To what end?" He sounded incredulous, confused.

Alicia hesitated. "I'm not sure," she said, not knowing how to share her suspicions with her husband.

"Because he wants future contact with her?" Justin's voice rose. "The daughter he's had no contact with whatsoever, and who is now *missing*?"

Feeling sick to her very soul, Alicia pressed a hand to her forehead. She had to talk to him, properly. She couldn't undo the lie she'd told, but she had to talk to him, try to explain. "I don't think that's his reason, no," she said guardedly.

Justin didn't say anything—nothing at all—staring straight ahead instead.

Alicia looked towards him. His face was taut and white, a telltale twitch tugging at his cheek. "Justin," she started, "I know you won't want to hear it, but—"

"I need to go," he said tersely, and started the engine. "You might want to tell him to have a rethink."

CHAPTER FORTY

SOPHIE

Waking with a jolt, Sophie sat bolt upright, looking frantically around. Seeing Paul coming through the door, she breathed a sigh of relief and then sank groggily back down.

"How are you feeling?" he asked, walking across to put a glass of Coke on the bedside table.

"Shitty," Sophie answered honestly, blinking up at him. She felt like she had the worst bug ever.

"Language," Paul said, smiling tolerantly as he looked down at her. He wasn't very impressed though, Sophie guessed, from the slight narrowing of his eyes.

"Sorry," she said, attempting to lever herself up. She'd have to watch her mouth, she realised. The fact was, though, she did feel like shit. It must be the worst superbug ever. "Do you think I should maybe go to the doctor's?" she asked him, as he reached to help her.

"I've rung them," he said. "They can't prescribe antibiotics for flu bugs, unfortunately. You need to drink plenty of fluids though. Don't worry, it'll be out of your system soon, I promise. I've had it myself."

Sophie nodded. She supposed he was right. And the fluids made sense. Her throat still felt like the bottom of a birdcage. She reached thirstily for her Coke.

Paul beat her to it. "Don't want to have to strip that bed again, do we?" He smiled and guided the glass to her mouth. "You should think about going without make-up," he said, watching as she took a huge glug. "Natural is so much nicer, don't you think?"

Sophie managed a small, indulgent smile. *Yeah, right*, she thought.

"You should lose the eyebrow stud, too," he said, nodding towards it as he placed the glass back on the table.

"Why?" She gawked up at him. She liked her stud. It had taken her ages to pluck up the courage to get it done, and it had hurt like hell, but she was quite proud of it.

"Just a suggestion," Paul said. "If you're hoping to get onto your veterinary course, they're likely to frown upon it, for hygiene reasons."

Oh. That gave Sophie pause for thought.

"Plus, it does look a bit juvenile, to be honest," Paul added.

"Does it?" Sophie frowned. "I thought it looked pretty cool."

Paul closed one eye and shook his head doubtfully. "Childish," he said. "I'd take it out if I were you, but that's just my opinion."

Not entirely convinced, Sophie reached for it, wincing as she pulled it out. He might be right, she supposed. She could always put it back in later.

"Better," he said, nodding approvingly. "Much. Trust me. Now, will you be all right for a couple of hours, do you think? I have a seminar I have to head up at the local office. I shouldn't be too long, though."

"I thought you were on leave," Sophie said, though she'd already guessed he was off somewhere, since he was wearing a grey business suit, crisp white shirt and red tie. He definitely looked dapper. Not as handsome as Justin though. She quashed an overwhelming sense of homesickness and wondered again where Luke's little pink elephant had gone. Paul had said he hadn't seen it but would ask his cleaner. Sophie hadn't seen a cleaner, but then she'd been pretty zonked out for a while.

"Seems I'm in big demand." Paul rolled his eyes. "My overseas investment knowledge is invaluable, apparently. There's more Coke in the fridge, but drink plenty of water, too. That fizzy stuff's no good for you. Way too much sugar. Don't want to get fat, do you? I'll make sure to get Diet Coke next time. Help yourself to anything else you fancy, obviously."

"Cheers," Sophie said. She actually was feeling marginally better—possibly well enough to have a potter around. She'd rather watch TV than lie around in here, and she could really use another shower.

"Shouldn't be too long," Paul said, heading for the door. "I'll bring some Florida brochures back with me. That should be worth getting better for. Oh, and don't forget to take your vitamins. I've left a couple next to your Coke."

CHAPTER FORTY-ONE

JUSTIN

"Christ, you look rough," Taylor observed, looking Justin over as he came into the station reception area.

"I need to talk to someone," Justin said, dragging his hands up over his face, exhausted and disorientated from endless hours spent searching for Sophie. He'd crawled the streets, checked shop doorways and car parks, trawled shopping precincts, and all the while, he hadn't been able to shake the thought rattling around in his head: *tall and dark*. That fitted Radley's description. He told himself he was being paranoid, counting how many tall, dark men he saw as he walked, but after his conversation with Alicia, he wanted Radley checked out. The man's interest, which he hadn't even tried to hide, was obviously more in Alicia than Sophie, but Justin needed to be sure he'd had no contact with her. He wanted the fucker out of his life, which might never happen, unless Justin did something about it. Sophie was his daughter. In his heart, he didn't need any proof of that. On paper, though… he had to do something about that. Go to the hospital and get the test organised. Today. Whatever the outcome, he would fight to make sure he stayed part of her life. He'd file for custody if he had to. First, though, he had to find her. He *would* find her.

Justin took a breath, knowing that what he was about to say might give Taylor more reason to class Sophie a low-risk runaway. It was possible that Radley had had no contact with her, but if he had any information regarding her whereabouts whatsoever, then Justin had to take that chance. "Paul Radley, the man who was at our house on the day of the break-in, he and Alicia, they..." He faltered, the words sticking in his throat. "They had an affair."

Taylor's eyes widened.

"Years ago," Justin went on, awkwardly, "around the time Sophie was conceived."

"Ah." Taylor's brow furrowed in consternation. "You'd better come through." He gestured for the PC behind the desk to release the security door. "So, am I to assume there's some doubt around her parentage?" he asked, leading Justin through to his office and nodding him towards a visitor's chair before seating himself at his desk.

Justin declined the invitation to take a seat. He was so wound up, he was finding it difficult to stand still, let alone sit. "Possibly," he said carefully. There was no way he wanted Taylor privy to the information about the test, which might sway his thinking in regard to whatever rights Radley had. "Alicia and I haven't really... Look, I don't know for sure, okay? For Christ's sake, do you need the details? Can you not just send someone to his—"

"Slow down, Justin," Taylor interrupted. "Take a breath and explain slowly. I can't do anything until I have the facts."

Justin sighed agitatedly. "You have them. There's a possibility Sophie might not be mine. This guy turns up out of the blue and—"

"He's had no previous contact with Sophie then?"

"As far as I know, no. Jesus, what does it *matter*?" Justin snapped. "My concern is that he might be in contact with her now."

Taylor looked puzzled. "Have you spoken to Alicia about this?"

Justin's frustration, which was already way off the scale, multiplied tenfold. "Not in great detail, no. It's a little difficult, as you might imagine."

Picking up his pen, Taylor began tapping it repeatedly on his desk, which was immensely annoying. "Do you think he might have taken her?"

Kneading his forehead, Justin sighed heavily. "I don't know," he said exasperatedly. "His interest seems to be more in my wife."

Taylor stopped tapping. "And was Sophie aware of this, shall we say, dilemma?"

"Yes," Justin said, guilt rising him. "She overheard me talking to Alicia's sister."

Taylor nodded slowly. "So, if Sophie is in contact with this... Paul Radley... it would be of her own volition?"

Justin clenched his teeth hard. "Yes, of her own volition," he said. "The point is, he might well know something about her whereabouts."

Again, Taylor nodded. "And the address?" he asked, poised to put his pen to its proper use.

"*Christ almighty!* I don't know! If I did, I wouldn't be here, would I?"

"I see." Taylor downed his pen and laced his hands in front of him. "So, let me get this straight. According to what you've told me, it would appear that, if Sophie has had any contact with Mr. Radley, it would be willingly. Do you agree?"

"Willingly?" Justin eyed him incredulously. "He's had nothing to do with her! Played no part in her life whatsoever. He doesn't give a damn about her. If he has been in contact with her, it's part of his plan to get to Alicia. I simply need to know whether he's heard from her, so I can get my daughter back. What part of this don't you *get?*"

Obviously unimpressed by the outburst of temper, Taylor glanced down at his desk and shuffled around some paperwork. "How old is Sophie, Justin?" he asked.

Immediately realising the significance of that question, Justin felt his heart go into freefall. Neither he nor Alicia had mentioned it when they'd spoken, but he hadn't doubted that his wife would have been thinking exactly what he was: that the milestone that marked Sophie's sixteenth birthday tomorrow would carry their daughter further away from them, that she might always remain low priority to everyone but them. Unless something happened to her, of course, and the worst-case scenario that had been haunting Justin day and night came to pass. Then they would mobilise all available bodies, or whatever it was police did when there was a *real* crime to solve. Someone raped and strangled, bludgeoned or knifed to death. Then they would cordon off areas, go house to house, investigate—while he buried another child.

Justin felt a cold shiver run through him. He didn't answer Taylor's question.

"A man eliciting contact with his sixteen-year-old daughter isn't a criminal offence, Justin," Taylor said regretfully.

Justin swallowed back a tight lump in his throat. "And if he's not her father?"

"We don't know, though, do we?" Taylor pointed out, confirming what Justin had already concluded: that they were going to do absolutely nothing. "If he's had contact with her and he's not, obviously we will want to speak to him," he went on, his expression now apologetic, as if impelling Justin to understand his hands were tied. "But there's nothing we can do without proof of parentage, other than make a general enquiry. Not unless Sophie herself actually comes forward with a complaint. I'm sorry."

"Right. Well." Justin shook his head, disbelieving. "Thanks for your help, Detective Inspector."

"Justin…" Taylor called after him, as Justin strode furiously towards the door. "Dr. Cole! Don't do anything rash."

CHAPTER FORTY-TWO

JUSTIN

Nice premises. Justin surveyed the Portland stone exterior of the 1930s art deco building from which Graham & Young Investment Advisers operated. The lease would undoubtedly be extortionate. Is that what Alicia had been impressed with, he wondered, his wealth? His emotions were swinging between disbelief that she would ever have got involved with Radley and gut-twisting fury. From where Justin was standing, the man had no redeeming features whatsoever.

They'd had an affair right under his nose. And this *wanker* had swanned back into her life and was resorting to threats, using *his* daughter as some kind of hold over her, presumably so he could pick up where he left off. That was a huge error of judgement on Radley's part, and Justin had decided to point out just how huge. He was obviously the type of person who got off on getting what he wanted, whatever the cost. Not used to being turned down. Justin recalled the challenge in Radley's eyes the first time he'd had the misfortune to meet him at the party, his obvious irritation when Alicia had turned down his offer of a lift to Jessica's after the break-in, the day she'd buried her child. And this was supposed to be someone who *cared* about her? About Sophie?

Bastard! There was no way he was going to have contact with

Sophie. Not while Justin still had breath in his body would he allow someone like that anywhere near her.

Curtailing his temper, Justin sucked in a breath and pushed his way through the revolving doors at the front of the building. Checking the list in the foyer, he ascertained the location of the company, nodded a greeting at the security guard and bypassed the lift, preferring to take the stairs up to the third floor. Counting the steady rhythm of his footfall against the stone steps did little to calm him.

Reasonably composed, he walked into the reception area and waited for the girl behind the desk to finish her call. "Paul Radley?" he enquired pleasantly, when she acknowledged him.

"He's in a meeting," the girl said, with a bright smile. "Do you have an appointment, Mr. . . . ?"

"Cole. Dr. Cole. I need to speak to him urgently," Justin said. "Is his meeting here, on the premises?"

"In the conference room." The girl pointed behind her, her forehead creased in obvious concern that a doctor was calling. "If you take a seat, I'll ring through and get someone to let him know you're here."

"No need. I'll go straight through. He needs urgent medical attention," Justin said, his tone serious, his gaze on the conference room doors at the end of the corridor. *Or he soon fucking well will.*

"Excuse me . . ." The girl twirled in her chair as he walked purposely around her. "Excuse me! Dr. Cole? You can't go in there."

Clamping his jaw tight, Justin walked on, shoving the double conference room doors open and walking straight across to where Radley had obviously been heading up the meeting. Plainly, he was some company bigshot, and Justin was about to bring the bastard right down to size.

His gaze shooting towards him, clearly registering who he was, Radley stopped mid-sentence, a startled look on his face in place of the smug expression Justin had seen what seemed like a lifetime ago. "What do you want?" he said, taking a step back. "You can't just walk in—"

"To break your neck," Justin cut across him. "But I'll settle for an arm or a leg. Maybe two."

Radley was scared, he noted, stopping in front of him. He searched his eyes—rich chestnut-brown, deceitful, dark eyes. Nothing like his daughter's.

"Look, I have no idea what this is about, but I'm sure we can sit down and discuss it civilly." Loosening his tie, Radley glanced around him, presumably wondering whether he could get past. *Not a chance, sunshine.*

"You threatened my wife."

"*Threatened?*" Radley laughed nervously. "Don't be preposterous. I rang her to ask if we could meet to discuss things going forward, that was all. I have no idea where you would get the idea that I—"

"Do your colleagues realise what a slimy piece of shit you are, Radley?" Justin cut him short. The "things going forward" business-speak really hadn't helped the man's case. He was talking about his *wife*, his *daughter*, his fucking life!

"This is ridiculous," Radley snapped irritably. "Rachel, call security," he instructed one of the employees Justin could sense hovering uncertainly behind him.

Justin's mouth curved into a scornful smile. "Good idea, Rachel," he said, his gaze never leaving Radley's. "Why don't you call the police while you're at it? Mr. Radley and I can have a nice cosy conversation with them down at the station about why he's stalking my wife."

"Mr. Radley?" the girl asked uncertainly.

Popping the top button of his shirt, Radley shook his head. "It's fine, Rachel," he said, coughing nervously.

"Tell them to leave," Justin said, working to hold on to his temper now he'd established the man was a spineless prick. He was as tall as him, and looked pretty fit, but he was shaking in his designer shoes.

Radley paled. "What?"

"I'm not asking you twice, you bastard," Justin bellowed. "Tell them to leave!"

Perspiration wetting his forehead, Radley swallowed, and then glanced at the audience behind them. "Can we have the room, please?" He smiled shakily. "Dr. Cole and I have some things to discuss."

Justin waited while people filed out.

"Satisfied?" Radley asked, as the doors closed.

"Not quite." Justin looked him contemptuously over. "Do those windows open?" He nodded behind him towards the long picture windows that gave a scenic view over the city.

"What?" Radley glanced confusedly in that direction. "No!" he said, his expression now petrified.

"That's a pity," Justin said, stepping towards him. "Means I'm just going to have to put you through one, doesn't it?"

Radley swallowed. "Look, I realise you're upset," he said, holding his hands defensively up in front of him, "I don't blame you. You should know, though, that I don't go around having random affairs with married women. Alicia was lonely, upset. She approached me, truth be known."

Justin narrowed his eyes.

"She contacted me when I got back from Dubai," Radley babbled on, spouting crap, his eyes all the while flicking nervously towards the window. "I tried to put her off, I swear I did. Obviously, now I can see how distressing this all is for you, I'll avoid any future contact. As for Sophie, I'm happy to back off. I'm not an unreasonable—"

His fury unleashing inside him, Justin seized Radley by the

throat, shoving him back towards the window before he could blink.

"Don't!" Radley screamed as he rammed him hard against it. "I'm terrified of heights. Please. God... *Don't.*"

Justin stared hard at him, his emotions swinging wildly as he realised, with a jolt, that he didn't actually care if the man went through it.

Twisting his collar tighter, Justin eyeballed him meaningfully. "Do not even breathe my daughter's name," he warned him. "And do not *ever* attempt to contact my wife again. If you do, I *will* kill you. Am I making myself clear?"

His eyes wide with fear, Radley nodded quickly.

"I didn't fucking hear you!" Justin lifted the man off his feet.

"Yes," Radley rasped, his Adam's apple bobbing in his throat.

Justin breathed in hard. "Good," he said, more quietly, and then, counting silently backwards, he gained a tenuous grip on his emotions and relaxed his hold.

Crumpling with relief, Radley almost slithered down the window. "Rachel!" he shouted croakily, as Justin turned away. "The police!"

Bad move. Justin turned back. "You'll want something more substantial than threats to report," he suggested, bringing his fist back, getting little satisfaction as he heard bone and sinew crack. "You're scum, Radley," he spat, turning to walk away as the man dropped to his knees.

CHAPTER FORTY-THREE

ALICIA

Recognising his ringtone, Alicia grabbed her phone.

"Hi," Justin said, as soon as she picked up. "I just wanted to check you were okay."

"Yes," Alicia assured him, amazed he cared enough to even ask after the news she'd given him. "Why?"

"No reason. I just thought I'd check." There was a pause on the line, then, "Radley," he said, almost spitting the word out. "If he gets in touch, will you let me know? Regarding Sophie, I mean."

"Obviously I will," Alicia said, wondering why he'd think she wouldn't. Then she thought of the paternity test, her heart aching for him as she imagined what his line of thinking might be: that she might decide her future was with Sophie's father.

"And you'll let me know if he bothers you? Assuming you don't want him to contact you unnecessarily, that is," Justin went on, sounding awkward now, uncertain.

"Justin…" Alicia paused. It would be so easy to just say it, to blurt it out. But then what? The endless questions, the disbelief. Him thinking she was incapable of doing anything but lying. Things were so clouded and confused in her mind now, she couldn't even be sure she wasn't lying to herself. She couldn't bear that Justin might think she had ever wanted to be with anyone but him. That she would entertain the thought of talking to Paul Radley now, unless through a solicitor. God forbid he should ever go down that route, but he well might now that he'd had the paternity test, meaning she would receive some cold, official letter in the post. "I don't want any contact with him. Not ever," she said.

She wished she could be with Justin now. Hold him. She wished there was something she could do to prove how very much she'd always loved and cared for him, even when she'd done the most careless thing in the world.

"Okay," he said, drawing in a tight breath. "I needed to check, for my own peace of mind."

His peace of mind? Alicia looked upwards, blinking hard… Would he ever have that again?

"I'd better go," he said, after another awkward pause. "I have some places to check out."

"Wait," she said urgently, wanting to at least check how he was. "Are you all right?" she asked him, stupidly. She knew how he was: a jaded, broken man. He missed Sophie and Lucas as much as she did: every minute of every waking day, in her dreams and her waking nightmares, she thought of them. Yet they couldn't reach out to each other, comfort each other. The void between them, where their children should be, was too vast.

"Tired," he admitted. "I've moved rooms. Renting nearer the area I'm going to check out later tonight."

"Is it clean?" she asked him, grieving for what they'd lost, for the ability to talk naturally that they'd once had. There was nothing between them now but stilted conversation.

"Reasonable," he said, then, "What about you? You're going to be staying with Jess for a while, I take it?"

"Yes, for now," she said, not sure what else she could say. She couldn't contemplate the thought of going back to a house where the ghosts of her family would haunt her. She hadn't even broached the subject of the house with Justin, whether he would want her going back there, whether he would ever want to go back.

"Jess is here now." She glanced towards her sister as she poked her head curiously around the kitchen door.

"Justin?" Jessica mouthed.

Alicia nodded.

Jessica nodded in turn, and then waggled her phone in Alicia's direction, indicating she was going to make a call.

"We're just back from distributing leaflets at district train stations," Alicia went on. "We have lots of shops and supermarkets putting up posters, too," she said, as if her efforts amounted to anything compared to what he was doing.

"Good. That's good." Justin sounded relieved. "Tell Jess thanks."

"I will," Alicia said, and then wondered what else to say. There was no subject that was safe. There was no future they could discuss, as Justin had pointed out. No present. No past. Every memory they'd made together had been tarnished.

"Right, I'll get off," he said, when it was clear they'd exhausted all topics. "Talk tomorrow."

"Okay." Alicia's heart fractured a little further. "Be careful, Justin."

"I will. You too," Justin said, and ended the call.

Alicia listened to the empty silence. There had been no coldness in his voice—he'd sounded like Justin—but it was as if he'd been talking to a sister or a friend, not his wife, not his lover. But then, she wasn't either of those any more.

Going to the fridge to pour herself a large wine, Alicia swallowed hard on the thought that one day he would stop calling. That would be the day she would stop breathing.

CHAPTER FORTY-FOUR

JUSTIN

Justin ended his call to Alicia. He'd been relieved to hear that Radley hadn't been in touch. Fury driving him, he hadn't been thinking clearly, hadn't considered what the consequences for Alicia might be when he'd stormed into that office. He hadn't been capable of anything beyond his fervent wish to do him permanent damage. He almost had.

Realising the man was a coward and likely to react in the way cowards did and pick on someone physically weaker than him, Justin had been worried he might retaliate and choose Alicia. He hadn't wanted to admit to her he'd been aggressive. In the normal run of things, he considered himself level-headed, and hated violence or confrontation of any sort. It rarely solved anything. Knowing Radley had threatened Alicia, though, that he thought he had a hold over her and was continuing to contact her when it was clear she didn't want him to, that had been beyond discussion of any sort. The man was pond scum, which begged the question again: what the bloody *hell* had she ever seen in him? He doubted he'd ever know the answer to that.

Pocketing his phone, he checked the time on the dashboard. Two weeks, he thought, his gaze flicking back to the windscreen. Fourteen days. He focussed, calculated the hours, the minutes, the seconds Sophie had been gone. The time he and Alicia had been apart. He tried to pinpoint the exact moment things had started to fall apart and he hadn't noticed. Or had noticed—he dragged a hand hard over the back of his neck—but had chosen to ignore it.

Why hadn't he quizzed her? Why had he ignored it and allowed her lie to perpetuate? His breathing suddenly shallow, indicating an imminent panic attack, Justin concentrated on the coping techniques he'd learned when he'd lost his family the first time around: breathing in to the count of four, holding for seven, breathing out for eight, repeating four times: re-oxygenating his body, attempting to get his anxiety back under control.

He'd conquered this once, found a way to get a grip on his emotions when the anger at their senseless murder, the guilt that he hadn't been able to help them, threatened to assuage him.

He didn't stand a chance this time. No matter how hard he tried, he couldn't get the images out of his mind: of Radley and Alicia together; of where Sophie might be, in some dirty, flea-bitten dive. On the streets. His fault. Whatever Alicia had done, he was the one who'd driven Sophie to run. He recalled the words he'd spat in anger when he'd found out. He'd played those words over and over ever since. And no matter how many times he did, what he'd said sounded exactly the way it would have to Sophie—that he no longer considered her to be his daughter. He would never forgive himself.

He should have done something when he'd suspected she might have overheard. He should have gone straight to see her. He wasn't able to even begin to process the knowledge that the child he'd brought home from the hospital, loved with every fibre of his being since before she'd been born, might not be his; that his wife had had an affair with another man, had sex with another man.

He missed her. Missed what he thought they'd had.

Missed his children, so much his heart physically ached.

He might never have a chance to tell Sophie how much he

loved her; that's what hurt most of all. Whatever a paternity test might prove, she was his daughter. No one could take that away from him.

Apart from Sophie.

Justin swallowed hard on that thought. He would give his life to go back and undo the damage he'd caused the day he'd climbed into his car exhausted, distracted. But he couldn't. All he could do now was pray. Pray and keep scouring the streets in the hope of unearthing some small piece of information that might lead him to her. He would keep searching. Had to. His past had been obliterated. He had no life now, no purpose, other than to keep searching. Without Sophie, without some knowledge she was safe, there was no future.

CHAPTER FORTY-FIVE

JUSTIN

Heading towards the canal towpath, planning to cover a section of the main line out of Birmingham, Justin stopped at the doorway of a derelict shop to talk to a guy who was tucked into his sleeping bag.

"Spare some change, mate?" the guy asked as Justin approached him. His look wasn't hopeful—more resigned. Any vitality he might have once had in his eyes had been dulled; by booze, Justin guessed, noting the several empty beer cans to his side.

Justin offered him a smile. "I'm looking for someone," he said. The guy recoiled, shuffling further into the doorway, assuming he was something to do with the police. "My daughter," he elaborated, drawing Sophie's photo from his inside pocket.

The guy looked warily up at him and then down to the photo. Looking at it for a second, he shook his head. Justin sighed. Even if alcohol hadn't addled his brain, the chances were the guy wouldn't remember anyway.

Sighing, he nodded his thanks and reached into his pocket again, this time for money, though it went against the grain. Maybe the guy would buy food; maybe he'd spend it on booze. The dog would get fed, though. Justin was certain of that. Checking his watch, he bent down to pat the animal, then headed for the towpath, hoping that this time he might get lucky.

The wind was bitter, channelled by abandoned factory buildings, converted warehouses and high embankments. It stung his face and sliced through his clothes. Pulling his collar high, chilled to the bone, he thought about Sophie, and the clothes she'd been wearing, which would do nothing to warm her. He walked on, speaking to homeless people as he went. Receiving nothing but negative answers to his questions, some incoherent mumblings, he searched all the likely places: benches located within walking distance of one-stop shops and garages, bridges that provided sparse protection from the elements, counting them off as he went.

He'd gone a fair distance when his phone buzzed. Pulling it from his pocket, Justin checked the caller display, and then furrowed his brow and took the call. "Jessica?"

"Justin, I have to be quick. Alicia doesn't know I'm calling you." Jess's voice was a hurried whisper, which immediately rang alarm bells.

"And?" Apprehensively, Justin urged her on.

"I wouldn't normally go behind her back, but I think she won't want to tell you, so—"

"Jess, can you just cut to the chase," Justin interrupted, his gut clenching.

"He's had a test. Paul Radley, he's had a paternity test, apparently, and I think you should know. I did suggest to Alicia that she should—"

"I do know," Justin cut across her.

"You do?" Jessica sounded surprised.

"We talked. She told me."

"Oh." Jessica went quiet. "Well, that's good," she went on, after a second. "That's she's finally decided to talk to you, I mean. It's a pity she didn't years ago. She's my sister and I love her to bits, and she's beside herself with remorse now, but I told her she needed to tell you everything from the beginning."

Justin ran his hand over his neck. He was too tired for repeat conversations. "I know, Jess. You said."

"She hasn't told you everything, has she?" Jess asked, sounding tentative.

"No," Justin said tightly. However well-intentioned Jess was, ringing him several times to see if he "needed a shoulder," he really didn't want to discuss this, not now.

"I have no idea why she saw him as many times as she did," Jess carried on regardless. "You can understand how she might have been—"

"Jess! I don't want to hear it," Justin snapped, images of his wife in bed with the bastard assailing him all over again, images that counting all the stars in the universe wouldn't make go away. "I really do *not* want to know."

"Oh God, I'm sorry," Jess said quickly. "I wasn't thinking. I just wanted you to know that I don't condone what Alicia did. I couldn't tell you, I was sworn to secrecy, and I had to be there for her. I still do, but I wanted you to know I'm there for you too."

Nodding tiredly, Justin drew in a breath. "I know. I just can't deal with it right now."

Ending the call, Justin felt the knife that had been plunged into his heart twist an inch deeper. A sharp, violent twist, made more painful by the knowledge that Alicia must have known this would all come out while he'd been burying his son. That cocksure bastard had been right there at the funeral. She must have suspected he would find out what had gone on between them, and still she'd kept the truth from him. Attempting some level of control, Justin tried to breathe through it. It didn't work. He didn't stand a chance of ousting the images now in his mind: Luke smiling at him on that fateful day of the accident, his little arms flailing delightedly. He'd sworn to keep his son safe. He hadn't. Justin breathed in, kept counting.

Sophie's words whispered on the wind as he walked. *He's nestled safe in an angel's wings now, but he will never leave me. He's here. He will always be.*

Where was she?

CHAPTER FORTY-SIX

SOPHIE

Still feeling lethargic and majorly bored, Sophie flicked through the channels, but nothing grabbed her. She wished she had her phone. She could at least download something to read then.

Heaving herself up from the sofa, she went to the kitchen. Nothing much took her fancy when she peered into the fridge, but she pulled out the Coke. She was halfway through filling a large tumbler when she stopped, debating. Should she? Had Paul been subtly hinting that she was getting fat? No, he was just pointing out that it wasn't very healthy to stuff herself full of sugar. He was probably right. She usually drank sugar-free. Maybe she could go and get some when she felt better. And when she had some shoes. Glancing down at her bare feet, she wiggled her toes, noticing her chipped nail polish as she did. There were a few things she needed, in actual fact—nail polish remover being one of them. She didn't want to ask Paul to fork out though. Then again, as he kept reminding her, he was her father, and he'd been pretty cool about buying her stuff so far.

She hadn't seen any evidence of a phone yet, but then, he had been busy looking after her. She'd remind him later—casually, though. She didn't want him thinking she was going to milk the situation. That would be a shitty thing to do when he'd already been treated so crappily by her mum.

Opting for water instead, she grabbed an apple and mooched

around the apartment. She hadn't liked to poke into too many spaces and cupboards while he was here—not that she'd been capable of nosing around—but she needed to know where stuff was and how it worked. The music system, for one. There was a fabulous wireless multi-speaker system. She really wished she had her phone. There was a turntable too, she noticed, going over to it. Not many CDs or vinyl records to choose from though—classical stuff, mostly. She guessed he probably used his phone with Spotify or something. And it wasn't his apartment anyway, she reminded herself.

The motorised shutters at the windows were something else. You really had to be making serious money to afford one of these places, Sophie surmised. Bored with opening and shutting them after a while, she ambled towards Paul's bedroom. Nothing much to see in there. Sophie hadn't thought there would be. Having noted his obsession with having everything in its right place, she guessed he'd have all his stuff put away in drawers and cupboards. She inched open the top dresser drawer. Yup, all neatly folded.

Feeling guilty being in his personal space, Sophie closed the drawer and then had a quick peek in the wardrobe, where his suits and shirts were all pressed and hanging with military precision, like soldiers on parade. His bed was made up with the meticulousness of a hospital. Fastidious, definitely. Still, if his obsession with tidiness was his most annoying habit, Sophie could live with it. She'd just have to remember to clear up after herself. It was no biggie.

Heading back out, she wandered towards the door furthest from the lounge area—his study—where she hesitated. But then, curiosity getting the better of her, she squeaked the door handle down and went on in. She wasn't really spying on him, she was just curious to know more about him, as anyone would be, having just learned that a complete stranger was their father.

Nodding righteously to herself, Sophie walked across to his desk, and then stopped as her eyes fell on the framed photograph there. It was of her mum, Sophie realised, astonished. She was less surprised by its presence than by the fact that it was a recent-ish photograph, taken by her at a hotel they'd stayed at in London early last year. Sophie remembered it distinctly. The London Eye had been lit up in the background. And wasn't Justin supposed to be in the photo, too?

How had Paul got it?

Plonking herself moodily down in his office chair, Sophie yanked open the top desk drawer and pulled out an envelope folder she found there. Her mum had sent him the photo, she supposed. Paul had been married in Dubai, and he was still grieving, Sophie had assumed. It might have been that her mum and him had started corresponding after he'd lost his family, which is why Justin might have suspected something. Her mum might have sent the photo and...

And Sophie had absolutely no clue why she was bothering to think it through. There was no point asking her mum about it—she hadn't been honest with anybody. Not that Sophie intended to speak to her anyway. She'd ask Paul about it. At least he seemed to think she had feelings worth considering.

Peering into the folder, Sophie knitted her brow, and then... *Shit!* Hearing the front door open, she almost died on the spot.

"Sophie?" Paul called.

Shit, shit, shit! Hurriedly cramming the folder back in the drawer, she shot to her feet, scrambling to think of an explanation as to why she was in here that would sound remotely feasible.

"Sophie?"

"Coming!" she shouted. She had no way of not being caught snooping. There was nowhere to go but out of the door, where she'd be on full view before she had a chance to nip back to her bedroom.

She snatched up a pen just before Paul came through the door. "Looking for something?" he asked her, his gaze travelling warily from her to the desk.

"Yes. I, um…" *Crikey.* Sophie's eyes grew wide. Had he been in some sort of fight? "Are you okay?" she asked.

Paul's fingers went gingerly to the definite blue-black bruise forming under his eye. "Fine. I had a fall, at the gym. Did you find it? Whatever you were looking for?"

"Paper," Sophie ad-libbed, holding up the pen.

Paul frowned, clearly not buying it.

"I thought I'd write to her, my mum," Sophie elaborated, her face, she hoped, the picture of innocence, though her heart was beating a rat-a-tat-tat in her chest. "I didn't want to text her or ring her," she went on. "I thought a letter might be better. You know, more personal. What do you think?"

Paul studied her for a second, then, nodding slowly, he walked towards her, and then past her, his gaze lingering on the desk drawers as he did.

Pulling a filing cabinet drawer open, he retrieved what she'd supposedly been looking for. "Paper," he said, handing her a sheaf of printer paper.

"Brilliant. Thanks." Sophie took it and beamed him a smile.

"No problem." Pushing one hand into his pocket, his other going to the bruise on his face, Paul considered her thoughtfully for a second. "Don't come in here again without asking, Sophie—please. I have client information in here. Data protection rules require me to keep that information confidential."

"Oh." Sophie looked suitably apologetic. "Sorry, I didn't think."

Again, Paul nodded and offered her a smile.

Not an overly effusive one, Sophie noted. There was something in his body language that made her feel uneasy, along with the wary look in his eyes as his gaze went once again to the desk drawers, the contents of which Sophie was now exceedingly curious about.

Come to think of it, she pondered, as she took her leave, why wasn't there a photograph of his family on that desk? His wife and his children. Why would he have a picture of Alicia instead?

CHAPTER FORTY-SEVEN

JUSTIN

"Can I leave now?" Justin looked up from his bruised fist as Taylor came back into the interview room. He had been left there while they waited for the officer in charge to report back on whether "Mr. Radley" was going to file charges. He'd obviously hit him harder than he'd realised. Should have hit the fucker harder.

At least he wasn't being held in a cell, Justin supposed, though that was where he might well end up, Taylor had warned him, if he didn't get his emotions under control. Justin wanted to challenge him to do the same, to remain perfectly calm while some bastard was using his missing daughter as leverage over his wife.

"Tell me something." Folding his arms across his chest, Taylor studied him curiously. "Did it make you feel better? Punching the man, did it solve anything?"

Justin noted the edge to his tone. "Not much, no," he admitted. He hadn't felt very proud of the fact that he'd given in to his base instincts. As to whether it had solved anything, that remained to be seen. If Alicia didn't want Radley contacting her, then the man needed to understand that. He also needed to know that if he even spoke Sophie's name, then Justin was very close to making sure he wouldn't ever again.

"Just so you know," Taylor said, "I get why you did it. I'd probably have done the same myself, to be honest."

Justin glanced at him.

"I have kids." Taylor shrugged, now looking sympathetic, at least. "I also have a wife. Ex, that is. I'll leave it to your imagination as to why."

Surveying him thoughtfully, Justin nodded, supposing that he would have some inkling of how he felt. It didn't really help.

"Look, Justin…" Taylor dragged out a chair and sat down opposite him. "I understand your frustration. I can't imagine what it must be like to lose a child so young under such tragic circumstances, to then to have your teenage daughter go missing. I promise you, we're doing all that we can."

Rubbing his eyes in exhaustion, Justin declined to answer. As far as he could see, that still amounted to nothing.

"He's not filing charges," Taylor went on. "I'm not majorly surprised, under the circumstances." He smiled wryly, and then drew in a breath. "In regard to your certainty that he may have had some contact with Sophie, we asked him the question, obviously."

Justin looked sharply back at him. "And?"

Taylor's expression held a warning. "He has."

What? Justin's first reaction was bewilderment. His second— gut-clenching fury that the bastard hadn't said. His third was overwhelming relief. She was alive. He'd *known* it. He could feel her. "When?" he asked throatily.

"Two days ago," Taylor said.

Justin sucked in a breath, buried his head in his hands and suppressed an overwhelming urge to cry.

"He phoned her," Taylor continued, as Justin struggled to formulate any words. "He didn't know she was missing, so he says. He was, and I quote, 'simply initiating contact with his daughter.'"

"My daughter," Justin managed to sputter.

Taylor didn't comment on that. "She said she was staying with a friend."

Justin nodded, trying very hard to do the simplest thing in the world and breathe. "She didn't say where?" he asked, and then coughed, attempting to clear the hard knot in his throat.

Shaking his head regretfully, Taylor sat back in his chair. "Apparently not." He paused while Justin attempted to compose himself. "I know this is painful, Justin," he said, after a second, "but possibly less painful than the alternative you were imagining, yes?"

Swiping a hand across his eyes, Justin nodded, vigorously this time.

"We're keeping our ears to the ground, Justin. We're still pursuing any leads we can in regard to the hit-and-run that took your boy away. What you need to do now, if you care to take some advice from someone who knows, is be there for each other. You and Alicia. Right now, you need each other."

Justin didn't respond. He doubted he could get the words past the fractured pieces of his heart, which still seemed to be lodged in his windpipe.

"You can leave as soon as you're ready," Taylor said kindly. "Just promise me you'll seek counselling if you need it," he added, as Justin got to his feet. "I would offer you some numbers, but I imagine you have access to people of your own. Think about it, Justin. You and your wife both."

Answering with another short nod, Justin swallowed and turned towards the door. What kind of counselling would best help Alicia, he wondered, bereavement or marriage counselling? His chest constricted.

What wasn't she telling him? How did Radley get Sophie's number? From Alicia? Was it possible he'd accessed it from Alicia's phone? Did she know he'd been in touch with Sophie?

CHAPTER FORTY-EIGHT

ALICIA

"He's leaving! Going back to Dubai," Alicia said, turning in disbelief to Jessica, having worriedly read her incoming text from Paul Radley.

Her wine glass halfway to her mouth, Jessica eyed her with surprise. "Really?"

"Apparently." Joining her at the kitchen table, Alicia hesitated, then said, "He suggested we should meet before he goes." She inhaled a tight breath.

Jessica furrowed her brow. "Why?"

"He has some things he wants me to give to Sophie, so he says. I have no idea what things."

"And are you going to meet him?" Jessica searched her face, her expression curious. She was probably wondering why she'd even read the text.

Alicia had almost deleted it, but as she'd actually been expecting threats in regard to Sophie, she'd thought better of it, thinking she needed to prepare herself as to what those threats might be. Some attempt at custody, or at the very least access rights, she'd thought. Now, she wasn't sure what to think. She felt utterly bewildered. And very wary. Would he really just go?

"I think I've said all I have to say to him." She sighed wearily. "I can't help wondering what the catch is. Why he would just decide to leave, after going to such great lengths to tear my marriage apart?"

"You don't know that he's done that yet, Ali." Looking at her sympathetically, Jess downed her glass and reached for her hand. "If you are thinking of meeting him, though, you should really let Justin know. If he finds out—" She stopped as Alicia's phone rang.

It was Justin's ringtone, as if he knew he was under discussion. Realising it was much later than he would normally call, Alicia immediately jumped up to snatch it up from the work surface. "Justin?" she said, glancing nervously back at Jess. "Has something happened?"

"Sorry," Justin said quickly, "I should have thought. Calling you at a different time was bound to worry you."

"It's fine," Alicia said, her eyes filling up. Only a truly special man would worry about her at all under the circumstances. "Are you all right?"

Topping up her glass, Jessica picked up her own phone and made a face at her, indicating she was off to make one of the many calls she preferred to do in private. Vaguely, Alicia wondered whether there might be a new man in her life. A man she was possibly avoiding bringing home, thanks to her sister moving in with baggage by the trunkful.

"As all right as I can be," Justin answered. "I just wanted to check you were."

Now Alicia was definitely taken aback. "Yes," she said. "Ish. Why?"

"No specific reason. It's just…" Justin faltered. "The things I see when I'm out walking—homeless people, young people," he went on tiredly. "It gets to me sometimes, to be honest."

Immediately empathising, Alicia's stomach wrenched as she imagined how affected he must be, the things that must inevitably go through his mind. Witnessing such things in her job, they went through hers too, causing her to tear herself from the warm bed in which she lay sleeplessly every night. And then, for fear of waking Jess, she would end up standing silently, gazing uselessly out of the window, where the images would only be starker. Justin was in the thick of it. She doubted he would even bother to lie down at night half the time. "Do you want to talk?" she asked him, tentatively, wondering whether there was anything specific troubling him.

Justin sighed. "No, not really. I think I just needed to hear a familiar voice," he said. And then went quiet.

Unable to bring himself to talk more, Alicia guessed, to someone he'd once trusted implicitly with his inner feelings and who'd so badly deceived him.

"So, are you back at work?" he asked her, changing the subject.

"No." Alicia sighed, despairing of her apparent inadequacy on all fronts. "I tried, but I couldn't handle it. The children..." She left it there, guessing he would understand what she meant. "I'm keeping busy though. I've set up a Twitter account and a 'Find Sophie' Facebook page. I thought it might be a good way for people to communicate anything that might help, any likely sightings. I also thought that if her friends wanted to message us privately for any reason..." She trailed off, realising Justin would gather what she meant there, too.

"Good idea," he said. And went quiet again.

Alicia waited, sensing there was something else he needed to say.

"Can I ask you something?" he asked, after what seemed like an eternity.

Alicia felt a prickle of apprehension run through her. "Yes, obviously."

"Radley," he said, causing Alicia's insides to turn over. "You said he'd had no contact with Sophie, right?"

"Yes," Alicia said quickly. "I mean, no. He hasn't, as far as I'm aware. Why?"

Justin breathed in long and hard. "It seems he has."

What? A million emotions assaulting her, Alicia felt her legs turn to rubber beneath her. "He's spoken to her?" she whispered. She had to see him. She headed for the hall. Went back for her keys. *Why* hadn't he mentioned—

"He rang her. Just once, according to Taylor," said Justin. "She's staying with a friend. She didn't say where."

"When?" Alicia asked, feeling desperate. She needed to do ... *something*.

"Two days ago, apparently," Justin said. "Alicia ... did you give him her number?" He paused, giving her a few seconds as she tried to assimilate the information. "Did you give him Sophie's number?"

"No! I wouldn't. Why would I have?"

Justin's silence spoke volumes.

"Justin, I didn't. I swear to God, I didn't," Alicia repeated, tears streaming down her cheeks, the phone clutched tight to her ear. "I don't want him to have access to her. He must have got it from my phone, or from someone else. Please believe me," she begged.

"I have to go," Justin said, over another tight intake of breath. "We should talk," he added.

"About?" Alicia asked fearfully.

"Things," Justin replied vaguely. "At some point, I mean. Take care, Alicia."

He signed off, leaving Alicia emotionally floundering. The "things" he wanted to talk about were presumably to do with their marriage. At "some point" soon, she would have to face the reality that they would have no future together.

Hesitating for a second, Alicia steeled herself and then rang Paul Radley's number, only to get his voicemail. After trying again minutes later, she grabbed the wine from the fridge. It would do nothing to anaesthetise her beyond the first alcohol-induced hour of total oblivion, after which she would end up going over and over things, until her recollection was more clouded than ever. Yet she needed it—needed somehow to try to numb the pain.

Did Justin believe she hadn't passed Sophie's number on to Paul? Why would he? He would never be able to trust anything she said ever again.

Draining half a glass in one, she topped it up again.

Why hadn't Paul Radley rung her?

CHAPTER FORTY-NINE

JUSTIN

After fruitless hours ringing around Sophie's friends again, hoping to find out the identity of the mysterious friend with whom Sophie might be staying, Justin headed to the hospital. He wouldn't stay. There was no way to concentrate. He couldn't possibly trust himself with people's lives until he knew his daughter was safe. Whether he would still have a job then, Justin felt didn't much matter without his family.

Picking up the results he'd come for, he went to the hospital restaurant, where he bought a coffee but didn't drink it. A colleague spoke to him. He hardly heard her. Dragging his hands over his face, he sat motionless, staring out over the car park, watching people coming and going, attempting to digest this latest news, until his coffee went cold. Then, sucking in a long breath, he left, going straight from the hospital to the room he was renting.

Weary with exhaustion, yet knowing sleep would elude him, he barely noticed the sparse furnishing as he dropped his keys onto the single chest of drawers. He'd stopped craving material things the day Sophie had disappeared and his marriage had disintegrated. Before that, when Luke had been cruelly snatched away from them, he'd begun to wonder how much one really needed in life. The fancy cars, flat-screen TVs, the latest in technology—they were just things, accumulated throughout a life. Stuff you couldn't take with you when you ceased to exist. It was all meaningless without someone to share it with.

Justin didn't miss those things. He didn't need them. There was no point in living luxuriously any more. He wondered whether there would be any point in living at all if he didn't find Sophie. Whatever the hell was going on with Radley, he knew Alicia felt the same: she was existing, rather than living, waiting and praying for news, for any shred of information that might lead them to her.

Refusing to entertain the thought that he might never find her, that she might choose never to contact him again, he pulled off his coat and dropped onto the bed. He should ring Alicia. He'd wanted to believe her—badly needed to—but how could he? How could he begin to believe anything she had to say when their whole life together had been a lie?

But would she really be carrying on with the charade if it was Radley she wanted to be with? Justin had considered that too, but had reached no conclusion. Part of him hated her for what she'd done, but part of him still loved her. It was pathetic, but there it was. He wanted to reach out to her. A couple of times he almost had, when he'd seen the tortured look in her eyes and felt her palpable pain, but he'd stopped himself. He couldn't take any more hurt. There just wasn't room inside him for any more.

He had to stay in touch, though. If he couldn't say what he wanted to, ask the endless questions going around in his head, they needed to communicate about Sophie.

Retrieving his phone from his pocket and selecting Alicia's number, his gaze strayed to the one thing he didn't want to be without—a framed photograph of her with Luke and Sophie, which he kept on the bedside table. He felt like it had been taken eons ago, in another lifetime, when they were a family, happy and healthy, a smile dancing in Alicia's dazzling cornflower-blue eyes. Despite the pain she'd caused him, he hoped she would smile again one day. That she would have a life beyond the purgatory they were living in now.

"Hi, Justin, it's me," Jessica said, picking the call up. "How are you doing?"

"Not great."

"I know." Jessica sighed sympathetically. "I honestly don't know how you're getting through each day."

"Willpower," Justin joked half-heartedly.

"*Yes*, it's a good job you're a strong man, that's all I can say," Jessica said dourly. "Some men would have walked away from it. Most men, in fact."

"I haven't always been, Jess," Justin said, reminding her of the time he hadn't been strong. Then, Alicia had had to be the strong one, while he'd learned how to feel normal again.

"You'd lost your family," Jessica said softly. "To have discovered them the way you did... To have had to bury them, try to carry on, never knowing who had been responsible, why someone would commit such an atrocious act of violence..."

She stopped. Justin was relieved when she did, every desecration of his family inevitably searing itself again on his mind.

"It's a wonder you didn't break down completely. The fact that you got through that makes you strong," Jessica went on forcefully. "You shouldn't be bottling your feelings up now, though, Justin, not when you're going through the same heartbreak all over again. I know you'd probably feel a bit awkward about it, but if you do ever want to unburden, I'm here. Just because I'm Alicia's sister, it doesn't mean I can't be a friend to you, too."

Justin ran a hand over his neck. Knowing exactly what had gone on, Jessica was possibly the only person he could talk to, but he wasn't about to do that. It wouldn't be fair on Alicia—or Jessica, come to that. There was also the fact that he didn't think he could talk about any of this without breaking down, and he was desperately trying not to do that.

"I know. Thanks, Jess," he said, wanting her to know he appreciated the offer.

"And if you don't fancy unburdening, we could just get drunk instead," Jessica suggested.

Justin smiled wryly. He didn't think that was such a good idea either. He doubted his problems would look much better at the bottom of a whisky glass.

"Has he been in touch?" he asked, bringing the conversation around to why he'd called. He should ask Alicia, and he would, but he'd taken to asking Jessica for information first, which didn't make him feel great.

Jessica hesitated. "He texted her," she said, sounding reluctant. "Apparently, he's going back to Dubai. He's asked to meet with her. And now I've said enough. I'd hate Alicia to think I was going behind her back. You'd do better to ask her about the detail."

"I'll do that," Justin assured her, already bracing himself. The fact was, he was scared. Terrified she would lie to him again. He had no idea what he would do, how he would react.

Whatever the future held for Alicia and him, he was hugely relieved Radley was scuttling off back to Dubai. He'd been shocked by the realisation he'd been an inch away from inflicting possibly fatal injuries on a man. Despite his assurances to DI Taylor, he wasn't certain he would be able to control himself if he found himself in Radley's company again.

"Is she around?" he asked, assuming from the tone of Jessica's voice that Alicia must be out of earshot. And then he immediately felt pig-sick as he wondered where she was—and with whom.

"She's busy. That detective guy has just arrived."

"Taylor?" Justin was surprised.

"He said he was passing, so he decided to call in to check on Alicia," Jessica said. "I'll get her to call you back as soon as she can."

"Cheers, Jess," Justin said, feeling wary. He wasn't sure why Taylor had decided to pay Alicia a visit. It certainly wouldn't be because "he was passing," but it wouldn't be to announce they'd suddenly decided Sophie was a high-profile case, that was for sure.

CHAPTER FIFTY

ALICIA

Hearing his ringtone, Alicia knew Justin had just called. She was desperate to call him back after the way their last call had ended, but first she needed to hear what the detective inspector had to say. "You're sure you won't have some tea or coffee?" she asked him, having already established that he wasn't here with news of Sophie and then gone through the awkward civilities.

"No, thanks, Alicia. I can't stay long." Giving her a brief smile, DI Taylor checked his watch.

"Something stronger possibly?" she asked him, making a supreme effort to be cordial, despite the fact that all she wanted to do was scream at him to do his job and bring Sophie home. She'd rung around all her friends, only to be told Justin had already called, and to receive the same news he presumably had. She'd supposedly been with this mysterious friend—whom no one had any idea about—two, getting on for three days ago, which meant she could be anywhere now. The nagging thought had also occurred to Alicia that this "friend" might not even be a girlfriend. A boyfriend would be worrying, but what if it were neither? What if it were some predatory adult?

"I'd love something stronger," DI Taylor smiled, regretfully this time. "I'm still on duty though, unfortunately."

"Right, well." Alicia smiled back. "What can I do for you, Detective?"

"Do you mind if we sit?" Taylor asked, and walked across to seat himself on the sofa anyway.

Alicia took the armchair, uneasiness creeping through her as she noted the troubled look on his face. He hadn't called by with news of Sophie. And Justin had just phoned, so what on earth was this all about?

"Paul Radley," Taylor said, and paused. Alicia's stomach turned over. "I believe he's an old acquaintance of yours?"

Oh no. Alicia dropped her gaze, feeling an immediate sense of deep humiliation.

"Mine's not to judge, Alicia." Taylor smiled kindly. "I'm merely trying to ascertain all the facts in regard to your daughter."

Alicia drew in a breath and nodded. "Yes, of course. Yes, he is," she confirmed falteringly.

Taylor nodded thoughtfully. "Justin came to see me," he said. "He was rather irate at the time—exhausted, clearly, having been searching for Sophie."

Alicia nodded, immense sadness settling inside her. She had no idea how Justin was pushing himself on. He wouldn't be sleeping. She could tell he was barely eating. He'd lost weight. She suspected the only thing keeping him going was his determination to find Sophie.

"He seemed very concerned about Mr. Radley having any contact with your daughter. I take it he told you Mr. Radley did in fact speak to her on the telephone?"

Alicia nodded. "Yes," she said tightly. "He did."

Taylor studied her for a second. "And what about future contact, Alicia? If Sophie turns up, which I'm quite sure she will, would you want Mr. Radley to be in contact with her?"

"No, absolutely not," Alicia stated categorically. "He's…a womaniser," she added. "Not the sort of person who would be a good influence on an impressionable young girl."

"I see." Taylor nodded. "Would that be why Justin would want to warn him off, do you think?"

"Warn him off?" Alicia's gaze shot worriedly to his.

"We had a call-out," Taylor explained, "from one of the staff at Mr. Radley's place of work. Apparently, Justin paid him a visit."

He let it hang, watching her carefully, then said, "He attacked him, Alicia. Quite aggressively, by all accounts."

"*What?*" Alicia stared at him, stunned. *Justin?* He'd never been violent in his life. He simply didn't have it in him to be violent. "Was he injured? Paul?" she asked, fear that Justin might be arrested causing her chest to constrict.

"He did have an injury, according to my officer's report. Sustained earlier at the gym, according to Mr. Radley. It seems he wouldn't confirm the initial report we received. Said there'd been some misunderstanding."

Now Paul's sudden decision to fly back to Dubai made sense.

"The strange thing is, the attack took place before your husband learned of this contact." DI Taylor paused. "A reaction to the difficulties he found himself in, no doubt. Understandable." He sighed expansively. "Nevertheless, Justin is still at fault. Please try to persuade him to stay away from Mr. Radley, Alicia. He could very easily have been charged with assault, which would have done no one any good, would it?"

Still uncomprehending, Alicia shook her head and nodded all at once. "He's leaving. Paul...Mr. Radley. He says he's going back to Dubai."

"Ah, right." Taylor's smile brightened. "In which case, hopefully that will be one less obstacle on the road to recovery, hey?" he said, getting to his feet. "I'll see myself out."

Walking him to the door anyway, Alicia maintained her composure. But when she'd closed the door behind him, she leaned against it and pressed a hand to her forehead. He'd attacked a man. But Justin wasn't aggressive. He'd never condoned violence of any sort. It was because of the paternity test, she realised. He was as determined to be a good father to Sophie as he was to find her. And Justin *was* her father—the person who'd nurtured her, loved her, laughed with her, cried for her. He would never give up on her, never bow out of her life. If there was anything positive to gain from this, it was that Paul Radley at least knew that now.

But what about Justin? What state of mind must he be in?

She picked up her mobile, unsure what she was going to say to him or how much she should reveal of her conversation with DI Taylor.

Justin picked up straight away. "Hi," he said. "Thanks for returning my call."

Hearing the formality in his tone, the politeness, Alicia felt another crushing wave of sadness.

"Obviously, I would," she started, and then stopped. He was keeping her at a distance. He'd hung a no-admittance sign on his emotions, one he wouldn't easily let her past, not now. "Sorry I couldn't get back sooner," she said, trying to keep the devastation from her own voice. "DI Taylor was here."

"I gathered. Did he have anything to say worth listening to?"

"Not in regard to Sophie, no," Alicia answered cautiously.

Justin sighed wearily. Clearly, he'd expected as much. "So, why the visit?"

Not sure what his reaction would be, Alicia hesitated. "He wondered whether I knew that Paul Radley had been in touch with Sophie. He was a bit concerned, I think."

"About?" Justin asked curiously.

"You. He said . . . He told me you attacked Paul Radley. He was—"

"He said what?" Justin sounded immediately agitated.

"He was worried about you, Justin. About the consequences. If you'd been charged with assault . . ."

"It would have been worth it," Justin assured her.

"It would have affected your job, Justin," Alicia pointed out, feeling scared that he didn't seem to care. "Your future."

Justin didn't answer immediately. "I don't have much of a future, though, do I, Alicia, without my family?" he said quietly.

Alicia felt fear pierce through her like an icicle. There had been no contempt in his voice, no accusation. Nothing. He'd sounded empty. Flat. As if he truly didn't care.

"I'm sorry if it upset you," he went on, drawing in a long breath, "but he had it coming."

"Sorry?" Alicia shook her head. "Justin, I'm only upset for *you*. I don't care about—"

"We need to talk," Justin said quickly over her, as though he had steeled himself to say it.

Alicia nodded, closing her eyes. He needed answers, none of which he would want to hear. "When?" she asked, gulping back the heavy weight of remorse.

"Tomorrow," he said. "At the house."

Surrounded by the ghosts of what had been, and the future that could never be. It would hurt meeting him there, seeing him there, being reminded of everything she'd thrown away. She didn't think that was Justin's intention, but it was fitting.

CHAPTER FIFTY-ONE

JUSTIN

Covered in a slick film of sweat from his efforts working in the basement, Justin wiped his arm across his forehead and checked his watch. It was early morning, he realised. Time he called it quits. He wasn't sure why he'd decided to come here, to carry on working on the studio. And then he realised it was because he saw Sophie and Luke wherever he went in the house; he would hear them. It was to be in touch with his children.

Tidying up his tools, double-checking he had all the equipment he would need, he turned his attention to the additional LED lighting he'd been installing. The soundproofing had already been done when he'd suspected the existing lighting wasn't sufficient. Wanting the studio to be finished for Sophie's sixteenth, he'd been planning to strip the insulation away and replace the spotlights. Her sixteenth had come and gone. The lighting had never been done. He'd come here on her birthday, but he hadn't been able to bring himself to disturb anything; not that day.

He would finish it. He was determined to. It was his way of keeping hope alive, he supposed. Hope that when she came back, it would be ready. When he'd finished it though, what then? What if Sophie didn't come back? He wasn't ready to contemplate that. Wearily, he climbed the steps back to the hall, where the melodic sound of a child's innocent laughter greeted him.

He'd heard it when he'd come once before. It had worried him then. Today, it didn't bother him. He found it quite soothing.

She'd learned to ride her bike, stabiliser-free, here in the hall, he recalled. It had been snowing that day. His gaze travelled the length of the long flagstone floor, where he could see her pedalling furiously, laughing delightedly when she'd realised he'd let go of the saddle and she was doing it all on her own. She'd abandoned her bike and run back to him, when the rug had slipped from under him and he'd ended up flat on his back, cracking his head on the tiles. "Is it hurting, Daddy?" she'd asked him, her beautiful chestnut eyes wide with alarm.

"It's hurting, baby," he said now to the wispy spirit of her. *So much, I don't think I can bear it.* Closing his eyes, he swallowed and headed for the stairs, planning to take a shower before leaving. Where he was staying, hot water was a luxury in the bathroom he shared with the other tenants. He didn't need luxury. He needed to function, to wash himself awake, wash the grime from his soul after endless days traipsing the bowels of the city, seeing things he'd always been aware of but could never have truly imagined.

The hallucinations, if that's what they were, were worse upstairs, where the smells of his family were overwhelming: Alicia's lingering perfume; the faded scent of the joss sticks Sophie burned. The sounds. Wherever he went, he couldn't escape them: Sophie's soulful singing; the butterfly wind chime Alicia had hung in the nursery to encourage Luke's hand movements; Luke's gurgles of pleasure as he batted it or managed to catch hold of it. That was the sound that haunted him most. Even in the basement, he heard it. In his single room, he heard it. It would haunt him for the rest of his life.

Hearing the chimes as he bypassed the nursery room door, Justin didn't try to block it out, accepting it instead as part of the insanity his life had become. It was possible, he supposed, that he might be going out of his mind. He couldn't seem to keep a rein on his thoughts—definitely not on his emotions. Everything seemed to mingle into one lately: days, nights, dreams, reality. He'd be thinking, only to realise he'd been verbalising his thoughts. Talking, only to realise he'd stopped and drifted off into some distant memory. When he counted, he sometimes found himself counting out loud, which earned him wary looks from people passing by.

Would it bother him, he wondered as he showered, if the only sounds he heard were those of his kids? If he simply stopped functioning in other areas of his life? He wasn't sure it would. He didn't want to let go of them. Couldn't.

Towelling his hair ten minutes later, he was halfway down the stairs when he realised there was someone at the front door. Justin quashed his irritation as he pulled the door open to find Taylor standing there. Was he doing follow-up calls now, checking up on victims of crime? As if they gave a damn any more who'd broken into their house. That was history. The here and now, the painful reality, was that their daughter was still missing. They still had no idea where she was. And this paragon of the law, what was he doing? Nothing.

Sighing, Justin draped his towel around his neck and eyed the man questioningly.

"We have the forensics team here." Taylor offered him his short smile—and a completely nonsensical explanation for his visit.

"Forensics?" Justin squinted at him, confused.

Taylor knitted his brow. "I left you a message, on your voicemail. I spoke with your sister-in-law, too. She said she would pass the information on to Alicia. I assumed she might have told you."

"No." Justin shook his head. It seemed Alicia wasn't in the habit of telling him very much at all. "No, she didn't. So, what is it you're looking for?"

"Anything we might have missed," Taylor supplied. "There's

been another break-in in the area. It's not exactly a crime wave, but we found some footmarks at the other property. I thought it was worth taking another look here. We'll be concentrating mainly on the gardens, but if it's inconvenient...? It's just, as we already have the men here..."

"No, no major inconvenience." Justin sighed, thinking he would need to call Alicia, assuming she didn't call first to postpone their meeting now the police were here. It occurred to him she might have thought this was a useful way to avoid facing him. It wouldn't be easy for her: explaining why she'd cheated on him, and then compounded that deceit with a decision that might ultimately crucify him. "Help yourself." He shrugged indifferently. "Have a field day."

Taylor looked mildly amused at that. "Am I to take it you're moving back in?" He nodded past him, to where Justin's tools made it obvious he'd been working.

Justin shook his head. "Under the circumstances, no," he said, holding the man's gaze. "We might well sell up. I just came to check the house over and attend to a few things."

"Oh." Taylor nodded awkwardly. "That's a shame. It's a nice property."

"A family property," Justin said pointedly. "Can I do something else for you, Detective? It's just that I'd quite like to get on with searching for my daughter."

Taylor glanced down and back. "We are looking, Justin," he said, with a heavy sigh. "Every one of my officers has her photograph."

"You're not looking hard enough," Justin said, attempting— and failing—to quell a rush of anger as he turned away. "Fuck it!" he cursed, managing to trip over the drill he'd left in the hall.

"Emotions not entirely under control then?" Taylor observed drily behind him.

"You know what?" Disentangling himself from his drill, Justin turned around, making no attempt this time to hide his anger. "No, they're not. Would yours be? I mean, look at it from my point of view: my daughter's missing and the people who are supposed to be out finding her are digging up my fucking front garden!"

Taylor drew in a breath and stepped inside, nudging the front door closed behind him. Obviously, he didn't want to be embarrassed in front of the officers whose resources he was wasting on a completely futile task. "You need to get some sleep, Justin," he said, his expression dour. "You're exhausted."

Justin laughed. "Shrewd observation," he said. "I can see why you're a detective."

"And make sure you stay away from Paul Radley," Taylor added, his eyes holding a warning. "He's leaving for Dubai shortly, isn't he? Just let him go quietly and try to get on with your life."

Dragging a hand over his neck, Justin smiled contemptuously. "I'd love to," he said. "Unfortunately, thanks to that bastard, I don't have one."

"I get that." Taylor nodded empathetically. "I've been there, remember, though not under such tragic circumstances. But you have to let it go, Justin. Let him go back, and then try to pick up the pieces of your life."

Justin said nothing. There were no pieces. Clearly, Taylor didn't get it.

"Violence rarely solves anything, Justin," Taylor went on, echoing what Justin had once thought—in another lifetime. "You could well have been up on a charge of grievous bodily harm with intent. How would that have helped anything?"

"Oh, the intent was definitely there." Justin couldn't help himself.

Shooting him a despairing look, Taylor ignored that. "Between you and me, I have no doubt he had it coming, but you don't deserve the repercussions, and nor does your wife. I might be completely out of line here, and you can tell me to mind my own business, but she cares about you, Justin. Don't let her go without a fight."

Justin eyed him with ironic amusement.

"Of the non-physical variety," Taylor added wryly.

CHAPTER FIFTY-TWO

ALICIA

Seeing Justin's car parked outside the house as she pulled into their road, Alicia felt an overpowering sense of heart-crushing homesickness engulf her, and then a flash of panic as she noted the police car beyond it. Parking behind Justin's car, she scrambled out, her insides twisting as she realised two white-suited officers were poking around in the soil of the garden. What on earth were they looking for? Her panic escalating, she hurried towards them and was surprised to see DI Taylor coming around the side of the house.

"Morning," he said, smiling as he came towards her. "Oh. I take it you didn't get my message either then? I left one with your sister."

"No." Alicia looked at him with a mixture of alarm and apprehension.

"We were investigating another property in the area," Taylor filled her in, "and we thought we might take the opportunity to check we hadn't missed anything forensically here. I did run it by your husband, obviously, when we arrived. I hope it's not going to cause you any inconvenience?"

The knot of tension in Alicia's stomach slackened. She'd been imagining all sorts of things in those few seconds climbing from the car. "No," she said, "not if Justin doesn't mind. So, have you found anything?" She nodded curiously towards one of his men, on his hands and knees brushing at the mud.

"Nothing much, no." DI Taylor followed her gaze. "Although I did spot your rather nice rose tree. Climbing Lady Hillingdon, isn't it, if I'm not mistaken?"

He was a gardener then? Alicia looked at him interestedly. She hadn't really considered the man beyond the policeman. "That's right," she said, an immediate sense of sadness overwhelming her as she glanced towards where the huge creamy butterscotch flowers would bloom come spring.

"I wouldn't mind a cutting sometime," DI Taylor said. "I have the perfect space for it outside my patio window."

"Of course." Alicia's eyes filled up, despite her best efforts. Would she ever see it bloom again? See her daughter coming through the front door again?

They'd painted the outside of the house together, she and Justin. They'd chosen a cheery yellow for the door with a white trim to complement the red brickwork. They'd wanted something bold and sunny to brighten up the grey days. She could almost see Sophie coming through the door now. Dressed in her jeans, puffer jacket and a furry bobble hat, earphones strung around her neck and her phone in her hands, she was turning to chatter nineteen to the dozen to Justin, who was coming through the front door behind her. Listening attentively, he was wearing his patient expression, as ever, an amused smile playing around his mouth as he glanced towards where Alicia waited in her car.

They'd been going Christmas shopping, she remembered. They'd made it a rule, even in the midst of the Christmas madness, to spend family time together. They'd go out for their own pleasure only, browsing the shops, pointing out things they hoped Santa would bring them. They'd do lunch, stroll, take in the sparkling decorations and twinkly bright lights, refusing, just for one special day, to put themselves under any pressure.

They would never have that again.

Pulling in a shaky breath, Alicia attempted to suppress the tears that would come if she held on to the memory for too long.

"I'll let you get on," Taylor said, his smile sympathetic. "He's inside." He reached to squeeze her arm, which, ridiculously, made her feel even more like crying. "You two should talk."

Alicia smiled faintly and then braced herself and headed towards the house. The locks had been changed since the break-in. Justin had organised it. She hadn't asked him for a key. In truth, she hadn't wanted to ask, terrified that he might suggest she didn't need one.

Answering it a minute after she'd rung the bell, Justin offered her a small smile. Alicia took some comfort from that, from the fact that he didn't appear to openly loathe her.

"Can I come in?" she asked him, smiling hesitantly back.

"Yes. Of course. Sorry. I, er…" Looking distracted, as he perpetually seemed to be, and utterly exhausted, Justin stepped back.

He'd been in the basement. Alicia noticed the door was slightly ajar, the tool bag outside it. He'd obviously been working on the studio—Sophie's sixteenth birthday surprise. Alicia's heart wrenched as she looked back at him. "How's it going?" she asked, for something to say.

"So-so," Justin shrugged. "It's something to do."

He didn't want to talk about it. Of course he wouldn't. He wouldn't want to talk about anything to do with the house. The material things and joint projects they'd shared in it. The memories. Alicia cursed her insensitivity.

Dropping her gaze, she turned and walked to the lounge. She didn't sit. She wasn't sure what to do. She felt bereft, a devastating sense of sadness encompassing her again as she stood in the middle of the room that was truly the heart of the home they'd built together, that they'd lived and laughed in together. Her breath caught painfully in her chest as her eyes fell on the TV remote, abandoned where Sophie always left it: on the arm of the sofa at the end she'd always claimed as her own.

Alicia squeezed her eyes tight shut and tried to breathe. If she caught sight of anything of Lucas's, her legs would fail her, along with her courage. She *couldn't.*

"Can I get you a coffee?" Justin said, his tone awkward as he followed her in.

Alicia shook her head. *Don't be polite. Please don't be polite,* she begged silently. She couldn't bear that he didn't know how else to be. "No," she said quickly, her throat tight. "Thanks. I'm... not thirsty."

Justin nodded, glancing down and back again. His eyes, finally meeting hers, were full of dark shadows, such insurmountable pain.

"I didn't realise DI Taylor was here," she said, again for want of something to say. The awful empty silence hung like a guillotine between them.

"Jessica didn't tell you he was coming then?" Justin eyed her curiously.

Alicia shook her head. "No. It must have slipped her mind."

His eyes narrowing briefly, Justin nodded, and walked past her to the window, where he stood with his back to her.

"Justin..." Alicia noted the stiff set of his shoulders, as if he too was bracing himself—for more hurt than had already been heaped on him, more weight that he couldn't possibly carry. "I'm sorry," she blurted, the same two stupid, ineffectual words she'd uttered before. Words that could never communicate how desperately sorry she was.

Justin drew in a tight, ragged breath.

The tick of the carriage clock on the mantel grew louder in the heavy silence between them, punctuated by the scraping of the officers at work outside. Alicia was uncertain what to do, whether to go to him. Should she stay? What could she say? It was too late. There'd been no way for her to explain it years ago, and there was no way to explain it now. Whatever she said, she couldn't undo the damage, the pain she'd caused him. She was supposed to be the nurturer, the carer for her family. She'd broken everything. And she couldn't fix it.

"Justin?" She tried tearfully again, needing a response from him—accusations, questions, a release of the fury that was surely stuffed inside him. Anything.

"Would you like me to go?" she asked him, after another hour-long minute ticked by.

Alicia waited, working to stifle the tears he wouldn't want to witness and with which he couldn't possibly sympathise.

But still Justin didn't answer.

He didn't want to hear it. That was his answer. As the tiny sliver of hope to which she'd dared cling began to fade, Alicia turned quietly to the door. He could never forgive her. She'd finally lost him. He would never know that she would never be whole again without him.

"Why, Alicia?" Justin said simply, as she reached the hall.

Alicia's heart lurched.

Stopping, she turned and walked slowly back. "I don't know," she said, her voice barely a whisper.

"I see." Justin shook his head.

"I didn't mean it to happen." Alicia took another step in. "I don't know why I—"

"How many times, Alicia?" he asked. "How many times did you not mean it to happen?"

And there it was. Alicia closed her eyes. The reason he could never, ever believe she hadn't meant to hurt him as cruelly as she had. It was impossible. "I'd been drinking. More than I normally would. I…" She trailed hopelessly off, the ominous tick of the clock growing louder still as she struggled for any way to explain herself that didn't scream her guilt.

"I think it might be an idea if you did go, Alicia," he said, his tone hoarse.

And Alicia felt her heart fold up inside her. Swallowing, she half turned to the door, and then wavered. "I thought she would save you," she murmured. "Sophie. I thought she would give you something to live for."

"She did," Justin said throatily.

But Sophie wasn't here any more.

And now he had nothing.

CHAPTER FIFTY-THREE

JUSTIN

Justin didn't even hear the door close as Alicia left. He was deep in thought, his mind going back to the time he now guessed it had all happened: the nights she'd supposedly stayed at a girl-friend's. To the first time she'd stayed, when she hadn't been very well. A hangover, she said. She hadn't looked well.

Painful though it was to be in there, Justin went up to their bedroom, feeling compelled to check their photo albums. He wasn't sure what for. A need for visual clarification of the mile-stones in their marriage, maybe?

They'd been to one of her friend's weddings a few days after; Alicia had been a bridesmaid. Justin remembered that bleak time in their relationship painfully well, because that was when he'd made up his mind he needed help. Seeing Alicia so closed in on herself, realising how badly he'd shut her out, he'd made a mon-umental effort to be more social, to be there for her. She'd been pale and drawn at the wedding and the reception, only half lis-tening to the conversation around her, to him. He'd been scared they might be about to split up, and he'd redoubled his efforts. Depression, like a suffocating grey blanket, was still pressing down on him, but he'd woken up to the fact that, while try-ing to deal with his grief, he'd been pushing her away for a long time. If he didn't do something about it, he was going to lose her. The day of the wedding, he'd desperately wanted to show her how much he'd loved her, and had prayed it wasn't too late. She'd still had the bug in her system, though, so intimacy hadn't been an option. He'd hoped that was the truth. That she'd still wanted him.

It had been the night after that when they'd finally talked, when he'd opened up to her about how he felt. Guilty. As guilty as hell. He hadn't been able to get it out of his mind, the image of his sister bleeding out from her knife wounds on the hall floor. She'd tried to run. She'd been breathing, barely. But she'd been alive. Might have lived, had his medical knowledge not deserted him. By the time the paramedics had arrived, it had been too late. He'd watched the lifeblood ebb from her body, powerless to stop it. There'd been no way to move on, to even begin to process his grief. He been stuck, unable to forgive himself, unable to shed the tears he'd desperately needed to.

He'd broken his bloody heart when he'd ashamedly confessed all that to Alicia, which had been therapeutic in itself, releasing the stop valve on his emotions. They'd moved forwards after that, been stronger as a couple. There for each other. Or so he'd thought.

Pulling open the drawer they kept the albums in, he pulled a few out, flicking through them. Realising the top few were more recent ones, where Alicia had painstakingly recorded memories of Luke, he placed them carefully aside, the pain of his loss far too raw. Delving further, he found another recent one: photos of Alicia, pregnant with Luke, radiant, smiling, never in her worst nightmares imagining she would be burying her son before his first birthday.

Swallowing emotionally, Justin placed that along with the others on the bed. He searched in the drawer for older albums, rifling through various bits of paper and certificates, and realised they were missing. Simply not there. Surely to God they hadn't been stolen? Hadn't Alicia kept her scan photos in here, too, for both Sophie and Luke? Where the hell were they?

He pulled his phone from his pocket and headed up to the third floor, where he knew their disorganised collection of older photos were still boxed in the spare room. The ones he'd been particularly interested in looking at would most likely be in there. In the meantime, he would very much like to know where the others were. He couldn't imagine why anyone would want to steal family photographs, unless they were a member of that family—namely Alicia. He knew this meant that she didn't intend to come back.

His thumb hovering over her number, he hesitated. Did he really want to speak to her now, after the conversation they'd just had? No, not yet. That was still too raw as well. Going into the spare room, he located the box he was looking for and began sifting through it as he selected Jessica's number.

"Hey, Jess, sorry to bother you," he said, pulling photos out and examining them as he spoke. "I'm guessing you're at work."

"Trust me, I'd rather talk to you," Jessica said brightly.

"Not that scintillating then?"

"The work? No. Talking to you, however..." Jessica joked.

Justin wasn't sure he'd ever been scintillating. "Can I ask you something, Jess?"

"Ask away."

"Do you know if Alicia brought some photographs with her to your house? Family albums?"

Jessica thought about it. "I'm not sure. Are they not there then?"

"No. Definitely missing. Most of them, in fact, apart from very recent ones and some older photos going way back. But I can't imagine anyone would want them."

"Apart from Alicia." Jessica echoed his own thoughts. "Oh dear, she probably has then." She paused. "Look, I wouldn't worry about it, Justin. That's not necessarily a bad sign, is it? That's she's taken them, I mean. She probably just wants some reminders of her children around her."

Or more likely she was taking things she definitely wanted to keep before they reached the stage of dividing their property. It was clear from what Jessica had said that she was thinking along the same lines.

"I take it you didn't get much chance to talk then?" Jessica asked. "With that DI Taylor being there, I mean. His timing wasn't great, was it?"

"No." Justin frowned. "No, it wasn't. You did let Alicia know they were due to arrive this morning? Taylor said he'd left a message with you."

"Yes." Jessica said assuredly. "I knew she was meeting you, so I made sure to. Why?"

So why the hell would Alicia lie about it, Justin wondered. She hadn't used it as an excuse to postpone. She'd met him there, as they'd arranged. She hadn't actually said very much—but then he wasn't very receptive to hearing anything she might have to say. It made no sense to him whatsoever. "No reason," he said, then, finding the photos he was looking for, added, "I'd better go. Thanks, Jess."

"No problem. I'm worried about you, Justin. I'm here if you ever need to talk."

"Er, yes, thanks." Justin's frown deepened as he ended the call.

CHAPTER FIFTY-FOUR

ALICIA

A deluge of freezing rain soaking through her clothes, seemingly to her bones, Alicia pulled her coat tight. Shivering as the wind whipped overhanging branches and fat raindrops plopped moodily around her, she wrapped her arms about herself and continued through the part of the cemetery where once-proud Victorian headstones had submitted to the elements. Walking on, past weathered stones and wingless cherubs, she avoided reading the inscriptions. She didn't need any reminders of how short life was.

Reaching her destination, a secluded spot surrounded by beech trees and overlooked by the church, she stopped. *I don't think a cup of tea's going to fix this, Mum*, she said silently, gulping back the lump like granite that was wedged in her chest. Swiping a tear from her cheek, she took a step closer, then looked to the pregnant grey sky and sank to her knees. "Sorry, baby," she said out loud to little Lucas. "Mummy's not crying, sweetheart. It's just rain. Just the rain."

Her jeans already saturated and heavy, she didn't care about the wet mud seeping through to her skin. She just wanted to stay here a little while with those she needed to hold her, those she needed to hold so badly.

She didn't hear her phone at first, buried deep in her pocket. A message alert. She felt sure it was Justin, but she didn't scramble for it. There didn't seem to be much point any more. There was nothing she could say to him. Nothing she could stand to hear him say. Not just now. They couldn't fix each other's hurt. They had been able to once. They'd talked all night, made love the next morning and she'd held him then, held him so tight that she'd been scared she might hurt him physically. He'd bared his soul to her. Told her how scared he was, how inadequate he felt after losing his family. She'd sworn she would do whatever she could so that he would never hurt like that again. She would extract herself from the situation with Paul Radley by any means possible. But then Paul Radley had extracted himself from her life—suddenly. Miraculously, she'd thought then. She'd truly thought it was a sign that not telling Justin the child she was carrying might not be his was the right thing to do. Her man was hurting, and she could help him. She could provide him a family.

Oh God. Burying her face in her hands, Alicia allowed the tears to come. How wrong had she been? Had she been mistaken about everything? Every time she thought about it, every time she'd listened to Paul talking about her deceit, her denying him the right to see his child, a new doubt crept in.

Going over it yet again, half of her screaming at her that she *was* right, the other half telling her she could have been so wrong, she stayed where she was for a while. Rain and tears dripping down her face, she told Luke she had a cold, that was all. That's why she seemed a little bit teary-eyed. A little white lie, this time to protect her child.

She checked her phone eventually. Justin had sent a text. *Did you take the photograph albums?* That was all it said. No sign-off. Nothing. She'd hoped he might have been trying to contact her to say he'd changed his mind and wanted to talk after all, to listen to what she had to say. Though what she could actually tell him she was growing steadily more unsure of. There was no hope now. She knew that. In looking for the albums, he'd obviously been seeking to salvage what memories she hadn't poisoned. Or perhaps he was trying to clarify in his mind that they were all fake memories, woven around the lie she'd told, the life they'd built based on that lie. It had all come crashing down. The foundations had been crumbling since day one, and now it was submitting to the elements, just like the forgotten Victorian headstones. She couldn't stop it. She was too weak. She always had been.

No. She texted back. And then she muted her phone. Not because she thought he might ring or text again. But because she thought he might not.

CHAPTER FIFTY-FIVE

JUSTIN

As Justin walked towards the pub, he passed a couple who were obviously worse for wear. Seeing the girl hunched under her boyfriend's arm, which was possessively draped about her, he couldn't help but notice the bruising on her arms. Justin felt his gut clench. He'd seen it too many times, in his work in accident and emergency, treating women with smashed faces, broken bones and bruises that had obviously been caused by a fist.

Pulling his attention away from where it very probably wasn't wanted, he attempted to focus on his own problems, on what he would do next in regard to Sophie, and his marriage.

He needed to talk to Alicia again—obviously he would need to do that. Unfortunately, she wasn't answering his calls or his texts. She was okay; she'd taken a hot bath and gone to bed early with a glass of wine and a book, Jessica had said. But after their conversation earlier, had she really? He couldn't see it. Just couldn't.

Following the couple into the pub, he noted the inside was much like others he'd been in in the area: decor circa nineties; depressing smoke; yellow and brown. Stepping into the lounge, which was much the same as the bar area, dark and dingy, he didn't draw much attention. Wearing jeans and a T-shirt, he made sure to fit in with the general clientele, rather than be mistaken for the law, which he had been once or twice. At such times, he'd found, people weren't very forthcoming.

Locating the man's whereabouts at a table at the back wall, Justin saw he now had his arm hooked around the girl's neck, yanking her towards him. Judging by the girl's body language, she wasn't a willing participant in the not-so-loving embrace.

"Dean...Get off!" she said, scowling and clearly upset as she attempted to pull away from him.

The guy only tightened his grip, his expression one of obvious contempt as he snarled something in her ear.

"I did not!" the girl refuted. "Dean, for God's sake, pack it in!" she shouted, struggling to break free of him and then scrambling hastily away.

The "boyfriend" was up in an instant, grabbing the girl's wrist and dragging her back. "Sit the fuck down!" he bellowed, shoving her hard onto the bench seat. "Where're you going, hey? To that tosser you've been having it off with, is that it?"

"No!" she screamed. "You're mental, Dean. I haven't been near anyone else, I keep telling you. Those drugs are doing your head in."

"You're going nowhere." The guy leaned in to clutch a fistful of her top and pull her up again. "You fucking *slut*."

It was the slap, a stinging blow across her face, that had Justin's temper snapping, launching him across the room in a second flat.

"Let her go," he seethed, as the man clamped a hand around the girl's throat, shoving her hard against the wall.

"Fuck off," the guy spat in his direction, and squeezed harder.

Justin looked from him to the girl's face. She was gagging—literally gasping for breath. What the hell was the matter with everybody, standing around letting *this* happen?

"I said, let her go!" Justin took a step forward.

"You want some an' all, do ya?" The man glared at him, his bloodshot eyes bulging with fury. "Back off!"

Seeing him turning his attention back to the girl, Justin

reacted instinctively. "I said let her go," he warned him. "You'll *kill* her." Intending to drag him off her, he moved meaningfully towards him, and the man turned on him like a rabid dog. Spitting obscenities, he seized Justin's shirt, pulling him forward and landing first one, and then two, heavy blows to his jaw.

Stumbling backwards into a table, Justin held his footing—just—as the man advanced towards him, his face puce and contorted with rage. "You really shouldn't have done that," he said. His own temper spiking, he righted himself, wiped the back of his hand across his mouth and stood to face him.

The man stopped, his chest heaving, his eyes full of violent malevolence, though Justin saw a flash of uncertainty.

A coward, Justin thought, standing his ground. They all were—cowardly scum, picking on people who didn't have a chance of fighting back.

"Tosser." The man's mouth curled into a snarl as he stepped towards Justin, and then shoved violently past him.

Cursing liberally as he went, the man strode on and banged out of the exit, and Justin breathed a huge sigh of relief. The guy was bigger than he was. Heavier. Justin wasn't sure he would have been able to hold his own. "Are you okay?" he asked, turning back to the girl.

She nodded shakily. "Yeah, thanks," she said. "He goes a bit mental sometimes. He'll cool off eventually."

Justin sighed inwardly. It sounded like she'd probably accept his apologies, which would no doubt be profuse—until the next time. "Do you want me to call anybody?" he offered. "Give you a lift somewhere?"

"No." She shook her head and indicated her phone. "I've called my brother. He's on his way."

Justin nodded. "I'll be at the bar," he said, intending to stick around until the brother showed up. "You might want to do yourself a favour and find someone who doesn't talk with his fists," he suggested. "You only get one life. Why waste it on someone like that?"

"I don't intend to," she assured him. "I'm going to college. Gonna get away from him."

"Sounds like a plan." Justin smiled, despite the sharp ache in his jaw.

Going back to the bar, keeping one eye on the girl until the brother arrived, Justin rang Jessica. He needed answers. If he wasn't going to get those answers from Alicia, then he needed to meet up with Jessica, in private—something, it was occurring to him, she seemed pretty damn desperate to do. She might not have all the answers, but she was Alicia's bloody sister. She would have some of them. Or she ought to. If she'd been "sworn to secrecy," as she'd repeated more than once, Justin wanted to know exactly what about. The affair? The pregnancy? If she'd known about the affair, and he was working on the assumption that she had, then he needed the details. He hadn't wanted to hear them before, but he did now, every single sordid one of them.

Arranging to meet Jessica the next evening, Justin ended his call, and watched as a man came into the pub and walked directly across to the girl. Seeing her jump up to meet him, he waited for her to pass by. Relieved when she gave him a thumbs-up as she did, he knocked the dregs of his pint back and headed out after them.

He'd gone no more than a few yards when his progress was cut short, by first one, then two, and finally three thuggish men. Justin didn't have time to consider his options before he was dead-legged from behind.

"Oh dear, poor sod's legless, ain't you, mate?" someone said tauntingly, close to his ear.

Justin felt his collar being clutched and tugged tight to his throat. An arm slid around his upper torso. They were obviously going to kick the shit out of him, he guessed, his gut turning over. He would stand no chance of fighting back against three of them. All he could do was pray they stopped before they killed him.

Justin guessed wrong.

Jesus Christ, no. Seeing the sharp glint of the blade in his peripheral vision, he felt sweat prickle his skin, saturating the shirt on his back, as he realised what was about to happen.

"Don't," Justin begged, swallowing against the arm now constricting his airway. *"Please,* don't..." His words died on his lips as he felt the knife going in, sliding slickly under his ribs, then a sharp, violent twist, before the blade was pulled out.

Please, God, no. Justin sank from his knees to all fours as the men backed away. This wasn't happening. *Please don't let this be happening. Sophie.* As searing pain ripped through his side, Justin blinked the perspiration from his eyes and struggled to get to his feet, only to find the use of his limbs had deserted him.

He stared at the pavement and sucked in a breath. It stopped painfully short of his chest. Nausea churned his stomach. His heart thudded, loud and sluggish in his head.

No! He started counting.

Tried to control his involuntary shuddering as the crimson stain on the hall floor seeped towards him. Shaking his head, he blinked against the bright light that shone through the cracked mirror. Then blinked again, hard, as blood seeped from the cracks, rich red globules, tears for his children. *Warm blood. His blood.*

His mind screaming, he attempted to shut out the sounds—melodic laughter, chimes tinkling. But they weren't chimes. They were church bells. And his baby was singing.

Justin jolted, gulping back the salty taste in his throat as the dark closed in around him.

CHAPTER FIFTY-SIX

JESSICA

Finally, Jessica thought, tearing the note of the address Justin had given her from the pad and slipping it safely into her handbag. He was a typical man, bottling up his emotions, trying to be macho when his poor heart was steadily breaking. But he'd reached the point where he needed to share, and she would be there for him.

She wouldn't tell Alicia, obviously. She had brought it all on herself, but she was utterly devastated, poor soul. She'd come home soaked through to the skin and covered in mud. Jessica's supposed-to-be-amusing quip about her having been rolling around with a rugby team hadn't raised even the smallest of smiles. Quite the opposite, in fact. She handed her their usual cure-all cup of tea, and Alicia had promptly burst into tears.

Pouring herself a glass of wine, Jessica supposed she ought to go up and check on her. She'd been worried she'd drowned herself in the bath at one point. Now, since she hadn't heard a peek from her—not so much as the squeak of a floorboard since Alicia had gone to her bedroom—she was worrying she might have taken more than the one sleeping tablet she'd suggested might help her rest.

Five minutes later, a tray in her hands, Jessica nudged the spare bedroom door handle down. "Only me," she said quietly, in case Alicia was sleeping, and then went on in.

Oh, not sleeping then. She saw her sister silhouetted against the window. What on earth was she doing standing there in only her skimpy pyjamas? She'd catch her death of cold after coming home soaking wet. She really was a worry.

"Ali?" she said, placing the tray on the dressing table. "Are you all right, sweetie?"

Alicia didn't answer. She simply continued to stare up at the stars, as if looking for the answer to the universe.

Uh-oh. She was swaying on her feet, Jessica noted, her gaze shooting to the bedside table and an almost empty bottle of wine. Oh dear, it looked like Alicia was attempting to anaesthetise the pain again—as if alcohol ever could, particularly if you didn't partake on a regular basis. And Alicia didn't. Or at least she hadn't for a very long time. Obviously, she'd snuck the bottle up in her bag. She really ought to let Justin know about this, Jessica thought. Alicia obviously wasn't coping at all.

Sighing, Jessica went across and placed an arm around her. "What are you doing, sweetheart?" she asked kindly. "You know drinking doesn't help anything. It only ever brings things into sharp focus."

"It doesn't," Alicia said, reluctant to let go of the glass Jessica was attempting to prise from her hand. "It just makes everything more fuddled."

"Muddled," Jessica corrected her, steering her gently away from the window.

"Blurry." Alicia nodded, allowing herself to be led to the bed. "It's like there's two voices in my head. One's saying, 'Stop doubting yourself.' And the other one's saying—"

"You've drunk too much, Alicia. You really shouldn't—"

"*Exactly.*" Alicia plopped down. And swayed. "I'm a lush. A drunken slush. Someone who gets para…paral…as drunk as a fish and then throws herself at the nearest man."

Oh God. Jessica sighed again, heavily. Now she was slurring her words. "A skunk, Ali."

"Sorry?" Alicia closed one eye and looked at her askew.

"It's as drunk as a skunk or drinks like a . . . never mind." Jessica smiled tolerantly. "Come on, tuck up under the duvet and have a nice sleep, why don't you? I've brought you some toast." She tried to tempt her in hopes of getting something down her to soak up the alcohol. "You'll feel better for a bite to eat and a nice cup of tea."

"No. Uh-uh." Alicia shook her head and got unsteadily to her feet. "I'm going on Facebook."

Jessica watched, perplexed, as Alicia groped for her phone and jabbed randomly at it. "Do you think I am?" She looked back to Jessica after a second, her eyes slightly unfocussed and full of uncertainty. "A drunken trollop, I mean. I bet Justin thinks I am. Do you think I am, Jess?"

Definitely worried now, Jessica felt her heart sink. She didn't want her going gaga on her. Justin was bound to ask how she was and she could hardly lie to him about that. He might well talk to Alicia. She couldn't tell him she was fine if she wasn't. "No, Ali, I don't think you're a trollop. And neither do you. It's just the drink, lovely. It's making you emotional."

"Justin will think I am though, won't he?" A tear spilling down her cheek, Alicia went back to her phone. "So, *c'est la vie.*" She shrugged and tried to focus on the screen. "I might as well live up to my reputation, mightn't I?"

"Right." Jessica heaved in a breath. "Alicia, what are you doing exactly?" she asked, as Alicia continued to squint at her phone.

"Picking up a man," Alicia supplied, with a determined nod, which was completely at odds with the tears now streaming down her face.

"From Facebook?" Shaking her head, Jessica eyed the ceiling. "I think you need a bit more practice, sweetie," she said, reaching to ease the phone from her hand as Alicia plopped back down on the bed—and almost missed it.

Damn. Jessica swallowed as a thought occurred. "You haven't taken the sleeping tablet I gave you, have you?" she asked worriedly.

Wiping her hand under her nose, Alicia shook her head. "No," she said, her voice full of anguish. "They make me feel ill in the mornings."

Thank God for that. Jessica blew out a sigh of relief. Having to ring Justin in his medical capacity to tell him his wife was popping pills and washing them down with wine wasn't something she would have relished doing. Then again, should she tell him, for Alicia's sake?

"You need to lie down, Alicia," she said firmly, as her sister leaned precariously to one side, "before you fall down."

Encouraging her to lie back, Jessica played mother—not that it was a role she wanted right now. "There we go," she said, making sure her feet were in and then fluffing up her pillows and tugging up the duvet.

Flicking on the bedside lamp, she fetched the tray and offered her the toast.

"I can't, Jess." Alicia shook her head, looking a little green around the gills. "I'm sorry."

Jessica huffed inwardly. She had her hair to wash and her nails to do. She didn't want to be playing nursemaid half the night. "All right," she relented. "But you have to promise to eat something in the morning. You need to stay strong for your family."

The last came out a little more stridently than she'd intended, and Jessica felt a bit guilty as she watched another tear slide down her sister's cheek.

"Come on, Ali," she said, holding on to her patience and

smoothing her hair away from her face. "Things will look better in the morning."

"Do you think?" Alicia emitted a strangulated laugh at that.

Jessica actually didn't think they would. And Alicia would definitely be feeling ill after drinking that lot on top of no food. She did hope she wasn't going to have a complete breakdown. Her eyes were bloodshot, red-rimmed and, frankly, looked like two peepholes in the snow against her pallid complexion. She'd lost an awful lot of weight—Jessica felt the tiniest bit peeved about that, having been struggling to lose even a pound over the last two weeks. She'd barely uttered a word since she got back, and when she did speak it was distractedly, with a glazed, faraway look in her eye.

Jessica sat with her a while. When, at last, Alicia's eyelids finally grew heavy, Jessica was hugely relieved. She had things to do.

CHAPTER FIFTY-SEVEN

SOPHIE

"What did you say this was again?" Sophie asked, referring to the classical music he was fond of playing while she helped him clear up after their meal. It had been pasta again—which it seemed he was also fond of—but without the meat. Garlicky mushroom penne he'd said it was, and it hadn't been bad.

"Beethoven's Moonlight Sonata," Paul supplied, wiping down the cooker, which he kept meticulously clean. Sophie stacked the dishwasher, making sure to put everything in the exact order he'd specified, since she'd apparently stacked it completely wrong last time. "I find this one particularly calming. It's scientifically proven that calm classical music is an effective way to alleviate stress. Did you know that? Listening to soothing music has a relaxing effect on the body and mind. It mesmerises you." He paused in his rigorous wiping. "Captivates you, almost. Allows you to explore your emotions, delve deep inside and…"

Sophie watched him interestedly as he narrowed his eyes, glancing off somewhere.

He obviously sensed her watching him. "And you don't really like it, do you?" He looked at her with a tolerant half-smile.

"I do," Sophie refuted. "I like most music, but…" She screwed up her nose. "It's a bit maudlin, isn't it? This particular track, I mean."

Paul sighed and shook his head, clearly despairing of her musical ignorance. "So, what mood-inspiring music do you fancy then?"

"Adele?" Sophie suggested hopefully.

He rolled his eyes. "Adele it is," he said, instructing Alexa accordingly.

"Brilliant." Sophie grinned and turned back to her task. "I've missed my music... without my phone." Dropping a subtle hint, she sneaked another peek at him.

Paul's sigh was longer this time. "Go on then," he said, retrieving a credit card from his phone wallet. "Go and order one online," he said, offering it to her.

Sophie stared at it agog. "Really?"

"Well, you obviously can't live without one." Paul shrugged good-naturedly. "But run it by me before you hit purchase," he said, as Sophie gleefully grabbed the card.

"Will do." Sophie smiled, delighted. "Cheers, Paul."

"No worries. Get yourself some shoes, while you're browsing. Can't have you running around in your socks forever, can we? It's not very hygienic."

"Yes. Right." Sophie furrowed her brow. She hadn't heard that one before. "Small problem," she said.

Paul arched an eye curiously.

"I don't have anything to browse on," Sophie pointed out.

"Ah. Of course you don't." Paul downed his cloth and went to the dining area, where his jacket was hanging on a chair. "You can use my laptop," he said, retrieving his study keys to go and fetch it.

"No dipping into files, though, Sophie," he said, coming back with the laptop and setting it up on the dining table. "I have confidential client information on here, remember?"

"I won't," Sophie assured him, her eyes straying to the jacket pocket he'd dropped his keys back into. He'd kept the study locked since he'd found her in there. She supposed it was fair enough, since he had all that confidential stuff. She still wanted to know what was in those desk drawers he'd been so concerned about, though, and why it was her mother's photo he kept on his desk.

CHAPTER FIFTY-EIGHT

ALICIA

Alicia couldn't shake the feeling that something was wrong. Justin had called every day since Sophie went missing, but today she hadn't heard a thing from him. Her useless attempt to explain why she'd taken a decision to ruin his life had driven him to some darker place than he had already been in. She would never forget the emotion in his voice when he'd confirmed that Sophie had given him something worth living for.

Had given him, was the thought that had been plaguing her. Assisted by far too much wine, she'd drifted off to sleep with that thought in her head. Her nightmares had been as bad as her reality. She'd found herself in an *Alice in Wonderland*, haunted distortion of her house, where she heard her family—voices and laughter and tears emerging from rooms she couldn't reach, no matter how hard she ran. Stairs—first one flight, then two—stretched before her like elongated rubber.

She'd left Justin in an empty house as haunted to him as hers was in her dreams, with nothing but the hope he might find Sophie. He'd been working on the studio to keep that hope alive. He would be so desperately lonely, so broken inside. She had to talk to him. If only to hear him say he didn't want to talk to her, she had to hear his voice, know that he was all right physically, if not emotionally. Hesitating for a second, she selected his number, and her anxiety increased as his phone went straight to voicemail.

"Any news?" Jess asked worriedly, coming into the kitchen as Alicia keyed in a text.

"No answer," Alicia said, fear that something had happened to him gnawing away at her insides. He might have simply decided to stop contacting her—he wasn't beholden to her now, after all—but the nagging voice telling her something was wrong just wouldn't go away.

"He's probably busy. Out searching, possibly?" Jessica suggested, looking as concerned as Alicia felt. "He might be in a bad reception area. Have you tried the hospital?"

"I'm doing that now," Alicia said, waiting for the hospital to pick up.

Finding out he wasn't there either, apprehension settled like ice in the pit of her tummy. He might not want to talk to her—might never want to ever again—but for him to remain uncontactable when there was even the slightest possibility she might be trying to get in touch with news of Sophie, that just didn't make sense.

"Give him another half hour," Jessica said, looking worried now as she checked her own phone. She knew, too, Alicia thought, that Justin wouldn't cut all contact under these circumstances.

He would call. *Please let him call.* Keying in a text to him, Alicia tried to quash the insistent niggle that told her he wouldn't. An hour later, she was half out of her mind with worry and incapable of sitting still. She had no idea where he was. He'd been looking for Sophie in the most godforsaken places. He could be anywhere. Lying injured in some backstreet. Unable to get help. Unable to call for help.

He was adamant he would find Sophie—or die trying. He'd said it. Alicia knew he would go wherever his search took him, with no regard for his own safety.

She was about to call DI Taylor when her phone rang. Terror gripped her stomach as the detective's number flashed up.

"Alicia, it's Justin..." he said, and Alicia reeled as even more of her world fell apart.

CHAPTER FIFTY-NINE

ALICIA

Yanked from a fitful sleep, panic flooding every pore in her body, Alicia's eyes shot to the monitor, and her heart rate returned to somewhere near normal. Reassured by the steady *blip, blip* indicating his vital signs were stable, she looked to where her hand still lay on Justin's, her fingers curled softly around his. He hadn't moved. No movement at all, apart from the rapid flicker of his eyelids as his eyes chased his dreams.

Or nightmares.

The cardiothoracic surgeons had worked relentlessly, and by some miracle they'd managed to control the haemorrhaging caused by the knife wound. And it *had* been a miracle. Even with fast surgical intervention, his chances had been slim. He was weak, but, God willing, he would recover physically. Mentally and emotionally, though, Alicia knew those wounds might be unlikely to heal.

He still looked deathly pale against the stark white of the sheets. Alicia studied his profile, a strong profile, which so often gave nothing away of the man inside. A good, dependable man, brought to his knees, by her. She desperately wanted to lie next to him, hold him, as he'd held her after the emergency surgery she'd had to deliver their baby boy. He'd been so gentle, so caring, both immediately after the birth and every day thereafter, until little Lucas had been stolen away. Until Paul Radley had walked back into her life and stolen Justin's happiness away.

Squeezing his hand gently, she leaned to brush his cheek with a kiss. "I never stopped loving you, Justin," she whispered. "Never."

Forcing her tears back, she prayed silently that God would find it within his mercy to bring his daughter back to him. Then almost shot out of her skin as Justin said, "Tell her I'm sorry."

"What?" Getting unsteadily to her feet, Alicia searched his face.

"Sophie, tell her, will you? I—" Justin coughed and then squeezed her hand hard.

Alicia wasted no time, jabbing buttons and calling for help, and when it came, even while they were checking monitors and tubes, Justin didn't let go of her hand.

Finally, his pain medication adjusted and as comfortable as he could be, he dozed. It was a fitful sleep. He would jolt painfully awake, perspiration beading his brow and confusion in his eyes. He spoke occasionally—incoherently, mostly. "Where's Sophie?" he'd asked several times. He'd asked where Luke was, too, which broke Alicia's heart all over again, for Justin. The nurse had confirmed that the morphine was feeding his confusion, but still Alicia worried. Justin needed help. Whatever kind of counselling he needed, she would support him, if he would let her. Whatever he wanted, she wouldn't fight him. She might not deserve to survive, but he did.

Alicia checked again. He was still sleeping. Knowing it might be the last time she would spend a night by his side, she brushed his damp hair from his forehead, pressed her lips lightly against it, and then settled back down to watch him. She wouldn't go, even if he didn't want her there, until he was out of danger.

CHAPTER SIXTY

JUSTIN

Drifting in and out of sleep, Justin opened his eyes as he heard a tap on the door.

"Only me," Jessica said, giving him a bright smile as she poked her head around it. "Bit of a drastic way to get out of our date, isn't it, Justin?"

Easing himself up in the bed, Justin smiled.

"I thought I'd bring you a few things." Jessica came on in, rattling a carrier bag and walking across to him. Or rather, clip-clopping across to him on heels that could definitely be described as vertiginous. She was a little overdressed, surely, for office or hospital visits. Noting the tight skirt and top, Justin made sure not to let his gaze linger.

"Cheers." He smiled. "You really shouldn't have bothered. I intend to be gone as soon as I can."

"Not too soon?" Jessica looked at him, alarmed. "I mean, I know you're a doctor, but you're not infallible. You should be resting, Justin, building up your strength. You're exhausted—emotionally traumatised, to say little of being severely physically injured." Her expression was almost tearful as she looked him worriedly over.

"Honestly, I could just shake Alicia sometimes," she went on, with a despairing sigh. "She's upset, too, of course she is. Devastated, poor soul," she added, her tone switching to sympathetic, which didn't ring quite true any more in Justin's mind. "But I do wonder why she couldn't just have been honest with you from the outset."

"It is what it is," Justin said, watching her warily. "She wasn't, for whatever reason. I suppose I'm just going to have to learn to deal with it."

"A mess is what it is," Jess said, delving into her bag and producing juice, fruit and tissues. "You two splitting up, poor Sophie missing, little Lucas...Not that I'm saying what happened to Lucas was Alicia's fault. Just so you know, I'm here, Justin. If you need someone to talk to, any time, just call me."

Justin nodded, glancing down at the hand she'd placed on his arm. "Have we?" he asked, looking back at her. "Split up?"

Jessica looked taken aback.

"Did Alicia say we'd split?" Justin pushed it.

"Well, not in so many words." Jessica busied herself with her bag, producing biscuits and a book.

"What words?" Justin asked. "What did she say exactly?"

"I haven't brought any grapes, you'll be pleased to know," Jessica answered evasively.

Justin kept his attention on her. "Jessica?"

"She didn't say *exactly*." Jessica arranged the things she'd bought on top of the locker. Stuff he didn't need, because there was no way he was staying. He'd haemorrhaged badly, but there was no major damage to vital organs. He would live. What he wanted to do was establish whether he had a life worth living. To find his daughter and get to the root of why he'd been lied to.

"She mentioned the house." Jessica's eyes flicked in his direction, after a pause, and then away again. "Something about needing to find somewhere to live. I—"

"On her own?" Justin cut in.

"Yes. A studio apartment, I think she said. She saw some somewhere. And with everything that's happened, I was assuming you wouldn't be rushing to get back with her."

"Where?" Justin said. "The apartments, where was it she saw them?"

Jessica looked flustered. "I don't know. I can't remember. The Moseley area somewhere, I think. I've had a lot on my mind, too, Justin. Luke was my nephew. Sophie's my niece. I'm just trying to make sure you're both all right. I'm not quite sure why I'm suddenly under interrogation."

Justin kneaded his forehead. "You're not. I'm sorry." He offered her a small smile. "I'm just a bit confused, that's all. Emotional, I guess."

Jessica looked him over uncertainly. "You're bound to be," she said, her tone back to sympathetic, her voice full of concern as she reached to fluff up his pillows. He didn't need his pillows fluffed. He needed to know what the hell was going on.

"Thanks." He forced a smile anyway. "Can I ask you something else, Jess? If you don't mind, that is?"

"Of course you can," she said, seating herself on the edge of his bed.

"She said she'd been drinking," Justin started cautiously. He didn't want to go in heavily. He simply needed to know how far Jessica was willing to go.

Jessica drew in a breath. Was that expression judgemental? Shouldn't it be guarded, for her sister's sake? "That's right," she said. "She's drinking quite a bit now, actually. Regularly, sadly. It's understandable, I suppose, under the circumstances, but it's a worry, as you can imagine."

Alicia wasn't teetotal. They'd both drunk more than was healthy on the odd occasion, but Alicia had never drunk regularly.

"How much? How much had she drunk, Jess?" he asked, running a hand across his neck. He didn't need to work at looking like a troubled man. "Was she drinking a lot back then?"

Jessica looked hesitant, then, "Yes," she said, "unfortunately."

"So she could have been paralytic then?"

Again, Jessica hesitated. "Not too paralytic to make her way to his room." Her expression was definitely disapproving as she glanced briefly away and back again.

"No, I suppose not." Justin heaved out a sigh.

He looked away then, appearing to ponder. "There's something else," he said, looking back at her.

Smiling caringly, Jessica took hold of his hand. Justin couldn't quite believe it. "Why didn't you tell her about the forensic search?"

Jessica looked confused.

"Was it because you hoped we wouldn't be able to talk with police officers poking around?" Justin asked her point-blank.

"No." Jessica snatched her hand away from his. "Why on earth would I do that?"

"The photographs I asked about," Justin went on. "Why did you tell me Alicia had them?"

Jessica paled, considerably. "I didn't. I just assumed, because of what you said."

Justin nodded slowly. "Making a lot of assumptions, aren't you, Jess?" he said, studying her carefully. "Tell me, how much bullshit have you been feeding me, precisely?"

Dropping her gaze fast, Jessica got to her feet, her cheeks flushing furiously as she collected up her bag.

"It never was a date, Jessica," Justin said quietly, as she walked to the door. All of this without once making eye contact with him.

Watching her leave, Justin cursed his naive stupidity. He really must be completely blind not to have seen what was right under his nose, he thought angrily, heaving his legs over the bed and pulling the tube from his arm. He didn't know how many lies he was being told, but one thing he did know for certain was that Alicia wasn't a closet alcoholic, as implied by her sister.

If her propensity was to hit the bottle in a crisis, wouldn't she have done that when Luke died? Would she have been capable of coherent, albeit emotional, conversation every day since?

He also knew that photographs didn't lie.

She'd said she wasn't well. The photos he had of her at that wedding told him there was a hell of a lot more to this than met the eye. Alicia was holding something back. And Justin intended to find out what. Why she would hold anything back now, he wasn't sure. But he intended to get to the truth, one way or another.

CHAPTER SIXTY-ONE

ALICIA

Rounding the corner of the corridor Justin was on, Alicia was surprised to see Jessica coming towards her. Shouldn't she be at work? Concentrating on her phone as she walked towards her, Jessica didn't appear to notice her.

"Jess?" Alicia said, eyeing her curiously. Typing out a text, she still hadn't seen her.

Jessica's head snapped up. "Alicia!" She looked surprised. "I didn't think you were coming until later."

"I had a few things I wanted to get for Justin, and then I had my doctor's appointment, but, to be honest, I couldn't face it. You know, having to go over why I'm not sleeping well."

"Ah." Jessica nodded, and pushed her mobile into her bag.

"I take it you came to see Justin?" Alicia asked, when Jessica didn't add anything else.

"I thought I would pay him a visit," Jessica said, glancing down at her shoes. They must be killing her, Alicia thought. They were a least six inches high, and definite toe-pinchers. Not the sort of shoes she'd want to wear to troop along hospital corridors. "He was a bit tired though, so I didn't stay long. I left him a few bits and bobs."

"Well, I'm sure he appreciated the visit, and the bits and bobs." Alicia smiled. "But shouldn't you be at work?"

"I had to deliver some papers to a client. I've wangled the rest of the day off," Jessica said quickly.

"Oh, right. Well, I'll see you back at yours then." Leaning in to give her a hug, Alicia noticed the troubled look in her eyes. "Jessica? Is everything all right?"

"Yes." Jessica said, her gaze flicking down and back. "It's probably nothing, but..."

"But?" Her antennae on red alert for the next bad thing to happen, Alicia urged her on.

"Justin seems a bit...confused," Jessica said, her expression now a mixture of sympathetic and guarded. "Mixed up," she elaborated, as Alicia looked at her worriedly.

"Mixed up how?" she asked apprehensively, praying that he wasn't heading back to the pit of despair he'd been in once before.

"It's probably just the stress of everything catching up with him," Jessica said. "He seems to think I've said things which I haven't, that you've told him things. He'll be fine after a good rest. Don't worry, Ali."

But Alicia was worried. "What kind of things?" She felt her eyes filling up all over again.

"Little things," Jessica said, seeming reluctant. "The missing photographs, for instance. He seems convinced that I told him you had them, and I distinctly remember I didn't. I mean, why would I when you don't? Like I say, it's nothing major. I thought I should warn you though." Jessica gave her arm a squeeze. "He's just a bit muddled. He'll be fine."

Alicia nodded bewilderedly.

"I'd better get back to work," Jessica said, kissing her cheek. "See you later, sweetheart."

Watching her go, Alicia ferreted in her pocket for the loo roll she'd grabbed from the patients' toilet, in the absence of tissue, and wiped her eyes. Earlier, she'd decided she would try again to talk to him. Not here, obviously, while he was so ill. She wasn't sure whether she would be able to talk sensibly, feeling as confused as she was, consumed with guilt, her heart fit to burst in her chest. And she wasn't sure whether he would ever be able to listen, but she knew she had to try. She'd even considered writing to him, because then she wouldn't have to see his face, read the expression in his eyes.

That would have to wait now. He needed to get well. And if he needed her to keep her distance until he did, then she would do that. At least he had Jessica to visit him, who clearly cared for them both.

She was pondering what Jessica had meant by *things she'd told him* as she went into Justin's room. Finding his bed empty, she frowned, puzzled. He was up and about but wasn't supposed to be walking very far yet with his drip. Perhaps they'd taken him for some test or other? Walking across to his locker, Alicia deposited her bags, and her heart stopped dead. His drip was still there, the cannula he'd had in his hand pulled out and abandoned on the bed. Holding her breath, she checked his locker. His mobile was gone. His clothes...

Oh God, no. "Justin!"

CHAPTER SIXTY-TWO

ALICIA

Alicia ran back to her car, ringing Justin as she did, only to get his voicemail again, which only increased the knot of fear growing inside her. Where on earth was he? Why had he left? He'd pulled his drip out, for God's sake, and not even discharged himself.

What was he thinking? His emotions were raw—all of the stages of grief and more. Alicia couldn't even imagine how he must be feeling. He'd been confused, Jessica had said. He'd already been bewildered and broken, stuffed full of pent-up anger. He'd snapped at her, but he hadn't once lost his temper, though he had every right to. But he had attacked Paul Radley. Icy fingers ran the length of her spine. Aggressively, DI Taylor had said. Where had he gone now, disorientated and in pain? What would he do? He wasn't capable of defending himself if there was a confrontation of some sort. Physically, he wouldn't be able to, but that might not stop him provoking that confrontation.

She had to find him. Please, God, before he did anything reckless. He wasn't *well*. Gulping back her mounting fear, banging the heel of her hand against the steering wheel and cursing the slow traffic, Alicia drove straight to the house, hoping she might find Justin there. Her heart plummeted another inch when she saw his car wasn't on the drive. After Justin was attacked, DI Taylor had organised the collection of the vehicle from where it had been parked. One of his officers had driven it here and delivered Justin the keys, so that could only mean Justin was driving it now. Was he even capable of driving? There were no signs of life when she knocked on the door, no signs of him through the windows. He wasn't here.

Justin, please, please answer your phone.

Driving straight to the house where he'd said he was renting a room—a single room, no bigger than a shoebox, with one tiny window and tobacco-stained walls, not fit for a dog—she found he hadn't been back there either, and her heart sank without trace. She had no idea where else to look. He obviously wouldn't be at work—the hospital he'd just escaped. Might he have gone back to trawling the streets, compelled to carry on searching?

Was he searching for Paul Radley? She didn't imagine he would cross the line for her sake, but for Sophie he would. For Sophie, in his disturbed state of mind, he might do anything.

Alicia drove next to Jess's, and sprinted to the house, almost falling through the door as she fumbled to open it. She was hoping and praying that Justin might have rung there, that there was some logical reason she hadn't been able to get hold of him, like his phone wasn't working, perhaps because he had dropped it. She was clutching at straws. Desperate.

"Jess!" she called, checking the answerphone and charging straight to the lounge, and then to the kitchen. "Jess?"

"Up here," Jessica answered from the top of the stairs. "I've just been speaking to Justin."

"You've been talking to...?" Noting the phone in her hand, Alicia shook her head, confused. "Where is he? I've been trying to get hold of him. His phone kept going to voicemail."

"I'm not sure." Jessica came on down. "He obviously needed some space to think."

"I see." Despite the fact that he'd clearly been avoiding her calls, her heart settled clunkily back into its moorings. Alicia nodded, looking worriedly at her sister as she met her in the hall. "Did he call you?"

"Yes. He said he's been trying to get hold of you."

Her phone had obviously gone to voicemail, too. Relieved, Alicia checked it, but found no message. Growing more confused, she scanned Jessica's face. "Is he all right?"

Giving her a small nod, Jessica glanced at her warily. "As he can be," she said.

"Are you?" Alicia asked, looking her over with concern. She looked pale and tearful. "Jess?"

Jessica took a breath. "There's something I need to mention, Ali," she said, seeming reluctant. "He asked me to meet him, before he was injured. I'm sure it was just to talk, but under the circumstances…" She hesitated uncertainly. "I told him I didn't think it was a good idea, when I saw him at the hospital. I thought you should know. I…"

Stopping, Jessica fixed her gaze on the floor, while Alicia inwardly reeled. Did Jess think…? No, surely Justin wouldn't…? Unless to get back at her? But he wouldn't do that. She knew him. He wasn't vindictive. He wouldn't do something out of spite. It wasn't in his nature to…her thoughts ground to a halt as it occurred to her that Jessica might possibly be embroidering the truth. She noted her sister's body language, the downcast eyes, the phone still in her hand. It was never far from her side. But why would she…

"I didn't want there to be any bad feeling between us, Ali." Jessica looked at her imploringly. "I didn't want to mention it, but…"

"It's okay, Jess. I'm glad you did. He probably did need to talk. He obviously has endless questions going around in his head." Giving Jessica a brittle smile, Alicia pulled in a breath. The "why would she," she realised, was becoming blindingly obvious.

"Exactly." Jessica looked hugely relieved. "I'm happy to lend a shoulder, of course I am. You know me, always willing to help in a crisis. But I didn't want to seem to be going behind your back."

"No, of course you wouldn't." Alicia smiled tightly again. "Did you go back to work?" she enquired casually.

Jessica looked at her blankly.

"It's just that you said you'd gone to see Justin because you were taking the rest of the day off."

"Yes," Jessica said uncertainly.

"And then you said you had to get back to work," Alicia reminded her.

Jessica's brow furrowed. "Did I?"

"Perhaps it's you who's a bit mixed up, Jess?" Alicia suggested.

Jessica looked somewhat po-faced. "I hardly think it's me who could be accused of that, Alicia. I only mentioned it because I thought you should be aware, but if you're going to start bandying accusations about..."

"Aware of what, Jess?" Alicia stopped her, as Jessica turned towards the kitchen. "That my husband's right up there alongside the 'bastards' you've had the misfortune to be involved with? That, even though he's injured, out of his mind with grief, he's engineering some plan to sleep with my sister to get back at me?"

"That was *not* what I said." Jessica whirled back around. "You're putting words in my mouth, Alicia, and that's not fair after all I've done for you. I really wonder why on earth I—"

"Why didn't you text me?" Alicia asked over her. "When Justin 'guessed' about Sophie, why didn't you alert me, Jess? Your phone is never more than two inches away from you, after all."

Jessica looked nonplussed. "I don't know," she said indignantly. "I don't remember. I was in a state of shock. Of panic. For you!"

"Right." Alicia narrowed her eyes. "Did you also forget to tell me you'd mentioned Sophie's sixteenth birthday to Paul Radley, therefore supplying him with the exact information I *didn't* want him to have—her date of birth?" she asked furiously.

"Oh, don't be bloody ridiculous," Jessica snapped, turning away again.

"He wouldn't have known!" Alicia shouted behind her. "He wouldn't have done the maths if you hadn't told him!"

Jessica turned back, two bright spots on her cheeks, her expression livid. "But Justin would have! He'd already done the maths, Alicia. He *knew*. And, if you ask me, it was about bloody time he did!"

Alicia stared at her, her heart feeling as if it was fragmenting piece by painful piece. "You wanted him to find out, didn't you?"

"Of course I didn't want him to find out." Jessica sighed short-temperedly. "But if you're asking whether I'm glad he knows, then yes, I am. You should have told him, Alicia. It wasn't fair to keep him under false pretences. You should have given him a chance at another relationship."

Alicia laughed—a short, disbelieving laugh. "With you."

Jessica notched up her chin. "If that's what he'd wanted, then yes. Why not?"

"Why not?" Alicia almost choked out the words. "He's my husband!"

"And you don't appreciate him!" Jessica countered angrily. "You had the perfect life, the perfect family, everything I ever wanted. You didn't deserve it, Alicia."

She was jealous. Alicia was utterly stunned. So jealous she would have risked Sophie's happiness? Justin's?

"You were so busy fluttering your bloody eyelashes and blushing the first time you saw him, it never occurred to you I might be interested in him," Jessica ranted on, obviously letting go of the frustration she'd bottled up inside for many, many years. "That he might have been interested in me. Oh *no*. You just moved in like a cruise missile, grabbing him for yourself, always getting everything you want because you're so obviously needy.

But you didn't want him, did you? You lied to him, deceived him, cheated…"

Realising she might have gone a step too far, she stopped suddenly.

Alicia clenched her teeth hard. "Did you give him Sophie's mobile number?" she demanded, her fury now bubbling white-hot inside her. "Paul Radley. Did you give him Sophie's number?"

Jessica held her gaze. "She's his daughter," she said, tilting her chin defiantly.

"*My* daughter!" Alicia's fury spilled over. "*My* husband!" She stepped forward to land a stinging slap on Jessica's face, who was even now unrepentant. "You're sad," she seethed. "A very sad, bitter woman, who I was fool enough to listen to for far too long. I hope you'll be happy on your own, Jess." Looking her over contemptuously, Alicia turned to fly up the stairs for her things.

"Where are you going?" Jessica shouted after her.

"To find my family!"

CHAPTER SIXTY-THREE

JUSTIN

Sitting with the heels of his hands pressed hard against his eyes, his chest heaving with a toxic mixture of raw anger and anguish that far outweighed his physical pain, Justin struggled to get a grip on his emotions. He needed to. Coping mechanisms weren't going to work. Nothing was going to work, but he needed to.

Picking up the photos from that long-ago wedding, several of which he'd now had enlarged, he studied them again. Her bridesmaid's dress was pastel blue; the colour suited her fair complexion and caramel-coloured hair. It was a sleeveless dress with thin shoulder straps. He recalled how she'd slathered herself in fake tan the night before—to hide her pale skin, she'd said. Her first lie, one of a succession of lies. How could he have been so blind? *How?* He was a doctor! He'd seen this type of bruising a thousand times. The concealer she'd also applied, some of which she'd got on the front of the dress—he vividly remembered her trying to sponge it off before she left the house—had clearly eventually worn off.

She'd worn a cardigan at the reception. Said she was cold. He'd been sweltering. But he'd also been preoccupied, too busy with his own problems to see the evidence that was right before his eyes. Bruises. Finger-shaped bruising on both of her arms. Livid, purple-black bruises—meaning they were only a few days old, inflicted, therefore, around the night she'd stayed with her friend. Got so drunk with her friend she'd been ill.

Had it just been drink, he wondered, his gut tightening, his jaw clenching. She'd been hungover the next day; that much she'd told him. She'd also been dizzy, her movements sluggish, her limbs heavy. She'd had an upset stomach. All the symptoms of a bug. They were also the after-effects of any number of sedative-hypnotic drugs: flunitrazepam, gamma-hydroxybutyrate, ketamine, Rohypnol. All available on the black market, the latter easily purchased in Europe for use as a sleeping pill—or to render someone helpless in order to carry out a sexual assault.

Swallowing back the bile in his throat, Justin pressed his knuckles against his temples and tried to think rationally. Was he going completely insane? Imagining this? Looking for explanations for the inexplicable that were in no way preferable? She'd seen Paul Radley more than once. She'd *said* she had.

Why?

And if he was right about this, why the hell would she have lied to him?

It made no sense. None of it. But going slowly out of his mind or not, one thing he wasn't imagining were those bruises.

Sucking in a breath, he glanced upwards and then pulled himself to his feet. Walking across to the drinks table, he considered his options, picked up the whisky, tested the weight of it, then—emitting a roar that came from his soul—hurled it against the far wall.

Sitting by and doing nothing simply wasn't an option.

CHAPTER SIXTY-FOUR

ALICIA

Alicia jumped as her phone rang.

Thank God! Alicia seized on it. "Justin, where are you?" she said immediately, unable to keep the wretchedness from her voice. "I've been so worried. I thought something might have happened to you. Are you all right?"

"Yes," he said. "Sorry, I didn't mean to disappear like that, or not to call you, I just..."

"Needed some space?" Alicia filled in sadly.

"Definitely." Justin drew in a breath. "I have to see you, Alicia. Can we talk?"

Alicia felt the familiar knot of tension tighten in her stomach. He didn't sound agitated. Drained, yes, but not angry. "When?" she asked him.

"Now. I'm outside."

Outside the house? Alicia went to the window, and sure enough, he was parked outside. Clearly, he didn't want to come into the house, which he would always normally do. Presumably because he wanted to avoid Jessica, which confirmed what her sister had said. Something had gone on between them, but not the something that at least one of them had hoped.

"I'll be one minute," she said, nodding as he glanced up at the window.

Debating whether to take her things out with her, Alicia

decided to leave them where they were. Appearing with her bags would only raise more questions, and she didn't want that. No doubt Justin wouldn't want to wonder about what she might be up to or where she might be going either. She actually didn't have a clue where she would go. A hotel, she supposed, at least for tonight.

"Alicia?" Jessica came out of the lounge as she reached the hall. "Can we talk?"

Alicia shook her head, incredulous. Did she honestly think they could? Now? Could she not see the damage she'd done? They still didn't know what had happened to Sophie. It was something Alicia tried hard not to imagine. She'd thought they were close—as close as two sisters with completely different lifestyles could be. That they would be there for each other in a crisis. She'd been so wrong. Jessica had never been the sister she'd thought she was. Instead, she was a twisted person, driven by jealousy. She'd wanted children desperately. She'd wanted what Alicia had, and was obviously prepared to go to any lengths to get it. Alicia felt for her, even now, but she couldn't ever forgive her for manipulating her own situation—or, more hurtfully, Justin's—to her own ends.

"I have to talk to Justin," she said, still not able to even look at her.

"He's not coming in then?" Jessica asked.

"No, Jessica. Are you surprised?" Letting herself out, Alicia steeled herself for the questions Justin was bound to have. She hoped this time she would be able to answer coherently, and that he would be able to listen. If there was one good thing that had come from her confrontation with Jessica, she supposed it was that she was determined now to tell Justin everything.

Breathing deeply as she approached his car, she pulled open the passenger door and slipped inside.

"Thanks," Justin said, glancing in her direction. "For coming out."

"You shouldn't have left the hospital, Justin," Alicia ventured, after an awkward second. "Your wounds won't be healed yet."

Justin grimaced. "No, they won't, not for a good while, I imagine."

His tone wasn't caustic or reproachful. If anything, it was subdued. "There are some things I need to ask you." He turned towards her, his eyes cautiously scanning hers. "I was hoping you could answer me honestly. If you can't... well, then I suppose I'll have my answer."

Nodding, Alicia closed her eyes. She would give him honest answers, however ludicrous they sounded. She would have her answer, too, then, to the question she'd asked herself over and over: *Would he have believed her?*

"You said you'd been drinking." He tugged in a breath, closing his own eyes briefly, Alicia noticed, possibly because of the pain in his chest. "Were you drunk?" he asked, looking back at her.

"Very," Alicia said, as she remembered it.

Justin waited a beat, then, "Not drugged?" he asked tightly.

The question hit Alicia like a thunderclap, instantly propelling her back there, to the hotel room where she'd woken up to the unfamiliar smell of Paul Radley—a cloying mixture of body odour, bitter lemons and alcohol—with only jagged memories of how she'd got there. She felt again the peculiar bruises on her body that she'd had to hide. The reason she'd lied and then compounded her lies.

"I...don't know. I..." she faltered. "I honestly don't remember. I've tried. I've gone over it a million times trying to remember, but I don't. I recall being at the bar. People drifting off. After that, nothing apart from hazy images, until the next morning."

"Jesus Christ!" Justin said, pushing the heels of his hands hard against the steering wheel and dropping his head back against the headrest.

A heavy minute ticked by. Alicia was sure she could hear her heart beating, the rustle of the leaves on the wind outside.

"Why didn't you report him, Alicia?" he asked throatily. He turned towards her when she didn't answer.

Her mouth dry, her throat parched, Alicia met his gaze. Here was the crucial question, the absurdity of the choice she'd felt she had to make. "You asked if I was drugged?" she said, as calmly as she could.

Justin looked confused.

"Would it have made any difference if I wasn't?" she asked him. "If I was *only* drunk, would that have meant it shouldn't have happened? That I could have stopped it in some way?"

"No," Justin said categorically. "I'm just trying to establish the facts, Alicia. I'm not judging you."

"Aren't you?" Alicia studied him. "What would you have done, Justin? Knowing you might not be believed, what would you have done?"

Justin raked his hands through his hair. "You went back, Alicia. You saw him *again*. That's the part I'm struggling with. Make me understand. For Christ's sake, I *need* to. Tell me."

Alicia swallowed, seeing the look in Paul Radley's eyes as clear as day: dark, intent, calculating. He'd told her she'd been insatiable. Justin would never have to find out, he'd said, gliding his hand down her back as she'd groped desperately for her clothes, sending a shudder of utter repulsion right through her. Though she'd had no idea what had happened between the bar and the hotel room—in the hotel room—she'd known with absolute certainty that he'd meant Justin *would* find out. She'd questioned herself over and over since, guilt overriding her anger, doubt clouding her recollection. But she *had* known. Justin's world had been falling apart, and, if she didn't agree to his terms, Paul Radley would make sure it did. How in God's name was she ever going to explain that, she'd thought then. She'd been young, naive, stupid, ashamed. Terrified. Finally, she'd been pregnant. No way to tell, no way to make anyone believe she hadn't known how to say no.

Alicia glanced down and then back, making sure to hold Justin's eyes this time. "He threatened to tell you," she said. "Obviously, it would have been his version of events. When he went abroad, I thought everything might be all right." She felt a tear wet her cheek and didn't bother this time to wipe it away. "I prayed it would be, every day and every night. I was wrong. I lied. And now I'm being punished. I only have the word sorry, Justin. There's no other way to tell you how I feel."

Justin stared at her, a myriad of emotions in his eyes: incomprehension, shock and pure, unadulterated rage.

He didn't respond initially, dropping his gaze and pressing his thumb hard against his forehead instead. And then, "You should go back in," he said gutturally, twisting to start the engine. "I have to go."

"Go? Go where?" Fear gripped Alicia's stomach. "Justin! *Where* do you have to go?" she asked frantically.

Justin breathed hard. "To finish the job."

"Justin, *no*." Cold foreboding sweeping through her, Alicia clutched his arm, immediately reliving the sickening impact on that dark day, when their little boy had been taken from them. "Please…" she begged him. "Don't, Justin. You're not well. Please, just let him go. I want him out of my life. Out of our lives. If you do this, he won't ever be, don't you see?"

Searching his face, she waited, her heart palpitating manically as she watched him suck in a long breath. "You should have reported him," he said hoarsely. "You should have told me, Alicia. You should have been able to. *Fuck!*" He slammed his hand against the steering wheel.

Alicia caught hold of his hand as he moved it again to his forehead. "I should have," she said hesitantly. "I know, now, that I could have."

He looked at her, his eyes awash with tears. "Jesus, Alicia."

He gulped hard. "I am *so* sorry." Moving his hand tentatively to her face, he grazed his thumb gently across her cheek. "So sorry."

"Don't be," Alicia said, pressing her forehead to his. "We don't have time for any more regrets. We have to find Sophie."

Blowing out a ragged breath, Justin nodded. "Can we talk more?" he asked her hesitantly. "Just generally, I mean," he added quickly, clearly noticing her uncertainty.

She wanted to talk to him, so badly wanted to reach out to him, for him to reach out to her and talk about all they were going through. Even to lie silently next to him, rest her head on his chest and listen to the reassuring thrum of his heart—that's when she'd always felt safest, able to shut out the world and all the bad things in it—would salve the raw pain inside her. To delve into this, though, to relive the memories she'd tried so hard to forget. . . She wasn't sure she would be able to do that.

"I don't need the detail, Ali," he said. "I'd like to think you could talk to me, but only if you wanted to."

Smiling tremulously, Alicia nodded. She hadn't been wrong about this man. She hadn't been wrong to love him completely.

Justin reached to wipe another errant tear from her cheek. "We'll find her," he said softly. "If you don't want to be at the house, I get that, but. . ." He paused. "I miss you, Alicia. Come back to me."

Alicia's heartbeat picked up in a different way as she saw the hopeful look in his eyes. Nodding again, she hesitated for the briefest second and then pressed her lips softly to his, possibly giving him a very snotty kiss.

"I have something urgent I need to attend at the hospital," Justin said, easing away from her. "I'll come straight back, if that's okay with you?"

Alicia hesitated, and then nodded. She didn't particularly want to go back inside, but she had her things to collect. "I hope you're going to get yourself checked over while you're there?" She gave him an admonishing look.

Justin managed a smile. "I will. I promise."

Alicia nodded, relieved, and then glanced back to the house. She would have to tell him she wanted nothing to do with her sister, possibly ever again, but there was another conundrum: how to explain that without seeming to be accusing him of anything or embarrassing him.

"Alicia, about Jessica," he said apprehensively, raising the subject for her. "I realise this is a big ask, but do you think we could maybe not share information with her?" He glanced awkwardly away. "I think we need to trust each other now. No one else."

Alicia scanned his eyes, as he turned back to her. His expression was definitely awkward, but it also held a warning, communicating all Alicia needed to know. He was aware, as she now was, of the hurt Jessica had caused, and still could.

Holding his gaze, she nodded resolutely. They had an understanding. There were no words needed.

"I'll ring you," Justin said. "As soon as I've finished at the hospital. It shouldn't be too long. Will you be okay until then?"

Again, Alicia nodded. "I need to get my things together," she said. It would never be whole without her children, but it was possible her heart might have started functioning again.

"One more thing, Alicia." Justin stopped her as she reached for her door. "Radley—he's dangerous. He's possibly a danger to Sophie, should she contact him again. I understand why you felt you couldn't say anything before, but…" He hesitated, studying her carefully. "I think Taylor needs to know everything now, for her sake."

Seeing the genuine fear in his eyes, Alicia felt a shudder run through her. He was right. Paul wouldn't hurt Sophie, surely? But even the slightest threat, in whatever form…Swallowing, she closed her eyes and took a deep breath. "I'll ring the station," she said. "I'll do it from my car, out of earshot of Jessica."

Justin sighed, clearly relieved, and then leaned towards her. "For what it's worth, I'm here for you, Ali," he said, brushing her lips with his own. "Just so you know."

Alicia immediately did what she'd been aching to do and threw her arms around him. "It's worth a lot," she assured him tearfully. "And just so *you* know, there was never a second I didn't love you. I always will."

Justin squeezed her back. "I'll call you," he promised, pulling away to kiss her forehead softly. "As soon as I can."

Watching him go, Alicia realised that Jessica really was a bad judge of men. Justin would never have got involved with her. Perhaps another woman, in time, possibly, if they'd had no future together, but he wouldn't have jumped at the first available female, particularly if that female was Alicia's sister. He just wasn't made that way.

Turning to the house, she was going over in her mind what she would say to DI Taylor—it was going to be one of the most difficult calls she'd made in her life—when her phone received a text. It was from Paul Radley, as if he'd known he was under discussion. Reluctantly, she checked it, and then froze, her stomach lurching violently as she stared down at the photograph: Sophie, lying asleep on her stomach, one hand resting on her pillow, her passport lying beside her. A single rose on the duvet. *A significant gesture*, that's what he'd said when he'd given one to her. He'd quoted something. Something to do with a rose bush growing in the pool of blood spilled from Aphrodite's slain lover, Adonis. He'd said it symbolised immortal love, love that would never fade, even through time or death...meaning they would be together forever.

She read the text.

Meet me. 8.00 p.m. Central Plaza, Apartment 153b. We need to talk about the future. Come alone.

CHAPTER SIXTY-FIVE

SOPHIE

Bored with the TV, Sophie wandered towards the kitchen for a drink. She quite fancied a huge glass of fizzy Coke, but guessed she'd have to settle for one of the fruit juices Paul made in his blender. The lime and cucumber was okay, but the apple, mint and spinach was foul.

"Won't be long," Paul said, sailing past.

Dressed in his gym clothes, Sophie noticed. He'd offered to get her a membership, but Sophie wasn't all that into gyms. She'd said she'd try it. Despite all this healthy eating, though, she'd been so exhausted lately, she wasn't sure she could be bothered to drag herself as far as the lift.

"Did my phone arrive yet?" she asked him, coming back with her juice and trying hard not to wince as she swallowed a mouthful.

"Afraid not." Paul smiled regretfully. "We'll see about chasing it later."

He still didn't trust her to use his laptop or his phone in his absence. He turned down her requests nicely, pointing out the importance of client confidentiality and all that crap, but it rankled that he didn't trust her enough not to poke around in his files. Like he'd got more to hide than boring old financial reports.

"Why don't you have a browse through the new Florida brochures I bought," he suggested. "We'll be going in a few days."

That was a little vague, Sophie thought. He'd said he hadn't confirmed the flights when she'd asked him, and, while she realised it would be him forking out for them, she still had to have some clothes if she was going on holiday. "I might," she said, yawning.

"Manners, Sophie," Paul reminded her, with a tolerant smile.

"Sorry," Sophie said, pressing a hand to her mouth as she yawned again, and then watching with interest as Paul checked his jacket pocket for his phone, bringing out his study keys as he did and then plopping them back in his jacket.

"Half an hour," he said, heading for the front door. "Don't forget to take your vitamins."

"I already did," Sophie assured him, yawning widely again.

Waiting until he'd gone, Sophie stopped yawning, nipped to the loo, flushed the vitamin tablets away—she was sure the bloody things were making her sleepy—and then flew over to his jacket to retrieve the keys. It was now or never. He'd kept that door locked religiously since the one time she'd been in there, even coming back an hour after he'd gone out once. He'd made some other excuse, but he'd come back to make sure he'd locked the study, Sophie was sure of it. Plus, she hadn't been able to get the photo on his desk out of her mind, and the fact that Justin had been cropped out of it. Then there was the envelope. Sophie had glimpsed more photos in there.

She'd bet those were of his family. She was hoping they were. He'd been okay to her—generous—but despite being under the same roof as him, she still didn't know that much about him. He didn't talk about his family, didn't have a single photo of them anywhere around the apartment, and to Sophie, who'd lived in a home where family photos were dotted about everywhere, that just seemed odd.

Two minutes later, she was in the study, fumbling to find the right key for the drawer in which she'd seen the envelope. *Bingo!*

Finally, she unlocked it, hurriedly extracting the envelope and peering inside. She squinted and tipped the contents out. These weren't photos of his family. Furrowing her brow, Sophie splayed them out on top of the desk. They were *their* family photos. Photographs taken mostly by Justin, of her and her mum. She recognised some of the backgrounds. Their bloody back garden, for one. Their lounge at Christmas. The holiday chalet they'd had in France. The boat they'd hired to tour Ireland. There were some later ones, as well, that she'd taken herself, of Justin and her mum, and Justin had been crudely cropped out of every one of them. Chopped out, with scissors. He hadn't even cut the photos in straight lines.

Why had he done that? How had he got them? Surely her mum hadn't given them to him?

Her heart like a big bass drum in her chest, Sophie shuffled through a few more and then stopped, a knot of apprehension tightening her tummy as she noticed that there were also much more recent photographs. Photographs that Luke should have been in—a family portrait, in particular. Sophie remembered that one so clearly. Her mum had had it framed for the hall wall. Justin had a copy of it in his office. In the photo, Sophie was sitting next to her mum on the sofa, her arm around her shoulders. Luke had been in her mum's arms, but now he was gone. Cropped out. Like he didn't exist.

There were more photographs in another drawer, all exclusively of her mum. Not posed, these photos hadn't been taken by Justin or her. They'd been taken by Paul, Sophie realised. Photos from over the years: Alicia walking along the street; loading her shopping into the car; coming out of the office where she worked. There was one of her painting their house, for fuck's sake. Hadn't he been in Dubai, time slipping by while he worked himself to death trying to get over the loss of his family?

Liar!

Scraping the photos together and furiously shoving them back in their envelope, Sophie put it back, slammed the drawer shut and moved to the last drawer.

It was stuck. *Shit!* Checking the time on the desk clock, she glanced worriedly towards the door and then yanked at the drawer. It was definitely jammed, not locked. Crouching down, pressing one hand against the desk for leverage, she tugged harder, and then fell back on her haunches as it gave.

Scrambling back, Sophie peered into it, and her heart skittered to a stop inside her. It was fairly obvious what had caused it to jam. Swallowing back a sick taste in her throat, Sophie reached for it: Luke's pink elephant toy. One of its floppy ears had got caught between the desk and the drawer and been torn clean off. He'd stuffed it in there as if it didn't matter. As if it wasn't the most important thing Sophie had ever, or would ever, possess in her life.

He'd taken it. Taken it from her.

A huge lump in her throat, Sophie lifted it to her face and sniffed it. His scent was still there—barely. Her little baby brother. Choking back the tears that stung the backs of her eyes, she delved further into the drawer. Feeling something smooth and cold towards the back of it, something with a chain attached, she fished it out. It was a locket. A gold locket, decorated with a flower motif.

Her mum's?

Sophie stopped breathing. With trembling fingers, she prised it open. Luke's little face looked back at her. His perfect cupid lips were curved into a delighted, gummy smile. His beautiful blue eyes, wide with the innocence of childhood, were dancing with glee.

Oh God, Luke.

Her mum hadn't given him this. She hadn't given him any of this. He'd taken these, too. Feeling the room shift around her,

Sophie tried to breathe slowly, like Justin had once taught her, when she'd had a major panic about her part in the school play. Calm—he'd always been that. Calm and measured. Suddenly, Sophie wanted very much to go home.

Having a final check in the drawer, she wasn't surprised, somehow, to find her old phone as well as the new one.

Breathe. Doing what Justin would, Sophie tried to focus. Sliding the phone into her back pocket, she fastened the locket shakily around her neck, making sure it dropped below her neckline. Then, resting pink Ephalump, as they'd christened him, on the desk, she used her foot to shove the stuck drawer back into place and then relocked the other drawers.

Checking everything looked as it should at first glance, her gaze snagged on something she hadn't previously noticed on the top of his in tray. Seeing the letter was from The DNA People, she snatched it up, quickly pulling the contents out.

It was a paternity test. The report included all sorts of indecipherable tables—Genetic System Table, Combined Paternity Index—and figures relating to "case number," "child, mother," "alleged father." Nausea almost choking her, Sophie hurriedly scanned it. She couldn't digest the information enough to understand it. It made no sense—until she reached the Paternity Test Conclusions, which clearly stated that "Paul Radley is excluded as the biological father."

Shaking, Sophie blinked at it, uncomprehending for a second, and then froze.

"Do you not understand basic instructions, Sophie?" Paul said, his face white with anger as he walked quietly through the study door and saw the letter in her hand.

CHAPTER SIXTY-SIX

JUSTIN

Justin had parked as close as he could to the apartment block he'd previously followed Radley to, and was now walking away from his car, his intention to have a quiet word with the piece of scum that walked around in the guise of a man. He thought of Alicia, his chest constricting as he pictured what she might have gone through, even without knowing the details. It still hurt that she had lied to him, but now he was pained because she'd felt she'd had to. That was on him, not her. He needed to put it right—or try to. To listen to her, if she wanted to talk. To be there, if she didn't. Assuming Radley didn't report him, that was. Justin had an idea he wouldn't, given the implications for himself. He wasn't quite sure how this would go yet, what he would do to him, though the temptation to give in to his anger was overwhelming—show the bastard what it was like to be raped with a very intrusive object and then castrate him and render him truly powerless.

Possibly not a good idea if he did want to be there for Alicia and find Sophie. But the threat might be sufficient. The knowledge that Justin could render him helpless any time he wanted to might give Radley an inkling of how he'd made Alicia feel. Had there been other women? Probably. It wouldn't be enough—not nearly enough—to quash the burning rage inside him, but Justin supposed it would have to do.

Hearing his phone ring, he checked the number. Not Alicia. Jessica. She'd already called once, leaving him a message: an attempt at an apology for misreading the signs. He'd rung her back and told her it wasn't a good idea to call him again, as reasonably as he could. And now here she was, doing just that. Sighing, Justin hesitated, and then thinking that it might actually have something to do with Alicia, he took the call.

"Justin, you need to do something. She's going to meet him," Jessica said immediately.

"What?" His stomach turning over, Justin stopped in his tracks.

"She's going to meet him," Jessica repeated frantically. "He said she should go alone. I don't know what to do. I've tried to convince her to let me go with her, to call you, but she won't. Justin, he has her."

Reeling on his feet, Justin told her to slow down. He couldn't keep up with her. Couldn't make sense of it. Couldn't breathe.

"Sophie!" Jessica cried. "Paul Radley has her! He has her passport, too. Alicia thinks he must have taken it from the house when he was there. You have to do something, Justin."

Sophie? Justin's heart careered to a stop in his chest—and then kicked back hard. "Where?" he asked, his emotions colliding, his adrenaline pumping, his mind focussing.

Breathe, he commanded himself, sucking air deep into his lungs. Ignoring the pain that seared through his chest.

"At his apartment—Central Plaza, 153b. Eight o'clock. He sent Alicia a photo of Sophie. It could only have been taken by him."

Justin's gut twisted violently. "What kind of photo?"

"Nothing explicit," Jessica said quickly, clearly understanding his meaning. "She was sleeping. He'd placed her passport next to her. He's obviously trying to tell Alicia that he'll take her away if she doesn't turn up. Oh God, Justin, I have no idea what to—"

"How do you know where he lives?" Justin demanded.

"I...don't. I saw it...on the text," Jessica stuttered. "The address, I—"

Right, and she'd just reeled it straight off. *Bullshit!* "How long have you been in contact with him, Jessica?" he asked her, barely controlling his temper. "How long have you been feeding information to the man who *raped* your sister?"

"I haven't!" Jessica denied vehemently. "I would never do that. I—"

"You're full of shit, do you know that, Jessica?"

"He's an old friend," Jessica said. "I could hardly lie to him if he asked me something outright."

Justin laughed, astounded that she was trying to justify what she'd done. "No, you couldn't lie to save your life, could you, Jess?"

"Justin, this isn't about me." Jessica tried a new tack. "What do you want me to do? Should I call the police?"

"I think you've done enough, Jessica," Justin pointed out contemptuously. "Stay out of it. As in, stay away from my family, full stop."

Attempting to regulate his breathing as he ended the call, Justin tried to think with the mind of an animal intent on its prey. Radley had dangled the bait: a photo of a lost daughter sent to her mother. *Bastard!* Justin clamped his jaw hard. Would he have Sophie with him, knowing there was even a chance Alicia might call the police? Possibly, but wasn't it more likely he would be holding her somewhere else? That he would want to get Alicia in that apartment alone?

That thought slicing through him like a knife, Justin made his decision. The police might do something; they might do nothing. Either way, they were unlikely to turn up here and arrest the bastard. They might ask Radley some questions, might even ask him to go to the station. Would he admit to having

Sophie though? To his perverse fucking intentions, which Justin had no doubt he had? Would he tell them where she was?

Not likely. At least not immediately.

And that, as far as Justin was concerned, was the critical factor. Assuming the police would even take any action, did Sophie have time on her side?

Justin checked his watch, calculating how long it might take Alicia to get here. It was the tail end of rush hour. Luck on his side, it might take her a while. He was already in situ. He needed to move. He needed to move now. Get to the bastard before Alicia arrived.

CHAPTER SIXTY-SEVEN

PAUL RADLEY

Listening to Rachmaninoff's Piano Concerto No. 2, which he preferred to the more popular third, Paul popped an olive into his mouth, rolling it around on his tongue and washing it down with a sip of cabernet sauvignon. He hadn't enjoyed what he'd just had to do to Sophie—it wasn't what he'd planned for her—but she'd left him with no choice.

He had been a touch disappointed with young Sophie, he had to admit. Their relationship had started so promisingly. He'd hoped she'd love him as readily as her mother had, but that didn't look like it would ever happen. Paul could see that now. He traced a drip of wine from the side of his glass with his finger, sucked it off and then scowled as he noticed another drop bleeding onto his natural wood worktop. Tugging a leaf from the kitchen roll, he moistened it at the tap and rubbed at the wine, and then, immensely irritated when he realised he would possibly have to have the surface stripped and resealed, banged his wine down, separating stem from glass, which made the situation ten times worse.

Temper, Paul, he cautioned himself. She would be here soon. Focussing on the calming music, he reached into his pocket, retrieving the lock of caramel-coloured hair he carried there, the smell of which—a woman's scent, with undertones of vanilla and innocence—he found soothed him.

Pressing it close to his face, he inhaled the sweet fragrance of her, and then glanced over at his ringing phone. Alicia. He'd guessed it might be. Paul breathed a deep sigh of satisfaction— and rejected the call. *Good things come to those who wait, my sweetest.*

He would bide his time. Soon she would be desperate enough to see him.

He'd been furious with her at first, but his anger had abated a little. He realised why she'd resisted his efforts to stay in touch, of course. She'd needed a father for her child, and who better than Justin Cole, who'd clearly been emotionally dependent on her, but also earned enough money to be someone she could depend on financially.

Yes, Paul could understand it, to a degree. It was clear she didn't want to hurt her husband now either; he was possibly still mentally unstable. That was admirable. A good quality in a woman. She shouldn't have deceived him though. He was Sophie's natural father. That was no way to treat a man she'd shared such intimacy with, was it?

CHAPTER SIXTY-EIGHT

JUSTIN

Taking another dose of fentanyl to take the edge off the nagging pain in his chest, Justin surveyed the apartment block from the opposite side of the road. He had no idea how he was going to get past the security guard. Ringing buzzers at random wasn't going to do it. The block was a new build, largely uninhabited. *Fuck.* Dragging his hand over his neck, he debated whether to try to bribe the guy. No. Too risky. He had no idea where this was going to end, but he definitely didn't want the man remembering he'd been here.

He'd considered the underground car park and had gone down there to take a look. He'd noticed there were two four-by-fours parked amongst a few other cars. Justin had tried not to let his mind go back to the day his son had been taken away, but it had anyway. Instantly transported back there, he'd felt the impact all over again, like a low blow to his stomach, and heard the cacophony of noise: horns blaring; people shouting; petrol spilling; sirens plaintively wailing.

Alicia. Screaming.

Sophie, her voice high-pitched, hysterical.

Luke…silent.

Not the car park, Justin had decided, his jaw tightening, his heart rate escalating, his mind refocussing. He had no chance of getting in without the security code.

Deciding his only real option was to go through the front entrance, he googled several local pizza parlours. Calling each of them, he ordered, prayed and waited. He needed to be in and out of there before Alicia turned up. He didn't want her involved in any of what he was about to do. And he would do whatever was necessary to get his daughter back. Once he'd established where she was, his inclination wasn't to leave the bastard capable of walking away.

Grabbing his overcoat from the boot, Justin fed his arms into it, pulled the collar high and then blew out a sigh of relief as two pizza delivery guys arrived in close succession, followed two minutes later by a third. It was now or never. There was no other way. He had no elaborate plan—he just needed to get to the lift, hopefully without providing a facial image on the CCTV. Pulling in a breath, he offered up another prayer as he sailed through the doors, the security guard being somewhat distracted.

"I've told you, there's no one here by any of those names." The guy splayed his arms in despair as he addressed the disgruntled deliverymen. "You must have the wrong building."

Shaking his head as one of the men insisted he hadn't, the guy sighed, picked up his phone, then cried, "Oh, for...!" He banged the phone down again as another pizza bearer appeared.

"Radley, fifteenth floor." Keeping his head down, Justin grabbed his chance, pointing his thumb towards the lift as he passed by behind them.

"Yeah, yeah." The guy waved Justin on, now looking considerably frustrated, as he picked up his phone again.

CHAPTER SIXTY-NINE

PAUL RADLEY

Paul was sizzling the bacon in preparation for his speciality—creamy courgette and bacon pasta—when his phone pinged. Setting the pan aside, he picked it up and checked the incoming text. It was from Alicia, as he'd expected.

How could she resist? His mouth curving into a smile, Paul went back to his culinary task. Patience was definitely a virtue, he decided. And he'd been very patient. Almost seventeen long years he'd been patient, living and working in a climate that didn't suit him. Not that that was Alicia's fault. Having sex with undesirable women rather than be unfaithful to her—that, he considered, was Alicia's fault. The last one had been particularly undesirable, making impossible demands on his time, imagining they were in a relationship. God forbid; the woman was a complete slut, leaving her underwear and feminine things—personal things no man would want to be aware of—all over the place.

He was back permanently now though. The wait would be worth it. Alicia would realise it. Now he was here in the flesh, she would recall—as he had every time he'd set eyes on her when he'd visited the UK; as he did frustratingly every night—how fulfilling their lovemaking had been.

Soon she would be here, where she should be: by his side, sharing the life they were meant to be living together, preparing meals together, experiencing the joys of making love to the soft strains of Rachmaninoff or Wagner in the background. She would be a good wife to him, keeping his house clean and lovingly pressing his shirts while he worked to put food on their table. Paul paused to ponder where they might live. In the country, possibly? A little cottage in Wales, perhaps—somewhere remote and cosy.

"Pass the wine, darling. I've let it breathe." He smiled tenderly at the image of her he frequently conjured up to keep him company in the kitchen. An image so tangible sometimes, he could see the tiny fleck in her mesmerising cornflower-blue eyes: a small imperfection, which he'd graciously overlooked.

"To us," he said, raising his glass in a toast and then taking a large glug of his wine, before turning to the preparation of the rest of his ingredients. He did hope she wasn't as faddish as young Sophie with her food. He knitted his brow as it occurred to him they hadn't had time to appreciate the delights of fine cuisine together.

Ah well, she'd just have to learn, wouldn't she? She'd soon realise how things worked. Nodding to himself, Paul chopped at the garlic with vigour. He really couldn't abide faddishness of any sort.

CHAPTER SEVENTY

JUSTIN

His mouth dry, sweat tickling his forehead, Justin willed the lift to arrive. Sighing with relief when it did, he stepped in and kept his head down until the doors slid closed. Hitting the button for the right level, he wondered what the hell he was going to do next. Radley was hardly likely to open the door if he knew it was him.

Steeling himself as the lift doors swished open, Justin scanned the corridor. Empty. So what now? Pose as a workman? The building was still being worked on. A power supply employee? None of the above, he decided. Without a high-visibility jacket, which he might have thought of if he'd had more time to prepare, he wasn't likely to pull that off. A buildings' inspector?

Would Radley have a security camera or just a basic intercom system? Justin had no idea. If it was the latter, then his plan might work. All he needed was to get Radley to open the door enough to ask for ID. That would be enough. It had to work. Justin hadn't known who his assailant was that night outside the pub. He'd assumed, when it had been established his wallet was intact, that it had been some kind of revenge attack by the aggressive bastard who'd been abusing his girlfriend. But the possibility that it was Radley had crossed his mind. Didn't he have every reason to seek revenge after his attack on him? Justin hadn't thought him capable of it then. Now, though, after learning the animal was a rapist, someone who used blackmail to wield his power over the woman he'd raped, a piece of scum who would lure or kidnap her daughter to coerce her further, he believed him to be capable of anything. The man obviously had money enough to hire people to do his dirty work for him, if he was too cowardly to carry it out himself.

If the attack had been something to do with Radley, then Justin would have the element of surprise. He should still be in the hospital. But he wasn't. He was here. Assuming Radley, who'd clearly been stalking Alicia, had continued to monitor her, thereby establishing they'd apparently split up, this was the last place he'd expect him to be. And if he didn't have that element of surprise and couldn't gain access through the open door, then he would just have to kick the fucking thing down.

Hitting the buzzer, Justin braced himself and waited.

CHAPTER SEVENTY-ONE

PAUL RADLEY

Alicia had arrived—a little bit late, but Paul would overlook that on the basis she'd had the good manners to text him and alert him to the fact that she would be. Clearly, their daughter had picked up her sloppy manners from her husband. Collecting up his homemade olive dressing, Paul placed it on the dining table alongside his Italian-inspired salad, and then, pleased with the table arrangement, went to greet his long-anticipated visitor.

"Darling," he said, his warmest smile in place as he reached to open the door, "I—"

"You *bastard*!" someone rasped furiously on the other side of it.

Sprawling backwards as the door was shoved violently into his face, Paul didn't stop to wonder what had just hit him. He rolled over, attempting to scramble away from the terrifying intruder advancing towards him.

Gulping hard, his bladder almost failing him, he pulled himself up onto all fours and then to his feet, almost losing his footing as he glanced frantically around for means of escape. He quickly realised his only exit was through the front door, but he stumbled away from there, where some madman, probably armed with a knife, was advancing towards him.

Paul felt sweat saturate his armpits as he imagined what

despicable crime this thug might be intent on, and then physically sick as he caught up with him at the patio window.

"Take anything you want," he spluttered, spittle wetting his cheek as the side of his face was rammed forcefully against the glass. "Anything," he gasped desperately. "I won't try to stop you, just . . . *please* don't hurt me."

The person behind him, clearly some lowlife, thieving thug of the worst kind, said nothing.

"I have money," Paul tried. "In my wallet. There's at least two hundred in cash. My credit cards are there, too. I'll give you the PIN—"

Fuck! He trailed painfully off as his face was forced harder against the glass. He was going to smash his cheekbone, deform him for life, the mad son of a bitch.

"What do you want?" he said weakly, when his attacker didn't answer. "If it's electrical goods, I have phones and—*Aaargh!* Don't, you're hurting me!" he screamed, finding his arm pulled back and jerked high up behind his back. "For God's sake, just tell me what you want!"

The man moved closer, his face right up next to his. "My daughter," he growled, close to his ear. "Where is she, you fucker?"

Shit! "I don't know!" Paul gurgled, as Justin Cole clutched a handful of his shirt, tightening it at his throat and yanking him back. "I have no idea!"

Cole didn't answer. Hanging on to him so tight he almost choked him, he reached for the locking mechanism on the doors instead. "You might want to have a rethink," he suggested, pushing him bodily out onto the balcony.

Oh God, no. Realising he was facing his worst fear, Paul struggled to turn away from the fifteen-floor drop, at the bottom of which was nothing but bone-crushing concrete. But Cole was on him, pressing his arm hard across his shoulders, pushing him towards certain death.

"Where is she?" he repeated, his tone now menacingly quiet.

God, please help me. He couldn't tell him. How could he? The mad bastard *would* bloody well kill him. "I don't know," he whimpered, blinking hard as the ground loomed up towards him. "I swear to God I don't."

He heard Cole draw in a ragged breath. Paul had no idea how he was breathing at all. Gulping hard, he waited. He wouldn't do it. He wouldn't stand a chance of getting away with it. And then getting out of the building unnoticed, if he did. Would he?

After a second, Cole relaxed, just fractionally, the arm he had locked across his back, to Paul's huge relief. He hadn't thought he would. He was bluffing. And Paul had called his bluff.

"So now what are you going to do?" he asked him, his voice shaky, despite his attempt at bravado. "Electrodes? Pull my fingernails—"

He stopped, emitting something between a squeak and a scream as Cole's arm snaked its way around his throat.

"*Shhh,*" he whispered, pressing a cold syringe to the side of his neck. "You wouldn't want to attract any attention, would you, Radley? Because if you do, I may be forced to drop you after all, and that really would be very messy."

Paul's eyes bulged as the man tightened his hold.

"Do you believe in karma, Radley?" he asked him, talking almost companionably, to Paul's disbelief. "You should." He squeezed still tighter. "Because I'm going to hurt you. I'm going to do to you *exactly* what you did to my wife. I imagine you have one or two kitchen implements that might serve my purpose. Or something from the bathroom, maybe? It will hurt, but then pain turns you on, doesn't it, you sick, sad bastard."

He let it hang, leaving Paul with a graphic image and his insides turning to liquid jelly.

"If I find you've hurt my daughter, in any way," Cole growled, "the pain is going to be so, *so* much worse. Last time, you fucker, where *is* she?"

"I don't know," Paul cried. "I swear—" He stopped, terror gripping him as Cole pressed the syringe closer. "Don't," he rasped, clamping his eyes shut.

Cole didn't answer, breathing slowly and heavily instead, like some lunatic psychopath.

He was insane, Paul realised, knowing with certainty that if he did tell him, the chances of the madman not doing him permanent damage were nil. "What are you going to inject me with?" he croaked, perspiration popping out on his forehead.

"Just ketamine, Paul," Cole said matter-of-factly. "Nothing harmful. Just enough to render you incapable. You know, unable to speak, move or control your own body? *Powerless*, Paul. As in, unable to fight back. I take it you're getting my drift here?"

"Please, don't..." Paul's voice came out a hoarse whisper.

Cole, though, just tightened his grip.

CHAPTER SEVENTY-TWO

ALICIA

Waiting in the foyer for the security guard to ring up and announce her arrival, Alicia felt every hair on her body rise with repulsion. She was nauseated at even the thought of being near him, the look of calculated triumph she would see in his eyes, the cloying, too spicy, alcohol-soaked smell of him. A cold knot of fear gripped her stomach, twisting her insides so tight she couldn't breathe, as she imagined what he might have done to her daughter. That's what was forcing her to stand there on legs she thought might fail her. That's what was compelling her to go up to his apartment, to beg him, plead with him, do whatever she had to do to get him to let her go.

"He's still not answering," the man said, having tried him for a second time.

"Did you see him go out?" Alicia asked, feeling more desperate by the second. Was he playing some sick, twisted control game, she wondered, her fear for Sophie intensifying as she realised that was very probably what he was doing: teaching her a lesson for being sloppily unpunctual. Like a child amusing himself by pulling legs from a spider one by one, until it had no ability to run, he'd played games with her from day one. How had he enticed Sophie? What sordid game might he have lured her into? Had she gone willingly?

The security guard frowned uncertainly. "Come to think of it, no. Mind you, there was a right kerfuffle here earlier. Umpteen bloody pizza delivery men trying to deliver pizzas to non-existent residents." He sighed despairingly. "Hold on a sec. I'll see if his car's still in the car park."

He turned to his monitors. "Useless twits," he muttered. "Call themselves security systems experts. If the circuit breakers don't need replacing, there's a bloody power outage. Could have done a better job myself." Finally, he banged one of the blank monitors, which flickered uncooperatively and then sparked into life, giving a visual of the car park. "Yup." The man squinted at it, apparently identifying Paul Radley's car. "His car's definitely here, at least."

Staring at the monitor behind him, Alicia's heart froze. Realisation hitting her with the full force of the impact that had occurred on the darkest day of her life, she gripped the reception desk hard. "I didn't know he had a new car." She forced the words out lightly.

The security guard glanced back at her. "That's his usual car. He's been driving a rental while it's been in the workshop. Prefers his Discovery though, he said. Personally, I prefer the Range Rover Evoque. Production's slowing off a bit now though, apparently, to make way for the new model." He twirled back towards her, obviously on a roll on the subject of cars. "It's a shame. I reckon the Evoque's more reliable. Mine's never been in the workshop yet. Then again, you won't catch me driving like a madman. Treat your car with a bit of respect and she'll run as sweet as a nut, that's what I told him."

"He does tend to hare around, doesn't he?" Alicia's smile was too bright, her voice tight. "He's a bit of a stickler for punctuality."

"Better to arrive safe than not to arrive at all, that's my motto." The security guard sighed piously.

"A man after my own heart." Alicia nodded in agreement and

tried to keep breathing. "He's probably in the shower," she said, desperate now to get past him. "He takes ages in the bathroom. Fastidiousness is in his nature, I'm afraid."

"Tell me about it. He had a go at me for there being dust on the reception desk the other morning, like there wouldn't be, with builders all over the place. I mean, do I look like the cleaner? I wonder why I stick this job sometimes, honestly."

"That sounds like Paul." Alicia laughed. "Sorry about that. I'm trying to train him out of it. Do you mind if I go on up?"

Narrowing his eyes, the man looked her over. "Go on then," he said, his face creasing into a smile as he nodded her towards the lift. "Good luck with that training."

"Thanks." Alicia waved behind her as she walked away. Then she fixed her gaze forwards, hatred for Paul Radley coursing through every vein in her body as she headed determinedly for the fifteenth floor.

CHAPTER SEVENTY-THREE

JUSTIN

"Don't!" Radley pleaded, as Justin allowed the sharp point of the needle to pierce his flesh. "Please. Stop. I'm begging you. You'll kill me."

Not yet, you bastard. That would be way too merciful. "When you've told me what you need to, Radley, then I'll consider it," Justin said tightly. "Possibly."

"Oh, sweet fucking Jesus." Radley squeezed his eyes shut. "You really are mad."

"As a hatter," Justin assured him. "The opiates I've been taking after someone attempted to have me knifed to death won't help my state of mind, of course. They tend to affect my concentration, I find. It's probably best not to struggle while I'm holding a syringe next to your jugular."

"I don't know where she is!" Radley repeated the same bullshit he'd already spouted. "How can I tell you something I don't know?"

"Wrong answer, you piece of shit. I'm running out of patience. And you're about to run out of time."

"For God's sake!" Radley screamed, as Justin tensed his thumb against the plunger. "Wait!"

Breathing in hard, Justin paused. He guessed from the gulp sliding tellingly down Radley's throat that he was considering his options, imagining his brains spilling out on the concrete below, and realising he hadn't fucking well got any options.

"There are some keys," he blurted, "in my jacket pocket, hanging on the dining chair."

"Keys to where?" Justin tightened his hold around his throat.

Radley gagged hard. "Her bedroom," he rasped, his hands seeking to release Justin's hold on him. "The door on the right, in the hall. That's where she is."

She was in the apartment? Silent? *Subdued?* Justin could feel sweat tickling his eyelashes, prickling his spine. It took every ounce of his willpower not to plunge the syringe deep into the bastard's temple.

"I just wanted to talk to Alicia. I know she loves me. She had my *child*. She wanted to be with *me*."

Justin's jaw clenched, a new image assaulting him: Alicia, with this *thing*, who had no respect whatsoever for women. Being touched by him. Raped by him.

"*My* child. *My* wife." A small tic tugged at his cheek. His hand shaking badly, he pressed the syringe home.

Calmly, Justin counted, forcing himself to wait the one to five minutes it would take for onset of symptoms. Once, he would have been shocked by the realisation he was an inch away from killing someone. They were fifteen long floors up. His skull would smash like an eggshell. He'd imagined, in his darkest hours, when dreams of his wife in the arms of another man had come to haunt him, how lost love could drive someone to acts of despair or even madness. How cold-blooded murder might have its basis in love, or unrequited love. In being unloved, spurned or wronged.

This man, gagging on his Adam's apple, a man who'd begged for his life, had wronged him. He'd wronged his family. His children. He had to pay. Left to the law, he wouldn't. He *wouldn't*. There was no other way.

But what about Alicia? Sophie? Would they ever be able to live with the fact that he was a cold-blooded murderer?

Sucking in a breath, he allowed Radley to slide to the ground and then banged the terrace doors closed and raced for the keys.

Heading for the bedroom, he was in the hall when his gaze snagged on something he recognised. Stunned, Justin walked towards it and picked it up from where it sat on an occasional table against the wall: Luke's pink elephant soft toy. Two images immediately emblazoned themselves across his mind: Sophie sitting on her bed after they'd lost Luke, the toy clutched tight to her, her eyes those of a frightened child; and Luke chuckling delightedly, his little arms flailing, as his big sister bobbed the toy in front of him.

Bastard! Justin clenched his jaw hard.

His limbs heavy, his heartbeat sluggish, he located the locked bedroom. Faltering for a split second, his hand shaking, he pushed the key into the lock and pressed down the door handle.

Seeing the light was off, he opened the door slowly and stepped tentatively inside. "Sophie?" he said, only half daring to hope she would answer. That she would be capable of answering.

His eyes adjusting to the light, he saw a movement—a shape stirring on the silhouette of the bed.

"Dad?" she said weakly.

And Justin's heart damn near exploded inside him. "I'm here, Pumpkin," he said, his voice cracking. "Close your eyes, sweetheart. I'm going to turn on the light."

Oh Christ, no. Justin felt the walls slam into him as he looked at his baby girl, her long sable hair hanging over the hands she had clamped to her face. She was trembling, shaking all over.

"He's here!" Sophie screamed suddenly, stopping him in his tracks. "He's here!" She prised her eyes open and then squeezed them tight shut.

"No, Sophie, he's not!" His gut churning, Justin spoke forcefully but calmly. "It's me. Just me, Pumpkin."

"I can smell him! Garlic," she cried, tears streaming down her cheeks. "Garlic and lemons."

"It's all right, Sophie. I've got you." Justin moved fast. With one arm supporting her as he sat beside her, he eased her towards him. "I've got you," he said throatily, pulling her gently into his arms.

"I tried not to fall asleep. I tried really hard, but…the vitamins… they were floating. He didn't like it. The study," she mumbled, her speech slurred, her eyes wide as she looked up at him. Unfocussed, Justin noted immediately, the pupils constricted.

"I've got you," he said again, hot tears of frustration and anger wetting his own cheeks. "Breathe for me, Pumpkin," he urged her. "Big breaths in, long breaths out. Can you do that for me?"

It was the item hanging around her neck that caused his gut to turn over: a yellow gold locket, enhanced with a white gold floral motif.

Justin breathed with his baby girl, tightened his hold around her. It was obvious. Blindingly obvious. He closed his eyes against the image that would be ingrained forever on his brain: *SORRY FOR YOUR LOSS*, scrawled in red lipstick on the mirror. He'd known it. Deep down in his gut, he'd known it.

"The study," Sophie said again. "The photos. We have to get them. You have to see."

"Later, Sophie," Justin tried to soothe her. He needed to get her to the hospital, flush out whatever drugs she'd ingested. "We'll get them—"

"No! Now." Sophie attempted to pull away from him. "You need to see. We need to—"

"Whoa." Justin stopped her as she tried to climb off the bed. "Wait," he said, standing carefully, easing her back down, making sure she stayed sitting. "I'll get them. Promise me you won't move."

Sophie nodded firmly. "The door at the end of the hall," she said. "Desk drawer. Top and second."

Justin moved fast, cursing as he reached the study door and tried a key that didn't fit. Finally finding the key that did, he thrust the door open and went to the desk. More *fucking* keys. Justin searched for the right one. His gut clenched as he glanced at the contents of the envelope he extracted from the top drawer, but he wasn't surprised. Radley's reality was skewed. He was a sick individual who hadn't been about to let the proof that Sophie wasn't his daughter change his plans. He wasn't surprised at the contents of the larger envelope he found there either—nauseous, but not surprised. Their family photographs. Stolen. Desecrated.

The photographs in the second did nothing to quell the rage burning like a fire inside him. Radley had watched her, stalked her. The torture he'd put Alicia through fuelling his twisted fantasy, he'd waited like a viper until they'd been weak, and then chosen his moment to strike.

Sophie was right: they needed these. It was all evidence should he be arrested, which Justin had no doubt he would be. Stuffing the photographs furiously into the envelope, he headed swiftly back to Sophie. She wasn't sitting on the bed. Strong-willed as ever, she was on her feet, weaving as she walked to the door.

Justin caught hold of her, easing her again towards him, holding her steady.

"You're my dad. You know you're my dad, right?" Sophie looked uncertainly at him.

"I do." Justin nodded firmly. "Just so you know though, I didn't need the piece of paper. Whatever the biology, I've loved you from birth, Sophie. And I always will. Nothing can change that."

Relief flooding her features, Sophie leaned into him. "Can we go home now?" she whispered into his shoulder.

"We can go home now, baby," he promised hoarsely, holding her trembling body a second longer before passing her the envelope and then lifting his beautiful daughter into his arms.

CHAPTER SEVENTY-FOUR

JUSTIN

The blue lights sweeping the road outside told Justin the police had arrived. He didn't stop to ponder who had called them and why. His focus was all on Sophie—his aim to get her to his car and straight to the hospital. No one was going to stand in his way. No one!

Pulling her protectively closer in his arms, he shot a warning glance at an officer approaching him, who stopped uncertainly a yard off.

"Get an ambulance here, *now*!" someone yelled. *Taylor*. Justin kept going towards his car. Even as Taylor's car careered to a stop alongside him, he was determined to keep going.

"Justin!" Taylor called. "Climb in."

Justin didn't pause.

"For God's sake, man, climb in!" Taylor yelled. "We'll get to the hospital a lot quicker with blue lights."

Justin stopped. His breath short, his chest thudding, he watched Taylor spill out, yanking the back door open and gesturing him inside. Nodding shortly, Justin made up his mind, turning towards the car to ease Sophie carefully into it and then climb in beside her.

Taylor threw himself into the front passenger seat, slamming the door closed behind him. "Go!" He turned to the driver and then twisted to face Justin. "Is she all right?" he asked, glancing at Sophie as Justin slid across, wrapping an arm around her as she burrowed again into his shoulder.

No, she's very much not all right. He looked down at her. "She will be. We'll all be, hey, Pumpkin? Together."

A slight nod told him Sophie was hearing him. She understood his meaning. He was her father. He would always be there for her.

Radley. His mind went to him, briefly. Should he just leave him? If the police presence here was anything to do with him, wouldn't they already be up there, rather than here? Justin shut it down. *Not now.* He needed to focus on his family. "Alicia," he said gruffly. "I need to call her."

Guessing he couldn't access his phone in his pocket, Taylor nodded, twisted back around and pulled out his own mobile. "Number?" he asked him, keying it in as Justin reeled it off. "Alicia?" he said a second later. "I have Justin with me. He has Sophie."

Turning back, he handed the phone to Justin.

"Sophie?" Alicia asked, incredulous, her voice choked, as if she was squeezing the word out through all the pain she'd been holding in.

"She's here," Justin assured her. "She's—"

Hearing the wretched sob that escaped her, he stopped and waited. "She's all right, Alicia," he said softly, after a second. "She's right here."

Sophie eased her head up as he spoke. "Mum?" she asked, her beautiful chestnut eyes, dulled by drugs, seeming, at last, to focus.

Justin nodded. "Hold on," he said. "Alicia, she wants to speak to you."

Cradling Sophie, he held the phone gently to her ear.

"Mum?" Sophie said, and caught her breath. "Mum? I'm sorry. I'm so sorry. I didn't get it. I still don't get all of it, but—"

"Hey, hey." Justin squeezed her closer as she, too, broke off with a sob. "No apologies, Pumpkin. They're not necessary. We'll get through this. I promise you we will."

Pressing the phone back to his own ear, he spoke to Alicia. "We're on our way to the hospital," he said. "Just to check Sophie over," he added quickly. "She's okay, I promise. I'll meet you there."

"Okay," Alicia managed emotionally. "How?" she asked. "How did you know where she was?"

Justin hesitated, his gaze flicking towards Taylor. "Jessica gave me his address. I went there to talk to him," he said, hoping it sounded feasible to Taylor. Whatever happened, he wanted to keep Alicia, and the fact that she was supposed to be seeing Radley, as far out of this as possible.

Taylor held his gaze for a long, hard minute, the look in his eyes dubious at best. "Strange coincidence, that," he said. "We were just about to pay a visit to Mr. Radley's apartment too. We had a 999 call from this geographical location. Cut short, unfortunately," he went on, as Justin eyed him questioningly.

"Me," Sophie said. "That was me."

"Ah." Taylor nodded and smiled—for Sophie's benefit, Justin guessed. "Well, that clears up the mystery. Don't worry, Sophie, we can have a chat later, when you're feeling better. We'll be having words with Mr. Radley in the meantime. I have officers on their way there now."

Shit! Justin squeezed his arm around Sophie a fraction tighter.

CHAPTER SEVENTY-FIVE

SOPHIE

Finally at home—her real home—Sophie sat on her bed, not quite able to believe she was here. Everything was exactly as it was when she'd left. Normal. The bedroom, which her mum and dad had decorated, knowing who she was, was *hers*. She was an individual, with a mind of her own. The only thing out of place was her notebook. She couldn't remember where she'd left that. In her drawer, she'd thought, but certainly not neatly placed on the dressing table. Her dad had done that. Not her mum. Her mum rarely touched her things. She'd once said she'd hate her to think she'd been snooping. Though she doubted her dad had been snooping. More likely it had been pulled out by that freak when he'd come in here, touching her things.

An involuntary shudder running through her, Sophie pulled her knees up to her chest, closed her eyes and rested her head. And then she snapped her eyes open as her mind conjured up an image of him, the look in his eyes changing from fondness to fury like the flick of a switch.

Sliding off the bed, she walked across to her mirror, her arms wrapped about herself as she examined her reflection. She couldn't believe how stupid she'd been. How utterly naive. How badly she'd misjudged people. She hadn't listened to her mum or her dad, just made assumptions and then charged off to nurse her own wounds. She'd listened to Paul Radley instead, been impressed by him, completely taken in by him. She wasn't sure she could ever trust herself again. She'd acted like a moody, selfish brat. And there she'd been yelling at her mum and dad because she'd wanted to be treated like an adult.

"Knock, knock," her mum said behind her, tapping on the open door. "Penny for them?" she asked, coming to place an arm around her shoulders.

"Just thinking." Sophie shrugged.

Her mum eyed her warily. "About?"

Sophie hesitated, and then decided that maybe getting through this together meant being truthful with each other whatever. "That maybe I'm not as mature as I thought I was."

Her mum moved around her. "We go through life growing up, Sophie, trust me. Learning from our mistakes. And we all make them. My gran used to say something, I don't think I really got it until I'd suffered true loss, but when I was young, crying over something or other, she used to say, 'Beautiful things make life worth living. Pain and sorrow turns to wisdom in time.' I think she was right. If you're beating yourself up because you're imagining any of what happened is your fault, then don't. You have nothing to reproach yourself for." She locked her eyes firmly on hers. "You're fine just the way you are: individual, quirky, caring and beautiful. You make my life worth living. Okay?"

Sophie's mouth twitched into a smile. "You forgot the super-intelligent and hugely talented bit."

"And that." Smiling back, her mum took hold of her shoulders. "You're okay, Sophie. A normal, well-balanced teenager."

"Apart from the odd moody moment," Sophie pointed out.

"Um, well, there are those." Her mum furrowed her brow and then laughed. "They're normal, Sophie. Allowed. It's called being human. Trust me, you're an extremely loving and much-loved person," she said forcefully. "I've loved you from the second I felt you growing inside me. I love everything that you are.

And what you are is good, through and through. No one can take that away from you. The only thing people can rob you of, if you let them, is your confidence. Don't let him do that, Sophie."

Sophie nodded, but dropped her gaze. She was trying, but she just didn't feel confident any more. Her mum had done it though. Somehow, she'd managed to find the strength to move on with her life, despite what had happened to her at the freak's hands. She hadn't been honest with Justin, something she clearly bitterly regretted, but she'd always been there for him. For her, too. Maybe her great-gran's saying was right. Her mum had learned from her mistakes. Sophie would do the same. She would certainly be wiser in the future and value those people who really did love her.

"Did he mention your surprise?" her mum asked her.

Sophie looked back up at her curiously.

"Your dad, did he tell you about your surprise sixteenth birthday present?"

Sophie's smile widened. "No," she said, betting it was something really cool. Her dad always got her cool stuff: her Red or Dead boots; the puffer jacket he'd seen her drooling over in Miss Selfridge. Her heart dipped again, though, when she remembered the luxurious things Paul Radley had tried to tempt her with, which she'd actually thought were cool.

"Well?" she asked, as her mum eyed her teasingly.

"Sorry." Her mum held up her hands. "I can't say. Your dad will kill me if I tell you before he does."

"Yeah, right." Sophie rolled her eyes. "I very much doubt that. Dad wouldn't hurt a fly. That's why he's a doctor."

Her mum glanced down. "No," she said, smiling sadly now. "No, he wouldn't."

Noticing a tear plop down her cheek, Sophie looked at her, startled. "Mum," she said, pulling her into a hug, "I thought we weren't supposed to be letting him win."

"We're not." Alicia squeezed her hard back. "They're tears of relief, that's all. That you're here. *God*, I've missed you. Come on," she said, easing away and running the back of her hand under her nose. "Let's go and find your father. He can give you the guided tour."

"Tour?" Sophie's mind boggled. "What's he got me, Buckingham Palace?"

Following her mum to the door, Sophie quashed another bout of guilt as she realised how upset they both must have been on her sixteenth. They'd always pulled out all the stops on her birthday—having her friends over, buying a cake. Her mum had even made one once. It had taken her hours. She was rubbish in the kitchen, she'd always said, making no excuses for what she called her deficient domestic goddess gene. Sophie's thoughts swung again to Paul Radley. She'd had no friends while she'd been stuck in that apartment, not realising she was actually stuck in it. No phone. No contact with anyone. She doubted whether he would ever have let any of her friends in it, so OCD was he. Whatever happened to him, after what he'd done to her mum and dad, he deserved it, she decided.

"It's not quite Buckingham Palace," Justin said, looking rueful as they met him on the landing. Obviously, he'd overheard. Sophie felt bad about that too. She hoped he wasn't thinking she rated material stuff over what really mattered. Because she didn't, and now she never would. She'd make sure to tell him that. "A bit smaller," he added, allowing them to pass.

"A shoebox?" *Preferably containing new Red or Dead boots.* Sophie glanced hopefully over her shoulder, noticing Justin's hand going to the small of her mum's back, which she'd managed to strain somehow.

"Any better?" he asked her.

"A bit." Alicia replied. "Still painful though."

"Bend at the knee next time," Justin advised, as they followed Sophie down the stairs. "So, when did you do it exactly?"

"I'm not sure," Alicia said vaguely, stopping at the basement door.

"What? You can't remember when you shifted the furniture?" Justin sounded dubious.

"Not exactly, no. Not to worry." She waved away his concerns. "I'm sure it will be fine once I've rested it."

Noticing they were both loitering at the basement door now, Sophie back-stepped. "A tiger?" she said, looking bemusedly at them. "Must be, if you're keeping it chained up in the basement."

"Try again." Alicia smiled, swinging the door open.

"My very own vat of vintage wine?" Sophie peeked down after her as her mum led the way.

"In your dreams," Alicia called back. "Well, come on then. Your dad will be having a nervous breakdown wondering whether you like it."

CHAPTER SEVENTY-SIX

ALICIA

"You have to be kidding me." Standing in the middle of the studio, Sophie's eyes grew so wide, Alicia was sure they would pop right out of her head. "You mean you did all this yourself?" She turned in disbelief to Justin. "The man who puts his foot in paint trays?"

Justin ran a hand over his neck. "Yes, thanks for that reminder, Sophie," he said, smiling embarrassedly.

"He's been working on his DIY skills," said Alicia. She stepped towards her husband, sliding a hand around his waist.

"Obviously." Sophie glanced around, clearly awestruck, though Justin didn't seem entirely confident she was impressed.

"So, do you like it?" he asked her tentatively.

"Like it?" Sophie's eyes boggled wider. "It's like, wow!"

"I take it that's a yes?"

"Yes!" Sophie said effusively, launching herself at Justin. "It's totally cool. I *love* it," she assured him, almost strangling him as she threw her arms around his neck, and then promptly took off, inspecting the various bits of equipment Justin had installed: microphones and stands, recording software, headphones . . . Alicia didn't have a clue what half of it was.

"You got me a Macbook Pro." Sophie turned to him, her eyes filling up. "And a digital audio workstation." She trailed a hand over it. "It must have cost a bomb."

"I'm selling my body to pay for it." Justin shrugged, definitely looking pleased.

God, she loved this man. He'd never given up hope, not once. Whatever the future held, Alicia knew with certainty she would have had no future without him. He'd never been selfish or controlling. In his lovemaking, in every aspect of his life, he was generous—a giver, not a taker. She would always be grateful for every precious day she had with him.

"Is it okay, the DAW?" he asked her.

"Perfect," Sophie beamed. "I can't wait to show Chloe."

"What about the monitors? I was shopping in the dark a bit."

"The man done good," Sophie assured him. "You even got an audio interface. It's phenomenal."

"I'll go and get the cake. Don't worry—it's not homemade." Alicia smiled, leaving them to the technical jargon.

CHAPTER SEVENTY-SEVEN

ALICIA

Candles blown out and wishes made—hers perhaps an impossible wish—they'd decided on a family afternoon as a treat for Sophie's postponed birthday. It was the first workday they'd all been home together that wasn't tinged with unbearable sadness, and being with each other seemed fitting. Clearing up in the kitchen, Alicia went to join Justin and Sophie in the lounge, but stopped short of the door, wanting to simply listen to father and daughter talking, as they used to.

"So what do you fancy?" Justin asked Sophie, picking up the TV remote. "A film, *Homeland* or a rerun of *Game of Thrones*?"

"Not fussed," Sophie said. "You choose."

"A film," Justin decided, flicking to Netflix. "Something cheerful, hopefully, that your mum will fancy too."

"Okay?" Alicia heard him ask softly a second later, as he browsed.

"Better," Sophie answered, her voice sounding so young, so vulnerable, it almost wrenched Alicia's heart from inside her.

Paul Radley had tried to steal her daughter's identity. She'd suffered at his hands, because of her own mother. Alicia had been trying to keep their family together, yet she'd almost torn them apart. She'd worried that Justin and Sophie might never be able to forgive her, but she'd underestimated them both. What Sophie needed to do now was what her mother had felt unable to: talk about what had happened, not allow it to fester inside her, asking herself "what-ifs." *What if I hadn't...? What if I'd done this differently? Or that?* From that came self-doubt. That was the negative emotion that ultimately destroyed people, stifled them and robbed them of all they could be. If anyone could help Sophie get past that, realise she wasn't responsible for other people's actions, it was Justin, who'd loved her unquestioningly. Who always would. Alicia had made a mistake all those years ago in not telling him, yet she'd made at least one good decision in her life, of that Alicia was sure. There was no father more loving than Justin. He would always be there for his daughter.

"Dad...I'm sorry," Sophie said hesitantly, "about taking off like that at the shopping centre. About being so angry with you. I think I was a bit screwed up. After Luke, I mean. And then, when I heard...what you said...and realised..."

"You and me both," Justin assured her, as she trailed off. "We all say stuff, Sophie—heat-of-the-moment stuff, when we're hurting or angry, which doesn't reflect what we really feel inside. I think the best thing we can do now is move forward, don't you?" he asked her tentatively. "Be there for each other?"

Sophie paused. "Just so you know, though, I never stopped thinking about you as my dad, no matter what I tried to tell myself. Not in my heart."

"Looks like you're stuck with me," Justin joked. "So...are you going to eat the rest of that cake, or am I going to have to help out?"

"Ditto. For your sins," Sophie answered, her tone sounding less uncertain and more like herself. Alicia felt hope rise inside her that she wouldn't be too affected by the monster who'd tried to control her. "And, no you can't have my cake," she added. "It's, like, chocolate."

"More than I dare do to go near that then." Justin chuckled.

"Do you still love Mum?" Sophie asked, just as Alicia was about to go in.

Alicia stepped back, fearing his next words might truly kill her.

"I never stopped loving her, Sophie," Justin said, after a second that seemed to last an eternity. "Why would I have?"

"Can you forgive her for what she did?" was Sophie's next question. "For not telling you about me, I mean?"

Again, Justin hesitated. "I wish she had told me," he said eventually. "I wish she'd felt able to." He paused, drawing in a breath. "I think she did what she did with the best intentions though. It's not easy to accept, if I'm honest—not easy to accept my own culpability in why she felt she couldn't—but yes, I think I can. Can you?"

"Uh-huh," Sophie said thoughtfully, after a second. "Her decision-making was a bit shit, but I do think she made the choices she did for the right reasons."

Sophie would heal. In time she would be whole again. And if she faltered in the future, Justin would always be there to catch her. Alicia swallowed back a different kind of lump in her throat.

"I've brought you an extra slice," she said, going on in. "I think we deserve to indulge—" She stopped as Justin's phone rang, an uneasy feeling of trepidation washing over her.

Placing his cake on the coffee table, she sat down next to where Sophie was parked on her favourite spot on the sofa.

Glancing worriedly at her, Justin got to his feet, nodding towards the hall to indicate he would take the call there.

"You forgot a crumb." Alicia smiled at Sophie, who was dabbing up the last of the cream from her plate with her finger.

Justin came back into the lounge a minute later, his face pale, Alicia noted—worryingly pale. "DI Taylor." He smiled, for Sophie's sake. "He wants to have a chat."

Alicia nodded slowly. "When?" she asked him, trying to remain calm, though her stomach knotted inside her.

Justin kneaded his forehead. "He's on his way."

CHAPTER SEVENTY-EIGHT

ALICIA

Justin had been like a cat on hot bricks. He was trying to keep his emotions under control, for Sophie's sake, but he was pacing endlessly, breathing slowly, trying to stay calm. He was concerned, as he obviously would be, that DI Taylor's visit was to do with what had happened to Paul Radley.

"Are you warm enough, sweetheart?" Alicia asked Sophie, who'd gone quiet, also anticipating DI Taylor's visit with apprehension, for her own reasons. Alicia knew she would be struggling with her own confused emotions—guilt being one of them. She just hoped Sophie would be able to talk more about how she was feeling as time went on, that she would realise she—and Justin, in particular—understood.

Sitting in the middle of the sofa, her legs tucked under herself and a faraway look in her eyes, Alicia guessed Sophie was going over things now, the chain of events since the day her dear baby brother had died, as they all would for a long time to come. Alicia made a mental note to try to encourage her to put the bad memories behind her and cherish the good ones, the time she did have with Lucas, as Alicia and Justin would try to alongside her.

She would never truly be able to forgive herself for her naivety in imagining the whole mess would go away the day Paul Radley had. That he wouldn't come back to haunt her. She'd never dreamed it would be her daughter he would haunt. If she had...

But it was too late for that now. She would die to undo it, but she couldn't. All she could do was be there for her daughter.

"Sophie? Are you all right, sweetheart?" She reached to squeeze her hand.

Sophie nodded again, and then looked worriedly towards Justin, who was gazing out of the window.

"It's probably just a routine call," Alicia tried to reassure her. "Don't fret too much about it, Sophie. You're not obliged to talk about anything unless you want to."

Sophie smiled distractedly at her, and then turned her attention back to Justin. "Dad? "What's up?" she asked him, clearly feeling his anxiety too.

Alicia followed her gaze to where Justin was still standing at the window.

"Dad?"

"What?" Justin turned around, looking preoccupied. "Oh, sorry, Pumpkin." He dragged a hand over his neck, smiled tiredly and came towards her. "I was miles away."

"I gathered," Sophie said, her forehead furrowed with worry. "What's wrong?"

"Nothing," Justin said, glancing quickly at Alicia. "That is..." He took a breath and sat down next to Sophie. "There is something I need to tell you before Taylor turns up. You too, Alicia."

Noticing the nervous look in his eyes, Alicia swallowed hard, feeling hot and clammy suddenly, as she imagined what he might be about to say.

"Dad, what?" Sophie urged him, looking as wary as Alicia felt.

Justin took hold of Sophie's hand, twisting around to make sure he had full-on eye contact with her, which sent a fresh wave of apprehension down Alicia's spine. "I need you to know that I've loved you from birth, Sophie," he said firmly. "And before that, when you were just a tiny heartbeat on the monitor."

He looked again at Alicia, whose heart was now thudding frantically. His expression was deadly serious. It was bound to be, under the circumstances, but Alicia prayed he wasn't about to announce something that would rock Sophie's world further. Her world. They needed him, both of them, now more than ever, if they were going to get through this.

"There was never a second I didn't love you," Justin went on. "There will never be. No matter what the future may bring."

Justin hesitated, glancing briefly at Alicia.

"Dad, what do you mean 'no matter what the future may bring'? You're starting to scare me."

Justin took a breath. "I, er…" he started, and stopped. "If I should have to go away for any reason…"

Now Sophie looked extremely nervous. "Away, as in something work related?" she asked, doubt clouding her eyes.

"Possibly." Justin's gaze flicked again towards Alicia and then back to Sophie.

"Like fictitious conferences because you don't want to be here?" Sophie attempted to pull away from him.

"What?" Justin looked confused, then, "No," he said quickly. "God, no. I'd rather be here than anywhere. I'm not even sure I'll need to go away yet. I just wanted you to know that my love for you never wavered, Sophie. It never will. I needed you to know that, that's all."

He squeezed her hand, took another long breath and waited.

Sophie's gaze travelled between her parents. "So you're not telling me you two are going to split up then?" she asked him suspiciously, the anxious look now in her eyes almost splitting Alicia's heart in two.

"No, Sophie, we are definitely not going to split up," Justin said adamantly. "I'm… not doing this very well, am I?" He eyed the ceiling, despairing of himself. "I was simply trying to tell you that no matter where you are, how old you are, where I might be, that I'll always be there for you. And you will always be right here."

Pressing a hand to his heart, he smiled encouragingly. "Both of you," he said, reaching for Alicia's hand.

Alicia looked at him, emotion climbing inside her. She knew what he was trying to say, and why he'd needed to say it now, before DI Taylor arrived: he thought he might not be around to afterwards. "I love you," she mouthed, squeezing his hand hard. *And I will, always, whatever the future may bring.*

Looking somewhat reassured, Justin nodded and turned back to Sophie. "Sorry I scared you, Pumpkin," he said. "I'll try not to be so clumsy in the delivery of my next emotional speech. I'll write it on my cuff or—" He stopped as the doorbell rang, his gaze shooting fearfully towards Alicia.

Alicia didn't need to see the police car outside to know who it was. Was DI Taylor accompanied by uniformed officers, she wondered, bracing herself for whatever news he'd come to deliver.

"I'll get it," Justin said, getting quickly to his feet. Alicia guessed from his steely expression that he was also readying himself for bad news.

CHAPTER SEVENTY-NINE

JUSTIN

"Justin." Taylor's smile was inscrutable as Justin pulled the front door open. "How are we?"

"Disorientated, tired," Justin answered truthfully. "Trying to pick up the pieces."

Taylor nodded understandingly. "It will be a case of taking it one day at a time, I suspect."

"Definitely." Trying not to look obviously nervous, Justin scanned his face, searching for some indication of why he was here. The small talk, along with the fact that he appeared to be on his own, didn't point to an imminent arrest.

"Do you mind if I, er..." Taylor nodded past him to the hall.

"We were actually about to go out. A belated meal for Sophie's sixteenth," Justin said, testing the waters, hoping the man might say it could wait. A forlorn hope, he guessed. Taylor obviously wasn't here on a social visit to enquire after their welfare. "Sophie was looking forward to it. Can it wait?"

"It's important, Justin." Taylor smiled again, but still his expression gave nothing away. "It's probably better if I have a quick word now, if I may?"

His stomach tightening, Justin nodded and stepped back to allow him access. It had to be about Radley. Why else would he be here? The ketamine he'd injected into him would have been easily tested for. Justin had handwritten the prescription requesting some from the pharmacy. He'd been right outside his apartment block with his daughter, Taylor as his witness. There was no way to deny what he'd done.

"Ah, Sophie." Taylor's mouth curved into a warm smile as Sophie came through from the lounge, heading for the stairs, "I'm very pleased to see you looking brighter, young lady," he said, extending his hand.

"I'm feeling brighter, thanks to Dad." Sophie glanced at Justin, beaming him a smile that would sustain him. It would have to. Justin had thought he was ready for this, that he was mentally prepared. He wasn't. His daughter was safe, he reminded himself. She had a future with the person most important to her— her mother. That was what mattered here.

"I'm not so sure I'm pleased to see you though," Sophie added, looking the detective guardedly over.

Taylor chuckled at that. "Such is a policeman's lot. We grin and bear it for the greater good." He sighed stoically.

To her credit, Sophie didn't quite roll her eyes at his obvious theatrics.

"Do you mind if I have a brief word with your parents in private, Sophie?" Taylor asked her. "I gather you have a dinner engagement, so I won't keep them too long."

Justin felt a little of his anxiety dissipate. If it really was only a quick word he wanted, then hopefully he hadn't come to read him his rights.

Looking relieved that it wasn't her he wanted to speak to, Sophie shrugged easily. "No, it's cool. I was going up to ring Chloe anyway," she said, giving Justin an impromptu hug and then turning for the stairs.

Justin watched her go, grateful that she seemed to be getting back to somewhere near normal, wanting to get in touch with her friends and pick up the threads of her life.

"I take it she's glad to be home," Taylor observed, as Justin led the way to the lounge.

Where she would have been a long time ago, if you'd followed up my suspicions, Justin wanted to say. He decided it was probably better not to point that out.

"DI Taylor." Alicia smiled brightly, turning from the window—though Justin could see that beneath the smile she was as nervous as he was. "I was just about to boil the kettle. Would you like something? Tea? Coffee?"

"No, thank you," DI Taylor declined, his expression serious. "I won't take up too much of your time. I've actually come with some news regarding Paul Radley."

And there it was. Justin could almost feel the cell door clanging shut behind him.

"What is it?" he asked, swapping worried glances with Alicia. He'd known this would come. He'd resigned himself to prison the second he'd started out on the path to extract information from Radley regarding Sophie's whereabouts. He'd wanted to scare the bastard as much as he'd terrorised his wife. Once he'd known for certain that his instincts were right, that Radley actually had her, nothing had mattered other than finding out where he was holding her. When he'd realised what Radley had done to her, on top of the torture he'd inflicted on Alicia, his instinct had been to kill him. He'd convinced himself that being locked up for life was a small price to pay.

Taylor looked him over, taking his time. Justin wished he'd bloody well get on with it. "Paul Radley is dead," he finally announced.

Dead? The news hit Justin like a sledgehammer.

But he hadn't…? He'd *stopped*. It had taken every ounce of his willpower to pull back from tipping the man over. Even knowing the bastard might never be brought to justice, he'd stopped, unable to condemn his daughter to living the rest of her life with a murderer for a father and causing Alicia's nightmare to go on forever.

And now…the evidence all pointed to him having killed him anyway. Justin felt sick to his soul.

"Or fortunately, depending on your viewpoint," Taylor added blandly.

Justin stared at him, uncomprehending. *But…* "How?" He choked the word out, his gaze shooting towards Alicia. Her face was hard, resigned, almost knowing. He noted the straight set of her shoulders, the defiant tilt to her chin. She looked indifferent—satisfied, almost. *Jesus.*

"Suicide," Taylor supplied, as Justin attempted to focus and failed miserably. "Not long after we left the vicinity, it seems, which puts you in the clear, Justin. A detective inspector's sworn statement is about as cast iron an alibi as you can get, I imagine."

Justin felt his blood stop pumping. "By what means?" he asked, swallowing hard as his mind raced through all sorts of scenarios.

"Plunged fifteen floors from his balcony. Made a bit of a mess on the concrete." Taylor had just confirmed what Justin really did *not* want to hear. He'd left the door open. He hadn't bothered to close the front door when he'd charged in there. Knowing he was in no fit state to take the man on physically, his aim had been to get to Radley before he'd realised what was happening. Alicia had been due to arrive. The door had been open the whole time—and Radley had been on the balcony, incapable of doing anything other than realise what was happening to him. *Jesus Christ.*

Justin pinched the bridge of his nose hard. He couldn't speak. He felt as if he might actually vomit. But…she *couldn't* have. He tried to still his ludicrous imaginings. Panic gripping his chest like a vice, he wiped a thin film of sweat from his forehead and tried to think rationally, rather than follow the insane road his thoughts were going down.

"Do you have any suspects?" Alicia asked, seating herself on the sofa, her tone calm, her movements tense but composed.

Taylor shook his head. "Not yet, no. The circumstances surrounding his death are not being viewed as suspicious. Looks like he took his own life."

Alicia nodded.

Justin looked back to Taylor, wishing he could read what was going through the man's mind.

Taylor locked eyes with him, studying him hard for a long, petrifying moment. "There's something else you should know," he said, his gaze travelling to Alicia and back to Justin.

His thoughts all over the place, Justin tried to concentrate as he waited for him to go on.

Taylor spoke, eventually. "You might recall we didn't have much to go on in regard to the road traffic accident, apart from the colour and model of the car?"

Struggling to keep up, Justin nodded. "A black four-by-four, as driven by half the population of the country."

"A Land Rover Discovery," Taylor said guardedly, and waited.

"The same car Paul Radley drives," Alicia added quietly, after a second, her gaze now on the fingers she was knotting and unknotting in her lap.

"Apparently, yes." His expression grim, Taylor looked from her to Justin. "We made some enquiries, concentrating on body shops in the area and the suspected damage to the vehicle. One of the shop owners was reluctant to impart details of such a repair. The owner of the vehicle paid cash, it seems. The job was never logged, for tax-avoidance purposes. Obviously, we can't say for certain whether Paul Radley was involved without further examination of the car, but..."

"So the car he's been driving was a rental?" Justin asked, attempting to get his head around what Taylor was implying.

"It would seem so," Taylor confirmed.

Justin dropped heavily down to the seat behind him. He'd known it. Deep in his gut, he'd known Radley had been involved in the murder of his son. He hadn't figured out how or why, but when he'd seen those photographs, Luke and him cut crudely out of them all, he'd been sure. The only thing he hadn't been able to fathom was why Radley would have taken the risk that he might have killed the woman he was obsessed with, too, along with the child he'd truly believed was his. But now he realised that he wouldn't have cared. In Radley's mind, Alicia and Sophie belonged to him. If he couldn't have them, then no one could.

Alicia knew it too. She'd just said so. She'd known Radley owned a Discovery before Taylor had confirmed it. Yet, she *couldn't* have. Unless…it had been one of the vehicles in the underground car park. He'd looked right at it. What state of mind would Alicia have been in if she'd seen it there too?

"I'm afraid there's more," Taylor said, as Justin dragged his hands through his hair and tried to stop their incessant shaking. He didn't dare look at Alicia.

"We've been waiting for a forensics report to come back in regard to footmarks retrieved from the garden of your house, which bear a significant identifier, allowing us to narrow a specific pair of trainers down to brand, possibly even batch number."

"And?" Justin held his breath.

"We were a bit stuck at that stage," Taylor continued. "More often than not, it's impossible to identify the actual wearer unless we have them in custody, other than by information already held on the database or divine intervention."

"Is this leading somewhere, DI Taylor?" Alicia asked, still sounding quite calm, where Justin felt as if his chest was about to explode.

"It seems the divine did intervene," Taylor went on. "We can't be one hundred percent sure at this stage, but it seems Paul Radley was the owner of a similar pair of trainers, thereby indicating that it might well have been him who broke into your home. We'd need other substantiating evidence, of course—"

Justin exchanged glances with Alicia. *Leave it*, was the clear message he read in her eyes. They had the substantiating evidence: the locket, the photographs. Did they really want to share that with Taylor, thereby supplying further motive for possibly being involved in his death?

"I'm afraid it does look likely though," Taylor concluded, with a heavy sigh. "I'm so sorry. This must all be very distressing for you both."

"I see." Kneading his temple, Justin forced himself to look back at Taylor. He needed to maintain eye contact. He needed the man to go.

"Did you recognise him, Justin? Or his car?" Taylor asked him curiously. "Did you get a look at him after the accident?"

Realising the man was looking for motive, Justin shook his head. "No," he stated categorically, making damn sure to hold eye contact. "Do you think I wouldn't have mentioned it, if I had?"

Taylor narrowed his eyes, scrutinising him carefully. "No, I don't think for one minute you wouldn't have mentioned it—volubly," he said, his expression…conspiratorial?

His emotions now way off-kilter, wondering whether he dare read into this what Taylor seemed to be communicating, Justin looked bewilderedly back to Alicia. Her expression unreadable, she glanced briefly back at him before turning her attention to Taylor. "Were there any extenuating circumstances?" she asked him, causing Justin to do a double take.

Taylor's expression went back to grim. "There wasn't a lot left of the body to examine, to be honest," he said. "I doubt the post-mortem will produce anything that suggests it wasn't suicide."

"No security footage?" Alicia pushed, causing Justin's stomach to drop like a stone.

"Nothing," Taylor confirmed. "It seems several power outages had damaged the security feeds, which basically means we have nothing to go on."

Looking back to Justin, he held his gaze for a long minute, nodded almost imperceptibly and then glanced down at his watch. "Right, well, I've taken up enough of your valuable time. I'll leave you to go out for your meal. No doubt you have a lot to discuss. One or two fences that might need mending, possibly?"

"A few." Nodding, Alicia stood to see him out.

"I'm sure they'll all be fixable," Taylor said. "It never ceases to amaze me how strong a family unit can be when everyone pulls together."

Turning to Justin, he reached to shake his hand. "Sorry we weren't much help to you in your painstaking search for Sophie, Justin," he said, now wearing his apologetic smile. "All's well that ends well, though, hey? I'll find my own way out," he said, turning towards the door with a wave—leaving Justin inwardly reeling.

CHAPTER EIGHTY

JUSTIN

Too shocked to move, Justin stayed where he was as Alicia went to the kitchen. She was making tea. *Tea?* She'd just learned that the bastard who'd raped her, killed their son and taken their daughter had fallen fifteen floors to his death, his insides undoubtedly splattered all over the pavement, and her reaction was to go and put the kettle on?

Christ. Running his hands up over his face, Justin took several slow breaths and then stood to follow her.

Seating himself at the kitchen table, he clasped his hands in front of him and watched her retrieve two cups from the dishwasher, wincing as she straightened up. She'd strained her back, she'd said, moving furniture.

When? She hadn't had a bad back when she'd met him in the car. And she would hardly have gone back into the house and started shifting furniture with the sister she wasn't exactly on very good terms with after certain events. Plus, there was the matter of Radley's twisted text. Was she likely to have been moving furniture after reading that?

"This heavy weight you lifted..." he ventured, mentally calculating Radley's weight, which he reckoned to be at least that of Alicia, plus half again. "Did Jessica help you with it?"

Alicia didn't answer immediately, appearing to ponder as she poured hot water into the teapot to warm it.

Turning to him, eventually, she looked at him, her gaze long and searching. "Yes," she said. "I was adamant I could do it on my own, but Jessica insisted on helping."

"Right." Justin studied his hands—hands that had come so close to committing murder. He would have done, if not for his wife and daughter, whose lives Radley had almost succeeded in destroying.

"How do we tell Sophie?" Alicia asked, her voice worried now.

Justin took a second to digest this, and then looked back at her. She was holding her breath. Her beautiful, cornflower-blue eyes wide with fear, she was waiting for his reaction.

Tugging in a tight breath, Justin got to his feet. "Together," he said softly, walking across to her. He needed to hold her, to be there for her, to try to the best of his ability to keep his family safe.

LETTER FROM SHERYL

Thank you so much for choosing to read *The Affair*. I have everything crossed, hoping you will enjoy it. If you would like to join a mailing list for alerts on my future novels, please sign up here. You can unsubscribe at any time, and your email address will never be shared.

www.bookouture.com/sheryl-browne

I have to say, this wasn't the easiest story to write. Sadly, I suffered a family loss as I set out on this particular journey, which threw me. I'm not sure I could have continued to write without the wonderful support and professionalism of Bookouture behind me. I will be eternally grateful for that.

In the writing of this book, I struggled with Alicia: firstly, to get in touch with her emotionally; and then, once I had, once I felt her every emotion, I struggled to live them alongside her. Without going into great detail, I would like to add another dedication here: to any mother who has had to grieve the loss of a child at any stage, from pregnancy and beyond. When the daily pace of life takes over, when you are perhaps striving to be the best parent you can to other children, a short life lived and lost is often grieved silently. That life though, grown inside you, is never forgotten. This isn't my story but, yes, some of it is based on experience. Alicia was a little bit scared to admit how emotionally broken she was at first. I think we have given her a voice. This, then, is a story of a woman who was lost, and a man who was lost alongside her, trying to come to terms with their grief when their relationship was under threat. I think, with every milestone in life, we look back and reflect, and we remember those we've lost personally and those who were there to help us over life's obstacles. For me, those are the people who believed in me, even when I didn't quite believe in myself.

To all of you, thank you.

If you have enjoyed the book, I would love it if you could share your thoughts and write a brief review. Reviews mean the world to an author and will help a book find its wings. I would also love to hear from you via Facebook or Twitter or my website. If you would like to keep up-to-date with my latest book news, please do sign up at the website link below.

Keep safe, everyone, and happy reading.
Sheryl x

 sherylbrowne.com

 SherylBrowne

 SherylBrowne.Author

ACKNOWLEDGEMENTS

Once again, I would like to offer a massive thank-you to the team at Bookouture, without whom *The Affair* would never have happened! Special thanks to Helen Jenner and Peta Nightingale for their skill in making this book the best it could be—and for their tremendous patience and support through a family loss, which threw me completely off track. Special thanks also to Kim Nash and Noelle Holten for their unstinting support and amazing marketing skills. For your shoulder, too, Kim. When I needed it, it was there. That meant a lot. To all the other lovely, friendly and super-supportive authors at Bookouture, I love you! Thanks for the smiles!

I owe a huge debt of gratitude to all the fantastically hard-working bloggers and reviewers who have taken time to read and review my books and shout out endlessly for me. I so often say I couldn't do this without you. Trust me, I couldn't. Your passion, as always, leaves me in absolute awe. Thank you! Huge thanks, too, to Shell Baker, without whose support and encouragement my previous book might never have been submitted. You're all awesome!

Final thanks to every single reader out there for buying and reading my books. Authors write with you in mind. Knowing you have enjoyed reading our books and care enough to say so is the best incentive in the world for us to keep writing.